# BLACK OCEAN: MISSION PACK 1

## MISSIONS 1-4.5

### J. S. MORIN

# CONTENTS

Mission Pack 1

Missions 1-4.5 of: Black Ocean

Magical Scrivener Press 22 Hawkstead Hollow Nashua, NH 03063

www.magicalscrivener.com

Publisher's Note: This is a work of fiction. Names, characters, places, and incidents are a product of the author's imagination. Locales and public names are sometimes used for atmospheric purposes. Any resemblance to actual people, living or dead, or to businesses, companies, events, institutions, or locales is completely coincidental.

Ordering Information: Special discounts are available on quantity purchases by corporations, associations, and others. For details, contact the publisher at the address above.

J.S. Morin — First Edition

ISBN: 978-1-939233-93-6

Printed in the United States of America

# SALVAGE TROUBLE

MISSION 1 OF THE BLACK OCEAN SERIES

## SALVAGE TROUBLE

THERE WAS something unsettling about being inside a dead ship. Darkness filled corridors where emergency lighting should have glowed. Anything to be seen existed within the claustrophobic radius of the hand lamps. Bare steel corridors devoid of air snaked their way through the inert hulk. Mag-boots snapped against the floor at each step, the pull to break them free keeping the pace slow, but safe.

It could have been worse. With a ship dead in the Ocean, sometimes they lost gravity as well, but whatever wizard set the ship's internal gravity had done a better job of hardening it than the engineers who built the onboard systems had. The mag-boots were just a precaution for all the places where the passenger freighter had been blasted open to space; without them, Carl and his crew could still have walked against the floor—but also might get thrown out into the void if something structural gave way.

"Got another one," Chip's voice came over the comm, popping and crackling with static. The voice filled the EV suit helmet and was starting to give Carl a headache. "Gimme a hand."

Carl backtracked and found Chip with one of the door panels pried open and a tangle of wires hooked to a handheld power supply. With the lock powered open, the two men were able to manhandle the door. Inside, a bunk and a footlocker were wedged into a ragged hole in the wall with the stars showing beyond.

"Must've lost everything else when the hull failed," said Carl. Fortunately his own voice merely echoed within the shell of his helmet.

Chip stomped into the room—he couldn't help stomping with mag-boots on—and gave the footlocker a tug. It fell from the hole and slammed to the floor. There was something Carl never could wrap his head around—the silence in vacuum. He felt the little tremor in the deck plates, but that was it. Chip struggled and dragged the footlocker to the door.

"I'm gonna pop a gut moving this thing," said Chip. "Can't we just get Mort over here and kill the gravity?"

"Can you even picture Mort in an EV suit?"

"Naw, guess not. Wouldn't want the cranky old bastard along anyway," said Chip. "He'd manage to find some way to make this corpse a bigger hazard than it already is."

Tanny's voice popped over the comm. "You know this is an open channel. Mort can hear you."

"Dammit," said Carl. "He's not in the cockpit with you? Get him the hell out of there before we have to—"

"Relax," Tanny said, her voice calm and measured. "I'm down in the galley making some lunch. I keyed the comm to ship-wide. Mort's right here, eating a sandwich. Want to say anything to him?"

"Um, sorry, Mort?" Chip said. "You're not a cranky old bastard? Except that you are and you damn well know it."

"Can you all shut up?" Mriy interrupted. Her voice was scratchy even without the interference over the comm. "The sooner we finish, the sooner we eat."

"Beer's on me," Roddy's high-pitched voice agreed. "I'm not seeing anything worth salvaging among the mechanicals. Ship was unarmed; engines are slag. Computers might have seen an EMP, might not have; I'll let Chip figure that out back home. We've already cut them out and made a trip back with them."

"Hear that, Tanny?" Carl asked. "We're hard at work over here while you're chowing down bacon cubes. Grab something quick and get back to the cockpit. We've got an asteroid coming in a couple hours and I want someone watching for it. I got better things to do than become a decorative splotch on a space rock."

"Two hours, four minutes, thirty-one seconds. I've got a timer set. Twenty minutes out, you're either back on board or I leave without you. And I'm having the chicken cubes. The bacon's three months past expiration."

"You wouldn't," Carl replied. "And the bacon's fine. Those dates are just rules and regs. Total bullshit."

"Yeah, the bacon's fine," Chip agreed.

"I don't see what you find so appealing in that dry, bloodless meat," said Mriy.

Carl waved his arms for quiet, even though Chip was the only one who could see him. "Wait, wait, wait. First, bacon is humanity's crowning achievement in food. Second, you're not leaving without us. Mort would never let you get away with it."

"Mort's always liked me better than you," Tanny replied.

Carl could picture the smirk on her face without needing to see it.

"Everyone likes you better than me," said Carl. "That doesn't mean he's going to let you strand us here to get dusted. Besides, you can't just take my ship."

"I'm still listed as your next of kin."

"Fuck." Carl just mouthed the word, not wanting to admit over the comm that she was right. Sometimes avoiding paperwork caused the most inconvenient problems. "Fine, but give us until ten before the asteroid."

"Twenty."

"Fifteen?"

"Twenty."

"OK, twenty. Give us a heads up at ten and five before then, so we're not caught with our pants down."

"The *hell* are you doing over there?" Tanny asked.

"Is there atmo in your section?" Roddy asked. "What are you and Chip—?"

"Nothing!" Carl snapped. "Just, everyone get back to work. And thanks for the extra time over here, sweetie."

"You *don't* get to call me that anymore!" A thump over the comm cut out halfway through as someone switched hers off with a fist. ,

"School drama's over, kiddies. Back to work."

"Yes, sir," Mriy and Chip answered in discordant unison. Carl didn't need to hear Roddy's reply. He would just get back to work. Roddy was good like that.

They went door to door, overriding locks where they could and going through with plasma torches where they could not. The salvage team kept in contact, giving a running account of the dregs left behind when the survivors abandoned ship. Standard issue footlockers with standard issue locks—some weighed more than others, but none was heavy enough to be stacked with gold or any other form of hard currency. It was like visiting relatives off-world for Christmas, except the presents were a uniform matte stainless steel. No one knew you well enough to get you what you really wanted, so what you ended up with was a crapshoot of ill-fitting clothes and knickknacks that would get tossed in a corner or sold off the first chance you got. Best case, there might be magic in one of those knickknacks, but there was no way to tell until Mort had a look. Odds ran against finding anything enchanted though, since the passengers had abandoned ship—most magic was worth the space in an escape pod.

Carl was panting, fogging the bottom half of his helmet's mask with each breath before the recirculator cleared the moisture. His back was aching from dragging plunder back to the *Mobius*. Thirty-two was too young to have an old man's body, creaking and protesting after a few hours of manual labor.

"That's it," Carl said over the comm. "No more holovids until I get back in fighting shape. How long have we got left?"

Tanny's voice squished and chomped. "Just over half an hour until the asteroid makes a sweating, scruffy paste out of you." The sound of her chewing made Carl's stomach grumble.

Roddy's comm opened. "I didn't know you navy boys even *had* a fighting shape. 'Fits in the seat, fit enough,' right? *Eee, eee, eee.*" Carl gritted his teeth.

"Captain!" Chip's use of his honorary title caught his attention. It meant someone was taking things seriously. "There's a pod jammed over here."

"Hey now! There's a bit of a break. Bulky, but portable if we can get it out of the ship's gravity. Nice work."

"There's *people* in it!"

"Of course there's people in it. You don't eject an empty—oh shit! We've gotta get them out of there quick."

"On it!" Chip replied.

"Mriy, Roddy, get back to the *Mobius*. Ready a winch and tethers for full EV. Me and Chip'll take care of things from inside."

"But Captain, we just spent five minutes cutting into the med bay—" Mriy whined.

"Anything not in your hands or your packs now, leave it! We can make another run in if there's time." Carl knew there would be no time to spare.

Carl flipped off the switch for his mag-boots and ran down the corridor, hand lamp creating a jiggling spotlight along his path. They had been on the ship for hours, and he had an idea where the hull was open to space and what sections were largely intact. He rounded a corner and found the wall of escape pod cradles, the safety doors all closed in a neat line, keeping the ship safe from the vacuum left when the pods were launched. Chip had already cut the hinges off one of the doors. He stood bent awkwardly over where it lay on the deck, the stance of a man whose mag-boots were stuck where he last set them and had neither the time nor inclination to move them. The bright flare of the plasma torch in his hand bit into the docking clamps that secured the pod to the ship.

"What've we got in there?" Carl asked, hanging back far enough to keep out of Chip's way. Two could work side by side with plasma cutters, but most times just got each other's elbows to the ribs.

"Locking clamp didn't release. Probably software, but it's quicker cutting than debugging it."

"Inside. I mean inside."

"Woman and a boy. Saw them waving from the window.

Shit, if I'd have been looking the wrong way, we'd have left them here and never known it."

Carl peered through the entry hatch window. "Don't see them in there."

"I think I got across that they needed to belt in. Who knows if the grav in there is any good? They might be on ship's—"

Chip's next words were lost when a jet of compressed gas burst from a ruptured line. It looked like nothing more than an aerosol spray, scaled up to a size that would send an escape pod clear of a doomed vessel. As the pod snapped free of the half-cut docking clamp, Chip was bent over backward by the blast until his mag-boots came free of the deck. He slammed into the far wall of the corridor head first and slumped to the floor in a heap, the lit plasma torch burning into his leg with no reaction. The only sound had been a *thump* heard through Chip's open comm.

"Chip!"

"What happened?" Tanny shouted into the comm.

Carl rushed to Chip's side, pulled the plasma torch from his hand, and shut it off. "Chip took a blast from a launch jet." The EV suit had sealed around the skin where the torch had burned, keeping it from losing air pressure. It was a good sign. He looked to the life support panel on the chest of Chip's suit, and the heart rate and respiration indicators were reading zero. Damaged in the blast? No, they would have been dark; they had a reading on Chip and the reading said he was meat. "No pulse, no breathing."

"I'll double back to the med bay and—" Mriy growled into her comm. She always sounded angry when she was nervous.

"No." Captain felt around under the back of Chip's helmet, below the base of the skull.

"But captain—"

"His neck. Nothing in the med bay's gonna help him."

"Oh God, Carl," said Tanny, her voice choking off in a sob before the comm closed.

Carl's own vision blurred as he looked down at Chip's body. He blinked away the saline build-up, unable to wipe it away from behind his helm. "Get that pod on board the *Mobius*. I'll get Chip out with me."

Whatever treasures the last pair footlocker might have held, Carl would never know. It was just an obstacle away as he carried Chip out, slung over his shoulder, back aching the whole way back to the *Mobius*.

---

The cargo bay doors closed, sealing the crew inside the belly of the *Mobius*. The dull grey of the painted steel walls was bathed in a flashing red strobe of the warning lights. Until the air pressure returned, the klaxon blared in silence. The cargo hold had no windows, and now that they were closed in, there was no way to view the destruction of the derelict ship that had so recently been their workplace.

"Nice to have real gravity again, eh, boss?" Roddy's voice crackled through the comm, despite him being within arm's reach. At just a bit over a meter tall, with prehensile feet and elongated arms, the laaku was a closer descendant of his chimp-like forbearers than Carl was of his hominid ancestors.

Carl just grunted in reply. Gravity was always nicer on the *Mobius*. It was a perk of keeping a proper merlin aboard and not some puffed up star-drive repairman. Didn't mean he needed to hear about it every time they came aboard. He always liked that there was no weather to talk about in space. It made spacers a bit more interesting than planetside folk—until some four-handed mechanic decided to start yammering about the gravity.

Mriy cuffed Roddy upside the helmet, sending him stumbling—not that Roddy ever fell, with four limbs so close to the ground. She slouched against the wall, waiting out the pressurization cycle with her usual ill temper. It was her usual posture, leaving her eye to eye with her captain. Drawn up to full height, standing tall on her backward-bending legs and throwing her shoulders back, she could tower over any of the crew.

"You're at eighty percent," Tanny called over the comm from the door. She caught Carl's eye and gave a tight smile that was probably meant to be supportive, but just looked sickly. Tanny looked like a wreck. Against the pale contrast of her spacer's skin, it was easy to make out the telltale redness in her eyes.

Along with the air rushing back in to fill the cargo hold came the klaxon's repetitive honking. It kept up its monotonous, headache-inducing chant until air pressure was back to standard. The red lights stopped spinning, and an eerie quiet was left in the hold.

Mriy was the first to tear off her helmet. She shook loose her fur and smoothed it back with a gloved hand. She was azrin, and appeared to be a humanoid house cat with a shock of longer fur on the scalp reminiscent of a lion's mane. She was white, with splashes of orange, an unusual coloration among her kind. Chip had looked it up on the omni once and told her that made her a harlequin orange—he got a claw scar for his troubles, and they never spoke of it again.

Carl gave his helmet a weary twist and broke the seal, letting his ears pop and allowing the stale, familiar smell of hydraulic fluid and recycling purifiers in before taking it off completely. He sighed as he let go of the minty freshness that the scent infuser line added to his suit. Best thirty terra he ever spent. He no longer had to smell his own sweat and breath for hours on end every time he wore it.

Roddy was the last to start removing his suit, helmet and gloves, but the first to finish, thanks to having quadridexterous hands and feet working in concert. Laaku, Roddy's people, were closest species that humans had found to themselves, descended from chimp-like primates instead of the great apes. He ambled over toward where the escape pod sat with the window facing them. There had been no sign of the two occupants while the hold re-pressurized. "We should see about our passengers."

The door to the rest of the ship opened. Tanny came through with her head down, making straight for Carl. He braced himself, knowing it was coming, but she still squeezed the breath from his lungs when she wrapped her arms around him. Carl had a few centimeters on her, and a couple dozen kilos, but Tanny had arms like the marine she used to be. He held his helmet away and pulled her head against his shoulder with his free hand. She sobbed.

"It's my fault," Carl whispered to her. "Never should have let the kid work on that pod. Roddy could've done it right, with no one hurt."

Tanny's head twisted back and forth under his hand. "He was always ... too sure ... thought he knew it all."

The door burst open again and a gawky middle aged man strode in. His hair was black, except for a few insidious grey hairs that lurked here and there. His face wrinkled around a congenial grin and a pair of hazel eyes that focused like lasers wherever he aimed them—not that he was the sort who would have any luck with lasers. He wore battered old denim pants and a loose, hooded pullover, both stained with splotches of condiments and meaty juices, spit-scrubbed with a cloth and still deemed "more or less clean."

"What have we got?" Mort asked, slapping his hands together and rubbing them like he was trying to start a fire.

Carl shot Mort a glare as Tanny continued to sob more quietly against him. Mort stopped in his tracks and ducked, grimacing as he nodded and met Carl's eyes. "*Oops. Sorry,*" he mouthed. He cleared his throat. "Real shame. The Dyson boy wasn't half bad, as techsters go. Still, when you wrangle daily with technological forces beyond your understanding, it's a risk you have to accept. He'll be missed."

A clunk and a hiss of released sealant gas echoed across the hold. Roddy had convinced the escape pod that it had finished escaping and could let its charges free. Carl patted Tanny on the back. "I've gotta go. Captainy stuff. Can't let them go thinking Roddy's in charge here, or they'll climb right back in."

As Carl walked across the hold, Mort took over the task of comforting Tanny. "Oh, you should have stuck around to watch. Tumbling across the cosmos like Lucifer's own bowling league. Smashed that little pile of gizmos and contraptions to confetti. Reminds you just how little tech can really do, once you pit it against the powers of creation."

Carl shook his head and checked to see who was stepping out of the pod. First out was the boy, older than he had guessed. Chip had called him a boy, but Carl might have credited him with ten or twelve years, more a lad than a boy by that age, for all the good semantics did. He was skinny, which meant he either ate little, ran around a lot, or was just that sort of skinny, wimpy kid that gets picked on wherever they pop up. Carl knew that type well. The lad had mop-cut blond hair, tousled and streaked with bits of a darker shade. His eyes were a mystery, since he kept them aimed firmly at his feet. The clothes on his back were all midnight blue, cut in the style of some sort of school uniform.

Following him out was a young woman dressed in a black, shapeless robe that covered her from hair to ankles, leaving only the oval of her face and her hand uncovered. That face was alabaster white and straight from an artist's sketch. Smooth. That was the word for it. High cheekbones, thin nose, and the rest pulled close and smoothed like clay. If it were not for the vivid blue of her eyes, she would not have looked much different on a monochrome display. The only decoration she wore was a pendant shaped like a lowercase $T$.

"We're no threat to you," were the woman's first words. She looked straight at Carl while she said them. "Please, don't harm the boy."

"Dunno who said anything about harming," Carl replied. "We just saved your asses from an asteroid. A few minutes more on that wreck, and you'd have been dusted."

"Far be it from me to question altruism, but I think the ship might have gotten out of the way fine on its own if you hadn't blasted it full of holes."

Carl watched her face as she spoke, listened to inflections. He heard the words and they registered somewhere, but he did not expect to get much out of them. Her accent sounded Martian, one of the snootier cities at that, drawing out the end of the last word in every sentence. Carl would take a girl with an accent from any of the old Earth languages over a silver spoon Martian.

"You got us wrong, lady," said Carl. "We got your distress call, found a pirate picking over a fresh kill, drove him off. Wasn't us shot your ride full of hot plasma."

"All plasma's hot," Roddy muttered out the side of his mouth from Carl's elbow.

"Anyway, we could have left you there to die, and we didn't," Carl said. "That's gotta put in a good word for us. Lost us a man in the doing, too." Carl hung his head.

The fear in the woman's face softened. "Peace to you and yours. May I be of aid in your time of grief?"

Carl grimaced, realizing he should have recognized the pendant. "You a priestess?"

"I'm Sister Theresa Richelieu, of the One Church."

Tanny had composed herself, and she and Mort came over to join the welcome party. "Thought the One Church wasn't the Seeker type; uppity-ups not too big on travel," said Mort. "If the past won't come back, beat the future with a stick until it cries 'uncle?'"

"Some branches are like that," Sister Theresa agreed.

"How's it a One Church if it has branches?" Tanny asked.

Carl whistled, a quick burst with his fingers between his lips to draw everyone's attention. "You can get into theology on your own time. We got us a few tasks left before we can kick up our feet. Let's get the introductions out of the way.

"This is Tanny, our pilot. Roddy's our mechanic. Mriy ... well, what Mriy does around here's not important right now. Mort's our ship's wizard. If you have any a-tech with you, I'd set it aside before getting too close to him. And I'm Carl, Carl Ramsey, Captain of the *Mobius*." He pulled off the EV suit glove from his right hand and held it out. Sister Theresa looked down at it a moment as if trying to decide whether to take it. When she finally shook Carl's hand, she had the grip of a child and skin as soft as peach skin.

An hour later, everyone had changed into their daily clothes, the cargo hold had been tidied, but far from inventoried, and they had reconvened in the hold.

"Thank you for doing this," Tanny whispered to Sister Theresa. They stood in a circle around Chip's body, still in his EV suit. As a small grace, they had left his face obscured by the darkened glass of the helmet.

Sister Theresa spoke at length about life and death, using ancient, dusty allegories and solemn assurances of the life beyond. Much of it was spoken in Latin, and Carl was tempted to pluck the earring from his ear so it would stay that way. The enchantment Mort had put on it turned everything into Earth Standard English—though it left Martian accents alone. Latin was one of those tongues that was clunky in translation, like Temerling or Straaka. It was meant to have a sound to it, like something you would recite to conjure demons, or to send them away. Instead, it sounded like a xeno trying to act tough in broken English.

Carl found himself fixated on the clumsiness of the words and not the message. He was unprepared when it ended.

"...Amen. Would any of you like to say a few words?"

Tanny nodded and took a half step forward. She looked at the helmet as she spoke. "Chip, I'm sorry. I'm not sure how I'll tell Aunt Sara and Uncle Bart, but I'll let them know you died saving two people's lives." She stepped back into the circle.

Everyone looked to everyone else. Sister Theresa caught Carl's eye and raised an eyebrow at him. Carl swallowed, knowing he really ought to say something as well.

"Charles Bartholomew Dyson, known as Chip because you thought it made you sound like you knew computers. Well, name or no name, you did. I was your captain. I was supposed to watch over you. Dammit, I should have made Roddy give you lessons in using a plasma torch." That was not the tone he was looking for. He needed something more profound. "Um, we are all dust in the wind, just drops of water in an endless stream. There is nothing to fear but fear itself. Don't fear the reaper. Um, Amen."

He glanced sidelong at the priestess, and Sister Theresa gave him a tight little smile and a nod.

"And now, in the tradition dating back to the sailing ships of Earth, we commend this body to the deep," said Carl. He leaned toward Tanny and muttered. "We on course?" She nodded.

With that, Mort muttered beneath his breath and lifted a hand; Chip's body rose from the floor. The old wizard led a short procession to the airlock and they shut the body inside. A moment later Chip was on course for the sun at the center of the Seles System.

"Tanny, get us a new course before we follow him in. Mriy, take our guests to their temporary quarters." Carl added under his breath: "We've got a free bunk."

---

Carl trudged up the steps, boots ringing on the steel mesh treads, heading for the common area. When he arrived, Mort was already there, slumped on the couch in front of a holovid— a detective story set in the early 2200s by the costumes. Carl grunted a greeting as he passed by on his way to the kitchen. Digging in the cupboards, he found a ham rod and a cheese rod, and fed them into the processor. After a quick check of the bread and mustard levels, he keyed in his order.

"What're you watching?" Carl asked as his lunch was

being prepared. He shivered. The chill in the *Mobius* was always refreshing after sweating his ass off in the EV suit. With his sweat cooled, it was time to find something warmer than a thin kevlex shirt. A battered leather jacket hung on the wall, and Carl slung it on as he waited.

"Some claptrap Tanny's been nagging me to watch," said Mort. "It's all drivel. I had the murderer figured out from the first scene. Not like yelling it to them will get it solved any faster, either."

"I think they usually do that on purpose. You're supposed to watch how they figure it out."

"Bah, load of ass-backward mind candy. All sweet, no savor. Be a lad and find me something worth watching." Mort tossed Carl the remote. Carl slipped it into a jacket pocket without giving it more than a glance.

"Sure thing." The food processor dinged, and he grabbed the ham sandwich that came out, along with a beer from the fridge. "Just wanna talk to you about something first."

Mort patted Carl on the arm as the captain sat down beside him. "Good enough words. No one's expecting a captain to be Marcus Antonius. Metaphor's a clumsy tool in the hands of a—"

"No, not that. Our guests."

Mort's face twisted in a sneer. "I'd steer clear of that one. There's a sniff of foul science on her. Those aren't the looks she was born to have."

"Figured as much. Some sort of knife-work."

"More knife than fork to her, that's for sure," said Mort. "Odd for a pious girl to be so vain, wouldn't you say? Ought to have spent more time on her Latin, less on keeping her looks. Dreadful pronunciation. Keeps a charm, too, just so you know."

"It's a holy cross. Don't see many of those outside Sol."

"Carl, I'm not a blithering idiot. I grew up in Boston, remember? I've seen a crucifix or two before. She's got something else, hidden beneath those robes. Might just be more cosmetics. Got hit bad with an ugly-stick, decided to come after it from both ends, science and magic. Then again, maybe it's a death charm, ready to end her life if she gets captured. I'll know piss-all until I can get a closer look."

Carl nodded. "I'll keep my guard up. What about the boy?"

"What about him?"

Carl held up an open beer and a sandwich as he shrugged. "You tell me."

"Boy's a boy. Get back to me in ten years, and I might have an opinion of him. He's just had a nasty scare on one starship, now he's on another. Might be technology's scarred him for life." Mort turned aside and furrowed his brow. "Hmm, might be that we can make a wizard of him," he murmured to himself.

"I'd settle for him being a computer prodigy. But we're not that kind of lucky."

Carl pulled out the remote and flipped through the ship's library as he ate. They were out of range of the omni, and it wasn't worth firing up an astral link to connect from the middle of nowhere. Most of the files were Chip's or Tanny's, but the rest of them had a few favorites logged as well. He found one that might keep Mort amused for a while.

"Here you go. Zero-G cage fighting. You can thank Mriy."

---

Sandwich comfortably digesting in his stomach, Carl climbed

down the steps to Chip's old quarters, keeping hold of both handrails. At the bottom he reached for the door handle but caught himself. He knocked.

"You may enter," said Sister Theresa, muffled by hull-rated steel.

Carl let himself in. The quarters were mostly how Chip had left them, with the soiled laundry moved from the bed to a neat pile on the floor. It was stacked with electronics and outfitted with more communications gear and computing power than the *Mobius's* main systems. "Getting settled?"

Sister Theresa gave him a wan smile. "We'll manage. When the world stops spinning around me, I'll help arrange Charles's things. I'm sure his family will want them."

"Tanny is family. And no one called him Charles. Speaking of, what's the boy called?"

"His name is Adam."

"He yours?"

For the first time, Sister Theresa showed some color on those pale cheeks. She flushed a pale pink. "Heavens, no! My vows forbid me from—"

"Yeah, sorry. Skip it. You look a little young for one that age, though I've seen stranger things," said Carl. To the boy, he said, "Hey, Adam, head on up those steps, go find yourself a bite. Just help yourself. I gotta have a talk with your friend here."

Adam nodded and slipped out the door. Before he got three steps, Carl called after him. "Hey Adam, you any good with computers?"

The boy turned and looked down the steps. He seemed a normal young boy for the first time since he left the escape pod. "I'm the best. I can beat anyone at Neptune Squad, Death Arena, and Omnithrust Racer."

Carl nodded. "Great kid. Good for you." He slammed the door shut.

Sister Theresa looked at Carl with wide eyes and clutched her crucifix tight in her fist. She swallowed. "So, this is the price of passage?"

"Whuh?" Carl furrowed his brow. "No! Hell no!" He waved his hands in front of him and backed himself against the closed door. "Nothing like that. Shit, and sorry about my language. No, we've just got a few things to discuss, seeing as you're with us until our next stop."

"What sort of things? I promise you; we won't leave these quarters."

Carl wiped a hand over his face. "What'd Mriy tell you? Never mind, just forget her. You aren't prisoners. Just stay out of the engine room, the cockpit, and the cargo hold. Rest of the ship, feel free. Just mind that you don't go into someone else's quarters, they're liable to get the wrong idea about you."

"Thank you," Sister Theresa smiled. "So was that all?"

"Hell, no. That wasn't even the preamble. I want to know what you were doing with the boy. You had hours to come up with a story, maybe even had something cooking for days before that. I expect it to be a good one. After that, you're going to tell me the truth."

"Captain Ramsey, it's really very simple—"

"Carl. Port authorities call me Captain Ramsey. And I'm damned sure this isn't simple. Priestesses aren't known for traveling much, and I should know because I'll take just about any kind of passengers I can get. You lot swear off children, and you don't make house calls to go picking up orphans. I'll let you continue, but just bear in mind."

The priestess's eyes searched the room for escape. The quarters aboard the *Mobius* doubled as the ship's escape pods

—palatial by pod standards, small for bedrooms. To one side was an arrangement of glassteel panels forming a window looking into the Black Ocean—the last frontier of mankind, infinitely vast. To the other side was a closed door with Carl leaning against it, blocking the only exit.

"Let me make this easy on you," said Carl when she didn't respond. "Everyone here's got secrets. That's why they aren't someplace better than this old bucket. I got 'em, too. I keep 'em safe. I keep 'em *all* safe. Everyone's. How can I do that? I gotta know what I'm protecting. I can't be having shit rain down around me over stuff I can't see coming. Too many lives are at stake. You level with me; I don't judge. Play it straight up and the worst thing I'll do is feed the both of you, loan you a bunk, and drop you off at the next stop. Understand me?"

Sister Theresa nodded.

"Then let's start with something basic. You kidnap that boy?"

The priestess looked away. "No."

"That's strike one," said Carl. He took a finger and aimed her chin back in his direction. "You slip up twice more, and you spend the rest of the trip in the escape pod we found you in, and that's how we deliver you to the law. So you have a good reason taking the boy?"

"Yes." She nodded.

Carl let out a sigh. "Good. You're a shitty liar, so this is going to go easy if you just keep sticking to the truth. So you had a good reason...what was it?"

Sister Theresa sat there a moment, chewing at the inside of her cheek.

Carl came and sat down beside her on the bed. "I'm counting that as your second strike. Let me put this into terms you maybe understand a bit better. This here, this is my ship.

It's like my church, and you're in it. It's time for you to confess your sins, but instead of repenting them, we're going to make them right; we're going to find a way to live with them.

"Or you can go right in the escape pod," said Carl. "Your call, but confession is good for the soul. Start at the beginning: are you even really a priestess?"

"Not officially, not anymore," Sister Theresa said. "I'm sure they've defrocked me by now, and I was only probationary to begin with. Before that I taught fourth grade at the school on Bentus VIII, at a church school. Adam was one of my students."

"I'm with you so far. What made you run off with him?"

"It's a small planet, mostly corporate. There's not a lot going on that Harmony Bay Corporation doesn't own. It was a research facility for them. In my class, there were a dozen like him...Adam, Benjamin, Caleb, David, Elijah, Felix..."

"They're cloning?"

Sister Theresa nodded. "Not just cloning, they're trying to rewrite the boys' minds, make them into customized people, data storage couriers, what have you. It's not just one plan; it's experimentation to see what they can do."

Carl ran a hand over his scalp, digging his fingers through hair that was five hours in an EV suit past needing a shower. "I get it now. You managed to rescue one of them."

"Not just one of them—Adam, the original. He's the one they cloned from. They're all in school together so they can judge the clones against him, see what they do better and worse. The scientists' children attend as well, but more than half my class were Adam's clones."

Carl nodded along, trying the pieces and seeing where they did not fit. "And how did you know what they were doing. Picking up on the clones, sure, I buy that. What about those plans for them? Doesn't seem like the type of stuff they'd tell the local schoolteacher."

"Are you a God-fearing man, Captain Carl?"

Carl leaned away, straightening from his seated position. That question caught him off guard, but fair was fair. He was asking a lot about her. "Me? Naw. If God was still the smiting type, I think I'd have gotten dusted years ago, back in my Navy days. He had plenty of chances after that, too. I'm a believer, don't get me wrong, but I've got plenty of time to settle up with Him before I'm done. I'm sure picking up one of his young minions on a mission of mercy won't look too shabby for me, either."

"Well, not every man of science is deaf to God's word. Dr. James Augustus Cliffton was one of the top scientists for Harmony Bay. He was an old man, and worried about his standing in the eyes of the Lord. He wanted to make amends for what he helped create. He helped us: access codes, transport schedules, a little money. Without his help, I'd still be wondering what was going on with all the identical boys in my class."

"What're you planning to do with him? Raise him as your own?"

"I ... I hadn't thought that far ahead. Just getting away seemed like such a ... such a ..."

"Herculean task?" Carl suggested. She nodded.

"I have to ask, now that I've told you," said Sister Theresa. "That ship you said you drove off, could it have belonged to Harmony Bay?"

Carl waved off her concern. "Naw. That heap wasn't corporate. Bigger question, would they call in a kidnapping, or would they handle it themselves?"

"I ... I couldn't say."

"Well, either way, we can't be having a defrocked priestess going around in a getup like that. Head down to the cargo hold and find yourself something inconspicuous in the luggage we salvaged. If you find your own stuff, great. If not, just pick something that fits. You got a name from before you joined the church?"

"Esper. My parents named me Esper Theresa. And I thought you said I couldn't go to the cargo bay."

"That was before I knew you."

---

Carl headed down before Esper got herself settled in enough to want a change of clothes. The interior of the *Mobius* looked like someone had set off an explosive charge in an open-air bazaar. Footlockers lay in poorly stacked heaps, while their contents were strewn across the floor in rough piles by type. One of the footlockers had been repurposed to collect currency found among the luggage. P-tech was jumbled into a rough pile while A-tech was laid out neatly to keep it from getting damaged. Sentimental items were clustered near the bay door, unsettling reminders that everything had once belonged to living people with families and friends of their own. Clothing had the largest share of the space—a two-meter high mountain of cloth made from every sort of plant, animal, and chemical known in ARGO space. Roddy and Mriy were hard at work cutting open the remaining footlockers.

"First impressions?" Carl called out as he crossed the hold. He fished a pair of dark glasses from his jacket pocket to protect against the flare of the plasma torches.

Roddy cut through a lock and flicked his torch off. "They seem harmless enough. Might be nice having a blessing on the ship." He threw back his head and downed the rest of the beer in his hand, tossing the empty can into the pile with the personal items.

"If we end up killing the woman," Mriy said, "may I keep the little one as a pet? I can make up a bed for him in my quarters."

"I meant the loot," Carl replied. "Anything worth keeping?"

"Take your pick of the boutique," Roddy said, jerking the thumb of one foot at the pile of garments. "Everything looks human in there. Nothing my size."

"Mort been down yet?"

"He took one look and said to let him know when we were done," said Roddy. "If you're looking for him, he's probably filling his burger-hole in the lounge, gaping at the holovid."

Mriy shut off her plasma torch. "Carl, come look!" Her pupils were wide behind her welding goggles, nearly circular, her fangs bared in a grin. Roddy beat Carl to Mriy's side, curiosity lending speed to his low-slung body. "This symbol is like the Earth woman's pendant."

Mriy pointed to a book lying atop a pile of folded clothes in the footlocker she had just cut open. Carl was tempted to protest that Esper was Martian, but he was more interested in seeing what her belongings contained. The book's title was *The Holy Bible*, which went along well with the Sister Theresa story. Carl pushed past Mriy and rummaged through the rest. A children's datapad, well scuffed from use. Several articles of women's clothing, all drab and conservative, even the undergarments. A silver box with a few pieces of costume jewelry. Two school uniforms. A tiny case containing toiletries.

"Airlock," Carl said.

"But wait, this is all her stuff, isn't it?" Roddy asked.

"She's on the run with that boy of hers. She's Esper, he's Adam, and there was never a priestess on board. If anyone asks, the boy is her half brother; I'll work out some details if he needs a better cover later."

Mriy pointed to the bible. "Bad business defiling a holy book. I want no part."

Carl pursed his lips and stared down at the book, lying atop the sloppily repacked belongings. The fake gold lettering stared up at him accusingly. The synthetic leather cover was worn from handling; someone had loved that book. He held it up and riffled through to see if anything fell out. The dingy grey paper held no secrets trapped between pages.

It was temping to throw all the problems away at a go. Carl's hand twitched toward the footlocker, to throw it back. "Here, take it back to your quarters if you don't want the bad mojo." He pressed the book into Mriy's hands. "I sent Esper to shower before coming to pick out new clothes from the heap here. You've got 'til she gets out to hide it. Roddy, I'll give you a hand venting this thing to vacuum."

He pointed to each of them, his best captain's glare in his eyes. "Not a word of this. She already mourned this junk once already. No point getting her hopes up, just to smash them. It's gotta go."

"What do I do with this?" Mriy asked, turning the book over in her hands. "I barely read ape."

"Stow it or give it to Mort when Esper's not around. Mort loves books."

---

The cockpit always had the best view, even when there was no view to be had. The Black Ocean went out to infinity, but the eye made you think that the stars were right there just out of arm's reach. Between star systems there was nothing. Lots and lots of nothing. There was more nothing than all the something in the galaxy combined. And it was beautiful. Peaceful.

The inside of the cockpit, however, was anything but. A faint rush from the air circulator never let it get completely silent. Indicator lights demanded attention, even when they had nothing important to show. The navigation display showed an icon representing the *Mobius* surrounded on all sides by void, even with the scale set to maximum; a line still spun around though, constantly updating the lack of anything to see. Jazz poured softly from the speakers. Tanny slouched in the pilot's chair, her feet up on the console, a datapad in hand.

Carl crept up under cover of a Miles Davis piece he could not put a name to. He peered over the pilot's seat and read the datapad Tanny held. He took one more quiet step to the side and threw himself into the copilot's chair, slumping with his legs over the arm. "A hundred men you should never date?" he asked, quoting the article title from the datapad. "How many times am I in there?"

"You keep those hands of yours off the controls or I'll break your wrists," Tanny replied, eyes wide and brow low. Carl held up his hands in the classic bank robbery victim pose. "What do you want?"

"I'm still sorry about Chip."

That took the edge off Tanny. She settled back into her seat and flicked the datapad off. "I'll write something to his folks tomorrow. Not like they have any reason to be expecting anything."

"I can have Mriy come up and watch the void for you, if you'd rather take the night off."

"Someone's gotta cover Chip's shift," said Tanny. "Might as well be me."

"I wanted to talk to you about the priestess we picked up."

"Oh yeah, the prom queen of Uncanny Valley."

"I'm trying to ignore that, but she does sort of have a weird look to her. Almost familiar."

"Did your sisters ever collect dolls?" Tanny asked.

"Holy shit!" said Carl. He slapped a hand gently against his forehead. "Susie Sunshine. Yeah, Jamie collected those. She's a dead ringer."

"Actually it was the Vicky Valentine doll I was thinking of. Same collection though. I used to collect those."

"So what, we've got a doll fanatic aboard?"

Tanny's expression soured. "Nah, those were a while back. I was on the young side to still be playing with those, and I bet I've got eight or ten years on that priestess." Tanny had never been shy about her age—or anything much, really. Carl always liked that about her. "It's probably her mother."

Carl's nose wrinkled as his brow scrunched. "That's sick. How many times you think she had to go under, to look like that?"

Pieces. That was why Carl liked talking to people. No one figured out a whole puzzle on his own, at least not someone like Carl. Different people picked up on different things. It helped being able to tell who was full of shit and who was telling it straight, but talk to enough people and you can get to the bottom of almost anything.

Tanny shrugged. "I'm no vanity surgeon. A dozen, twenty, a hundred? More than she could stomach is a good bet."

"Shitty childhood, runs off to join the church?" Carl asked. Tanny nodded. "Might explain why she took the boy."

"They're not related, are they?"

"Nope, just one lost soul rescuing another."

---

A torrent of water washed over Carl's bare skin. It was tepid, just warm enough not to make him shiver. Still, it felt good to wash away the grime from helping Roddy in the cargo bay. He opened his mouth and gargled the water that filled it. There was a metallic aftertaste when he spat it into the shower drain —the reprocessor was just one more thing for Roddy to fix.

From outside the shower, Carl heard the muffled sound of the ship-wide comm. He reached for the controls and shut off the shower flow. "Carl? CARL? Get your ass up here, pronto!" Tanny shouted over the speakers.

Carl hustled through the ship with a towel around his waist, his hair dripping and his bare feet slapping against the steel deck plates.

"Go find out what's she blathering about," Mort said from his seat on the couch in the common room. Mriy glanced up from the game of Death Arena she was playing against Adam, and the boy did not even flinch from the holovid screen.

Esper poked her head up from the stairwell to Chip's old quarters. "What's going on?" Her cheeks were flushed, and she was short of breath.

Carl did not stop to answer, but continued along the short corridor and up to the cockpit, one hand holding his towel closed.

"What's wrong?" he asked Tanny when he opened the cockpit door.

"Look." She pointed to the console.

It was a text-only communique: UNIDENTIFIED

VESSEL, POWER DOWN AND PREPARE TO BE
BOARDED. ARGO AUTHORITY: (ENV) TALLY-HO.

"What should I say?" she asked after a pause to let Carl
process the message. She leaned away from him. "And stop
dripping on me."

"Full stop. Transmit our coordinates," Carl replied. "Not
like we've got anything to hide. Rather let them rummage
around than risk finding they've started outfitting customs
ships with top-line engines."

"You *sure* we're clean?" Tanny asked. "Like, Navy inspection clean?"

Carl furrowed his brow and ran his fingers through his
dripping hair. "Mort's got our unmentionables sealed up tight.
We've got legit salvage in the hold ..."

"She means me," said Esper from the corridor just outside
the cockpit. She had changed into clothes from the salvage pile
in the cargo hold. Baggy black pants brushed the floor, held in
place by a wide belt. A sleeveless pink blouse covered her to
the neck but left her midriff exposed. At a glance, Carl could
not tell if she wore her pendant beneath it, but she looked
nothing like a priestess.

"You hotter than you let on?" Carl asked. "What
happened to that story about a rescue?"

"The boy's not mine. Even if Harmony Bay didn't report
Adam kidnapped, we can't explain why *we* have him. He's got
parents on Mars."

"Your call," Tanny said, her hands hovering over the
controls.

Carl looked Esper in the eye. She was scared; that much
was plain. But what did it mean? Was she concerned for her
own skin, the boy, or something else she failed to mention?

"Send it," he said, nodding to Tanny. "Wait. On second thought, open a comm."

"Might take a minute. Who knows how far they are behind us? They're not even in sensor range."

Carl ran a hand over the stubble on his face, options whirring in his head. He nodded absently. "You," he said, pointing to Esper, "are the only survivor of that wreck. We pulled you out during the salvage after your escape pod jammed, except you were the only one in it. Got that?"

"I think so."

"I want you to *believe* that's what happened. I'll try to keep them from asking you too many questions; you just had a major shock after all. But if they do, you've gotta keep them off Adam's trail. Now go back and tell Mort to stash Adam in his quarters. Clean out Chip's bunk and take anything Adam touched and send it with Mort, too. Go."

Esper nodded and hurried back down the corridor.

Tanny closed her eyes and shook her head. "You never change."

"The easy way's never the best one. Once you start running from every little thing, you can't ever stop."

The console beeped. Tanny keyed the comm. "Unidentified ship, this is Earth Navy Vessel Tally-ho. Coordinates received. Hold position and prepare for customs inspection per ARGO transportation code 97312.3.1." The voice was smooth and professional, as bland an Earth accent as you could get, shy of a computer.

Carl smiled. There was something familiar about that voice. He reached for the button to open the mic. Tanny slapped his hand away. He reached around her on the other side, and she slapped his hand again. "Stop that."

"Get out of my cockpit and dry off."

"Just ... key it for me, then. Would you?"

Tanny pursed her lips, but held down the button as requested. *"Tally-ho,* this is *Mobius.* Your signal checks out. Can't be too careful this far out in the Black Ocean. You won't get any trouble out of us. Thanks for keeping the borderlands safe. *Mobius* out." He nodded to Tanny and she closed the comm.

"What?"

"What what?"

"That grin."

"I thought you liked surprises," said Carl. He slicked back his dripping hair and flicked droplets of water in Tanny's direction as he left the cockpit.

"I hate surprises," she called after him. "You *know* that."

---

Carl came up the steps from his quarters two at a time, bending in half at the waist to keep from hitting his head on the ceiling of the narrow stairwell. He was dried and dressed, wearing denims and his battered leather jacket. Once he reached the common room, he had the overhead clearance to pull on an equally battered old Earth Navy dress cap. He stopped and blinked to take in the scene before him.

"The hell's all this?" he asked. Esper sat at the edge of one of the dinner table chairs, back straight and hands clasped as if they were keeping each other from running away screaming. Mriy was lying spread full length on the couch, asleep to all appearances, her bare feet twitching. On the kitchen counter, Roddy was four-fisting cans of Earth's Preferred. The tables in the kitchen and rec areas of the common room were both arrayed with the personal weapons the crew kept on board, from blades to blasters—it was the only thing Carl could see that was right about the picture.

"What?" Esper asked, jerking her head around at the sound of his voice.

"I asked you all to be ready when they got here," said Carl, spreading his arms.

Roddy belched. "You expect me to be civil while I'm sober?"

"Relaxed. Amiable. Helpful. What I see is scared shitless, sleeping, and half-drunk." He grabbed two of the beers away from Roddy. He plunked one of them down on the table by Esper, between a stun rifle and one of Mriy's bone dueling knives. "Drink up."

"But I don't—"

"Can it," said Carl. "And I mean *can* it. You can't be tight as an E-string when the inspection crew gets here."

He took the second beer over to Mriy and held the can as if to pour it over her face as she lay snoring softly. There was no flinch; she really was asleep. Much as he hated *ever* waking her, he took a swig of the beer himself and kicked the couch. Mriy stirred and opened one eye in a squint.

"They here yet?" Mriy asked. She yawned, revealing a mouth full of fangs the size of Carl's fingers—and stinking of rotted *taru*.

"Tanny's feeding them candy glass down in the hold," Roddy replied. He took a chug of his beer. "They've Navy though, so there's only so long she's gonna be able to put up a smiley for them."

"We had candy left?" Carl asked.

"Hell, no," Roddy replied. "Figurative ... you know."

Hearing footsteps coming up from below, Carl threw himself against the nearest wall, feigning a casual slouch. He pulled his navy cap low and crossed his arms. A grin worked itself onto his face, but he fought it back and relaxed his facial muscles before the footsteps reached the common room.

"Which one of you is captain of this ship?" The navy officer who spoke was soft and doughy, with a crisp navy blue uniform making his build appear solid rather than sloppy. He carried a datapad and wore a blaster sidearm at his hip. He scanned the room with professional annoyance.

"Hey, Dingo? What're you up to out past nowhere? They punish you for something?" Carl asked.

The navy officer's eyes narrowed. "Who the hell are—?" Carl pushed up the brim of his cap and smiled. "Blackjack, you bastard! How've you been? Wait, don't answer that; must be shitty if you're flying this heap of castoff parts."

"Hey, don't talk about my crew like that," Carl replied with indignation. He addressed the crew scattered around the room, including Tanny, who lingered in the doorway. "This is an old buddy of mine, Ted Wellington. He used to be a half decent fighter pilot before he put on twenty kilos and those scrambled eggs on his collar."

"Hey, I outrank *you* now, hotshot," Wellington replied.

"I promoted myself to captain when I bought *Mobius*," Carl replied.

Wellington snorted. "You retired as a Lieutenant Commander though, and that's what really counts. You can call yourself emperor of this tub for all I care."

"Retired?" Carl scoffed. "Do I *look* retired to you? You were the in the hold. I was on that transport, hauling salvage right along with the rest of my crew."

"About that ... I'm going to need records of that salvage op. Your first officer told me ..." Wellington trailed off. He paused to look at Tanny. "I thought you looked familiar. Tanny?"

She smiled. "Hey, Dingo. I didn't recognize your voice over the comm, but Carl did, apparently."

"Carl?"

"My middle name. I stopped going by Brad when I mustered out. Keeps things compartmentalized. Anyone who calls me Brad's from back home. Don't hear Blackjack much these days."

"So what's Carl do with a hodgepodge old diplomatic shuttle with more scrapyard parts than original?"

Carl shrugged. "Little of this and that."

A pair of marines entered with blaster rifles at the ready, as if Carl and his crew were going to ambush them. Behind them, a small squadron of techs tromped in with scanning equipment.

"Hey, watch it with that stuff," Roddy said from the counter. He gestured with a beer can at the navy scanners.

"Ahh, yes," Wellington said, as if noticing the other crew members for the first time. "She mentioned you had a couple xenos aboard."

"Wait a minute, now. Roddy's a full citizen. Phabian Two is an ARGO member."

"I'll verify that, but *that* isn't," Wellington said, hooking a thumb at Mriy. Her eyes tracked him, but no other part of her moved. "You running a ship or a zoo?"

"C'mon Dingo, ease off," Carl said. "What're you boys doing tossing a little freighter like we were big bad pirates?"

Wellington raised an eyebrow. "I'm just hoping you're not smuggling anything. For an old pal, if you want to mention anything I might find that ... shall we say ... might not look good in an official report, I might be able to take care of it discreetly."

"I'm clean as your service record," Carl said with a grin.

There was no objecting to that one with four of Wellington's own crew in the room. One of the techs cast him a surreptitious glance to check for a reaction. Wellington just frowned slightly.

"Have it your way."

"Just a 'so-you-know-it,' my ship's wizard is in the forward port cabin. I told him to stay there until you were done your inspection."

Wellington gave Carl a beleaguered glare. "You *know* I'm going to have to search his quarters. The old 'my wizard hates scanners' bit got old years ago."

"Mine's a little rough on A-tech," Carl replied. "You just might want to watch out for your shiny toys when you interview him."

"Another dreg in a crew of dregs?" Wellington glanced over at Tanny. "No offense. A grav-jockey who can't keep his magic in check for a simple scan?"

"Mort? Mort's not my star-drive mechanic. He's more like a partner—old family friend who comes along to see the sights. Keeping 'dark science' from invading his innards is a reflex. Just a warning, do whatever you want. I'm not the one who'll be stranded out in nowhere's back garden without a scanner and trying to explain it in a report."

"Fine. Give me his biographicals, and I can at least run a manual check in the system."

"His name's Mordecai The Brown, from Boston Prime, born—"

"Wait, I need his official name, not his professional title," said Wellington. Roddy snickered.

"That *is* his given name. Whole family's got "The" as a middle name; it's traditional. He's got a sister who married into the name Sarajah The McGowan."

The two techs exchanged a worried look.

———

Mort sat on the edge of his bed with his hands tucked into opposing sleeves of his sweatshirt. It was, all things considered, a dignified, wizardly pose. At his elbow sat a ten-year-old boy trying to mimic him, fingers trying to worm their way into sleeves to snug for them to fit. Mort elbowed Adam in the side to get him to stop fidgeting. One of the two techs scouring the room glanced over at Mort, but the wizard glared at her until she went back to her work.

"You know," the tech said to her colleague, "when the commander said we'd be checking a wizard's quarters, I expected more ..."

"More magic?" the other tech asked.

"Yeah," the female tech replied. "This stuff's all phony. The staff, the robes, it's like costume wizardry."

Adam looked at Mort with a question plain in his eyes. Mort put a finger to his lips and winked.

The techs opened the closet door, revealing Mort's drab wardrobe, as well as a hastily piled assortment of military-grade blaster power packs. They looked it over, each using their scanning equipment. Mort could only guess, but he assumed one was checking for magical objects, and the other for more mundane contraband.

"You sure you're a wizard?" the female tech asked. "Not just a street magician or something?"

Mort tapped his index fingers together, producing a spark. He graced the tech with a genial smile, but said nothing. She went back to her work, opening the cover to Mort's bookshelf and scanning the volumes. Mort squinted at the scanner, trying to make sense of the red blinking lights and flashing text that the tech was ignoring.

"Well, that'll do it," the male tech said.

"Yeah, I'm finished here, too," the female tech replied. "Sorry for the inconvenience."

When the door clanged shut behind them, Adam let out a long breath and slouched. "How did they not see me?"

Mort shrugged. "I don't know what those scientists left in that noggin of yours, but remember this: never fight a wizard on his own turf."

"The scanners *did* find stuff though."

Mort tapped a finger to his temple. "I de-attention-ified them. They could have been in a navy surplus yard or the grand chamber of the Convocation, they would have found the same thing: jack squat."

---

Esper sat frozen to her seat, staring at the back side of Commander Wellington's datapad. She could not look up into his eyes; couldn't even say what color they were. He held the scanning wand in front of her eye and a soft light shone briefly over her face.

"Miss Esper Theresa Richelieu," Wellington addressed her, butchering her last name and adding an extra syllable to it. "Says here you're from Mars. Where about?"

"New Singapore," she replied. The datapad must have said so. If that was the commander's idea of a test, maybe this wouldn't be so bad.

"There's no occupation listed. What is it you do for a living?"

"I'm currently between jobs," Esper replied.

"I understand you were the lone survivor of the *Regulon*," Wellington said. It was not a question, exactly, but he paused for a response.

Esper nodded. The back of the datapad was a light grey, the color of a pigeon's feathers, or a storm cloud. The hand that held it was thick-fingered, and one of those fingers bore a wedding band. It was simple in style, like the one Carl wore.

"Can you describe the events leading up to your ship's destruction?"

Esper swallowed. Wellington's cuff was starched stiff, and there was a comm built into it. It had false cufflinks with brass naval insignia. "I was just a passenger. First I knew of it was when the horns sounded that we were under attack. The ship shook a number of times, and there was an announcement to get to the escape pods. I got to mine late. I ... I had to launch it myself. I don't know if it was damaged or I did it wrong, but I got the pod stuck. Carl and his crew rescued me; a man named Chip died cutting me free." A fresh pang of guilt jabbed her in the stomach.

Esper's eyes strayed to Carl, sitting on the arm of the couch with the two armed marines looming over him. Immediately she focused on the back of the datapad once more. There was a scratch on the corner, perhaps two centimeters long. Parts of the back were worn smoother than the rest, near where Wellingon's fingers rubbed.

"And the identity of the attacking vessel?" Wellington asked. His tone hardened. This was what he really wanted. Esper relaxed, but tried not to show it, remaining stiff in her seat.

"I have no idea. Carl would know better than I," she replied. "I wasn't in any position to find out who attacked us."

"You're sure?" Wellington pressed. "No one rushing for

the escape pods said anything? Mentioned a ship name? Described it?"

Esper shook her head. "No. Nothing."

"If you want, you can come aboard my ship. They can't hurt you, you're an ARGO citizen, and you're under my protection."

Esper's eyes darted to Carl for a fraction of a second, but Carl was gazing off into space, watching the stars through the glass panels in the common room roof. "I really have no idea."

Wellington tapped something on the datapad and it beeped. "Very well. I've recorded that as your official statement. You can go if you like."

Esper nodded and headed for the stairwell to her borrowed quarters, treading the line between unseemly haste and lingering a single moment longer than she had to.

"You're an ass, Dingo," she heard Carl say just before shutting the door and buying herself enough privacy to sit down and cry.

———

Half an hour later, and with all the crew interviewed, the inspection and scanning crews reported in. Carl had lost count of them, but apparently there had been a dozen junior naval officers swarming through his little ship like bees in a hive. Wellington let Carl sit and listen to the officers' reports.

"... parts all have IDNs, none in the database as stolen ..."

"... this tub has a heavier shield generator than the *Tally-ho*. I don't think the engines even throw enough juice to fully power it ..."

"... guns check out. This thing is armed like an escort

frigate, but all the readings are in the approved civilian range ... just *barely* ..."

"... no contraband, including the salvage. Looks like this lot wasted a lot of time cutting out the computer cores. No data anywhere. Must have been a hellacious EMP ..."

Carl swore under his breath. He had been counting on selling the cores with the data intact. Blanked and possibly EMP damaged, a transport's computers were worth only their spare-parts value.

"... no sign of stowaways, unreported crew or passengers, and no unauthorized plant or animal life. The two xenos have been IDed as Rodek of Kethlet, ARGO citizen from Phabian II, and an azrin from Meyang VII. We can't verify her claimed identity until we get signal from the core, but she says her name is Mriy Yrrsis ..."

Wellington nodded along with the reports as they came in, each officer departing for the airlock as he or she was dismissed. When they finished, just Wellington and his two marines remained with Carl, Tanny, Mriy, and Roddy in the common room.

"You people seem to be looking for trouble," Wellington observed, giving a nod to the pile of weapons spread on the table. He picked up a sword from the pile and drew it from its scabbard, revealing a black graphite blade with a graceful curve. "This isn't the sort of thing they taught in that fencing elective in flight school. You even know how to use one of these?"

"Not really," Carl replied. "But I'm a shit aim with a blaster, too, so what's the difference? It's sharp, won't ricochet off energy shields, and works around active magic." He shrugged. "I like to be prepared."

"Prepared ..." Wellington said. He slid the sword back into

its scabbard. "Prepared like having engines running on three different fuel sources, guns that I'm lucky you're not aiming at my ship, a shield generator that you can't even get up to full power on a dinghy like this, and more obsidian-hardened systems than I've seen in a space-faring vessel."

"I heard obsidian keeps the gravity nice," Carl said sheepishly.

Wellington bounced on the balls of his feet. "Well, I'll say that much for you. This *is* nice gravity. You wouldn't believe how many times we get stuck combing through zero-g heaps. Crazy spacers who never set foot in a gravity well." He shook his head.

"You're welcome," said Tanny flatly. She sat with her arms crossed on the couch, willing Wellington off the ship. She had a special talent for making someone feel unwelcome. She had never gotten on with Wellington, even when they had first met.

"I've gotta ask, or it'll kill me wondering: what do you *do* with this thing?" Wellington asked. "I can't cite you for anything. You're a millimeter from breaking a dozen regulations, but you haven't. Why go to the trouble?"

Carl smirked. "I like feeling safe, but I want to see the sights in the galaxy. I don't want to be stuck where Earth Navy can protect me. Some folks pay good money to deliver things interesting places. I like good money."

"And yet you're cutting dead computer core from derelict transports?"

Carl raised his palms. "Work's been a little scarce."

"And what about your crew? No offense to any of you," Wellington added hastily. "But what the hell, Blackjack? You used to be an ace, now you're ... and these ... you let your ex-wife fly your ship for you?"

"They threatened to mutiny if I kept flying *Mobius*," Carl replied. "He may be mine, but the crew aren't. Tanny flew troop transports, and that's the sort of ride my crew prefers. They kept thinking they were going to die with me flying, so it was either let Tanny pilot, or watch everyone leave *Mobius*. Speaking of which ..."

Wellington nodded. "Yeah. So long, Captain Ramsey. Blackjack's a long way in your ion trail, huh?"

That evening, the crew and guests of the Mobius all gathered in the common room, under a ceiling that showed the stars above. The ship was on auto-pilot, limping out of ARGO controlled space. The *Tally-ho* had gone back to its own patrol route. The food fabricator was churning out dinner after dinner as everyone settled in to eat.

"I can't believe you did that for me," Esper said. "Thank you all so much."

"Mort did all the hard work," said Carl. "I nearly gave myself a hernia not laughing when those two wet-eared techs came out of your quarters like they'd just wasted their time."

"Think nothing of it," Mort replied. Roddy tossed a hamburger across the room, and it slowed to a drift as Mort collected it and reassembled the pieces that had drifted apart in flight. "I enjoy practicing the subtler arts once in a while. Their scanners were no match for my magic."

"You could have let me do all the hard work," Mriy said, slumping back on the couch with Adam tucked under her arm. She had eaten first and quickest, and was already finished.

"We'd have two ships and plenty of money once we sold theirs."

"Last thing we need is ARGO hunting us down," said Tanny. "Don't we have enough enemies as it is?"

A quiet hung in the air as everyone carefully avoided delving into that particular subject. The only sounds were of eating and the ding of the food processor finishing meals.

"Guy was an asshole," Roddy said, breaking the silence. "Can't believe you were friends with that xenophobe."

"Friends?" Carl scoffed. "We called him Penny-Toad until he earned his wings. One of those spoiled navy brats who shows up to flight school with an admiral's last name. I made his life hell for a good two years."

"Should have done it my way," Mriy muttered, flexing a hand and extending her claws.

Carl winked at her. "I was tempted."

---

That night, Tanny sat alone in the cockpit, reading. There was no guessing the *Tally-ho's* sensor range, and they did not want to do anything but a slow drift until they were sure *Mobius* had some privacy. No matter their speed, the view outside the glassteel windows remained the same. There were times when she stopped to contemplate the dissonance of the ship. Outside, the majestic infinity, separated from them by a void so vast it defied imagination, with nothing but stray hydrogen atoms for light years. Inside, the sweat and stink of a half dozen sentients, the thrum of the engines through the ship, and the sound of Caro Jay and the Brainwaves trying to drown out Mriy and Mort's holovid blood sports.

A soft knock on the cockpit door startled her. Tanny

juggled the datapad she was reading and pulled her feet off the co-pilot's armrest. "Who's there?" It was a stupid question, she knew. None of the crew knocked.

"It's me," Esper replied through the door. "Can I come in?"

Tanny opened the cockpit door. "Just don't touch anything."

Esper sat down gingerly in the co-pilot's seat and closed the door. "You know the captain well, right?"

Tanny opened her mouth to say something scathing. Something about Esper's earnestness gave her pause. "Not as well as you might think. But yeah, I guess I know Carl well enough."

"Please, if this is too personal, just tell me," said Esper. "I mean, you were married to him after all. But—"

"But what?"

"Can I trust him?"

Tanny burst out laughing. Esper paled, which was a trick considering how pale she started out. Tanny held up her hands to placate the priestess. "I'm sorry, but you just asked the trillionaire question there, didn't you?"

"He explained how to deceive that commander so simply. I ... I can't imagine I got away with it. He must be a lot better himself."

She was a delicate creature, inside and out. Tanny had known girls like her; maybe not ones that looked so mannequin perfect, but ones that got by on looks and trust and luck. "Listen to me. You're a big girl now, and you can do whatever you want. But if you give that man your heart, he will put it in his back pocket and forget about it when he sits down. I can already see the little twinkles in your eye when you look at him. Snuff 'em out quick, or it'll hurt. I used to think I knew him better, that I could tell when he was being honest. Well, I've divorced him three times."

"Three times?" Esper asked, gaping at Tanny. "How the h — why would you do that?"

"The man can talk a pretzel straight, and be sweet enough to rot your teeth."

"Why do you still fly with him?"

"He's a good man and a good boss, just a shitty husband. Don't go breaking any vows over him; he's not worth it."

---

The stairs clanged beneath Carl's boots as he took them two at a time up to the common room. Mort sat on the couch with Adam, the two of them engrossed in a game of Omnithrust Racer. Carl hadn't even known they had a copy of it in the ship's computer, but right then he didn't care.

"We're good," said Carl, catching his breath. "Roddy's got everything back the way it belongs and Tanny just got me on the comm to say that the Tally-ho's been out of our sensor range for six hours—hopefully that puts us out of theirs."

Mort grunted.

Carl turned his attention to the racing game and saw that the two of them were neck and neck in the final straightaway of a course called "Tri-star Deathway," according to the in-game display. Mort rarely played active games, but was faring surprisingly well. With any luck he wouldn't get steamed and accidentally fry the controller if he lost.

"Yes!" Adam shouted, jumping from his seat. "That's five in a row!" The game played a victory theme as Adam's racer crossed the line in first place. Carl didn't know if he was better off congratulating the kid for winning or making fun of him for beating an old wizard who couldn't work a datapad.

Carl took the remote and shut off the display. "We're good for astral any time, Mort."

"Kid's lucky, that's all," he grumbled. He threw the controller across the room. Just before it smashed against the wall, it slowed to a drift and set itself gently into its recharger. "How deep you need us?"

"Nothing fancy," Carl replied. "Just someplace with a little zip, and none of the standard depths."

Mort disappeared into his room and returned with a gnarled staff of authentic, Earth-grown oak, older than everyone on board the *Mobius* put together. Carl had never thought to ask, but he had always assumed it pre-dated the ban on cutting trees in Earth's preserves. As Mort took up a position in the center of the common room, Carl keyed the comm panel by the door. "Keep out of the common room for a minute. Mort's taking us astral."

It was easy at times to think of Mort as just a grumpy old man who hated science. But watching him plant his staff in the center of the floor and begin his chant, it was hard to think of him as anything but a wizard. The words *felt* old, even though he had no idea what they meant. If God were the swearing type, Carl imagined that He would use some of those words in doing it. As the chant continued, symbols around the periphery of the common room floor began to glow a dull green.

"What are those?" Adam asked in a whisper, gaping at the sight.

"Nothing to worry about," Carl whispered back. Mort didn't get distracted easily, but it never hurt to be cautious. "We just do astral drive the old-fashioned way around here."

"I mean on the floor."

Carl shrugged. "Glyphs. Mort knows what they all do; ask him when he's done if you want to know."

Adam nodded absently, still staring at Mort.

When the chant ended, the glow in the glyphs faded and disappeared. Mort slouched down with a sigh and headed back to his quarters with the staff. "I need a nap."

"How deep did you put us?" Carl asked. While the thrusters of the *Mobius* could send them in any direction through real space, it took wizardry to move perpendicular to reality. Wizards had dubbed the region where space compressed the "astral plane," and the deeper a ship went, the faster it traveled relative to normal space. There were industry and guild standards that kept astral drive users slotted into standard depths, forming "lanes" and keeping communication and rescue efforts organized.

Mort just pointed over his shoulder at the speaker for the comm. A few seconds later, as Mort left the room, it crackled with Tanny's voice from the cockpit. "We're at a depth of six point eight, two, two and holding. Is Mort done?"

Carl hit the comm button with the butt of his fist. "Yeah, he's going to nap it off. We're good to go."

"Soon as I convince the nav computer that this depth is legit, we'll get underway. We should be at Willamette Station in a little over three hours."

Adam's head snapped up. "How's that possible? It should be days from here."

Carl gave the boy a sidelong glance. "You some expert on astral travel?" he asked with a chuckle. "We don't keep Mort around for his personality."

The Kearny system was just outside of what ARGO officially claimed as protected territory. None of the worlds were inhabited, but three of them showed promise for future terraforming. Kearny III and Kearny IV were two planets in the habitable zone with liquid water but no breathable atmosphere. The only ones living there were part of tiny colonies dedicated to scientific research. Set in a solar orbit between the two was Willamette Station. It was a floating outpost of commerce and civilization amid the lifeless system.

It also looked like a scrapyard that had developed its own gravity. There was no grand plan for the station's layout or architecture. It had been founded when a pre-fab orbital habitat was hijacked by pirates and placed in orbit in the system. From there, it expanded when opportunistic businessmen convinced the owners that it could make money as a fueling station, then as a supply depot, and later as a refuge for those looking to do their business free from the overbearing eyes of ARGO patrols. Earth Navy designated the station and the surrounding system as lawless, but Willamette Station had plenty of rules.

Tanny guided the *Mobius* into the hangar they'd been assigned by Willamette traffic control. A faint blue haze parted for them as the ship pushed through the air lock force field. Dingy yellow overheads gave the hangar bay a sickly look, but the structure appeared solid. As they set down with a soft thump, barely noticeable due to the ship's gravity compensator, a set of doors slid into place to cover the air lock. Carl hated in-hangar berths on space stations for that reason; watching from the cockpit, it made him feel like his ship was being devoured.

"We're secured," Roddy's voice came over the comm.

Carl keyed the ship-wide comm. "We're down, everyone. Enjoy the amenities while we're here, but be back by oh-nine-hundred ship time tomorrow."

On his way down to the cargo hold, he nearly ran into Esper and Adam. Pulling up short of the startled former priest-ess, he stuck out his hand. "Nice having you aboard. Good luck with the kid." He tousled Adam's hair, which prompted a flinch and a grimace from the boy. "You take good care of her, too. I find out you given her any trouble, I'll sic Mriy on you." He winked, in case Adam couldn't tell he was joking.

The cargo bay door was open when Carl arrived. Roddy had just finished loading crates with their haul onto an anti-grav sled. It was too quick a job for Carl's liking. A few pulsed computer cores and an assortment of semi-valuable personal effects weren't much to refuel a starship on. He just hoped he could get enough for the escape pod to make up for the damage to the transport's computers. They were leaving the pod in the ship, because it was either that or leave everything else behind; it would have taken the whole anti-grav sled to haul it. It was easy enough to describe to anyone who'd buy that sort of thing.

"Hop on," Roddy said, jerking the thumb of his right foot toward the passenger seat.

Carl climbed aboard, smiling ruefully that no one even let him drive a grav sled—not that he'd have wanted to. It was just the principle of the matter. The sled sagged momentarily under Carl's weight before it readjusted to the imbalance, but never came back fully level. "Shitty rentals. We should buy one of our own one of these days."

"Maybe you should stick to vegetables," Roddy replied. "Your species isn't cut out to be omnivorous."

"It's not me; it's the sled!"

Roddy shook his head and cracked open a can of beer. "You keep telling yourself that." The sled needed just two hands to drive, and that left Roddy free to drink and pilot at the same time.

The sled whizzed past the rest of the crew as they disembarked, and Carl held up a hand to wave. Esper noticed and raised a hand in reply. Adam just stood with his arms folded and his jaw set, eyes scanning the landing zone. There seemed something shrewd in the look, but Carl passed the notion off as the work of his imagination baiting his natural paranoia.

Tanny and Mriy would probably be off to find a holo-relay to watch—something with a bigger viewer than the *Mobius* boasted, and with new vids in from civilized space. If he was lucky, they'd poke around for a job while they were out. Mort would stay in the ship; Willamette Station wasn't the sort of place that appreciated wizards. It was self-contained, fully sci-dependent for life support, with no outside atmosphere to fall back on. A magic-related mishap was the last thing anyone aboard wanted.

He hoped Esper and Adam managed to find a cheap ride back to ARGO space, but it didn't seem likely. One of the downsides of living outside civilized space was that people charge extra to take you to and from it. They'd claim it was because of security worries, or because of concerns over having a passenger who was the sort who dealt outside the law, but it mostly came down to supply and demand. There weren't a thousand transports leaving every hour, like the Earth-Mars shuttle service. Ten departures taking passengers might be a good day, and that was if you weren't picky about getting to your destination directly.

"They'll be fine," Roddy said, catching Carl looking back.

"How can you be sure?"

Roddy chuckled. "They survived being with us. It's all auto-pilot for them from here."

---

Sprokytz was a typical junker. The equipment was all franchise-bought, the decor gaudy, with too many flashing lights and oversaturated colors. The three laakus working behind the counter passed items from one to the next, turning them over and examining each in detail. They muttered to one another in low voices, cognizant that Carl could understand their language—and of course, Roddy was one of their own kind. Outside in what passed for a road within Willamette station, two more laaku techs scanned the computer cores.

Carl browsed the shelves, daring any part of the oddball collection to catch his eye. A set of analog binoculars. A few well-worn kids' toys. A datapad twenty years out of date. A little statue of someone's idea of a well-endowed frog. Crap, the lot of it. Roddy was at the inventory kiosk, poking through the ship equipment Sprokytz kept in the warehouse.

"Anything worthwhile?" Carl asked, looking over Roddy's shoulder. He had to bend down, since the screen was placed at a height that was a compromise between human ergonomic standard and laaku common accommodation.

Roddy didn't look up. "I could build us a new ship from this stuff."

"Anything we can afford?"

"Not unless you've been holding out on us," Roddy replied.

"I wish," Carl said, eyes drawn to the 2D image of a pair of XK-80 ion thrusters with fifty percent higher power output than the *Mobius's* main engines. They were meant for an in-system racer, but that sort of detail had never stopped Roddy before. The *Mobius* was a testament to his ability to force disparate components into a working vessel.

Roddy cleared his throat. "You know, I never saw Chip spending much of his own share ..."

Carl gave him a dirty look. "And you never saw him digitize it as fast as he earned it? You know he didn't trust hard currency."

"Well, maybe if you ... or maybe Tanny happened to know his encryption code ..."

"Even if I did, I'm not robbing my own crew," Carl replied. "That money goes to his family ... assuming anyone can even get at it. He never left *me* any codes."

"Tanny's his cousin."

"Just drop it."

Roddy sighed, looking longingly at the XK-80 ion engines. "That pile of shit we brought in won't come close."

"Maybe with the escape pod," Carl said. "It's in perfect working order. That's gotta be rare as rain around here."

Jekjo walked in from inspecting the computer cores. The laaku wiped an upper hand on his coveralls to clean away some of the grime and offered it to Carl. "Thanks for stopping by," he said as he and Carl shook. Of all the non-terrestrial races, the laakus had most thoroughly adapted to live according to human norms. They learned Earth Standard English in primary school, watched human-made holos, and generally tried to act as human as their physiology allowed. Jekjo and his gang were old-fashioned, living outside ARGO space and keeping the old language, but Earth had rubbed off on them anyway.

"What're you going to give me for the lot?" Carl asked.

Jekjo looked to his crew behind the counter. A series of

looks and subtle gestures passed between them. Carl didn't bother trying to puzzle any of it out; it was their own signaling system. Carl exchanged a look of his own with Roddy, and didn't like what he saw. Roddy could read Jekjo's body language better than he could, and Carl could already feel the pain in his bank account. He was disappointed before Jekjo even came back with a number.

"Eight hundred for the personals, thirty five for the cores," Jejko pronounced after the conference concluded.

Carl's eyes shot wide. "You can't be serious. I was upfront about the cores being blanked; you don't have to put the screws to me over it. Those are worth at least five-k to you."

"I'm being generous on the personals because I like you, Carl," Jekjo replied, lifting his hands in a helpless gesture. "You bring me stuff I can turn around pretty easy most times. This lot though ... it's a dud."

"I also got an escape pod, came through in good shape, just needs a recharge on the life support." Carl had hoped the pod would be icing on the cake. Now, he was just hoping to eat the icing.

"You said that it was a Berring class passenger transport?" Jekjo asked. Carl nodded, and Jekjo laughed. "There's more escape pods for those heaps than you could ever fit onto the working ships. Those things are death traps. That thing'd be taking up space in my warehouse for years."

"Someone could use it for a refit," Roddy suggested.

Jekjo ignored him, and Carl felt a brief pang for his friend. Roddy did better dealing with laakus who didn't know him personally. "How much can you give me?" Carl asked, firing the thrust reversers on his expectations.

Jekjo shook his head. "I can shove the jewelry and knick-knacks on a shelf and let them take up space, but I can't afford to waste the room a worthless escape pod will take up. Can't do it."

"Rryzgat!" Carl swore, continually amused that his translator charm never converted the curses Mriy had taught him from her language. It certainly gave its best effort when he heard her use them.

"What's that?" Jekjo asked, narrowing his simian eyes.

"Nothing," Roddy said. "We'll take the forty-three hundred for the lot."

Jekjo picked at something in his teeth as he sized them up. "OK. You've got yourself a—"

"What if we threw in the grav sled?" Carl asked. Forty-three hundred was cutting things close. Even splitting things one fewer way, the ship's share plus his own was barely going to cover fuel.

Roddy shot Carl a panicked look, which Carl pretended not to notice.

"That's a rental," Jekjo said with a frown.

"Bought it refurb," Carl replied. "Got sick of renting one in every port. Figured I'd save a few terras having my own."

Jekjo exchanged some gestures with his gang behind the counter, who had kept a respectful vigil as their boss negotiated. "I assume you've got documentation to back that up?" Jekjo asked.

Carl grinned. "Of course not. Same as you, I don't keep anything on file that I don't have to produce for an ARGO inspection."

Jekjo stared at him for a moment. Carl could imagine the math at work in the laaku's head. They both knew it was theft, but on a station the size of Willamette, it was something that could get done. Jekjo could sit on the sled until Dynamik

Transport wrote it off and forgot the whole matter; Carl would steer clear of the Kearny system for a while.

"I'll give you thirteen thousand for it," Jekjo offered. The crew behind the counter bobbed their heads in concurrence.

"Fifteen," Carl countered.

Jekjo scowled. "Why can't you people ever take an offer at face value?"

"Because I know you take the haggling into account. Besides, you'll turn it around for a solid thirty."

"Fine. That's ninety thousand eight hundred," Jekjo said. He stuck out a hand again and Carl shook it.

"Hard cash, of course," Carl said with a wink.

---

They returned to the *Mobius* on foot, picking their way through the crowds on the pedestrian overpasses as anti-grav vehicles sped by beneath. The smells from the restaurants tugged at Carl's stomach, begging him to enter with scents of grilled meats and fresh bread. But there was a heap of money in his pocket, most of it belonging to his crew, and Carl felt the weight of it sagging his pockets. He needed to get back to the ship and at least stow Tanny, Mort, and Mriy's shares. Roddy insisted on skimming his cut before they left the Sprokytz.

"You know we lose our deposit on that grav-sled," Roddy reminded him.

"Yup."

"You know we're in a heap of trouble when we leave port without returning it," Roddy added.

Carl shrugged. "We report it stolen, we apologize ... they'll get over it."

"What're we gonna do with that damn escape pod? Air-lock it once we get out of system?"

"Nah," Carl replied. "We'll keep trying. Someone's bound to take it off our hands."

As they approached the *Mobius*, they saw Esper pacing the hangar outside. She was still dressed in the clothes she had taken from the haul; Carl had assumed a clothing store would have been one of her first stops. She was wringing her hands and watching the entrance. When Carl and Roddy approached she perked up instantly.

"He's gone!" she said. She hurried over to intercept Carl. "I don't know what to do."

Carl shrugged. "He's got to be around somewhere. He'll turn up. Have you considered asking the local cops? They're not the most pleasant bunch, but they oughta have a soft spot for a lost kid."

Esper pursed her lips and frowned. "I'm not his legal guardian. I can't get help from anyone official ..."

"She's right on that one," Roddy said. "They'll probably think she's after a bounty."

Carl snickered and glanced up and down the wispy priest-ess. "Her?"

"Some of 'em are pretty good actors," said Roddy, wagging a finger.

"Well, what do you expect us to do?" Carl asked. "We're not cops. Hire someone local to help you."

"I don't know anyone local," Esper protested. "Everyone seems so ... sinful. I don't know who to trust. You treated me and Adam like guests."

"I guess by local standards, we *are* pretty respectable," said Roddy.

Carl cast him a sidelong we-just-sold-a-rented-grav-sled

look, and Roddy gave a subtle shrug in reply.

"I imagine his parents can reward you if you help me get him home," Esper said. She looked at Carl with such pleading hope in her eyes.

Carl sighed, his resolve no match for a girl in trouble. "Fine. Lemme get Tanny and Mriy on the comm." He pulled out his pocket comm link. "Hey, why didn't you ask Mort to help? You wouldn't have had to wait outside for us."

"I'm a little afraid of Mort."

Roddy's shoulders shook in a silent chuckle.

Carl spoke into his comm. "Tanny, are you with Mriy? ... good, get back to the *Mobius* ... yeah, it's urgent ... Adam's missing ... yes, I agreed already." He flicked the comm off. "They're on their way."

Carl and Tanny jostled their way through the crowds of Willamette Station, past noodle shops and tattoo parlors, palm readers and black market drug smugglers with their own store fronts, courier services and holo-vid parlors. It wasn't the sort of place most people brought children, especially not their own. The ones who did were mostly hardened sorts, the ones that didn't expect anything more from their offspring than to take over the reins of their own ill-won criminal enterprises. Adam ought to have stood out like a puppy in a pigsty.

"Have you seen my nephew?" Carl asked a clean-cut man in a navy surplus coat. "Ten years old, light brown hair, about yeah high."

The man in the navy coat jerked back like Carl had a skin condition that looked contagious. "Human?" he asked.

"Of course he's human, gene-spliced mule, what do I look

—never mind."

Carl took Tanny by the hand and led her away. They were posing as husband and wife, a micron-thin cover identity that she hated, but agreed to in order not to raise suspicion when looking for a child. Her grip just about cut off circulation to Carl's fingers, warning him that he was getting too close to his cover story.

Tanny flagged down a young couple who seemed like they might prove sympathetic. "We're looking for a lost boy: human, ten, skinny with brown hair. Have you seen him?"

They looked at one another. "I think so," the woman said. "Blue eyes?"

Tanny froze. Carl bit the inside of his cheek to keep from crying out at the pain in his hand as she tightened her grip reflexively. "Uh, yeah."

"I saw him with a couple mercs in body armor," the woman said. "I think maybe they're station security. I couldn't say for sure; this is our first time outside ARGO space. Isn't it exciting?" She smiled, revealing all gold teeth—body-mod fanatic. When Carl looked closer, he noticed that her ears were slit to look like flower petals, and there were diamonds set into the whites of her eyes.

"Thanks," Tanny said. She let go of Carl's hand and headed off. Carl rushed to keep up with her before she disappeared into the crowd. His hand tingled as blood returned to its normal flow.

"Where you going?"

"Hangars," Tanny replied. "Willamette doesn't hire mercs; everyone's uniformed who works for the station."

Esper followed close behind Mriy, thankful that someone else was clearing a path for her. She had grown unaccustomed to crowds. The Harmony Bay settlement on Bentus VIII had been wide open. There was none of the forced closeness resulting from having a fully artificial atmosphere; the planet was designated Earth-like, and she could go outside and see clouds and birds in the sky. Aboard Willamette Station, everyone fought for enough room to breathe. But nobody got in Mriy's way. Strange xenos were usually given a wide berth, just as a general precaution. Anyone familiar with the azrin race would have kept even farther from her path.

There had been little to do aboard the *Mobius*, so among other things, Esper had looked up whatever she could find on Mriy's people. Despite being bipedal, they were evolved from her world's equivalent of tigers and lions and house cats. There was no direct correlation to Earth species. They weren't a technological people, only discovering space flight by having human explorers land on their world and explain the concept at gunpoint. They were an ARGO protectorate, not actual members, and most of their population preferred to live on-world. Those that left usually worked grunt jobs in personal security or mercenary companies.

Knowing all this, Esper had mixed feelings about enlisting Mriy in the search for Adam. "You sure this is a good idea?" she asked Roddy quietly.

Roddy plodded along in Esper's wake, just as Esper used Mriy to clear a path for her. "Sure, why not? She likes the kid. She catches a whiff of him, we'll have him back in no time."

Mriy garbled something, but Esper had no magic earring to tell her what the azrin was saying. She looked to Roddy, who gave a long-suffering sigh. "She says she'll find the little warrior." He beckoned for Esper to lean close, so he could whisper. "I think she figures the fighting games are a sign he's got a vicious streak."

Esper nodded, wondering if there was any truth to it. Adam had never struck her as violent, but he was an excitable boy and seemed competitive.

Suddenly, Mriy stopped in the middle of the pedestrian walkway. Esper bumped into her from behind, but the azrin didn't seem to notice or care. She growled something, and her head snapped to the left.

"She's found him," Roddy said. "Or at least a scent."

"What are we waiting for?" Esper asked. "Let's go."

Mriy said something else. "She wants you to stay behind. Meet us at the ship. She'll handle it from here."

Esper drew herself up tall. "I most certainly will not! He's my responsibility, and I'm the one he'll be hoping to see."

Mriy nodded. That needed no translation.

They plowed through the crowd, Mriy's snarling demeanor keeping station-goers from hindering them. The azrin danced the tight line between efficient bullying and getting station security summoned to arrest them. They left the commercial district where they began their search, and continued into the maintenance bays, station subsystem access points, and finally to the far end of the hangars from where the *Mobius* was berthed. Mriy pointed a palm at one of the personnel doors.

"This is the place," said Roddy.

Esper's heart raced. If they had gotten to him, he could already be aboard a ship back to Harmony Bay. "Open it!"

"You keep back," Roddy said.

Mriy shoved the door open and stalked through. Inside, a sleek, modern interceptor ship sat with its cargo bay door open. Metallic crates lined the wall, some of them still on the grav-sled that had brought them. Two mercenaries in glistening black body armor stood over the merchandise, one reading from a datapad, the other poking through the crates' contents. Their helmets were perched on the seats of the grav sled.

"Hey, what're you doing in—?" one of them began to ask.

"They must be after the kid," the other one cut in. The datapad clattered to the floor, and both mercenaries grabbed for their helmets. Mriy growled something that Roddy didn't bother to translate, and both men drew clubs from hooks on their belts. Esper hadn't actually gotten around to reading the station rules, so she wasn't sure how lax they were on weapons inside a rented hangar bay. The clubs looked like metallized plastic, and there was a device built into the end of each.

"Just give us Adam and no one needs to get hurt," Esper shouted, seeing the conflict about to play out in front of her.

"We got a job to do, ma'am. We ain't handing that boy over to you or anyone else," the mercenary who dropped the datapad replied. "Maybe you just want to call off your cat, and let us do our job."

Mriy's natural slouch made her appear short by human standards, but physiology is a strange thing. As she snarled in defiance, she drew herself up to her full, two-meter height, towering over both mercenaries. The mercenaries exchanged a look from behind the black, featureless helmets, then looked back to Mriy. They spread out and came at Mriy from the sides. Crackling blue arcs snapped at the clubs' ends as they swung toward the azrin.

But neither had ever fought an azrin; that much was plain to see. She caught first one, then the other by the wrist, her own arms moving faster than any human could react without cybernetic limbs. She twisted her right wrist, and the mercenary in her grasp dropped his stun club. She yanked on the mercenary to her right, lifting him as she drew him close, and tore his throat out with her teeth, forcing her way beneath the helmet. Dropping the body, she extended her claws and slashed out the throat of the other.

The whole encounter took perhaps five seconds.

Esper swallowed. She clasped her hands together to stop them shaking, and found herself in need of prayer. "I run to you, Lord ..."

"Yeah, she has that effect on me sometimes, too," said Roddy. "But let's go check the ship for the kid."

---

"This should be it: hangar eighty-four" Carl said, huffing for breath. They had crossed the full length of the station to reach their destination, the hangar that three witnesses had identified. If the two armored figures with him were the kidnappers, this is where their ship was berthed.

"We should have brought a weapon," Tanny said, putting a hand to the door controls.

"*Praesertim virtute*, right?" Carl asked with a smile. The translator charm didn't correct his Latin either.

Tanny frowned at him quoting the marines' motto back at her. She hammered the door controls with a fist and burst inside. Even unarmed, Carl liked her odds against two flash-and-polish mercenaries. No one walked around a space station in armor unless they were assaulting it, or they needed people to think they were bigger badasses than they really were.

Carl poked his head in after giving himself a five-count. There had been no signs of trouble, just the sound of Tanny's boots on the steel plates of the floor, but even those had stopped. What he saw was Tanny staring back at him with her arms crossed and a scowl on her face. He also saw Mriy and Roddy by the cargo ramp of the mercenaries' interceptor, two dead bodies, and his erstwhile passengers. With a shrug of apology to his ex-wife, Carl strolled into the hangar, checking over his shoulder as he closed the door behind him.

"Well, it looks like you all made quite a mess in here," Carl remarked, giving a slight frown. It was the same look his commanding officers used to use when inspecting something and needing to make up a flaw for the sake of feeling useful. "Lucky for you, I think I see how to fix this. By the by, you all right, kid?"

Adam nodded.

"I think we have to let the authorities know what happened here," Esper said.

"Um—" "Yeah, maybe not—" "I see no reason—"

Carl just smiled and held up his hands. "No need to be hasty. This sort of misunderstanding happens in places like this. We just need to make sure no one gets sore at *us* until we're a few systems away. Mriy, thanks for taking care of those two." Mriy grinned, showing her fangs. "Now, drag that mess you made into their ship and dump them in the crew quarters." Her grin turned into a hiss. "Oh, and clean up when you're done. You've still got a bit of human ... right ..." Carl pointed a finger to a spot on his cheek, and mirrored Mriy until she found the spot on her own cheek that was still bloody.

"You want me to check if they had surveillance on the hangar?" Roddy asked.

"Station won't—that sort of snooping's bad for business— but you can check the ship," said Carl. "Pocket anything you see that you like."

"I'll get Esper and Adam back to the ship," Tanny volunteered.

Carl's eyes drifted over to the anti-grav sled parked to the side of the hangar. A mischievous grin betrayed his idea even before he said a word. "Not yet. Help me load up that sled."

"We can't afford to waste time stealing a grav sled," Tanny argued.

As he climbed the cargo ramp, Roddy stuck his head back down. "Well, he sold the one we rented, so maybe a replacement isn't a bad idea."

"You're kidding me."

"The cut'll drop from thirty-three hundred to under three grand if we don't get our deposit back," said Roddy. "I'm not a charity."

"You can't just—" Esper began.

"Let's get this thing loaded," Tanny barked. Adam snapped to attention like a raw recruit and pitched in. Carl and Tanny started heaving crates back onto the grav sled without even looking. Noticing the datapad on the floor, Carl tucked it between two of the crates.

Esper looked on with a helpless, horrified expression.

"Mind giving us a hand?" Carl asked. "This'll go quicker, and we'll get out of here."

"I can't ..."

"Listen, Sister," Carl said. "We just ended up with a double-homicide grabbing Adam back for you. Maybe if they investigate, we'll get our names cleared. More than likely, they'll dust us just to keep their law-and-order reputation appearances up. Now, grab a crate and pitch in."

---

Two hours later, the *Mobius* was deep in the astral again, leaving Willamette Station behind—possibly for good. Mort had put them shallow this time, letting them have the time to think about their next move. Something wasn't sitting well with Carl, a nagging thought buzzing in the back of his brain. He needed some time to think, to throw ideas in a heap, sort them into piles, then kick the piles over and start again. Esper and Adam were back in Chip's old quarters as if the *Mobius* had never offloaded them. Tanny was at the controls, probably reading. Mriy and Roddy were in the hold, sorting through the mercenaries' cargo. That left Mort.

Digging through his quarters, Carl found a battered cardboard box with lettering too faded to read anymore. He gave it a cursory dusting with a shirtsleeve, and headed up to the common room. The box was older than Carl or even Carl's parents. It had belonged to his grandfather, and it had been passed down through the generations. One day, Carl was going to have to find a new box to replace it, but until it crumbled to confetti, he was going to keep using the original packaging. Carl removed a plastic housing, three hundred centimeters on a side, and placed it on the kitchen table. Tucked beneath it were two stacks of composite plastic datacards, each bundled together with an elastic band. Glancing at the two bundles, Carl set one down across the table from him, and removed the elastic from the other.

"Mort," he called out, loudly enough for the wizard to hear from his quarters. "Up for a game of Battle Minions?" There was a chronometer on the common room wall, set to Greenwich Mean Time. Carl watched the seconds blip by.

Eight seconds later, Mort's door opened. "You're what now?"

"Come on, it's been weeks," Carl said. "I still owe you one from last time." He flipped through his stack of minions, trying to decide how best to prepare for facing Mort's.

Mort stopped by the refrigerator and pulled out a pair of beers. He tossed one to Carl and the other opened of its own accord in his hand.

"Watch it," Carl chided him, not for throwing the can, but for magicking his own open. "I actually want to *play* a game, not spend hours trying to log into the omni from a random depth to restore our minion data."

Mort waved away Carl's concerns as he took a sip of his beer. "I'm careful. So, what're you in the mood for? Standard game, gladiator, or one of those flaky custom setups you keep pestering me about?"

"Just standard," Carl said as Mort unbound his minion datacards. "I need to talk something over with you."

Mort squinted one eye at Carl, a look that sent some men clutching for charms of protection. Carl had seen it too many times, and just smirked back. "Tanny trouble again, or something with those two?" Mort asked, pointing with his nose in the direction of Esper and Adam's temporary quarters.

"The kid," Carl confirmed. He finished his selection of minions and fed the eight chosen datacards into his side of the game board. "Something just seems off with him. You talk with him much? I see you two gaming enough."

"Enough, I suppose," Mort replied. "Nice kid. Got his head on straight. Miracle after what they probably did to him."

"He doesn't seem ... I don't know ... a little phony?"

"I'm no expert on kids, but I'm a fair judge of minds. Don't know what the scientists did to the kids at that school the plastic girl taught at, but the teachers have done well by him. Politics, religion, music, he's got a pretty broad set of interests."

"And you two just sit around playing Omnithrust Racer, talking politics?" Carl asked.

"Adam and I see eye-to-eye on the Mitchell Administration, AGRO membership expansion, and Earth preservation. He's a bit too pro-science for my liking, but I blame the schools for that."

"I'll let Esper know you disapprove of her curriculum," Carl joked.

"Bah, she taught math," Mort replied. "Best thing I can say about her, really. The One Church's 'magic for Him, not for you' stance sours the lot of them." Mort slid his own minions into the machine and the game began. Little holographic monsters rose from the game board and sized each other up. Carl and Mort keyed in last-second modifications to their minions' orders as a holographic clock counted down seconds until the battle started.

The two of them watched the battle unfold. The cherubic, colorful creatures with their absurd and oft impractical-looking weapons clashed in the middle of the board. They grunted and squished as they attempted to hack one another to pieces. Carl's squad was big and brutish, and tried to occupy the center of the battlefield. Mort's squad spread out and picked at the edges of Carl's defenses. There was nothing to do but watch and wait, as the commands were preset prior to the game's beginning.

"Come on ... come on ..." Carl breathed, clenching his fists. Every creature of his was stronger and tougher than any of Mort's, yet Mort was gaining the upper hand. When the last of Carl's minions expired with a melodramatic "Euuuaaa!", the game played a happy little tune and pronounced Mort the winner.

The old wizard chuckled. "You try that plan every few battles you know. All big dumb brutes just doesn't work against a competent opponent."

Carl tipped back in his chair and sighed. "I just wanted

something straightforward to work for once. Why does everything need to be complicated?"

Mort twisted his lips; it was a facial shrug, as far as Carl could tell. "Just the way the universe works. You got no business complaining; you think you got where you are today by playing it straight?"

"I know. I know. I just feel like I deserve a break now and then," Carl said. "Something with someone shooting at me, and I can shoot back ... not that I want to get shot."

"Navy's always recruiting," Mort said with a grin.

Carl yanked his datacards out of the game board and began sorting through them. "Yeah, and have them put me back on Earth, teaching twitchy teenagers how to fly? And another thing, how'd I end up playing ferry to those two again? I've never taken a job with such a sketchy payout."

"You'd just gotten short-ended on our last haul, plus a few glandular inconveniences clouding your thinking."

"She's not my type," Carl replied.

Mort snickered. "Dark science or no, she's any man's type who hasn't got himself situated. Plus, there's Adam. Man can't feel like a proper man if he can't look after a kid."

"Even if the kid's comet cold when you rescue him? Mort, I tell you, the kid's not right in the head. You'd think we picked him up from school, not a kidnapping."

Mort shook his head. "Dark science, my boy. It's not pretty. Speaking of which, you should go talk to her and get it out of your system. Oh, and if you want the boy out of the room for say ... an hour or two, just tell him I wanted to try Neptune Squad."

"You're incorrigible."

"Why would I want to be corriged?" Mort asked with a wink.

Carl knocked softly on the door to Chip's old quarters, wondering how long it would be until he stopped thinking of it as Chip's. Since each of the crew quarters on the *Mobius* was a separate escape pod, it was possible he could just trade it in for a new one; Carl had been thinking a lot about what to do with escape pods of late. It was a shame that the one in the cargo hold was incompatible. Even Roddy was unlikely to be able to force it to fit.

There was no answer from inside, and Carl had lifted his knuckles to knock louder when the door opened. Esper peeked out before opening the door wider to let Carl inside. "Captain?" she whispered. Adam was sleeping on Chip's bed, still dressed with shoes and everything, on top of the blankets.

"Yeah, thought he might be sleeping it off," Carl whispered back. "Rough day. Can you join me ..." Carl paused. He was about to suggest his quarters, but with Mort's teasing fresh in his mind, he changed his course. "... down in the cargo hold? We need to talk."

Esper didn't question him, but followed Carl up the stairs and through the common room. Mort gave a disapproving scowl as he fought with the holovid controls, but said nothing. Down in the cargo hold, Roddy and Mriy were prying and cutting the lids off the stolen crates, many of which were sealed shut. They both looked up at the sound of footsteps on the landing.

"You two take a break," Carl called down as he descended. "Give Mort a hand with the holovid and find something to watch."

"C'mon, we were just getting to the fun part," Roddy

griped. "These Grayson & Wesson locks took forever to bust open."

Mriy nodded in agreement. "Go mate in your own quarters."

"What'd she say?" Esper asked quietly.

"She wants to see what we got," Carl lied softly, "same as Roddy." He got down to the cargo floor and peered over Roddy to see what they were excited about. "What *do* we have?"

"Manifest's encrypted, so we only know as we open them," Roddy said. He lifted the lid on one with a lower hand. "This one's just a sniff of the ion trail." Inside, there was a rack of disintegrator rifles, UniDef Systems' Adjudicator Mk VII series.

Carl let out a low whistle. "That crate's worth almost as much as this ship."

Roddy snorted. "Sure, and anyone missing a shipment of these babies gets word we boosted them, we're not just dusted, we're particles."

"Problem for later," Carl replied. "Now, go grab a beer and watch some *Samolith* or something with Mort."

"The Tri-Annual Hunt might be on relay," Mriy said.

Carl held up his hands and ushered Mriy and Roddy toward the stairs. "Whatever the three of you can agree on. Hell, grab Tanny and make a party of it; not like there's much to watch for in the shallow astral. Just get a move on."

Roddy fixed Carl with a glare and a meaningful look at the crates as he departed, adding the rubbing fingers gesture humans used for "money."

Carl replied with a less couth gesture after making sure Esper wasn't looking.

"So what did you want to talk to me about?" she asked once the door to the main crew compartment closed.

Carl ran a hand through his hair as he tried to decide how to put it. It was odd: he could lie to a man with a gun pointed at his head, or a ship with its guns trained on the *Mobius* and never so much as stutter over his words. But the truth and a pretty pair of eyes looking back at him and he turned into a blathering idiot.

"It's Adam."

"Yes ... I've been thinking about him, too," Esper replied, crossing her arms. "I don't think I'm telling you where to bring him until we get to Mars. I don't trust you not to leave me stranded somewhere along the way if I tell you before then."

"You think I'm above knocking on two billion doors to get my reward?" Carl asked. He closed his eyes and shook his head; he couldn't afford to get pulled into a contest of clever one-upsmanship. "That's not the point. How did they find Adam?"

Esper blinked. "What do you mean?"

"How did they know he was on Willamette Station? We don't exactly publish an itinerary. The only ship that even knew we were in this sector was the Tally-ho."

"Maybe Harmony Bay has connections inside Earth Navy ..."

Carl pointed a finger at her. "Ah HA! I thought of that, but we hid Adam from them. I don't think those techs of Penny-Toad's were faking when they said they found nothing out of the ordinary. Mort fooled them good."

"Maybe they have scanners installed at all the starports ..."

"At every starport in the quadrant? Including Willamette Station, which isn't even in ARGO space? No, I'm thinking he might have a tracker planted in him."

Esper opened her mouth, aghast. "No, he can't. Doctor Cliffton said Adam's had been removed."

"That scientist who helped you smuggle him out?"

Esper nodded. "Doctor Cliffton got his doctorate from Oxford in cellular genetics. I don't think he'd miss something like that."

Carl nodded. It was time to dig into the background of Doctor Cliffton. "Well, we're going to get ourselves somewhere planetside and have Adam checked out. Nothing we've got on board is going to find a tracker if someone wanted it hidden."

"Wouldn't it be safer heading straight for Mars?" Esper asked.

Carl pinched his chin between thumb and forefinger, feeling the scruff of not having shaved in days. "Depends how good a tracker it is."

---

The descent into an unfamiliar atmosphere always put Carl a little on edge. Delos was the only habitable world in the system of the same name. The others got numbered and forgotten, but the fifth world from their sun was just Delos. It was a dry world on the Earth-like spectrum, with just a quarter of its surface covered in water. Most inhabitants of Earth didn't care for the weather, so the population centers were all domed in. The starport looked like a produce market, with pea-pod hangar bays, each berth having its own retractable hemisphere that split to allow entry and egress. Yet another landing point that wanted to eat his ship. One day, Carl figured he ought to talk to a professional about that imagery, before he went nuts (or as Tanny would have told him, any *more* nuts).

While most people still considered Delos to be the frontier, it was clean and safe compared to Willamette Station. Companies had corporate offices in places like Delos; whereas, the only organizations who sought out Willamette were the ones who didn't want the competition from legitimate businesses—or the oversight that went with it. One of the benefits of respectability was attracting doctors with valid medical licenses. You could get a hole patched up, or a parasite removed on just about any outpost. Delos had facilities that employed people who had done those sorts of things before, had gone to school to learn how, and had equipment designed just for that purpose. Carl still had a few scars from encounters with the other kind—sometimes you just had to take what you had available.

Their hangar was in the city of New Melbourne, one of the mid-sized settlements that dotted the sea of the southern hemisphere. While Delos catered to a mix of tourists and explorers, New Melbourne leaned toward the latter. Traders, cartographers, diplomats, smugglers, and pirates came and went from nearby xeno space; not many of the locals could tell them apart, and the smart ones just kept their heads down and counted the credits that flowed into their accounts.

As the crew filed down the loading ramp and into the hangar, Carl doled out assignments, such as they were. "Tanny, you go with Esper and Adam. Make sure they get to the med facility without any trouble." Carl didn't need to spell out the sorts of trouble she needed to look for. Tanny was better qualified to identify those than he was. "Mriy ... just don't kill anyone while we're here. Mort, you can do whatever you feel like ... not like I could stop you anyway. Roddy, you and me are taking another shot at getting rid of that escape pod."

"Shit, Carl," said Roddy, "First real port in almost a month, and I'm stuck haggling with scrap dealers again?"

"I don't want them bullshitting me on tech details," said Carl. "I'll do the haggling."

"Yeah, but—"

"We'll find a good pub around here after. Drinks are on me," said Carl. "That goes for everyone."

New Melbourne Starport was bright and cheerful, with glossy white surfaces, colorful holovid displays showing departures and arrivals, and smiling personnel in teal uniforms. There were plenty of skylights looking up into the atmosphere as well, allowing bystanders to watch the ships taking off or landing. The glitz and polish were for the customers of the starliners; Carl and Roddy didn't see anything but utility corridors and cargo haulers until the private and commercial wings of the starport merged at the central hub.

"Look at the rubes," said Roddy, shaking his head. "All looking up, like they never saw a ship before."

"Maybe some of them haven't," Carl said. Looking around, it was the usual mix. Over ninety percent human, about half the rest Roddy's kind, and the other half a sprinkling of ARGO races. Nothing exotic. There wasn't even the typical vibe of a swagger and ego that came with a spacers' port. New Melbourne was tame, and Carl would have bet that there were people arriving by passenger liner that had never been outside the Terran system before.

As they walked the concourse, Roddy kept up a non-stop chatter. Sometimes he denigrated the false shine on everything in ARGO-secured space; other times he pointed out the people who weren't what they were dressed to be. Carl had heard it all before and auto-piloted some supportive responses to keep Roddy from demanding too much of his attention. Carl wanted to look in the shops. As with anyone possessed of a Y chromosome, he hated shopping unless it involved a device that converted power into forward motion, explosions, or entertainment. But he was fascinated looking through the windows of shops as they passed by. Most of the clothing stores catered to women's fashions and accessories. But there were also a number of shops hawking Delos-themed curios: shirts with images of the famous Angelic Falls, EV helms with the Delos "nine-planets, one Delos" logo and motto, and mugs boasting that the owner had flown the Zephyros Canyon Run. Other shops catered to basic necessities, perfunctory gifts, and personal entertainment.

Roddy's voice grew quieter and distant, petering away to nothing but the general hum of a thousand conversations bouncing around the concourse. Carl had stopped. Amid the coffee shops, sushi bars, and chain barbecue restaurants was one establishment that enveloped him, sight, sound, and soul: Duster's Dogfight Diner. They must have pumped something through the ventilation system, because amid the scents of grilled beef, fried chicken, and hot cakes, Carl smelled starfighter fuel rods. It was the largest restaurant they had seen on the concourse, and through the glass he could barely make out the giant holovid globe suspended above the patrons. Signs by the door didn't allow anyone to pass by without knowing what went on inside.

INTENSE STARFIGHTER ACTION!

FOUR-ON-FOUR TOURNEYS NIGHTLY!

CHAMPIONS EAT FREE!

NOT A PILOT? PLACE YOUR BETS ON THE ACTION!

Carl blinked when he felt a tug at his coat hem. Slowly, he returned to New Melbourne, the concourse, and his impending trip to find a salvage dealer. "Come on, flyboy," said Roddy. "If you wanna come back later, I'll drink anywhere."

"Yeah," Carl said, staring over his shoulder as Roddy towed him away from the diner. "Yeah, we'll come back later."

---

Carl sat on a molded plastic bench, meant to look and feel like stone. No matter how hard the chemists tried though, they could never make plastic feel *old* the way stone did. Real stone had a comforting eternal feel to it; it made your troubles seem fleeting and petty and helped put things in perspective. Carl had sat on real stone before, back on Earth, so he knew. Parked on a plastic bench next to a genetically perfect potted ficus tree, he felt the full weight of being at the mercy of a laaku's skill with the help kiosk. They had already tried every likely salvage yard within local tram distance and were back at the starport, looking to widen their search.

When Roddy returned, he was shaking his head. "I looked at other scrappers on Delos, and it's the same song. They'll melt it down for us for beer money. Starport's offer's as good as any. I say we just dump the thing and be done with it."

Carl stood up, shaking his head. "Naw, we've put too much effort into this to cut and run now. We'll hang onto it, maybe find a system running older transports and see if we can palm it off on them."

"It's really not worth the trouble, you know," Roddy said, falling into step beside Carl as they headed back toward their hangar.

"Yeah, probably. Now it's a matter of principle, though."

"Principle doesn't pay."

Carl stuffed his hands into the pockets of his jacket. "I know, but principle's what keeps you going when the galaxy seems hell-bent on siphoning every terra out of your wallet."

"Come on," said Roddy. "Let's grab everyone and go out for that drink. That ought to cheer you up." Whether Roddy intended him to or not, Carl heard the muttered afterthought. "It'll sure cheer *me* up."

---

The lighting was low enough that the holovid globe could be seen from anywhere in the diner. Along two separate walls were banks of old flight simulator pods, four to a side. From those simulators, eight pilots controlled the action taking place above. Represented in the three-meter diameter globe was—according to displays built into the surface of each table—the Gespen Ship Graveyard, a man-made asteroid field of orbiting wrecks. Voice comm blared from overhead speakers, directionally oriented so that the knowledgeable observer could tell which team was talking.

Blue leader to Blue Two, you've picked up a tail.

Copy that Blue Leader, taking evasive.

"Noobs," Carl muttered, glaring longingly up at the holovid globe. The whole crew of the *Mobius* sat together at a round booth, along with Esper and Adam. The boy's scans had come back clear, and it looked like they had stopped at Delos for nothing but a bit of peace of mind.

"Shouldn't we be in the wizards' section?" Esper asked quietly. Anything below a shout was unlikely to be overheard. In addition to the comm chatter, bettors shouted encouragement to the teams they were backing, and a few beleaguered wait staff tried to run a restaurant.

"Young lady," said Mort. "It is a layman's misconception that wizards are inherently hazardous to scientific devices. It is

the mark of a true wizard to refrain from magic at his will.
I can—"

Tanny shushed him as the waiter with their drinks
approached. He was dressed in a stylized Earth Navy cadet
uniform, just obviously fake enough not to offend visiting
naval personnel. Carl, Mort, Mriy, and Tanny had all ordered
local Delos brews. Given limited options, Adam had requested
a Cherry Hydro-Blaster. Esper went the safe route and
ordered a caramel soda. For all his griping, Roddy just wanted
Earth's preferred from the tap, which tasted hardly any
different from the cans they kept aboard the *Mobius*.

"Well, so it turns out Adam's in fine health," Esper said,
starting the conversation anew in a different direction.

Tanny shrugged, lifting the local approximation of an old
Earth stout to her lips. "What would you expect from a
lab rat?"

"I'm sitting right here," Adam protested.

"Hey kid, we all start somewhere," Tanny replied. "Not all
of us are proud of where."

*Viper Four, come about to two-six-oh mark one-five, and
intercept.*

*Roger that, Viper One.*

"Those guys aren't half bad," Carl remarked, staring up at
the holovid globe. He absently tipped back his drink, never
taking his eyes from the action.

"They're just little hologram flies buzzing around each
other," said Esper. "How can you tell?"

"The blue squad's just faking it," Carl replied. "Bunch of
passengers getting a chance to sit up front for once, and play-
acting being pilots. They're flying around like cockroaches,
not thinking, just reacting to their environment. The red
team, the ones calling themselves Viper, is the real deal. I'd

bet my take from our salvage job that these guys fly together."

Roddy snorted. "Big spender."

"No takers," Tanny added. "I can kind of see it, too. They either fly together, or they practically live in this joint."

"Pack hunters," Mriy agreed.

"So who's with me?"

They all looked to Carl.

"You didn't ..." said Tanny.

"We've got winner," said Carl. "It's going to be that Viper team. Look, they just went ahead by a ship. Anyway, I put Team Mobius on the list for tonight, but I need a roster. They'll come up with odds for us once I tell them who I'm flying with, and we see who we're facing."

"Can I?" asked Adam, looking to Esper, not Carl.

"Sure you can," Carl replied.

Tanny gave him a withering look. "You can't seriously think the kid can fly against those guys?"

"Think you can do better?" Carl asked. As soon as Tanny opened her mouth to reply, he cut her off. "Good, because I'm counting on you as my wingman."

Roddy held up his lower hands. "Don't look my way. Those human-sized cockpits are no place for me."

"Fair enough," Carl replied. "How about you, Esper?"

Esper choked on her drink, spluttering half a mouthful back into the glass.

"You OK?" Carl asked. "I was just joking. Come on, Mriy. It'll be like hunting, but without all the running and mess to clean up."

Mriy yawned and stretched, her arms spreading wide enough to span the whole table. "This looks better than the games on the ship."

As his squadron extracted themselves from the table, Carl took advantage of the momentary distraction to lean in and whisper to Mort. "Bet everything you can scrape together on us. This'll make up for the scrawny haul."

---

Carl's eyes glazed over as the referee gave them instructions on both the battle setup and the basic controls of the simulator. He resisted the urge to tell the jumped-up waiter where he could shove his "new pilot tips," but he needed to keep his cool to let the odds drift up. Besides, Adam probably needed the help, possibly Mriy, too. Tanny would be fine. Piloting a marine transport wasn't like handling a starfighter, but she'd been through flight school—at least what the marines passed off as flight school.

As he climbed into the cockpit of the simulator labeled Blue Two, he felt a wave of nostalgia. Underneath the scent of beer and the rickety canopy whose hydraulics could have used an overhaul, it was still a Typhoon III simulator. It took Carl back to his academy days, not the first go-round as a cadet, but the second time, as a flight instructor teaching dirt-booted pilots how to fly the Typhoon IV. The differences between the two ships only mattered to sticklers and bureaucrats; it was even running the same UI and training programs.

Analog toggle switches were scattered across the inside of the cockpit. Without even giving it a second thought, Carl flipped through them in a standard pre-flight check. Most were stiff with disuse, a few sticky. It took Carl until he was halfway through the check before he noticed that none of them were functioning. Someone had dumbed down the simulator to diner-patron simplicity. The flight yoke was loose and free though, and had just the right amount of resistance to feel stable. Reaching behind him, he found the helm for Blue Two and plunked it down over his head with a grimace. He hadn't watched who had last flown in the unit, but now he smelled the foul chili-pepper concoction his predecessor had eaten prior to playing.

Once he had his helmet on, Carl was bombarded with comm noise.

This is great! We're going to win!

My ears are squashed against my head.

What'd she say?

Never mind.

All right, when we start, just follow my lead.

The comm was low-end and fuzzy and flattened the voices so badly that he could only tell the speakers by context. He should have realized that Adam wouldn't be able to understand Mriy. Mort could have loaned him his translator charm; the old wizard understood azrin well enough without it. In the end, of course, it didn't matter anyway. Let the diners laugh themselves silly until the fighting actually started.

Contrary to whatever instincts screamed in his head, Carl kept silent. The betting period would close once the simulated fighters launched. Hopefully Mort was letting the odds drift to their high point before placing his bet. It wouldn't have surprised him if Mort was the *only* one placing a bet on the Blue Squadron.

The heads-up display showed a countdown, starting thirty seconds out. Carl cracked his knuckles.

At twenty seconds, he tilted his neck back and forth, working loose any kinks.

At ten seconds, he took a long, slow breath.

Then the countdown hit zero. Carl punched the throttle to

full and was first out of the simulated hangar. In flight school, it had always been a point to brag about. The simulators didn't accept any inputs before the countdown finished, so a partially opened throttle was a recipe for a slow start. His Typhoon III rocketed out into the hologlobe battlefield, which was different from the one the *Mobius* crew had just watched. Carl didn't need the nav display to know that it was Frontier Station Bravo, an unusual place for a dogfight. A working (albeit fictional) space station, Frontier Station Bravo was swarming with civilian traffic at the start of the simulation. In flight school runs, it was meant to be a defense against a raid, with the defense of the civilians paramount.

All right, everybody, you see them on radar? Let's get there before they know what hit them. Full throttle, and everyone aim for the guy on the far left. Adam's strategy was straight out of the pre-adolescent belief that heroes were bold and brave.

Mriy's ship followed as Adam continued to pour ions out of his thrusters, but Carl hung back, easing off his own throttle. Tanny was smart enough to follow suit. Shield flashes marked the opening salvos from both sides, Adam hitting several times from beyond his cannons' optimal range, and Mriy connecting once or twice with marginally effective shots. The Viper squad waited until they closed range with Adam and Mriy, and Blue Leader and Blue Four exploded in short order.

"Blue Two to Blue Three: Tanny, mind taking up position on my six. Let's show these guys some flying."

Roger Blue Two. Try not to get us both killed.

Carl laughed over the comm. "Don't worry; it's just a game." He opened the throttle and veered toward the civilian shipping lanes, where a thirty-four ship convoy was headed for the safety of the station's docking bays.

Carl, what are you doing?

The Viper Squadron turned to give chase, but their lines of fire were spoiled by congested ship traffic crossing between the two squads. Carl fought with an under-used switch on the side of the flight yoke, one not too many civilian sim-jockeys would bother with even if they realized it was there. He flicked it on and off, working the switch loose, the simulator's hydraulics bucking to mimic the shuddering that alternating the flight control assist on and off would cause. He left it in the "off" position and pivoted his typhoon to aim the guns back at Viper Squadron. Starfighters were complicated enough to fly without needing to perform advanced physics calculations on the go. The flight control system made the ship compensate for existing momentum in executing turns and rolls. With it turned off, Carl had the freedom to spin his ship and fire his lateral and vertical thrusters to angle in any direction he liked —but he had to worry about managing the ship's momentum himself.

Of course, now he was flying mostly backwards and a bit to port.

Tanny dove out of his way as Carl opened fire. He tracked one of the Viper Squad, shooting it just before it passed behind a medical evac ship, then again once it emerged on the far side. The target's shields sputtered and died out, as Carl's shot hit at the spot where the generator was most vulnerable. Tanny swung around and put in two quick shots to destroy it.

"Nice shooting."

"You're a fucking maniac!"

Carl grinned, turning his flight controls back on and slinging his ship through the station traffic. He headed for the far side of the station, Tanny taking up position behind him.

"Where are we going? They're the other way."

"I'm a good shot, but there's still three of them. Rather string 'em out and pick 'em off."

The station's defense cannons fired, but it was all for show. Unless someone had really monkeyed with the programming, they would never aim anywhere near the combatants. They were just meant to make cadets feel like they were in a live-fire situation. Avoiding a fleeing passenger liner, Carl swung through the interior of the ring-shaped station. Checking his radar, he saw that the three remaining members of Viper Squadron were closing in, spread wide to take up multiple firing angles.

As soon as he broke line-of-sight with them, Carl switched off the flight assist again and spun his typhoon.

Stop doing that!

Tanny looped around in a standard turn, but didn't have her guns around by the time Carl opened fire on the first of the Vipers to emerge from behind the station's bulk. Using his vertical thrusters and pitching downward simultaneously, he maneuvered his craft to keep its aim on the Vipers while backing out of the path of their turn to intercept him. One exploded in a hail of withering fire from Carl's cannons, but the other two changed tactics and focused their fire on Tanny. Her long, looping turn had left her exposed with nothing but her shields between her and the two Vipers. Twisting and rolling, she tried to keep them off target, but she was blasted out of space.

Carl found himself alone against two opponents. He breathed a sigh of relief, careful not to have his comm open. With a growing grin, he fired his directional thrusters and looped around to give chase.

There was any number of ways that flight school cadets would react to unexpectedly finding themselves on the defensive. Carl had seen them all. The ones destined to wash out just panicked and froze. Others would scatter for cover, which was always a low-percentage play in deep space; not many real battles would take place in congested regions like the simulator. The good ones regrouped with their squadron and adapted to the flow of the fight. Carl had found a pair that wanted to go out in a blaze of glory; they both turned to fix their plasma cannons on his typhoon.

Carl turned on his comm and laughed out loud. He knew they couldn't hear him inside their simulator cockpits, but he taunted them anyway. "You lunar ferrymen couldn't hit your own mouths with a toothbrush. What are you even aiming at? Are you trying to blow up the station or me?"

Frontier Station Bravo had innumerable contours, from sensor arrays to small ship docking arms, gun ports to reactor nacelles. Carl knew them all as if he had built the place with his own two hands—not that it actually ever existed. He wove his way along the surface of the station with his ship's momentum carrying him along backward, firing his guns at the pursuing Vipers and his thrusters to keep from crashing. It was a failing grade in any simulator run to splatter on an inanimate target, so he had always loved challenging cadets to chase him through the hazardous region.

"If you haven't already, can someone please set the display area to a quarter kilometer? You'll get to see what I'm flying through up here."

Carl spun around forward and pulled up, leaving the vicinity of the station and re-entering the traffic flow. The two Vipers were keeping a cautious pursuit, wary of Carl's free-form flying and reverse angling of his guns. He slowed to allow them to close the distance, and plowed head-on into the line of ships headed for the station. In his imagination, the two enemy pilots were swearing up a storm in their cockpits, and were probably to the point of blaming one another for their inability to finish off the lone survivor of Blue Squadron.

There was a point in the simulation coming up that was meant to test cadet reactions to unexpected turns of events. There was a corvette in the middle of the convoy that was supposed to get frustrated at the slower ships blocking its way to safe harbor. Carl angled his ship right into the impending path of the corvette, and ... he passed through as the corvette veered ... *now*. One of the two Vipers slammed into the corvette as its pilot swerved from the orderly line of fleeing ships. The trailing enemy ship flew through the debris field and right into Carl's gun sights as he spun again and hammered a full five volleys into the Viper ship before its pilot could bring its own guns to bear.

The simulator went quiet, and a humble "VICTOR" appeared on the heads-up display.

Carl tossed the reeking helm on the back of the seat and hopped out of the simulator as all the cockpit canopies opened in unison. Mriy was busily unmussing the fur around her ears. Tanny had the disapproving-but-unable-to-form-a-legitimate-complaint scowl that she'd had during most of their time as husband and wife. Adam looked up at him in awe. The Viper Squadron, across the diner, was less diverse in their opinion of Carl's flying.

"You filthy cheating ass!" one of them shouted. The three pilots storming across the establishment in the walking equivalent of squadron formation appeared to share his view. "There's no way a typhoon handles like that." He turned to the referee. "I want him disqualified."

Carl was a rich man now—at least by his personal standards. He was in a jovial mood and more than willing to rev up a hotheaded loser. "Funny, none of my wingmen think I can set a chrono by myself."

"You had a collision avoidance hack, auto-hit targeting, and I'm pretty sure decoupling the maneuvering thrusters isn't allowed in combat."

"You're just sore because you're used to picking off tourists and freighter jockeys," Carl replied. "I bet you've played dozens of battles in that thing. You learn the tricks of each simulated combat zone, and take advantage of pilots who don't know any better."

"Dozens?" the Viper leader scoffed. "Try hundreds of hours logged in these things. There's not a pilot on Delos with more flight time in a typhoon simulator."

Carl smirked. "I've never set foot in a Typhoon III simulator before today."

"Bullshit."

Tanny slid up beside him. "Are you looking to start a fight here?" she asked Carl. "If so, you can fight it yourself."

He looked to Mriy for backup. She yawned and looked away. There was always Mort, but admitting he'd brought a wizard with him was as good as admitting that he *was* a cheat. Carl held up his hands in mock surrender.

"Fine, you got me," he said. "I've never flown a Typhoon III, but I have seventy-two confirmed kills in my old Typhoon IV, plus another few thousand hours teaching advanced techniques to cadets on a Typhoon IV simulator. Only differences between it and this one here are about five percent more thruster power, an updated targeting computer, and the Naval Academy's simulators didn't smell like barbecue sauce."

"You think you're some hot shit, liar?"

"Love to stay and chat, boys, but I don't care if you believe me or not."

"Ref, who'd this guy sign in as?" the Viper leader asked.

The referee consulted his datapad. "Says here: Manfred von Richthofen."

Carl fell in with the rest of the *Mobius* crew and headed for the exit. "I'll save you the trouble. That's not my real name," he called over his shoulder.

"Ooh, you lit a fire under that rube," Roddy said. "He's gonna be bitching to all his friends on the waste reclaim freighter that he got robbed."

"Speaking of robbed, Mort, how'd we do?"

Mort cleared his throat, but said nothing.

"How much did we make?" Carl pressed. "What kind of odds did you get on us? We must have been at least ten-to-one underdogs."

Mort patted him on the shoulder. "Let it go."

Carl stopped in his tracks. The rest of the crew kept walking. "You didn't place the bet."

They stopped. "Tanny caught my eye, reminded me about our little talk."

"You know you shouldn't be gambling," Tanny said, using her wife scold. "And you were planning to bet *our* shares from the last haul?"

"It was a sure thing," said Carl.

Roddy gave him a friendly swat in the chest. "I believe in you, buddy. If it'd been up to me, I'd have let Mort bet our hard-coin on that game." He took a swig from a glass mug of Earth's Preferred that he had smuggled out of Duster's.

"Come on," said Tanny, "We've got somewhere to get. Somewhere with real money in it."

Esper gave Carl a pitying look, and he knew he was on his own. It was time to be responsible and go bring Adam home.

The *Mobius* drifted through space, on their way to the edge of the Delos system. Of course, drifting was relative. Looking out a window, there was no sense of proper scale, nothing like the blood-pumping speed of the combat simulator. In actuality, the *Mobius* was traveling a thousand times the speed of the digital Typhoons that Carl and the other pilots had flown.

Carl reclined with his feet up on the common room couch, a bacon bar in one hand, datapad in the other. Roddy and Adam were watching an animated holovid comedy, but Carl was fixated on researching Berring LX-4 transports, trying to figure out who might be interested in buying surplus escape pods. He had hardly spoken a word to Tanny since lifting off from New Melbourne and had said even less to Mort. His pockets hurt just looking at either of them.

The prospects for dealing away the escape pod were looking remote. What he found was that the Berring series was all but decommissioned due to fundamental systems flaws, a number of key systems up for recall, and a counterfeiting scam fifteen years back had flooded the market with substandard parts. Anyone who owned or operated one was more likely to be *using* the escape pods than buying replacements. It was getting damned tempting to shove Esper and Adam back in it and let someone else pick them up.

Making Adam squadron leader had been a test. Not that he expected any great strategic thinking of a ten-year-old, but for all the complexity of the subsystems, the simulator was just a fancy computer game. Kids come preprogrammed to win at those. Beating Mort at Omnithrust Racer was just proof that the kid had basic motor skills; Carl didn't even bother playing against the old wizard at anything that required quick thinking and basic tech aptitude at the same time. The fact that the races were even close called into question Adam's claims of prowess at the game. Then again, kids were stone-faced liars, the lot of them. He could respect that. It didn't make sorting the mess out any easier.

On the bright side, nothing had gone terribly wrong on Delos. Sure, his crew had murdered his hopes of scavenging three jobs' worth of cash out of one paltry haul, but that wasn't the sort of trouble he had been worrying about. If someone else had shown up to recapture Adam, Carl would have known Harmony Bay had found some way to track him, implant or no. You just couldn't trust galaxy-wide scientific syndicates not to come up with new ways of screwing people over. Maybe they had turned his DNA into an astral antenna, broadcasting his location; maybe they had a computer that could predict how his rescuers would behave; or maybe ... just maybe ... they had gotten the boy away free and clear.

Staring up through the glassed dome ceiling of the common room, he watched as Delos IX came into view. There had been no sensation of deceleration, thanks to Mort's artificial gravity being top-notch. Mort was a bastard, a backstabber, and a weasel, but he was good with gravity. Delos IX had a green atmosphere; Carl couldn't say what chemical made it that color, but it made the planet look sickly. The view was marred by the structural supports, and the presence of the manually operated dorsal turret dead center in the top. Maybe he could have Mort glass the steel supports one of these days. That bastard.

Any minute now, Mort would chase everyone out of the common room so he could plunge them into astral space. He could have done it hours ago, but on the off chance anyone was paying too close attention to the *Mobius*, Carl didn't want them to see a ship disappear from the astral sensors that watched the standard depths. As soon as they were on the far side of Delos IX, they could sneak into astral space with no one the wiser.

The ship shook, and Carl saw the flash of the ship's shields taking a hit. Dropping the datapad to the floor, he ran for the cockpit. The ship-wide comm crackled with Tanny's voice, "Mriy, take the turret. We've got incoming!"

Carl reached the cockpit at a sprint and slammed into the back of the co-pilot's seat to stop himself. "What've we got?" His eyes were already scanning the instruments.

"Hostile dropped out of astral right in front of us. Titan Nine frigate ... launched four Komodo fighters and backed off." Tanny jerked on the flight yoke, running through a basic evasive battery straight out of the marine flight manual. The ship shook with another hit.

Carl reached forward and opened a comm on an unsecured channel. "Unidentified ship ... stand down. Repeat, stand down or we will return fire."

"I just sent Mriy to return fire," Tanny said as soon as Carl closed the comm.

"Whatever. It never stops anyone from firing, but it might get them to tell us why."

"Mobius, this is the Viper. Power down your weapons and engines, and prepare to hand over the boy."

"Well, that answers that," said Carl. "Harmony Bay has it in for me personally."

"Yeah, sounds like it," Tanny agreed. The ship took another hit. "So what, hand him over or fight it out?"

"We give them Adam, and they'll just dust us anyway," said Carl. "You just slide over and let me handle the flying for this one."

"Like hell I will, after that stunt you pulled," Tanny replied, turning a shoulder to block Carl from getting past her to the flight yoke. The ship took two more hits, causing Carl to stumble. "If it weren't for you rubbing those dogs' noses in their own shit, they might not be looking to hollow us out right now." Another impact rocked them.

"Would you *stop* letting them hit us?" Carl asked.

"We have plenty of shield reserves, and Mriy needs to aim," said Tanny. "And I'm not *letting* them hit anything. Those are Komodos. They're twice as maneuverable as we are."

"Leave that to me," said Carl. "You go back there and kick Mriy off the turret controls. You're the better shot."

"Carl, just—"

"That's an order!" Carl snapped. "This is *my* ship, and I'm not ready to go down with it over a few upset stomachs."

Tanny snarled at him and slipped out of the harness. "Fine!" She shouldered past Carl and headed toward the common room and the turret. "If you get us killed, I'm coming to Hell to personally torment you," she called back.

The pilot's chair was still warm from Tanny's occupation. Sharing the warmth of a seat was about as close as they got to one another these days, but it was still comforting. As soon as Carl's hand gripped the yoke, it hit him: everyone's lives were riding on him. His palms began to sweat as he pulled them into a twisting climb. He hit the selector for the maneuvering thrusters, just as he'd done in the simulator, but nothing happened. He flipped it to the off position and back on—still nothing.

He jabbed a finger to the ship-wide comm button. "Oh, Roddy, dear," Carl singsonged through gritted teeth. "Please come up to the cockpit and *fix my goddamn ship!*"

Carl maneuvered as best he could with the computer flight assist active. They took a few more hits, with Carl juggling power to the aft shields as he kept the Komodos behind him. *"Not so smart now, tough guy?"* a voice came over the ship-to-ship comm. It was the squad leader from Duster's—possibly the sorest loser Carl had ever encountered. He felt an urge to snark back, but it was hard to come up with something clever to say when you were losing a fight.

"What's wrong?" Roddy asked, vaulting into the co-pilot's chair as soon as he entered the cockpit.

Carl's attention snapped back to the cockpit. "Manual thruster control's gone," Carl said. He saw bolts of high-energy plasma lance past the cockpit as he dodged fire.

"Yeah," said Roddy, "Safety feature at these speeds. Tanny had me upgrade it to military code."

"That's bullshit," Carl replied. "Tear out those safeties."

Roddy opened his mouth, but Carl glared plasma bolts of his own. "Sure thing, boss." The laaku stuck his head under the control console and removed a panel. Carl lost sight of him down there, but could hear the mechanic at work. He felt like a shuttle bus pilot with the way *Mobius* was handling.

"I cobble-jobbed a quick bypass," Roddy's voice echoed from inside the console. "Try now."

Carl flicked the switch for manual control, and suddenly the *Mobius* leapt at his command. He felt the rise in his stomach as the ship's movement fought against the dampening effects of Mort's gravity enchantment and snuck some force through to the crew.

Roddy moaned from below. "I'm not going to enjoy this, am I?"

"Nope, probably not," said Carl. He was panting for

breath, his heart racing. "Just head for the engine room and get ready to fix anything that breaks."

As soon as Roddy was gone, Carl squeezed his eyes shut, fighting down a wave of panic. It had been a long time since he'd flown in a live dogfight. He opened his eyes. That was it: *dogfight*. Keeping one hand on the flight yoke and twisting the ship through maneuvers by muscle memory, he opened file clusters on the *Mobius'* computer. Carl opened an archive and scanned through sub-clusters, burrowing down until he found what he was looking for.

The cluster title was "Dogfight 7" and it dated back to his navy days. He selected "play" and slid the volume indicator to maximum. In seconds, the growl of distorted guitars thundered through the cockpit. By the time the snarling vocals came in, Carl's hands had stopped shaking. He seethed out a deep breath and opened the ship-wide comm. "This is your pilot speaking. Please strap in and prepare to kick some ass. That is all."

Even with the maneuvering thrusters at his disposal, the *Mobius* was a hulking brute compared to the Komodos. It handled like the diplomatic shuttle it had been born as. In combat, it was the snapping turtle of vessels—all shell, with just enough bite to make someone wary of getting too close. Four medium-weight fighter craft were the perfect foil to use against it. Carl couldn't outrun them, and Mort couldn't take them astral while they were under fire. It was time for a new plan.

Carl dove for the planet.

Tanny's voice crackled from the turret comm. "What the hell are you doing? I can't get a track on these things with the ship jerking around, and you're going to crush us hitting atmo' at this speed."

"When was the last time they hit us?" Carl asked. "Just keep shooting. A couple lucky shots is all it'll take."

"Atmo," Tanny reiterated.

"Leave that to me."

Carl preferred to do most of his navigating by feel while under fire, but one task he always left to the computer was reentry vectors. The navigation computer blinked red with the words "No Valid Trajectory." Carl feathered back the throttle until it relented and plotted him a safe reentry angle. Just before the *Mobius* hit the atmosphere of Delos IX, Carl reached for a set of switches he had hardly ever needed. The shields were washed in flame as the gasses that swirled around the planet ignited, setting off beeping alarms that temporarily interrupted the music blaring through the cockpit.

He hit the switches, and the shields reshaped. Instead of an egg-shaped blob around the ship, they stretched, sharpened, and took on an aerodynamic profile, tied into the flight yoke. Roddy had given him a barrel of grief over installing it, but Carl had wanted it for just this sort of emergency. The *Mobius* bled speed as it forced its way through the clouds of the uninhabited world. The beeping alarms stopped as the ship's momentum was no longer enough to burn the atmosphere around them, and the next song came on. This time it was a heavy instrumental piece with a hammering bass line and primitive synthesizer.

On the radar, the four Komodo ships were slowing down and entering the atmosphere well behind him. *Mobius's* shields were sturdy enough to allow them to come in with more speed without burning up. Carl continued his dive, watching through the murky green haze for signs of terrain. He pulled up when he saw a mountain range, which might have been eerily beautiful had he stopped to enjoy it. Rocky spires shot into the emerald heavens, larger than the greatest peaks of Earth or Mars.

He keyed the comm to the turret. "I'll try to string 'em out through the mountains. Atmosphere should slow them down more than us."

"How much of our shield power did you just throw away?" Tanny asked.

Carl shrugged, even though he knew she couldn't see him. "Some. Just keep those guns warm."

He banked as he pulled the *Mobius* through a valley between two enormous peaks. He saw flashes of plasma slam into the mountainsides to the starboard side of the ship. The Komodos were behind him and trying to close in, thrusters plowing their semi-aerodynamic hulls through the atmosphere. The *Mobius* took three hits in rapid succession; Carl crested one peak and dove down one behind them.

One of the Komodos disappeared from radar. "Got one," Tanny shouted over the comm. Another shot hit the shields, causing the aerodynamic shape to fluctuate. A momentary panic came over Carl as the ship lurched toward the ground, but the shields reformed and he was able to pull up.

Another blip vanished from the radar. Carl opened the ship-to-ship. "Not so fancy now, huh, you burger-hustling sim-jockeys? Stick to the restaurant circuit; the ocean's too deep for you boys."

The last two fighters broke off pursuit, but Carl was past the bygones point. There came a time in any battle when letting the other guy go just sat wrong in a pilot's stomach—when the fight got too personal, the ramifications too complicated to think of in the heat of the moment. Maybe the other guy would never want to think about the incident again; maybe it would turn into a vendetta. With those angry red blips still flashing in the radar screen, the solution seemed obvious. Caution demanded fiery wreckage, and mercy seemed like a fool's plan.

Carl pulled up, rolled, and twisted the *Mobius* around to give chase. The cockpit shuddered as the shields took the brunt of the high G-force maneuvering, straining the generators to maintain the shields' shape. Ignoring the warning lights of impending shield overload, Carl hammered the throttle open, blood still pumping in time with the rhythm of the bass. For once, he took Tanny's need to aim into account and held a steady course, taking a gentle hand to the yoke as he kept on the tails of the two remaining Komodos.

Carl clucked his tongue. "Not even splitting up?" he muttered, not even able to hear his own voice. He was tempted to open fire with the *Mobius's* forward guns, but he could see Tanny's shots tracking them, now that the battle was taking place in front of him. She had everything under control. First one, then the other Komodo burst into a cloud of shrapnel and plume of ignited oxygen.

Carl shut down the music and let out a whoop. When he caught his breath, he keyed the ship-wide comm. "All clear everyone. Roddy, run a quick check, make sure we're not leaking anything important. Mort, get ready to drop us astral as soon as I bring us back to our departure point."

He climbed out of the atmosphere, disengaging the aerodynamic shielding effect. As he did so, he took his first close look at the shield status readout: five percent. It was closer than he had meant to cut things, but the engines seemed intact, and they would power back up while the *Mobius* traveled between systems.

"Carl!" Tanny shouted over the comm. "You forgot the carrier!"

His eyes first widened, then shot over to the radar. Around the far side of the planet came the *Viper* on an intercept course. The *Mobius* was only a third of the *Viper's* displacement, and outgunned, but they had speed on their side. Carl fired the maneuvering thrusters and swung them full about, aiming out to the deep ocean between stars. The safety harness bit into his shoulder as the inertia tried to throw him across the cockpit despite the ship's gravity spell. Once more, Carl opened up the throttle to full, thinking to get far enough ahead that they could escape astrally. Even if the *Viper* had scanners that could sweep between standard astral depths, he doubted they could go deep enough to keep up. The *Mobius* would just need to—

The ship shook, and Carl's neck whipped forward. Spots swam before his eyes. When he blinked his vision back to working order, they were adrift. The shield indicator read zero. Main thrusters had gone out. The *Viper* hailed them.

"Mobius, stand down and prepare to be boarded. Resistance will be met with deadly force. Turn the boy over unharmed, or you're all as good as dead."

---

The floor bucked under Carl's feet as he ran for his quarters. The *Viper* had latched on with capture claws. "They're coming for us!" he shouted on the way. Realizing that not everyone could hear him, he hit the common room ship-wide comm. "Arm yourselves and prepare to repel boarders."

In his quarters, he dug through the hastily stored weapons that had been unearthed as if from an ancient tomb during the Tally-ho's inspection. He belted on a holster with the blaster already in. He drew the weapon, popped the power pack out, checked that it was full, and snapped it back into the grip. Three more power packs slipped into his pockets. Turning to leave, he had a stray thought and returned for his runed graphite sword. If the power packs ran out, he didn't want to go unarmed.

A klaxon blared, letting everyone aboard know that there was a hull breach. Carl was only marginally worried about losing pressure. They wanted Adam alive, and that meant cutting through the hull someplace where the *Viper's* people had life support latched onto the far side. He brushed aside the idea of grabbing his EV helmet and rushed to the cargo hold.

He got as far as the doorway.

The *Viper* had cut through the cargo bay door near the center, and invaders were firing up at the walkway, where Mriy and Tanny were already armed and returning fire. The corner of the common room by the refrigerator had become their bunker. Carl ducked as splats of low-energy plasma whizzed through the open door. He bent in half as he slunk up beside Tanny to get a status.

"How's it looking?" he asked.

Tanny was armed with a blaster rifle, and was poking it around with a blind scope to lay down suppression fire. "Oh, just peachy. Ship that size, they've probably got us outnumbered four to one. The only grace we've gotten is that they're trying not to vent the ship to space; otherwise, they'd have shot right through the walls."

"I cannot reach them," Mriy said. "Perhaps we let them advance?"

"That's the backup plan," Tanny replied. "For now we keep firing and hope we hit a few. They're here for the money; they might not like their payout if they see a few buddies die."

Carl tried to think as the klaxon blared, but all he could

come up with was to join Tanny and Mriy in firing back at the boarders. Standing above Tanny's crouch, he reached his blaster around and squeezed off three shots. He pulled his hand back before someone took a shot and blew it off.

Tanny checked in her scope. "You barely hit the wall they breached."

"Where's Roddy?" Carl asked. "Maybe he can rig up something to power those disintegrator rifles from the power packs we've got."

"The rifles are halfway between us and them," Tanny said. "We can't even *get* to them. I sent Roddy down to see if he can get us engine power for a breakaway."

"Good idea," Carl said, nodding.

Plasma bolts continued to come intermittently, the invaders conserving their power, trying to time a shot as someone poked a weapon at them. They had nothing but time on their hands, as far as they knew. Carl snapped a few shots around the doorway, then winced as a bolt of plasma caught his blaster. Composite plastic shards sprayed from the shattered weapon. He clapped a hand to the side of his neck where it felt like a bee had stung him.

"Carl!" Tanny shouted. "You're hit."

He gritted his teeth as he put his back to the wall and slid down to a seated position. "I noticed that."

"Shit, you're bleeding," Tanny said. She turned toward the crew quarters, just a few meters away. "Esper, get out here and help him; he's cut bad."

Mriy's ears flattened against her head, and she hunkered back against the side of the refrigerator. "Death comes."

"Come on," said Carl. "Let's not write me off just yet." Mriy shook her head and pointed.

There was a thump of wood on steel, and then another, a

drumbeat of calm menace playing counterpoint to the frantic shriek of the klaxon. They turned and saw what Mriy had seen. Mort emerged from his quarters clad in black robes, a chain of heavy silver links around his neck, bearing a graven pendant. The thumping was the staff he carried as a walking stick. His scowl carried the weight of storms; his eyes promised fire. With casual disdain he slammed the head of his staff against the wall, and the klaxon stopped.

"Mort," Carl grunted as he tried to hold back the flow of blood from his neck. "What are you doing?"

"Mort, no!" Tanny warned. "We've talked about this. We need the ship's tech to stay alive."

"Mordecai The Brown will not meet his end cowering behind the paltry protections of science. If this is to be our end, let there be a reckoning in blood and fire. I'm going to show these fuckers something very, very old."

He strode past the three defenders at the door. None tried to bar his path as he presented himself in full glory before the open door. He leveled his staff at the invaders that only his vantage allowed him to see, and cursed in that harsh, guttural language that spoke of demons and angels. From the staff came fire, and the lights in the common room went dark. By the time the soft, red emergency lighting came on, Mort was gone, disappeared down into the cargo hold, and perhaps beyond, to do battle with the crew of the *Viper*.

The door to Chip's old quarters opened. "Stay put," Esper said, speaking back inside as she peeked out. "What's going on out here?"

"Carl took a piece of shrapnel to his neck," Tanny replied. "Go find the med kit."

Esper closed the door behind her and hurried to Carl's side. She saw the blood seeping from between his fingers where they covered his neck. Kneeling down beside him, she turned to Tanny. "I don't know where it is. You go; I'll stay with him."

"I need to cover the—"

"I heard Mort's little speech. And I don't hear any more shooting. Just go."

Tanny glared at Esper, but didn't argue the point. Carl managed a weak smile as she left. "She hates getting the fun taken out of her hand ... I mean gun."

"Just you relax," Esper said. "Now take your hand away." To reinforce her point, she tugged gently at the hand that was staunching the blood. Instantly it spurted forth, but she covered the wound with her hands. Carl grimaced, and grunted in pain as she pressed down.

Through squinted eyes, Carl saw her lips moving. She had her eyes closed. In the dim crimson light, she looked unhallowed, like someone had come and replaced Sister Esper Theresa Richelieu with a creature of magic and darkness, performing a foul ritual. For a moment, Carl thought it was his imagination, exacerbated by blood loss. Then a stabbing pain clenched at his stomach and latched on. He doubled over in pain, and Esper let go of his neck.

"Get him something from the fridge," Esper ordered Mriy. The azrin looked at her with narrowed eyes, uncomprehending. "He needs food; his body just used up its reserves healing itself."

"Gah," Carl grunted. "What'd you *do* to me?"

"I sinned, but I may have saved your life," Esper replied.

---

The crackle of flames and a whiff of brimstone in the air hearkened back to the battlefields of Mort's ancestors. Too often he felt bottled up, squeezed into a tin can in the vast Black Ocean, unable to unleash his magic for fear of fouling the bedratted technology that kept them afloat. Putting on his formal Convocation robes had seemed like vanity at first, but as fire leapt from his staff and his voice boomed thunder, the old confidence returned. A pained groan from the floor told him that one of his would-be killers was still alive. Mort jabbed the butt of his staff down at the half-burnt pirate; the wood tip never touched the man, but the deck plates beneath buckled at the force of an unseen blow. He left the corpse in a shallow depression newly formed in the floor.

He stumbled. One footstep was too light as the ship's gravity wavered for a moment, then reverted to normal. Mort's eyes narrowed. Someone was fiddling with the ship's gravity stone, and he had a fair guess of who it might be. A ship the *Viper's* size ought to have had its own mechanics aboard for both scientific and magical devices. The poor slob of a science mechanic could have been any of a number of corpses littering the ship, but he had yet to run across anything resembling a wizard.

In theory, Mort knew precisely where he was heading—the ship's gravity stone, nestled somewhere below him and roughly fifty feet to his right. The problem was that the ship was made by engineers. The layout was nonsense. Mort spent the better part of five minutes punching buttons on a door-side control panel to no avail. After melting a hole through the door made from a not-quite-metal scientific material, all he found beyond was a lavatory.

"What bumbling nutter locks a loo from the outside?" he muttered.

Three melted door-holes later, the found the stairs down to

the lower level. The air was growing foul with acrid smoke from dead bodies and the strange substance the doors were fashioned from. Despite the stale, processed smell below, it was easier to breathe as he went down. Fortunately, once he was on the same level as the gravity stone, it was easier to find his way. One door opened at his approach, startling Mort, and one more yielded to magical coercion.

The room inside was thick with science, but arcane energy thrummed beneath. At the far wall was a set of crystal and stone rods held together in a lattice of wires—the *Viper's* star drive. In the center of the room, set atop a scientific steel pedestal, was a sphere of pure, Earth-quarried granite—a gravity stone. It was not the decorative, mineral-veined granite found in bar-tops and decorative flooring, but the plain, serious sort used in ancient headstones. Standing between these two wonders of modern magic was a sniveling excuse for a wizard.

"Stay back," the *Viper's* star drive mechanic warned, his hands resting on the gravity stone. "I can crush you where you stand."

Mort felt a twinge. *You are heavy*, the universe told him. *You are being crushed into a tiny ball centered just behind your navel.* The sensation was that of a giant mitten closing around him—soft, smothering, and firm. It was a sign that this pissant wretch of a grav-jockey was adept at his business—Mort was surprised to feel anything at all.

*Like hell I am*, Mort replied to the universe, asserting his own self-image through an act of will. *Quit bothering me if you know what's good for you.* He had never shied from threats made by the greater universe around him, and was not about to stand idly by while it tried to convince him he was a source of gravity.

Mort jabbed a bony finger down on the surface of the

gravity stone. The granite split in twain with the crack of a sledgehammer's strike. "Care to try that again?" he asked with a smile of feigned sweetness.

"Wh-who are you?" the star drive mechanic asked, backing away from the ruined stone. Though the *Viper's* gravity still functioned, it was bleeding away and in no shape to be used as a weapon. When Mort took a step forward instead of answering, his staff thumping on the deck like a funeral bell, the mechanic threw up his hands in surrender. "I'll serve; two years indentured. You've got me." Mort took another step. "It's bad luck to kill a wizard."

"That's because the Convocation used to send wizards like me after the ones who killed them," Mort relied. "I am Mordecai The Brown, former holder of the Eighth Seat, Guardian of the Plundered Tomes, and current *persona non grata* with the higher-ups in the Convocation, so I'm not registering any apprentices. But if you mention my name in the afterlife, I'm sure there's a support group for wizards I've killed."

The star drive mechanic gave a choked gasp. Without the *Viper's* gravity stone objecting, it was a simple matter to convince the universe that it was the mechanic whose body was the wellspring of gravity aboard. The mechanic crumpled into the fetal position in mid-air, while a datapad and the contents of a toolbox leapt to press against him. Mort didn't drag things out; this wasn't personal, after all. He squeezed, and the lights went out in the ship. A few crackles and pops, and he allowed the mechanic's body to flop to the floor with a wet splat. "*Kirash,*" he whispered, and the end of his staff glowed with enough light to see the mass of twisted and broken limbs at his feet.

Mort coughed. The air was getting worse. The whoosh

and hum that was the undercurrent of any ship's environmental controls had gone silent. It was not the sort of thing Mort typically took note of, but its absence shouted alarm to him. Stumbling through a haze of magically illuminated smoky corridors, he made his way back to the *Mobius* before he passed out.

---

In the wake of most battles, the smoke cleared. When Mort stumbled back into the common room, coughing and batting the smoke from his robes, there was no functioning life support system to disperse it. Carl slammed the common room door closed behind the wizard. Everyone who had EV suits had already changed into them. Tanny, Mriy, and Carl were waiting in the common room for Mort to return, while Roddy was down in the engineering bay, trying to see what he could patch back together. Esper, Adam, and now Mort were all without environmental protection.

"Boss," Roddy came over the comm in Carl's helm. "We got a whole lot of nothing. Good news: nothing looks beyond repair. Bad news: this isn't gonna be quick."

"You've got to come up with something for the life support," Carl replied. "We're short three EV suits for a long-term plan. Even the life support in the crew quarters aren't—"

"I'm the one who told you, remember?"

"Just ... go fix something," Carl replied. "Life support first ... salvage stuff from the *Viper* if you need to."

"It safe over there?" Roddy asked.

Carl relayed the question to the wizard. "How would I know?" Mort replied. "Starships are inherently *unsafe*. I tell you this much, there's no one over there in enough pieces to point a weapon at you."

"Yeah, Roddy. It's all clear."

"Wait," said Tanny. "What if we stashed them in that damned albatross of an escape pod you can't get rid of?"

It was hard to give a withering look through the smoky plastic visor of an EV helmet, but Carl gave his best effort anyway. "After all Mort just did ... you can't tell me that piece of junk took all that?"

"Do lights and blinky things mean it was working?" asked Mort. It was an astounding observation on his part, on par with the time he managed to use the ship-wide comm. "Because it had things blinking."

"Let's get Adam and Esper something to cover their faces to make a run for it," said Carl.

"... and speaking of things not working," Mort continued. "I thought you were bleeding out your last drops just a few minutes ago."

"Ask Esper about it," Carl said. "You three might be cooped up in there a while."

"Me?" Mort scoffed. "But I don't—"

"I offered you an EV suit years ago, and you didn't want one. Time to live with that decision. Now get moving; air's a wasting."

---

The door swung shut and latched with a quick hiss of compressed air. They were sealed in. Mort slumped down into one of the four seats in the escape pod with a huff, folding his arms. He brought with him more of the smoky smell that had only started to dissipate as the pod's life support system worked to filter the air. He harrumphed.

"Looks like we're stuck here a while," said Mort.

Esper nodded. She couldn't think of anything she wanted to say to the wizard. She kept as far from him as the tight confines of the escape pod allowed.

"How comes this thing still works?" Adam asked. "Just about everything else broke."

Mort scowled. "How should I know? Far as I can tell, most of this stuff shouldn't work in the first place. It's all plastic and wires and whatnot with tiny sparks of lightning chasing each other around inside. But then, that's science at work for you; never makes a lick of proper sense."

"Don't you go filling the boy's head with nonsense," said Esper. "Science works, and if you took the time to study it, you'd see how, too."

Mort waved a hand in her direction and looked away. "I've heard it all before. The professors, the researchers, the would-be science evangelists. They pull out Newton and Einstein and Hawking, and tell me those tidy little equations make it all work. I counter with del Braham, Miang, and Copperfield. It all goes round in circles 'til everyone's hackles are up and no one's convinced anyone of anything."

"But science works," Adam said. "I mean, there's proof."

Mort shrugged. "Never said it didn't. Just not my preferred modus."

"No, you prefer blasting things with fire," Esper snapped.

Mort chuckled. "Is *that* what has your snoot in a snit? I figured a science fanatic would approve. I took a big problem and reduced it to smaller pieces."

"I'm not a science fanatic," Esper protested. "But misusing God's power is a sin."

"I used my own power. God's got plenty of His own," said Mort. "And like hell I sinned. I saved all of us. From what I've gathered, *you* have a bit of your own."

Esper swallowed. She had hoped to avoid this conversation. "I learned that trick a long time ago, before I heard the calling. Even for good cause, it was a sin, and I'll do penance for it."

"Long time ago? A long time ago your parents hadn't met. You haven't got a long time in you, period," said Mort. "You saved Carl's life, and you're ready to throw yourself up on a cross for it. I killed nineteen people just a few minutes ago, and I'm feeling pretty damned heroic, if I must say. Which one of us has his priorities straight?"

"*Their* priorities," Adam said.

"Huh?"

"You presupposed an answer with the masculine pronoun," Adam replied. "It's a nasty trick. You asked a question with just one answer."

"He didn't mean to—" Esper said, but Mort cut her off with a laugh.

"Guilty, I admit. We could make a wizard out of you yet, boy."

Adam frowned, but that just caused Mort to laugh anew.

"So how's a sweet, spoiled thing like you learn a bit of magic, anyway?" Mort asked. "Your parents have retrogressive views on education, or something?"

"I'd rather not talk about it."

"Suit yourself," Mort replied. "But we've got nothing to do but wait out the repairs, and if Carl's in a helpful mood, it might be a while. If you ignore the boy, you could even consider it confession. Not like you're going to find a more sympathetic soul when it comes to magic."

"Confession isn't about sympathy; it's about compassion and understanding the temptation of sin, and the cleansing of the soul afterward."

"There are only seven real sins, you know," Mort said. "Convince me which you broke, and I'll admit you sinned in saving Carl."

Esper remained quiet. He was baiting her. Wizards were devilishly clever by training and by nature, and Mort wouldn't have asked if he wasn't prepared to counter her answers.

Mort leaned forward. "Did you know that Earth is the only world to hear God's word and think he meant for us not to use magic? The Seekers have shown it's all the same religion, all the same root, and yet Earth is the only place where you're a heretic for practicing the ancient ways. Among Mriy's people, you'd be revered. Roddy's would consider you duty-bound to use that power of yours to help people."

"I've never met a Seeker," Esper replied, hanging her head. "I was raised in the One Church. We didn't consort with those sorts."

"You should," said Mort. "Otherwise, you're doomed to self-loathing and self-flagellation for doing what your heart tells you is right. A man who tells you he has all the answers is lying to himself and to you. A man who admits he knows nothing is a man you should turn to for advice. Whoever taught you that trick of magic was a proper saint."

Esper snorted. "I never thought I'd hear anyone called Tamra Dawson a saint."

Mort raised an eyebrow, and Esper sighed. "We were just kids, really," she said. "I was fourteen, maybe fifteen at the time. I'd just gotten these." She bared her perfect white teeth in neither a smile nor a snarl. "Mine weren't straight, and even if they got straightened, they weren't shaped just right. My mother had them replaced with ceramite implants. They only let me use painkillers the first few days, but the pain lasted weeks. Tamra's parents were the same way with her; she'd gone in for more upgrades and adjustments than I ever had. She'd picked up this trick, you see—never told me where. It speeds up your body's own healing. I didn't even realize it was magic at first; I just thought it was one of those hokey ancient get-well-by-thinking-well mantras. But it worked. I got good at it. I'd come back from the cosmo half patched up—natural healing's supposed to make the results look smoother. Next day, I'd be fine, but I'd eat my way through a week's meals."

Mort nodded. "I wouldn't mind learning a trick like that. Sounds damned handy."

"I practiced. I got good at it. I needed to, since my mother was never satisfied. Teeth, irises, ears, cheekbones. I've had my nose reshaped three times because she changed her mind about what looked best on me. Breasts, hips, buttocks, feet, fingers, and ribs, all adjusted to her liking. It took six tries shaping my vocal chords and soft palette until she liked my voice. Every follicle on my body has been replaced or removed. But it was when she decided to take me in for personality softening that I ran."

Mort reached across the pod and put a hand on her shoulder. She flinched, but his touch was gentle and warm. "And you did the right thing."

"My body barely has any fat cells left," she said, sniffing. "I can't go long periods without eating because my body can't store it."

"I meant with Carl," Mort said. "But running away was right, too. Everyone here's running from something. It's the sort of place for people who don't belong."

"Chocolate bar?" Adam asked. Producing one from his

pocket. Leave it to a ten-year-old to take provisions for seques-
tration of unknown duration and pack candy.

"Yes, thank you." Esper snatched the bar, perhaps too
violently to be considered polite, and tore the wrapper off. She
bit into the bar and savored not just the flavor, but the gritty
texture of the chocolate. "Where'd you get this?" she asked
after swallowing her first bite.

"They're Tanny's, I think," Mort said. Esper stopped cold.
There was no feasible way to un-eat a bite of chocolate and put
the wrapper back around it, but if there were she would have
done it in an instant.

Mort just laughed. "Don't worry. I won't tell her. For all
she'll know, Adam ate it. I'm a fair hand at keeping secrets. For
instance, I haven't mentioned to anyone about that pendant
you wear ... and I don't mean your order's cross."

Esper felt her face warm. There was no way he could
know. Or could he? He was a wizard after all. "It's just sentimental. I've had it forever."

"Forever, or since you were ... oh, eleven, maybe twelve or
thirteen? Helps you out once a month, give or take? I can sniff
out an enchantment as easily as you smell chocolate in the air.
But like I said, I can keep a secret. I imagine you must be able
to, too. The One Church is rather particular on that subject."

Esper offered a weak smile. "None of them noticed, so I
never said anything. It's not against the vows."

"What vows?" Adam asked.

Mort cleared his throat. "So, how long you think those
repairs are going to take?"

---

Carl wished he had sent Tanny over to the *Viper*. She had the stronger stomach. Other navy officers, active and retired alike, kept up a stubborn rivalry with the marines, but Carl would never begrudge them the ability to walk through a pile of bodies without getting sick. There was no unseeing the things that Mort had done to the crew of the hostile vessel. All he could say for the wizard's work was that it didn't look like any of the mercenaries suffered long, and that with a strong enough alkaline solution, most of it would clean up. But Tanny was helping Roddy get the *Mobius* spaceworthy again, and Carl's errand was less than vital in that regard. In the near term thereafter, what he was looking for could be crucial.

The *Viper* was roomier than the *Mobius*, the interior all colored in garish spray-art; probably the work of one of the crew. It was hard to imagine any captain *paying* to have that sort of thing done to virtually every interior surface of his ship, but then again, some captains had strange tastes. The haze of smoke made the air murky and caught the light from Carl's hand lamp. There was no emergency lighting on board, but here and there an indicator blinked, showing that there was power at work somewhere to supply it. It was as good a sign as Carl could hope for. He headed toward the cockpit.

It was strange at times, being a fighter pilot by trade. His destination was, by all standard parlance, a bridge. Yet any enclosed space dedicated to flying made him revert to Typhoon jargon. The *Viper's* bridge was abandoned. It appeared as if all hands had been called to battle Mort. Aside from the haze of smoke and the lack of ambient light, it looked serviceable. He sat down in the captain's chair and hit a button at random on the armrest console. It lit.

"Hey Roddy," he called over the comm. "How's things?"

"You know," the comm crackled, "This really isn't the time

to be riding my ass. Just leave me the hell alone to do my job. When the ship's fixed, you'll be the first to know."

"Sorry, just thought you might be interested to hear that the *Viper* has power to her bridge."

"You gotta be fucking kidding me," Roddy replied. "Mort fried the *Mobius* worse than their scrap heap? I installed all that obsidian for nothing?"

"We planned ahead for gravity and astral drive," Carl replied. "We didn't have a contingency for Mort impersonating Genghis Khan."

"I'm going to have to tell Mort that one," said Tanny. It was an open comm among the EV helms and the cockpit, so Tanny and Mriy heard everything they said. "He'd get a kick."

"Who is Genkis Khan?" Mriy asked.

"Human from about a million years ago," Carl replied. He didn't know exactly, and Mriy probably didn't care. "He killed half a continent's worth of people using tech like the azrins had before the rest of the galaxy discovered you."

"I think I like him," Mriy replied.

"So how 'bout it Roddy?" Carl asked. "With the two ships joined up, could we use the *Viper's* life support to clear both ships?"

"You owe me a beer," Roddy replied.

"I what?"

"Not you," Tanny replied. "I bet him you'd be more trouble than help."

"Thanks."

"Anytime."

Carl settled back in the captain's chair and fiddled with the controls until he got the main screen to display the communications logs. It was reverse chronological and had both voice transcriptions and text communiques intermixed. It was fancy.

If Carl wanted to keep records of his comm traffic, he had to link a datapad to the *Mobius's* computer. After skipping past the conversation between himself and the *Viper's* captain—which carried a strange sense of deja vu—he found what he was looking for:

0832:05:15:2560 C.B.DYSON: 75000 NOW, REST WHEN ADAM DELIVERED SAFELY.

DESTINATION TBD. ADAM WILL INFORM YOU AFTER RETRIEVAL. TRANSMITTING COURSE DATA.

"Gotcha."

"What's that?" Tanny asked. Carl had spoken with the comm still open. It was damnably inconvenient to turn off and on while wearing the helmet.

"You three, change of plans. Get over to the *Viper's* cockpit. I need you all to see something."

---

The hours passed, and the inside of the escape pod grew ever smaller. The walls stayed where they were of course; it was Esper's need to be on the other side of them that kept growing. She kept looking out into the cargo bay through the pod's tiny windows, looking for a glimpse of one of the crew in their EV suits or for some sign that the smoke was clearing. The problem was that the lights were so low outside the pod that the glare from the ones inside kept her from seeing much. To his credit, Mort had kept up a lively conversation to drag her mind away from their predicament.

"... and that's when I knew that we were going to be stuck with Mriy on board," Mort said, finishing what must have been his twentieth anecdote.

"So it was all a misunderstanding?" Adam asked. "She didn't mean to kill him?"

Mort twisted his face and scratched his chin with one finger. "I can't say for certain. Oh, I'm sure she didn't start out meaning to kill her brother. Her kind fights for dominance in the family as a matter of course. It's just ... well, there are rules for that sort of thing, she didn't follow them, and it happened. Azrin don't think much is wrong with killing in general, but within the family they don't put up with it."

"Hopefully, the longer they're exposed to human—I mean civilized—cultures, the more they'll respect life," Esper said. "Mriy doesn't seem as bad as I've heard her kind are, but she's still a savage."

"No one's as bad as the stories about their people," Mort countered. "You should hear the stories they tell about us, especially in regards to dark science. I mean, just look at the two of us; then, consider those bastards who mucked up Adam's brain, not to mention cloning him."

Adam frowned. "My brain's not mucked up. The doctors even said so."

"Well, now there's a—"

A thump from the door ended the debate abruptly. With a hiss of equalizing pressure, Esper's ears popped and the door opened. Carl stood outside, still in his EV suit. He pressed a helmet into her hands, and tossed another to Mort. "Put those on and come out here. Adam, stay put."

"What's this all about?" Mort asked.

"We're wasting the pod's air. I'll explain outside."

Esper put hers on with some trepidation. The helmet had to have come from the *Viper*. She could only pray that it had not been taken from the dead. The rubber membrane sealed against the underside of her chin, and she took a deep breath.

It was stale air, but the purified, sterile sort of stale, and there was no smell of anything unsavory having happened inside it recently.

Mort glared at Carl from beneath one raised eyebrow, but crammed the helmet over his head. "I feel like an idiot."

"You look like one," Carl said. "Now, get out so we don't let Adam's air out."

Mriy was standing by to close the pod door and seal Adam safely back inside.

"So, what's this all about?" Mort asked. "Why am I dressed up like some medieval motorcycle knight?"

"Sister Theresa, I think you have a holy duty to see to," Carl said. "We're about to inter nineteen men and women on Delos IX, and that ship is their coffin. We've cleared the ship; it's safe. Go do what you need to do."

Esper nodded. She found herself wondering whether it was pious to be thankful for such a grim duty. Alone among heathens and heretics, she was being asked to be a priestess once more.

"What about me?" Mort asked. "What am I out here for?"

"As soon as she's done, you're going to turn that place into a pyre."

Esper walked away down the boarding tunnel and into the *Viper*. It was a scene she was never going to forget. She had seen death before, but it was the whispering sort: age, disease, or more commonly a combination of both. This was death that howled. Bodies burnt like candle wicks lay shoved against the walls. Others had been torn to pieces by forces she could not imagine, drenching whole corridors in splattered blood, through which trails of footprints tracked in both directions. There was little doubt that the *Viper's* crew died in poor standing with the Lord. There were no mortally wounded to be brought back into grace before the end. It was all she could do to intercede on their behalf in death.

She wept, and prayed, and hoped fervently not to be sick inside her borrowed EV helmet.

---

"Fine," said Mort, "Now that she's out of earshot, can you tell me what's going on? Like hell you want me using more magic in that ship."

"Of course not," Carl replied, pulling off his EV helmet. He pointed a finger to Roddy, who flicked on a plasma torch and tack welded the door to the escape pod shut.

Mort scowled, but Carl could see the water-wheels turning the wizard's brain. "You got me. What's the punchline?"

Carl handed Mort a datapad with a transcription of the *Viper's* log. Mort took it gingerly by the edges and squinted down at it. After a moment, he straightened. Balancing the datapad in one hand like a serving platter, he tore the helmet from his head and threw it at Carl. "Air's fine out here."

"Yeah, Roddy got life support back up a couple hours ago. We needed you to see this first, before Esper."

Mort scanned the datapad for a moment. "This doesn't make any sense. C.B. Dyson is Chip, I presume. But why would Chip sell us out? How would he even have known about Adam? Was Chip in on this from the start?"

"Look at the date," Carl prodded.

Mort squinted and held the datapad closer. "What on this infernal thing is supposed to be a date?"

Carl grabbed the datapad out of the wizard's hands and pointed. "Right there. Those numbers, that's a date. Today's date."

Mort's eyes widened in dawning comprehension. "Chip's still alive! Or back from the dead. Either way, he seems hellbound on avenging himself on Adam, whom he probably blames for his—"

"Mort, it's not Chip, it's someone using Chip's ID," Carl replied. "This message was sent from the *Mobius* after we set course out of Delos. Using Chip's rig. From his quarters."

"From his quarters ..." Mort repeated. "Not Esper!"

"No," Carl replied. "Adam."

"Why would the boy kidnap himself?"

Carl led Mort by the arm away from the escape pod. There was no way Adam should have been able to hear from inside, but he was beyond the point of taking those sorts of risks. "He's not. He's buying himself free. Esper's plan to rescue him is naive; it's going to get him picked up by Harmony Bay again. He wants a clean break, to disappear, all witnesses disposed of."

"That means us," Roddy clarified as he walked over to join them.

"How? Where would the boy get that kind of money?" Mort asked.

"Doctor James Augustus Cliffton," Carl said with a smug smile.

Mort shook a finger in Carl's direction. "Now, wait just a minute. Esper said that dark scientist was dead. We had a long talk in that infernal pod, and she mentioned checking up on him while she waited on Adam's tests at the hospital. Was that a trick, or is this some elaborate scam?"

"The most elaborate scam I can think of. I'm convinced that Adam *is* Doctor Cliffton."

"But that's ... now wait just a minute ... you're saying that little boy is a one-hundred twelve-year-old man?" Mort asked.

Carl nodded. "It explains everything. Adam's tried ditching us at Willamette Station, but we 'rescued' him. He saw some unsavories at Duster's who looked like they might be for hire and had a grudge, and transmitted our coordinates and heading. I bet he even arranged for that escape pod to jam in the first place; he's been trying to lose Esper since before he met us. Who knows what else he tried that we never saw; all the records on our end are encrypted or destroyed. Doctor Cliffton *is* an expert with Chip's stuff. I had to dig into the *Viper's* computers to find proof."

"And he put the Tally-ho on our trail, too, I bet," Mort said.

"Maybe, but I'm guessing it was just Penny-Toad doing his job, policing the smuggling lanes. Getting picked up by a Navy patrol wouldn't do him much good."

"So what now?" Mort asked. "We toss him out a window in that pod?"

Carl chuckled. "It's tempting, but no. I've got something better in mind. But first I needed to know I had you on board. Now? Now, I've got the hard part."

---

It was as embarrassing as it was sad, losing count of the dead. Esper could have convinced herself of anywhere from seventeen to twenty. She was no forensics expert to say whose remains were whose, and where one began and another ended. The few who died alone were easiest. The filter on the EV helm kept away the smell and put a barrier of translucent plastic between her eyes and the horrors around her. It was all that kept her from being sick at the sights around her. Through the visor, she could imagine that it was all just a vivid simulation. A vague worry gnawed at her that she wasn't praying for real men and women, but for mere holograms.

The footsteps startled her into a gasp. Could there have been a survivor? As it turned out, it was just Carl in an EV helmet. The nonchalant swagger that he took wherever he went was absent. She almost wished he had been flippant about the carnage, just so she could chastise him for his part in it. Mort had been so ... proud wasn't the right word ... righteous, perhaps? It had been hard to argue with him. After all, she was only alive because of his intervention; so were the rest of them. Barring a miracle, the crew of the *Viper* would have killed them, and demanding a miracle was the epitome of Pride.

"You good here?" Carl asked, sweeping a pointed finger around the floor.

"No," she snapped, finding the opening she needed to vent her frustration. "There's nothing good here at all. Vile men or not, these deaths are on your hands, and you should treat them with a little more—"

"Easy; easy. I'm sorry," Carl said, holding up his hands. "But it's not me who brewed this batch of vinegar. Wasn't Mort either; he just cleaned it up ... well, clean maybe isn't the right word. But come up to the bridge and I'll show you who's to blame."

"Who?" she asked.

"I need you to see this for yourself," Carl replied. "I seem to recall bragging about being a lying sonofabitch, so I think the *Viper's* computers have a bit more credibility."

Esper followed Carl toward the front of the ship. "And you couldn't have altered this ship's records?"

Carl looked over his shoulder as he walked, the EV helmet masking his expression behind six millimeters of smoky black plastic. "You've been bunking in our computer guy's quarters; you performed his funeral yourself. Maybe it's your turn to show a little respect. These sim-hustlers were trying to kill us; Chip was family."

Esper followed quietly after that. It was true, everyone in the crew knew Carl was a gifted liar; they seemed oddly proud of it. But there was something in his voice that she had to believe was genuine—unless that was just how good a liar he truly was. At some point, she had to trust to her own judgment and decide whether he was the man he claimed to be, lies and all.

When the cockpit door closed behind her, Carl took off his helmet. "Air's clean enough to breathe. Just didn't want to smell Mort's handiwork." He pointed to the captain's chair. "Have a seat."

Esper obliged and set her own EV helmet at her feet. "What am I looking at?"

"Pull up the ship's comm log, starting with today and working backward."

"What am I looking for in there?"

"It stands out a bit. Don't worry."

The armrest console was simple enough to operate that she had no trouble with the unfamiliar system. For a mercenary vessel, the buttons and screens were all bright, cheerful, and helpful. In moments she had brought up the most recent communications to and from the *Viper*. She read the past day's entries with particular attention to detail as a hollow feeling welled inside her. Hoping she had missed some crucial detail, she read them once more. And when that reading failed to change her mind, she went through a third time, poring over one word at a time, trying to find double-meanings, mistaken identities, or unclear motivations.

"Now you see why I needed to show you, not just tell you?" Carl asked. His voice was soft and compassionate. She had already pieced the puzzle together, no doubt.

"I can't believe it was him all along."

"Old man is a blasted good actor; I'll give him that much," Carl replied. "He never ... you know ... tried anything, did he? I mean, you shared quarters and all."

Esper gave a sad, halfhearted smirk. "I made him turn away when I changed, and he never tried so much as a peek. You never would have known he was a grown man inside there. What are we going to do?"

"Well, we're certainly not letting him run loose," Carl said. "We locked him up in the escape pod. And we certainly can't deliver him to some poor, unsuspecting couple on Mars."

"You're not going to kill him, are you?" Esper asked, seeing where this line of logic was headed.

Carl scratched at the side of his head, losing his fingers in the mop of helmet-sweated hair. "Well, you see, we talked that one over, and none of us can kill a kid, even if he's not really a kid."

"So what, then?"

"We're turning him over to Harmony Bay," Carl replied.

Esper gasped. "But they'll—"

"Yeah, probably," Carl said, not even letting her finish. "But if we don't, and they get wind we had him, they'll dissect our brains to figure out where he went. We give him back; we wipe our hands clean of it. Tanny's already put the call in. They had a ship not too far off, be here in a few hours on a deep run."

Esper swallowed. There was a detail that Carl's plan was overlooking. "But they'll want me, too."

"That's why we have to kill you first."

Roddy sat on the floor of the cargo bay with a portable power supply and a multitool, all four hands working inside a panel of the escape pod. While the laaku worked, Adam knelt on one of the pod's seats, glaring out one of the windows. If looks could kill, his would have, but those sorts of powers were the province of wizards, not scientists. Without the tools of their various trades, men of science were just animals, left to the defenses of tooth and limb ... or voice, if they were lucky enough to find an adversary who could be overcome by reason or threat.

"That ought to do it," Roddy reported.

"Hey, Adam," Carl called out. "Can you hear me in there?"

"Let me out of here," Adam whined. "This isn't funny."

"You're not supposed to find it funny, Doctor Cliffton," Carl said, walking over to stand face to face with Adam, with just the window separating them. "None of *us* are laughing out here. You've left a lot of men dead in your trail and gotten their blood on our hands. But we've found you out."

"What do you mean? I'm not Doctor Cliffton; he's *old*. My name is Adam. It's Sister Theresa who's trying to get rid of you. She made me promise not to tell; she said she'd send me back to the Harmony Bay people if I didn't go along with her. I'm sorry. Please don't kill me."

Carl offered a reassuring smile. "Don't worry; we're not going to kill you. You're valuable. Your accomplice, on the other hand ..." Carl pointed outside Adam's field of view, and Tanny brought Esper over, wrists bound behind her back in a pair of duramite shackles they had found aboard the *Viper*. Though of similar heights, the difference in build between the two women was apparent in the ease with which Tanny manhandled the disgraced priestess.

"Adam, tell them I had nothing to do with this!" Esper pleaded, twisting around to face the escape pod. "Doctor Cliffton, don't let them kill me!" Carl had considered letting Esper think they were really going to go through with it, but he couldn't bring himself to be so cruel. Her acting was believable at least. It didn't hurt that Tanny had told her to give her best effort at breaking free. That much wasn't an act.

Within the escape pod, Adam grew quiet. "What do you want? I've got money, friends. I can get you things."

"If I believed a word of your promises I might consider it," Carl replied. "But considering you've tried at least twice to kill us, I'll take the bounty from Harmony Bay instead."

"Adam, *please!*" Esper shouted. Tanny forced her head down as she pushed Esper through the boarding tunnel. A moment later there was the thump of a door closing, and only Tanny returned.

"You're bluffing," Adam replied. "You aren't that cold blooded."

Carl put on his EV helmet, and then the rest of his suit. In full view of the escape pod, Roddy did likewise, and Tanny left for the common room. A klaxon sounded as the air was pumped from the cargo hold, quieting when no air was left to carry the sound. With Adam watching, Roddy cut the *Viper* free of the *Mobius*. Through careful maneuvering, the *Viper* stayed in view through the hole in the cargo bay door. Bolts of violet plasma from the *Mobius's* turret slammed into the drifting ship, carving holes in the hull until one ignited the ship's oxygen in a jet of flame. Several more shots and the *Viper* headed for the atmosphere of Delos IX.

Roddy began welding a plate in place to seal the cargo door.

"Show's over," Carl said through the comm in his helmet. Reaching down, he ripped the external power supply from the pod, ending communication with the furious and terrified occupant.

At the back of the cargo bay, outside the view of the escape pod, Esper stepped out of the personnel airlock in a poorly-fitted EV suit from the *Viper*. Carl held a finger to his lips, winked, and helped her up the stairs to the common room without tripping over boots five centimeters too big for her feet.

---

The *Bradbury* dropped from astral, gleaming in the light of the distant sun. It was no standard class that Carl was familiar with, but that wasn't surprising. The design was probably new since the last time he'd been in truly civilized space. Sleek and pristine white, it looked like a piece of medical equipment had been launched into space. Within seconds of arrival, the ship hailed them.

"*Vessel* Mobius, *this is the* Bradbury. *Hold position and prepare for docking.*" The voice was clear, crisp, and female, but whether it was human or computer, Carl couldn't tell.

"Friendly sorts," he muttered.

Tanny nodded and rolled her eyes, reaching for the comm. "*Bradbury*, this is *Mobius*, message confirmed. Holding position and releasing docking locks." She slumped back into the pilot's chair—her chair, Carl had to remind himself—and crossed her arms. "You feeling good about this?"

"Dumping the kid on them? Yeah," Carl said. "Because I

can tell myself that if that ever really *was* a kid, the only ones who can get him back are the Harmony Bay scientists. If he was just a clone, and there's nothing more than an asshole scientist in there ... well, he's getting what's coming to him. Now ... if you meant whether I liked our odds of survival, I'm a coin-toss still."

Tanny grimaced. "That bad?"

Carl chuckled. "Naw, I think Mort'll pull us out of this just fine. You just stay up here, watch those instruments, and hit the throttle the second we're in astral. Oh ... and be careful, I had Roddy remove most of the safeties." Carl scurried from the cockpit before Tanny could retaliate against him.

Mort and Roddy were waiting for him in the cargo hold. Esper was hiding with Mriy in Mort's quarters. Carl had always been wary of the azrin around scientists, more for their safety than hers, and Esper obviously had to remain hidden. The spells in Mort's quarters ought to have been plenty to conceal them both.

The docking hatch opened in the center of the cargo hold floor, and a contingent of five climbed up one by one. The first two were security goons in pressed black uniforms that showed off bulging muscle beneath; they carried blaster pistols, but didn't look like the sorts who used them much. Next came a technician who juggled a scanner as she climbed the ladder into the *Mobius*. After her, an officer in a navy-style uniform, less the badges and rank insignia, scampered smartly up behind the technician; she was older, possibly close to Mort's age, with grey hair and an easy air of authority around her. Last came a hard-eyed man in an untucked shirt and denim pants.

"I am Captain Yasmira Dominguez of the *Bradbury*," the officer greeted them.

"Carl Ramsey," he replied, holding out his hand. "*Mobius* is my boat." To his surprise Captain Dominguez not only took the offered hand, but gave him a firm shake. It was the most respect he'd gotten out of anyone on as official a ship as the *Bradbury*. Maybe the corporate types weren't as bad as he gave them credit for.

"Where is the boy?" Captain Dominguez asked.

Carl pointed to Roddy, who flipped down a pair of protective goggles and flicked on a plasma torch. In seconds, he cut through the weld that sealed the pod shut. The two goons didn't need telling, they marched forward in lock step; one yanked open the door, the other grabbed Adam around the waist and hauled him out.

"Is this him?" Captain Dominguez asked. The tech and the hard-eyed man came forward; the tech fiddling with her scanner, the hard-eyed man staring at Adam intently.

"James," the hard-eyed man said. "If that's you in there, you'd better explain yourself. You're a crowning success if you are. If not, the team's prepped and ready for when we get you back; they'll figure out what's in that skull of yours."

Adam could not have looked more undignified without serious effort. He was slung beneath the arm of one of the goons, arms and legs dangling, squirming ineffectively. "Call them off, Alvin. Call them off. I'll show you everything."

"Where is your accomplice?" Captain Dominguez asked. "Where is Sister Theresa?"

"No one said anything about wanting her back," Carl put in. "We sent her down with the ship your friend here called in to dust us."

"She's dead?" Captain Dominguez asked. "You people executed her?"

"If you want to get technical," Carl replied. "We *told* her not to go into the *Viper*. But she didn't listen, and we cut it loose with her inside." It was a lie to cover a different lie, and Carl made no effort to sound sincere.

"Alvin, these people are monsters," Adam said. "If they didn't think they could get paid for returning me, they'd have sent me right along with her. Don't give them a single terra."

"We don't want any money," Carl said. Everyone stopped a moment to look at him like a zoo exhibit. "All I want is a guarantee that this little shit never bothers any of us again."

The lips of the man called Alvin twitched. "Oh, no worries of that." That sealed it; the *Bradbury* was going to dust them. Alvin lied like a ... well, like the ten-year-old Adam appeared to be. He probably thought he was being clever and coy.

"Well, we won't keep you any longer," Carl said. "We've got an appointment in the Orion cluster. We'll be heading out just as soon as you drop astral."

Carl waved as the delegation from the *Bradbury* climbed down to their own ship. As soon as the docking hatch closed, he sprinted up the steps to the common room and shouted to the wizard. "Get us astral now, and get us *deep*."

Carl ran to the cockpit as Mort chanted the spell to send them between stars. He was panting as he came up behind Tanny and looked at the displays. "They're just disengaging now," she reported.

Carl nodded. "Mort's ... got this." He hoped Mort had it.

He lost sight of the *Bradbury* through the cockpit windows and turned his attention to the radar, focusing on the distance between them and the Harmony Bay ship. They were still in the sensor shadow of Delos IX, hidden from view by the observation posts on Delos. In areas of unobserved space, there was no law, no rule, no witness. The *Bradbury* backed away to a safe range to blast them to dust.

An indicator light perked up, showing the *Bradbury* powering its plasma cannons. Tanny's finger was already over the button to raise their own shields. But before she even had to hit it, space dropped away around them. Delos IX took on a ghostly aspect, no longer green, but a wispy grey monochrome. The *Bradbury* was gone.

Tanny reached for the throttle, and they sped from the scene at a speed that the *Bradbury* couldn't hope to match. They didn't have Mordecai The Brown to send them 11.42 standard astral units deep.

---

Esper sat in the middle of Chip's old quarters, surrounded by boxes of his things. Despite the clutter, the room felt empty. The walls had been stripped bare of pictures. The floor was no longer supplemental storage for half the ship's communications systems. Chip's clothes were folded neatly inside a footlocker, along with a few datapads, a stack of Battle Minions datacards, and a threadbare plush elephant. Carl had repatriated Chip's private stash of booze to the common area fridge, but the rest was bound for Mars and Chip's family, to be shipped at the next stop the *Mobius* made. Carl hadn't said yet where that would be.

With her hands folded in her lap, she found herself with nothing to do. The window view out into the astral void showed pinpricks of distant stars, barely drifting but passing at a phenomenal rate. It was all out there—all of it. The good, the bad, the in-between, and in all of it, nowhere to go. Maybe she would take Mort's advice and become a Seeker. She certainly hadn't found any answers yet, not to anything important.

Going back to the One Church seemed ... unwise. Harmony Bay had likely reported her dead, if not to the proper authorities, then at least to the Church on Bentus VIII. Going back to her family was out of the question. Maybe some of her friends had broken free of the insidious grasp of New Singapore high society and left Mars for a simpler life.

Whatever she decided to do, it wouldn't be resolved sitting amid all Chip's belongings, fretting over it. Taking a deep, soul-cleansing breath, she resolved to park herself in front of the ship's holovid and wait to see where Carl decided to drop her off. She marched up the steps to find out what everyone was watching.

"Hey," Mort greeted her with a smile. His feet were up on the couch beside him, and he had a can of beer in hand. Roddy and Mriy acknowledged her as well, as they sat watching an old episode of Springwillow Valley. It just figured that of all the things they'd pick to watch, they chose a program she knew by heart. Mort reached over and grabbed another can. "Want one?" he asked.

Esper was about to refuse his offer by reflex, but instead paused to consider. She decided that she didn't want a beer, but she really *wanted* to want one. It had been years since the last time she was drunk, or even had anything more than a sip of wine. "Thanks, I think I will." She panicked when Mort threw it to her, holding out her hands in an awkward cross between a cradling motion and snatching something hot from a stove top. But the can stopped in mid-air, within easy reach. Before she could get mad at Mort for the prank, he smiled—it hadn't been a prank at all; it was just Mort's way of dealing with the world.

Esper popped the top and tipped it back. It was swill, the cheapest, hoppiest sewer water Earth exported: Earth's

Preferred. She fought down the mouthful and gasped. Her mouth and throat burned. At Mort, Roddy, and Mriy's looks of concern, she offered a weak smile. "Before I came here, I hadn't had beer since I was ..." she fought to remember back, "... sixteen."

"When you think you can manage, Carl wanted to see you down in the cargo hold," Mort said.

"Oh?" she asked. "Did he say why?"

"Nope." The wizard's attention was clearly more focused on the soppy drama on the holovid than on whatever Carl was up to.

"Thanks," she replied. So instead of finding a place among the holovid viewers, she wove her way past them on her way to the cargo hold, jostling Mriy, who deigned not to say anything. Esper muttered an apology anyway.

She felt silly carrying a can of beer with her, but she didn't want to offend anyone by abandoning it with just a single sip gone. As she put her hand on the door, she heard strange, muffled music coming from the other side. When she opened the door, it hit her like an avalanche. Carl sat on the crate of expensive military guns, the ones they had taken from the first men Adam had hired to steal him away. He was playing the top half of a double-guitar, but it sounded broken. There was interference on the built-in speakers, making everything sound fuzzy and scratchy. It was a tune Esper had never heard before, and she had obviously come in the middle of it, because Carl kept playing after noticing her. He just gave her a quick nod, then lost himself in the music again. A few times she caught him wincing at an off-key note, but the whole thing sounded a bit off to her ears anyway. At the end, she gave an awkward clap around the can in her hand.

"I didn't know you were a musician," Esper said, coming down the steps to talk at a more comfortable distance.

"Not much of one," Carl replied, lifting the guitar strap over his head and resting the instrument by his feet. "This is Roddy's. He can play both sets at once. He'd have been a musician if he wasn't such a good mechanic."

"You should get it fixed if you're going to play it so loud," Esper said.

Carl chuckled and reached for a half-empty beer by his feet. "It's not broken, that's just my playing. It's old classical rock music. My parents raised me on this shit. It seeped in. But that's not why I called you down here."

"Why did you?" Esper felt herself sweating, even though the environmental controls were working just fine.

"You give any thought to where you want to go, now that you're done with Adam?"

She had been right, it was time for *that* talk. "Some. But I had just figured I'd get off wherever you put down next. You're not a shuttle service, and I don't have money to hire you anyway."

"You give any thought to staying?"

"You mean ..."

"Yeah, once we ship Chip's things off to his folks, those can be your quarters, not just a borrowed bunk. And you wouldn't be stuck with a ten-year-old roommate."

"But what would I do around here? I'm not exactly crew material."

"It's not a matter of what you do," said Carl. "It's who you are. Have a seat and quit looking so nervous. Listen, you saved my life. I—"

"I didn't," Esper replied. "If Tanny had gotten back with the med kit first, you'd still have been fine."

"Maybe she would have saved my life if you didn't, but you did, not her," said Carl. He took a long chugging drink. "That counts for something around here. That makes you family. And I already know a secret that you need kept."

"Now, wait a minute," Esper said. The can in her hand made a metallic crinkling noise as she tightened her grip on it. "Don't think you can blackmail me into working for you!"

"Working for me?" Carl asked. "Maybe you haven't noticed, but no one around here seems to work for me. We just pitch in and keep this boat floating. I mention secrets because everyone has them. Some ugly ones, too. I don't care what you've done out there." Carl waved his beer in the vague direction of the universe. "But I know that the One Church thinks you're dead, and they've got to keep thinking that for your own good. If I didn't know that, I couldn't do anything to protect you from them. Same goes for Mort, for Tanny, for Roddy, and for Mriy. You saved my life, so I'll do the same for you."

"You have secrets, too, or are you just their keeper?" Esper asked.

Carl gave a rueful smile. "Tons. The most obvious one is that I'm an unrepentant liar."

Esper frowned. "Everyone knows that."

"Everyone *here* knows that," Carl corrected her. "But if you join the crew, I swear I'll *never* lie to you."

She stabbed an accusing finger at him. "That ... right there. That was a lie."

The cargo hold echoed with Carl's laughter. "And you see? That's why I'd take you on. You're quick. You can learn."

Esper still wasn't sure. It sounded like a scam. That was Carl's stock in trade, by his own admission. "But I'm not—"

"You're not what?" Carl cut her off. "You're not a priestess. You went to them looking for answers, but did you find them?

No, they stuck you in front of a bunch of ten-year-olds to teach them long division."

"I taught fourth-grade algebra," Esper corrected him, but Carl kept barreling on. He was truly something to behold as an orator.

"You're not a spoiled rich girl, at least not anymore," he said. "The universe had a crazy notion to give you all the money in the world and an insane mother."

Esper's eyes went wide. "Mort said he wouldn't tell!"

Carl waved her objection away. "Tanny and I figured it out your first day on board. She pegged it that your mother was a doll collector, and thought you should look like one, too."

"I never thought of it like that ..."

"I don't know what you are, frankly," Carl said. "You're like new clay, still able to be anything."

"What if I'm not good at anything?"

"You think Tanny's the best pilot I could find? You think I like my mechanic being drunk off his ass eighteen hours a day and sleeping the other six? You think I need a bodyguard who sleeps the eighteen?"

"Or a wizard who can ruin your ship?"

"It's a bit different with Mort," Carl said. "He was friends with my parents. I wouldn't trade him for ten wizards just as good."

"I'll agree, under one condition," said Esper.

"What's that?" Carl took a sip of his beer and waited.

"You tell me the *real* reason you want me on your crew."

Carl was silent for a moment. He set his drink on the floor and leaned back with a thoughtful expression on his face. "All right ... no bullshit. You need us. Same way the rest of us need each other. They don't know it yet, but they'll need you, too. I already needed you; you saved my life. This is sort of a roving colony of misfits and outcasts."

Esper huffed, unsure whether to follow though. It *sounded* like a bull-poo answer ... no, it sounded like bullshit. But it made sense, too, in a Carlish sort of way. A chance to make herself over. A chance to start fresh, with people who had some idea where she had been and didn't hold it against her. A chance to fit in.

"What do I need to sign?"

"Nothing," said Carl. "You're in. We don't have a lot of rules around here. No one goes in anyone else's quarters without their say-so. Most of us waive that, but Tanny's not allowed in mine and vice versa. When we get a paying job, the split goes even to each of us, including *Mobius*."

"The ship gets a share?"

"Pays for fuel, repairs, upgrades ... yeah, he gets a share. And before you ask, *Mobius* is a 'he.' I was originally going to name him Star Ghost, but Mort made a better case. Way he put it, a mobius loop only has one side, so there's no place to be *but* all on the same side. And no matter how far you travel on it, you'll eventually come back."

"How often do you come full circle?" Esper asked, still smirking at the thought of a ship named Star Ghost. It was something one of her students might have come up with.

"I'll let you know the first time it happens," Carl replied. "Next place we stop, instead of leaving you there we'll get you your own EV suit, so you won't have to flop around in one that doesn't fit." He glanced at the can clutched in Esper's hand. "Oh, and there's one other rule around here."

"What's that?"

"We don't waste beer. Bottoms up."

# A SMUGGLER'S CONSCIENCE

MISSION 2 OF THE BLACK OCEAN SERIES

## A SMUGGLER'S CONSCIENCE

With an impact that drove the breath from her lungs, the cargo bay stopped spinning around Esper. An uncomfortable pressure released from her shoulder socket, and her arm slapped limply to the mat. Overheard lights shone down into her eyes, forcing her to close them. She heard footsteps, and a shadow passed over her; a hand grabbed hers and hauled her to her feet.

"You try scratching me in the face again, I'll dump you even harder," Tanny said.

Esper slumped forward, hands braced against her knees as she caught her breath. Tanny was dripping with sweat, but otherwise seemed unbothered by the exertion of throwing her around. "Sorry," she replied. "It's an old habit. I never got into fights as a schoolteacher. I mostly just broke them up."

"It shows," Tanny said, putting her hands on her hips. She wore padded fingerless gloves and a padded helmet, along with aerobic workout gear and bare feet. Esper was unprotected, but trusted Tanny not to actually *hit* her. "You fight like a little girl. I'm guessing you only had sisters."

"Nope," Esper replied between breaths. "Two older brothers. Never laid a hand on me."

"Must have been a lot older."

"Eight and twelve years," said Esper. She took one huge breath and forced herself upright.

Tanny nodded. "Usually it's the only children who never learn how to fight, or the ones who grew up in space aboard ship. Spend enough time around kids your own age, you learn how."

"I'm not sure I'm cut out to be a marine," Esper said.

Tanny cracked her knuckles and settled into a defensive stance. "Well, no shit. This isn't about making you into a boxer; it's about keeping you from being a liability." Esper threw a punch, but Tanny caught her by the wrist. Poking a finger inside Esper's fist, Tanny popped her thumb out. "You'll break your thumb if you hit someone like that. And use an open palm trying for my jaw. You'd bruise your knuckles if you hit someone like that."

"You didn't care about me being a liability when I was a passenger," Esper pointed out. She bounced on the balls of her feet like Tanny had shown her and threw another punch, which Tanny batted aside.

"I'd written you off. I knew if anything happened, I'd have to save you," Tanny replied, throwing a slow punch meant to force Esper to duck out of the way. "Now that you're part of the crew, it would be nice if you weren't such a pushover. It's bad enough how often I had to bail out Carl or Chip."

"I thought Carl was in the navy," Esper said. She swung her foot around in a clumsy kick that Tanny accepted to the side with a grunt, not even bothering to defend herself. "Shouldn't he have learned all this stuff?"

"Navy and tough don't belong in the same sentence; at

least not without an 'ain't' thrown in somewhere," Tanny said. "Carl was the biggest wimp on board until you showed up."

Esper pulled up short, taking a tap on the cheek from Tanny's gloved right fist for her lapse. "Even Roddy? I mean he's so—"

"Stronger than he looks, and quicker, too," Tanny finished for her. "Chip wasn't much better, but he was ten years younger." Tanny's expression went flat for a moment, and her shoulders slumped. "Anyway, me and Mriy are the ones who keep everyone safe planetside."

"You had all this equipment on board," Esper noted, pointing to the protective padding Tanny wore. "Do you and her fight like this?"

Tanny laughed. "I could maybe take her in a points-only boxing match, but marine conditioning can't make up for azrin physiology and a lifetime of hunting her own meals."

Esper sighed and stepped back off the edge of the mat, the cold steel of the cargo hold floor icy against her bare feet. "It just makes me wonder what I've gotten myself into. I mean, Carl said I'd find a way to fit in, but I just don't see anything I can do that you need."

"This really isn't a ship," Tanny replied. "This is an asylum where the patients all pitch in to fly."

---

Carl and Mort sat on the couch with Roddy as the laaku introduced them to one of his species' greatest cultural exports—the action holovid. While human audiences had tended to move either up or way, way down the scale of sophisticated entertainment, the laaku people had been turning out the best unapologetic, mind-numbing adrenaline pumpers for decades. Carl had seen real-life laaku fight—even Roddy once or twice—but it looked nothing like the physics-defying acrobatics filling the holovid field. Quadridexterous bare-fisted masters were slugging it out with some sort of demons taken from the mythology of a lost subdivision of the laaku species. The battle was playing out at a temple perched on the edge of a smoke-belching volcano, giving Carl a hint as to why this particular people might have died out.

When the door to the cargo bay opened, all heads in the room turned to look. Tanny and Esper stumbled through, their workout clothes and hair soaked with sweat. Carl looked from Tanny and her glistening bare arms to Esper with her shirt plastered against her skin, then back again. Without taking his eyes from them, he leaned close to Roddy. "Think you could install some security cameras in the hold? I think we've been watching the wrong feed."

Roddy made a rude, flapping noise with his lips. "Face it; you blew all your chances with Tanny. She's probably warned Esper off by now, too."

"Whatever they were doing down there's still better holo than what's on now," Carl replied.

"What are you kiddies whispering about over there?" Tanny asked, inclining her head in Carl and Roddy's general direction. She grabbed a can of ReCharge from the fridge and cracked it open, then offered a second can to Esper.

Esper's face was flushed from exertion, but the redness deepened and she turned and whispered something to Tanny.

"No shit," Tanny replied loudly enough for everyone to hear. "I just want them to cop to it. I don't care if you watch us or not, but I catch any cameras in the shower or my quarters, I'm airlocking you ... both of you." She added a pointed look in

Roddy's direction. It wasn't as if Carl was likely to manage any modifications to the ship without the laaku's help.

"The humors spilleth over," Mort said with a chuckle. "Been cooped up too long in this little box. When we get planetside, take care of yourselves, the lot of you."

"Yeah," Tanny replied. "Whenever *that* might be. We've been floating aimlessly for five days. Be nice if our *captain* would do some captaining and get us some work."

"I'm working ..." Carl replied with an easy smile. His statement at odds with lounging on the couch with his feet on the base of the holovid.

"Yeah, bullsh—" Tanny said.

"He found something," Esper interrupted, perking up. "Didn't you?"

Carl pointed a limp finger in Esper's direction. "Give that lady a cashier's chit. Yeah, I'm waiting to hear back from a guy, but we're headed his way."

"What guy?" Tanny asked, her brow furrowing. She took a long swig of ReCharge as she waited for his reply.

"Well, technically not a 'guy' guy, but she's—"

Tanny spluttered, spitting half a mouthful back into the can. "Not that creepy old bitch!"

"Lay off. She's fine. And she pays," Carl replied. "Mriy's already punched in the heading, just in case."

"You let Mriy—"

"Mriy can work the nav computer," Carl snapped. "It's not yours. Roddy can work it, too. Hell, even I know how to use it. Mort's the only one on board who ..." Carl turned to Esper. "You know how to plot a course in the navcom?"

Esper shrank back from the sudden attention. She shrugged.

"Everyone but Mort and Esper can work it," Carl said.

"Fine," Tanny replied. "But you can go meet her by yourself. Or just take Mort; she likes *him* well enough."

Mort cleared his throat. "Not this time. I've got something to look into when we set down."

"Since when have you got business?" Roddy asked. "Not that it's any of mine."

"Whose business is any of this?" Esper asked. "Who is this mystery person you might be meeting?"

A few notes from an ancient song chimed from Carl's datapad. "Speak of the devil," he said. "This is her." He turned the datapad in Esper's direction as he hurried to his quarters.

The name on the screen read: Keesha Bell.

---

The call was voice only, and the audio was heavy with static. Carl knew it was part of the encryption that was keeping their conversation private, but it was pissing him off all the same.

"Can you repeat that?" Carl asked. He was hoping what he heard was a result of the encryption's interference.

"Ms. Bell will not buy your disintegrators," Hobson replied, his crisp, old-Europe accent distorted by a whining squawk and pops of static. "She does invite you to discuss a job well suited to your talents."

"I was more hoping for an off-world merchandise exchange," said Carl. "Maybe one of the moons, or ship-to-ship out in the Black Ocean somewhere."

"Ms. Bell can arrange for your ship to land with no customs inspection, if that is an impediment to your meeting with her."

Carl whistled. It was one thing to have her own little outpost carved out in the wilderness. It was another to have pull with planetary authorities. Keesha Bell was bigger on Champlain VI than he had realized. "If she can pull that off, yeah. OK. But you sure she doesn't know anyone who might take a shipment of—"

"Captain Ramsey, this connection may not be perfectly secure," Hobson cut him off. "I have no idea what one would do with the types of goods you are peddling. If that is all you wish to speak to Ms. Bell about, then I suggest you—"

"No!" Carl shouted into the datapad, hearing his lead slipping off the hook. "No, I'll hear her out."

"Very well, Captain Ramsey," said Hobson. "I'll transmit a landing permit and coordinates." The connection went silent.

Carl flopped back onto his bed. "Why is it that no one ever wants what I have?" he asked the ceiling. "It's amazing the galactic economy hasn't collapsed by now. How's a guy supposed to make an honest living if no one buys the junk he steals?"

***

The orbital space around Champlain VI teemed with starcraft, satellites, and sundry high-altitude habitats. It was nothing like the man-made clutter around Earth or Mars, but it prevented a pristine view of the pretty little blue-green world below. The Champlain system was pastoral by ARGO standards, but it was the sort of pastoral a great many people paid good terras to experience firsthand. Real soil under your feet, a domicile disconnected from the adjacent buildings (if that was what you liked), and the ability to look off into the untamed wilderness and see no sign of human habitation—provided you didn't turn too far to either side. All that and the cozy knowledge tucked away that if anyone came to spoil that peace, ARGO warships would be on hand to stop them.

Carl watched through the cockpit window as they descended leisurely into the atmosphere. Tanny had keyed in the pre-clearance code, and orbital security had spared them the drawn-out process of explaining where the *Mobius* had been and why they had come from outside ARGO's suffocating swaddling of protection.

"It's not too late, you know," Tanny said. "We can land, find some other job, and you use that forked tongue of yours to get us out of working for Bell."

"Yeah," Carl said absently. "I bet we could."

"No job she's given us has turned out like it was supposed to."

The corner of Carl's mouth twitched. "Just like everyone else who hires us."

"You do realize that if they board the ship while we're down there, and Mort isn't around to hide things, they're going to find those disintegrator rifles."

"Better argument for my plan than yours," Carl replied. "Besides, she also pays better than anyone we've worked for. Maybe we'll make enough to afford to just pitch those disintegrators out an airlock so we can all breathe easy in civilized space."

Tanny snorted. It was all the reply she needed.

The comm blinked and Tanny keyed it open. "Vessel *Mobius*, this is station Charlie Foxtrot Eight Zero Niner. We have you on an approach vector to a reserved landing site with no clearance. Please transmit."

Tanny held down the transmit button. "Champlain ground control, this is *Mobius*. Stand by for landing permit code." She punched several more buttons and waited.

"Fucking bureaucrats. Getting to be as bad as Sol out this way."

"We'll be fine," Carl said softly. He reached over the pilot's chair and kneaded the muscles of Tanny's shoulders and neck. They were rock hard—even by her standards. "Far as anyone knows, we're clean."

Tanny sighed and relaxed for just a moment. Then something clicked in her head and she shrugged him off. "Quit that. You're not—"

"*Mobius*, you are cleared to land. There is ground transport waiting for Captain Ramsey upon your arrival. Charlie Foxtrot Eight Zero Niner out."

Carl grinned. "See? We're VIPs."

"Volunteering Ignorant Patsies?" Tanny muttered.

"Something like that."

The Champlain VI countryside rushed by in a blur. Scrub grasses poked up amid the broken landscape. Here and there a jut of red rock provided a landmark, making it feel like the hover-cruiser was actually getting somewhere. Carl turned in his seat to look back at the Jefferson Landing starport, receding over the horizon behind them.

"Likes her privacy, huh?" he remarked.

"Ms. Bell prefers the security of a vast stretch of land between her and unsavory elements," Hobson replied. He sat across from Carl, the only other one along for the ride besides their driver. It hardly seemed fitting to call the operator of a ground-hugging vehicle a pilot.

"Present company excluded?" Carl asked.

"You are aware of Ms. Bell's less public activities," Hobson replied. "She casts no aspersions."

"Just wondering why now she's all gung-ho to meet in person," Carl said. "She was always big on intermediaries."

"Perhaps she merely thought that it was past time to meet one of her more promising agents," said Hobson.

"We've met before," Carl said absently, watching out the window as they passed a lumbering herd of bison.

"Of course, sir," Hobson replied. It was the genteel way of telling Carl that he was full of shit. That was fine. Hobson didn't matter.

Carl let the ride pass in silence. Hobson was exactly as much of a conversationalist as etiquette required, and had all the personality of a public relations kiosk. Carl wasn't going to worm out anything about the job, Keesha Bell, or anything else of value from the starch-suited assistant. He watched the landscape instead, trying to imagine life sucked down by gravity to a single ball of rock. It was horrible.

"What's that?" Carl asked at length, pointing toward the oncoming horizon.

"Ms. Bell has her own shield generator," Hobson replied. "You are seeing the atmospheric distortion from the field."

"Um, we're still a long ways off, aren't we?" Carl asked. "How big's this place?"

"The dome of the shield covers an area one point two kilometers across."

Carl ran a hand through his hair. "What's she need *me* for? She can afford to run a generator that size; she can hire whole mercenary fleets."

"Not every job calls for a show of force. She will explain how you and your ship fit her vision."

As they drew near, Carl made out the concrete wall that

defined the lower edge of the shield. The perimeter was dotted with ground-to-space gun emplacements, tucked just inside the shield's protection along with sensor towers and maintenance drones. Trees rose up, lush and green, protected within the confines of the shielded estate, their canopy reaching just higher than the concrete.

The hover-cruiser sped on, the shield dome growing like a mountain at their approach. A packed strip of dirt led to a massive steel gate that opened as they drew near. By the time they arrived, it was just wide enough for the vehicle to zip past at full throttle without leaving paint scrapings on either side. As soon as they were past, it began to close.

"Not the friendliest of places," Carl remarked, watching the estate seal shut behind him. He lurched forward as the hover-cruiser decelerated. It had taken only a few seconds inside the shield dome to reach the main residence.

"If you will follow me," Hobson said, stepping down even before the door finished opening.

"You folks don't like to waste time," said Carl. He hopped to the ground, expecting to find barren, dusty ground beneath his feet. But when he landed, his boots sank gently into a thick carpet of manicured grass. Hobson was already making his way toward the residence, which struck Carl as more castle than house.

As he entered the foyer, Carl's practiced eye appraised the architecture. He was no historian, but years of practice had taught him enough to spot the difference between the pretentious and those with actual taste. Keesha Bell lived in a structure that would not have felt out of place in sixteenth century Earth, but had dragged it spotless and new through space and time to modern day Champlain VI.

"If you would wait in the study," Hobson said, escorting

Carl into a posh side room off the main foyer. All the furnishings were authentic; either real antiques or replicas of the sort that cost nearly as much. The fireplace was lit, the only other light in the room besides the sun streaming through the windows; no artificial illumination at all. The pleasant woodsmoke scent mixed with wood polish and floral perfume in a way that made everything seem ancient, like a museum exhibit brought to life.

Carl considered sitting in an ancient-looking chair, and was running a finger along the velvet upholstery when a voice startled him.

"I see you came alone," Keesha Bell said, standing behind him with her hands clasped behind her back. She wore an eighteenth century gentleman's suit, with long tails and gold embroidery at the cuffs and lapels, cut to hug a figure that had no business on a woman who was Mort's age with room to spare. Her braided white hair stood in stark contrast to her dark skin, and was the only hint of her true age aside from a few wrinkles at the corners of her eyes.

"Ms. Bell, it's been forever," Carl replied, extending his hand.

Ms. Bell looked Carl over, head to toe, before presenting a hand of her own and shaking Carl's. "You have your mother's looks, except for that nose."

"You sure know how to puff a guy up," Carl replied. "Thanks for meeting me in person this time."

"I hadn't expected you to come alone. I had thought that perhaps Mordecai might have wanted to come along."

Carl slumped into one of the ancient chairs, drawing a wince from Ms. Bell, but one which she suppressed instantly. "I'm sure you've heard about his situation. You're just a bit too 'Convocation' for his tastes these days."

"A pity," Ms. Bell replied. "I'm the last one he'd need to worry over. If they knew half what I did out here, they'd want more than just my eyes for it. But if Mordecai would rather cower inside a starship than enjoy my hospitality, it's his loss. I trust that he and the rest of your crew can keep out of trouble while we discuss business?"

"Of course," Carl replied. "We're professionals."

---

A sweat-slicked body crashed against the plastic mesh just in front of Mriy's face. She slammed her paws against the cage, along with a dozen other spectators, jostling the dazed fighter as he staggered to escape his opponent's onslaught. Both fighters were human, as were the majority of the spectators around her. The crowd was raucous, most of them drunk. Mriy had never understood the appeal of dulling the senses to watch combat, if such a display could be called combat. These humans fought like children with their claws tucked away.

"Fall upon him," she snarled, not caring what her shouted advice sounded like to human ears. Hardly any of their kind spoke azrin. "Take his throat!" Fighter Lyang had shown such ferocity when the two met at the center of the cage, but now he reeled from the punishment that fighter Drahos was inflicting. When Lyang lumbered into a clumsy blow by Drahos, Mriy pounded her fists against the cage and hissed. "You steal my money, you weakling coward!"

"Hey, who let the zoo out?" a human to Mriy's side asked. While she spoke little English, the charm earring she wore translated it with perfect clarity. The insult followed a common theme among xeno-hating humans, equating sentients with their non-sentient cousin races of Earth. Little did they realize that cute little proto-hominids were kept as pets on her home planet.

Mriy hissed out a breath, and focused her attention on the fighting. Carl had made it clear that they were to keep out of trouble while planetside. It was Carl's pack, Carl's ship, Carl's rules. Mort and Tanny had claws in him, but cross him too often and Mriy might find herself marooned on a human world. She glanced at the insulting human, and slaked her anger on imagined acts of violence against his person.

"Maybe we should toss him in the cage, see if he can do better than Lyang," the insulting human said. He was intentionally loud enough for her to overhear him, even if her ears had been weak as a human's.

"I ... female," Mriy grumbled in English.

"Hah! It speaks. How about that," the insulting man said.

"Dumb as a sack of hotdogs though," one of his companions added.

Mriy cursed them in her own language, then punched the cage as she watched Lyang take a brutal kick to the abdomen. Her own blow lacked conviction; her bet on Lyang was as good as lost, and she had could muster no more enthusiasm to chide him.

"What's that, kitty?" the companion asked. "I don't speak meow."

It was a more philosophical question than he realized, no doubt. Azrin languages contained concepts foreign to humans. Her limited understanding of English made a proper translation all the more difficult, but in this case, it seemed worth the effort.

"You ... prey ... taste bad. Piss ... fear ... no good eat." She snarled in frustration. She was failing to properly convey the disdain she held for them, and the unworthiness of their fear and urine-soaked flesh as spoils of her inevitable victory over them. To help overcome the language barrier, she flattened her ears and showed them her teeth. Wracking her brain, Mriy struggled to recall an insult that would have teeth the humans would feel. "Your mate ... seeks ... *kthizz-ka.*" The English word wouldn't come, and it was the only human language she had any familiarity with. The azrin word she had used was the term for a male who fathered children for impotent relatives. It was a quiet arrangement, and cause for great embarrassment if it became public.

"Ooh, tough kitty," the insulting man said in a sarcastic tone, one of the subtle human mannerisms she had picked up from studying Carl. "Ain't no weapons got past security, and you're outnumbered. So how about you just pack up and get lost, before you get hurt."

Mriy scanned the crowd, looking into the eyes of the bystanders, gauging each according to their will to fight, their build, their health. Her hunter's instincts sized each up at a glance. Taking the insulting man by the collar, she drew herself up to her full height, towering over the human. As his friends and other drunken rowdies closed in around her, Mriy leaned in close. "Hunter fears no prey."

They fell upon her, and the lopsided bout in the cage became a sideshow.

---

Mort kept his hands in the front pocket of his sweatshirt as he walked the streets of Nephrim. It wasn't one of Champlain VI's largest cities, but it had a quaint feel reminiscent of the Back Bay district of Boston Prime. Wrought iron lamps lined the streets, ready to spring to light when dusk settled in. Parks and strips of lawn broke up the monotony of stone, brick, and concrete that plagued more modern cities. Scientific vehicles buzzed among the pedestrians, but once he left the tram station, there were few other overt signs of science.

Not everyone in Nephrim was magically inclined, but much of Champlain VI's magical community congregated there. There were no holovid parlors, no gadget emporiums, no flashing advertisements using every psychological science in the book to soften minds until they bought what they were told. The residents liked it that way, wizard and retrovert alike.

Painted signs at every corner gave the names of streets and boulevards, but Mort was a stranger in Nephrim. For his current business he was wary of asking directions, and only knew his destination by name, not location. Though it shamed him, he found himself wishing for a voice-interaction kiosk to help find Confabulous, the wizards-only shop that might have what he was looking for.

After a footsore hour spent wandering, Mort stumbled across a civic map of Nephrim. It was wooden, hand-carved and painted, rendering the city in bas relief with tiny numbers referencing a legend on the side. Confabulous was listed, and it was only a few blocks from his present location. Mort memorized the turns and the compass direction, and looked to the sky. A pale white sun stared back down at him, reminding him that he was not on Earth, and solar navigation might not be the best idea. He checked the nearby street signs and oriented himself by those instead.

When he reached Confabulous, he paused to read the warnings on the door. There were standard legal disclaimers in plain English, warning patrons of the dangers of interacting with unfamiliar magic; Mort glossed over those. In smaller lettering, carved into the stone above the door, were the words:

"RARA MAGICAE POSTULATUM." Just what he was looking for. It was considered poor form to dangle rare magics before the public, and foolish to display them where scientific sorts could lay their sterile, latex-covered hands on them. But a place with a reputation as oaken as Confabulous would have strange and wondrous things hidden away where only special patrons might peruse them.

Mort pushed his way through the door, which caused the tinkling of a brass bell, announcing his arrival. Two other patrons browsed the shelves, and a tidy man in adept's robes behind the counter glanced up at the sound of the bell. Mort wanted some privacy with the shopkeeper, so he bided his time among the mundane magics and wizardly accoutrements kept out for common shoppers. There were the usual candles and pungents, making the shop stink like an old lady's sitting parlor. Bins of semi-precious and common stones lined one shelf, while the shelf opposite was stacked with branches and twigs fit for making staves and wands respectively—presuming the wizard was of limited means and no discerning taste. Mort grimaced his way through the aisle of pipes and hookahs, the crutch of a wizard whose mind could not let go the concrete world without imbibing.

After the other patrons finished their shopping, the clerk left the counter and came to see about Mort. "Can I help you, sir?" he asked, his tone hinting that perhaps Mort was lost, or in need of a washroom, and not actually shopping with intent to purchase.

"I'd like to see your back room," Mort replied, setting down a sphere of glass the size of an orange.

The clerk looked over Mort in his jeans and shabby sweatshirt, the gaze doing a great deal of talking without so much as a spoken word. "Sir, I'm afraid the back room of Confabulous is only for members of a certain rank in the Convocation. It isn't for idle browsing. Now, if there isn't anything further—"

Mort clapped a hand down on the clerk's shoulder. "I'm sorry. I really am." He guided the startled clerk around behind the counter. "I just need to look through, and see if there is one particular item in your collection. After that, you're going to consent to a memory wipe, and forget I was ever here."

"Sir, I'm not sure who you think you are, but there's no—"

"I'm Mordecai The Brown," Mort replied. "And I don't mind telling you that, because in an hour you won't remember it."

Mort stopped before a stone door with a complicated arrangement of moving panels, some straight, some semi-circular, others square but bearing glyphs. It was a puzzle lock, meant to keep out the rabble and riffraff. It had the unfortunate side effect of keeping out disgraced wizards of the Convocation—after a fashion.

"You can't threaten me," the clerk replied, though a tremor in his voice suggested otherwise. "I won't open it."

"Listen," said Mort. "Here's how it's going to work. You have a choice. You open that door for me, let me look around, and let me wipe your memory. If I find what I'm looking for, you'll wake up with a hand full of hardcoin for your troubles. If I don't, you'll just wake up confused. Now, if you don't want to help me, I'll have that door off its hinges, I'll *still* look around inside, and they'll find you a drooling imbecile because I had to wipe most of your mind to make sure you forgot me. *Intelligas?*"

The clerk nodded. His fingers began tracing the patterns required to open the lock.

Half an hour later, Mort departed empty-handed, leaving a

befuddled adept of the Convocation staring into an hourglass, wondering where his afternoon had gone.

---

Keesha Bell's home was an imitation of the Earth History Museum in Stockholm Prime. Smaller in scope, lesser in the prestige of each exhibit, it was nonetheless an overwhelming display for a private collection. Ms. Bell had spent hours parrying Carl's requests for information about the job as she showed him around.

"Your eyes are glossing over," she observed. "This ought to bring back memories. Do you recognize this piece?"

Carl blinked. It fit in so perfectly with the surroundings, he hadn't even taken note of it. "That's the violin we picked up for you on Janus II. It cleaned up nice."

Ms. Bell arched an eyebrow. "Indeed." Carl and his crew hadn't exactly delivered it in pristine condition, but there had been extenuating circumstances. "I have someone procuring an authentic bow to pair with it, though I can't imagine finding one by Stradivarius. The display just lacks something without the bow though."

"Yeah," Carl muttered. It was hard to think of the museum as lacking much of anything.

"The parcel you delivered from Roger Krause is here as well," Ms. Bell said. "Care to guess which it is?"

"I don't look in the package," Carl replied. "I wouldn't know where to start guessing."

Ms. Bell smiled and gave a nod of acknowledgment. "Of course you don't. Your father was never good with that one."

"Well, me and him aren't much alike."

Ms. Bell walked around Carl, looking at him from all

angles. "In looks, no, but you sound just like him. He was always quick with his tongue. Impatient, too. You lasted perhaps ten minutes longer on this tour than he did, before your mind wandered off completely."

"Real observant. You want my attention, tell me what you need me for," Carl replied.

"In time," Ms. Bell replied. "But I see no reason to rush into things. You're going to be acting with my reputation in hand, and I want the full measure of you before I allow you to leave with it. For instance, I was pleased to hear about your remarriage. You and Tania seem suited to one another."

"And here I thought you had spies," Carl said with a snicker. "That's old news. Married ... and divorced again. It's fate, I think."

"Perhaps I misjudged you, then," Ms. Bell said.

"Now, wait just a minute—"

"Your father may have been many things, but he was reliable. He could put his problems aside and get a job done. The fact that he was a stable family man was reassuring. I knew he had a reason to succeed. But if you can't even—"

"It was a misunderstanding," Carl snapped.

"Misunderstanding ..." Ms. Bell echoed, prompting him to elaborate.

"Not that it's any of your business, but yeah," Carl replied. "It was all part of a job. Strictly business. I only lied to Tanny about it to keep things from getting complicated."

Ms. Bell stopped. For a moment the wrinkles hidden beneath that smooth complexion showed through. "You lied to your wife about sleeping with another woman?"

Carl shrugged.

"And you consider this a misunderstanding?"

Carl lowered his head and offered a weak smile. "Yeah?"

"I'll send Hobson to take you back to your ship," Ms. Bell said. "It appears I have wasted your time and mine." She turned to walk away.

"Hey, hold on," Carl said. He reached to grab her by the arm, then thought better of it. He hustled to get ahead of her as she left the room. "You think I don't judge people well?"

She stopped. "Prove me wrong, then?"

"You're bustle is off kilter because Mort didn't come," Carl said. "You two haven't seen each other since Mort was my age, and you liked the idea of taking a renegade wizard to your bed. But Hobson let you know in advance it was just me coming. You changed your plans and set your sights on me, but you were disappointed when I got here; you expected a young version of my dad." Carl grimaced at a disturbing image that snuck up on him. "Which I'm guessing means you had a thing for him, back in the day. He probably cheated on my mom with you. You spent the afternoon trying to decide whether to settle for me, delay me until Mort came looking for me, or just give up on the whole mess. But you don't get a lot of visitors, so you were in no rush to call things off. Same way you're *still* in no rush to send me off on this job of yours."

Ms. Bell stood motionless, save for the smoldering eyes that bored into Carl's forehead. He tried to remember the signs Mort had taught him to tell if anyone was fiddling with his mind using magic, but all he could feel was the weight of her scrutiny.

"Your mother was a trusting woman," Ms. Bell replied. "Your father was the scoundrel who kept his word when it suited him. You've inherited nothing of his looks, but you are so much like him otherwise."

"Fuck you," Carl replied. "My father was small time. A coward. He went behind people's backs because he couldn't lie to their faces. Anyone pulled a blaster on him, he folded faster than a busted straight. If my mother had half the brains Tanny does, she'd have blown his head off herself."

"How do you do that?" she asked.

"Huh? Do what?"

"I can't read you at all," Ms. Bell replied. "I've made a great deal of money by knowing when someone is lying to me."

Carl grinned. "My father was a saint. Well, he was a thief and a con, but he never did any wrong by my mother. You never got him into your bed, but not for lack of trying. If you did, it was by magic."

"I *know* you lied," Ms. Bell said, her perplexed frown deepening. "I heard the contradictions, but I can't *tell* that you lied."

"You're an old friend of Mort's, so I let that much slip," Carl said. "That's all you get though. I don't pull back the curtain on the puppet show for anyone. Mort pounded that one into my head with thunderbolts.

"But if you want to know why you should still give me the job, it's this: *Mobius* is a ghost ship. We ever get stopped by a patrol, our cargo hold is empty, our ship's log is boring, and my crew knows nothing. That's how we get jobs done, and that's how we're going to get your cargo delivered, whatever the hell it might be."

Carl was still smirking in self-satisfaction when Hobson interrupted. He whispered something Carl couldn't make out, and handed a handwritten note to Ms. Bell. Hobson departed without a word to Carl or so much as a glance to catch his eye. Carl waited with his hands clasped behind his back, rocking between his heels and the balls of his feet as Ms. Bell read.

The handwritten page ignited in her hand, crumbling to ash in seconds. "It seems your azrin crewman has gotten herself arrested. Some anti-xeno hooligans attended the same combat sports exhibition and there was an altercation. Normally the authorities would just let the sentient non-human free, but there was excessive property damage and two serious injuries, injuries that would have proved fatal without the medical staff on site for the combat sports."

"Yeah, that sounds like Mriy," Carl said with a shrug. "We gonna have a problem there?"

A sly smile spread on Ms. Bell's face. "I could smooth out any snags by ... morning, perhaps?"

"You like a man who's hard to get, huh?" Carl asked. He didn't wait for a reply. "Well, you're going to like me a lot. Now, don't get me wrong; I like games, but I don't like being the prize. Hell, I'm no prize, and I know it. But I'm done with this little game. If you've got pull with the locals—which I'm sure you do—then get Mriy released, give me the contact I need to do this job of yours, and let me get to work. If you won't help, I'll find a way to get her out myself, and we can call the whole deal off."

She took him by the chin. Startled, Carl let her guide his face down until his eyes were level with hers. *"Never look a strange wizard in the eye,"* Mort had taught him, along with *"all wizards are strange."* But it was too late now, and as Carl stared into the swirling depths that lurked behind Ms. Bell's eyes, he found himself unable to blink or turn away.

He straightened and blinked a moment later when she released him. "What'd you do to me?" he demanded.

"A coded message for your contact on Vi Tik Naa," Ms. Bell replied. "That will serve as both introduction and confirmation of your identity. No scientific scanner can intercept, decode, or even perceive it. Hobson will transmit a location to your ship."

"That doesn't sound like ARGO territory," Carl said, referring to the bizarre system name. ARGO space was filled with mythological references, esteemed historical figures, and Greek letters, with a smattering of self-aggrandizing modern explorers thrown in.

"It's in-Tik territory. I don't expect that will be a problem for you."

It was too late now even if it was. Carl played along. "Course not. Guess I'll be on my way then."

"Stay for dinner," Ms. Bell said. "I've had the cook outside grilling authentic Earth-style burgers made from local bison."

"Mort's favorite," Carl noted. He chuckled. "Yeah, sure."

---

Carl stumbled into the common room of the *Mobius* at nearly midnight local time. He was met with the wailing symphonic soundtrack to a weepy holovid drama. On the far side of the holographic romance unfolding in the middle of the room, a strange woman reclined on the couch. She was dressed in form-fit kevlex with ablative armor plates, with a midriff length leather jacket on over it, too small to zip closed. Her hair was a nest of braids wound into a knot at the top of her head. Black, marine surplus boots came up to her calves, with clasps every few centimeters. In one hand she held the remote for the holovid, in the other a bottle of something that was undoubtedly alcoholic. With a long, hard, second look, Carl realized it was Esper.

"The hell happened to you?" he asked.

"Tanny," Esper slurred, holding the bottle up as she shrugged. "We shopped."

"Where's she now?"

"We drinked ... drank? Drinked. She met a friend ... old friend. He said he knew her somewhere. She said yeah but I don't think she knew him. He was cute so she lied for sex. That's where she is. Getting her brains sinned out. Ditched me."

"Oh," Carl said, working his way through what Esper said to figure out what she meant.

Esper raised the bottle, but instead of drinking she brought it to eye level. "You know, I'm sinning too now, dammit. Tanny's fault. But ... you know ... the more of this sinning I do, the less guilty I feel about it. Like a vicious sickle. Except it tastes like peaches."

Carl pointed a finger from each hand in Esper's direction. "I know you're new at this ... but you're drunk."

Esper spread her arms and looked up at the ceiling. "No ... fucking ... shit."

Carl fought back a fit of laughter. "I like the new look."

"Oh, you like this?" Esper asked, gesturing up and down her outfit with her bottle hand. She snorted. "Typical." She took a swig from her bottle of peach liquor. Carl noticed that there was a six-pack with five more like it; she wasn't even a full bottle deep. "Tanny dressed up me like a soldier. Let's pick out something comfy, maybe a nice dress or three or four. *No, no dresses for you. You're just gonna get kidnapped and raped and we'll have to rescue you. Gotta look tough.*" Esper managed an overblown impression of Tanny, deepening her voice. "How about we get our hair done. *Sure, short hair makes more sense on a ship.* No, I like my hair. Argued about it for like an hour maybe two. Well, maybe a few minutes. Ended up with braids. Gonna take me like an hour to redo it every time I shower. *How often you need to shower?* Tanny's some kind of barbarian woman."

"Kinda," Carl agreed, grinning. Weary as he was from his day, he leaned against a wall to let Esper's rant to play itself out.

Someone in the holovid moaned and professed an undying love. Esper frowned at it and shut the holoviewer off. "I see you looking at me, all grinning. I know what you're thinking."

"That'll put you one up on Keesha Bell."

"You're thinking you want me."

Carl closed his eyes and took a deep breath. When he opened them, he pointed to the five-pack on the floor. "Look, I appreciate the effort—I really do—but you need to cut back and learn your limit on that stuff. Stick to beer for a while maybe."

Esper hugged her bottle close. "Beer's yucky."

"Go get some sleep."

"Or she can come down and learn to weld," Roddy said, causing Carl to flinch.

"Dammit!" Carl said. "Where'd you come from?"

"Door wasn't shut. I just came in behind you while you were ogling Esper."

"See?" Esper said. "You were."

"Welding sober's too easy," Roddy said. "Learn drunk and you'll never have any trouble sober."

"Bed," Carl said, jabbing a finger Esper's way. He turned to Roddy. "And you, stop encouraging her."

"Hey, we got a job or not?" Roddy asked, changing the subject. "Cuz I found some sweet stuff in Andrews Station this afternoon. Real sweet. More cash than we've got going, but maybe coming back ..."

Carl grabbed two beers from the fridge and handed one down to Roddy. "Yeah, yeah. We've got a job. Won't know the details until we meet our contact though. Keesha Bell's just brokering this one. She didn't even front us an advance."

"When we leaving?"

"Soon as Tanny and Mriy get back. Bell's popping Mriy from lockup for a bar fight."

"At least both of them are getting something out of their system," Roddy said. "Better than dragging that shit out to the Black Ocean with us."

Carl threw back his beer. "Helluva way to start a job. Sooner we're off this rock the better."

---

Esper slumped over the kitchen table of the common room, forcing spoonfuls of wheat puff cereal into her mouth. The room throbbed. The dim overhead lights burned like individual suns. The reconstituted milk of her cereal couldn't wash away the dank-washcloth feel of her tongue fast enough. Even after changing into her baggy new coveralls, the dried sweat built up from sleeping in kevlex armor clung to her.

"I deserve this," she mumbled to her cereal. This was the penance for indulging in drink, not just the physical discomfort, but the guilt of remembering the things she had said the night before.

She was nearing the end of the bowl, weighing her hunger against the sour lump her stomach had become inside her, when a thump startled her. The door to Mort's quarters slammed shut, and the wizard stalked across the common room. Esper clenched her jaw and winced with every hammering step.

"Who are you?" Mort demanded. "What are you doing here? Did the Convocation send you?"

"Mort!" Esper exclaimed, dropping her spoon and shrinking back from the enraged wizard. She hardly recognized him.

"No, that's me," he replied with a curt shake of his head. "I won't fall prey to such juvenile misdirection. Now tell me ..." Mort squinted and rubbed his eyes. "Wait. I know you ..."

"Esper."

His face relaxed. "Oh yes. Yes. We have an Esper now, don't we? You look different somehow."

Esper flicked the disheveled snarl of braids on her head. "New hairstyle. New clothes. Same me."

Mort hunched down to put his face level with Esper's. "No, that's not it. You're hung over."

"I'm trying not to be," Esper said. "But it's God's way of punishing my sins from last night."

"Naw," Mort replied. "It's the alcohol making your head pulsate and your eyes burn from the light. The guilt is His punishment. You ought to get some coffee in you. Tanny'd tell you lots of water. Roddy'd tell you beer, but I convinced Carl of the wonders of a good cuppa, and it'll help you, too."

Mort prepared a mug of hot coffee for her. Once he had filled it with water from the reclaim spigot, that was the last technology he used. The water boiled of its own accord, and after pouring in an eyeballed helping of freeze-dried coffee crystals, the mixture spun itself until stirred. The wizard handed her the steaming cup.

Esper chuckled weakly as she accepted the drink. "Thanks. That's just amazing how you do that."

Mort took another mug for himself. "What's amazing is that I hurled us so deep into the astral plane last night that if we broke down no one would ever find us, a feat I doubt ten wizards in the Convocation could manage, yet you're impressed by some handmade coffee."

"Sorry," Esper replied. "I wasn't awake for that."

"You ought to have been. I was brilliant."

Esper smiled.

"You see? Coffee's already doing its work. Thanks for taking care of Tanny last night, by the way."

"Taking care of her?" Esper asked, sipping her piping hot coffee. "I let her drag me around, boss me around, and ditch me at a bar."

"Took one of the team," Mort replied. "Just what she needed."

"Wasn't me," Esper replied. "She met some guy at Fuego de la Noche, and they scooted off to ... well, you know."

"Worked a charm, by my reckoning. Magic all its own. You don't have to put up with getting bossed around though. Next time you're out, *you* ditch *her*. Got it?"

"Was Mriy okay? Carl mentioned something about a fight."

"Nothing she can't brag about, now that it's over."

"Where are we headed?"

"Some gibberish-named system outside ARGO space," Mort replied. "Nothing you or I need to bother with." He took a sip of his drink, wrinkled his nose, and added a pinch of extra coffee crystals.

The door to the cargo hold cracked open. "Hey, Sunshine," Roddy called. "Time to learn a trade." The door clanged shut.

Mort stood, taking his coffee mug and heading for his quarters. "He wasn't talking to me," he said in a cheery voice at odds with everything Esper felt in her head.

"I'm in no condition," Esper replied.

The door opened again. "Today, maybe?" Roddy asked.

Mort snickered. "Go on. Penance, remember?"

The plasma torch was the size of a flute, with a bend that terminated in a tapered nozzle. It had been awkward at first, but after several passes, she had made her first clean, straight cut. The protective goggles fogged as Esper sweated from hauling her practice pieces around.

"How many more of these do I need to do?" Esper asked.

Roddy shrugged and sipped at his beer. "You saw what happened to Chip, right? How bad you want to avoid ending up like that?"

Esper sighed, and the tip of her plasma torch flared to life. She bit her lip in concentration and started cutting another thin strip off the edge of a steel plate, trying to keep the width as uniform as possible.

"We're not a ferry service," Roddy said as she worked. "And we're not pirates. Cargo runs don't always fall in our laps, at least not ones that pay worth taking. So we make do with a lot of salvage work. That torch in your hand can get you through a door or bulkhead, cut open a lock, disconnect high-price equipment from the junk around it. It's the omni-tool of a salvager. Best friend you'll have on a derelict, aside from your EV suit."

"I want to pull my weight, but—"

"You don't weigh much," Roddy said. "Not for a human. You're gonna have to pull more than that around here. There's only six of us, and any work that don't get done, we don't get paid for. Mort ... well, he's Mort; he gets off on the grunt labor. Wouldn't trust him with a torch if he offered. The rest of us work for a living."

Esper whispered a prayer.

"What's that?" Roddy asked. "You bitching about me? Laaku aren't deaf you know, despite what you might've heard."

"I was just asking for strength to get through the day," Esper replied.

"Sister, you ain't gettin' off that easy. Only way to get strength is to work for it. I'd offer you a beer to make it go by quicker, but after seein' you last night, I don't think you'd handle it too well."

"It was peach. I didn't think it would be that strong."

"About twelve beers a bottle," Roddy replied. "I checked the label."

"Really? It stopped burning after a few sips, so I figured ..."

"Numbed. Listen, kid, if you're going to drink, you're going to need to be careful," Roddy said. "Don't watch yourself, you'll wind up like me. If you weren't human, you probably already would have."

"I didn't want to say anything."

"Yeah, I've heard it all, sweetie," Roddy said. "Laaku can't hold liquor. Ain't quite true. Stuff's banned on the homeworld because we can't stop ourselves. Just physiology is all. Livers and brains and pancreases and whatnot. Azrin almost never get addicted. Your kind is hit or miss. Me? I'm a victim of biology." He tilted back his beer can, draining the contents. Even before he finished, his walking hands were popping the top on another can.

Esper set back to her cutting, and tried to let the subject go away.

---

The trip to Vi Tik Naa was shorter than it had any business

being. Tanny had marveled at how deep Mort had put them into the astral, but the wizard had told only Carl just how close he had come to the inflection point. Though Carl was fuzzy on the specifics, if Mort had pushed much farther, the *Mobius* would have emerged into a different universe than the one it had left. Keesha Bell had given him five days to reach the contact on Vi Tik Naa before the message she had planted in him wore off. Mort had gotten them there in two.

Vi Tik Naa was neither a member nor a protectorate of ARGO, though there was a human presence on the planet. It fell into the grey space between a wilderness preserve, a colonization prospect, and a sovereign world. The inhabitants were a sentient but primitive race known as the in-Tik, evolved from avians. They had radios and chemically-propelled ground vehicles, but had not discovered powered flight. Reading through the computer files on the in-Tik, Carl chuckled at the thought of birdmen needing machines to fly.

Of course, Vi Tik Naa had heard of all the modern sciences now. Humanity was nothing if not prolific in the spread of technology, even if ARGO laws prohibited sharing the science with primitives. They were more concerned with keeping the dangerous wildlife from being exported off world.

The ship shuddered. Tanny's voice came over the ship-wide comm. "We're atmospheric. I'll have us on the ground in ten."

Carl shut down his datapad as the rest of the crew congregated in the common room. "This is it everybody. We're going to keep it tight. No shore leave, no sightseeing, no shopping. Roddy, we desperate for any supplies?"

"Nope," Roddy replied. He slouched back on the couch and crossed both sets of arms—or a pair of arms and a pair of legs, depending on human versus laaku perspective.

"Right then," said Carl. "No one goes down but me and Tanny. We're taking a megafauna safari at one of the tourist parks and rendezvous there with our contact. I don't know what it's going to take to move this cargo, so keep an ear to the comm if we need someone to bring the ship around. Mriy, you handle in-atmo pickup if we call."

"Fine," Mriy agreed. She slumped down on the couch and threw an arm around Roddy. Within seconds, her eyes had closed and her breathing slowed. Her part of the planning acknowledged, she wasn't going to waste time listening to the rest.

"Anything you need me doing?" Mort asked. "Wouldn't mind a peek at some dinosaurs if there's nothing pressing."

"It's not the dinosaurs sort of megafauna," Carl replied. "And no sightseeing."

"I had assumed you meant the rest of them," Mort replied with a frown. "It's not like I can't keep out of trouble."

"Sure, just like Champlain," Carl snapped. A dull thump sounded, and the omnipresent hum of the *Mobius's* engine died down. "Keesha got news of a break-in at a wizards' shop in Nephrim. She put two and two together, you know, but since nothing was taken, she shrugged it off."

"I just—" Mort began.

"Since when did you start calling Ms. Bell 'Keesha?'" Roddy asked.

Carl jabbed a finger in the laaku's direction. "Can it. I can call her whatever I want. Mort, I don't need you doing anything on this pickup. I just need you *not* doing things. Things go right, this'll be our first big payday in months. We're not taking any chance. *Any* chances. You got me?" He scanned the room, looking for signs of dissent, or at least a bit of shame or contrition. He settled for all of them paying attention, save for the sleeping Mriy.

Tanny walked in from the cockpit. "I set us down at the safari park's landing site. Vi Tik Naa traffic control is more of a concierge service than any authority. They just wanted to give me landing coordinates to wherever we were headed."

"It's not ARGO space, and not even ARGO fugitives running the place like most of our borderlands runs. They can do whatever they want. *Unlike* you lot."

"Laying down the law?" Tanny asked.

"Something like that," Carl muttered.

"Working?"

"Nope," Roddy replied.

"Get changed," Carl said to Tanny. "Standard tourist couple getup. Nothing elaborate."

Tanny grinned. "Not this time."

Carl gave her a puzzled look.

"Take Esper."

Carl held up an objecting finger. "No. We can't look suspicious. Who's going to believe—"

"That a guy like you'd marry a girl who looks underage," Tanny said. She leaned around to address Esper briefly. "No offense, sweetie, but you look eighteen as much as I do, coming the other way. No one's going to question whether you're a couple, just your character."

"But I've never done anything like this," Esper protested. "Plus I'm—"

"Gotta earn your keep somehow," Tanny said. "Maybe this is it."

"... hung over," Esper finished in a quiet voice. She swallowed, and Carl saw the resignation in her slumped shoulders.

He sighed. "You pick up anything on Champlain that

would work? I saw the combat getup, and I'm not sure the coveralls are tourist guild approved."

"There's no such thing as ... oh," Esper said. "Yeah, we got some casuals, too. Nothing *nice*, but I can look like a normal person."

Mort shuddered melodramatically. "What a horrible thing to be."

"Or ..." Tanny said, letting the word hang as everyone focused on her. "You could take Mort with you. Sort of a spring/autumn couple. You two would be cute together."

Carl scowled at Tanny. "I'll take Esper. Mort's not my type."

Mort huffed and turned his back with an air of offended dignity.

"Go get changed ... darling," Carl said to Esper.

---

The safari hover-cruiser was open air, with a tent-like canopy overhead but sides unobstructed by either glass or shield. They were higher than most ground-transport hover vehicles, with a good ten meters altitude between them and the savanna below. The sky was brilliant blue, with just a few fluffy white clouds and a yellow-light sun in the sky above. It was one of the true Earth-like worlds, nearly indistinguishable from ground level if the nighttime stars weren't out. Carl didn't get to the Earth-likes very often, and it always made him stop and wonder about the God's Seeds theory of the galaxy when he did.

But it was no time to be philosophical. Despite the warm climate and fantastical creatures promised by the tour officials, the safari was a means to an end. Their contact was on the hover-cruiser—supposedly—but had yet to identify himself. Or herself. Keesha Bell had withheld even that level of information about their target.

Esper sat beside him, nestled in the crook of his arm, staring out at the passing scene through dark-tinted lenses. They'd had a brief but pointed conversation on faux-marital boundaries before leaving the *Mobius*. Kissing, but no tongue. Touching, but ass, breasts, and thighs were off limits. Pet names were fine, but no phony boasts about their physical relations or her anatomy beneath the loose blouse and trousers combo she wore. All in all, it was a more reasonable set of demands than Carl had anticipated. She felt different beneath his draped arm than Tanny did—less substantial, certainly less muscular. It prompted an unfamiliar protectiveness in him.

"To your right, about half a klick, you'll see a pair of short-haired mammoths with a calf," the tour guide said over an amplified comm, with speakers scattered throughout the craft. He was human, mid-twenties, with an easy manner and casual familiarity with the alien world. "In a few minutes, we'll come up on Mount Jixhau, where we'll see the nests of floral raptors, birds with no Earthly counterpart, but with kaleidoscopic feathers and a wingspan of nearly eight meters."

The rest of the crew was comprised of in-Tik waitstaff, sliding about the rocking hover-cruiser with plates of local delicacies and human-friendly drinks. The in-Tik were avian humanoids, covered in such tiny feathers that they looked like short fur. They had huge eyes and hook-beaked mouths with nostril slits instead of noses. Their hands were two long fingers and a shorter, opposable thumb, each ending in a stubby talon. The waitstaff each wore a speaker around his or her neck— Carl couldn't tell their gender—programmed to translate in-Tik to English. With his translator charm earring, it was amusing to listen to the differences.

"Hey ape, you want a drink or not?" a waiter asked.

*"Sir, would you care for a beverage?"* the speaker echoed.

Carl looked over the platter. "I'll have a beer. Lemonade for Mrs. Ape here."

The feathers on the waiter's face bristled and he ducked his head. "Buddy, I didn't mean anything by it."

*"Sir, I meant no offense,"* the speaker echoed.

"Please don't tell hair-head over there," the waiter said.

*"I beg you not to inform my supervisor,"* the speaker echoed.

Carl waved the waiter's worries away with the hand draped across Esper. "No problem. By the way, what do I owe for the drinks?"

The waiter took the hint. "Hospitality gift. No charge."

*"No charge,"* the speaker repeated, curiously leaving out the in-Tik idiom.

With their drinks in hand and the waiter scuttled off to elsewhere on the cruiser, Esper leaned close. "I need one of those charms."

Carl put his lips to Esper's ear and whispered. "Could have had Mort working on that while we're here. Remind him when we get back."

As the safari continued, their guide pointed out dozens of animal species, some familiar, others reminiscent of Earth creatures long lost to history. A few were unique to Vi Tik Naa. Whenever he could spare a moment, Carl twisted around and looked at the other passengers. They were a mix of hardened spacers and wealthy travelers out to see the galaxy. Not the usual weekend holiday-goers, but neither did any of them scream "I'm the one you're looking for," to Carl's eye. Which was just as well; a contact who stood out was bad for keeping business on the deep-astral band.

He noticed Esper fiddling with her borrowed wedding

band, and put a hand over hers to stop her. "Cut it out. You're breaking character," he whispered.

"Sorry," she whispered in reply. "It's just I'm not used to wearing one. It's loose, too."

"Cuz it was Tanny's."

Esper made a fist, preventing any possibility of the ring slipping off. "I thought it was a fake! Why would she give me the real thing?"

"Hey, ask her. I'd just be guessing. Just ... stop acting like it doesn't belong on you, ok?"

As they passed over a lake, the safari guide pointed out a group of sauropods grazing along the bank, bodies submerged while their long necks reached onto the shoreline trees. The hover-cruiser gained altitude, ten meters being insufficient to stay out of reach of the creatures as they passed close by.

"I thought you said there weren't any dinosaurs," Esper said.

Carl chuckled. "I couldn't have kept Mort off this thing if I'd said there were. Not like he's going to scour the omni looking up Vi Tik Naa's wildlife, though I'd love to be there to watch him try."

A tower appeared on the horizon, slim and sleek, with a bulbous top. It grew rapidly as they approached and ascended. The top, it turned out, was an observation deck, and the hover-cruiser pulled up alongside. The tour guide disembarked, and passengers started doing likewise.

"Welcome to Observation Post Olympus," said the tour guide, using that voice all tour guides had, just loud enough to carry across a group of semi-attentive tourists. "For those of you who are taking the Man Eaters' Big Game Tour, your transport will arrive shortly. Just remember, animals over twelve tons are protected by in-Tik law, and your rifle's targeting assist will not allow you to fire at larger animals. For those of you staying on the safari tour, please enjoy the buffet. Lindsay will be along with the transport for the second leg of your journey."

The group broke up, most heading for the buffet. A few headed for the far side of the tower platform, where a smaller hover-cruiser was arriving.

"Mriy would love this place," Esper said, watching the hunters queue up for their transport.

"Nah," Carl replied. "Armed hunting is for older azrin. This place would be a retirement commune for them. Come on, now's our chance to ferret out our contact."

The buffet was at the hub of the tower, well away from the railings. Carl glanced at the dishes as he mingled with his fellow safari tourists. They all had little placards beside them, identifying what they were made from. It was all familiar human fare made from ingredients native to Vi Tik Naa. Carl took a handful of hors d'oeuvre pizzas and took half of one in a bite. He choked down the sour, over-spiced morsel, and returned the others to the platter, discarding the half piece under a napkin.

Esper followed on his heels, sampling the food and finding it better to her liking than Carl had. Martian upbringing. Rich parents. She had probably eaten alien foods before. For all his travels, Carl had never developed a taste for anything that didn't taste like home.

"You see anyone?" Carl asked.

"I'm not even sure what I'd be looking for," Esper replied.

"Excuse me," the tour guide said, placing a hand on Carl's shoulder. "I understand you had some complaint with the service on the tour."

"I didn't really—"

"Not to worry, sir," the tour guide assured him. "Your waiter confessed everything. If you would just step this way, I'm sure we can make amends for your treatment."

"It's all right," Esper said. "We—" She stopped short when Carl gave her a nudge with his elbow.

"We didn't want to make a scene earlier. That's all. Thank you," said Carl. He leaned close and whispered to Esper. "I think we found him."

"Him?" Esper asked, incredulous.

The tour guide was young, smiley, tanned golden as fresh-baked bread, and perfectly hidden in plain sight. Carl followed him onto the hover-cruiser. As soon as Esper was aboard, he disengaged it from the tower.

"Sorry about the delay," the tour guide said. "Gotta keep my day job happy, ya know?"

"So, where's the cargo?" Carl asked as they zipped across the savanna, soaring over a herd of what looked like shaggy oxen.

"We're heading for it now," the tour guide replied. "I've got it stashed in the preserve. You got your ship on comm?"

"Yeah," Carl replied.

The guide handed him a slip of paper. "Read them these coordinates. Have them meet us there?"

"Ships aren't allowed in the airspace over the preserve," Esper said.

The guide shrugged. "Hey, air-traffic gives you a hard time, just apologize. Not like they want any trouble with a human ship. Human tourists are single-handedly funding the advance of their civilization. They won't stop you unless they *know* you're up to something."

"If it's so easy to get stuff off-world, why'd Keesha Bell make this sound like a big deal?" Carl asked.

The guide smiled. "Out's not so bad. It's getting it through ARGO space. You don't want to get caught with this cargo."

"Just what are we—" Esper's question ended with a muffled, indistinct noise from behind Carl's hand.

"We don't wanna know. All I want is a location to deliver it to, and a partial payment up front."

Carl took his hand from Esper's mouth. She glared at him, but kept silent on the subject. He suspected he was in for a rash of shit—or at least some whining—when they got back on board *Mobius*.

Carl keyed his pocket comm and relayed the coordinates to Tanny. "How big are we talking?" she asked. "We need to get equipment ready to haul it in and stow it?"

Carl held out the comm to the tour guide, who chuckled. "Naw, it's carry-on sized. No worries."

They set down in a depression on the downwind side of a hill. Carl wanted to call it east, based on the sun, but he wasn't sure which way Vi Tik Naa spun. The soil was soft when he stepped off the hover-cruiser, covered in sparse, dry grass that came up to his knees. A lone tree stood atop the hill, casting a long shadow across their ride.

Their guide dug with his hands, easily displacing the loose soil until he exposed a metal box. As the guide pulled it out and brushed most of the dirt away, Carl saw that it was covered in glyphs, and also sported a sophisticated digital lock. "Here's your cargo." It was no larger than a med kit and weighed maybe ten kilos by Carl's guess.

"That's it?" Esper asked.

"How about our money," said Carl. "It's a nice enough little box, but without a pile of hard-coin, it's not leaving this rock."

"Sure. Sure," the guide assured him. He dug in the soil in

the same spot but deeper and pulled out a small leather knapsack. It jingled. Carl foisted the box off on Esper and snatched their payment.

"Do I need to count it?" Carl asked.

The guide shrugged. "Your call, buddy. Fifty large, rest on delivery. But that's not coming from me. Delivery instructions are in there, too."

Fifty thousand was Money, with a capital M. It wasn't Buy-Your-Own-Moon money, but it was certainly Stop-Worrying-About-Fuel-Costs-For-a-While money. Carl played down his excitement. He hefted the bag. "Feels about right. I know where you live."

The *Mobius* arrived shortly thereafter, lowering the cargo bay door to let Esper and Carl aboard. Mriy and Roddy were waiting there, blaster pistols in hand, just in case.

"By the way," Carl said to the tour guide from the cargo ramp. "I can tell you're new at this. If I wasn't such a nice guy, this would be the part where my crew dusts you and buries the body in the middle of nowhere in your safari preserve. Remote exchanges favor the guy with more guns. It'd be worth it just for the fifty, even if we left the cargo."

"You'd piss away two hundred fifty and pass on the job?" the guide asked.

Carl clenched his jaw and told himself that two-hundred fifty was chump change to a rogue of his standing. Otherwise, he might have left his mouth agape. "Yeah, maybe. But I'm a nice guy, and you might have a future in this business if you smarten up."

He turned and walked up the ramp. "Come on. We've got a delivery to make."

If there was trouble with Vi Tik Naa's traffic control, Tanny took care of it without telling anyone. Esper watched the planet recede through the glass canopy of the common room's dome ceiling. When it faded from view she slumped onto the couch beside Roddy and Mort, who had just turned on the holovid and were flipping through the library of shows.

"What do you think is in it?" she asked. The box sat on the kitchen table, in easy view. Roddy had used the compressed air hose and scrubbed it with cleaning solvent, leaving the metal gleaming clean.

"Dunno," Roddy replied absently, his eyes focused on the holovid listings. "For the price and the size, I'd bet on some new narcotic the in-Tik discovered. You can always count on primitives to find some creative, low-tech shit to blast their brains out with."

"Could be," Mort said. He glanced over and gave the box a glare. "Glyphs are professional. Quite good. Can't tell a thing about what's inside because of them. I admit my bias, but someone with that sort of prowess is likely smuggling arcana. The in-Tik aren't very scientific, but their magical reputation isn't shabby. Convocation never had much dealing with them, but they're believed to be of human-like magical potential."

"Keep rubbing that in, peach-fuzz," Roddy griped. Laaku were notoriously inept wizards.

Mort made a rude noise. "The lady asks my opinion. I give a reasoned, logical reply. You accuse me of species bias. If I wanted to malign you, I'd have referred to your lack of stature or your foul hygienic habits. If I really wanted to hit below the belt, I'd have pointed out that there isn't much to hit below a laaku's belt ... but all I mentioned was that in-Tik are about as magical as humans, give or take."

"How's this?" Roddy asked, gesturing to a highlighted entry in the *Mobius's* holovid collection. He ignored Mort's goading with an air of long practice. Esper wondered how long it would be before she felt the same level of comfort around them.

"Too long," Mort said. "Tanny's going to have us far enough out to sneak into the astral soon. How about one of those kidsy adventure shorts?"

Roddy rolled his eyes. Tossing the remote to a startled Esper, who juggled it before grabbing hold, he slipped down from the couch. "Knock yourselves out. I'll go find some work to do."

Esper hadn't browsed the ship's library extensively. She'd mostly stuck to Tanny's favorites; despite their outward differences, they seemed to share a taste in multimedia entertainment. Flipping through categorical selections, she found a small file cluster of children's animated shorts. Knowing nothing about them, she picked the first one that struck her fancy and loaded it. The screen came up in two dimensions.

"Sorry," she said to Mort. "I must have done something wrong. Let me—"

"No, leave it," Mort said. "These are Carl's—first-run historical theater clips. Harmless slapstick humor. He found some that have been remade as proper holovids, but they lose something. Typical overtechnologizing ... have a seat." He patted the couch beside him.

The shorts were slapstick, but she didn't see the humor. And they were anything but harmless. There were no voices—probably lost in old-timey archival storage—but the plots (if you could call them that) involved an anthropomorphic mouse tormenting an equally humanized cat who wanted to eat him.

The mouse's brutal and scientifically dubious tricks and traps were graphically inhumane. "These were shown to children?"

Mort lifted his hands. "What can I say? It was a brutal era. They had to toughen up those little buggers for wars and plagues and whatnot. Earth wasn't safe like it is now."

"Still ..."

After sitting uncomfortably through three episodes, amid Mort's giggles and snickers, Tanny's voice came over the comm. "Drop us in, Mort. Nothing crazy like last time."

Mort reached over, and with a self-satisfied air, hit the off button on the remote.

"Time to get to work," he said.

"Mind if I watch?"

"Depends why."

Esper bit her lip. She hadn't really given it much thought. "Curiosity?"

"Admirable reason. If you were just bored and figured I was as good as a holovid, I'd have kicked you out. I *had* somewhat hoped that I cut a dashing figure and you wanted to see me in all my glory."

"You're wearing a sweatshirt with a grease stain by the collar and a hole in the front pocket. How much glory were you hoping for?"

"*Vobis*," he replied with a nod and a spread hand, conceding the point.

"How about you just go ahead now?"

"Since we're not going deep, apparently, I've got to show off a *little*. No staff, no chanting. Just little old me," said Mort. He took up a position at the center of the common room, closed his eyes, and bowed his head.

The glyphs that lay dormant around the periphery of the

room began to glow green. Esper watched through the domed ceiling as the stars faded away.

"Good enough," Tanny said over the comm. "Leave us right here."

Mort's eyes snapped open. "Buggery." The glyphs faded, but the stars stayed gone outside. "Waste of my time."

"How'd you do that?"

Mort scowled. "*You* could have done that, I'd wager. I hardly moved us."

"No, I mean without the gibbledy-jabbering and the staff? I thought you needed those."

Mort sighed and his expression relaxed. Esper knew it wasn't her that he was miffed at. "Belief is a funny thing. It's all an argument with the universe, convincing it to bend to your command. The more strongly you believe, the more potent an argument you can make. It's not all literal, mind you, but believing that you can win plays a huge part in success. I might not like to admit it, but the words and the staff help. I feel more wizardy."

"So the words don't matter? You could just say anything?"

"Not anything," Mort cautioned with a raised finger. "But the right thing. You taught children, so maybe you can relate. Imagine the children all had some half-cocked notion, nanobot-osis or phalangeopelia or whatever you want to make up. You want to convince them of ..." Mort waved hands, searching for the word, "... electrons. Can you just tell them any old thing?"

"No, but I just can't will them into believing in atomic theory, either," Esper replied.

Mort scratched his chin. "Well, that's where the analogy breaks down, I suppose. Point is, if you're going to *make* the argument, you damn well better get it right. The universe isn't a toy."

Esper nodded, but remained silent. She didn't have an argument to make against that.

Mort scowled once more. "Oh, fine. It *is* a toy, dammit. We should have gone deeper, just because we can." And he stormed off to his room, muttering to himself.

---

"I don't like it," Tanny said as soon as she closed the shipwide comm. The view outside the cockpit windows had gone grey, and the astral depth meter read 0.98, very nearly a standard travel lane.

"What's not to like?" Carl asked. "We're not in a rush anymore. That time-lapse spell of Keesha's did its job."

"Mort could put us below even the crazy depths that black ops use," Tanny replied. "We could sneak by half the ARGO fleet. Why dangle ourselves as bait? We're limping along like ... like ..."

"Like anything but smugglers?" Carl ventured.

"Like bait."

"Well, that's the point."

Tanny pinched the bridge of her nose. "We don't *need* to get cleared by border security. They don't even have a record of us leaving ARGO space. What do we gain by dangling our cargo under their noses?"

"Mort's great and all," Carl said. "But one of these runs, we're going to get snagged on some bullshit experimental sensor net or just be in the wrong place at the wrong time, and we're going to look *really* guilty. Won't matter what we've got on board, they'll take us in just for astral travel violations, and with *Mobius* in impound, they'll find everything. How'd you like to end up back in the marines as a front-line grunt with a memory wipe?"

"They don't do shit like that, Carl," Tanny replied. "It's just nutjobs spreading rumors."

Carl paused. "Really? I've been giving those meat-brains too much slack, then. Either way, how good are we gonna get it when they figure out half the stuff we've done? I've run the math. I'm due about six hundred years hard labor, and I don't think I'd *want* to live to finish a sentence like that. We let a few hapless clipboard carriers onto *Mobius*, let Mort play the aggrieved grav-jockey, and they put a check mark next to our ship ID ... cleared for customs."

"Why would they—"

"Because those guys live oatmeal lives with no cinnamon on top," said Carl. "They're bored stupid, and if they find something, that's gonna make them happy. They're not Planetary Security or Earth Interstellar Enhanced Investigative Org. Someone back home asks them what they did today, they can tell 'em they helped some poor derelict freighter with a busted astral drive. That's all any of them need. They're not out to meet an arrest quota."

Tanny sighed. "Why do I get the feeling you make this shit up as you go along? Did you even have a plan before we started arguing?"

"It's really starting to come together," Carl replied. "You've always been a great help with working out the kinks."

"Yeah ... figured as much."

It was the UNV *Gallivant* that found them. Spluttering into ARGO space just outside of a standard astral depth set off alarms, and had a patrol ship on them in short order to investigate. There was not even a request for them to drop into real space. The captain of the *Gallivant* had his ship maneuver into the sub-standard 0.98 depth to meet the *Mobius*. Esper waited for someone to tell her what she should be doing.

Carl jogged into the common room from the cockpit as everyone was gathering to prepare for a nice friendly boarding. "This is your show, Mort." The wizard stood with his staff in hand, ready to recount the harrowing tale of how their star drive was beyond his ability to repair, and how he had used manual wizardry to get them limping back to civilized space.

"Why do we have to use this tired old gimmick?" Mort asked. "Makes me look like a bargain-bin Oxford drop-out. I got my doctorate in wizardry, I'll have you know! I've got a sheepskin made with real sheep skin to prove it."

"This is for your benefit, you know," Roddy said in an aside to Esper. "We've all heard this spiel before."

"Cork it, techie," Mort snapped. "No one's asking you to put on an apron and claim you can't bake the engines back into working order."

"If people are after you personally, wouldn't it be nice for them not to know you're a big bad wizard?" Esper asked.

"My dear girl, there is a fine line indeed between demurring when occasion arises to display my might and debasing myself while astral-obsessed adept lectures me on proper maintenance of the *Mobius*," said Mort. He frowned a moment as everyone looked on. "Imagine standing there while Tanny lectured you on fashion."

"Hey!" Tanny and Esper exclaimed in unison, then looked

to one another with a mutual understanding of a common object of annoyance.

"Besides, it's not like the Convocation gets diddly-squat for information out of the navy," said Mort.

"Oh?" Esper asked, looking to Carl.

Carl held up his hands. "I mustered out as a Lieutenant Commander, but anything doing with the Convocation was still above my pay grade. Even the whiny little bitches that kept the star drives going on the carrier ships were off limits. Didn't answer to anyone but the captain and the XO."

"Terms are cordial," Mort said. "Navy gets terramancers delivered to barren worlds. Convocation sloughs off their dead weight into navy service. Nobody *likes* one another, though."

Carl shrugged. "I gave the *Tallyho* Mort's real name. Easier than making something up that would pass scrutiny. Not like the Convocation has a wanted list on the navy's radar."

"I'm ... shocked," Esper said. "You gave Mort up to the navy and just hoped they wouldn't tell anyone?"

"Welcome to the real world, kid," Tanny said. "Government isn't this big, friendly blanket over everything. It's just a shitload of underpaid quarter-day desk pilots and a billion loosely interconnected computer systems."

Mriy growled something Esper couldn't understand.

"That, too," Carl said.

"What?" Esper asked. She turned to Mort. "I really need one of those translator charms."

"She just said the government's also got a military," Tanny said. "So there's that."

"I've made up my mind," said Mort. He took two long steps and thrust his staff into Esper's hands. "I'm promoting Esper to ship's wizard."

Esper opened her mouth, but words eluded her. The common room grew suddenly warm, and the voices around her grew fuzzy. Everyone wobbled ...

A moment later, Esper found herself sitting on the couch, Mort's staff still clutched in one hand with a death-grip. Someone tugged at the staff, and she loosened her grasp. Carl took custody of the unwelcome symbol of her newfound cover identity.

"Mort was kidding around," Carl said, crouching down to Esper's eye level. "Weren't you, Mort? He's always a baby about this routine."

"Sorry," Mort muttered, snatching his staff back.

"Kid," said Roddy, "You gotta learn to take a joke, or at least roll with it. Come on, we got company coming any minute."

The crew dispersed to their respective stations. As Tanny passed by the flushed and flustered Esper, she leaned down and whispered. "Mort would've let you try. Don't let them fool you."

Esper found herself alone in the common room a moment later. The feel of the sinful wood in her hand still fresh in her memory. She absently wiped her hand on her trousers, telling herself she had done nothing wrong. Mort gambled with his soul's health every time he plied his twisted profession. She had a duty to look out for him. But one question nagged at her.

Why did she regret letting go?

---

Roddy sat on the *Mobius's* gravity stone as he watched Mort put on a show. The star-drive mechanic from the *Gallivant* was a pot-bellied jackass with a permanent squint to his eyes, but he knew his business. He had a tool belt dangling with half regular tools, half nonsensical wizard toys, and was jabbing and prodding the star-drive with a mix of both.

"How long you been without astral?" asked Rybakov, the star-drive mechanic.

Mort scratched at his scalp. "Couldn't say. I mean, we were on the ground a couple of days. Could've gone kerflooey anywhere along the way. We weren't using it at the time, if that's what you're asking."

"That's not what I'm asking," Rybakov replied. "I was wondering how long you've been limping around the galaxy at non-standard speeds. You should have had this looked at straight away."

Mort leaned against the wall and wagged a finger at Rybakov. "I get it. You're just jealous. Old coot like me knows how to get things done when the gizmos go all ... scientific on you. We were stranded, with no Convocation repair crews within shouting distance. I dragged this carcass back to ARGO space. Bet *you* couldn't have managed that."

Rybakov pulled his head out of the star-drive and raised an eyebrow at Mort. "I wouldn't have needed to find out. Proper maintenance and these things don't happen. Listen here, old timer, while your improvisation may be fine for emergencies, we can't condone this reckless astral diving in ARGO territory. Now if you don't want this to happen again ..."

Roddy watched Mort's eyes glaze over. It wasn't his fault, really. Not only had he heard this spiel before a dozen times from various ARGO maintenance gremlins, but he had another task nagging at him. The *Gallivant* had brought an actual investigative wizard on board, and Mort was fighting a war of misinformation on two fronts.

Carl hadn't counted on the *Gallivant* having an actual wizard aboard. Mort had been jerking the strings on navy star-drive mechanics for years. It had become routine. The young woman in the sapphire blue uniform and Convocation crest stalked the cargo hold with a permanent furrow in her brow. Carl watched with arms folded, a practiced look of ease presented for the *Gallivant's* first officer, Commander Jeanine MacDougal.

Without taking the effort to convince himself that he had nothing to hide, Carl kept his worry from his features by concentrating on the two women who had commandeered his ship for the moment. Commander MacDougal was pushing forty, if he had to guess, with soft features and a few locks of grey in her single braid. She had the sort of hard, trim body the navy preferred in its sailors. Sorceress Tia Ramirez was probably the same age, but didn't look it. Mort had warned him years ago not to trust the looks of anyone who knew transformative or illusory magic—Keesha Bell was a prime example. The *Gallivant's* investigative sorceress had jet black hair that fell plumb-line straight to a uniform length at her jawline and a figure her unisex navy outfit couldn't hide. It was the eyes that kept drawing Carl's attention though, not just because they were trying *very* hard to see a crate of disintegrator rifles she was nearly tripping over, but because they were an unnatural share of turquoise. The faint glow in them might have been an affectation, or a function of whatever magic she was rooting around the cargo hold with.

Commander MacDougal's fingers danced across the surface of her datapad, making a series of bleeps and bloops.

"Your travel records are spotty," she said, not looking up as she addressed Carl.

"Spend a lot of time outside ARGO space," Carl replied. "We're armed and shielded. No harm seeing a bit of untamed space for ourselves."

"To call your logs inadequate would be doing them a service," Commander MacDougal continued. "I've arrested pirates with better record-keeping."

"Yeah, I know," Carl said, trying to sound contrite. "I just hate the way my voice sounds in a log. I sound fine in my head, but playback always makes me out to be this pompous, reedy-voiced ass."

Commander MacDougal looked up from her datapad. "I can't imagine how that happens ... I see you were stopped in neutral space by the *Tallyho* recently. They cleared you at the time. Care you explain your whereabouts since then?"

"You make a guy feel awful guilty for just a blown star-drive," Carl said. "You know that?"

"Something's definitely wrong here," Sorceress Ramirez said. "I just can't put a finger on it."

"I can see why they don't saddle you guys with Convocation help too often," Carl said in an undertone to Commander Ramirez. "She piss someone off Earth-side? Girl's got no business in space if she can't either clear me or say what she's found. This innuendo business is bush league. I'm ex-navy myself."

"Commander," Sorceress Ramirez said. "He is hiding something here. I just can't find it."

Carl scratched behind his ear. "Listen, I don't know what to tell you. You're not going to find anything because there's nothing to find. You're welcome to keep looking, but I don't want this to turn into an archaeological dig site. Once your mechanic gets my star-drive up and running, I was hoping to get under way."

Sorceress Ramirez looked to MacDougal. "Commander—"

"Look," Commander MacDougal said. "You can get your ship under way as soon as my scanning crews and wizard give the all-clear. Not before. You have problem with that?"

Carl snorted. "Yeah, your wizard's pissing me off. She could end this any time she wants. You guys aren't searching for contraband, you're looking for some pretense to write me up and pad your fine quotas. I've got rights, you know!"

"Yes, you do," Commander MacDougal agreed. She slid her sidearm free from its holster and pointed it Carl's way. "But we have broad discretionary powers out here in the border regions. You want this wrapped up? Fine. You can tell us under truth scan what's going on with this ship, and what's bothering Sorceress Ramirez."

Carl laced his fingers behind his head and headed for the docking hatch at an easy saunter. "You want the truth? Let's do this. I've got all the truth you can handle."

---

Mriy came in just as the techs were packing up their gear, having found nothing out of the ordinary. She had a look on her face that few humans would have recognized. Her upper lip twitched, and her ears kept trying to swivel back despite an obvious effort to keep them facing forward. She was nervous, and with two scanner-warmers from the navy still in the room, Tanny was worried the azrin was going to go bloody on them.

"Thanks for the once-over, boys," Tanny said, speeding the techs on their way. "Nice knowing there's nothing else wrong aside from the usual we already knew about." The two techs were customs enforcement, not mechanics. While their scanners might have found major hull breaches or radiation leaks, they were looking for plants, animals, and weaponry that didn't belong in ARGO space—at least not among civilians.

"Thank you for your cooperation," one of the two replied in an Old Earth accent, something quaint and western-European. Straps for scanner carrying cases were slung this way and that over the techs' shoulders as they trudged out of the common room and into the cargo hold, where their ship was connected to the *Mobius*.

As soon as the door closed, Tanny whispered urgently to Mriy. "What is it?"

"The captain," Mriy said. "The patrol ship commed us. They took Carl aboard their vessel."

"Oh, shit!"

"Yes," Mriy agreed. "Dung, excrement, and shit all in the same pile."

"All right, let's stay calm," Tanny said, putting her hands out to calm the azrin. "We need a plan. Where's Mort?"

Mriy turned up empty paws. "I was in the cockpit. How would I know?"

"Must still be down with the *Gallivant's* star-drive guy," Tanny said. She nodded to herself as a plan began to form. But first of all, she needed to make sure that Mriy was with her. "They pull Carl's brain out through his ears, we're cooked. They find those disintegrator rifles, we're doing cold time. When they find out what our cargo is, there's a good chance things go worse for us. So ... blood or water?"

It was an azrin expression Mriy had taught her. An ancient legend among their kind said that a hunter's blood would turn to water if he abandoned a packmate in the wild. There was more to it than that, but Mriy wasn't much of a storyteller. The key point that Tanny had retained was the question to ask before a hunt.

"Blood," Mriy agreed. "Lots of blood. We wait for Mort?"

Tanny rubbed her face with both hands, squeezing her eyes shut and willing away distracting thoughts. Mort might wreck both ships, like he had with the *Viper*, but they might get lucky once again with the damage being reparable. If they waited, the interrogators on the *Gallivant* might break Carl. At that point, it would be blaster-rifles in the corridors until one side couldn't fire back. Of course, the *Gallivant* could always release the docking collar and blast *Mobius* from space, leaving a shattered hulk not quite one standard unit deep in the astral plane. Roddy was with Mort ... a non-factor until the wizard showed up. Esper ... well, she was something.

"Let's get Esper," Tanny said.

"Um."

Tanny knew the objection. Esper was no hunter. She wasn't much of anything, really. But she could man the comm from the cockpit and coordinate their movements. She could also probably maneuver the ship if the *Gallivant* broke free. Hopefully if it came to that, one of them would be able to man the turret for a final showdown before Earth Navy's finest dusted them.

Tanny ignored Mriy's halfhearted objection and pounded on the door to Esper's quarters.

"What is it?" Esper asked as she opened the door. "All clear?"

"Not hardly," Tanny said. She drew her blaster pistol and pressed it into Esper's hands. "We've got us a rescue mission. Carl's stepped in it again."

There was a clunk as the magnetic locks of the restraints held Carl's wrists to the arms of the chair. A technician in a white medical smock pressed his head back against the headrest as probes telescoped in, surrounding his cranium in a sparse forest of stainless steel spikes that prevented any movement.

Carl flapped his hands. "You don't need the restraints. I've got nothing to hide."

"You'd be surprised how many exhaust-sniffing space cases I've had in that chair who changed their mind midway through. Those 'beat the machine' articles in the bowels of the omni catch me more criminals ..." said Commander MacDougal, shaking her head.

Something cold pressed against the side of Carl's neck, and there was a puff-hiss as some drug was forced into his bloodstream. "The hell'd you just fill me with?" he demanded through gritted teeth as a warm feeling spread from his neck into the rest of his body.

"Just something to relax you," the tech said, adjusting a set of tiny cameras on an armature so that they aimed at Carl's eyes.

"You ever consider people might not need relaxing if you didn't put pointy objects a few centimeters from their eyes?" Carl asked.

"If you'd rather, I could go first," Sorceress Ramirez said flatly. She stood at the edge of Carl's field of view, her hands tucked into the opposite sleeves of her uniform shirt. Only a wizard's uniform had sleeves loose enough for that maneuver to work.

"No need to fight over me," Carl said. "Plenty of Carl to go around. Play nice and take turns."

"We ready to baseline him yet?" Commander MacDougal asked.

The tech made a few minor adjustments. Near as Carl could tell, it was just to make him more uncomfortable, puttering just out of view on stuff jabbing at his brain. "You're all set, Commander."

"State your full name."

"Bradley Carlin Ramsey," Carl said. "Carlin was one of my dad's favorite comedians. Never got a good answer why the hell the picked Bradley. Mike got the normal name, and he—"

"Enough," Commander MacDougal snapped. "Date of birth."

"July one, twenty-five twenty-eight," Carl replied.

"Place of birth."

"Depends who you ask," said Carl. "Officially Warwick, Boston, Earth. Really my mom popped me out while we were still on approach, aboard the *Madison Squared.*"

There was a pause, and Carl imagined the commander, sorceress, and tech conferring silently behind him. The tech was a bland little spud that Carl had forgotten the instant the man left his sight, but he could imagine in the details of his two female captors.

"We ready for real questions yet?" Carl asked. "I probably should have mentioned this earlier, but I need to piss. I mean, I'm not gonna piss in your weird inquisitor chair, but ... well, it would be nice if we moved things along here."

"How long have you owned and operated the *Mobius?*"

"About four years, give or take, and about four years, give or take," Carl replied. "Unless by 'operate' you mean 'fly,' in which case: all too fucking infrequently."

"He's muddling the baseline," the tech said.

"Mr. Ramsey," Commander MacDougal said. "Please stick to the questions asked. Let's start over. State your full name."

"Oh, for fuck's sake."

"State your full name."

Carl played along, answering their bland and mundane questions until they reached the point they had left off.

"Mr. Ramsey, do you have anything on board your ship which is prohibited from civilian transport by ARGO regulations?"

"Nope," Carl replied. At that moment, he could not imagine what they might be talking about. The *Mobius* might take a questionable job once in a while, but they were squeaky clean and had been for months.

"Any passengers or crew with outstanding warrants?"

"Nope."

"Any passengers or crew that you did not disclose?"

"Nope."

"Any plant or animal life from an alien world outside ARGO control?"

"Nope. Unless we lost Meyang VII while I was traveling, in which case Mriy would qualify."

"Does your ship have any systems, magical or technological, that might interfere with our scans?"

"Damned if I know how your scans work," Carl said. "But nothing that I know of."

Carl strained to make out the whispered conversation going on behind him. It was bugging the hell of out them, he knew.

"Mr. Ramsey, are any of your systems running outside of legal specification?"

"Yes!" he said. He allowed them a moment, judging how long they'd wait before pressing him for details and beginning just before they demanded he elaborate. "Our star-drive is busted."

"Your gizmo is worthless," Sorceress Ramirez said. "Leave the restraints, but get the rest of that junk away from him."

"You sound so beautiful when you're angry," Carl said. "It might just be the drug you gave me talking, but if you want to get together once we're finished here, I won't hold any of this against you."

"Mr. Ramsey, do be quiet," Commander MacDougal ordered. "You will only speak in response to the questions put to you."

"Sorry Commander," Carl said. "I saw by your ring that you're a married woman. I didn't know you'd get jealous over me and Tia. I mean, I saw you checking her out, licking your lips with that hungry look in your eyes while she was searching my ship. I just figured it was pent up. What happens in the Black Ocean ... you know. So if you two ladies want to—"

"This machine is worthless," Commander MacDougal shouted. A thump behind him told Carl a fist had been pounded against a display panel.

"I'm sorry," Carl said, hoping they couldn't see his smirk. The indicators *had* to be showing him lying just then.

"Commander?" Sorceress Tia Ramirez asked, leaving her actual question unspoken.

"This is awkward," Carl said. "Maybe I should be going."

"Get him out of here," Commander MacDougal ordered.

"It's nice meeting you all," Carl said, no doubt setting off the truth detectors once more. Commander MacDougal and Sorceress Ramirez left the room, and Carl heard a heated argument muffled by the door.

The technician set to work briskly, disconnecting Carl

from the machine. "You got a ring yourself, there, sir," he said. "You just trying to wind Ramirez up just then?"

"It's your machine," Carl replied. "You'd know if I was lying."

"I just mean ..."

"So she's a wizard. What's wrong with that? I'd have her in a second and keep her for hours. I love my ex-wife to death, but we're not exactly saving ourselves for one another. You know?"

"Yeah, but how would you ever get comfortable around her? None of us turn our backs on her, even Rybakov. He's more like one of us than a real wizard."

"Some of my best friends are wizards," Carl replied indignantly.

---

Carl passed the star-drive mechanic in the docking collar as the two men returned to their respective ships. Mort and Roddy were there waiting for him.

"How'd things go?" Carl asked.

"What were you doing over there?" Roddy asked.

Carl shrugged, wincing and working loose a kink in his neck from sitting so still in the interrogation chair. "Aw, just clearing up a few things. Mort wasn't sly enough for that fine piece of sorceress they sent over to check our cargo. She couldn't pin it, so I had to talk them around to my way of thinking."

"Sure," said Mort. "You go being Mr. Clever while I'm trying to convince the limp wand brigade that I'm stupider than he is. *You* try fuddling things for two wizards at once."

"I got a wizard and two Earth Navy officers," Carl replied. "Plus their tech."

"He's got you, I think," Roddy said.

Up above, the door to the common room opened. "What's going on down there?" Tanny asked. She had a blaster rifle in hand.

"Nothing," replied Carl. "We're good to go as soon as we're off the tether."

Mriy's head appeared in the doorway. She looked down at Carl, then to Tanny. "I thought you said—"

"Never mind," Tanny snapped. "Rescue's off."

"I'm glad you're OK," Esper's voice carried down into the hold from unseen behind Mriy and Tanny.

"Thanks," Carl shouted up, just before the door slammed shut.

"What was that all about?" Roddy asked.

Carl rubbed his chin between thumb and forefinger. "I think the girls were about to come rescue me. How sweet."

"Without me?" Mort asked. "Are they daft? That Navy ship has Navy sailors on it, maybe even marines. I don't know one science gun from the next, but numbers alone favor the Navy."

Carl just shrugged. "Well, Mort, we'll cruise for an hour at standard depths, then you can tear the star-drive to shreds and drop us nice and deep."

Mort clapped his hands and rubbed them together with glee. "Can't wait."

---

In a past life, the *Mobius* had been a diplomatic vessel. That was the reason that every crew member had their own living quarters instead of shared bunks, and it also accounted for the fact that the *Mobius* had a conference room. Esper had been aboard over a week before the room's existence had come up in passing. Up until that point it had been the scary door halfway between the common room and the cockpit that no one seemed to use. Now that she looked closely, there was a discolored rectangle on the steel of the wall next to the door where someone had pried away the placard that said what lay beyond.

Of course, what lay beyond was nothing a self-respecting diplomat would ever have tolerated. Without apparent need for a meeting room that didn't have a holovid and refrigerator, Carl and his gang had piled it high with every useless object aboard that they couldn't bear to part with. It was a teenager's closet, stuffed to bursting, except that instead of a square meter of floor space, the conference room comfortably seated twelve. Esper rolled up the sleeves of her coveralls, took a fortifying breath, and set to work.

Within a few minutes, the corridor to the cockpit was barely traversable and Esper was out of breath. She had already removed a guitar case, a hammock, several plastic crates stuffed with exotic clothes, a set of four lawn chairs, the mat and padded protective gear Tanny used for sparring, several outdated datapads, and an easel. The pile just kept going, but she was working on creating a path, not a wholesale excavation.

The cockpit door opened and Mriy stuck her head out. "What are you doing out here? I thought you were asleep." It all came through in clear English, with a funny growling accent. Her new translator-charmed earring was working.

Esper sighed and slumped against the wall. "Couldn't

sleep. We almost got caught today. I got my first taste of being a real live criminal."

"You kidnapped a boy," Mriy replied. "You made yourself a criminal that day."

"But that didn't *feel* criminal," Esper said, brushing a stray lock of sweat-stained hair out of her way. Her braids were coming loose. "I was rescuing Adam, even if I didn't follow the law to do it."

"You broke a law, and your old pack shunned you," Mriy said. "You have a new pack now, and you don't need to worry anymore. But why dig in the spare room? Go watch a holo if you can't sleep."

"I'm worried we're not doing the right thing with that box we're transporting," Esper said. "I'd feel better knowing what was in it."

"Probably not," said Mriy.

"Well, that's just it!" Esper said, pointing a finger at Mriy. "Everyone thinks there's something horrible and illegal in it, and wants to just stuff their hands in their pockets about it. Not knowing doesn't make it right. What if it's a bio-weapon, or plans to a space station's defenses, or stolen military tech, or—"

"Or someone's museum piece, or a sculpture, or an heirloom dagger," Mriy countered. "If we don't open it, it can have anything inside."

Esper furrowed her brow. "What kind of twisty-brained notion is that?"

"Carl's." As if that explained everything.

Esper crossed her arms. "You *do* realize that Carl's tongue is a shovel for tossing around huge piles of bull-poo?"

Mriy gave a halfhearted swipe with one paw and withdrew to the cockpit. "Do whatever. You won't open it without

Mort's magic, and I wouldn't wake Mort if the ship was on fire. Roddy climbed in and buried the box; let him climb in and get it out in the morning."

"I just need to look at it," Esper said.

"Just keep the noise down. I'm trying to sleep." The cockpit door clanged shut.

They were drifting along at an astral depth of 7.72, and their pilot was sleeping. At that moment Esper discovered one benefit to ignorance. If she knew just how many kilometers the *Mobius* was leaving in their wake every second, she might throw up. Instead, she trusted that the ship had some sort of warning thingy that was loud enough to wake Mriy if they ended up aimed at a planet or a star. She made a point of remembering to ask Mort one day whether hitting planets or stars was even possible where they were in the astral. Then she reminded herself pointedly *not* to talk to Mort about any such thing, just in case it was.

With a crawlspace along the top of the pile, Esper squirmed into the erstwhile conference room. The overhead lighting was just centimeters above her as she made her way across boxes of plastic, cardboard, and various metal and composite materials. No two boxes were quite the same size or shape, so the stacks were irregular and often precarious. After one slid beneath her weight and dropped her half a meter onto an upturned polycarbonate canoe, she suddenly wished she had worn her combat getup instead of coveralls.

"There you are," she said to their mystery cargo when she caught sight of the box. It was wedged in between a broken holo-projector and auto-walk exerciser. "You're coming with me." She wouldn't have blamed the scanning techs if they hadn't even tried to check the cluttered room.

It took nearly half an hour to extract the box. Light as it

was, the passage had been awkward enough forward and empty-handed. Wriggling backward, carrying the box, and favoring her ribs where she'd fallen on them, Esper felt lucky to have made it out in one piece.

She was sitting at the common room table, staring at the box, when the rest of the crew began to wake.

Roddy was the first up. He stumbled bleary-eyed into the kitchen area, cracked open a beer, and poured it into the coffee machine before he took note of Esper. "Bleeding Christ, kid, what're you doing with that thing?"

Esper opened her mouth to chide him for blasphemy, but gave him a droopy-eyed smile instead. "Thinking. Thinking what we almost got busted for."

"You mean besides a shipment of black-ops grade military weaponry?" Roddy asked as the coffee machine gurgled and protested.

"That's disgusting."

Roddy shrugged, poured himself a mug, and took a long draw from it. "Takes getting used to. I'll give you that."

"And it can't be good for the machine."

"Who do you think fixes the damn thing?" Roddy asked. "Or anything around here, for that matter?"

"Well, Mr. Fixit, how about a hand figuring out how to open this thing?"

"Not on your life," Roddy replied.

"What?" Esper said. She found a respite from her sleep-deprived sluggishness as she straightened in her seat. "I mean, after yesterday, you've *got* to be wondering."

"Nope. That was reasons one through a hundred why we *don't* wanna know. If Carl wasn't such a slick-talking glove-salesman, we'd all be locked up about now. Or the commando squad would have most of us dead in a firefight. No thanks. I'll stick with keepin' my head down and waiting to get paid. Besides, that things got a molecular lock on it. No opening it without the code."

Esper rinsed the coffee pot three times before daring to brew another batch with water. She settled back in to stare at the box. Her eyelids slouched as she followed the lines of the glyphs, wondering what impossible magic Mort would declare them to be to get out of helping her. Fuck Roddy. A sudden guilt swept over Esper as she realized how malign her thoughts were turning. She needed sleep; she wasn't herself.

The rest of the crew trickled in, asked about the box, and went about making their breakfasts around her. She could barely recall the conversations as they occurred.

"Morning everyone," Carl announced as he emerged from his quarters, last to wake. "The day is fine, and we are fast, free, and ... profitable. Damn, blew it there."

"Fortunate?" Roddy offered.

"Fully funded?" Mort suggested.

"Felons," Esper muttered.

Carl looked to the box on the kitchen table. "What's that doing out here?"

"She wants to open it," Roddy said.

"No way," Carl replied. "Bad business. One of the reasons we're getting almost *forty ... thousand ... apiece* for this job is that we're not asking any questions. The only thing that box can have inside is a bunch of questions."

"I'm with Carl on this one," Tanny said. "Business is business."

"Thirty-five, seven," Roddy interjected. "That's the cut, not forty."

Carl turned to Roddy. "Our last job didn't clear half that *before* the split."

Roddy held up three hands while standing on the fourth. "Don't look at me. I'm with you on keeping our eyes out of that thing."

Mriy yawned, revealing bloodstained teeth from her breakfast. "Open it. Don't open it. As long as we get paid I don't care."

Mort pursed his lips and tapped them with a finger. "I admit I'd like to know."

"Come on, Mo—"

"But I don't see a pressing need," Mort continued over Carl's objection. "Besides, looks like a bloody mess of science sealing it shut."

---

Esper woke with a kitchen towel under her head and a pool of drool by her mouth. The box had been pushed to the edge of the table where she had fallen asleep. She didn't remember dozing off, but the evidence was overwhelming that she had. The common room was quieter than she could ever recall it being; it was eerie.

A finger rubbed across paper—the turning of a page in a paper book. Not many people would have recognized the sound, but the One Church had always favored paper Bibles. Blinking back the gummy feeling in her eyes, Esper glanced around to find Mort sitting on the couch, a huge tome spread across his lap.

"Oh, you're awake," he said, stating the obvious. He took a red cloth ribbon and tucked it between the pages before shutting his book.

"Since when do you read books?" Esper asked.

"My dear girl, I'm a wizard," Mort replied. "I just normally keep my reading to my quarters, where there are fewer jelly stains. You'd been acting peculiar though, so I shooed everyone out and kept an eye on you."

Esper wiped at her mouth with a sleeve, wondering just how undignified she had looked sleeping at the kitchen table. Then she considered her present company, and wondered why she worried about that sort of thing anymore. "I'm fine. Thanks."

"Oh, I know that, but you needed the sleep and I didn't mind having both quiet and a couch at the same time," Mort replied. "Besides, I recognized the symptoms instantly. The rest have grown a bit dense about this sort of thing, but I still know the signs."

"Symptoms?" Esper asked. "What is it you think I've got?"

"A conscience."

"Oh."

"It's treatable," said Mort. He waved his hand around, indicating their general vicinity. "They all manage. Beer treats the symptoms, but money pulls it out by the roots."

"You think getting paid will stop me caring what we're delivering?"

"Do you think we wouldn't deliver it if we knew?"

Esper swallowed. "I hope it would depend what's inside." She studied the wizard a moment, wondering what bait she could put on a hook to snag *his* conscience. Conscience and guilt were the surest weapons against evil. They compelled a good person to do the right thing when the wrong choice seemed easier. They made righteous actions feel good and immoral ones feel bad, and kept souls on the path of salvation better than any amount of coercion or fear ever could. But this time, the sin of Pride might serve better. "But it doesn't matter anyway, since we couldn't open it if we tried."

Mort snickered. "Don't give me that hangdog look. Reverse psychology, the scientists call that one. But wizards learn that trick young. The simplest of magics is turning someone's own mind against them. You think I'm so desperate to prove myself that I'd open it just to show that I could? Of course I could figure a way into it. I don't doubt that for a moment. The challenge holds no thrall over me."

"It's a dinosaur egg," Esper blurted.

Mort narrowed his eyes. "What's that now?"

"That safari park had dinosaurs," Esper said. "The guide was—"

"Carl told me there were no dinosaurs," Mort said. "Just run-of-the-mill megafauna. Stupidly huge animals, but just regular ones."

"Technically 'dinosaurs' are from Earth. That was Carl's excuse. These were Vi Tik Naa sauropods, just like dinosaurs in every way ... except technically not dinosaurs. Anyway, our contact was the safari guide, and the box was hidden buried in the park. I can't be sure, but my guess is that it's a dinosaur egg."

Mort eyed the box. He eyed it long and hard, and Esper let him do so in peace. If scientists held that the human brain was a biological computer made of neurons and lobes and cortices, what did wizards think went on inside their heads? Whatever alchemy was gurgling inside Mort's skull, it reached some conclusion.

"If it's a dinosaur egg ... you got any problems with us delivering it?"

Esper sighed. "I think when you agree to deliver something no questions asked, you know you're hauling something illegal. Unless someone's making the galaxy's most expensive omelet, we're basically just taking it from one zoo to another."

"Let's have a look, then," said Mort.

Esper nodded and didn't say a word. She kept the smirk off her face until Mort was looking the other way, bent over inspecting the carved glyphs on the box. He squinted as he examined them, traced them with a finger, and muttered to himself beneath his breath. Esper wondered how much of it was for show.

"Professional job," Mort said, sitting back and scratching his chin. "I'll give them that much, whoever warded this thing."

"That a problem?"

Mort snorted. "Look up on top of the fridge, there's a black marker up there. Grab it for me."

Esper did as he asked, and found a disreputable old marker atop the *Mobius's* refrigerator, sticky with some food-based substance. On a hunch, she looked close at the refrigerator door, and noticed faint remnants of old messages scrawled on the stainless steel and mostly wiped away: "Out of cheese," "Touch the cake and die," "Green bottle is for med scan, DO NOT DRINK," and several others. She handed the marker to Mort.

Mort popped the cap and sniffed the exposed tip. "Love that smell. Nothing natural about it, but science gets one right once in a while." He proceeded to start drawing on the box.

"What are you doing?" Esper demanded, horrified. She hadn't given it much thought, but she had assumed he was going to take notes or work out whatever wizard's did for magical mathematics. Defacing their cargo had somehow not occurred to her.

"Making a few modifications," Mort replied. His tongue poked out the corner of his mouth as he worked. The lines held no meaning for Esper. The patterns of the glyphs were one sort of gibberish; the graffiti Mort added were another sort. The result looked like a street map of an old Earth city, before enlightened city planners discovered grids and right angles.

"There we are," Mort said, capping the marker, which he slapped down onto the table with a satisfied grin.

"Now what?" Esper asked. "It's still sealed."

"I gave that some thought," Mort replied. "I could break it open, but damn me if I have any idea how I'd get it back into one working piece. But then I realized ..." Mort lifted the box, which turned wispy and insubstantial in his hands. " ... that I don't need to harm it at all."

Left on the table was an egg, resting atop the towel Esper had used for a pillow. It was cream-colored, flecked with blue, and the size of a loaf of bread. She reached out a hand to touch it but stopped short. Whoever was to receive it might scan the egg, and she might leave traces of her DNA on it.

Mort set the box down, which turned solid once more, and hefted the egg. "Lotta trouble for this little critter," he said. "Lighter than I'd have imagined for a dinosaur egg, but what do I know about dinosaurs."

Esper looked on in horror as Mort casually turned the egg over, looking at every side of it and running his hands across the surface. He could drop it. He could break it. He was leaving his DNA all over it like a bear rubbing on a tree to leave its scent. "Wipe it off. Put it back in the box, quick."

"So, it was an egg," Roddy said. Esper and Mort turned to see the laaku mechanic loitering by the cargo bay door.

"How's it that you can open and shut that door without us hearing you?" Esper demanded, flushing with embarrassment.

Roddy waggled the fingers of his upper hands beside his head. "Magic," he replied. "Or maybe I've got a bunch of secret tunnels only I know about. Or maybe ... I'm not a stampede of elephants through the ship like y'all are. For a hunter/gatherer species, you humans are shit all at moving quietly."

"Don't tell Carl," Esper implored. "We're going to put it right back. No one else needs—"

The door to Carl's quarters opened. "Mort, what's going on out here? Lights in my bunk went out and I can't get them back on."

"Probably temporary," Roddy said. "Mort's done some shit with magic that *Mobius* wasn't shielded for."

"Is that an egg?" Carl asked.

"I'm not supposed to tell you that," Roddy replied. "But yeah."

Carl shrugged. "Could be worse." The door to his quarters slammed shut.

"That's it?" Esper asked.

"What'd you expect?" Roddy asked. "That he was going to airlock you or something?"

"I ... I don't know," Esper said with a huff. "I expected him to be mad at least."

"If Carl blew a fuel rod every time something went sideways around here, he'd be in a mental ward as a permanent guest," said Roddy.

"The thing Carl understands is that he's not really all that in charge," said Mort. "He's captain. *Mobius* is registered in his name. But when you boil the skin off the tomato, we outnumber him."

The intra-ship comm opened. "What's going on back there?" Tanny's voice crackled. "I'm showing power distribution malfunctions."

"Now, there's a bit more of a problem," Mort said in an

undertone, leaning close to Esper and pointing to the comm speaker.

---

A council was convened in the common room, unlike any seen in the halls of the great kingdoms of ancient Earth. Esper and Mort sat on opposite sides of the kitchen table with the egg and its empty box between them. Roddy lounged on the couch with a bowl of cereal held in his lower hands, the upper two being occupied with a spoon and the remote for the holoviewer. Tanny stood at the entrance to the forward corridor with her arms crossed; the *Mobius* was at idle, stopped but still deep in the astral. Mriy waited by the food processor as it thawed a raw lamb haunch. Their would-be king, Carl, sat in his flannel boxers and a sleeveless undershirt with his battered leather jacket on over it.

Carl raised one hand in half a shrug. "What're you going to do? You knew it was bound to happen."

"We had the perfect chance this time," said Tanny with the resigned exasperation of a schoolteacher who came back to find the class pet had been set free in the wild. "They locked it six ways from Sunday. All we had to do was *not* bust our brains figuring out a way into it."

"Ah," said Mort, raising a finger. "But I didn't get into it. I got it out from around the egg, not the other—"

"Can it, Mort," said Carl. "None of us could have gotten into that box except you. I wouldn't be getting all professorial right about now."

"Pfft. You were all assuming we were up to something horrible for the money we were getting," said Mort. "Turns out we're nothing but zoo recruiters."

"From a world where they let you hunt dinosaurs," said Mriy. "I could see going back to Vi Tik Naa for a vacation someday. They just don't want anyone else opening a hunting park like theirs."

"Either way, now we've got to get that egg cleaned up navy-like," said Carl. "Spit and polish, except don't go getting any DNA on it, and don't use any polish. Just clean. Like we never touched it. Mort, I assume you can get it back inside?"

Mort shrugged, then nodded.

"Roddy, I want it cleaned up good as new," said Carl. "No trace of the marker on it."

"That shit's a pain to get—"

"I'll take that as a 'yes,'" said Carl.

"One of these days," said Tanny. "*One* of these days, we'll take one of these don't-open-the-cargo jobs and *not open the cargo*." She strode off down the corridor, leaving them to clear up the mess of the egg. The cockpit door slammed.

Esper broke the awkward silence that followed. "I thought she'd have been in a better mood since ... you know."

"You kidding me?" said Carl. "She pulled a blaster on Roddy last time *he* opened one. Roddy, find us something comedy on the holo. We'll deal with the egg after lunch."

---

Esper sat in her quarters, cross-legged on the bed. The pod was filled with the sound of Mindy Mun's peppy, high-pitched vocals as the speaker system fought to drown out the sound of the loudest, most obnoxious 23rd Century comedy she had ever heard, coming from the common room. Esper bobbed her head along with the beat and let the gibberish lyrics of one of Earth's heritage languages wash over her. She had experienced quite a shock when her earring translated the words for her, so she'd taken it off while she listened. Mindy Mun was a talented singer, but the song sounded better without understanding the words.

The datapad in her hand was borrowed. Or pilfered. It had been in the pile where a conference room should have been. She didn't own one of her own, and she needed data. Stranded at a weird astral depth, she couldn't connect it to the omni to get better answers, so she had to settle for what was stored in the *Mobius* computers.

SEARCH> EGG> DINOSAUR

A brief listing came up for ancient paleontological records, modern dinosaur theory, and a serial drama about teenagers who traveled back in time to bring home a dinosaur egg. She ignored the fossils and fiction and looked up what modern scientists said about the creatures. Instead of the kilometers-long flood of information she was accustomed to when connected to the omni, all she got was a synopsis slapped together for children to read. Her students on Bentus VIII would have demanded better than this.

"If Mort likes dinosaurs so much, you'd think he'd have looked them up ..." Esper realized her error when she said it aloud. Why would the *Mobius's* computers have anything about dinosaurs stowed inside? Mort never used it.

With a touch of the datapad, Mindy Mun went silent. The muffled guffaws and shrieking laughter from the comedy holo and its viewers in the common room intruded, but Esper took a steady breath and pushed them aside. She looked to the ceiling of her quarters. "Lord, I don't know what to do. I keep trying to follow the righteous path, but it twists and doubles back and I don't know whether I'm even on it anymore. I'm lost in the darkness ... the real, super darkness of the Black

Ocean, and I can't tell whether there's even light enough to see it by.

"They all seem like such good people, until you consider what they do. Am I any different? I don't want to fall prey to their easy trap. Lord, grant me the wisdom to ask the right questions, so that I can see which path is which. I realize that knowing what sort of dinosaur comes from that egg won't change anything. I just don't know what else I can do. Show me the way so that I can keep my path, and show the others the way as well. Amen."

"*Skiffy, look out*," came a muffled voice from the holovid outside. There was a crash that sounded like hundreds of dishes falling. Mort, Carl, and Roddy hooted and laughed.

Esper sighed. Through the window, she could see the endless void of the Black Ocean, which looked a bit greyer than black down in the astral. Mort could probably explain why. Everyone was so helpful, so nice, so loose and friendly with one another, and they had extended that to include her. The *Mobius* was a tiny speck of life amid the bleakness all around. She remembered the words of Saint Ashleigh, the first saint of the interstellar era: "Lost in the endless ocean of black between worlds, the same stars shine that touch the Earth. Each of us carries that light within us."

The datapad was in easy reach. The temptation to bring back the soothing, saccharine melodies of Mindy Mun beckoned. The idiocy outside her quarters would just fade away. Too easy. She recalled Matthew: "For the gate is narrow and the way is hard that leads to life, and those who find it are few."

Esper clenched her fists and set her jaw. It was time to stand up to Carl.

"I thought we already said we're packing it up," said Roddy, peering through the frozen, translucent image of two men in chicken costumes being chased through a shopping plaza by dozens of policemen.

Carl shrugged. "We've already gone and paused it. Might as well hear her out."

"We bring the egg back," said Esper. "We make an anonymous drop-off, let the local wildlife officials know where to find it, and everything is back the way it belongs."

"Except we don't get paid," said Carl.

"You already got paid," Esper said. "We still get to be criminals, but we only robbed someone who was breaking the law."

"Who's to say the little dino isn't better off with this new zoo, or as a pet, or wherever it's going?" asked Carl. "Vi Tik Naa lets people pay to hunt them. Maybe this is one of the small ones. I can't imagine anything huge growing out of an egg that size."

Roddy furrowed his little brow and tilted back a beer. "You know ... maybe we can make a play. We know what the thing is now. Maybe we can angle for a bigger payout."

Carl stretched up and reached the comm panel. "Mriy, Tanny, come on down here. We've got a can of worms open and I'd hate for you two to miss out."

Esper flushed. This wasn't going as she'd imagined. In her heart, she had seen Carl with his face grim, nodding his understanding that it was the right thing to do. In her head, she had pictured Carl laughing and Roddy unpausing the holo-viewer.

Mriy came in from the cargo bay. She was shirtless—which due to anatomical and cultural differences was nothing unusual for a female azrin—and out of breath. Her pupils were wide, nearly round. "What?" she snapped.

Carl waited for Tanny to arrive from the cockpit. "Esper's got a plan half baked, and we're debating whether to finish baking it or bin it," he replied.

"What? Does she expect us to turn around and bring it back?" Tanny asked.

"Yup," said Roddy. He squeezed an empty can in his hand and dropped it on the floor at his side. He called across the room to Mriy. "Hey, beer me?"

The azrin grabbed a beer from the fridge, and Roddy caught her toss with a foot—hand? Esper was still struggling with laaku terminology. One or the other was supposed to be considered rude.

"Why would we bring it back?" Tanny asked. "If we were going to refuse the job, we should have done it before we left the Vi Tik Naa system."

"We didn't know what we had," Esper replied.

"Sweetie," Tanny said. "If I had my guess when we picked that thing up, a dumb egg was nowhere near the top. You always gotta worry a little picking up black-box cargo, and if I'd have known we were hauling *that*," she pointed to the egg, still resting on the table atop a towel, "I'd have slept like a baby the night we picked it up."

"But what if whoever we deliver it to decides to kill us instead of paying us," Esper said. It was a valid point, she knew, but not one that came from pious thinking. Doing the right thing out of cowardice or caution was no path to redemption.

"She's got a point," said Roddy. "This is a bigger job than we're used to. Maybe we need a secure exchange. Let's load up a few heist holos and get some ideas."

"Or we could hatch it," said Mort. Everyone turned to look at him.

"Thanks Mort," said Carl. "We needed someone to put together a worst-case scenario, where we don't get paid *and* can't return it like nothing happened."

"At least we'd know what kind it was," said Mort. "You don't have any scanny thingies to look inside, and all I can tell is that whatever's inside is still alive. Hatch it, and we'd know."

"And knowing wouldn't do us a damn bit of good," Tanny said. "For once I'm with Carl. We gotta get that thing to its new owner, get our money, and get the hell out of there. Maybe we can rig up a secure drop though."

Carl waved his hand in front of him. "Negatory. No changing the plans. We've got a delivery location. We've got an amount to collect. We start fiddling with our end, *that's* what'll get things turning wet and red when it comes time to get paid. Reliable. Quick. Professional. Rich guys like having a few crews like us around they can count on."

"And rich women," Tanny noted, an obvious reference to Keesha Bell.

"Exactly," said Carl. Esper watched for any sign that he had picked up on the venom in Tanny's voice, but he seemed oblivious. "One good job leads to another."

"Is that why all our jobs lead to shit?" Roddy asked.

"I have an idea," said Mriy. "If it is a small one, we keep it. Train it. Make it a mighty guard pet. Let Mort hatch it."

Carl turned to Mort. "I owe you an apology. Your idea *wasn't* the worst case. Mriy's got you beat."

Esper considered the idea that if it was a truly harmless creature, a pet might be just the thing to teach the crew a little responsibility. Math class was no place for pets, but the science teachers at her school all kept hamsters or gerbils or fish.

Caring for a living thing built empathy. The odds of a random dinosaur egg being from a harmless species, especially the kind that someone would dole out hundreds of thousands of terra for, seemed remote. Maybe it was especially cute ... two hundred fifty thousand terras worth of cute?

"I was just—" Mriy began.

"Yeah," said Carl. "I know. Listen, if you and Tanny want to put together an oh-shit plan for this one, be my guest. It's not plan 'A' though. Esper, I want you to do something."

She nodded. There was going to be no return trip to Vi Tik Naa.

"Grab a beer or one of your peach-flavored things from the fridge, park it on the couch, and we'll find something to watch that we can all agree on. Spacers go nuts spending too much time by themselves, and you're wearing a little thin, I think ... err, no pun intended."

And that was the afternoon. Peach liqueur and pretzels that were more preservative than food. A kid-friendly animated adventure on holovid. Then Mort and Roddy left to take the egg and seal it back up like they never opened it. Carl stayed with her and they watched an Abbey Stanton mystery. It didn't seem like the sort of thing he would choose, but he was trying so hard to be nice to her.

They were all trying to do right. And they were all failing. Especially her. Esper should have known better, but the wide highway to hell was too inviting. It tasted like peach, spouted bland, childish clichés about love and friendship, and ended with the guilty man going to prison. Prison was where Esper was going to belong on her long wait to hell, the way things were going.

Hadrian IV. It was technically in ARGO space, but mainly because all the systems surrounding it were. Officially it was uninhabited. The system's two green-belt worlds were on the list to terraform, but nowhere near the top. It might be centuries before any official effort was made to colonize either of them. Unofficial efforts, apparently, were a different story.

"This is vessel *Mobius*, requesting landing clearance and coordinates," Tanny said into the comm. As soon as she keyed it off, she turned to Carl, who was standing beside the co-pilot's seat, leaning over to watch the sensors. "I've got nothing. No settlements. No ships. No relay beacon. If someone's out there, they—"

"Vessel *Mobius*, this is Gologlex Menagerie. Stand by for landing instructions," said a female voice over the comm.

"Mountain range in the southern hemisphere," Tanny said, tapping one of the sensor panels. "Can't pinpoint it."

"I guess we wait for those instructions," Carl replied. "Whoever these guys are, they've got one helluva sensor jammer up."

Tanny shook her head. "Maybe, but look out the window. It's a green/blue world. It may not be an Earth-like, or have an air mix we can breathe, but that's a living planet and I get no readings for life."

"Natural phenomenon, then?" Carl asked. "Might be why someplace that looks like an easy terraform got bumped to shitsville on the colonization plan. Who'd want to live somewhere you can't even use basic sensors."

One of the computer screens flashed a scrolling field of numbers as a data feed came in from the planet. Detailed approach vectors. Visual-landmark orientation to set a coordinate system on a world with a haywire magnetic field. Temporary pass-codes to a planetside shield generator. It was presented in an easily-digestible format for the *Mobius's* computer, but at the same time the feed contained a boiler-plate greeting tacked to the end, where the feed stopped and stayed on screen.

*Welcome to Gologlex Menagerie, the galaxy's most comprehensive multi-xeno wildlife collection. All our animals are bio-quarantine safe and provided with habitats that mimic their home world ecosystem as exactly as possible. Hadrian IV has a 22.8 hour day, and our exhibits are open on a rotating basis depending on the activity cycle of the animals. Please find a local-time conversion and schedule of exhibit open times in your visitor's package. You are welcome to follow the approach vectors provided, but we encourage you to open your navigation controls to Gologlex Menagerie Flight Control to guide you to a safe landing at your designated pad. Thank you, and enjoy your stay.*

"I assume I'm taking us in manually," said Tanny.

"Hell, yeah," Carl agreed. "We *know* this place can't be trusted. They hired *us*."

---

They landed under open skies, on one of a row of pads nestled against a mountain range. The valley was over a hundred kilometers across, with lush jungle vegetation. Even on approach, the landing site had been difficult to spot due to the surrounding trees. But once on the ground, the facility took on a modern look. The pad was dura-crete, marked with ARGO regulation lights and signage in English and Atik, the dominant language of the laaku. The area around the pad was walled in with glass supported by steel. Scattered around the interior were poles with nozzles that forced a jet of oxygen into the landing zone.

There was a delegation waiting to meet them as the cargo bay door of the *Mobius* opened. Two were obvious security types, with their black uniforms, dark glasses, and comm earpieces—the readied blaster rifles helped too. The woman in the sky blue uniform with the name badge appeared to be the welcoming committee. Carl assumed she must be good at her job if they expected anyone to feel welcome with the thugs to either side of her.

"Welcome to Gologlex Menagerie. My name is Celeste, and I'm here to escort you to see Mr. Gologlex."

"Carl Ramsey," Carl said, holding out a hand. Celeste smiled but declined to take it. "This here's Tanny and Mriy. They're uh ..." Carl looked to the thugs, first to one side, then the other of Celeste, "... my security. Rest of my crew is staying aboard."

Celeste nodded. "Of course, Captain Ramsey. I assume you have the cargo."

Tanny patted a knapsack slung over her shoulder. "Right here."

"Please leave any weapons on board your ship," said Celeste. "We take complete responsibility for our guests' safety on Hadrian IV. I'll give you a moment."

Carl held up a hand. "No need. We didn't bring any. Let's get going." In some systems, Carl's statement would have been legally inaccurate. Those closest to the Meyang system generally considered azrin armed and dangerous with their own anatomical weapons. When the security thugs didn't chime in and mention muzzles or locking mittens, Carl suspected that Hadrian was too far removed for the azrins' reputation to have reached them.

Celeste piloted an open-top shuttle that hugged the walled-in strip down the center of all the landing zones, never topping 20 kph. Carl watched the speed gauge. He had to fight the temptation to lean past the thugs and bump the throttle to at least half-way. The landing zones they passed were all vacant. The staff must have had their own parking.

"The walls to either side allow us to oxygenate the guest areas," Celeste said, her cadence that of a tour guide. "Hadrian IV had breathable air, but the low oh-two content generally makes breathing uncomfortable. We have similar arrangements in the habitats. One of the keys to maintaining a multi-xeno facility is being able to provide each species with an environment in which they can thrive."

"On hand-tossed meat and chemical supplements," Mriy muttered.

"I'm sorry," said Celeste. "I didn't quite catch that." She didn't understand azrin, Carl realized, and didn't have a charm to translate it.

"She was just wondering whether the predator species hunted their own food," said Carl, giving Mriy an elbow to the ribs to keep her from contradicting him.

"Oh, they hunt all right," Celeste said with a grin. "We're expecting feeding-time tours to be popular. Release an entertaining prey item, then follow the predator in a discreet manner while still giving guests an up-close and bloody view of the hunt."

Mriy's pupils began to dilate. Carl chuckled. "You might have yourself a customer once this place opens," he said. Celeste looked over her shoulder with a puzzled frown. "You've got no one parked here. It's not astral cartography to figure out you're still finishing this place up. Plus everything looks too new."

"Any reason we couldn't have just gotten our pay on the landing pad?" Tanny asked. "Why does Mr. Gologlex want to see us?"

"I can't confirm delivery of the cargo," Celeste replied. "Mr. Gologlex takes care of those kind of details himself. He's very ... involved."

Carl and Tanny exchanged a look. In that look an unspoken conversation took place. Carl pointed out that he was right, and that Tanny's idea to set the terms of the cargo exchange was futile. Tanny countered that this was exactly the sort of scenario her plan would have avoided. Carl replied that she was being paranoid, and she countered that paranoid smugglers lived longer. The look ended with neither of them having convinced the other of anything.

The shuttle slipped into a tunnel, speeding down the gullet of the mountainside. It had been easy to ignore under the skies, with a clear view of the path to orbit, but now that they were inside, Carl was keenly aware that the safety of the *Mobius* was growing more distant by the meter.

It must have been a kilometer or more before Celeste stopped the shuttle. The retractable bay doors along the way had unhelpful names like K-2, and L-45, codes that no doubt meant something to the facility's residents, but kept Carl and his crew in the dark. Celeste leaned down to allow a retina scanner to swipe a beam of light over her eye, and a security door popped open with a hiss of released pressure.

"This way," said Celeste, waving them through as the security thugs subtly herded them from behind.

The corridor was a shock to the system. Gone was the utilitarian access tunnel with its grim steel and bare rock, lit by hard white light. The floor was carpeted and ate the sound of their footsteps. The lighting was soft and warm. A melody played over unseen speakers, just loud enough to ward off any eerie silences that might otherwise plague a deserted luxury hotel. As they followed Celeste, Carl glanced at the artwork on the walls, wondering how much—or rather, how little—of it came from Earth or any human colony.

Celeste glanced over her shoulder and caught him looking. "It's a scattering of art from across the galaxy," she said. "Most of them are replicas or modern pieces. A few are from non-sentient worlds, native materials worked by human artists. Nothing worth stealing, if it came down to it. Most of our resources are poured into the wildlife care and acquisition."

"Which I can appreciate," said Carl with a tight smile.

They passed into a main foyer area that looked like a cross between a museum entrance and a planetside transport hub. The vaulted domed ceiling was an inverted holographic map of the region—or maybe it was better to think of it as a map seen from the underside. Tunnels ran off in all directions, with friendly overhead signs designating them: Tropical, Temperate, Arid, and Aquatic. They had sub-heading and directions to restaurants and washrooms; to all appearances, it was a regulation ARGO-approved facility. There were information boards everywhere, but most of them were inert, or displayed a Gologlex Menagerie logo.

"This looks like the entrance," Carl remarked, his voice echoing. "Why'd we come through the ass end of the place?"

"Because for now there's no way to get here. Construction has the tramway shut down between here and the landing zone," Celeste replied. "Come on. We're going to the employees only section."

"Lucky us," Tanny leaned close and muttered.

Behind the scenes, the glitz, flash, and fakery vanished. The corridor past one more retina-scanning security door was bare, white-painted steel. 2D image boards showed construction schedules, safety admonishments, peppy slogans, and corporate organizational announcements including a native-species hunt.

What sort of criminal organization was this? Most people who went into a life below the notice of law and order did so because of some fundamental disagreement with both concepts. A marine conforms for a few years' service, decides she's sick of getting shipped from one shithole to another, signs on with a smuggler. A navy pilot wears his welcome thin with the higher-ups when he's not out topping the squadron kill lists, takes a buyout and becomes that smuggler. He knew of kingpins and warlords who ruled little kingdoms of their own, but most took the 'organized' part of organized crime with tongue in cheek. He'd never seen one with company outings and workplace safety vids on loop.

Mr. Gologlex's office was at the end of a hallway, but was otherwise unassuming. At least on the outside. Inside, Carl didn't quite know what to make of it. He'd met with gang heads and admirals, eccentric wizards and corporate middlemen. None of them had quite the mix of office flunky, corporate ad man, and mad scientist as Mr. Gologlex had going on. The walls were plastered with info panels and paper posters touting the wonders of the Menagerie in overblown terms and loud, demanding lettering. Carl's boots squeaked on the lab-shiny floor that gleamed in the soft blue overhead lights. Mr. Gologlex sat behind a steel-tube desk piled with datapads and disposable coffee mugs. At the front of the desk, where it couldn't help being in a visitor's field of vision, was a line of skulls, all pristine and medical-school perfect, starting with human and working its way through a series of other hominid skulls that Carl didn't have the background to identify.

Gologlex was thin, with rounded shoulders and a round face covered by a sparse white beard. His eyes were blocked by a pair of data-display glasses, the back sides of the screens all Carl could see. He stood and offered Carl his hand across the desk, his beard parting to display a bleached-white smile. "So, this is the infamous delivery man Keesha Bell scrounged up for me. Now that you're here, I don't mind telling you I had two couriers fail this task already."

Carl shook the proffered hand. Gologlex had the grip of a man who did some of his own work; not a strong grip like a laborer or a soldier, but firm enough to see he wasn't just a behind-the-scenes sort. "I hate the idea of getting locked up, so I make a point of not getting caught with stuff I shouldn't have."

"Yes, of course you do," Gologlex said, the smile never wavering. "Now, let's see about that package." As Tanny retrieved the box from her knapsack, Gologlex touched a datapad and spoke into it. "Irindi, report to my office. Time to earn that extortion I pay you." He pushed another button and winked at Carl. "Wizards. So much trouble. But then, you ought to know. Yours wanted a tour of the unopened exhibits. Of all the nerve."

Carl winced. "Sorry about Mort. He just wanted to see dinosaurs. He didn't get into the safari park on Vi Tik Naa. I'll call my ship and let him know to lay off. If you don't mind ..." Carl reached for his comm.

"Oh, he's not there. He and two others from your crew are on their way into the habitats right now. I didn't see any reason not to show them around. Might help getting fresh eyes on things ... see if we've overlooked something before we start taking paying guests."

"Oh," said Carl. He didn't need to look over to know

Tanny was panicking. She might be keeping it together, but this was the scenario she had worried about. Gologlex had everyone off the *Mobius*, and separated.

Mort felt better with stationary ground beneath his feet again. The *Mobius* gravity made it feel like a planet's surface, but the shuttle had a harrowing lack of stability as it wobbled along a few feet above the ground. The bare artificial stone of the tunnel was a comfort, despite the eyesore lighting that forced him to squint.

A plain, low-sci door cranked up and pulled into the ceiling, and their guide beckoned them through. "This isn't quite what a tourist would see," said Murray, a fresh-faced smiley little twit who seemed good-natured enough. "We're still working on construction. A few exhibits still aren't in viewing shape."

"Just so long as I can see some giant, extinct lizards," said Mort. He had learned his lesson with Carl's semantics. "Extinct from Earth, that is. I don't want to see any necromancy, scientific or otherwise."

"Cool it, Mort," said Roddy. "I don't think anyone's wasting their time making a zoo of dead animals. I mean, who'd pay to see that?"

"You'd be surprised," said Esper. "There are some twisted people out there." Mort and Roddy both turned to give her puzzled expressions.

"We do have dinosaur-type lizards," said Murray. "Species equivalents of animals believed to have once inhabited Earth from the Triassic through Mesozoic Eras. None are Earth-native, of course, but we've gotten specimens from

Earth-likes that never had extinction level events to wipe them out."

Mort gave a curt nod. "Well, let's have at 'em, then."

"Well, the tour starts in the tropical region, where we have a number of breathtaking—"

"If that next word wasn't going to be dinosaurs, don't bother," said Mort. "I've seen animals before, even weird, strange, and downright grotesque ones. But I've only seen them here and there, and by chance. If I had my druthers, I'd have found some on my own, but this is the first time that giant lizards and Carl's backroom deals have smacked heads."

"Technically," said Murray, "they're not lizards. They're reptiles."

"Listen here, son," said Mort. "I appreciate a good pedantic correction as much as the next fellow, so I'm going to level with you. I've wanted to see a dinosaur since I was a wee nipper. Best fire for a young boy's imagination, if you ask me. I don't begrudge the breath of God's wrath breathing meteors down onto them all, because if He didn't wipe them out, mankind surely would have by now. So when I say I've been waiting all my life to see one, I only depart from the literal truth by the margin of the five years or so of my life before someone saw fit to mention them. Now, if you don't take us to see them, I'll start my own blasted tour and show myself around."

"I'm ... I mean ... it's dangerous out there. I was just ... you know, you're right. But first just let me—"

"Buddy," said Roddy. "Maybe you oughtta just let this one go. If you've got dinos, I'd rather get this over with. I was half expecting you guys to have some slick tech if you could jam all sensor readings from this place, but you ain't got squat for A-tech around here. You just found a planet with some sort of fucked up magnetic field."

As Murray turned back to face Mort's best stern-wizard face, Roddy slipped a keycard from his pocket and handed it to Esper. Murray nodded. "Sure. It's a bit of walking, but I can take you."

Mort winked at Esper, and with a few whispered words her clothes transformed into a uniform that matched Murray's. She slunk away from the group, and Mort planned to make sure that Murray forgot she was ever along.

---

Irindi was older than Carl had guessed, probably almost Mort's age. His first inclination was to assume that Gologlex kept a few pretty wizards around for prestige and his own ego, but Irindi didn't seem cut out for prestige. She had a ruddy face and a mop of short, curly grey hair. She arrived with rolled up sleeves and a furrowed brow.

"I was working on the water supply. Does this have to be now?" she asked.

"Irindi, meet Captain Ramsey and his crew, Tanny and Mah-riy," said Gologlex, stumbling over the azrin name. "They finally managed to get a specimen out of Vi Tik Naa." He patted the box on his desk.

Irindi's expression softened into one of surprise. "Oh, really?"

"Yes," said Gologlex. "But before you open it, I was hoping to settle our wager. Captain Ramsey, I have a bet with Irindi that you would open the package to check its contents. If you can tell me what's inside, I'll split my winnings with you. Your share would be an additional fifty thousand."

Carl let out an involuntary whistle. A hundred-thousand terra bet? Over whether he'd open the box? That was a quick seven in his pocket if he split it, and he might have grounds for keeping the whole bundle, considering it was all *him* doing the work, not the rest of the crew. All he had to do was tell Gologlex what was inside, and the old bastard would be *happy* to fork over not only the extra fifty, but their promised two hundred as well.

"Sorry, boss," said Carl. "We don't open cargo. This was no questions asked, and I'm good to my word."

"Pity," Gologlex replied. He opened a desk drawer, counted out a hundred thousand terra, and handed it to Irindi.

"How about ours?" said Tanny. "We did our job. We got no involvement with what's inside. Pay our share, and we don't need to be around when you open it."

Irindi frowned. "I don't trust them. She's being evasive, and his mind is like a sack of confetti that used to be a book."

"Truth charms?" Carl asked. He clucked his tongue. "Amateur hour. Worse than not knowing, from what I've been told. False positives, false negatives ... you second-guess good decisions and feel good about bad ones."

"Open it," said Gologlex. "And we'll see if you've been as good as your word or not."

Irindi traced her finger along the glyphs, leaving a glowing trail. Partway through, she scowled and washed away the glowing lines with a wave of her hand, and started over. It took her four tries, but on the fourth the glyphs sank into the surface of the box, leaving it smooth. "Blasted Cortez and his impossible puzzles," she muttered.

Gologlex pulled a device from his pocket. It emitted a high-pitched whine as the eccentric zookeeper punched in a code that must have been forty digits. With wizardry and science bypassed, the box top came free and Gologlex lifted out the egg.

Carl cocked his head. "Was that all? We went through this whole hoopla over an egg? You got a critter there that eats rock and shits computer cores or something?"

"Well, since we're being cautious," said Gologlex, "let's just have a look and see what *is* in here. Can't be certain you haven't swapped eggs on me until I scan it."

"We played square," Carl insisted. "Do what you gotta so you can pay up."

Gologlex exited the office via a side door, with Irindi hanging back to herd Carl, Tanny, and Mriy into the next room. The med-lab floor continued, and it had a med-lab to go along with it. Gologlex had a fully-equipped scientific rig, with scanners and probes, things Carl could identify only by vague type. All Carl knew for certain was that it was exactly the sort of equipment he'd expect someone like Gologlex to use to look inside a simple egg.

Gologlex placed the egg under the armature of one of the machines. It looked like a blaster cannon aimed to make a messy plate of scrambled eggs as soon as it fired. Gologlex worked at a console, and an info panel on the wall flashed with numbers and geometric shapes, overlaid atop an image of the egg.

"Well now, ready to see what you brought?" Gologlex asked, twisting around to grin at Carl, his finger poised above a button. If he was looking for some sign of worry from Carl, he was going to have a long wait.

With the push of a button, the cannon-like machine shot a cone of amber light that resized itself until it enveloped the egg. There was a faint humming as the armature swiveled around, scanning the egg from all angles. On the screen, a new image overlaid the egg, showing its interior. There was no dinosaur inside, nor any other sort of lizard. The little creature curled up within, large enough to be ready to hatch, looked more like a parrot.

It was in-Tik.

---

Esper kept her lips pursed and her gait stiff as she walked the corridors of the Menagerie's back tunnels. Her false uniform came with a matching short-brimmed cap, which she pulled low over her eyes. Workers in uniforms just like hers rushed by, everyone seeming in a hurry to be somewhere or do something. She drew cursory nods of acknowledgment from some; others ignored her. It took an effort to keep from clenching her fists, but she had brought nothing to carry. Esper snagged a datapad the first time someone set one down and looked away.

The datapad made her look like she was in the middle of something important. It also had a connection to the facility's mini-omni, including a rough-plan layout of the tunnels. There were no labels—someone obviously still had some programming to do—but it did know her current location. She could infer some landmarks based on the landing pads she knew to be located outside the mountain.

Things had been bothering her. Details didn't fit together. Why go to so much trouble for one egg? For a huge zoo like Gologlex Menagerie, acquiring rare species for such crazy prices would take mind-boggling amounts of money. Plus, why hide a zoo? Even a zoo with creatures from outside ARGO space could get permits and be completely legal. And why the box? Half the spacers on the wrong side of the law wouldn't bat an eye at transporting an egg as cargo. There was something at work besides what they had discovered by opening that box.

She hurried past doors with innocuous signs like Maintenance, Cafeteria, and Gym. She sped her pace past one listed as Security. Poking her head inside the Medical wing had shown nothing out of the ordinary, just a few workers being treated for minor injuries.

"You there, give me a hand with this," a voice called out. Esper looked up to find a man with gold stripes on his uniform sleeves. She hurried over and saw that his name badge said "N. K. Jameson." He was standing beside a repulsor-cart that was resting on the ground, piled with equipment.

"Yes, Mr. Jameson?" Esper asked.

"Repulsor's dead on this thing," he said, clutching his lower back. "Get this down to Sub-Humans. This is for the new exhibit."

Esper hesitated.

Jameson gave her a hard look. "You new around here? I don't remember seeing you."

Esper smiled and gave him a doe-eyed look, hoping she wasn't playing it up too much. "I'm still learning my way around."

He snatched the datapad from her hands, muttering. "Here," he said, handing it back. There was a route displayed from her current location to an unlabeled spot on the facility layout.

"Thank you, sir."

"Thank *you* ..." he glanced down at Esper's name badge. "Richelieu. That thing's about busted my back. I'm heading to Medical if anyone asks about me." Jameson limped down the hallway, still clutching his back.

Esper looked at the overloaded repulsor cart with apprehension. Jameson might have been past his prime, but he was also twice her size. The cart had little wheels on the bottom, but a test push barely budged it. Esper set down her datapad and pried the access cover free. Inside there was a tangle of cables connecting an array of circuit cards.

"Need a hand?" a young mechanic asked as he passed by.

"Yes!" Esper said. "It looks like the repulsor control board is fried; do you know where I can find a replacement? Jameson asked me to bring this load to Sub-Humans, and I don't want to be late."

"You have access to the maintenance bay?" the mechanic asked with a skeptical frown.

Esper held up Murray's keycard. "Don't know. I'm still lost around here."

The mechanic smiled. "It's OK. This place is a maze, but you get the feel for the layout after a couple weeks. Here. Take my card, it's two bays down that way. Just leave it with Mickelson. I'll grab it when I get back from lunch."

Esper took the card from him. "Thanks!"

"I'm Garret. Chad Garret. Catch you around sometime?"

Esper nodded.

As soon as he was gone, Esper hurried to the maintenance bay, where she looked up repulsor cart parts and grabbed one of every circuit card it used. Mickelson wasn't around, so she left the keycard on a desk and headed back to fix the cart.

Esper had never been much for mechanics, but her father had been a local-transport pilot before he moved up in the world. She had seen him work on vehicles enough that she wasn't afraid to poke around inside one, even if she had no idea how this repulsor cart worked. She pulled out and replaced the circuit cards one by one until the machine coughed and sputtered to life.

"Yeah, Roddy, I didn't need you for this," she whispered. The fact that Roddy wasn't there was beside the point. As was the fact that keeping the *Mobius* flying and brute-force repairing a repulsor cart were light-years apart. She had bested the little monkey and his patronizing plasma-cutter lessons.

Datapad in hand and the repulsor cart drifting along with a gentle push, Esper made her way to the Sub-Humans department. The name alone set her teeth on edge. Polite society didn't use that term, let alone plaster it on overhead signs and across doorways. It was a term relegated to xenophobic corners of the omni, she had thought, where human supremacists argued over genetic destiny and whether ARGO should bomb primitive worlds or round up alien races as workers.

She pushed her cart through the door with the faint worry that she would burst into flames as dark powers rejected a pure soul. It was a silly thought; she knew it even as it popped into her head. But as the cart crossed the threshold she secretly hoped some supernatural force would keep her out, spare her from seeing what lay beyond. Even if such a force existed, who was she to be judged so pure and precious? She was a criminal now, and if she differed from the Gologlex Menagerie employees, it was only by type.

The hall was well lit, the walls lined with inert info panels on both sides that acted as black mirrors, showing Esper reflected ad infinitum. Infinite darkness. Never a good sign.

Her breath caught when she came to the first exhibit. The perfection of the glassteel made it look as if the squat, rat-faced creatures could reach out and grab her. When one of them slammed against the transparent barrier, it clawed at her with dexterous hands sporting opposable thumbs. Esper had taken basic xenobiology in school. She knew that the opposable thumb was near synonymous with the development of sentient life. The rat-faced creature's mouth moved, and she could hear something faint through the heavy muffling of the glass.

Swallowing back her fear, Esper edged closer. "Let us out!" the creature screamed. "We've done nothing wrong! I want my advocate!" Esper clutched her hands to her ears, unprepared to hear the plea translated. She was still growing accustomed to Mriy speaking intelligibly.

Esper continued down the hall, face forward but eyes constantly flitting to the sides. The habitats had beds and chairs, blankets, food bowls with utensils. Some had primitive altars, showing that the occupants were not only sentient but spiritual. Several were empty.

"You there," someone called out. Esper nearly dropped her datapad. "Is that for the in-Tik exhibit?"

Esper's heart stopped. Her soul curled up in a corner to weep.

That was the missing piece. It *was* too much trouble over a dinosaur egg. It *was* too much trouble for a simple xeno-diverse zoo, even one that got its animals illegally. It was quite in line with a zoo that included sentient creatures, one that catered to that xenophobic segment of humanity that might pay a lot of money to gawk at "sub-humans" from safely behind glassteel.

She had to get out. She had to tell Carl. A plan would come later. "Yes, sir," Esper said after an awkward pause. With a quick naval salute, she backed away. "Got to get back to Medical. Jameson hurt his back."

At a walk that bordered on a jog, she hurried from the Sub-Human department, clutching her pilfered datapad. First things first: get back to Mort and Roddy.

---

As soon as the cargo bay door clanged shut with a hiss of pressurization, Carl let his shoulders slump. For the first time in hours, he allowed himself to remember that he wasn't the ruthless, hard-hearted sonofabitch that he wanted Gologlex to think him. All at once he felt both relief and sick to his stomach.

Tanny shook her head. "I don't know how you could *eat* with that piece of shit."

"And that food ... I'll be in the washroom," said Mriy. She had choked down the turtle soup and collard greens. Gologlex had raved about their homegrown imported species, but Carl suspected he had chosen the meal just to discomfit the azrin.

"Block it out," said Carl. "Not like he was poisoning us." He glanced after Mriy as she hastened up the steps to the common room. "Well, not you and me anyway."

"What do you think got into Mort?" Tanny asked. She still had the knapsack slung over her shoulder, heavy with hardcoin terras, all two hundred thousand they had been promised. "He's not usually this reckless."

"Dunno, but I've got my suspicions," Carl said. "Esper's not much of a liar, but she can play on a man's conscience—or a wizard's curiosity, maybe." He scratched the back of his head. "Might have done better leaving Mriy here and taking Mort with us. At least that way I could have kept an eye on him."

"And Mriy away from that xenophobe," said Tanny.

"I'm not even sure that's quite it," Carl replied. "I don't think he's a blister pack xeno hater. His flunkies maybe, but not him. I think he's ... well, Mort's sort of scientist, you know? The kind he's always kicking dirt on."

"I don't care what you want to call him. That shit's evil, plain and simple," said Tanny. "He's kidnapping sentients, and he got us to do his bio-transport. And we took his money." She hefted the sack. The coins inside were tightly packed, so there was no jingle or rattle.

Carl headed for the stairs. "I don't think we were getting out of there with the egg. It was either with the money and an understanding, or without and we turn into a liability. We're accomplices, which means we can't just rat him out. If we'd refused, I don't think we'd have had a ship to come back to."

"I'm throwing this sack through the clothes cleaner, coins and all," said Tanny. "I'm tempted to jump in there myself."

"Shower's less painful."

"I'm not sure any of us deserve less painful," said Tanny.

Carl continued up the steps. "I gotta get Roddy on the comm. Sooner we get them back on board, the sooner we can forget this place even exists."

---

The shuttle puttered and wobbled along though a tunnel of glassteel. The lack of science in the steel was its saving grace, clear and perfect, and not distorting the view much at all. Murray had told them that the animals could not see through in the other direction, which Mort found more than a bit disappointing. He rather fancied the idea of staring down a tyrannosaurus, the two of them sizing one another up. But they hadn't seen anything so grand as the king of lizards, and even if they had, it would be oblivious to them.

"When are we going to see something *big*?" Mort asked.

"Those stegosaurs were three tons apiece," Murray replied. "Fully grown, they'll be close to five. In five years, we'll—"

"I don't care about five years from now," said Mort. "Where are the huge ones? Fully grown. Mouths full of fangs.

Huge. Not these plodding half-grown lizards. I've seen elephants, Murray. You're going to have to top that."

"We have sauropods a little bigger than those," said Murray. "But we only import juveniles. Transport of adults is prohibitive and, frankly, dangerous."

"Turn this serving-platter of a vehicle around," said Mort. "I came to see fearsome reptiles of a bygone era, not to be disappointed by a bunch of underfed dino-larvae."

"Some of the little ones are pretty cute," Murray offered.

"Hold up," said Roddy. "Turn around and have a good look at me and him. Where do you see someone who looks like they came here looking to see cute?"

"You're not supposed to be drinking in the shuttle," Murray said, unable to offer an effective counter to Roddy's retort.

Roddy held the man's gaze as he drained his beer and flicked the empty can away. It bounced off the glassteel tunnel wall with a hollow ring. "The man said to take us back. Haul it, peach-fuzz."

Murray scowled. "I don't need to take this from a drunken halfwit chimp! Walk for all I care." Murray reached for his comm.

Mort waved a hand, and the air rippled.

"Security," Murray said into the comm. "This is Murray, out in sector Baker Nine. I've got two guests from the cargo ship causing trouble. Send a team. Over." He gave them a smug look. "Mr. Gologlex doesn't take kindly to ill-mannered guests."

Roddy fought back a smirk when Mort winked at him. The silence loomed over them in a way that the dinosaurs had failed to manage.

"Security, do you copy?"

...

"Security?"

"Roddy, think you can fly one of these contraptions?" Mort asked.

Murray scrambled out of the shuttle. "What are you going to do with me?" he asked. "I just work here. I'm sorry. I didn't mean anything. I've got nothing against laaku."

"How long a walk is it back to your headquarters?" Mort asked.

Murray's eyes went wide. "It'll be dark in two hours. I'd never make it by then. Please ..."

Mort climbed down from the shuttle. Murray backed away from him, but ran out of room with an ill-considered retreat toward the arched glassteel of the tunnel wall. Mort took him by the collar and pushed. The glassteel was as insubstantial as it was transparent. A faint gleam shone around Mort's shirt-sleeve where the barrier passed through him.

"Murray old chum, I am sorely tempted to leave you out there with those harmless little dinos you spent the afternoon wasting my time on."

"You wouldn't!"

"You know Mort, this doesn't seem like the sort of place where security sends troublemakers off with a warning," said Roddy. He hopped into the driver's seat and adjusted the settings until the controls were within comfortable reach.

Mort harrumphed. "Roddy's probably right about that one, isn't he?" he asked. Murray grabbed Mort's forearm in both hands and tried to pull it away, but the sleeve was slick and his fingers slipped off; the cotton-synthetic blend was supernaturally slippery at the moment. Mort gave a quick shove and released Murray. When the Gologlex employee lunged for the tunnel, he struck solid glassteel.

Roddy winced. "Ooh, that's gotta hurt. But whatever. He didn't seem like the sensitive type anyway. Hop in, Mort. Where do we find Esper?"

"Not the foggiest," Mort replied. "Let's head back to the ship. If she's not there, we'll come up with a plan to look."

---

Esper kept her head down and her eyes on the datapad's map. It was a puzzle where no one had bothered to check whether all the pieces were in the box. The labyrinthine system of tunnels had a distinct pattern to it, a sort of architectural logic that would probably be mind-numbingly simple if there were only a few notations to hint at the logic behind them. Every time she passed a labeled door, tunnel, or corridor, she added a quick comment on the map. Eventually she started to get a feel for the layout.

"Big animals outside the mountain, little ones inside," she muttered. "But where outside would they put dinosaurs?" It wasn't that Esper didn't suspect them of being in a tropical or jungle climate, it was that there was no mention of the surrounding terrain. She slipped into a power distribution room for some privacy and browsed through the datapad's files on Hadrian IV, hoping to get a geographic survey to overlay onto her facility map.

"Richelieu?" a familiar voice called out.

Esper quickly flipped the datapad back into map mode. A head popped around the corner and she allowed herself to relax just a little. "Oh, hi, Chad. Didn't know you were back there."

"What are you doing back here?" Chad asked. "Did you get your repulsor cart working?"

"Yeah, thanks," Esper replied. "Sorry I didn't leave your keycard with Mickelson. He wasn't there."

"I got it back. No biggie. So what's with the datapad? You lost or something?" Chad smiled, trying to be reassuring. He was also clearly flirting with her. He had a kind face and broad shoulders. If she wasn't planning a hasty escape, she would have liked to get to know him. There were certain hardships of the clergy that she was beginning to feel less obligated to follow. How binding was a vow once the terms were broken by the other party, anyway?

Esper remembered her need, the one of circumstance and not of flesh. "I think someone's having some fun at my expense," she replied. "I'm supposed to bring a snack out to a group of test tourists looking at dinosaurs. I guess we had some delivery people ask to see them. But that's just silly, I mean—"

"No, we've got dinos," Chad replied. "We don't call 'em that officially. Reptilian Megafauna is the zone you're looking for."

"Which way is it?" Esper asked, handing over the datapad.

Chad worked poked here and there on the datapad and handed it back. A route was highlighted. "There you go. Don't go getting lost now, though. All right?"

"Thanks," Esper said with a goofy smile that was intended to be endearing.

"Listen, if you get back in time for dinner, I wouldn't mind showing you around the place," said Chad. "Holotheater is test running some of the aerial footage for the promo campaign tonight."

Esper blushed and nodded. She hurried away, wondering why he was having such an effect on her. Maybe Tanny was right, and a girl needed to take care of herself once in a while. She couldn't be acting like an idiot whenever a cute guy threw himself at her. Things were so much simpler at Harmony Bay, surrounded by stern priestesses and children.

Still, she felt badly, knowing that she wasn't going to see Chad again. He'd be sitting alone at dinner, wondering why she hadn't come.

An hour later, Esper sat in the pilot's seat of a hover-shuttle under the roof of a clear steel tunnel. She had a covered platter filled with pastries, in case she needed to reuse her cover story about bringing refreshments to the tour group, but there was no tour group to be found. The end of the tunnel was in sight, a simple dead end, walled off for construction, probably some sort of rest area or observation platform like the one on Vi Tik Naa.

"Where'd you guys run off to?" Esper said aloud. There was no one within kilometers of her. She took a deep breath to calm herself, and thought things through. "OK. Mort and Roddy are gone. If they'd been captured, I'd probably have heard an alarm or something. But they're not in this tunnel, either, and the branches are still closed. They must have backtracked, and since there's no way I didn't see them, they must have done in a while ago. Unless Mort used magic. Darn it, that *would* be just like Mort, too. But if they *did* leave already, would they have gone back to the ship, or another exhibit?"

Mort didn't give two shakes of a tyrannosaur tail about the other animals. He wanted his dinosaurs. If he and Roddy weren't going to wait for her here, they'd have gone back to the *Mobius*. A coldness rushed through Esper's body. What if they didn't wait for her? If they were in some sort of trouble—

always a possibility with this crew of Carl's—they might not have been able to wait.

Of course, waiting wasn't going to do *her* any good, either. She swung the shuttle around and hit the throttle, blasting down the clear steel tunnel as fast as she dared. The jungle trees passed by outside in a blur, along with occasional glimpses of animals, though nothing on the scale Mort was hoping for. At one point she thought she saw a man in a blue uniform outside the tunnel, in the jungle with the dinosaurs. She glanced over her shoulder but couldn't catch sight of him again. The tunnel was mostly straight, but there were enough twists and angles to require her eyes on her driving. She sped on.

When she reached the mountain facility, she slowed down and drove with one hand on the steering yoke as she referenced her map. She must have scared the willies out of several Gologlex employees as she blundered down corridors barely wide enough for people to dive out of her way. There were angry shouts and a few colorful swears left in her wake. It was only a matter of time before someone got security involved. Esper was willing to chance it though, lest she miss her ride.

The tunnels had a familiar look. They ought to have, since she had traipsed up and down most of them in her search. But these had a look from early in the day, when she had just arrived. She was on the right track—the map was guiding her true. She plowed onward, just slowly enough for people to get out of her way without injury.

Except one.

He stood in the middle of the tunnel and held his arms out. "Richelieu, what are you doing?" Chad asked. The expression on his face was worried, not angry. "Half the place is in an uproar. Comms are warning people we've got a brain-fry on the loose."

"Move aside, Chad," Esper said. "I'm in a hurry."

"No shit," said Chad. "But I'm not moving until I get an explanation."

Who was he, to be demanding anything? Esper's hand itched on the throttle. He'd move if he knew she was willing to run him down. The problem was that she wasn't. He seemed to know that. "I've got to get out of here. I can't explain."

"Claustrophobia?" he asked, his arms dropping and his expression turning puzzled.

"Dear Lord, you're dense," Esper muttered. She took advantage of his confusion and yanked the yoke to one side. The shuttle veered and she feathered the throttle, edging past as Chad stumbled for cover. The shuttle scraped the rock with a cringe-inducing squeal until she straightened her path and followed the tunnel once more. "Sorry!" she shouted over her shoulder. To herself she muttered: "And to think, I would have had dinner with that neutron brain."

It wasn't far. The exit to the landing pads was half a kilometer ahead with just two turns remaining. A call echoed over a public address system. "*Be on the lookout for a runaway shuttle. Pilot is inexperienced and possible intoxicated. Please clear the tunnels until further notice.*"

It was a small blessing wrapped within a blanket of bad news. At least the tunnels ahead would be clear while security tried to round her up. She pushed the throttle and careened onward. Time was against her, but distance was in her favor. The shuttle sped toward the exit, the little green indicator triangle on her datapad showing she was almost home free.

That was when she noticed the forcefield. It hadn't been active on the way in. She could see past to the landing pads, and even make out the shape of the *Mobius* in the distance. But a telltale sparkling shimmer in the air told her that there was no way between here and there. Esper slammed the thrust reversers for the shuttle and came to an abrupt halt that nearly ejected her from the craft. She hopped to the ground.

The controls for the forcefield were right in front of her. A console with a single seat stood right beside the entryway, displaying the field status, and a number of other bits of data that weren't important just then. She pushed a button that looked like it ought to have released the field, but nothing happened. There wasn't even an annoying little noise to accompany the machine's refusal. It just did nothing. She tried again. She tried other buttons. Nothing. She noticed that there was a retina scanner set into the console, and that was when she knew she was going to get nowhere the easy way.

Looking under the console, where the operator's legs would tuck beneath it in his or her chair, she found an access panel. She tried to pry it loose, but it held on stubbornly. She could get her fingernails into the groove where the panel and console met, but she had no leverage. With a sigh of frustration, she realized it made sense. This wasn't the motor of a repulsor cart, this was a security station. It wasn't meant to grant easy access. Only someone with proper maintenance clearance would have the tools to get inside.

Chad. He worked in maintenance. He would have the tools she needed.

"Oh hell no," said Esper. She wasn't about to go back and attempt to smooth over those ruffled feathers. She needed another plan. She didn't have a comm with her, but the console would have access to the ... no, that had the same problem. If she could get a message to Roddy, maybe he could talk her through it. Of course, if she had Mort along, any old magic of his would befuddle the tech making the forcefield work.

"Any old magic?" Esper asked herself. She glanced to the platter of pastries in the shuttle. They'd had a rough ride, but she was willing to overlook some smooshed cupcakes and frosting on the wrong treat. She had no time to lose. Rushing over to the shuttle, she tore the cover off the platter and began stuffing herself. Chocolate cupcakes, cinnamon danishes, jelly donuts, she wolfed them down with wanton disregard for propriety, wiping her hands on her pants and her mouth on a sleeve as she plowed through the platter until she was stuffed.

Hobbling from the onset of an upset stomach, she made her way to the forcefield. To the best of her knowledge, she was in fine health. But her trick of metabolic healing magic didn't technically require her to be injured. She calmed her thoughts and pumped her heart faster. Blood rushed through her veins in a torrent. Her adrenal glands emptied. Her whole body warmed and sweat. The food in her stomach was digested at a phenomenal rate to fuel her metabolic riot.

The forcefield wobbled and spluttered out. With a victorious grin, Esper turned to get back onto the shuttle, but its repulsors had failed along with the shield. It crashed to the floor and Esper winced. There was nothing to do but run.

She had not been much of an athlete as a girl. Nice girls—pretty, delicate girls—didn't run track or play sports. Her mother would have forbade it if she had ever wanted to. At Harmony Bay, she worked on her feet much of the day, but it hardly counted as exercise. But now, with a kilometer or more of ground to cover and who knew how many security guards en route to apprehend her, Esper ran. She ran like her life depended on it, because it very likely did.

Her eyes went wide when she saw the *Mobius* lift off.

They were leaving without her! Or were they? The ship stopped climbing just above the height of the environmental walls. It turned and headed her way, drifting backward and angled nose-up. The turret turned and pointed in her direction —well, her general direction. It was pointed past her, toward the entrance to the mountain. The *Mobius* opened fire, and Esper didn't look back to see what damage they had wrought.

The cargo bay door opened as the *Mobius* closed in. Roddy and Mriy were there. Roddy at the winch controls, Mriy ready to throw her a line. Esper caught hold, finding a looped end and putting her arms through. It tightened around her chest, just beneath her arms, and when the line pulled taut she was snatched from her feet.

She screamed, but it was surprise, relief, and the terror of a rather precarious flight all rolled into one. The *Mobius* was over a hundred meters up by the time she was pulled inside. There was a strange moment when the ship's gravity took custody of her from the planet, and the world turned. As she climbed to her feet in the open cargo bay, the direction of the planet below was sideways, even though it quite clearly looked to be down.

"They've got sentients down there in that zoo," she said as she tried to catch her breath.

"We saw," said Mriy. "The egg was in-Tik."

Esper untangled herself from the makeshift harness and stumbled for the stairs.

"Where you off to in such a rush?" asked Roddy. "You about to lose your lunch? Sorry about the ride."

"Gotta get to Carl," Esper said. "We've got to go back. We can't just leave them."

Mort was already in the center of the common room, staff in hand, when Esper arrived. Any minute, Carl would give the order to drop into the astral plane. She didn't have much time.

The wizard gave her a tight smile. "Good to see you made it. Find what you were looking for?"

"Yes," Esper replied. "No time to explain though. I've got to talk to Carl."

"He's flying right now," Mort said.

"Figured," said Esper. She paused a moment and put her hands on her knees to catch her breath. "Crazy plan like that, it had to be." She gave Mort a nod as she passed, not wanting to spare breath that could be used to get to Carl in time.

She found him in the cockpit, the front windows filled with stars. They were heading for orbit and beyond. He turned at the sound of her footsteps. "Welcome aboard. Don't say we never did anything for you." He winked.

"We've got to go back," said Esper. "And thanks."

"This is the part where we take the money and run," said Carl. "Once we're deep, I don't plan on coming up out of a bottle until I don't remember where this money came from."

"Can you forget the money for ONE. BLESSED. MOMENT?" Esper asked. Her fingers dug into the headrest of the copilot's seat and she shook it with each word.

Carl locked their heading and twisted in his seat to face her, meeting Esper eye to eye. "Fine. You've got my attention."

"They're slavers!" said Esper. "It's a zoo for sentients. Sure, they've got exotics from half the galaxy, too, but those are thinking, feeling beings locked up in there who know what's happening to them."

Carl's eyes slid away, toward one of the cockpit displays. "It was just an egg. Maybe there was something wrong with it, and it was never going to hatch anyway. You can never be sure."

"They had a whole *wing* of sentients. Half the exhibits were full," said Esper. She grabbed hold of her translator-charmed earring. "I could *hear* them through the glass, pleading for help. It broke my heart."

Carl reached out a hand. "I know it's hard, sometimes—"

Esper slapped the hand away. "Can the fake sympathy. I don't want to feel better about what I saw down there. I expect us to do something about it."

"Not much we *can* do," Carl said. "We call the authorities and this gets big. The kind of big that puts a few clues together and notices little old us. Gologlex knew he had us before he let us go. Once we were down there, it was either play ball or get buried. We played ball, and now if anyone gets caught, we all do."

"Well, then we're just going to have to do it ourselves," said Esper. She crossed her arms and fixed Carl with a you-just-cheated-on-a-test glare.

Carl chuckled uneasily under Esper's scrutiny. "Brave idea, kid, but I'd think you had your fill of brave for the day. That shit's addictive as any alkaloid, and just as likely to kill you. Besides, they've got a lot more firepower than we do."

"Oh, really?" Esper asked. She reached down and keyed the ship-wide. "Roddy, mind coming up to the cockpit?"

"Just whose ship is this, anyway?" Carl smirked, but it vanished under Esper's glare.

"Near as I can figure, everyone's."

Roddy came in on all fours, which was a quicker mode of travel for laaku. Esper had known other laaku to use the technique, but it was the first time she had witnessed the mechanic use it. "What's up?"

"What if I said we needed to go back and free those slaved sentients in the Gologlex zoo?" Esper asked.

Roddy cupped a hand to his ear. "I hear you right? You wanna go back?" When there was no sign of Esper wavering, he shrugged and continued. "Be crowded as hell in here. I don't know how many we could even fit. I mean, even with just us, it's—"

"Forget getting them out for now," said Esper. "What can you do to help us break in?"

"Don't know where I'd even start," said Roddy. "We don't know anything about their numbers or equipment. What sort of power they're running on. The sensors and scanners they've got."

Esper reached into the pocket of her coveralls—her illusory uniform having faded when she wasn't watching—and drew out the datapad. It clattered to the cockpit console, Gologlex Menagerie logo proudly displayed at the edge. "It's missing stuff, but I think you'll find most of it on here."

Carl's eyes drifted to the window. "You know ... that fucked up magnetosphere must work both ways. They didn't know we were up here until we called them. They probably already lost track of us."

"You two willing to hear me out?" Esper asked.

"Sure," said Roddy. Carl nodded.

---

"First off," said Esper, "how many of you think you're going to hell if the *Mobius* were to be blasted to bits right this instant?" The crew was gathered around her in the common room, with Esper leaning against the holo-viewer's emitter. She looked to Carl and Roddy lounging on the couch with beers, to Mriy squatting on her haunches with the refrigerator door open, to Tanny leaning at the forward corridor entrance with her arms crossed, to Mort sitting with his head down at the kitchen table. Through the domed glassteel above, the color distortion of astral space rendered Hadrian IV in greyscale.

Esper waited. "None of you? You all feel righteous after what we just did? You think this all gets overlooked because you can convince *yourselves* that there's nothing you can do, that you were all victims of circumstance?"

Tanny broke the uncomfortable silence that followed. "I know it was bad, but ... well, no one but you is a member of the One Church."

Roddy cleared his throat. "Well ... technically ..."

Carl gave the laaku a puzzled look. "Really? You never mentioned it."

"'Til the kid showed up, it wasn't exactly a topic we got into around here," Roddy replied.

"And what would your priest say, if he knew what you'd done here?" Esper asked. "You're unrepentant. Would he take your confession?"

Roddy held up his beer can and waggled it, sloshing the contents. "Him and me aren't on speaking terms these days."

"And you, Carl," Esper said, turning. "You told me that you were a believer, but you figured you had squared your ledger. This isn't a balance sheet; these are real people suffering because of your inaction, and ones that will suffer their fate because of your actions."

Before Carl could answer, Mort let out a single, bitter chuckle. "You know ... you use the One Church's words, but that's a Seeker's attitude. You should be praying and confessing. We should turn ourselves in and let the authorities clean up this mess. That's what you should be telling us. Never heard a priest or priestess advocating an armed rescue."

"I'm not saying we need to use force," said Esper. "We can find a way to bypass their systems and sneak into—"

"Never happen," said Tanny. "You caught those second-rate shopping plaza patrolmen with their pants around their ankles. Place like that usually has someone ex-special forces as security head. You can bet that he's having a parade right about now, marching up and down those guys with his boot up one ass after the next."

"They can't keep their eyes stapled open forever," said Carl. "Maybe we wait 'em out. Let things die down, then try in a week or two. We can run a job or two out this part of ARGO space, maybe a few quick terra. Maybe we can just find a place to spend the terras we just—"

"No," said Esper. "Carl, don't take this wrong, but the minute we leave this place, we forsake it. You won't come back. I can't let you weasel out of this, for your good as well as those poor creatures down there."

"She's gotcha there," Roddy agreed.

Tanny held up the stolen Gologlex Menagerie datapad. "You're overlooking the fact that we're outnumbered, outgunned, and we'd need to get into the bowels of that mountain and out again with we don't even know how many sentients. Different languages. Different foods. Some might even need different atmospheres. We can't just run out of there with everyone."

"We have Mort," said Esper.

"I'm sure Mort's flattered," said Carl, "but they've got a wizard of their own. Probably more than one. That's heaping a lot on Mort's shoulders. Even if he—"

"I'll do it."

They all looked to Mort. The wizard stood from the table and cracked his neck. "I have been responsible for some awful things in the past, but this one I have a chance to set right. The rest of you don't need to come. Set me down in the jungle near that misbegotten zoo, and I'll make my way inside. Just pick me up when you see the mountain collapse."

Tanny's lip curled in a lopsided grin. "I see what you're doing, Mort. Shame us into coming along to help. You're not a one-man orbital bombardment."

Mort straightened and held his chin high. He appeared haughty, if one could overlook the stained sweatshirt and the spot of ketchup at the corner of his mouth. "I most certainly am!"

"We're not bombing anything from orbit!" Esper shouted. "And we're not having Mort simulate bombing things from orbit. We're not blowing up a mountain. By all that's holy, people, this is a rescue mission. Haven't any of you rescued hostages or ... I don't know, pulled off a jailbreak or something?"

Carl raised a tentative hand. "No, but I've actually bombed things from orbit."

Esper shot him a glare and looked around for signs of anyone being more helpful.

"Don't look at me," said Roddy.

"I flew ground assault missions," Tanny added with a shrug. "Deliver boots to planet. Head back and pick up more. Repeat."

"I've pulled Carl's ass out of several fights," Mriy said. "But we never let him get put into a jail."

"Mort," said Esper. "You *must* have done this sort of thing before."

Mort cleared his throat. "I imagine ... well, I think we're all fine with the theory. It's just ..."

Esper held her arms out to her sides, mouth and eyes gaping. "What kind of outlaws *are* you people?"

"I can field that one," said Carl. "We're the kind who do what we need to do to get paid. I make sure we don't keep records around, but maybe we can start a group story night, get you up to speed. We can take turns telling—"

"Roddy, throw me that remote," Esper ordered. The laaku mechanic complied, lobbing the device to her with a foot. "This seems to be the only thing any of you listen to around here." She played around with it for a few moments, flashing through file clusters and search results until she had a short list of holovids.

"I didn't even know we had some of this shit," Carl muttered.

"Waiting a day is probably a good idea," said Esper. "Tanny had a good point about them being on alert. I'm going to show you all what being an outlaw is supposed to be about. Mriy, do we have popcorn in the pantry?" The azrin nodded. "Well, settle in. We're all going to watch holos and eat popcorn, and learn what a hero really is."

---

"That's it," Esper said. The credits were rolling by on the last of their holovid marathon as inspirational music rose in crescendo. "Now, do you see? This is what being outlaws is supposed to be about. You can do things no law-abiding person could get away with. It's your duty to use that freedom to help other people."

"Didn't seem to work out that well for most of them,"

Roddy grumbled. "Robin Hood never actually made good. Derrius Miles got spaced by his own crew ..."

Esper frowned. "I had forgotten that bit at the end."

"These were mostly set on old Earth," said Tanny. "Only a couple looked close to modern."

"Aha!" said Mort. "But one wasn't. They snuck it in at the beginning that it was actually set in the distant past in some other galaxy. Technically even older than the others, I'd wager."

"I think you guys are missing the point," said Carl. When everyone stopped their individual arguments, he continued. "Esper won. She got us drunk and happy, filled our heads with tales of the little guy winning out, doing the right thing. Fuck it. I want some guy a hundred years from now writing shit like that about us ... and I want Jack Plantier to play me."

"That Douglas Fairbanks was a looker," said Tanny, drunkenly attempting to be helpful.

"Sure," said Mort. "And in a hundred years *both* of them will be dead."

"You saying I look like Douglas Fairbanks?" Carl asked.

Tanny squinted. "Maybe," she said with a sly grin. "After six of Earth's Preferred, at least."

Roddy tried squinting at Carl. "I'm at fifteen, and he's still lookin' like a washed-up, sim-hustling fighter-jockey. We seriously going to follow this guy into a war zone tomorrow? Shit ... I need a good night's sleep. Mriy, beer me. Two for the sack."

"What about you, Mriy?" Esper asked. "You haven't said what you think."

"The one with the feathered hat should have kept the money," said Mriy, lobbing two cans in Roddy's direction. Even drunk, he caught them fluidly. "The masked one should have slain all his foes and claimed rule. The smugglers were admirable hunters in the end. I think I liked the spacers in the stolen ship best; they sought revenge and got it."

"I would have *sworn* he retired to a life back on Luna," said Esper. "But you're missing the point. It's all about finding something deeper than just money. You can live it up outside the law, but when the calling comes, they heed it."

"Holovid drivel," said Mriy. "People aren't like that."

"Who says 'heed?'" Roddy muttered.

"We've got to be all in this together, or—"

Mriy hissed, and the translator charm did nothing to offer a meaning. Esper shrank back, despite being across the room. "I don't care what those holo-people want. My pack hunts, and I go. I don't lead, so 'why' doesn't matter."

Esper was quiet. "It does."

"Listen, kid," said Carl. "Don't throw the fish back in because it took an unbaited hook. Might not catch it twice."

"How ... how you do that?" Tanny asked. Carl gave her a quizzical frown. "You're drunker as I am, but you're still pretty slick that tongue of yours." There was a look in her eye, and Esper was growing worried about it. It was that barroom look all over again.

"Once you get good at something," Carl said. "A couple beers can't stop you." Carl had the mirror of Tanny's look. There was a point-to-point laser comm going on between them, a direct line-of-sight uplink that Esper was hacking into and decrypting without meaning to.

"Well, I think I've given everyone enough to think about for one night," said Esper. "Let's all get a good night's rest and wake up ready to right some wrongs. Remember," she emphasized, "we *need* our rest."

"Sure, kid," said Carl. "G'night." He lurched to his feet and sauntered off in the direction of his quarters. Esper breathed a silent sigh of relief when Tanny headed for her own.

---

Carl awoke in the past. Through some trick of temporal magic, it was years ago. It had to be. He remembered movie night, but after that, things got hazy. Now, here he was, probably two or three years in the past, waking as he often did in those days, pinned beneath the surprisingly heavy dead-weight of Tanny's slumbering body. It wasn't all of her atop him, but her head was pillowed on his chest, her hair filling his nose with the scent of the military-surplus brand of shampoo she loved. One arm was curled around him, tucked under his neck, effectively trapping him.

She was still snoring, oblivious to Carl having awakened. He took a moment to just enjoy her warmth, the smoothness of her skin, the ... well her warmth was actually a small inferno, thanks to her amped-up marine metabolism, and there was a thin layer of sweat between them that kept him from appreciating most of her smoothness. Still, he had no idea how long his little bout of time travel might last, and having Tanny back as his wife was comforting, even if it wasn't quite comfortable. A thousand arguments faded to echoing whispers. The dozen of thoughtless, hurtful acts on both sides seemed less egregious now that he had some perspective on them.

Tanny choked off a snore with a snort and shifted positions. She slid off and came to rest in the crook of his arm, with her head on his shoulder. The arm that had had served as his pillow dumped him rudely back onto his pillowcase. That arm ended in a hand, and that hand had a ring finger. That ring finger had no ring.

"Shit," Carl mouthed. His time travel delusion was just the fancy of a half-slumbering mind. Maybe he let himself believe it, but it was just to enjoy the moment and pretend.

Tanny stirred again, and pulled herself up to his lips. Carl indulged her, tasting the warmth of her tongue. She moaned and rolled, pulling Carl atop her, obviously intent on resuming whatever activities they'd enjoyed overnight. Depending on her disposition when she woke, he was more than willing to indulge her in that, too. But when her eyelids parted, and she caught a glimpse of him through those thick, dark lashes, it was all over.

Her eyes shot wide. "What the hell?"

Carl was airborne before he could formulate a response. He hit the floor at the side of his bed, saved from a potentially serious injury by a heap of unwashed clothes. "Whaddaya mean, what the hell? *You* came on to *me*."

"Bullshit," Tanny replied, pulling the sheets up to cover herself. She scanned the room. "You got me drunk last night."

"Esper got us *all* drunk," said Carl. "And that's about as tough as selling beers at a ballgame. What you do when you're drunk is what you'd do sober if you weren't uptight about it."

"You're as bad as Roddy," Tanny snapped. She stood from the bed and yanked the sheets free to form a rudimentary toga. "This didn't happen. And it's not going to happen again."

"Yes, dear."

Tanny stabbed a finger in Carl's direction. If it had been loaded, he would have been a dead man. "Don't you start with me."

"I think we finished."

"I'm serious," Tanny snarled. "Now, help me find my clothes in this landfill."

Carl held up some flannel garments. "Yours, I believe." He

dangled the pajamas in front of her. "Methinks you didn't come straight here under my spell. I'm thinking someone went to bed and decided that she'd rather sleep with Douglas Fairbanks than alone. Hmm?"

"Give me those," said Tanny, flushing. She snatched the nightclothes from Carl's hand, and he obligingly turned his back to her.

He listened to her changing, his mind drifting back to bygone days when she liked him watching. "You know, for just a few seconds there, I forgot when I was. It was in that little snippet when you're done dreaming but not thinking right yet. Right then I'd have sworn we were still married." Carl had been keeping track of the sounds. She had just finished dressing. He turned and looked her in the eye. "It was nice."

He watched the anger melt away from her face, jaw relaxing, brow unfurrowing. She closed her eyes and sighed. "God dammit, Carl. We're not doing this again."

"I know."

"Good."

"But it was still nice."

"What'll be nice," said Tanny, "is if no one sees me coming out of your quarters this morning. You go out first and make sure the common room's clear before I sneak across." She caught Carl snickering. "This is serious! No, I'm not acting like a ... oh, forget it. Just get out there."

Carl gave her a nod and a thumbs up, and exited his quarters barefoot and in just boxer shorts. Tanny pressed herself against the wall to stay out of sight of the doorway. Mort and Roddy were sharing breakfast with Esper at the kitchen table. Presumably that meant Mriy was minding the helm. The door thunked shut behind him.

"Morning, everyone," said Carl.

"You're late enough," Roddy replied with a mouth full of cereal. "Esper wouldn't let us cook anything until everyone was here. It was bullshit. Where does she get off ... well, we compromised on cereal in the meantime."

"Fire up the egg-maker!" Mort proclaimed, holding a milk-dampened spoon aloft as a battle standard.

"Hold that thought, guys," Carl said, pausing to yawn. "Tanny wants you lot to clear out of here for five, give her time to sneak back to her own quarters with no one looking."

"That's daft," said Mort.

Roddy laughed, hastily swallowing his cereal to avoid spitting it out or choking on it. "You're an ass, you know that? A class-A, grade one-hundred ass."

"Yeah, only if anyone tells her," Carl replied.

---

The Rescue Council convened around the holo-viewer. Tanny had linked Esper's stolen datapad to it so that everyone could see the display at once. She cast suspicious glances at everyone, especially Carl, but Esper kept her mouth shut. There was no gain in strife just then, and a sin kept secret is a sin that could still be confessed by the sinner.

A map hovered in the air, the 2D image from the datapad rendered fully in three dimensions on the holo display. It showed an intimidating network of underground passages, complete with Esper's impromptu annotations. Tanny held the datapad in hand, running down through a list of questions.

"OK, then," said Tanny. "I'm just going to change 'two guards at desk,' to 'Security Checkpoint (2).' And what the heck does this mean: 'Chad?'"

"Chad was a ... contact ... I made," said Esper. "He helped me navigate the facility. You can delete that, though."

"Can we make any use of this Chad guy?" Carl asked.

Esper felt everyone's eyes on her. She could just imagine they could all see right through her. "Probably not. I think I used up all my good will with him in my escape."

While Carl and Esper spoke, Tanny had been tracing out a route from the jungle to the Sub-Humans. "I've got us an assault plan," Tanny said. "We can use the *Mobius's* guns to blast a hole in the glassteel tunnels into the jungle, enter from this point here."

"They must have *some* aerial defenses, even if they'd be on visual targeting due to the interference," said Roddy. Ever-present beer in hand, he was the only one not showing signs of a hangover.

"Agreed," said Tanny. It was amazing how she transformed when the subject had fit into military paradigm. Esper wondered whether she saw things skewed as well, and what that skew might look like to the rest of the crew. "I think we can count on some element of surprise on the way in. On the way out, we need to be sure they can't blast us out of the sky."

"I hate sky," Carl muttered. "It's like space, but half-assed."

Tanny snapped her fingers in Carl's direction. "Focus!"

"I'll handle the flying both ways," said Carl. "I'll know all the evasives."

Tanny brought up the tactical view of the facility. "This file doesn't list model numbers or anything specific about personnel; I think it's two-part security with the facility main computer. But I recognize the silhouette on these gun emplacements. They've got four Raijin series ion cannons, plus a few smaller emplacements, probably automated. Those Raijins mean trouble getting off-world."

"What kind of trouble?" Carl asked.

"*Mobius* won't take that kinda punishment," said Roddy. "Shields just ain't designed for weaponry like that. We need to stop them firing before we high tail it."

"Main power is located here," Tanny said, rotating the map and zooming in on a location at the heart of the mountain. "They're tapping a magma chamber for geothermal ... and before you ask, no, we're not trying to make it erupt."

Mort gritted his teeth and clenched a fist.

"*Anyway*," Tanny continued. "If we disrupt main power, they won't have the juice to run those guns. Emergency backup and localized generators will keep environmental systems and probably some lighting on. Wouldn't surprise me if they had sensitive equipment on battery power as well. It's going to be hell getting in there, but we need to shut down that generator if we want to make an escape."

"It would be nice if we could just convince them to surrender," said Esper. Carl and Mriy chuckled, while Roddy splurted his beer.

"Look what you made me do," Roddy said, giggling.

"Well," said Esper. "I'm sure we can figure out a way to pull this off, and if *they* knew that, they should just let us, so none of them gets hurt."

Carl rubbed at one of his temples. "Yeah, nice theory. But this whole business counts on a lot of surprise. We can't just transmit our attack plan and have them toss all their guns in a pile. To get someone to surrender you gotta show you've got 'em outgunned, and outgunned bad."

"What about those stupid disintegrator rifles you keep trying to sell?" Esper asked.

"No power packs for 'em," Carl replied. "No way to power those things without a power pack."

"Um," said Roddy. "Technically?" He was still wiping beer off the front of his coveralls.

"What?" Carl asked, turning to the laaku.

"Well, I mean we can't power them *right* without power packs, but those things use a pull charge," Roddy explained. "They hold enough mojo to fire once or twice. They backfill power from the packs."

"Fine," said Tanny. "But how does that help? They're not charged in the first place."

"I can cross-wire something to plug them into the *Mobius's* engines," said Roddy with a shrug.

"Holy shit," said Carl. "What the hell's that going to do to them?"

"Nothing good, I'll tell you that much."

"How'm I gonna sell those disintegrators after you—"

"Do it," said Tanny. "Nothing those Gologlex security doofs have is going to compete with those things. Those are top-of-the-line infantry ordnance. They can't even take cover against them."

Carl raised a finger from each hand. "Problem. You can only fire once or twice."

Tanny shrugged. "Esper wants a surrender. Point that shit at me and *I'd* surrender."

"We've still got the problem of transporting refugees," said Carl. "I'm not signing off on a trip in unless we've got our exit worked out. And we need to make sure that those Raiju fuck-my-ship-up guns stay out of commission after we lift off."

"I'll handle that," said Mort. "Be a shame if someone used magic around all that pretty A-tech." He gave Esper a knowing look, and she realized he noticed her trick with the forcefield.

"That stuff's military-grade. Probably hardened against magic," said Tanny.

Mort sniffed. "Not against mine."

"I think we have a plan, then," said Esper. "Roddy will get the guns charged. Tanny will lead the breach and get to the sentients exhibit. Mriy, Roddy and I will go with Tanny."

"You never answered how we're going to—," said Carl.

"I figured you'd stay behind, where it's safe," said Esper, not allowing Carl's question to poke a hole in their plan. "Keep *Mobius* ready for a quick getaway." They were doing the right thing; an answer would come to them. It was more important not to lose their courage over it.

"How soon do we leave?" Mriy asked. Esper smiled at the azrin. Mriy had offered no input to the plan, no objections. Esper wondered if it was some azrin custom that kept her from questioning a battle plan, or if she just didn't care for the details.

"When Carl says," Esper replied with a smile at the captain. "He's in charge."

———

The deck of the cargo floor lurched under everyone's feet. Esper stumbled, catching herself against the handrail for the stairs. Tanny seemed prepared for the rough ride and just shifted her balance. Mort fell onto his backside and hit his elbow on the steel floor.

"Blast that boy!" Mort said. "This is why we never let him fly. Off to battle forces unknown and I'm going to die in transit."

"We know all about the forces we're—" Tanny said.

"They've got a wizard," Mort snarled, clambering to his feet. He wore his black robes and a heavy silver pendant that hung from his neck proclaiming his once-esteemed position in the Convocation. His staff lay just out of reach. "Might be there's more than one. Irindi isn't a name I know, so either she's an up-and-comer or some cut-rate piker, selling herself to this dunce-cap outfit. Either way, I'd like to survive to find out. Can one of your ladies go up there and wring his neck? A little air-loss might calm his flying to non-fatal levels."

Roddy came in from the engine room, dragging the crate of disintegrator rifles. The ship lurched again, but the laaku seemed unbothered as everyone else braced themselves or hung on to something solid.

Tanny lunged for the comm panel. "You trying to kill us down here?" she shouted.

"We don't know if they have aerial drones, patrol craft, sensor towers ... I'm keeping us below the tree line," Carl replied over the comm.

"You mean 'just above,' right?" Tanny asked.

"Nope," Carl replied. "I've got the forward shields cranked up just in case, but we're sub-canopy. Now, if you don't mind, this isn't easy."

"I used to wonder how bad he could be," Esper said to Tanny. "Now I see why you're the pilot."

"I should have flown the approach," Tanny muttered. "Let Ace Kill'em'all fly us out."

The comm echoed through the hold. "We're coming up on the facility. Hang on."

Esper clung to the railing for dear life. If Carl only saw fit to warn them *now*, she could scarcely imagine what he might be planning. The *Mobius* swung around, and Esper's arms felt like they would be wrenched from their sockets. Her feet lifted from the ground, and the crate of weapons slid across the floor, Roddy in tow.

The cargo bay door opened and a rush of humid

jungle air blew in. Outside, there was one of the menagerie's glassteel tunnels with a hole large enough to fly one of the facility's shuttles through. Branches cracked and snapped, and leaves shushed against the hull as Carl backed them toward the hole. Mriy sprinted through the door from the common room, no longer needed in the gun turret. She vaulted the railing and landed in a crouch beside Esper.

Tanny grabbed a disintegrator from the crate and slung it over her shoulder by the strap. She took another and tossed it to Mriy, who snatched the weapon from the air and did likewise. Another flew to the azrin and she handed it to Esper. Given the way the two of them handled the rifles, she expected it to be lightweight, but the unexpected heft nearly caused her to drop it.

"Lord, these things weigh nothing," Tanny said, shaking her head as she tossed Mriy a second rifle and took another in hand for herself. "I wonder what they make these out of."

"You're kidding, right?" Esper asked. "This thing must be ten kilos!"

"Proprietary polymerized carbon steel," said Roddy, "And they're eleven point two two kilos apiece without the power packs." He took the last disintegrator rifle and gave Esper a cockeyed glance. "You're as bad as Carl whining about your flabby human muscles."

"Helmets on," Tanny said. "Enough chatter. Comms open and keep it business."

"Yes ma'am," Esper replied. She was already wearing her ablative armor suit and feeling like she was at a costume ball. Who was this woman in her boots, carrying a disintegrator rifle and being admonished about comm chatter? Putting her EV helmet on only amplified the effect. The world on the other side was just a vivid holo-game. With one exception. "I've never shot anyone."

"First time for everything," Roddy replied.

"I won't."

"You shouldn't need to," Tanny replied. "We want showy and explosive. They need a reason to surrender."

"The deaths of comrades would do best," Mriy added.

Esper closed her eyes. "Please Lord, don't let this end in bloodshed." She had whispered it, but the sensitive mic in her comm broadcast it.

"These things don't shed blood," said Roddy. It wasn't what she needed to hear.

The *Mobius* hit the ground with a gentle thud, cargo bay ramp pointed right into the ragged, still-smoldering hole in the glassteel tube.

Tanny made a beckoning hand signal. "Let's move."

---

Mort stood and watched them go. Tanny and Mriy toting spare weapons like they were children's toys, Esper struggling to keep pace even at the outset while lugging hers. Roddy took up the rear. Mort hoped that the laaku was going to look after her. There was neither the time nor the manpower to spare, or he'd have done so himself.

He set a leisurely pace. Just before entering the mountain, he cast a glance over his shoulder on the off chance there was a creature worth seeing out in the jungle. Carl had forewarned him that he wasn't setting the ship down anywhere near where dinosaurs might be, and Mort begrudgingly acknowledged the wisdom in that.

The butt of his staff echoed in the empty corridors, much

louder to his ears than the distant booted feet of the rest of the crew. He fished a folded piece of paper from his pocket and tucked the staff under his arm. It bore a map of the facility, transcribed from the holo-viewer image by Tanny. It was light on detail, but covered his intended route to the heart of the mountain. Mort bitterly wondered whether its scant detail was intended to discourage him from wandering or just because Tanny was lazy. In either eventuality, he disapproved.

It wasn't long before his path diverged from the route already taken by Tanny and company. Personnel that had scattered before the oncoming rush of would-be and former soldiers had left those corridors empty, but now Mort was going to have to clear his own path.

A pair of workers rounded a corner into his path, and slumped to the floor before raising any alarm. They were distracted, surprised, easy prey to fall into slumber at Mort's silent suggestion. Until things got scratchy in the under-britches, Mort was willing to give Esper's don't-blow-up-the-mountain plan a try, even the part about not killing slaving bastards in the process. He had to admit, sleeping mechanics didn't raise a stench like burning ones would have. Quieter, too.

With his hand-drawn map in one hand, staff of Earth-hewn wood in the other, he must truly have been a sight. If anyone managed to get close enough to engage him in conversation, Mort resolved to grumble about crusaders and ask directions to Babylon ... or perhaps Atlantis. This warren of ultra-modern tech was no fit place for a wizard.

A wall blocked his path. It had neither sprung from noth-ingness, nor moved into place by any scientific means he was able to notice. It was just there when he arrived, stubbornly disagreeing with the map in Mort's hands. He growled a few syllables of the ancient tongue of angels and devils, leveling his staff at the offending barrier. A gout of flame poured forth, and the stone glowed and turned molten. A metal support beam caught in the blast boiled away to smoke and soot. When a minute and more passed, the universe suggested that perhaps enough fire had flowed at Mort's beckon and he let off with a gasp for breath. He had carved a deep pocket into the rock, but the promised network of corridors beyond did not manifest.

With a frown and a glance to either side to make sure no one was observing him, Mort turned the map ninety degrees and retraced his last several turns. When he resumed his trek, the corridors did a better job of playing along with the map, and he found his confidence growing as he drew ever nearer the power thingamajig he was supposed to disable. With every pace, he pounded the end of his staff against the smooth rock of the man-smoothed tunnel, announcing his approach.

"*Warning. Intruder alert. Warning. Intruder alert ...*" a voice blared from the echoic depths of the warren, unseen and cowering. It kept repeating, along with a honking noise that grated on Mort's nerves.

"Shut the hell up!" he shouted down the hall behind him, his best guess as to where the voice and horn originated. "I'm right here, you plastic-sniffing atom-worshipers! Come and get me."

"Blasted racket," he muttered to himself. "How's a fellow supposed to feel wizardly when he's got some inane computer yammering over a squawking flock of electric geese?"

Mort emerged into what the map said was a maintenance hangar. There were vehicles of all sorts—or at least several sorts—scattered around, many in pieces. There were no people around at all. Probably seeking shelter from the noise, he reckoned. The echoing was more pronounced in the large empty space, but there also seemed to be additional sources of the noise.

While Mort was still puzzling out why anyone would want *more* of those gibbering voices besetting them, a side door opened and a squad of five guards poured through. "Throw down your weapons! Get on the ground!" their leader ordered. They leveled blaster rifles in Mort's direction.

Mort scoffed and walked straight toward them. "I'm already *on* the ground, you mole-sighted ignoramus. And as for the—"

"Fire!" the air lit with blood red bolts of scientific energy, but the space around Mort distorted like a pane glass that had cooled as someone spun it. The bolts slowed and curved, struggling through heavy air and losing their way. They circled around Mort like flies until one by one they slammed into objects around the hangar.

"As for the other thing," Mort continued. "I can't throw down my weapon. I *am* the weapon." Esper be damned, but those guards burned, and quickly. Mort could be a forgiving man, but with the strike of serving slavers already marked against their names, he was ill-inclined to extend further clemency when they tried to shoot him.

Mort wrinkled his nose as the map's instructions took him out the door the guards had entered by, forcing him to pass through the worst of the smell. "Why do I always waste the grand, crowd-pleasing lines for the ones about to die?" he said through an improvised mask made of his robe's sleeve. "Memoirs, I guess. Gotta write that down later."

By how far he had come already, it should not have been much farther. Tanny had scratched a quick little scale in the corner, but she'd used kilometers, which was about as useful as telling Mort how many crow's-flights it was. While Mort wasn't opposed to miles or feet, he preferred Mortsteps when making his own maps.

On his route, he found himself passing through a room labeled Power Distribution. The door had crumpled like tin foil with the application of a bit of gravity, but the room itself gave him a chill. It was packed with coils and gadgets, wire and glass filaments. The whole room had a dull hum that carried up through the floor and right into Mort's knees. Everywhere he looked were signs that warned of mortal peril. Even had Mort not grasped the English language, he would have known the hazards by the cartoons that accompanied the signs: thunderbolts striking men down, a struck-through flame, the skull and crossed femurs used by pirates and scientists alike. There was no telling what scientific powers his magic might unleash; it was worse than the engine room of the *Mobius*, which he had ventured into just once, and swore never to return. He crept through the room, clutching his staff before him in both hands.

Once through the hellish sci-scape, the rest of the way was easy. Two more deserted corridors, two more labels that checked against the signs along the way. Tanny's map had its flaws, but oriented just right, it worked well enough. It brought him as far as a steel door wide enough for ten wizards to walk through abreast. Above in block letters it read: Main Power.

Mort glanced from map to sign and back again. "This must be the place," he said to no one in particular, and stuffed the map into a pocket, heedless of crumpling it. A panel on the wall probably controlled the door, either holding it closed, awaiting orders to force it open, or prolonging its continued existence. Since two of his three options suggested that destroying the panel would allow him passage, Mort plied his magic against the controls.

He suggested in his head that it curl into a ball of twisted scrap, but it declined. He told the box that it was very, *very* heavy, and out to be collapsing under its own weight, but it seemed skeptical. Mort insisted aloud, in the ancient tongue, that it was grasped in the fist of demons, and it relented with a crunch and spray of sparks.

Mort scratched his chin and gave the panel a suspicious look. Not only had the door not opened for him—rotten luck with a two-in-three chance of working—but it should not have resisted him like that. Someone else was at work here, reinforcing the facility's belief in its own existence. It was entirely likely that someone had headed him off, and was holed up inside the main power room, ready to ambush him.

"Mustn't disappoint," Mort muttered.

He chanted low and slowly in the language of creation, words predating mankind and even the creatures of the netherworld. It was a puzzle of logic that he put forth, a twisted, intentionally convoluted set of premises that would, upon their release, strike a fearsome blow upon the door's belief system. By the point that Mort unleashed his syllogism of destruction, the door gave way and ceased its existence as anything more than dust and the memory of a once-mighty portal guardian.

The room beyond was mostly cavern, with a vast contraption of scientific metals at its center, stoppering the larval volcano and sucking at its veins. It was thrice his height and thrice *that* distance across, with umbilical pipes and wires webbing out to all sides, stretched well overhead. Were he alone, Mort might have balked at entering such a room, so infested with technology.

But there was a woman beyond. And Mort had his image to think of. Man might have thought better of many a crazy idea, had not woman been looking on with a skeptical eye.

This woman was a businesslike sort, with a pudgy face and rounded shoulders, not the type of sorceress who bothered altering her looks with magic. She had her sleeves rolled to the elbows, and a staff of her own clutched in two hands. Mort might have taken her for a proper foe if not for two factors. The first was the gaping eyes that tried to cower behind that staff as if it were a bulwark. The other was the pipe clutched loosely in a half-gape jaw.

"Who ... who are you?" she asked, taking a step back.

Mort opened his mouth to begin a speech, but stopped himself short. What was the point? "Listen, if I thought you were going to live out the minute, I might bother. But if you've got a name, I'll pass it along to the Convocation so they can notify your next of kin. Of course ... if you surrender, I might keep you around long enough to bother with introductions."

The staff clattered from her hands.

He smiled with an admixture of disdain with reassurance that only a wizard can pull off properly. "I'm Mordecai The Brown. Pleased to meet you."

She took another step back. "Irindi ... Irindi Ciera Branson." The look of fear did not wither.

"I see you've heard of me, Sorceress Branson. Now, if you'll be so good as to show me how to shut this infernal thing off, I won't have to erupt this volcano."

---

Tanny pulled up short at a corner and peeked around, whipping her head back immediately. She held up a hand with three fingers raised. This was it. Esper was going to have real live people shooting at her. Not at a ship with her in it. Her.

"Throw down your weapons," Tanny ordered. After a few

seconds of silence, she poked the butt of her disintegrator around the corner and jerked it back. A volley of plasma bolts flew past, slamming into the far wall.

"You were warned," Tanny said. She reached the business end of her weapon around the rocky edge of the hallway wall and squeezed the trigger. Esper had never seen one fire before, but she had assumed it would make a loud fuzzy squirting noise like most blasters. It didn't. A soothing hum emanated from the rifle, lasting just a few seconds until Tanny pulled back. "Now, throw down your weapons and come forward with your hands on your heads or you *will be disintegrated.*"

There was a scuffle of booted feet, but it grew fainter rather than approaching them. "I think they retreated," Esper said.

"Come on," said Tanny. "Stick to the plan. We can't give chase."

Esper followed as the squad scurried down the corridor like mice. Tanny slung the spent disintegrator rifle over her shoulder as she ran, readying her backup. Esper marveled at how effortless it appeared for Tanny. Esper's own rifle was an anchor around her neck, the strap biting into the spot between her shoulder and neck; her arms were already too tired to keep holding it up.

"*Warning. Intruder alert. Warning. Intruder alert ...*" a voice echoed down the corridors. Someone had raised a proper alarm, and it was accompanied by a klaxon that tried to impersonate a duck's quack. Fortunately the EV helm muffled the worst of it.

"That fucking thing going to keep up the whole time?" Roddy asked. "I wouldn't mind a side-trip to find the off switch."

"Cut the chatter," Tanny snapped. "We're in for more company."

"Bring them!" Mriy snarled.

"Next left," said Tanny. "Double-time. Clock's against us."

"I thought we wanted ... to scare them into ... surrendering," said Esper, huffing between words as she struggled to keep pace.

"That was plan A," Tanny replied. "Plan B is to haul ass and get out with those hostages before we get overrun."

Booted feet were closing in. Someone had come up a side tunnel behind them. Esper turned, but saw that Roddy was well ahead of her. The laaku was a ludicrous sight, hefting a gun nearly as large as he was. If any of the approaching guards with their little blaster pistols were amused, that impression was permanently wiped from their faces as Roddy pulled the trigger and swept a translucent green beam across them at head height.

Four bodies toppled, headless. It had taken less than a second. Four lives, decades in the making, ill-spent and morally adrift, but with friends and family and loved ones uncounted, undone between two beats of her heart. She stood staring in macabre fascination as blood leaked from the stumps of necks and one lower quarter of a head. Roddy had been wrong about disintegration being bloodless.

The rifle was pulled from Esper's grasp and the strap lifted over her shoulder. Another weapon was shoved into her hands in its place, and reflex alone made her grab hold of it. "Come on, kid," said Roddy. "You don't need to fire it. That one's dry. Just keep moving." A sudden blow struck her aside the helmet. The jolt restarted her brain.

"Yeah," she said. "Got it." She didn't even have the mental energy stored up to object to the killings.

"This way," said Tanny.

Everything looked different through the EV helmet's visor. Tiny symbols and numbers at the edge of her vision told her the ambient temperature and $O_2$ levels, comm channel, and relative distance and direction of her squad mates. But when she made an effort to ignore all those, and the tinting that made everything a shade darker than it should have been, things began to look familiar. She had been down these corridors, pushing that repulsor cart she had fixed.

The lights went out. The klaxon and public address warnings stopped. A second later, red lights blinked on, dimmer than the normal lighting, but enough to maneuver around by.

"Looks like Mort did it," said Roddy.

"We're here," Esper said, pointing. The Sub-Humans wing was just ahead.

---

Carl paced the *Mobius* from cockpit to cargo hold and back. He had a comm headset on, but his mic off. He could hear the squad's progress, but there was nothing he could say that wouldn't be a distraction. It was maddening, but the best thing he could do was listen, wait, and keep his mouth shut. As luck would have it, those were three of his weakest skills. The news that Mort had killed power in the mountain had been welcome, especially after the realization that Tanny wasn't having any luck convincing their security force to surrender.

The cargo bay ramp was down, affording Carl a look into the ruptured tunnel and the jungle on the far side. Thus far, no wildlife bigger than an insect had dared to come in. He suspected that most of them had been scared shitless by the arrival of the *Mobius*. Give them enough time though, some critter was bound to happen by out of curiosity, territorial defense, or just plain old hunger. Carl had his blaster sidearm ready, just in case.

The common room was vacant. There was no one else to be there but him. Carl fought back the temptation to park himself on the couch and put holos on to take his mind off everything. It would be just his luck that someone would call for help, and he'd miss it over the sound of a hover-bike chase or a shootout.

The cockpit was awash with natural light, which made everything look weird and alien. The UV filters were practically offline, letting the atmosphere filter out the worst of the harmful solar radiation. The mountain loomed to one side in his view, the jungle treescape hemmed them in on the other. The *Mobius* needed to be there, waiting for everyone to return. He needed to be on it, because they couldn't risk leaving it unprotected and Carl was the least help in a raid. He was a big boy; he could admit that much to himself. Still, he felt like a star drive on a sailboat—useless. He was just sitting on his ass (or pacing aimlessly), waiting for news over the comm. He was no good in a firefight. He had never been in the facility. He couldn't puzzle out machinery or zorch his foes with wizardly fire. All he was good at was flying and fast talking, and neither was going to do them any good right that minute.

The comm. It was a generic term. The one on the *Mobius* was as modern as anything on board, which was to say only fifteen or so years out of date. It was separate from the comm system that Tanny and her squad were using, though it could patch them in if need be. But it could also host an entirely separate conversation. A grin eased its way onto Carl's face. "Well, shit. Why didn't I think of this before?" The comm panel blinked with a listing of available channels with signal traffic.

Carl slouched down into the pilot's seat and removed his headset. After a quick pause to clear his throat, he keyed a channel from the Recent Contacts list. "Gologlex Menagerie, this is the ENV Beowulf. Come in," he said in the smooth, confident tones of a naval officer. He'd never used that voice when he actually *was* a naval officer, but he'd heard it enough times to mimic the cadence.

There was silence in response. Carl wasn't going to let them off that easily. "Gologlex Menagerie, this is Captain James Hendrix of the Earth Navy Vessel Beowulf. We have a ground force that has infiltrated your facility and relayed the coordinates for a firing solution. I will accept your unconditional surrender. You are charged with illegal detention of sentient hominids per section four, eight, six, stroke four, paragraph seven of the ARGO code for xeno-relations. Evacuate all personnel, unarmed, via the equatorial tunnel out of your facility. Orbital bombardment will commence in 30 standard minutes. Starting ... now."

Carl closed the comm. "Yeah, fuckers. Don't answer *my* call, will you?" He pulled his headset back on, folded his arms, and waited.

If possible, the sentients behind the glass walls were more frightened than the last time Esper had been through. The Sub-Humans section was a chorus of muffled shouts and pounding against the insides of those walls. With the murky red light, filtered through the tint of her EV helmet, it was hard to make out anything more than indistinct shapes inside the exhibits.

Esper pulled off her helmet. "It's OK. Everything's going to be OK." She could make out faces where they pressed close to the enclosure glass. Wild eyes, raised hackles, puffed cheeks, and bristling feathers were all signs of aggression, agitation, or fear as best she could tell. Some exhibits appeared empty at a glance, but only because the occupants were hiding, not trying to draw attention.

A faint voice sounded from her hip. Esper glanced down and realized someone was talking over the comm. She lifted it to her ear like a seashell.

"Put that back on," Tanny ordered. "This is not a secure area."

"I can't see a thing with this lighting."

"Jesus, kid," said Roddy. "Turn off your UV filtering, or switch to gamma correction. If any of these primitives get physical, you don't wanna get your face chewed off."

"We're here to save them," Esper replied. "They're sentient, not animals. They won't bite the hand that feeds them."

"Where do we unlock them?" Mriy asked, feeling along the wall between exhibits, looking for control panels.

"Must be on the far side," Esper said. "This is where the visitors would be."

"Makes sense," said Tanny. "Let's look for an 'employees only' area."

The hall of sentient creatures took a right-angle turn, and tucked unobtrusively in a corner was plain door with no markings. Tanny gave it a push, but it didn't budge. Mriy shouldered her out of the way and used both hands, extending her claws to dig into the seam where door and wall met for extra grip. Her wordless snarl of exertion made Esper hold the helmet away from her ear.

"Stand back," Tanny ordered. She swung her disintegrator into line with the door.

"Hold up!" Roddy said, raising his arms. "Could be anything past there. You hit a coolant line, a bio-hazard unit, or anything explosive and we're dusted." He eased the barrel of Tanny's weapon out of the way and fished a plasma torch out of his pack. "Finesse. See kid?" he turned to Esper as he flicked on the cutting beam. "Comes in handy."

In just a few seconds, Roddy had cut away the locking mechanism, allowing Mriy to force the door open. Inside was a narrow passage that ran along behind the exhibits in both directions. There was no emergency lighting, so Roddy passed out hand lamps to everyone.

"Roddy, you're with me," Tanny said. "Mriy, look after Esper. We'll split up and start opening enclosures."

"No offense," said Roddy, "But I like my chances with Ms. Congeniality."

Tanny huffed into the mic of her comm. "Fine, Mriy come with me." She stormed off down the left passageway.

"Come on kid," said Roddy. "Let's go be saviors." They took the right passage.

There was no security on the exhibits. They were already inside the security perimeter, it appeared, and no further effort was made to stop them. Esper knocked firmly on the door to the first and put her head against it. "Hello in there. Stand back. We're opening the door. You can come out." She had no way of knowing whether they understood English, but the occupants of cell H-1 would get the idea soon enough. Esper popped a catch and pulled the door handle, leaning back with all her weight to drag it open.

The door flew wide. Esper was thrown to her backside, helmet clattering out of reach, as three porcine humanoids careened past clad only in loincloths. They paused to sniff the air with flat, upturned noses, gazing down at Esper with blank, black eyes. She wondered momentarily whether they knew she was the one who released them, but they ignored her and hurried off. The creatures hesitated when they came to the intersection where Roddy had cut through the door, then ducked into the visitors' hall and disappeared from sight.

Roddy pulled off his helmet. "You OK?" He offered her a hand to get up.

"I think so," she replied. "They were in more of a hurry than I imagined. Strong, too."

"Maybe we need a better plan than just opening all the doors. Maybe some of them speak English?"

Esper nodded. "It's worth checking."

The two of them hustled down the passage, calling out, asking whether any of the sentients understood spoken English. They heard plenty of responses, and thanks to translator charms, understood most of them as well. Unfortunately, not one of them conveyed the least sense of comprehension, and some were downright troubling to hear. With only a limited exposure to non-human cultures, Esper had a lot to learn about metaphor and threats.

"What the hell?" Roddy asked. When Esper looked where the light from his hand lamp shone. It illuminated one sign that said "Genetics" and another that said "Specimen Storage."

"We should check those out," Esper said. "If they're doing genetics work here, that would explain a lot. There might be sentients trapped in those rooms. We should split up. You check—"

"Oh, *hell* no," Roddy said. "We're not splitting up again. Fuck that horror vid crap. You're not even armed with a charged weapon. We'll check the genetics lab first. I'm really not looking forward to what might be in that other one."

"Fine," Esper agreed. The door to the genetics room wasn't locked, nor was it as heavy to move as the exhibit door. Inside, the room was dark, but there was someone inside. Clinking glassware and a heavy plastic clatter of a storage case drew two beams of hand lamp light.

A skinny, hunched-over man was stuffing glass jars into foam-lined round pockets in a shock-proof carry-all. He looked up at them and crouched down behind the safety of the table. All they could see were the bald scalp and the reflection off a pair of data-display glasses. "This is all a misunderstanding!" he shouted. "I was given informal permission to set up my menagerie here. You have no right to bomb it."

Roddy and Esper exchanged glances in the dark. She saw no hint that he knew what the mad scientist was talking about.

"Stand away from that case, and put your hands where I can see them," Esper ordered. She pointed the disintegrator rifle in the man's direction, but pointedly not at him. She didn't want to chance that there was any charge left in it, even if her finger wasn't on the trigger. It was dark, after all. How would he notice?

The man stood slowly, and with a pained grunt of exertion. "My name is Elmer Gologlex. If you're willing to give me a ten-minute head start, I can see that you're both very wealthy men—people," he quickly amended. "Omicron Squad might give you a pension when you're forty and wondering whether you can afford genetically restructured knees or cybernetic ones, but I can save your that wear and tear."

Esper didn't need to look to know that Roddy had to be as puzzled as she was.

"Hey, slimeball," said Roddy. "I'm proud to earn my pay serving my planet. I didn't join Omicron Squad for the money. Now, keep your hands up and move toward the door."

She had heard of Omicron Squad, of course. Mentions of them popped up in the sort of holovids she usually didn't bother seeing. But the ads always described them the same way. Best of the best. Secret, elite unit. No one knew its members. Answerable to no oversight committee. ARGO's go-to team for black ops. It was vid-biz bull-plop, she had always assumed.

She looked down at Roddy, and he winked. Maybe it was bull-plop they could use.

Gologlex crept along at a slug's pace. Esper kept her gun sort of pointed at him as he walked by. When he was within a step of her, the old man surprised her. Moving with a young man's agility, he snatched her disintegrator rifle by the barrel and yanked it out of her hands. The strap caught her in the back of the head as he pulled the weapon away, and Gologlex used that opportunity to grab hold of her.

Seconds later, it was a standoff. Roddy held his disintegrator aimed at Gologlex. Gologlex held Esper's gun pointed at her head, and had an arm around her neck, pulling her close and using her as a shield.

"Step back, chimp," Gologlex ordered. "I'm taking the girl as insurance. Lower that weapon this instant, or she loses her head."

Roddy aimed his disintegrator aside, but didn't drop it. He was no fool, but he obviously shared Esper's worry that there might be a tiny bit of oomph left—plenty to vaporize her head. "Easy there, buddy. No one wins if you pull that trigger."

"Girl, close that case and pick it up," Gologlex ordered.

Esper complied. It struck her right then that this is what Tanny had warned her of. She had turned into a liability, being unable to defend herself. The case was heavy in her hands, but nothing compared to the weight of her failure. She realized that she might very well be about to die, and closed her eyes to pray. A warm wetness rolled down her cheeks as she did so.

"You aren't any sort of commandos," Gologlex said. "Are you?"

"We're a bit irregular is all," Roddy replied. "And if you don't let that girl go, you're going to find out what not having a head feels like."

Gologlex twisted, turning Esper to shield him more fully. When he spoke, she felt his hot breath on her ear and cheek. "You a ... a marksmonkey? Huh? Take the shot! No, you don't dare." He stepped back, and Esper choked as she stumbled to keep up with him.

It was the time for desperate measures. If Gologlex had a ship ready to make an escape, Carl might not be in a position to notice, let alone give chase. She could wind up as his hostage, or worse, his slave. Gologlex has already shown that he wasn't above the notion. Mass murderers often gave hints of their derangement in their treatment of xenos; could slavers be much different? There was a coin-flip of a chance that the disintegrator Gologlex had taken from her was well and truly dry. If Esper could just jerk free of him, Roddy could take the shot.

She tried one last prayer for deliverance, but couldn't finish the thought. It was asking for murder. If she was spared her own death when the gun didn't work, her hope was for Roddy to kill Gologlex. Esper couldn't ask God for such a terrible thing. But she wasn't ready to die either, she discovered. Remembering the forcefield, she drew upon her meta-bolic magic. Her body had no need of healing, as before, and the gnawing hunger overwhelmed the sensations of heat and dizziness that accompanied speeding up her natural processes.

Using one of the techniques Tanny had taught her, she stomped down on Gologlex's instep. The slaving zookeeper gave a cry of pain through gritted teeth, and Esper jabbed one elbow into his stomach while using her other hand to pull his arm away. She tumbled to the floor as she broke loose from his hold.

*Click.*

Nothing happened. No disintegrator beam bored through her head—not that she expected to feel such a thing had it done so. "Roddy, shoot! I borked the gun with magic." Then she curled into a ball on the floor, grimacing at the stabbing sense of starvation that her magic had wrought on her.

But Roddy didn't fire either. Gogoglex must have sensed the laaku's hesitation, grabbed the case, and fled through the back door of the lab. From the other room, they heard Gologlex scream. It was a short, astonished shriek that ended abruptly.

Even from the floor, Esper could appreciate the poetic irony of the porcine xenos stumbling across their captor and sating their vengeance. It was downright biblical. "For all who draw the sword will die by the sword," she murmured.

Her illusion was shattered seconds later when Mriy entered via that same back door. Her disintegrator rifles both hung idle around her neck. In one hand, she carried Gologlex's case, in the other, Gologlex himself. Her grip was the only thing keeping his head from lolling at a grotesque angle, and the hand that held him aloft like a rag doll was drenched in blood.

Tanny followed her in a moment later. "Well, no wondering where this piece of shit ended up."

"Hungry," Esper gasped. "Food."

"He hit her with some sort of stupid-ray?" Tanny asked.

Mriy held out the dead scientist. "Fresh kill?" she offered.

"Don't worry, kid," said Roddy. "It might be kibble, but I'll find you something."

---

There were hundreds. Humanoid and non-humanoid, life forms from ARGO protectorates and species from far-flung star systems, Earth-like beings and strange creatures whose anatomies were bizarre. The exhibits viewable from the public side did not begin to cover the variety of sentient life forms that inhabited the mountain. They might even have outnumbered the facility's personnel.

"It'll be chaos if we let them all loose," Esper said in a whisper, meant only for herself but overheard by keener ears than humans had.

"So we have chaos," said Mriy with a yawn. "We've killed or chased off their caretakers. Even if they were kept prisoner, they were kept alive. We'd starve them if we left. Or maybe we just allow them to be re-slaved?" The azrin cocked her head at Esper. This was a challenge. Would Esper stand up for principle or flee?

Tanny had her EV helmet off; they all did. She fished a headset comm from a pouch on her combat gear and donned it. "Carl. Carl, come in." Esper couldn't overhear Carl's side of the conversation. "Yeah, we're getting a crowd estimate on the slaved xenos ... No, we're talking estimates, unless we find records ... Yeah, that many ... No, I was hoping you'd have some thoughts, smart guy ... You *what?* ... Is Mort back there yet? ... Good, send him our way, then take the ship, go around blasting all the entrances but the one we came in by."

"What was that all about?" Esper asked.

"Carl bluffed the station personnel into surrendering. They think the place is getting leveled by naval fire in the next few minutes. That's why we stopped meeting resistance."

"Explains that kooky shit Gologlex was spouting, too," said Roddy. Tanny gave him a puzzled frown. "He had me and Esper pegged for Omicron Squad."

Tanny and Mriy both laughed. "Their standards must be slipping," said Tanny. "Nothing personal, you two, but the holovids don't do those brutes justice."

"Did Carl have any ideas about the refugee problem?" Esper asked.

"No, but he's sending Mort."

"What, is Mort going to shrink them all to the size of mice?" Esper asked.

Roddy smirked. "Like Cinderella, in reverse. Turning coachmen into mice."

"No," Tanny said. "We need a translator, or we're going to get overrun when we open all these cages and enclosures."

"Hmm," said Roddy. "Not a bad idea. Maybe he can whip up a shipload of charmed earrings and pass 'em out. Still doesn't find us a place to put them."

"Gologlex was planning to leave," said Esper. "There must be at least one ship on-world."

"If not, there's at least going to be supply ships coming," Tanny added. "We can wait and ambush one."

"Roddy, come help me find it while Mort plays peacemaker," Esper said. "I have an idea, even if it's not big enough for everyone."

There was a shuttle hangar with its own concealed exit, tucked up a series of ventilation shafts and hidden corridors that didn't appear on Esper's map. They had, however, shown up on Gologlex's personal datapad. The ship was a one person courier vessel with its own star-drive. There was room for cargo or a couple passengers, but probably not both. It was one man's last resort, and had Esper and Roddy not stumbled across Gologlex when they did, he might have gotten away in it.

"Well, kid, if plan A was stuffing this thing full of xenos, it's time for plan B," said Roddy.

"Don't you feel strange calling them that? I thought most non-humans considered it offensive?" Esper asked.

Roddy shrugged. "Far as I'm concerned, you humans are just tall, bald-faced laaku with clumsy feet. Up to when you and us met, your species' best friend was the dog. When I think xeno, I think non-laaku, and I don't include you guys."

"Thanks?" Esper ventured. "Anyway, plan B involves getting on board. Hop in." She climbed into Gologlex's ship and slid into the pilot's seat.

"Whoa there," said Roddy. "You know how to fly this thing?"

"It's a personal craft," Esper replied. "I've got my pilot's cert." Roddy traced the sign of the cross in the air in front of him and climbed in behind her. "I saw that. You'll be fine."

The ship handled like the hover shuttle, with the added ability to go upward. Esper had no trouble navigating the narrow shaft that led them out of the mountain. The view was nothing spectacular. The claustrophobic forward windows barely afforded any field of vision. It was a vessel meant to be flown mainly on instruments, and as they rose through the atmosphere, all they could see was a sky filled with clouds, then a clear blue sky above, then the darkness of the Black Ocean, pinpricked with stars.

"So what are we doing up here?" Roddy asked.

Esper scanned the comm controls, selecting her way through sub-menus and inputting a recipient ID. She hit the switch to engage the astral antenna for long-range communication. "Keep quiet and you'll see."

"*This is Sister Agatha of the Nineveh, vessel of the Lord,*" said a voice on the comm. The signal was clear and crisp, conveying a dignified, middle-aged speaker with African-Earth accent.

"Sister Agatha, I bring word of a horrible crisis," said Esper. "My ship and crew have stumbled upon an unregulated colony where humans have taken our cousins as zoo animals. They have kept animals and children of our Lord alike in cages and exhibits. My comrades have secured their release, but we have no means of rescuing them or returning them to their homes."

"*My child, this is troubling news. I don't mean to disbelieve you, but can you provide proof of these claims?*"

"Yes, Sister," Esper replied. "I'm transmitting the contents of a datapad confiscated in the raid. It belonged to the founder of the facility. He was a geneticist and entrepreneur, looking to profit on xenophobe tourists and illegal gene splicing. Would it be possible for me to speak to the Bishop?" The *Nineveh* was a missionary mother-ship and had to have at least a bishop aboard, if not an archbishop.

"*I'm sorry, but the Bishop is a very busy man. I will pass your data along, and get back to you.*"

"Thank you, Sister Agatha," Esper replied. "We'll be waiting for your reply." She keyed off the comm.

"So what now?" Roddy asked. "We just sit here? This thing doesn't even have a holo-viewer."

Esper yawned. "I don't know about you, but I'm exhausted. My soul finally feels clean enough to sleep without nightmares, and my shoulders ache from carrying that awful gun all day. I'm taking a nap."

---

Mort's words carried a strange echo. Neither the initial sound, nor the aftereffect made any sense, but Tanny was left with a keen understanding of what he had said. It was as if the wizard were sitting down and painstakingly explaining each word, each sentence, and how they combined together to create meaning. The creatures from the menagerie understood him just as well. The growing throng in the warehouse filed out toward the jungle, many muttering thanks or offering blessings upon their rescuers. Tanny and Mriy moved along the walls of cages, breaking the occupants free one by one or in small groups, however they had been confined.

"We are working our way through," Mort's shouted words conveyed. "Everyone will get released. You owe us your lives and freedom. All we ask in return is your patience."

One particularly sturdy cage required a quick burst from Tanny's disintegrator. Inside were a mated pair of stuunji, two-and-half meter tall creatures, descendant from rhino-like ancestors. Either of them could have crushed Mriy in one fist, but they folded their meaty hands and bowed. "Blessings upon your home and children, small saviors," they spoke in unison with grumbling bass voices. Stuunji were native to Garrelon II, an Earth-like world and ARGO protectorate.

Mriy was working the opposite side of the aisle and was having trouble with one crate that was fully enclosed aside from a series of tiny air holes. "Need me to blast that one?" Tanny asked.

"No, look," Mriy replied. She extended one claw and pointed. The cage was protected with glyphs.

"Mort," Tanny called out over the buzz of conversations and requests from the captives and newly released sentients alike. "We got a magicked-shut box over here."

"Keep calm," Mort imparted. "We just have a magic cage to pry open. I am fully qualified. Nothing to worry about."

Mort wove his way against the tide, which parted respectfully, but could only do so much in the cramped aisles. "What have we got?" the wizard asked in plain English.

"Binding charms on the enclosure," came a sibilant voice from within. Whoever was inside had understood him.

"Merciful Merlin," Mort breathed. "Hold on. I'll have you out of there in a jiffy." He dragged a fingernail through a glyph, and it left a ragged gouge in the steel. A shudder emanated from the other glyphs, almost as if they knew their existence was measured in minutes, if not seconds. Several scratches, he gave a tug and the door to the crate fell away. Two cobra-like sentients emerged. Their heads were as large as Roddy's, if not a human's head, and were at least four meters long, perhaps five. Mort pressed his palms together and bowed low. "I am deeply sorry for this incident. The Convocation had no part in this." He lowered his voice and glanced around to see who else might be listening. "Even if we have to take you personally, I will see that you are delivered home."

The two snake creatures departed, slipping easily through

the crowd, both due to favorable anatomy and the fact that many of the other sentients seemed wary of them. "What were those?" Mriy asked.

"Ssentuadi," Mort replied. "Not on the best terms with ARGO, but the Convocation does business with them. The non-wizardly ones are considered invalids. Bygone days they used to let them starve. Whole race of them with magic, pretty much. Now, unless you've got more glyphed boxes for me, I've got refugees to shepherd."

Tanny's next crate was a sorry sight. A single dog-like creature lay inside, four feet up, displaying its belly. It had an oversized cranium and large green eyes, but otherwise reminded her of a Rottweiler. The door unlatched with no trouble, and the creature twisted and sprang to its feet in an instant.

"Thank-you-thank-you-thank-you-thank-you-thank-you," it garbled at her, nearly bowling her over as it plowed its head into her and rubbed against her side. "Hungry-hungry-hungry-hungry-hungry."

Tanny smiled and scratched the creature behind the ears. It flopped to its side and rolled over, its heft pinning her feet to the floor. "Good boy," she told it, continuing to scratch. Its gender was made abundantly clear by its pose.

Those too-large green eyes looked up at her. "Kubu loves! Mommy?"

Tanny stopped scratching and shook her head. "Sorry Kubu. I'm not your mommy. I'll see about getting you something to eat though." There was no sign the dog-like creature understood her, but his ears perked up at the mention of its name. Her tone seemed to reassure him though. Tanny broke off the rescue momentarily to get Kubu something to eat. In sharp counterpoint to the English-comprehending ssentuadi, Kubu didn't seem too bright.

Esper set the courier vessel down not far from the *Mobius*. There was a crowd gathered outside, with non-human sentients spreading out into the jungle, erecting makeshift shelters. It seemed counterintuitive, given that the mountain had been designed as a shelter for them and many more, but she could see the emotional reason for them to want to distance themselves from it.

Roddy was already scampering down the steps even as they descended toward the jungle floor. The laaku had not been keen on the wait, and was even less keen to hang around while she delivered their news to Carl. That was fine. Esper was at peace with the decision, and it was just going to have to do. If he wanted to strand her on Hadrian IV, she could always hitch a ride on the *Nineveh* or just take Gologlex's courier shuttle. It was strange how casually the thought of theft fit in among her options, but she could muster no guilt over this particular crime—even if its theoretical commission still lay in her future.

"Hey!" Carl shouted, waving from the near edge of the throng of sentients. "Welcome back!"

Esper trod down the underbrush, glancing back over her shoulder in vague dread of some off-world creature following her in from the jungle's edge. "It's all covered. We can leave as soon as everyone's settled."

"How's that?" Carl asked. "You place a comm to the navy while you were up there? We'll have to do a little purge work to make sure no one traces this back to us."

Esper shook her head. "Not the navy. The church."

A light of amusement shone in Carl's eyes and one side of his mouth curled in a half-smile. "You don't say ..."

"They're sending a ship," she continued. "I uplinked Gologlex's personal datapad to them. They know who came from where, so they can return them home. I think we should find that egg, though, and return it ourselves."

"I'll cut you short right there," Carl replied. "We've got no business going back to Vi Tik Naa. The One Church wants to be neighborly and bring back a hundred sentients, give or take, they can make it a hundred one. Mriy found it safe in an incubator back in there, and it can stay there until the Sisters of Zoological Repatriation show up."

"I figured as much," said Esper with a sigh. "But it was worth trying." Small steps. She had won her victory, and the bad news was yet to come. Best not to stretch her luck to its breaking point ahead of time.

"Well, Mriy and Tanny are cutting the last of these folks loose," said Carl. "We can get going in probably an hour."

"There's one last thing."

"What's that?"

Esper cleared her throat and made an effort to look Carl in the eye.

"What?" he repeated.

"The care and feeding of so many sentients isn't cheap," Esper said.

Carl rolled his eyes. "I see where this is going. They're hitting us up for a donation, right?"

"... and it *was* fairly ill-gotten," Esper said. She noticed Roddy sneaking up behind Carl, a datapad in hand. He had the built-in camera aimed in Carl's direction.

Carl's jaw hung slack and his eyes gaped at her. "You didn't!"

"No one felt good taking that money," Esper countered. "Including you. The One Church can use that to pay for food and fuel as they crisscross the galaxy taking these poor lost souls home."

Carl set his jaw and stared at her, chest rising and falling in great heaves. Esper held her ground, staring right back at him. After minutes of this, Carl closed his eyes, let out a long breath, and turned away. "Fine. Just ... don't let me see you doing it. It'd break my heart."

There were two refugee camps on Hadrian IV, one populated by a xenobiological potpourri of races with a makeshift tent city and access to all the supplies in the menagerie, the other a huddled and frightened collection of humans who found themselves trapped between the feral creatures who might eat them and the angry former prisoners who might do just about anything in vengeance. Opinions seemed mixed among the refugees, but eating them was still counted among the options for a few of the more predatory species.

There would be tense days ahead for both groups, and there was every possibility that by the time the *Nineveh* arrived, the two populations might have decreased. But the crew of the *Mobius* would not be there to see how it played out. They were preparing to depart.

Mort stood by the ramp to Gologlex's shuttle with Irindi, who had runes scrawled on her forehead in black marker. They would wear off in time, but until then, she was no more a threat than any of the humans in the refugee camp. Beside them slithered the two ssentuadi, heads drawn up to human height for conversation. "This one will pilot you home. She's an idiot when it comes to scientific powers, but Esper assures me that this bucket is idiot-proof. All I ask is that you remand her to the custody of the Convocation, and keep her safe on your homeworld until she can be handed over."

"Wizard Mordecai The Brown, we thank you," one of the ssentuadi said. "We shall respect your wishes, and make sure that the Synod of Justice speaks honorable words to the Convocation on your behalf."

Mort pressed his palms together. "I ask no more. Have a safe trip, and try not to run into any naval patrols. You're better off riding with this pipe smoker than getting processed through official channels." He hooked a thumb in Irindi's direction. She seemed too dazed to care, and tromped up the steps into the ship.

Across the camp site, Carl and Mriy were packing the last of the supplies they had commandeered from the menagerie. The refugees had insisted the crew supply themselves, even though they might be in greater need. Carl humored them and took some of the less healthy (but better tasting) foods, most of the alcohol, and made the bulk of their supply trips in and out of the facility dragging luxuries. None of the artwork was particularly valuable, but it would add up. They also took a number of lab gizmos that looked expensive, a multi-game flat-vid table from the rec room, and one of the hover shuttles.

The refugees were crowded around the base of the cargo ramp to bid them farewell. Kubu, who had been following Tanny around from a meter away since his release, jumped up onto the ramp.

"Sorry, boy," Tanny told him. "You can't come with us." He didn't understand a word, and she had to lean down and push him by the shoulders to evict him from the ship.

He jumped right back on. "Mommy! No leave!" Tanny winced, but pushed him out again. She gestured to one of the hefty stuunji to hold him back, and Kubu was unable to re-enter the ship as the cargo bay door raised.

"Mommy! Mommy! No Mommy! Don't leave Kubu! Kubu be good! Kubu love Mommy!"

Tanny fumbled with the translator earring as she unclasped it and threw it across the cargo hold. There were tears in her eyes as she took the stairs two at a time up to the common room. Carl was at the fridge, trying to find room for some of the newly acquired beverages. He was starting by removing beers and tossing them to Mort and Roddy. "You ready to take us out of here?" Carl asked.

"You fly us!" Tanny snapped. The door to her quarters slammed shut behind her.

"What was that all about?" Carl asked as Esper emerged from the cargo bay.

Esper gave a sad smile. "I think I grew a conscience in someone. Careful. They might be contagious."

---

The *Mobius* lifted off into the evening sky, a departing hero riding into the sunset with Carl at the helm. Below on the planet, the refugees watched them until the ship was no more than a speck against the night sky, engines a pair of shooting stars, heading up. There were feelings of anxiety among the sentient creatures left behind, but for the first time since any of them had been there, a sense of hope as well. The saviors had promised a ship would come. A larger ship, one big enough to carry them all. The slavers had taken breeding pairs whenever they could, so they would be returned two by two to their home worlds, long before the substandard atmosphere of Hadrian IV did them permanent harm

For those lonely creatures captured individually, they would not speak to another who could understand them until they returned home. Most bore this knowledge with a grim understanding that it was of necessity—that they would have their turn and be brought back to those who loved them. Nearly three in four of the refugees were juveniles, most just past the barest minimum breeding age, but some were even younger.

———

Kubu was perhaps the loneliest of all. He had no memory of a time before the menagerie. He remembered the cage, the mean man with the black eyes, the noises and smells of the other creatures all around him. He remembered Mommy, too. But now she was gone. She had turned into a great big bird-thing and flown away into the sky. Kubu lay down in the jungle grass and whimpered in the direction that Mommy had gone.

Sunset turned to nighttime, and the grumbling in his stomach told Kubu he needed another meal. He didn't care. He watched the night sky, waiting. He fell asleep waiting, dreaming of a dark place where he was all alone and no one would feed him ever again.

He woke when a noise caught his ear. It was a hum that grew louder. With eyes raised to follow the sound, he saw it. The bird-thing was back!

It landed in the grass, right where it had left him behind. The back was open, and it had a ramp waiting for him. Mommy stood there. Her eyes were red and she was sniffing because she was sad. *"Blah blah blah, Kubu."*

Kubu didn't need to be told twice. He bounced through the jungle grass and sprang up the ramp. He knocked Mommy to the ground and licked her face. Two of Mommy's friends stood by watching, and the small fuzzy one hit a button and the ramp closed up, making the jungle go away.

Little did he realize at the time, but Kubu had just joined the crew of the *Mobius*.

# POETS AND PIRACY

MISSION 3 OF THE BLACK OCEAN SERIES

## POETS AND PIRACY

Tanny popped the pills into her mouth in little squadrons. Two blues and a pink. A yellow with black stripe, a squarish red, and a clear amber. Four clean white ones shaped like torpedoes. A pair of chalky hexagons and a trio of half-brown, half-yellow capsules. The last to go was a single pill in a metallic casing, printed with a red letter R in gothic script and a standard ARGO hazard marker. She chased each swallow with a mouthful of ginger soda, both to settle her stomach and to kill the bitter aftertaste from the chalky pills. The whole conglomeration fizzed and churned in her stomach as they set out on their assigned tasks.

Centrimac boosted her immune system. A constant presence of it in her system had kept her from so much as a sniffle since she joined the marines. Carl and Roddy came down with something every second or third trip planetside, but not Tanny. She had heard that it took the edge off a hangover too, but she wasn't about to abstain to check for herself.

Plexophan improved her balance and reflexes. There was some weird enzyme in it developed by the yishar that altered her muscle fibers. They no longer used the same chemical process as most humans. Once she had tried research how that all worked, but no explanation made sense unless you had a degree in biochemistry—preferably an advanced one, focused on xenobiology.

Adrenophiline altered adrenaline production and consumption in the body. Any marine with a year's service had adrenal glands twice the size he enlisted with, and they replenished at six times the normal rate. It also eased the jittery feeling that came after the rush wore off.

A few of the pills were simple mineral supplements. Most humans didn't need a lot of molybdenum, selenium, or cobalt, but anyone with a daily regimen like Tanny's required them. The identical white pills were compacted mixes of auto-release hormones, designed to keep her mood level—she had never found them that effective, but she was worse off without them.

Some of the drugs were just included to cancel out side effects of the others. Plexophan increased her metabolism, but also spiked her appetite out of proportion to the increase. Pseudoanorex counteracted that effect, but resulted in light-headedness that Zygrana balanced out. Cannabinol was there to reduce the anxiety and nausea that Adrenophiline induced.

The centerpiece of the whole cocktail was Recitol, which saturated every marine's system. Though the drug's maker used a soft C sound in the recipient-care video, the marine nickname "Wreck-It-All" came to be the more common pronunciation. It allowed the body to use quick, efficient bursts of adrenaline at will, hyper-oxygenated the blood, and slowed the perception of time by an estimated 11 to 12 percent. It also suppressed activity in the ventrolateral frontal cortex, the part of the brain responsible for morality and conscience. Tanny had been taking Sepromax to counteract the latter effect since re-entering civilian life, but she was unwilling to give up the other benefits.

The water from the faucet shocked Tanny alert as she splashed her face. Leaning heavily on the sides of the sink, she watched her reflection in the mirror. Staring into her own eyes, she waited until the stranger lurking there faded away and she could connect the image with a sense of self. The scrawled red lines receded until the whites were clear; the pupils contracted in reaction to the glare of the mirror light.

There was a knock at the door. "What?" she snapped. It hadn't been an invitation, but the door opened anyway.

"Sorry," Esper said. The hangdog expression and the apologetic duck drained the venom from Tanny. Suddenly embarrassed, she reached over and snapped shut the case where she kept her pills. *"What was that?"* Esper never said it aloud, but her furrowed brow and the tilt of her head to get a better look said it for her.

"What?" Tanny repeated, holding the case behind her. The Adrenophiline must still have been digging its claws into her brain. She rationalized that if anyone on the *Mobius* was incapable of threatening her, it was Esper. With a conscious effort, she set the case down on the side of the sink and dared Esper to ask about its contents.

"Roddy sent me," Esper said. "It's Kubu. Roddy says there is 2.6 kilos of sub-grade fertilizer in the hold. He says if you don't clean it up, he's delivering it."

"Like to see him try," Tanny muttered.

"... through the faucet," Esper added.

Tanny glanced to the sink and the churning froth in her stomach soured. The last thing she needed was to vomit up a thousand terras worth of marine biochemicals. Recitol was a weekly, and there weren't many pills left in her stash. She wasn't ready to go without until she could buy more.

Esper seemed to notice her discomfort. "He didn't *actually* do it ... yet."

"I'm surprised he didn't make you clean it up," Tanny said. "Aren't you his assistant these days?"

"Not today," Esper replied. "I've just been in and out of the hold, moving stuff from the conference room. I'm converting it to passenger quarters so we can make actual money on fares. Carl and Roddy both seemed pretty keen on the idea, so—"

"Fine," Tanny snapped. She didn't need an affidavit. It was a simple enough question. "I'll get right down there."

Once the door closed behind Esper, Tanny reopened the pill case. Supplies were always hit or miss. Sometimes she'd find a dealer with a glut of Plexophan, or a fence would have a load of boosted Recitol. It was rare to find things in balanced ratios to match her regimen. Since her recent change to a higher dose of Sepromax, she had run her reserves dangerously low, and a few other pills weren't far behind.

An hour of cross-referencing the itinerary of the *Mobius* (a work of optimistic fiction at the best of times) against known gray-market pharmacists, Tanny concluded that she wasn't going to stumble across anyone who had what she needed. Her finger hovered over the button for the intra-ship comm as she decided whether she could afford to wait and hope to get lucky along the way, or if she really needed to make this particular call. Deciding that withdrawal symptoms were worse than asking for help, she closed her eyes and pressed.

"Yo!" Carl's voice came through from his quarters. "To what do I owe the—"

"I'm running low," Tanny blurted before Carl could get any farther.

The flippant joviality was gone. "Esper came by and mentioned you were a bit worn thin. I told her not to worry. How low we talkin'?"

"A week," Tanny replied. "I'd feel better with four days, plus some wiggle room."

"Gotcha," Carl replied. He sounded relieved. "We can reroute to Tau Ceti. Ought to be plenty of options there." Why did he have to be so goddamn understanding? He'd tried to get her to detox more times than she could count. Tanny had hoped he'd be put out, that he'd argue with her about it again, that he actually cared where they were headed and found a detour inconvenient.

But once again, Carl was just going to have them drop everything and head off to find her a seller. All she could think to say was, "Thanks."

---

The first day of their side trip to Tau Ceti IV was winding to a close as Esper and Roddy returned to the *Mobius*. Her borrowed datapad was filled with items and their associated prices from their day's window-shopping. Esper held the screen so that the laaku mechanic could follow along as she explained her vision. "There's plenty of room for a washroom, mini fridge/food-processor combo, and a holo-projector, not to mention a bed, dresser, and all that other stuff. A tiny hotel room right here on the *Mobius*."

Roddy rolled his eyes. Esper was meant to notice, but she deigned not to acknowledge. She continued delving into details of plumbing fixtures and upholstery as they made their way through the cargo bay. But when Roddy opened the door to the common room, their conversation stopped abruptly as a wall of deafening noise from the holo-projector drowned them out.

Unlike most of the ancient fare that cluttered up the computer core, Esper recognized this one from the promotional vids from a few years back. She couldn't recall the name, but it was a Zach Spanner military-action vid. They were all alike, as near as she could tell; some misfit pilot nearly gets his squad killed—or he does get them killed early on and he's the only survivor—and loses his confidence, only to save the day in the third act. In the holographic field, little generic enemy spacecraft were blowing up at a mind-boggling rate as the hero spouted patriotic jeers at them—as if it were their fault for not being born human.

Carl sat slumped on the couch, watching the action with dead eyes. By his side, Mort appeared to be in much better spirits, munching on cheese-drizzled chips as he took in the show.

"Lousy fuckers," Roddy griped loudly enough to be heard over an exploding ship. "You loaded up *Last Stand at Zulu Seven* without me?"

Mort elbowed Carl in the ribs, and it roused him enough to pause the vid. The din ebbed to background levels. "Don't worry about it," Mort replied. "We can watch it again later. His eyes are open, but nothing's getting in."

"Yeah," Roddy replied, pointing at the frozen hologram. "But now I know how it's going to end."

Mort scoffed. "If you don't know how it's going to end, you haven't watched *Last Stand at Luna, Last Stand at Daedalus Colony,* or *Last Stand of Miracle Squadron.*"

Esper studied Carl as he slouched. It was unlike him to

remain silent. He wasn't normally the sort to let a conversation happen without him. "What's wrong with Carl?"

"Oh, that's right. You're still new around here," Mort said. "You're familiar with Carl the Starship Captain, Carl the Swindler, and Carl the Cocksure Ex-Fighter Pilot. You might even have met Carl the Drunken Ladies' Man, though that's none of my business. Well ..." He bracketed Carl with his outstretched hands, "Meet Carl the Just Lost All His Money at Poker."

"*All* his money?" Esper asked.

"Bullshit," Roddy muttered.

"He was smart enough to pre-pay his tram fare round-trip, or we would've had to send someone to get him," Mort replied.

"How'd we let him wander off on his own again?" Roddy asked.

Mort shrugged. "We'd already split the take from the Hadrian advance. It's *his* money he lost."

"And the ship fund?" Roddy asked. "I'm the one who has to deal with this bucket on no budget."

"Paid the fuel guy before I left," Carl muttered.

"Oh, so you're not catatonic over there, gamblin' man?" Roddy asked. "I spend the whole goddamn day trying to keep Esper's hotel idea below cost so there'd be enough left over to overhaul the power plant. We've beaten that poor thing to hell."

"So ... what?" Esper asked, waving the datapad. "We can't put in passenger quarters now?"

"Not unless we're converting the ping-pong table into a bunk," Roddy replied.

The scrabbling of approaching claws carried through the door to the cargo hold. Seconds later, the door opened and Kubu bounded through, followed by Tanny. He leaped onto the couch and forced himself between Carl and Mort, curling into a ball.

"I take it he didn't like the university?" Esper asked.

"I swear this animal is bigger than when you left with him," Mort said, edging away from the furry mass.

"I left him there a couple hours while they did some intelligence testing on him," Tanny replied. She raised an eyebrow at Kubu. "Apparently, he's not brain damaged, this is normal for whatever he is."

"Still no idea what species this sack of muscle is?" Roddy asked.

"That Dunkirk guy is still working on it," Tanny replied. "We might not have an answer by the time we drop out of here, so I left him a comm ID where he could contact me."

Roddy grunted. "Chip was always good for a secure false comm ID. You gonna be clean?"

"The guy's a university professor," Tanny replied. "What's he going to do?"

Just then a muffled chime emanated from Carl's pocket. It was an unfamiliar melody, but it sounded like one of Carl's classical rock pieces, with scratchy guitars making the lyrics incomprehensible. He dug a datapad from inside his jacket. "Knock it off, everyone," he said. "Unknown ID. Shit." He answered the call. "Hey, who you looking for?"

Whoever was on the other end of the connection was too quiet for Esper to hear.

"I might be," he answered. "Who told you that?... Never heard of him. ... Yeah, yeah, sure... You got a name?... Hope you don't mind me checking up on that ID... No, that's not a problem. ... Depends. How soon you need us there?... No, I'd rather work out those details in person. There's only so far I'm trusting this comm link. ... All right. It's a deal."

Carl shut down the datapad and slipped it back inside his jacket. "Which one of you was blabbing?"

He had asked the room at large, but his eyes were on Esper. "Why are you looking at me?"

"Tanny, did you happen to mention to anyone that we were getting into the passenger business?" Carl asked. She shook her head. "How about you, Mort?"

"I was bowling," Mort said. "Found a few lanes in the arcanopolis in Stevenston. Just a bunch of Order of Gaia blowhards. I could have flat out told them I was a Convocation fugitive and they'd have brushed it off. None of them have been off-world in his life, and most probably couldn't work a comm."

"How about you, Roddy? You go bar-hopping and spill our plans?"

"Piss off," Roddy replied. "I was with Miss Baroque here, picking out bed linens and furniture."

Esper gave a sheepish smile. "Maybe Mriy..."

"She's hiking," Carl replied. "And she's *such* a gossip, especially to people who can't understand azrin."

Roddy squinted up at Esper. "Wait a minute. You told them what we were outfitting, didn't you?"

Esper held up her hands. "Just the appliance salesman and the woman at the store where we found the bed I wanted. It was easier than trying to explain all the corridors we had to transport things through and the layout of the conference room. Once they knew it was a modified turtledove-class shuttle—"

"Wait, you told them we were a chop-ship?" Tanny asked.

"That explains how they ID'ed us, at least," Carl said, nodding to himself. "Someone in one of those stores did some digging and found a non-standard turtledove that landed recently. Not exactly astral cartography. It's beside the point now, anyway. Someone wants to hire us."

"I figured that much from your half of the conversation," Tanny said. "What's the job?"

"Passenger transport," Carl replied. "Pickup is in-system on Drei, one of Tau Ceti VII's moons. Drop-off details to be provided in person."

"That's a rough neighborhood," Tanny said.

"I imagine that's why they wanted someone like us."

"Hold on a minute," Esper said. "Since it seems to be something we need to ask around here, *who* are we transporting? We running slaves, kidnapped witnesses, escaped inmates ... am I getting warm?" After the incident at the Gologlex Menagerie, she felt the need to get the unpleasantries out in the open up front.

"It was the guy on the comm," Carl said. "Can't promise he hasn't escaped from anywhere, but he gave me an ID to run a background on him. Either he's clean or has a nice forged ID."

"Who's gonna run that background?" Roddy asked. By his tone, it wasn't going to be him.

Carl just shrugged. "Wasn't going to bother. Chip might have cracked a false ID, but no one here can do better than taking whatever bait he left us. I'll dig up the basics on the omni, just to see what he looks like."

Mort cleared his throat. "Where's he going to sleep?"

"Shit," Carl muttered as he threw his head back against the couch cushions.

---

Tau Ceti VII had three moons, all terraformed: Einer, Zwei,

and Drei; none was the sort of place that drew vacationers from far-flung systems. It was a hazard of being one of the first systems humans colonized; terramancers were more than willing to stick close to home and keep making every orbital body habitable, rather than traipse across the galaxy. Despite its potato-like shape, Drei was a warren of cities connected by tramway tunnels, clinging to a breathable atmosphere.

All the landing bays were of Port-of-St.Paul enclosed, which was just as well, because the air quality on the moon was notoriously rough on non-natives. As Carl stepped off the cargo ramp, he stumbled in the gravity change. Here and there you'd find an inhabited world with as much as a 10 percent variance from Earth's gravity, but moons threw a lot of those rules out the airlock. Drei had less than half of Earth Standard, and every organ in Carl's body shifted under the new, lesser pull.

"I hate that," he muttered. "Why can't you people just fix that shit when these moons get terraformed?"

Mort snorted. He strode past the bounding Carl as if the moon's gravity wasn't affecting him any differently. "Just ignore it. Besides, they built this place centuries ago. I doubt the locals would take kindly to anyone mucking about with their little worldlet. Locals are funny like that. Consistent too. Just about anything you'd like to fix is some sort of offense. Nasty buggers, locals."

"No, Kubu," Tanny said, holding the dog at bay. "Stay." Kubu was having no part of being left behind, trying to force his way past Tanny to follow Carl.

Carl turned back, regretting the sudden motion while his mind and body were still struggling to assimilate to the gravity shift. "Maybe you should just stay on board. It's not like we can't handle this ourselves. Besides, Kubu might get into just about anything."

"I'm not a dog-sitter," Tanny snapped, despite having her arm wrapped around Kubu's chest in a wrestling hold.

"Hey, he's your responsibility."

Tanny fumed, but Roddy hit the release to raise the cargo ramp. Ex-wife, mechanic, and dog all disappeared from view.

"The dark beast shall be the death of us all," Mort said, his voice dry and sepulchral.

Carl shied away from him. "Was that supposed to be some sort of prophecy?"

Mort just snickered, his shoulders shaking gently. "Nah, I imagine the overgrown slipper-chewer will grow out of it. Tanny's just in for a rough go of it in the meantime."

"I didn't know you knew anything about dogs."

"What's to know? Simplest creatures on Earth. Probably simplest creatures on whatever planet Kubu's from. Not a bit of guile or malice in them."

"Well, odds are this guy we're meeting has plenty of both," Carl said. They walked from the hangar area into the public section of the spaceport. There were the usual shops and cafés, as if someone designing a spaceport figured anyone new planetside needed a memento shirt or a cup of overpriced coffee. The central hub of the plaza featured a decorative fountain with sprays and jets of water that drifted in the low gravity to catch offworlders' attention.

"What kind of a name is that, anyway? Bryce Brisson?" Mort asked. "It has to be a fake."

"Could be," Carl agreed. "Or maybe his parents just hated him. Didn't do him any favors in life, if any of that bio is real. He's done time—nothing major. A couple cons, a hold-up, shit that'd get you dusted on Earth but only a couple years' cold time in the borderlands."

"Wash the suds off the notion that any of that poppycock is worth a damn," Mort said. "Want to know if a man's a phony? Look him in the eye. All a matter of observation and a keen understanding of the mind."

"Try me," Carl said.

"Anyone *else*."

"Well, we're going to be in for a lot more keen looks into guy's eyes if we don't find another tech juggler," Carl said. "I've been thinking of asking Esper to take a course over the omni."

"Whoa there, cowboy," Mort said, holding up both hands and waggling them. "I like that girl. Got a head between those ears of hers. In all the time you've had the *Mobius*, we haven't kept anyone in that job who hasn't either come to a bad end or stuck a knife in us when time came to share the spoils of our own cleverness."

Carl sighed. It was an old argument, but he pulled on his verbal boxing gloves once again. "It's all a matter of coincidence. There's nothing to say Esper will have anything bad happen to her just because she knows how to wrangle a computer core or slog through the muck in the back alleys of omni. And can you honestly picture her turning on us? She won't even fire a blaster at a target dummy that's shaped like a human."

"We're damn fools if we let her," Mort replied. "Time and again the universe tells us we're not supposed to muck around with that garbage. How many times do you have to burn your hand to stop sticking it in the fire?"

"Maybe this Bryce guy will be a computer Einstein," Carl said. "We can have him run a check on his own fake ID."

Mort sighed. "You're doing that mocking little sing-song thing again. I win the argument."

"Fuck you and your argument rules! The universe is *not* trying to send me a personal message about who I can hire for my crew."

Mort grunted. "Where are we supposed to find this mystery passenger?" The two of them passed the Chugga-Guzzle that marked the end of the shopping area. Overhead signage pointed out various outlets into the surrounding city of Tangiers Gamma.

"I wanted to scout this place out for a good meet-up spot and send him a comm." Carl took a moment to glance at his options and headed in the direction of the Galveston District. The subheading mentioned industrial processing, ore refinery, and freight transfer—not the sort of place many people would go by accident.

"So, we're just wandering?"

Carl took a bounding step and turned in mid-air to face Mort. "For now."

Mort glared sidelong at Carl, and might have raised some objection, had not someone beaten him to it. "Sir, if you'll step aside please," a helmet-muffled voice addressed Carl.

Two uniformed security officers separated themselves from the crowd and barred Carl and Mort's path. Behind the helms, they probably bore distinguishing features, but with the darkened visors, gloved hands, and regulation law-enforcement physique, it was impossible to tell one from the other.

"Sorry fellas; there must be some mistake," Carl said with an easy smile. It was a reflex. He hadn't given any thought to the response. "We just got here."

"Get back to us in an hour, maybe two if we're slow," Mort

added. That was when Carl knew the wizard was thinking along with him. They weren't going quietly.

The security officer tapped a finger on the side of his visor. "You are Captain Bradley Carlin Ramsey of the Earth-registered ship *Mobius*. There is a warrant for your arrest for an incident that took place on Orion Station Echo Nine. Please place your hands on your head."

Carl blinked in disbelief. His first instinct had been that Bryce Brisson had set him up. But this was legit. Someone with too much time on his hands had put together enough pieces to dump the mayhem on Echo Nine at his feet. The paltry blaster pistols in the officers' hands had every right to be aimed his way. From his vantage, Carl couldn't tell whether they were set to stun. If Mort wasn't quick, that little detail might make all the difference. Trusting that this wasn't a "he was reaching for a weapon" setup, Carl complied. The stream of factory workers and freight handlers that had filled the corridor a minute earlier dispersed with guilty haste, as if they all wanted to dissociate themselves from whatever Carl had done.

"I'm sure we can work something—"

There was a minor tremor in the air, and a sound like a faulty compressor coil just before it burnt out. One of the security guards dropped to the floor like dead weight. The tremor and sound repeated, and this time Carl saw the blue of the stun bolt just as it struck the second guard and sent him limply to the ground as well.

The man with the stun pistol in his hand looked familiar, just like his flatpic on the omni. Bryce Brisson wore a comm headset with the mic flipped away from his face, and carried a travel pack over one shoulder. "I'd hoped to meet under less urgent circumstances, but we can work out a payment once we're off this rock."

"Um, thanks," Carl said, his fingers still laced together, resting on his head.

"This is our fare?" Mort asked.

"You boys always this slow?" Bryce asked, waving the stun pistol in a beckoning gesture toward the hangars. "We've gotta get out of here."

Carl opened his mouth. Words were about to come out—something protesting the presumption on the part of one Bryce Brisson, prospective passenger. But there were two stunned security officers on the ground at his feet, and enough witnesses that there was a good chance one might decide he didn't have amnesia and ID Carl and Mort. The words on the tip of Carl's tongue transformed. "We've got to stash these guys."

"We can shove them in there," Mort said, pointing to a nearby door labeled "Grade Epsilon Clearance Required."

"Hacking that will take more time than we've—" Bryce began, but he stopped himself mid-sentence. Mort had already made his way to the door. With none of the wizardly trappings of spellcasting, he simply jammed a finger into the key-card reader. The metal of the device glowed red as Mort's finger pushed through, and the innards crackled and sparked in their death throes. The door popped open.

"Give me a hand," Bryce said to Carl, reaching down to grab hold of one of the security guards. Before he could reach the limp form, both guards slid along the floor, pulled by an unseen force.

"No time for mucking around with grunt work," Mort said. "And since we're past the point of subtlety ..." He muttered something guttural and pointed a finger down the corridor and upward. A gout of flame spilled forth from empty air, setting off alarms and sending the remaining bystanders scattering.

"Holy shit," Bryce said, throwing an arm up to shield his face.

"You're with us, I guess," Carl said. "Come on."

The run was awkward in the low gravity. Carl bounded along with Bryce as his heels. Mort outpaced them, taking advantage of being able selectively ignore the effects of gravity on his creaky old carcass.

"Can you call ahead to your ship?" Bryce asked, huffing as he ran.

Carl broke stride to fish his comm from his jacket pocket. He hit the transmit button, but the device failed to respond. "Nope," he replied. "Mort blew my comm with his little tantrum."

"You should have mentioned wanting to call the ship sooner," Mort said.

"Half the responders in the city are going to be heading this way to deal with that fire," Bryce said. "I was counting on us having a few minutes' head start before anyone knew what was going on."

"We still ... have it," Carl replied, beginning to feel the effects of a sedentary life aboard ship. The run was wearing on him already. A hover-shuttle headed their way bearing four red-garbed emergency personnel in full environmental protective gear, faces hidden behind breather helmets. "Fire! Back ... that way!" Carl shouted to them, pointing the direction they had come from. As soon as they were past, he slowed to a walk, then stopped. "Hold up. They're dealing with a fire, not us. Play this cool and we get back to the *Mobius* like nothing happened."

Mort slowed to match his pace. "Good enough for me. I'm too old for shit like this. What do you think they'll have done to keep us from flying off?"

"Probably a no-fly order to traffic control," Carl replied, still breathing heavily. "There's nothing between us and the Black Ocean, though; this is a moon, not a sealed station. We're likely to get patrol craft after us."

They entered the plaza, which looked like a different world with the chaos of commerce and idle snacking replaced by the chaos of fire response teams coming and everyone else fleeing for cover.

"Leave that to me," Bryce replied. "I've got claws in local computer systems. I can get them seeing false images on their sensors, enough to throw them off for an escape."

*Oh, really?* Carl remembered Chip saying something like that once. It had worked, but Carl had written off having that sort of technical help on board since Chip's death. Maybe this Bryce was worth more than just a paying fare. "Bryce, you carrying your fare in that pack by any chance?"

"Captain Ramsey, I'm carrying all my worldly possessions in this pack," Bryce replied.

"Good, because we still have to work out a payment for this trip of yours."

"Maybe now's not the best time to be negotiating," Bryce said.

"Look," Carl said. "We're about five minutes—maybe six—from blasting off this rock with a whole freighter of trouble left in our wake. If you don't want to be the one to clean it up, I think you're going to take whatever I offer."

"You're bluffing," Bryce said. "You wouldn't risk having half the planetary defense force after you."

"If there's one thing my crew can tell you: I never know when to back off a bluff. Your fare is that pack of yours and everything in it, and I'm guessing it's still not going to cover the fallout from this shit supernova."

"Anyone ever tell you you're an ass?" Bryce asked. When Carl just grinned in reply, he relented. "Deal."

---

The *Mobius* was still waiting for them when they got to the hangar. All along the retreat, Carl had a nagging worry that there would be an armed security unit waiting there for him, with an impounded ship and his crew already taken into custody. The cargo bay door lowered as they approached, and Roddy gave the fleeing trio a wave.

"Didn't expect you guys back so soon," he shouted across the hangar bay. "This our guy?"

"Fire up the engines," Carl called back. "Comm Tanny and tell her if she's not in the cockpit by the time I get there, I'm flying."

"We in some kind of—"

"NOW!"

"Sure thing, boss-man," Roddy replied. He hit the comm panel by the cargo bay door. Carl couldn't hear what he said, but Roddy held up his hands in a placating gesture that was lost on Tanny at the other end of the conversation. Apparently Carl's impromptu departure was an inconvenience.

A minute later, Carl, Mort, and Bryce were in the common room. Mort collapsed onto the couch, while Bryce stood with one hand on the strap of his pack, looking lost. "Where can I get a good signal?"

"Cockpit," Carl replied. "With me. Mort, you get ready to take us astral."

"Wait ... the wizard's doing it?" Bryce asked with a rising note of panic. "No offense, but I assumed you people used a star drive. I didn't sign on for—"

"I didn't sign on for any of this," Carl snapped. There was a telltale shift in the feel of the floor beneath his feet. The subtle shift in engine vibration meant that they had just cleared the ground. "We're past the point of leaving you behind. So suck it up and trust us to get you out of here ... our way."

Carl strode down the corridor to the cockpit. En route they passed the converted conference room. The door was open, and Esper was waiting inside, but there was no time for her just then. "Carl, what's—" she began, but Carl was already past the doorway and she let the question drop.

"Tanny, what've we got?" Carl asked as he leaned over the co-pilot's seat.

"How about you tell *me* that?" Tanny sniped back. "Where are we even heading?"

"They were waiting for us with a warrant," Carl replied. "Just plot us a course anywhere extra-solar. We'll worry about navigation once we're astral. Oh, and watch out for planetary security. By the way, this is Bryce. Bryce, Tanny. Tanny, Bryce Brisson."

"Where can I interface?" Bryce asked.

Carl stepped aside and allowed Bryce into the co-pilot's seat. "Work it."

"What's he—?"

Carl didn't let Tanny finish. "He's putting enough ships on the planetary sensor net that we can slip away in the confusion. I guess he's good at that sort of thing."

Bryce fished a device from his pack that looked like a miniature computer core. He took a cable that sprouted from one end of it and scanned the ship's main console until he found a matching port. "Give me a few seconds to get connected, and ... what the ...?" He gave the portable core a firm whack and squinted at the display. "It's dead."

"We're dead," Tanny said matter-of-factly. The *Mobius* was picking up five patrol class closing on their location. She looked up at Carl and shook her head in disgust. "You're as good with techies as you are with cards."

Carl scanned the sensor displays. They had chosen Port-of-St.Paul for its relatively remote location, so there was some slop in the patrol response window. "We've got time. Get us to orbit and park just out of atmo." He hit the comm. "Roddy, get the shields ready to take a pounding." Keying off the comm, he rushed from the cockpit.

"Where you going?" Tanny asked.

"To make Mort's day."

---

Esper sat on the couch with her hands folded in her lap. She had fled there after Carl and their new passenger flew past the guest quarters. Something was wrong, she had realized, and Mort had confirmed her suspicion. The wizard sat beside her, leaning forward to rest elbows on his knees.

Footsteps pounded down the corridor toward them, culminating in Carl's breathless entrance. "Mort, I need you to be ready. Drop us... soon as I say."

"How deep?" Mort asked.

"*Bury* us."

A glint flickered in Mort's eye as he replied. "As you command, Lord Ramsey."

Carl gave him a raised eyebrow. "Don't go archaic on me. Just get us astral enough that planetary security can't fire on us." He held up a palm to calm Mort's manic look, then headed back toward the cockpit.

"You!" Mort said, pointing a finger squarely at Esper. "Fetch my things. The staff is in plain view, the robe hanging in the closet, my chain of office is under the dirty laundry pile."

"But why can't—"

"Just do it!" Mort snapped. He leapt to his feet and paced the common room, hands outstretched. Esper edged past him and opened the door to his quarters.

She had poked her head inside Mort's quarters once or twice, but never set so much as a foot within. She had, in fact, avoided going inside anyone else's quarters but her own since she'd been aboard the ship. But she had made especially sure to steer clear of the living quarters of Mordecai The Brown. Issues of privacy and personal space aside, there was something unnatural about the air that wafted out the door each time it opened. It was anachronism embodied in a cloister of a bedroom, from the antique wrought iron candleholders to the shelves filled with paper books; it belonged in a museum or a retrovert colony, not aboard a starship.

But there was an urgent need, and Esper had no time to worry that she was stepping into the seventeenth century as she crossed the threshold. There was a musty smell inside, something that the ship's air filtration seemed unable to remedy, but she was otherwise no worse for her entry into Mort's domain. From the rugs thrown across the steel floor to the clutter that hung from every wall, it would have been easy to fool herself into believing she was in an old-Earth cottage from a holovid—if not for the massive window that showed the moon Drei rapidly falling away beneath them.

Esper found the staff first, resting against the headboard of Mort's bed, and she used the butt end of it to shift aside soiled wizard-wear on the floor until a silver chain emerged from the pile of cloth. The metal was pleasantly warm in her hand, reminding her that it was no ordinary substance. Each link was as thick as her little finger, and the pendant that hung from it bore the insignia of the Convocation—a letter 'C' struck through with a lightning bolt. Mort's closet was a jumble of sweatshirts and novelty sweaters from dozens of different worlds, but one leather garment bag stood apart from the rest. Unzipping it, she found a well-tended robe, cleaner and in better repair than anything else in Mort's closet.

Back in the common room, she helped Mort wriggle into the robe and then handed over the staff and chain. The blue atmosphere outside the overhead dome was tinged in red as the *Mobius'* shields ignited the oxygen and forced it out of their path. The fires gave way to the quiet, endless void of the Black Ocean as they achieved orbit. The ship shuddered.

"We're parking," Carl's voice came over the intra-ship comm. "Get us out of real-space before the satellite defenses pulverize us." As if to emphasize his point, the ship shook once more.

Mort pointed to a seat on the couch. "Silent. Still. Understood?"

Esper nodded, keenly aware of the first of Mort's commandments.

With a flourish that sent the voluminous sleeves of his robe fluttering, Mort spread his arms, staff held clutched in one hand. Raising Earth-born old wood over his head, he grabbed hold of it with his other hand as well and slammed the butt end to the floor. The ship convulsed, and Esper couldn't tell whether it was Mort's doing or the work of Drei's defense force. Either way, the Black Ocean's eponymous color soon faded to the now-familiar grey of astral space as Mort chanted.

She had heard his spellcasting before, but this time there was an urgency in his voice, something plaintiff and raw that made her curious what sort of argument he and the universe were having. Being magical itself, it was strange that the earring charm she wore couldn't—or wouldn't—translate it.

Esper expected Mort to stop at any moment, but he kept up his chant. He gestured with his hands and shook his staff as if some rival debater threatened to win the day. The flat gray outside the domed glassteel ceiling deepened, not darker but rather acquiring an element of depth that it had previously lacked. Esper dug her fingers into the couch cushions to hold on as vertigo swept over her, but she couldn't bring herself to look away or close her eyes. It seemed an affront to the wonder before her not to witness it. An iridescence swirled in as Mort's chanting grew frantic. Soon the whole sky shifted in swirls and whorls of purple. The purple darkened and reddened as Mort screamed primordial syllables. Esper spared a glance from the astral miracle outside to see Mort's face dripping sweat. With a final shout and the slamming of his staff once more against the steel floor, the sky settled back into purple and stayed that way.

Mort stood panting, leaning on his staff for support. "That ought to do it."

"So..." Esper said, not quite sure what to say after such a display. "Where are we?"

Mort managed a weary chuckle. "Damned if I know. We're not dead. The rest can wait. I need a nap." Without any further comment he shambled off toward his quarters.

Soon after the door thumped shut, Carl peeked into the room from the cockpit corridor. "What the *hell* was that?"

Esper felt drained. Her fingers were stiffened into claws from gripping the fabric of the couch, and whatever worries had welled within her had been siphoned out by Mort's simple pronouncement that they were still alive. "Well, Mort purpled the universe, but I'm guessing you could see that up front. He almost redded it, which I gather would have been bad, but he managed to convince it to be purple for us instead. If you want a better answer, you're going to have to wait out Mort's nap. How deep did he put us, anyway?"

Tanny walked in behind Carl. "We've got no way to tell. The astral depth sensors work by scanning progressive depths back to real-space to pick up E-M radiation. They can't find real-space from where we are."

"So..." Esper said.

"We could be five minutes from any system in the galaxy," Carl said, "but with no way to navigate."

"Does this happen often?" Bryce Brisson was out of sight down the corridor, but Esper knew his voice by process of elimination.

"No," Esper replied with a sigh. "It's something different every time."

Roddy walked into the common room to find the rest of the crew sitting around in an uncomfortable silence, along with their new passenger.

"I know I'm not gonna like the answer," he said, "But what the hell just happened? The engines went into an overload lock and restart, and that's about the best news I've got."

"I'd have called down to tell you," Carl replied, "But the comm's down."

Roddy lifted his palms to the ceiling. "You couldn't have, maybe, *yelled down* or something?"

"Didn't think you'd take this long coming up."

"I'm the mechanic, and the *Mobius* is falling apart around me," Roddy griped. "Either Mort fucked something up, or the planetary defenses got us and this is hell."

"Pretty sure this isn't what hell would be like," Esper replied.

"Although ..." Carl said, taking aim with the holovid remote and pressing several buttons with no response. "Adrift with a blown holo-projector would be a good start."

Roddy frowned. "Gimme that!" He took the remote and ambled over to the holo-projector, pressing buttons all the way. "What the ..." he muttered to himself. Prying open an access panel, he peered inside. One of the circuit cards popped out after a brief wiggle. "*This* shouldn't be possible. This thing's right in the middle of where Mort always stands to send us astral; it's packed with more glyphed obsidian rods than ... well anything I've ever worked on. That's for sure." He shoved the circuit card into Carl's hands.

He took it gingerly, as if it would be hot, but it was just cool, hard plastic. Holding it up to his eye, he squinted at the surface and noticed the striations across the whole length of the card. "What am I looking at?"

"Those ripples," Roddy said, "Those aren't supposed to be there at all. It's like ... I dunno, we went astral faster in some parts of the ship than others. Engines took a bit of roughing up —not as bad as this. But the *Mobius* just got pressed through a toothsoap tube or something."

Carl sighed. "Well, I guess no holovid to watch while we wait for Mort to wake up and get us back to a depth we can—"

"You're not getting it," Roddy said. "There's no more holovid until we buy a new one. Circuit traces are disrupted and cross-connected. The data matrix is scrambled eggs. This thing's nothing but an awkward table now."

"The main computer is still fine," Tanny said. "I mean, we can't compute a heading, but the nav-comp *knows* we can't."

"We're lucky fucks, then," Roddy replied.

"Well," Bryce said. "At least they stopped shooting at us."

Carl chuckled. "They did, at that. Gotta wonder what those trigger-happy bastards were thinking when we dropped off the far end of the astral sensors."

"Yeah," Tanny said dryly, folding her arms. "I feel much better knowing that we crippled our ship to confuse some pisspot lunar militia who wanted you for questioning."

"Better than taking a chance," Carl replied. He turned to Bryce. "Since there's nothing to watch, want to see your quarters?"

---

The converted conference room echoed their footsteps as Carl and Bryce entered. Aside from a cot and a rickety bedside table, the room was empty. The full-wall window cast everything in a hazy purple hue from the strange astral space outside.

"Cozy," Bryce said deadpan.

"Reminds me of a song," Carl replied.

"Considering the fare you're charging, I was getting a little embarrassed," Bryce said. He unslung the pack from his shoulder and pressed it into Carl's hands. "Now it seems like a fair trade."

Carl grimaced. After all they had just been through, it didn't seem right taking everything Bryce had left. "Sorry," he said. "I just can't—"

"Like hell you can't," Bryce replied. "A deal's a deal."

Curiosity piqued, Carl unbuckled the pack and peeked inside. A smattering of A-tech devices nestled among a change of clothes. He was no expert, but the brands were top-of-the-line: ClanCore, Nano Nano, Fylax, and one in laaku that he recognized by logo alone. "Lemme guess ..."

"Yup," Bryce said. He looked Carl up and down. "Clothes'll probably be a bit loose on you, but they're worth more than the pile of scrap circuits after your wizard's little stunt."

"He means well."

Bryce turned his back and meandered over to the window. "Not my problem, now. All I've got is a ticket to a system of my choosing."

"About that ..."

Bryce whirled, scowling. "You're not stiffing me."

Carl held up his hands. There was a good chance that the blaster in Bryce's holster was at least temporarily out of commission, if not permanently fried. Mort was asleep. Tanny and Mriy were too far to intervene. It was the sort of survival math that ran through Carl's head any time danger presented itself outside a cockpit environment. "'Course not! You just haven't mentioned where you're going."

Bryce nodded to himself and scratched beneath an ear. "Yeah. Guess I haven't. You know the Freeride System?"

"Sure," Carl replied. The official name was Syrbaat, or Syerbat or something tongue-twisting, but hardly anyone called it by that name. Certainly, no one who belonged there would use the scientific nomenclature. "The Poet Fleet's turf. We've been out that way before. Not the nicest neighborhood, but if you wanted to travel in the protection of ARGO's loving chokehold you wouldn't have hired us."

Bryce gave him a puzzled look. "You're not even going to haggle?"

Carl puzzled right back at him. "What do you mean?"

"I paid you with a sack of dead A-tech and my dirty laundry," Bryce replied, prompting Carl to hold the pack away from him. "And then I ask you to take me halfway across ARGO space to a system with black-level security."

"Like you said," Carl replied. "A deal's a deal. Besides, black schmack. Security is fine out there if you play by their rules. It's just not ARGO security. Hell, maybe we can find some work out there to pay for repairs."

"So ... you're not even worried about this?" Bryce asked, jerking a thumb at the swirling chaos outside the ship.

"Just looking at it makes me want to vomit," Carl confessed. "But Mort'll get us out of this. Don't worry. Just *whatever* you do, don't wake him up."

Bryce grunted. "Grumpy wizard. Tell me something new."

"Not grumpy," Carl corrected. "Forgetful. Might take him a minute to remember we brought you on with us. Last thing you want is Mort thinking you're an intruder."

"I'll keep that in mind," Bryce said. He flopped down onto the bed with a long-suffering sigh. "Does this bed smell like dog?"

"No," Carl replied. "Of course not."

---

Kubu sat on Mommy's bed. It was nice enough—the blankets smelled like her. She had left him a bucket of water and a pair of boots to chew on, but there wasn't much else to do in the little room. There was nothing to look at outside the window, just a lot of purple sky. The purple sky had stopped being interesting once Kubu realized there were no birds or animals out in it. It was just a boring purple sky.

Kubu was hungry. He was usually hungry enough to eat, but this was the bad kind of hungry that made him wish that Mommy's boots were just a little easier to chew. The dry slab of meat she had left with him was a faint memory in his tummy, already grumbled up and ready to drop somewhere later—but not in Mommy's room. Mommy had trouble getting her point across most of the time, but she'd managed to make that one clear.

Mommy had been gone too long. There was a chance that she might never come back. A rational part of Kubu's brain told him that was silly, and that Mommy would be back; that kept him from being sad about his temporary abandonment. The less rational part told him that he needed to eat something, even if it wasn't yummy.

Yelling at the door did no good. He'd tried it enough times to know that Mommy couldn't hear him through it. Mommy's ears weren't very good, because he could hear voices on the other side sometimes. He tried to open the door himself, but his paws couldn't work the handle. It was time to take matters into his own jaws.

Mommy didn't keep lots and lots of things in her room. There were her dress-up clothes, and the leash and harness he had to wear when they went outside the ship. There was a big box he couldn't get open, and a few funny-tasting things that were too hard to gnaw on. Kubu nosed around the room, sniffing everywhere he could find for something to eat. Here and there, he pushed aside one of Mommy's strange things or dug behind something to see if anything was hidden there.

He found a bunch of small boxes. They were tucked behind a piece of wall that had just enough room for Kubu to fit a claw into. Mommy ate from a little box just like that every morning. The box was metal, but it cracked open when he bit it and little bits of food fell out with a few shakes. They didn't taste good, but Kubu was hungry, and they were better than nothing—or metal boxes.

It was a lot of work for how little food was in each one, but on the off chance that Mommy might not be back for a long time, Kubu emptied them all. By the time he was finished, if it was possible, he was even *hungrier*. Mommy's little foods were broken. They didn't sate Kubu's hunger; they didn't taste good, and his tummy was starting to gurgle. There weren't a lot of things Kubu had eaten that made his tummy bubble. There was a bucket of bad water in the mean science man's big house that had made him sick. Some spotted mushrooms had made his head funny and his insides wobbly. And one time Kubu had eaten a bunch of little frogs without chewing them first; those felt so bad in his tummy that he puked them back up and didn't even bother eating them again.

This was worse than all of those put together. His head was wobbling, his legs had gone jittery, and the room was getting too hot around him. Kubu was *angry* that Mommy had left him alone. How dare she not give him enough food and make him eat the yucky tiny food in the metal boxes. Kubu's breath came quick and heavy. He bit the mattress from Mommy's bed shook it. It was dry in his mouth though, and Kubu was beginning to notice just how thirsty he was becoming.

With effort, Kubu stood on his hind legs and turned the faucet with a paw. Jamming his face into the sink, he lapped up the water as fast as his tongue would flick. *Mommy, where are you? Kubu isn't feeling good.*

Compared to the homey comfort of the pilot's seat, the co-pilot's side of the *Mobius* felt weird. Tanny hated having Carl there while she flew, and Mriy wasn't much of a conversationalist. The only times he sat in the cockpit were the few occasions when he got to fly. There was a perspective shift that made everything look wrong, like trying to fire a blaster left-handed or sitting on the wrong side of a holovid field.

Of course, the lack of holovid entertainment was the main reason Carl was up front in the first place. The nav computer wasn't much of a pastime, but it beat sitting in a quiet common room with a dead holo-projector.

"This is pointless," Tanny griped. "It's not like anything we plot will be worth a damn once Mort brings us up. The course will change depending on our depth."

Carl rubbed his eyes with his fingers. "I just wanted an idea how long this trip was going to be. If you'd rather just sit here and talk, though, fine."

Tanny cast Carl a narrow glance, then returned her attention to the computer. "If he brings us down to anything around ten astral units, you can figure on a week and a half to get there."

"What about fifteen?" Carl asked.

"Jesus, how deep do you think we *are*?"

"Can't say for certain. All I know is we're in a ..." he reached for a button on the console.

"Not again! Just—"

"*Purple haze, all around* ..." the computer managed before Tanny could squelch the audio playback. Carl giggled.

"You just don't get tired of that joke? How is it that your shitty old music has something for every occasion? We're lost at the deep end of astral space, and some fucker 600 years ago wrote a song, just in case."

"Esper said it got red for a few seconds before Mort settled us in," Carl replied. "If it had stayed red, I didn't have a song for that."

Tanny snorted. "You'd have forced something to fit."

"Hey, how often do you find yourself in a ..."

This time, Tanny caught Carl by the wrist as he reached for the audio controls.

"Purple haze?" Carl sang the line himself.

"I wish Mort had fried the song library," Tanny muttered.

"Hey, at least *you* had your holovids stored in the ship's computer. Me and Roddy lost everything."

"What a shame," Tanny deadpanned.

"Hey, I'm just trying to keep a rosy outlook here, but ..." Purple haze, the ship supplied, "is actually freaking me out a little. Is that what you wanted to hear? Mort can't wake up too soon to fix this, far as I'm concerned."

"You warned the fare?"

"Yeah, Bryce got the standard warning. I don't think he'd dare go near Mort at this point, let alone startle him awake."

———

Sybil and the Sunspots blared a tinny melody from the built-in speakers on Esper's datapad. She kept the volume low so that no one would hear through the walls with the eerie quiet that lingered throughout the ship. It had been years since she'd listened to the group, one of her favorites growing up. It seemed naive and immature now, but when she was twelve it had been profound. Still, it was a comfort, something familiar like the deep black that usually filled the window of her quarters. Esper mouthed along with the words, not quite daring to ask her questionable singing voice to follow the melody out loud.

*Every sky is a blue sky,*
*If you raise yourself above the clouds,*
*If you want your soul to fly,*
*Just sing and raise your voice up loud.*

Esper swayed as she lip-synced, remembering the concert her friend Novembra's mother had taken them to on Phobos. It had been her first trip off Mars, and she could still remember feeling queasy in the unfamiliar gravity until the music started. Sybil and the Sunspots had been on the downside of their popularity by then, but it hadn't mattered; the whole day had been magical, one new experience after another. The little datapad sitting in Esper's lap was struggling to compete with those fond memories, failing to wash away the constant reminder outside her window that all was decidedly not right in the universe just then.

The purple radiance in the deepest reaches of astral space was hypnotic. As much as she tried to push it from her mind, she found herself staring into it once more, as if some great mystery would unfold before her eyes and make sense of the cosmos. There was motion within the radiance, not objects trapped within the deep astral but a movement of the colors themselves. Light and dark hues swirled like oil droplets in water, never mixing to form a uniform shade of violet. Esper's childhood perception tests had placed her within half a standard deviation from the mean on color identification—she had no artist's eye for colors. But staring into the astral depths, she began to note an overall brightening, and perhaps a hint of too much red creeping in.

Her stomach churned as she watched, wondering if she

was the only one paying attention to the ship's plight as it teetered on the edge of astral space so deep they might never return. She moved to stand, to run and shout throughout the ship that they were dropping deeper, but forced herself to sit. It was just her imagination, she convinced herself. Mort went to take a well-deserved rest, and he never would have left them in such peril.

But what if he didn't realize?

Esper clasped her hands in her lap, her grip growing ever more desperate as she watched out the window. Doing nothing might get them all killed. She had to go wake Mort. He could be angry with her all he liked, but the time for peaceful napping was over, wizard or not.

She tore open the door to her quarters and rushed across the empty common room to Mort's. It was doubly odd: once for the emptiness and quiet instead of the every-present holovids, twice for the purple illumination from the domed ceiling. She didn't bother knocking, just opened the door and peeked inside. Mort snored softly, sleeping fully dressed atop his blankets. He had the look of a vagrant with his stained, worn clothes and unshaven face, mouth hanging agape. He stirred at the opening of the door, but did not wake.

"Mort?" Esper whispered, seeking a gentle waking. "Mort ..." she tried once more, in a normal tone of voice. The snoring carried on uninterrupted. With a glance behind her for gossiping eyes, she slipped into the room and closed the door behind her. Tiptoeing across the room for reasons she would struggle to explain if asked, she crept to Mort's bedside. "Mort," she crooned, in her best imitation of her mother's summonses from dreamland when she was a girl. "Time to—"

Mort's hand shot up and caught her by the upper arm. "Who are you? What ... how did you get in here?"

Esper's whole body tensed. "It's me, Esper," she replied. "I came in by—"

"You can't fool me," Mort said, sitting up but not relinquishing his grip. His fingers dug into Esper's bicep and triceps, and she gritted her teeth. She was only thankful he didn't have Tanny's strength or Mriy's claws. "Esper is in the reliquary. I left her there not ten minutes ago. Now speak, or I'll tear the secrets from your mind." With his free hand, Mort took hold of Esper's chin and tried to look into her eyes, but she averted her gaze in time.

With a leverage technique she had learned from Tanny, Esper wrenched herself free of Mort's grasp. "It *is* me," she insisted. "You were dreaming. This is the *Mobius*. We need your help. We're slipping deeper into the astral plane."

"*Mobius* ..." Mort repeated, then nodded slowly. He looked around the room for the first time since waking. "Of course it is ..." He cleared his throat and blinked several times. "Sorry about that. Didn't anyone mention never to wake me when—"

Esper pointed out the window. "There's no time."

Mort followed her finger's indication and looked out upon the purple void. After a moment's inspection, he asked, "How can you tell?"

"Can't you see it? The color is changing?"

Mort gave a twitch of a shrug and a tilt of his head. "Not really, no."

"It's getting darker and redder," Esper said, shaking her pointing finger at the purple. "I'd tell you just to keep watching, but if we *are* drifting, that seems like a bad idea."

"Well, your supposition would be correct if the color were changing," Mort said. "I just don't see it, though."

Esper's eyes went wide. "No! You have to believe me."

Mort shrank back and furrowed his brow. "What?" he asked. "I never said I didn't believe you. Best to bring us back up, before it gets worse. Half a nap's better than none."

Esper folded her hands together and closed her eyes. As she began a silent prayer of thanks, a gentle tug separated her hands. "Don't go giving Him the credit. It's my help you asked for. If you wanted a miracle, you should have asked for one. But you wanted magic, so it's me you came to. If you want to be useful, just tell Him to keep out of the way and let me do my job." As Mort stepped around Esper on his way to the door, he paused and leaned close. "And if I fuck this up, *then* you can pray for help."

When Esper and Mort entered the common room, they discovered that they weren't the only ones there. Carl and Tanny stood with backs turned, staring at the door to Tanny's quarters. A thump issued from the door, and the sound of a muffled growl.

"What's going on?" Esper asked.

Carl twisted around, frowning at the open door to Mort's quarters and the two of them standing just outside it. "Were you two just—? Never mind. Something's wrong with Kubu. He's flipping out in there."

"It's OK, Kubu," Tanny called through the door. "Just ... calm down, and I'll open the door and let you out." She looked over her shoulder. "You guys might want to keep back, just in case."

"If he's gone all zoological, I can—"

"No!" Tanny and Carl shouted in unison, then exchanged a frowning glance.

"Sorry, Mort," Carl replied. "*Mobius* is just a little fragile right now. You zorched the holovid and gave the engines the hiccups. Roddy's pulling his fur out down in the engine room as it is. Aside from bringing us up to a traversable depth, I think you might want to ease off the magic for a while."

"No holovid?" Mort asked.

Carl shook his head.

Mort folded his arms and let out a disgusted sigh. "Blast and be bothered. Was the fridge affected?"

"Beer's fine," Carl confirmed.

"Well, there's that at least."

There was a howl from inside Tanny's quarters. "If you ladies wouldn't mind, get behind cover."

Carl scurried over to join Mort and Esper behind the couch. "Were you two just ... alone?" he asked as he hunkered down.

"Limit your filthy mind to its own affairs," Mort warned. "Esper noticed we're still drifting deeper and came to find me."

"What do you mean, we're—"

Carl's question was cut short by an ear-splitting howl as Tanny opened the door. Kubu bounded from Tanny's quarters like a canine avalanche, bowling Tanny over as if she were a child. She fell back, struck her head on the steel floor, and lay still. Kubu ignored her and headed straight for the refrigerator. "Hungry, hungry, hungry, hungry," he said. Jaws like a hydraulic clamp latched onto the door handle and yanked the fridge open before the handle broke loose and Kubu spat it onto the floor.

Kubu's single-minded assault targeted foodstuffs indiscriminately. He gobbled down leftover meals from the food processor and a half wheel of cheese that had gone so moldy that no one wanted to touch it. Carl let out a quiet yelp as

Kubu bit into can after can of beer, sucking out the fizzing spray of liquid before chewing and swallowing the cans themselves.

Esper moved to approach the canine, but Carl put a hand on her shoulder. "He's hurting himself," Esper said. "Look, his gums are bleeding from the cans."

"What do you think those teeth would do to *you?*" Carl asked.

The door to Mriy's quarters opened, and the azrin emerged, yawning and rubbing an eye with the back of one paw. "What's all the—" She looked toward Kubu.

"Watch out!" Carl shouted across the room. Kubu turned from the fridge and looked right at him. The eyes were vacant, bloodshot, and glassy. A froth of saliva, beer, and blood dripped from the corners of his mouth and from the tip of his lolling tongue. His chest heaved for breath, but his head remained motionless, fixed on the shouted challenge. A bass growl rumbled in Kubu's throat.

The languorous vestiges of slumber evaporated from Mriy as she sprang forward. Before Kubu could leap at Carl, she had her arms around his neck. Kubu thrashed in her grasp, trying to twist loose, but Mriy bore him to the floor under her weight. As the canine struggled to regain his feet, Mriy used her elbows to knock his legs out from under him.

In the momentary reprieve, Esper rushed to Tanny's side. Putting a finger to her throat, Esper felt a pulse. A small puddle of blood was forming beneath Tanny's head. Esper opened one of Tanny's eyelids with her thumb, and found wide pupils and no sign of reflexive response. Esper was no doctor—she hadn't even taken an emergency aid class. All she had to rely on were the scenes from the holovids she had seen countless times. Tanny either had a concussion, a brain aneurysm, or had seen a nebula demon—and they weren't in any sort of nebula, plus she had seen Kubu knock Tanny to the ground. Odds were, she would recover in time, possibly with amnesia or a weird speech condition. In any event, she had to do something.

Esper placed her hands on either side of Tanny's face, putting Mriy's struggles with Kubu from her mind. The skin was already cool to the touch; there was no time to waste. Her lips moved, but she gave no voice to the little rhyme she and her friends had learned to work the spell of healing. "*Cuts close, bruises fade; three weeks healing done today; bones knit, pains ease; cleanse the body of disease.*" She repeated it over and over, and felt Tanny's skin warm feverishly beneath her palms.

Tanny sat up suddenly with a gasp, clutching her stomach. She grunted in pain. "What did you do to me, Esper?"

Esper let out a sigh of relief. "Good, no amnesia. Kubu knocked you out cold. Your head was bleeding, and you weren't waking up."

"But my stomach is on fire," Tanny replied with a grimace. "And what's Mriy doing to Kubu?" She tried to stand, lurching for the wrestling match by the refrigerator, but doubled over instead.

"You need food," Esper replied. "The healing takes a lot out of you."

"And here I thought Carl ... was being a baby about the hunger pangs ... that time you healed him."

"Is it safe to get in there?" Esper called across to Mriy.

"I can hold him away from the food long enough for you to get in," Mriy answered. For all Kubu's compact strength and frenzied struggles, Mriy was nearly twice his mass. She kept him pinned to the floor as he tried to squirm loose and reach the open fridge and what little remained untouched within.

Esper hurried past the struggling pair, tiptoeing around a splatter of ketchup from a ruptured bottle and a small lake of spilled beer. The shelves inside the fridge were in shambles, and not much was left inside that was either edible or potable. Esper grabbed whatever she could lay hands on and returned to Tanny.

"Here," she said, dumping the armload beside Tanny and beginning an inventory. She found the first filling-looking thing in the pile and pressed an eggplant casserole E-Z-Meal into Tanny's hands.

"Who the hell bought this?" Tanny asked accusingly as she tore open the package.

"That would be me," Esper replied. "It was our first stop after I joined the crew. I ... I hadn't remembered how good bacon cheeseburgers were, and I just never got around to—"

"Fine," Tanny replied. "Whatever ..." she muttered as she shoveled the self-warming pasta into her mouth with her fingers. Her head lifted at a canine yelp and subsequent whine. "Mriy, get off Kubu! What do you think you're doing?" At least, that was what Esper imagined she said through a mouthful of eggplant, cheese, and pasta.

"He fights!" Mriy replied. "You were already defeated when I came out."

Tanny cast a suspicious eye into her quarters and the shambles inside. Esper pressed a bottle of peach liquor into her hands and Tanny popped the top with her thumb and sucked half of it down in a few continuous chugs. All the while, she drifted cautiously into the wreckage left in her room. "Shit," she said, wiping her mouth on the sleeve of her jacket. "Esper, where'd the med kit from the conference room end up?"

"It's down in the—"

"Go grab it. Quick. We need to tranq him."

Esper nodded and edged past Mriy and Kubu, still struggling on the floor. Mriy had the canine under control, but that didn't stop his constant efforts to get free. He seemed wild, too far past rational thought even to put words to his frustrations any longer. He snapped at Esper's ankle as she came near, but Mriy got a paw under his jaw and held it shut.

"Should we do anything?" Mort whispered from the corner.

"Hell no," Carl replied in kind, peering over the arm of the couch. "They've got it under control. Plus it's like a full-room holo-projector. Best thing I've watched all day."

---

Esper knocked on the door of the guest quarters, using the butt of her fist. It was a sturdy door, and any other knock would be either too quiet, or hurt her hand. The door's thickness, and perhaps some trick of its design as a conference room door, prevented her hearing the telltale noises of someone coming to answer.

"Is it safe to come out?" Bryce asked as he opened the door a crack.

"All clear," Esper confirmed, trying to sound as perky as possible. No one else seemed inclined to look after their paying customer's happiness, so it had fallen to her.

The door opened all the way, and Bryce slumped against the opening. "I don't know what the deal is with you people, but astral space just was purple for the last three hours, and I thought I heard a wild animal out there."

Esper pursed her lips and frowned. "I'm not sure how

much I can do about that. We might have a spare rug or blanket around somewhere that we can use as additional soundproofing. I'll see what I can—"

"Was there?"

"Was there what?"

"A wild animal."

Esper gave a nervous chuckle. "No, Kubu's domesticated ... sort of. I mean, we don't know what he is, exactly, but he is *very* dog-like. And usually he's pretty friendly, but we cooped him up too long while you were settling in, and he got rowdy." It wasn't the whole story, Esper knew, but it was as much as Tanny had been willing to share on short notice.

Bryce nodded along like someone who was hearing information but failing to absorb it. "Rowdy ..."

Esper nodded exuberantly. "All taken care of. Poor little guy's sleeping it off—erm, behind a locked door."

Bryce swallowed and licked dry lips. "You guys got any food aboard? I was getting a bit between meals when we tucked our tails back on Drei."

It was a subject that was guaranteed to come up sooner or later, but Esper had been hoping it would have leaned toward the later end—when someone else might be around to answer. "Sort of. That is ... I mean ... don't worry, none of us are going to starve or anything like that."

"What's that supposed to mean? Something happen to your supplies?"

"Kubu ... I mean. Yes. But don't worry."

"Listen," Bryce said. "You've got food or you don't. What's to eat around here?"

"We've got sandwich bread we pried out of the food processor along with a dozen centimeters of salami, some salsa dip, and a jar of huckleberry jam."

"That's it?" Bryce asked with a note of alarm in his voice.

"It's a good-sized jar," Esper assured him. "And don't worry, we're due planetside in eighteen hours or so. We'll get some real food there."

"Where we stopping off?"

"Freeride," Esper replied.

"No, I mean on the way? Freeride's weeks from here, even if this thing's flying below military courier depths."

"No, just about eighteen hours," Esper said. "I think if you look out that window some more, you'll see that the gray's still got a tinge of purple in it. So just relax, grab yourself a jam sandwich, and we'll have you to Freeride in no time."

---

Bryce emerged from his rented quarters like a rehabilitated animal being returned to the wild. He looked poised to bolt at any moment for the relative safety of his room. The veneer of cocksure swagger he'd displayed on Drei had rubbed off to reveal a timid tech jockey underneath.

"Come on and join us," Carl offered, beckoning him over the heads of Mort and Roddy. "Pull up a chair. The cards are analog, so they're still working fine. We're playing for dibs on the last bottle of anything drinkable that isn't water." Carl cast a sidelong glance to Roddy, who he knew kept an emergency supply of Earth's Preferred under his bed, but didn't see the point in mentioning that in front of Bryce.

They were gathered at the kitchen table in the common room, next to the refrigerator with its door held shut by mechanics' tape. At the center of the table was the last bottle of Esper's peach liquor. She had donated it to the cause of intra-ship harmony, and declined to play for it, along with

Tanny who had drunk the second-to-last bottle already. Mriy was back in her quarters, exhausted after her prolonged struggle with Kubu.

"What are you playing?" Bryce asked, pulling out a chair and settling in beside Mort.

Carl pushed a pile of loose hardware in Bryce's direction. "Poker. Five card stud. Old school as hell, to humor Mort. You know it?"

"Yeah," Bryce mumbled, looking down at the assorted steel hardware in front of him. "What's all this for?"

"Since we're playing for the booze, we're using those instead of hard-coin. Nuts are fives; washers are ones. Those broken rivet heads are twenty-five apiece."

"Um, sure," Bryce replied. "The girl mentioned something about sandwiches."

Roddy reached back for a plate stacked with square-cut bread designed to feed into the loader of a food-processor. "Knock yourself out. Jam, salami, and mustard are in the freezer. I turned the reducer down to act as a fridge."

Bryce sat out the first two hands as he made himself a sad little meal. Carl didn't mention that the salami was three months past expiration, and that Roddy had hacked the food processor to accept later and later dates to keep it from auto-dumping it.

"Fancy grub," Bryce muttered through a mouthful of dry bread and spoiled salami as he sat down. "Listen, Carl, you and me gotta talk. Is it true we're less than a day out of Freeride?"

"It's all right there in the computers," Carl replied. "Shit, if we could make contact with anyone official, we'd probably be up for some sort of record. Fella could get used to crossing the galaxy at these speeds."

"Don't go getting used to it," Mort interjected. "You're only smug about it because you can't wrap your science-filled head with just how close we all came to oblivion."

"How close *did* we come?" Bryce asked.

Mort raised one eyebrow and squinted at Bryce with the other eye. "I'll tell you how close, tech-boy. We came within the length of a dragon's whisker, the breadth of a silkworm's sigh. There was time, perhaps, for one syllable of the Cladis Grimoire to pass a fool's lips before creation itself snuffed us like a birthday candle."

"Oh," Bryce said.

"Ante up," Roddy said, tossing in two washers.

Bryce tossed two of his own into the middle of the table and cleared his throat. "So anyway ... thought I'd have more time in transit, but we need to talk."

"Can you talk and play at the same time?" Carl asked. Bryce nodded. "Then shoot."

Roddy flicked cards around the table with casual precision. Aside from a peek at his facedown cards, Carl didn't bother moving his from where they came to a halt. Mort tidied his cards manually, pointedly not using his magic. Bryce packed his tight and lined them up like inventory on a store shelf. Secretive. Organized. Obsessive. Carl filed the traits away in case they ever became useful.

"Well, I don't have a job lined up when I get there," Bryce began.

Roddy let out a quick burst of shrieking simian laughter. "Boy, you're pumpin' from a dry well here."

Bryce waved a hand. "No, nothing like that. I've got a line on a job, see? It's just I could use a reference. You know, some sort of good word to get a foot in the door."

"Sure, I guess," Carl replied with a shrug. "You didn't get a chance to show off with the defenses at Drei, but if that had worked... *Man* would that have been something to see. All those defense cannons and ships with their heads spinning, chasing after phantom ships. If you're half as good as you can promise people in desperate need without actually delivering jack shit, then you'd be a credit to anyone looking for one of whatever you actually are."

"He's a doorstop salesman, right?" Roddy asked. "Had a whole pack filled with samples."

"Can it, banana-brain," Bryce snapped, jabbing a finger in the laaku's direction. "Ain't my fault the A-tech I bartered for this hay-ride got wizard-twisted. I'm not asking for charity. I'll make it worth your while."

"How much you thinking?" Carl asked. It was about time to try pinning Bryce to a sum of terras expressed as an actual number, with digits and everything, rather than vague promises and mystery gear.

"Well, I've got ten grand in digital terras, but I might be able to do better in barter," Bryce said.

"In case you hadn't noticed," Roddy said, "We might be in need of repairs. Repairs in a place like Freeride won't come cheap, and they prefer hard-coin terras. Digital might get us somewhere, but chickens, or booze, or whatever shit you're hoping to trade us better convert into a payment to a starship-grade garage."

"There is that," Carl agreed.

"What if I got your criminal records expunged?"

Carl looked to Roddy, then to Mort. Mort and Roddy exchanged a glance of their own. The same skepticism was on every face. "How exactly you planning to pull that shit off?" Carl asked.

"Same way techsters have been beating encryption for

centuries: human weaknesses in the system," Bryce said. "All the best have heartbeat ins at anyplace they want to breach. Some careless, some on the take, mostly just idiots who don't even know they're getting used. It's not all strings of zeroes through fifteens in a computer core. Those are just the accessories. It's the people who service and maintain the systems— they're the real weakness."

"So, who've you got who can alter ARGO law enforcement records galaxy-wide?" Carl asked, discarding a bum hand as the bet came his way.

"That's my value: I know and you don't. I send the right message *from* the right guy *to* the right guy, and some terminal data-entry drone processes the request."

"Just like that? Won't that look a little suspicious?"

"Please ... he'll see your record update right in between entering a court date for an assault trial and authorizing a petty cash expenditure to pay off an informant. You're nothing special; just another box to check off before he can go grab lunch."

"Yeah, smart guy?" Roddy asked. "If you can do all that, why do *you* still have a record?"

"The banana-brain's got you on that one," Mort said.

Bryce shrugged. "I've done my time. Sure, I could wipe it out, but what good's that do me? Guy that's been in, you know he's made of something tougher than some pansy who might piss himself if he ever got wind of a little heat. People I'd want to work for would appreciate that."

"What kind of people you talking?" Carl asked.

"Janice Rucker," Bryce said.

There was a long silence. The card game stood still. "So... lemme guess. It's not a coincidence you tracked us down for transport?" Carl asked. "You know who Tanny is."

"Tania Louise Rucker, daughter of Donald and Sue-Ellen Rucker," Bryce replied. "It's sort of my business, figuring out who knows who. Nothing personal. I'd lump you in under 'on the take' for this job. You're no patsy."

"I say we airlock this weasel," Roddy said.

Bryce knocked his chair over as he leapt to his feet and backed away. "Woah! Hear me out!"

"Go on," Carl said with a smirk. "Roddy's just a mean sober; don't mind him."

"We land. I find a terminal, work my mojo, and your records get cleared. You confirm I done my bit, and that's my resume for Janice Rucker."

Carl scratched at the back of his neck. "What's Janny doing out that far? Don likes keeping business close to Mars." It was annoying to have to find out family news from a stranger. Even if Carl was legally divorced from the family, there was no legal force strong enough to entirely remove him from The Family.

"She's branching out, with Don Rucker's blessing," Bryce said. "I haven't been able to sniff out the terms, but she's on her own in exchange for a kickback."

Carl turned to Mort. "See what I have to put up with? If Tanny would talk to her father, we wouldn't have to learn this shit secondhand. We could've hit Janny up for work."

"Which one was she, again?" Roddy asked. "I have trouble keeping Tanny's cousins straight."

"At the wedding, she was the one with the finger-bone earrings," Mort said. "And the five-terra amulet of Kali."

Roddy shuddered. "Ugh. That one's bad news."

"Most of Tanny's family is bad news, if they don't like you," Carl said. "But Janice isn't half as tough as she tries to look."

"That's still twice as scary as I'd want to turn my back on," Roddy said.

Bryce returned to his seat and tossed in a small bet, though the game was quickly becoming an afterthought. "See why I want someone to smooth my intro?"

"Makes sense," Carl admitted.

"So, think Tanny will do it?" Bryce asked. "I mean, even if she's on the outs with her father, you're her captain, and—"

Roddy burst out laughing, and Mort snickered. "Yeah, as if Carl could *order* her to do anything," Roddy said.

"Not to mention, Janny and Tanny don't exactly get along," Carl said. "Nicknames sounded too much alike. Janny's older, but Tanny's Don's daughter, so she was always on a bit of a pedestal. No, it's *me* you want making the introduction, not Tanny."

"You're smooth with Janny?" Bryce asked.

"You're the people researcher," Carl replied. "Janice Rucker seeing anyone?"

Bryce's brow knit for a moment, then he shook his head.

"Then I can be as smooth as I need to," Carl said, tipping back his chair with a smug grin.

---

"So how do we plot a course change, if we needed to?" Esper asked from the co-pilot's seat. She was sitting with her hands folded in her lap, pointedly not touching anything. The jacket, the coveralls, her hair in a tight bun at the back of her head; everything was just as Tanny had instructed her for getting actual work done aboard ship.

"You don't have to pretend to be interested in this stuff," Tanny replied. "It's sweet that you're worried, but I'm fine now. Thanks." There wasn't even a lingering pain from the blow to her head when Kubu had trampled her. The dumb brute was sleeping off his triple-dose of tranquilizer in her quarters, which had the added bonus of hiding the evidence of what he'd eaten. How could Tanny explain to Esper that the concussion was the least of her troubles.

Tanny's stomach churned, not quite satisfied with the "meal" Esper had scrounged, and even less happy with the alcohol that had washed it down. But those were mere side-effects. The trouble was that Esper's magic had sped her metabolism. She wouldn't know until symptoms started manifesting, but she had burned either hours or days out of her drug regimen, and Kubu had consumed all her recent supplies. The dog-like creature had a digestive tract that a vulture would envy. Had anyone told her a seventy-kilo animal had eaten a two month supply of marine biochemicals, she'd write the creature off as a corpse. Kubu's reaction to the drugs aside, he didn't seem in imminent danger of death.

"I know," Esper replied with a faint smile. It was a trick Carl used. Just agree to shut someone up, and keep on acting like neither of you said anything. "Could I try plotting a heading, and just not confirm?" She reached a finger toward the nav computer.

Tanny batted the hand away, already noticing that her own hand was jittery. "Leave it alone! At this speed, I don't want to touch anything." For at least the hundredth time, she glanced at the astral depth gauge. It read 30.88, with the analogue needle over the digital display pegged at maximum. Before she met Mort, Tanny had figured those gauges only went to up to ten to make ships seem faster than they really were.

"You don't look so good."

"Don't you start that with me," Tanny snapped. Esper had that patronizing look in her eye—pity and sympathy, mixed with a bit of holier-than-thou, I-told-you-so crap.

"Start what?"

"Being a priestess at me."

Esper slumped back in her chair with a sigh. "I don't think I could if I wanted to. I mean, look at me." She gave a two-handed gesture up and down herself. "Who'd come to *me* looking for spiritual solace? I look like an outlaw spacer, because that's what I am, now."

"Worse things to be," Tanny muttered. "But you still act like a priestess, sometimes. You've got a vibe."

"Do I?" Esper asked. "Do I really?" She fished at her collar and drew a chain out from under her shirt. Dangling from the end was a stone in a silver setting; it was bone white except for a bit of pink toward the bottom. "Do you know what this is?"

Tanny shrugged. "A necklace. What, did you steal it from the One Church or something?"

"No, it was a gift from my mother for my twelfth birthday. It's magic."

"What's it do?"

Esper regarded the pendant a moment before answering. "It gets darker toward the end of the month. Swoosh it around in water, and it goes white again, and the water turns red. How'd my mother put it... ? 'Keeps away cramps and boy problems.'"

"Sounds handy."

Esper gave a delicate snort. "Handy... yeah. I gave it a workout, that's for sure. I should have given it up when I joined the priesthood, but I couldn't part with it. Just a little inconvenience now and then, but I'd gotten so used to it that I was scared what it might be like quitting. I was supposed to be putting my faith in the Lord, setting an example. I mean, I didn't totally hide it, and I had to swear it was for the side benefits and not because I intended to break any vows, but sometimes it felt like an anchor around my neck."

"So?"

"Sound familiar?"

Tanny glared at Esper. What was she getting at? The imbalance of biochemicals in her system was making it hard to concentrate. She had a constant ringing in her ears, and her eyes kept losing focus. There were few enough times when she was in the mood for riddles and innuendo, and this was certainly not among them.

"Kubu didn't get sick eating cosmetics or foot cream," Esper said when it became clear Tanny had no ready reply. "I must have burned something out of your system when I healed that bump you got on the head."

"That fucking bastard," Tanny muttered. Esper had probably confronted Carl and he must have told her. "It's none of your business, and I don't like you going behind my back." Esper flinched back, and that was when Tanny realized she was not only shouting, but leaning toward the co-pilot's chair. She settled back into the pilot's seat and took a calming breath.

"It wasn't Carl," Esper said. "You're coming down off something. You all act like I was born and raised in a convent, but my parents were broke when I was young. We lived in Neo-Rotterdam, and not even the OK part. I saw burn-outs, vapes, glass-eyes, 'roid-mutants, tweakers, and schizoids. The school shuttle pilot had a stim addiction, but no one else would take the job, so they kept him on."

"So that's what you see? A tweaker on a crash?" Fuck Esper. Even when she was trying to act like she grew up tough, she came across like a ... well, like a priestess.

"Everyone's heard about the stuff they give marines. It doesn't take a xenogeneticist to figure out you kept taking it. You can pass it off as lingering effects of the stuff you took while you were in, making you stronger and tougher than everyone. But if you're reacting like *this* to metabolic healing, and sweet, dopey Kubu turned into Cerberus all of a sudden. Come on, I'm not an idiot."

Tanny swallowed. "No, I guess you're not." She let her head loll back against the headrest and closed her eyes.

"You don't have to show me how to navigate if you don't want to," Esper said. "But I'll stay right here, in case you need me."

---

"Bring us to a halt at the edge of the system," Carl said, resting a hand on the back of the pilot's chair. His stomach was undecided between gnawing hunger and wanting to eject the huckleberry and salami sandwich that was the only thing he'd eaten in the past eighteen hours.

Tanny turned and looked up with a question in her eyes. For a split-second, Carl thought it might stay there, but he was disappointed yet again. "What for? It'll take days to cross the system in real-space." There was an edge in her voice, and Carl knew he was walking across springtime ice on a sunny day. Whatever she was feeling from the lack of her stash, Tanny was in a bad way—pale and glistening with sweat on her brow even in the cool 16°C cockpit.

"Yeah, we could blow by them and they'd never see us," Carl agreed. "But this is the Poet Fleet's turf, and I want to play nice. We'll hail a patrol ship and say 'hi.' They've got intra-system astral gates we can use after that."

"Mort'll be pissed."

"Mort's a big boy," Carl said. "Besides, everyone'll be fine once we get the holo-projector replaced."

Tanny snorted. "Just like that, huh? With what money?"

Carl took a casual step back and out of Tanny's reach. Her attention was back on the ship's controls, so he didn't try to hide his grin. "I figure Janice can spot us."

"Janice ...? Janice who?" Tanny's voice held a note of slow menace.

"Janice Rucker," Carl said. "You know, Jay and Carly's oldest. Seriously, I keep better track of your family than you do. Maybe I can make you a chart or—"

"What's Janice doing out here?"

"Hiring Bryce, hopefully."

"What?"

"Bryce wants a job working for her," Carl said. He shrugged even though Tanny wasn't looking his way. He explained Bryce's plan, and rehashed Mort and Roddy's interrogation of their passenger and his responses. He skipped the part where he implied he might seduce her cousin, but otherwise left nothing out.

"I don't like it," Tanny declared at the end of Carl's story. "Seems too polished. How's this penny-ante data hustler know so much? And if he did, why's he pulling out the overdrive to work for *Janice* of all people? You'd think anyone with three working brain cells would be trying to get *off* her crew, not on it."

"I don't think she's working a crew anymore," Carl replied. "Your dad doesn't like things getting too far out of his sight. This is her own gig, being her own boss."

"You think that's going to make her cupcakes and taffy to work for? That hulking she-beast's probably going to rip people's hearts out with her bare hands when they piss her off."

"Probably good money in it, though," Carl said, stuffing his hands in his pockets.

"Don't you even..." Tanny said. "Didn't you hear a word I said?"

Tanny slowed the ship to a stop. The *Mobius* was at the outer limits of the Freeride System. They were too deep in the astral to pick up anything on sensors—far too deep—but the concealment worked both ways. Nothing should have been traveling this far down; Mort had described the *Mobius* as an elephant walking a tightrope, but Carl figured *anyone* would be able to see that. Mort had tried changing to a non elephant-centric metaphor, but Carl had admitted that he really didn't care, so long as Mort didn't get them stuck in a purple haze again.

"Janny isn't a—"

"Janice," Tanny insisted.

"—isn't a problem at the moment. We've still got to deal with the pirates." Carl keyed the intra-ship comm. "OK, Mort. Set us back in real-space, nice and gentle."

A shout echoed through the corridor from the common room. "Don't tell me my business!"

Carl double-checked to make sure the comm was off. "Geez, who'd have thought the fridge was the key to everyone's mood on this ship," he said to Tanny. Then he caught a glimpse of the bloodshot glare she was giving him. "Present company excluded, of course. Don't worry. Recitol might be tough to find out here, but you can bet the rest is for sale."

"You'd like that, wouldn't you?" Tanny asked with venom.

He shouldn't have mentioned the Recitol. He knew it even as he'd said it. Those pills had been at the center of more arguments between them than any subject except for who should fly the ship. "Just being realistic. Farther you get from Sol, the scarcer it gets."

The gray of astral space darkened into the familiar Black Ocean. Stars perked up against the backdrop of the void, and a tiny speck of yellow light was the Freeride System's sun, Syrbaat—or Syerbat, whichever. Carl could never keep it straight which was a star system and which a cheap brand of recreational land-cruisers. The cosmos was not the only thing to be seen; Tanny had dropped them out at an unofficial check-point, a place in-the-know spacers could pay their respects to the Poet Fleet and her commander before venturing into the core of the system. A small fuel depot, a pirate-owned astral gate, and a lone patrol ship waited for them. Just by stopping there, the *Mobius* had shown that they weren't rubes blundering in unawares.

"Weapons lock!" Tanny shouted.

"Shields!" Carl snapped, but Tanny was already lunging for the shield controls.

*"Vessel Mobius, power down and prepare for scan,"* a voice ordered over the comm.

Carl reached down and hit the button to reply. "Hey there, this is Carl Ramsey, captain of the *Mobius*. No problemo. Powering down. Just... don't shoot us, OK?" Some hasty gesturing ensued, and Tanny shut down the ship's engines and shield generator. Their weapons were already offline, and no one meant life support when they told you to shut everything down. It was just one of those quirks of ship-to-ship communication.

*"This is Commander Anabel Sanders of the We Are Pariahs Because We Speak Unpleasant Truths. How were you able to evade our astral sensors?"*

"Shoot, I'd have to know a lot more about astral sensors to answer that," Carl replied. "We're a bit non-standard in the star-drive department though, so that might explain things. Didn't mean to spook you. I mean, we stopped at your check-point and all."

*"Yes, you did. What is your destination?"*

"Third planet. I forget the local name," Carl replied.

*"Sybaat III is called Carousel,"* Commander Anabel replied. *"Your business there?"*

"Passenger drop off."

*"Length of stay?"*

"Until we find a job that pays us to go somewhere else."

*"Who can vouch for your ship?"*

"Shit," Carl said. "I've been here before. Doesn't that count?"

*"New security measures. Your ship will be limited to high-security docking if you don't have a sponsor."*

"Janice Rucker," Carl replied. Tanny whirled in her seat before he could wipe the grin from his face.

*"What philosophers do you follow?"*

"Pardon?"

*"For example, I follow the tenets of Bushido, and the writings of Nietzsche. Whose philosophies guide you?"*

Carl scratched his head. "I don't get that one often, I gotta say. I guess Miller and Stills. I'm a complicated guy, though. I could list off a few dozen, mood by mood. Is there a wrong answer to this?"

*"Not as such. I just like knowing whom I'm allowing through. I'm not familiar with either a Miller or Stills though."*

"That's a shame," Carl said. "I can transmit copies of their seminal works."

There was a brief silence on the comm. "You just had to do

that," Tanny whispered, as if the ship would transmit without an open comm if she spoke in a normal voice.

"*Very well, Mobius, proceed to the gate. Refrain from using any onboard star-drive systems, regulation or otherwise. I look forward to perusing the works of your philosophers.*"

"See?"

"They're as fucked up as you are," Tanny muttered as she powered up the engines and set a course for the Poet Fleet's astral gate.

———

The trip through the Poet Fleet's astral gate was uneventful. It was set to 1.5 astral depth, just to keep it separate from the traffic of ships operating under their own star-drives. In the whole two-hour slog through the Freeride System, they only passed two other vessels, one a Saddlebag-class trader broadcasting no ID, the other an interdictor like the *We Are Pariahs Because We Speak Unpleasant Truths*. Its name was *There Is No Soap to Cleanse the Soul*, and was probably set to relieve the *We Are Pariahs Because We Speak Unpleasant Truths* on gate-guard duty. Carl tried to condense the names into something that rolled off the tongue a little easier, but after two hours, all he had was the acronym W.A.P.B.W.S.U.T., with no pronunciation he could manage. TINSTCTS started off with some promise, but ran smack into a reinforced carbon-laminate hull midway through.

Carousel was what most travelers referred to as one of "the dregs." It wasn't an Earth-like, hadn't been terraformed, but was still habitable—at least at the tropics. Ice caps covered nearly a quarter of the planet, and much of the rest was in a state of near-permanent winter. The equatorial belt hovered in the 5-15°C range, with little seasonal variance, and that was where Carousel's residents clustered.

The *Mobius* arrived at a communal landing field outside the town of Calliope, located on the horse-shaped landmass (if you squinted just right, or were drunk, or both) that inspired Carousel's name. It was a barren, dry patch of land, the native wild grasses trampled under feet and landing gear of countless interstellar visitors. Those grasses got crushed down by a few more of each as the *Mobius* set down and the crew disembarked.

"Back in the cold, dry armpit of the galaxy," Roddy said, the last one off the ship. He took a huge, audible breath and let it out. "And smell that de-icer and coal soot."

"Hey, coal's cheap and local," Tanny snapped. "You don't like it, you can crawl back inside." She climbed into the hover-cruiser the *Mobius* had stolen from the Gologlex Menagerie, shoving Carl out of the driver's seat.

"Thanks, but no thanks," Roddy replied. "I'm finding a bar with a three-meter holovid and an omni link that can get ARGO Athletic Broadcast, and I'm not crawling out until I'm seeing double."

"You coming, Paycheck?" Tanny called to Bryce.

"I thought I'd head into town, look for a solid data terminal," Bryce said. "You know, get started on my end of the deal."

"Nope," Carl said. "You're with us. Me and Tanny talked it over, and we figured we'd trust you on your end. You're meeting Janice Rucker in about ..." Carl paused to check the chrono on Tanny's wrist "... about twenty-eight minutes."

They had talked it over, but it hadn't been some grand agreement. Carl had wanted to trust Bryce just enough to allow him access to a data terminal unsupervised. Tanny didn't even want that much. Janice and her crew were getting the full story, and Bryce was using a hook-up from their local base of operations. The details would get worked out later, since the comm call had only wrapped up while they were on approach to the surface. Carl negotiated with Tanny's nephew Zack, who through the wonders of sprawling, multi-generational families, was two years older than her.

She took the hover-cruiser along the outskirts of Calliope. The buildings were dingy, utilitarian, mostly pre-fab. Aside from places with prominent signage, it was hard to tell corporate offices from apartment complexes, and factories only stood out by virtue of the chemical tanks and smokestacks that clung to them like parasites.

The thought of seeing Janice again dredged up old memories. There was the time they had gone to Luna together for a week with Aunt Cerise and had been forced to share a room. Janice had spiked her shampoo with day-glow dye, the same stuff used for construction work to mark off work sites. She had retaliated by adding UV-cured epoxy to Janice's hair gel; it had solidified seconds after she stepped outdoors. Years later, Janice had ratted out Tanny's first boyfriend to her father, lying that Landrew Mitchell had taken her virginity. No one ever saw him again. Tanny was fifteen by then, and her own viciousness had taught her some subtlety. Janice was the subject of a series of nasty rumors that prevented her dating seriously until Tanny left to join the marines—at which point those rumors mysteriously dried up.

The terrain shifted, growing hilly as they made their way through the city. Streets followed the topography rather than conforming to a grid like most colonies. It had an almost Mars-like feel, where the residents preferred natural geography to modern efficiency in city planning. Tanny swung the hover-cruiser through a near-empty shopping district in one of the valleys, then along a natural pass where more low-altitude traffic flowed.

How Janice would react to her arrival, Tanny could only guess. She had come to the wedding, but they had barely exchanged a greeting. A lot of time had passed since their childhood feud—and Tanny, for one, was old enough to consider anything prior to her enlistment to be "childhood." She could only hope that Janice felt the same.

Carl's snapping fingers startled her from her musings. "Hey, I said you missed the turn."

"Sorry," Tanny replied. She slowed and swung the hover-cruiser around in a U-turn.

"Sure you don't want me to drive?" Carl asked. "I can keep this tub under two-hundred," he added, and she could envision the lopsided grin that went along with it without having to turn.

Tanny checked the speedometer and they were only doing eighty. "Nah, I'm good. Just a lot on my mind."

"You just say your awkward little hello, and let me talk to her," Carl said. "In fact, the less you say, the better. Your mother told me the stories of you two spitting and scratching at each other growing up. I bet there's a lot she didn't know, too."

"Probably," Tanny muttered. If Carl was fishing for more bait, he was going to need a less obvious hook.

"This gonna be a problem?" Bryce asked. "I mean, maybe we can just get me to a terminal, and we can meet with your cousin later, once I've—"

"Nope," Carl said. "Well, I mean, yes it's a problem, but

no, we're not changing the plan. Janice is family; how bad can it get? Blood's thicker than water, after all."

"What's that even mean?" Bryce asked. "We're not at sea or anything. What's water got to do with it?"

"Hmm. That's a good question. Probably ought to change it up on circumstance. Thicker than opium for narcotics smuggling. Thicker than liquid nitrogen for cryonic kidnappings. Thicker than—hey, what is Janice up to, anyway?"

"Mining equipment, far as I know," Bryce replied.

"Shit. Not sure blood's any thicker than that stuff," Carl replied. "Some pretty dense gear involved in mining."

"It better be," Tanny said. "Or we're in trouble."

"Let's just leave a placeholder," Carl said. "Blood's thicker than somethingorother. Fill it in as needed. Today, let's hope it's thicker than hair gel."

Tanny felt her face warm, and wondered whether it was due to embarrassment or a lack of Pseudoanorex in her system. Possibly both.

---

There was no holovid to watch, but Mort sat on the couch looking in its general direction anyway. At his side, Kubu took up the remaining space on the cushions, his head resting on his front paws. An empty jam jug lay on its side by Mort's feet, the insides licked clean. Kubu didn't protest when Mort rested a hand on his back.

"Hope you've learned a lesson in all this," Mort said. "A beast of lesser intestinal fortitude wouldn't have survived those poisons you ingest." He made no effort to simplify his vocabulary, unlike the others. Kubu didn't understand complex English any worse than he understood the monosyllabic drivel they cooed at him. Esper was the worst of the lot; she must have told Kubu what a good boy he was a hundred times.

"Kubu's tummy hurts."

"Well, not shit, you Jörmungandrian eating machine," Mort replied. He wondered momentarily whether somewhere on Kubu's homeworld there were myths about a dog devouring the sun to end the world. "Those pills of Tanny's—Mommy's— aren't fit for human consumption, period. Loads of scientific swill, crammed tight as they can pack it into tiny capsules. They're no good for *her*, and she's built up a tolerance to them. You stick to the food we give you, and keep your damn muzzle out of the beer."

"Kubu's tummy still hurts."

"You are a master of conversation," Mort observed. "Still better than Roddy when he's sober, though." He scratched behind Kubu's ears, which caused his tail to start wagging weakly. "*That*, you understand, at least. Things would be so much easier if you could talk. Well, I mean you can *talk*, you just don't ... oh, good Lord, we've been idiots."

Mort extracted himself from the couch, where Kubu's bulk had been resting against him. The canine rolled onto his side and looked up with baleful eyes. "Stay with Kubu?"

Mort was two steps from his quarters when his conscience snagged him by the back of the collar. Kubu whined, and that was that. Such a pathetic, innocent creature, barely able to string three words together. With a sigh, Mort settled back onto the couch and resumed scratching behind Kubu's ears. "You'll feel better before Mommy will, I'll wager. Then, it'll be your job to comfort her. Hopefully, we can have a little surprise for her."

Esper strolled the streets of Calliope carrying bags from various food markets. It wasn't the sort of place that warranted strolling, but it had sky and plenty of room for her to stretch her legs. The sky was a dingy grey and the streets dusted with soot and scattered with litter, but she was willing to overlook those facts for the time being. As she walked, she juggled a peppermint soda and a bag of powdered sugar puffs, trying her best not to drop the ship's groceries while she ate.

"This cold is welcome, but the air tastes like ash," Mriy said from just behind her, where she was toting the more industrial foodstuffs that would reload the food processor. Though she carried twice the weight, Mriy seemed to have no trouble keeping one hand free for a ham hock to snack on.

"Is it cold on Meyang?" Esper asked.

"Near Rikk Pa, the best hunting season is winter," Mriy replied. "But the air is clear and the scent of prey carries for kilometers. The snow makes for easy tracking and keeps a flushed quarry slow. Nothing like this place but the cold."

"You can go back to the ship if you want," Esper said between bites. "I can get by on my own."

"Tanny said—"

"Tanny worries too much," Esper cut her off. "Look around. It's a grimy little nowhere town, but it's not exactly New Singapore." There were street vendors and mothers out with children in tow. They had chain restaurants like Choc-o-Barn, Speedy Burger, and Patty Mac's. There were more ground vehicles rumbling along the asphalt roads than hovercrafts above them, but there was enough traffic for the city to feel lived-in. Carousel might have been farther out than most people would consider civilized, but it had the trappings of civilized space.

"Strength is law here," Mriy said. "You won't even carry a blaster."

"I wouldn't fire it," Esper replied. "So why pretend? I'd be more likely to find trouble if I invited it."

"The greatest warrior fights the least," Mriy replied, taking a huge bite out of her ham. "His enemies fear defeat."

"I think I'm better off without enemies, thanks," Esper replied. "I don't mean this as an insult, but you seem ... well, a bit built to force people to have an opinion of you."

"What about that one?" Mriy said, shifting the topic and pointing at a nearby storefront with the remnants of her ham. "They ought to have a holo-projector."

Gladstone Entertaintech certainly looked like a place where someone could buy just about anything. Out in the midst of nowhere, diversion was at a premium. Miners, prospectors, and freighter crews had nothing better to do in their down hours than sedate their brains with drinking and holovids. Some of them, it seemed, might be willing to dump heaps of terras on top-of-the-line gear. "Out of our price range. They probably have holo-projectors that cost more than the *Mobius*."

"Not if you asked Roddy. He seems to think—"

"Speaking of Roddy," Esper said. "Why not guard *him*? Those scrap-peddlers he's dealing with are loads more dangerous than the consumer shopping district. Plus ... you know ... he's little."

"He'll fire," Mriy replied. "And he acts like he'll fire. For him, carrying a blaster keeps him out of most trouble. Few humans would chance a laaku's aim or reflexes."

"Here we go," Esper said. "This place ought to have something I can afford." Randall's Resale was, by all outward appearances, a pawnshop. The window display held an assortment of unrelated goods: a saxophone, a leather jacket, two tennis rackets, an out-of-date EV suit, a rack of jewelry, and several hats. Electronics didn't look like much in a window, but Esper had no doubt in her mind that someone must have sold them an old holo-projector.

Mriy bared her teeth. "Junker."

"We're not rich," Esper replied. "If we want something decent, we're going to have buy secondhand. It's not like something new would stay new long on the *Mobius* anyway." Esper's family had been poor before her brothers left home for fame and fortune. Samson and Napoleon had set up their parents—and by extension, Esper—in a comfortable lifestyle with money they sent back. But Esper still remembered her father bringing home and old broken holo-projector and tinkering with it until the image came in as clear as any off-the-shelf model.

She pushed through the door, setting off an old-fashioned three-note digital chime. Whoever ran Randall's wanted to know whenever anyone entered or left. Esper caught sight of a security camera pointed at the doorway, its little red "on" indicator staring accusingly from beside the lens. The shop was everything Esper had imagined from the outside. Poor lighting. Better for shabby merchandise. Narrow aisles. Made the store seem packed with things to buy. No price labels. Haggling was mandatory.

The chime rang a second time as Mriy followed her in.

"Hey!" a voice shouted. Esper craned to see around the shelves. The man behind the counter was dark-skinned, bald-shaven, with eyes hidden behind red-glowing scanner lenses. "We don't allow their kind."

"Huh?" Esper asked. In the moment it took her to process who the proprietor meant, he clarified for her.

"That fleabag of yours. It'll have to wait outside. Can't have it shedding all over my inventory or pissing on the floor."

Mriy hissed and folded her ears back.

"*She* understands English just fine," Esper said. She made a shooing gesture to Mriy, hoping that she could get the azrin to exit before things escalated. "I'll be fine. Just hold these and wait outside." She pressed her bags into Mriy's hands, thinking that being a tad overburdened might make her less inclined toward aggression.

The door chimed again as Mriy departed, glaring over her shoulder at Esper. "Anything you lookin' for in partic'lar?" the shopkeeper asked.

"Holo-projector," she replied.

"Aisle three."

Looking up, there were indeed plastic-board signs dangling from the ceiling by strings, each bearing a number. Aisle three was next over, and she found another patron already browsing the wares. He was probably a local miner, still wearing his hard-hat and soot-caked jacket. He looked up as Esper approached. Friendly eyes and a leering grin; not a combination she relished in tight quarters. He had bleached sideburns and stained teeth, all nearly the same shade of yellow. From where he was standing, he was on the market for a datapad.

Esper offered a tight, awkward smile, and made eye contact. The probably-miner glanced away and slunk around the corner into another section. She didn't need Mriy hovering over her. She'd been living with such unwanted attention since she was a teenager. Sober and in a public space, perverts were cowards. Putting the encounter out of her mind, Esper scanned Randall's selection of holo-projectors.

They had a Martian Vision 1-meter projector, which was similar to what the *Mobius* had been using before Mort's "incident." It had seen better days, but the model was only two years old, so there was probably a limit to how much wear and tear it could have seen. There was also a Reali-Sim 2655 that went up to 3 meters. They could always set it lower for everyday use, but for special occasions a display area that size could fill half the common room. It would be like living in the holovid.

But something nagged at Esper's mind as she inspected the projectors. On the shelf behind her was a wide array of data-pads. She had been using a borrowed one so old that it probably ran on whale oil. The data rate was akin to sending smoke signals, and it could only connect to the omni through the *Mobius*. It was also a little scuffed, and much as she hated to admit it, that fact bothered her to no end. The pawnshop's datapads weren't all pristine, but some were pretty close. She picked up several and handled them, trying to find one that had a comfortable mix of weight (not too heavy, but heavy enough to feel sturdy), texture (smooth, but not slick enough to risk dropping), and color (glossy white was nice, glossy fuchsia or chartreuse would be better).

But money was an issue. Unmarked prices aside, she had a good idea what things would cost, and she'd be lucky if she could get a decent holo-projector on her budget. Getting a new (to her) datapad would preclude any other purchases. And that was when an insidious thought crept into her head.

Datapads were small. She could fit one into the pocket inside her jacket. Cameras were watching, but that was nothing compared to the forcefield at the Gologlex Menagerie; her limited magic had proved more than sufficient to foul that up for a little while. It would probably get the lights too, and the shopkeepers data lenses. The inevitable hunger brought on by her magic use could easily be preempted by eating a couple of the raspberry-peach Snakki Bars she had in her pockets from shopping. She was no Mort. The devices would all be fine in a little while. Simple.

Esper was appalled. She was thirteen the last time she had shoplifted anything; it had been a datapad then, too. Her mother said she didn't need a new one, and that Esper wasn't going to blow all their money on trendy electronics. No one had caught her, and the guilt gnawed at her until she confessed to her priest, who made her return it. A hot wave of shame washed over her, and she set the datapads back on the shelf and left them alone.

Eyes met hers through the shelves. The next aisle over, the miner was watching her again. He coughed—a dry, rattling cough that bent him over at the waist—and looked away. That was the last straw. Esper hurried toward the exit; she could shop anywhere for a holo-projector, but things in Randall's Resale were getting a bit too personal for her liking.

The miner cut her off. "Can't keep your eyes off me, babe?" he asked, resting a hand on one of the shelves as he blocked her path. He reached a hand for her cheek and she slapped it away.

"Get out of my way," she snapped. The miner flinched back, and his jacket swung open just enough for her to see the top of a datapad peeking out of his pocket. He had just been looking at those datapads; obviously he'd found one he liked. Esper gasped. "You're a thief!"

She reached out and pulled open his jacket before considering the consequences. Esper might have felt the temptation, but she dismissed it. Calling attention to the miner proved to herself that she was the righteous one. Keeping silent would have made her complicit.

Of course, the righteous often face consequences.

"Hey!" the shopkeeper shouted. Though he made no move to come out from behind the counter, there was always the hope that he might intervene. And Esper felt the sudden need for a little intervention as the miner put a hand on her collar and shoved her against one of the shelves. She clung to his jacket—stupidly, she realized, but it was reflexive. Overbalanced, he tumbled down with her amid a shower of pre-owned electronics.

"Let go of me, you stupid bitch," the miner snarled. A fist to the jaw set a flash of light behind Esper's eyes. But Tanny's training had developed new reflexes in her, and as soon as her head cleared, Esper brought her arms up to shield her face, and the next blow caught her on the forearm. The miner was atop her and struggling to regain his feet in the unstable pile of plastic and steel electronics casings.

She couldn't let him get away with it—not just the theft, but the assault as well. Too much of her life of late was painted in gray; this was clear, crisp black and white. The right thing was to hold him, stop the thief from getting away, and wait for help. Taking hold of the miner's wrist as he grabbed for a shelf for balance, she called on the universe for aid. Heal him. Speed his metabolism. Cause that stabbing hunger than always comes along with it. Esper didn't bother with the mnemonic rhyme; there was no time for that, and the results didn't need to be pretty.

They weren't.

She had grown used to people doubling over or curling up when their body devoured all its reserves and demanded more sustenance. But the miner collapsed, wracked with agony, hacking and gasping for breath. Esper wrestled to get him off of her, but his convulsions made him too difficult to wrangle. The next moment he went limp and collapsed atop her in a heap. The miner lay still. His warm, dead weight pressed down, threatening to smother her.

All Esper could hear was her own ragged breathing and the tentative footsteps of the approaching shopkeeper. She was afraid to move. Her mind raced with possibilities, but looming over them all was the stark realization that the man draped over her was dead.

"What'd ya do?"

"I... I'm not sure."

"Ya done killed Gerry. And... shee-it, my merchandise is all busted." Footsteps pounded across the room. The slam of a hand, and red lights strobed overhead. A siren sounded.

Esper scrambled out from under the dead miner in the dark as the strobe provided scant help. All she could make out clearly were the door and front windows, where dim sunlight struggled to enter through dirty glass. She burst through the door to find Mriy preparing to go in after her.

"There you are," Mriy said. "What's going on in—"

"No time," Esper said. She grabbed a couple of their bags at random from the sidewalk. "Let's get out of here."

Picking a direction at random, she stopped short. A pair of black-clad security officers jogged toward the pawn shop, stun batons in hand. Mriy tugged her by the arm. "Wrong way."

Reversing direction brought them face to face with a second patrol pair. The four security officers spread out to hem them in. Through the speaker in his black, faceless helmet, one of them ordered, "Get down on the ground."

Mriy dropped their shopping bags, and whipped out a blaster.

"No!" Esper jumped in front of the barrel as the security officers drew weapons of their own. She had no way of knowing whether local law enforcement kept theirs on stun or lethal, but knew that Mriy had no qualms about live fire on city streets.

"Drop the weapon!"

"I said on the ground!"

"Last chance. Drop. The. Weapon."

Though they were surrounded, Esper ignored the officers and stared until she caught Mriy's gaze with her own. The azrin looked away at first, but couldn't focus on the security patrol while Esper's eyes bore into her, welling with tears.

Esper patted the air. "Put it down. It's me they want. I just... there was a... it's all my fault!"

Mriy hesitated, but couched and set her blaster on the ground before raising her arms in surrender.

Esper turned to face her arresting officers. "She's got nothing to do with this. It's me you want. I'll come quietly."

"Subdue."

Two of the officers holstered their blasters while the other two kept theirs out and aimed at Esper and Mriy. Esper held out her wrists and one of them snapped a pair of binders around them. The cuffs pulled her wrists tight together and squeezed until her fingers went tingly.

There was a electrical crackle as another of the officers jabbed Mriy with a stun baton. Mriy growled at the first jab, sucked in a hissing breath after the second, and fell limp after the fifth.

"I told you she had nothing to—"

But one jab of the stun baton was all it took to shock Esper into silence. Spots swam before her eyes, and firm hands grabbed her by the arms as she wobbled.

"Yeah, we heard you."

A second jab and Esper blacked out.

The Rucker Resort was a bold name for a hotel, since most of the galaxy knew of the Ruckers as a criminal syndicate. It was also questionably accurate, since Calliope was a shithole. Unless they had some amazing guest facilities on the *inside*, Tanny was going to call bullshit on the place. Twelve stories wasn't much in a heavily populated area, but out in the fringe of ARGO space it was bloated. It had a flat, gray concrete exterior highlighted with faux neon lighting. On the roof, a small but indiscreet gun emplacement kept it from having that home-away-from-home feel, unless you were from somewhere equally ugly and paranoid.

As a base of operations, though, Tanny had to give them credit. Plenty of room for guests of the syndicate, round-the-clock food service, and no one would wonder about the odd assortment of clientele. It was clever enough that Janice couldn't have been the one to think of it, though there was a good chance she was the one who decided to plaster the Rucker name all over it.

A valet at the front entrance took custody of their hover-cruiser. There was a familiar look in his face, more a type than a specific set of features. Bulging at the seams of a crisp red and gold uniform, he would have looked more at home in a dark alley with a knife. Just inside the hotel, there was someone waiting for her whose features she truly did remember.

He was dressed in an Earth-style business suit with dark glasses pushed up onto his thinning hair, revealing gray eyes. "Good to see you, Miss Tania," the familiar-looking man said, raising Tanny's hackles. Her father's lackeys had always called her that, and despite not recalling the man's name, she had little doubt he'd guarded her at one time or another when she was young.

"Looks like you've come up in the world," Tanny commented. To her mind, it was stating the obvious, but it brought a pensive look to the man's face.

"If you ain't never climbed to the top of a mountain, find one short enough what you can," he replied. Straightening and making a visible attempt to appear professional, he hooked a thumb Bryce's way. "This the guy?"

"Yup," Carl replied. "Bill, meet Bryce Brisson, would-be data-scoundrel-for-hire. Bryce, this is Bill Harker." Carl shook hands with Bill. "Nice place you guys've got here."

Bill shrugged. "Ain't Mars. Hell, ain't even Earth. But we brought a little class to this rock. This guy of yours talk?"

"I... I do," Bryce replied. "I just didn't quite know—"

"Wonderful," Bill said. "You can talk to Miss Janice. I ain't a talker." He turned to Carl. "So anyway, how's that family of yours?"

They crossed the hotel lobby and took a gravity-stabilized elevator ride to the top floor. All the while, Carl and Bill caught up on old times as if they had met more than twice in their lives. Tanny just couldn't understand how he did it. Carl was an imbecile of the highest order on subjects ranging from politics to gambling to basic ship maintenance. But he'd yak for hours with a total stranger until the two of them became the best of friends; he'd remember the poor sap until doomsday. He kept better track of her family and their various goons, lackeys, and middlemen than she ever could. To top it off they all *liked* him... even Janice.

The elevator door opened. "Well, look who Lady Luck brought me today."

The penthouse apartment was decorated more tastefully

than Janice's room had ever been back home. Tanny had expected pink everything and plush pillows scattered around just for cuteness' sake. Twelve or fifteen years had changed her cousin that much, at least. The decor was dark and glossy, with a cold look at odds with the 25°C climate inside. Janice lounged on a leather couch, dressed in scarlet. Her crop-top blouse was sleeveless, plunging down her front; it stayed in place by some clever, high-tech fabric trickery. The skirt she wore billowed into individual pant legs as she rose to greet them; heeled shoes clacked on the floor, hidden beneath the fabric.

Carl gave a lopsided grin. "Hey, Janice. Long time."

She swayed over toward them. Gone was the grim jewelry she once wore, as was the skull tattoo that used to grace her left shoulder. Instead she wore a pair of dangly diamond earrings with a matching solitaire necklace against her smooth, clinic-fresh skin. Janice's loose, flowing black hair stood in stark contrast to Tanny's close-cropped cut.

"I forget," Janice said, her attention fixed solely on Carl. "Are you and the princess currently married? I can never keep track."

"Not presently," Carl replied. With not so much as a hitch in her gait, Janice slunk up to him and wrapped her arms around his neck. The ensuing kiss lasted indecently long. It was all for her benefit, Tanny knew. Janice might have gained some class, and learned a bit of subtlety, but she was clearly still new at both.

Janice gasped for breath. "Hello, Tania," she said, her arms still encircling a grinning Carl. "Finally decided to pay a visit? Should have come while we were still on Mars. It would have been like old times."

"Who would've wanted that?"

"My mother, your father, probably a few hangers who still think you're their ticket to the big time, but that's probably about it," Janice replied, disentangling herself from Carl. "No one else misses you."

That last was bit probably an exaggeration, but not by much. Tanny had grown up a lot since leaving home. She could hardly look back on all the things she got away with in her teen years without embarrassment. Dealing with her on a day-in, day-out basis must have been exhausting for most of the family and the household staff, not to mention her security detail.

"Why Carousel? Why Poet territory?" Tanny asked. "Why not just stay cozy on Mars?"

"Cozy?" Janice scoffed. "Same reason you left, sorta. I wasn't anyone's plaything, and I wasn't going to be second string. I put together my own crew, but your father didn't like it."

"Lemme guess, because you wanted to take it outside Sol?"

"No, because your father doesn't trust non-humans in the business," Janice replied. She shook her hair and walked over the expansive windows overlooking the city. The Rucker Resort had a high vantage in the rocky terrain north of Calliope, and nighttime illumination glittered in the valley that spread below them. "All this is mine, just because your father decided to let me go 'crash and burn'—his exact words— trying mixed-raced crews."

"My father's no xenophobe," Tanny protested, unsure why that exact moment felt like the time to show filial loyalty. It probably had to do with the source of the accusation.

"Like *you* know your father," Janice said with a sneer. "Everyone else sees how he is around you. News-blurt: he's not like that with anyone else, not even your mother. Sure, he'll let a laaku do his accounting or draw up contracts, but he's not letting them into the business side of the business, and he sure as hell isn't letting any of the non-primate xenos anywhere near his operation."

Tanny shrugged. "Not a lot of xenos can afford Mars."

Janice snorted. "Yeah, like *that's* an accident. ARGO relocation taxes anywhere in Sol are designed to keep xenos out. But you're traveling with an azrin in your crew, I hear."

"Yup," Carl interjected.

"Figure that makes you at least a few neurons smarter than your old man," Janice said. She drifted over to a side table cluttered with glass decanters and crystal-ware and poured herself a drink. "So tell me about the quiet one. What's he got that I need to hire him?"

Tanny elbowed Bryce. She didn't know if it was nerves or hormones that had his tongue knotted up, but he needed to speak for himself if he had any shot of impressing Janice. There was no confusing her with a delicate flower, despite her current attire. That act fell flat after a minute of her opening her mouth. She didn't abide meekness. Never had. Probably never would.

Bryce cleared his throat. "I'm in data... digger mostly. I know you're in the market for some mining gear; portable, nothing huge, but a good-sized haul in smaller chunks from a fleet set to come through this way. You're set to start a mining colony somewhere bleaker than here; once you've got them though, you're going to want them free and clear, and that's where I can be of use." He stopped to catch his breath, barely having paused in his introduction.

"Jesus," Janice said. "Did you rehearse that or something? Where'd he find out about that job?" she asked Carl.

"Like I said," Bryce said. "I'm in data."

Janice bit her lip as she looked Bryce over for the first time since he arrived. Tanny turned aside so she could roll her eyes without her cousin seeing, pretending to notice the view of the grimy little town below filled with miners and the profiteers who supplied them with a livable world.

"Carl, I got you and the princess separate rooms on the tenth floor," Janice said, picking up a second glass and filling it with an amber liquid from an unlabeled decanter. "Yours has a view of the landing field where you parked. I'm going to have a drink with Mr. Bryce Brisson, and tomorrow he can try his hack to clear your warrants. He has until then to impress me."

Tanny had to learn where her own room was from Bill, who was waiting for them in the lobby. She was tempted to blow off Janice's hospitality and go back to the *Mobius* for the night, but she just didn't have the energy. It had taken all her focus and reserves of strength not to either pass out or vomit in front of her cousin. Instead, she thanked her lucky stars that her room wasn't directly below Janice's and proceeded to do both.

---

Mort sat beside Kubu, beer in one hand, a copy of *Daedalus and the Art of Artifice* in the other. Roddy had brought back a few essential supplies, along with spare parts for the ship, including several raw steaks. It had only taken two to settle the canine's stomach, but he was still exhausted from his ordeal. Aside from Kubu's snoring and the occasional mechanical clank from the bowels of the *Mobius*, everything was quiet.

"Mort," Roddy's crackly voice blurted from the shipwide comm. "Hey, Mort ... push the goddamn button labeled 'comm open,' you Iron Age relic."

Mort spared a glance up at the panel, rolled his eyes, and returned his attention to his reading. "You see, boy? There are things about being a wizard. You can't just go letting regular folk drag you around by their gizmos and whatchamacallits. Just you wait and see."

*Daedalus and the Art of Artifice* was an excellent resource. Mort's copy wasn't original, but it preserved the ancient Greek, making it both informative and a good mental exercise. It provided an escape into a world before technology, when artifice was more a product of imagination and willpower, and less a matter of money and robotic factories. Daedalus wouldn't have built a ship that needed an overhaul after a bit of magic was performed nearby. Then again ... he probably would have built it from a whale carcass with glued-on feathers, so there was a comfort factor to consider as well, not to mention that the *Mobius* passed a lot of suns.

In moments, the inevitable happened. The door to the cargo bay slammed open, and an irate laaku entered the common room. "I *know* you can work a comm panel, you bastard."

"I'm not dropping everything I'm doing the minute you decide—"

"It's Esper," Roddy said. "Call came in from local lock-up. They've got her in on charges."

Mort snorted. "She get picked up trying to shop for Tanny's misbegotten pills? Good Lord, that girl ought to have known better."

"No, murder."

Mort raised an eyebrow. Murder wasn't the sort of thing you could just drop on the floor at someone's feet without explanation. Even snide laaku mechanics had to know that.

Roddy sighed. "She went to some dung-bucket secondhand shop and got in a fight. Other guy ended up dead, and the local sheriff's deputies arrested her."

"I thought Mriy went along with her," Mort said. Mriy's only *real* job around the ship was keeping other people from having to kill anyone—or getting themselves killed.

"She's locked up too, as an accessory."

"I don't see it," Mort said. "Spend five minutes talking with her and anyone with half a wit in his head'll see that she hasn't got it in her. She won't shoot anyone, and she's hardly the sort to break necks. How do they think she killed someone?"

"Cancer," Roddy said.

"So wait, some wretch keels over and they pin it on the nearest offworlder?" Mort asked. "That doesn't make any sense at all."

"They said she used magic on him."

"Bah, Esper can't create cancer in ..." Mort's words drifted, swirling into nothingness as a new thought contradicted what he would have said. He spoke aloud, but to the universe at large, more so than Roddy. "He already had it. She sped it up, same as she speeds up healing. Body's natural processes. What's cancer but those processes run amok?"

"Nasty business," Roddy said. He shrugged and pulled a beer from the freezer. "Anyway, figured you'd deal with it."

"Me?" Mort scoffed. "I'm not a lawyer, and I'm not her captain. Why would they listen to ..." Mort chuckled silently. "Of course. This place is run by pirates. They don't care, as long as someone pays them off."

Roddy cocked his head, pausing mid chug. "You holding out on us? Thought pretty much everyone was scraping terras out of the couch cushions."

"Of course I am," Mort replied. "But that's not the point.

Shakedowns work both ways." He stalked off to his quarters to change.

---

Esper sat on the edge of a cot, chin resting on her hands. A lone, dim panel in the ceiling lit her cell, which was all of two meters by two and a half. The scant light was enough to see by, but allowed the disreputable features of the cell's uncleanliness to remain concealed. There was a toilet and water spigot within arm's reach; the latter didn't work, and she hadn't dared try the former in case it was likewise out of order. The cushion of the cot was some rugged synthetic leather with lumpy stuffing; there was neither blanket nor pillow. All she had were her boots and the form-hugging armor Tanny had insisted she wear in dangerous places like Calliope. Without the concealing shapelessness of the jacket she usually wore with it, she felt displayed, but embarrassment was the least of her shames.

Yesterday she could have said she never killed anyone, and the question would have struck her as preposterous. Now she could not. There was no malice in her use of magic, but she had not known about the miner's illness, nor had she imagined that her healing spell could nurture malignant growths. Kenneth Eugene Shaw. That was the name they had told her, the man she had murdered. Idly she rubbed her hand on the cot cushion, the hand she had touched him with, the hand she had killed with. There was no wiping away the unclean feeling though.

In time, Esper would pray for forgiveness, for understanding, perhaps even to wipe the incident from her memory. But for now she had no business asking anything from the Lord but mercy upon the soul of Kenneth Eugene Shaw, a man taken before his soul had a chance at redemption. Her encounter with him had lasted only minutes from their first fleeting eye contact, and he had left a sour feeling in her stomach. But she had to imagine that far worse than Kenneth Eugene Shaw had been brought back into God's grace. She had denied him the opportunity for salvation. Even if she could forgive herself for causing his death, she could not shirk that responsibility.

She had gotten Mriy arrested, too. Aiding and abetting— what a curious turn of phrase. All she had done was run when Esper told her to run, and drawn a weapon she hadn't used. Had Mriy actually managed to aid or abet, they'd have gotten away. But azrin weren't given the benefit of much doubt. If the sheriff's deputies hadn't known her species, five minutes with a connection to the omni would have been long enough for them to realize she was dangerous.

Worst of all was Esper's deep certainty that she was going to get away with it. The tidal wave of guilt wasn't enough to wash cold logic out of her. Carl was a master of talking his way out of things, and would talk his way around any punishment Esper might be in line for. Barring that, Tanny's cousin was a high muckety-muck in the local criminal clique. Tanny and her cousin didn't get along, but somehow strings would get pulled, someone would owe someone else a favor, and she'd get released.

Esper slumped back onto the bed with her arms crossed. One full wall of the cell was glossy black, mirror perfect. She knew it was see-through from the far side, and that the guards were watching her every second. As a prisoner, she had no expectation of privacy. Even her grief and guilt were subject to the amusement of her captors.

The door opened. "Come on," one of the deputies said. He

was the slouch-gutted blond who had told her of the "ameni-ties" when they put her in there, hours ago. His weapon was holstered, and his wrist-restraints dangled at his belt.

"Where are we going?" Esper asked, scooting out of the cell before he could change his mind and seal her inside once more.

"To see the Fleet Admiral."

Esper's head snapped around. Mort stood just a few steps away, dressed in his robes and chain, though he did not have his staff along. Standing beside two more of the Carousel deputies, he showed the sharp contrast between old and new. The local law enforcers had their kevlex uniforms and stun pistols, their bioactivated restraints and their ear-clip comm links. Mort was a peddler of fire and brimstone, a bottomless well of menace with a scowl and two day's unkempt beard.

"You disappoint me, apprentice," Mort continued, wagging a finger at her. "Kill when you must, but kill with intent, not lax control."

"I just—" Esper began, but Mort raised a hand in a curt gesture and cut her off.

"Save it for the Fleet Admiral. I'll not be subjected to hearing the story twice."

"If you'll just follow me," one of the other deputies said. They brought Mort and Esper outside to a waiting shuttle. It was just an old Integra-Cruise Sparrow, but the exterior was painted sky blue with twisting ivy wound about. The painted ivy parted around the vessel's name, the *What Goes Down Must Come Up*.

The air outside was biting, and the armor Esper wore was designed to dissipate heat, not trap it for warmth. One of the deputies handed her back her jacket, and she gratefully shrugged it on as she shivered.

The shuttle door popped open with a hiss of equalizing pressure, and the deputies stepped aside to allow them aboard. Mort slid his hands into opposing sleeves of his robe, never giving the slightest hint that he was cold despite there being no shelter from the stinging wind. He nudged her with an elbow and glared down at her arms, then wiggled his hands inside his sleeves.

Esper hadn't been given much chance to figure out what was going on, but Mort had called her his apprentice—to call that a stretch of the truth was like giving Carl credit for an occasional exaggeration. She wasn't quite comfortable with her own infrequent use of magic, which she had limited to life-threatening emergencies until today, and in retrospect, there had been a life at stake there as well, just not hers. But if Mort had gotten her out of that gloomy little cell (though to give it credit, it was much warmer in there), then she would play along for the time being. It was a snug fit, but she managed to get each of her hands into the jacket sleeve for the other arm.

The interior of the shuttle was partitioned. There was no access for the passengers—herself, Mort, and two deputies—to interact with the pilot. Four seats faced forward, and four others faced them, oriented backward to the direction of flight. Esper sat in a forward-facing window seat, and Mort settled in right beside her. The two deputies, for all their niceties, sat in the opposite corner, as far from Mort as they could get. He set his eyes on them, and with no magic Esper could notice, held them silent in their seats.

There was so much she wanted to ask, but without quite knowing what was going on, she didn't dare. Trust in Mort. It was all she had to go on. If ever there was one of the crewmembers whose plans she ought to trust, it was Mort. Tanny and Mriy were ruthless and might do more harm to her soul than good for her safety or freedom. Carl made up his plans as he went along, regardless what lies he might tell to cover the fact. Roddy, if he were ever to plan anything, the odds of him following through were no better than the flip of a coin—or the pop-top of a beer bottle.

Mort put a hand on her shoulder and leaned close. "Don't worry. I'll handle this," he said, his voice low, but not a whisper. Esper should have been more nervous, but what little doubt she had that she would see this through was washed clean. Was this what magic felt like? Some spell, not even perceptible, just evaporating her worries like dew before the morning sun? If it was, then she could not even blame Mort for doing it. If it wasn't, then she didn't know why it was working. Mort was, by all she had been taught, a tainted soul. Should solace come wrapped in a black robe and bearing the ill-gotten forces of creation?

The shuttle trip was only to orbit. It lasted mere minutes. The sky above filled with a single ship, blotting out more and more stars as proximity altered her view from the window. The *What Goes Down Must Come Up* was swallowed up by the Poet Fleet flagship. "Welcome to the Look On My Works, Ye Mighty, and Despair," one of the deputies said as the shuttle door opened.

"At least one of these bloody ships is named for a poem," Mort grumbled as he stood.

"Not exactly reeking of humility," Esper replied softly. She followed Mort a step behind and off to his left.

"On the contrary," Mort said. "Read the whole thing sometime. Remarkable sentiment for someone who owns a star system."

The *Look On My Works, Ye Mighty, and Despair* was large enough that there were transport vehicles servicing in the interior. A rubber-wheeled buggy pulled up alongside the *What Goes Down Must Come Up* with a man in a sleeveless gray shirt at the wheel. "Hop in," he said. "Admiral's all curious who the hell you both are."

Esper made eye contact with Mort, who offered a grin and wink, but no explanation. They both climbed into the buggy, and without preamble, the driver sped off. There was no time after that for thinking, worrying, or puzzling, just white-knuckle terror. The sleeveless-shirted driver tore through the corridors of the ship like a rally racer—or like Carl in anything that flew. They had a moment's respite when they stopped in a freight elevator to head up six decks, but then with a squeal of tires, they were off again.

Esper's heart pounded so that she could feel it in her ears, and when she climbed out of the buggy, her legs nearly gave out beneath her. "End of the line," the driver said. He gave Esper and Mort a lackadaisical salute and sped off. There were two officers waiting for them. Esper was guessing at the rank by the way they stood, for there was no uniform or insignia anywhere on their person. One was a woman in her early thirties with a shaved head and spikes through each ear. The other was from a race she didn't know—reptilian, shoulder-tall to his companion, and covered in dull, swampy green scales. If she had to guess his evolutionary origin, she'd imagine he was some Earth-like world's idea of an iguana.

"I am First Officer Hazz Shi," the iguana-like officer said. He gestured to his comrade. "This is Security Chief Indira Jackson. Admiral Chisholm is waiting on the bridge."

Esper found it curious that neither was armed. For the first officer, perhaps it might make sense, but for a security chief to go around without a weapon struck her as out of place. The only way that would make sense was if...

She tugged at Mort's sleeve to get his attention as their escort headed for a the door labeled "A throne is only a bench covered with velvet." He looked down and Esper nodded toward Security Chief Indira Jackson. A twitch of a frown graced his brow, but it faded quickly into an understanding smile. A gentle nod confirmed Esper's assertion: Indira Jackson was a wizard.

The bridge of the *Look On My Works, Ye Mighty, and Despair* was luxurious without being ostentatious. The consoles gleamed, with smartly-dressed officers at each station pillowed snugly into leather-upholstered seats. The floor was polished hardwood, or at least appeared so, and beheld a mosaic design in shades of brown. Standing with one hand resting on the back of the command chair at the center of the bridge was none other than the Fleet Admiral.

She turned at the opening of the door. "Welcome. I am Emily D. Chisholm, Admiral of the Poet Fleet." By all appearances, she was no older than Esper, certainly not more than thirty. She wore a jacket and slacks in a checkerboard of jester's motley, tailored to her tall, slim form. At her neck she sported a ruff like a Renaissance nobleman, and she wore her dark hair dangling over it in pigtail braids. For the moment, Esper was at a loss for words.

"Charmed," Mort replied, sketching a shallow bow with his arm across his waist. "I am Mordecai The Brown, former holder of the Eighth Seat of the Convocation and Guardian of the Plundered Tomes. And this is my apprentice, Esper Theresa Richelieu."

Esper ducked her head in an emergency bow, caught unprepared for Mort to take on her introduction as well as his own. "Ma'am," she mumbled.

"I am a great admirer of the truth," Admiral Chisholm

said. "It is as scant a resource in this galaxy as any gem, as any piece of artwork. In return for receiving so precious a gift as unblemished truth, I could forgive a great deal."

"What do you want to know?" Mort asked. Esper felt a knot of dread as to what Mort might say if he let loose with *too* much truth, and worse yet, what Admiral Chisholm might do if she caught either of them in a lie.

The admiral turned her attention to Esper and her face brightened in a condescending smile. "Are you truly his apprentice?"

Esper swallowed and shook her head.

"I thought not," Admiral Chisholm said. "The Esper Theresa Richelieu that I dug up was a priestess initiate of the One Church. I highly doubt such a dichotomy of soul exists that would allow one woman to serve such opposing masters. Certainly not a dead woman. Tell me, did you fake your death or steal Sister Theresa's identity?"

"Faked," Esper admitted. "I'm not proud of it, but I ruined my career in the clergy and... well, at the time it seemed like a good idea."

"And *you*, Mordecai Brown," Admiral Chisholm continued. "Are you the same Mordecai Brown who is wanted by the Convocation for a sum that temps even me to violate the hospitality of the Freeride System?"

"You wouldn't survive the attempt," Mort replied, lifting his chin. "If you like truth, let *that* one stick in your craw. We're here about that little scuffle in Calliope, not to trade threats."

"Very well." Admiral Chisholm took a step toward Esper, who flinched back a half step. "The miner had an untreated malignant tumor in his left lung. "You caused the rapid growth of that tumor until it killed him in a matter of minutes. Do you deny this?"

Esper shook her head.

"Do you *deny* this?" Admiral Chisholm snapped. "Answer me!"

"No," Esper said, looking down at the exquisite floor and imagining herself crawling beneath it.

"Are you a wizard? Was that why you faked your death?"

Esper shook her head and realized that wasn't going to be enough. "No. I just know the one spell."

"Why would you claim she was your apprentice?" Admiral Chisholm asked Mort.

A sly smile crossed Mort's lips as he paused before answering. "She won't get it out of me that way."

Esper's puzzlement momentarily overcame her shame. "What do you—"

Admiral Chisholm waved a dismissive hand. "Indira, enough. I don't know how you managed it, but she can't even contact me telepathically. Your reputation doesn't do you justice, Mordecai Brown."

Mort offered a helpless shrug. "You get out into the galaxy, you learn a few things. Those pointy-hatted old fools back on Earth must think my brain's gone to rot out here, but I get to practice an awful lot of *not* doing magic. Your Indira seems like a nice enough girl, but she's got all the ego of an assistant janitor. Universe isn't going to listen to her when I've got my boot on its throat. Sorry, if you two had a 'thing' going that I interrupted."

Admiral Chisholm's eyes brightened. "Excellent segue. Speaking of things that are going, that is the crux of the reason behind Miss Richelieu's arrest. I don't give a miser's pity about some thieving local miner, but the Rucker family is operating in *my* territory. I want to know why, and I want them dealt with."

"But you own this whole system," Esper protested. "Just kick them out."

Admiral Chisholm tapped a finger to her lips. At first Esper took it as a shushing motion, but quickly realized that the admiral was thinking. "There is, of course, that option. But I don't want Don Rucker to bear me ill will. Should any blood relative of his be harmed in the eviction, I would be looking over my shoulder till the end of my days. Better to work through an intermediary. Janice Rucker has some scheme at work here. I don't know what it is, but she's far too settled on Carousel for my liking. Miss Richelieu will be staying here until Janice Rucker and the rest of the Rucker Syndicate are out of Freeride."

Esper felt the hair rise on the back of her neck. Mort stepped forward, placing himself between the admiral and Esper. "I don't think so."

"I do," Admiral Chisholm replied. "You're going to go back to the surface, inform your captain of my terms, and use whatever wits you have to get Janice Rucker to leave Freeride. Until then, Miss Richelieu will enjoy the hospitality of the *Look On My Works, Ye Mighty, and Despair.*"

Mort squinted at Admiral Chisholm. "You don't look worried that I might just kill you where you stand."

"An act," the admiral admitted. "I've never tested my anti-wizard defenses against one of your presence."

"Mort, don't," Esper said, pulling him back by the arm. "I'll stay. Just ... fix this." She turned to the admiral. "What about Mriy?"

"I've already offered her a job," Admiral Chisholm said with a shrug. "She turned it down, and has been returned to that heap you so generously describe as a ship. Now, take your leave, Mordecai Brown. Miss Richelieu will come to no harm aboard my ship. Even should you prove unsuccessful, she will merely ... remain."

Mort nodded slowly and put a hand on Esper's shoulder. It had a warm, comforting weight. "All right. If you're willing to play along, I'll leave you with these... poets." Esper could only guess that he almost said "pirates" and thought better of it. He turned to the admiral. "If she *does* come to harm, you can bet I'll be back to test whatever traps you may have set up in here. Oh, and I appreciate the Shelley reference."

"So few do," Admiral Chisholm replied. With a flick of her fingers, the door to the bridge opened. The man in the sleeveless shirt waited outside, his ground-car idling a few meters down the corridor. The door closed behind Mort. There was a brief squeal of tires, and then she was alone, surrounded by genteel pirates.

---

Tanny paced her room at the Rucker Resort. It was a tenth-floor suite looking out on the ice-capped mountains to the North, but the glare from the holovid ruined the night view. The fight between Graccio and Martinez had seemed like a good plan to settle her mind. It was just a middle-weight bout; there was no title on the line, just distracting violence to numb her worries. The cool marble sucked feverish heat out through her bare feet, and her pacing kept the floor from warming in any one spot.

A knockdown in the fight momentarily captured her attention as the announcers went wild and the unseen crowd cheered. Graccio would have been Tanny's bet if she'd been inclined to place one, but he wasn't long for the fight by the look of things. Just one more bit of evidence that she was off her game. Normally she was the one to pick the winners when she and Mriy went to the fights in person. Mriy was good at sizing up azrin fighters, but Tanny was better at evaluating humans.

He was late. When Tanny had discovered that Janice hadn't put any restrictions on in-room communications, she had immediately gotten on the local section of the omni and dug until she found someone who could help. It had taken a debit against her future pension from the marines, but she had gotten a hold of enough digital terras to place a discreet order for some illicit chemicals. It wasn't everything she needed, but it was better than what she had. But that was two hours ago, and it should have taken her contact less than half that time to make the drop-off.

A melodious chime had Tanny rushing for the door. Thoughts of strangling the courier for making her wait were swept away in a floor of relief. She hammered the door release with her thumb. It snapped into the wall with an audible whoosh. As she opened her mouth to make a snide comment, she froze.

Bill was standing there, a rumpled brown paper bag in his hands. It looked out of place against the backdrop of his tailored Argozzi suit. "Good evening, Miss Tania. We had a delivery for you down at the front desk."

Tanny snatched the bag from Bill's hands. "Thanks." She pressed the door control once more, but Bill put a hand in the entrance, triggering the safety override that kept guests from getting slammed in doors.

"Miss Tania, didn't you learn nothing all them years with guys like me looking after you?" Bill asked. "You looked surprised to see me, which means you didn't check the security screen to see who it was. Could be it was anyone out here."

Tanny glanced to the screen by the door. It hadn't even occurred to her to check. Either she was getting used to the P-tech all over the *Mobius*, or she was getting sloppy. "I didn't want it recorded," she lied. "It's none of Janice's business who I see."

Bill held up his hands at stomach height, just enough not to be intimidating. "And Miss Janice don't care, neither. But it's all on recording, all the time, just in case—you know, nothing special in this case on account of it being you and all. Gotta tell you, we ran that shit—pardon my Earthy tongue—ran that junk through the chem scanner, just to be safe."

Tanny waved a hand in a circular motion. "And?" She wanted this conversation over, and Bill stumbling over himself wasn't getting any of the drugs into her bloodstream any quicker.

"Miss Tania, that tweaker who brung this stuff ... this is some serious stuff, you know?"

"Yeah," Tanny said. "I kinda knew that. I don't care, as long as it's all in here."

"Um," Bill said. He reached a finger inside his shirt collar and tugged. "You see... I can't lie to you, Miss Tania. I had to take some of them pills out."

"Which ones?" There were a few in her order that she could live without—in the literal sense, probably any of them. But she had already worked out in her head what the makeshift cocktail would do to her. Re-figuring what she could and couldn't afford to ingest wasn't part of her evening's plan. Drugs. Shower. Bed. That was all she was looking for, with emphasis on the bed.

Bill took a step back. Tanny could have snapped the door

shut between them if she hadn't wanted answers. "Just the Cannabinol."

"What?" Tanny shouted, not caring if anyone heard, or if the security cameras had an audio feed that might pick her up. "God dammit, Bill. That was the one I was *really* hoping you weren't going to say. Plus, of all the fucking things ... seriously? That shit's harmless compared to the rest." Cannabinol would calm her, and more importantly settle her stomach to keep her from vomiting up the rest of her purchase. In fact, until it had time to kick in, she wasn't planning on touching the rest.

"Hey, I made your dad a promise a long time ago to keep you off that kinda stuff," Bill said.

Tanny reached out, grabbed Bill by the collar, and hauled him back into the room. "Listen to me, Bill," she said quietly, her face centimeters from his. "I spent eight years in the marines. They gave us stuff to keep us on top of our game. I've been taking it all this time, even since I've been out. Look me in the eyes. Right now, I'm dry on all but the *one thing* that will let someone my size snap your neck like a dry twig. But I like you, Bill." She let go of his collar. "So I'm going to let you go downstairs and bring back that Cannabinol. NOW!"

---

In a back room behind the hotel bar, there was a gathering that wasn't open to the general public. The chairs were high backed, cushioned like a dream, and gathered in a circle around a table strewn with cards, chips, and glasses of booze. Four holovids played around the room, all sports, but no one was watching. It was all just atmosphere. The room Tanny's cousin had provided was nice enough, but Carl felt more at home surrounded by people.

"Hey, look who be back," Mikey Whistles hollered, grinning with his gap-toothed smile. Bill slouched and shook his head as he lumbered in.

"Told you," Carl said, draining the last of a bottle of Amberjack Ale. He tossed a taped-shut cardboard package to Bill, who snatched it from the air with a scowl. Carl pointed around the table. "Pay up, boys. Bill can lie his ass off all he wants, but that girl's getting high tonight or killing someone." No sooner did he set the bottle down, but one of the waiters scooped it up and replaced it with a fresh, cold one.

There were grumbles around the table, but a mix of chips and hard-coin terras made their way into Carl's pile, turning barrel-scrapings into a proper hoard. Carl pulled it toward him, just enough to make room for cards to settle in front of him. He might stack them; he might not. It all depended just how fast he started losing them.

"How'd you know?" Janice's cousin Veronica asked. She wasn't family to Tanny, being from Janice's mother's flock, but she had a coincidental resemblance to Tanny in her build that Carl was finding harder to ignore, bottle by bottle. "You'd think he coulda slipped one past her."

Two-Shot Pete chuckled from his belly. He hadn't lost so much as a terra betting on the ruse. "You ain't known Carl long enough, then. I think no one's got Princess Tania figured out but him."

"Maybe we just pity bet him," Gazlir said with a sharp-fanged smile. He was azrin, with ash gray fur and the tip of his left ear missing. He had given Carl a growl when introduced, and when Carl laughed it off, he had earned a bit of the azrin's gangster's respect. "Since his rusty ship's falling apart."

Carl laughed despite the sting. "Oh, that one hurts. Cheap shot, taking aim at my ship. Behind his back, no less. You come on board sometime and talk shit about *Mobius*." Carl pointed an accusing finger at Gazlir, using the hand that held his beer.

Bill slunk away to go deliver Tanny's Cannabinol as the poker game went on. Carl was determined to at least hang onto enough for a used holo-projector by night's end. All he had to do was play safe and... there was a second thing, but after four bottles of Amberjack Ale, he couldn't think what it was.

"Why you loopin' 'round the borderland in that heap, anyway?" Mikey asked. "Don would'a taken you any day of the week—twice on Tuesday."

Carl tipped his chair back and held up his hands. "What can I say? Tanny won't budge on it. If it were just up to me, I'd be wearing a cheap suit like Gazlir's and using terras to fill my swimming pool." He pointed to Gazlir, whose sleeveless suit probably cost as much as an engine overhaul for the *Mobius*. But he had to give the guy *some* grief for disrespecting his ship.

Two-Shot Pete raised his glass, half filled with twelve-year-old scotch and two ice cubes. "To Carl, the most henpecked, love-struck son-of-a-bitch between here and Andromeda. I'd put myself in front of a blaster bolt for Tania Rucker, and I wouldn't blame Carl one iota if he was the one who fired it."

"Here, here," a chorus echoed around the table. Glasses, bottles, and tankards clinked and clanged. Carl chuckled. There were times when he wondered...

The shush of the door sliding open brought Esper awake with a start. The unfamiliar surroundings confused her for just a moment before she remembered her circumstances. Security

Chief Indira stood in the doorway. "Good morning. I trust you slept well."

Esper pulled up her blanket, feeling underdressed in the nightgown the Poet pirates had provided. Her cell—if it could remotely be called that—was nicer than her quarters on the *Mobius*. In fact, it was nicer than her room back home on Mars, because whoever had decorated it had refined taste. It wasn't the frilly, garish explosion of self-expression from a girl whose parents had decided to give her whatever she wanted. The floor was wood-inlaid, warmed from beneath and polished to a shine. Her bed was four-posted with heavy velvet curtains on all sides. Books lined shelves on one wall; windows that looked out over the planet below took up most of another.

"Um, yes," Esper replied. "Fine, thank you." The mattress had been a pillow for her whole body, so soft she had felt weightless.

"Dinner to your liking?"

"Delicious," Esper confirmed. They had given her a menu, and she had picked everything chocolate that the kitchen had. It had been a day that warranted something sweet.

"And Raimi?"

Esper flushed. She had been preparing for bed when Raimi had arrived. He wasn't tall, but had arrived bare chested and glistening, with a smile that shone like pearl to offer his services. There had been a fair amount of beating around the bush before they settled on a massage being among her options. She had been skeptical at first, putting herself in the hands of a half-naked man, but Raimi's fingers had worked any lingering tension from her muscles, like a magic all his own. It had taken a fair bit of praying to keep her from suggesting any more than that.

"He was nice," Esper said, and cleared her throat. "So ... what now?"

"Your clothing is being laundered and will be returned to you," Indira said. "However, you will have a wardrobe provided by this afternoon, at the admiral's direction. There is a bathrobe in the washroom if you feel a chill in the meantime. Breakfast will arrive shortly. You may amuse yourself however you like. The holovid is omni-connected and has an extensive in-core library of classical works. Most of the books are written in English. So long as you handle them with care, you may read any you like."

"And ... that's it?"

"That's it. You are our guest for the time being."

"Not that I'm complaining, but why treat me like I'm staying in a New York Prime hotel?"

Indira's face grew stern. "Admiral Chisholm believes that Mordecai The Brown has more than a passing interest in your well-being. The cost of pampering you is insignificant compared to the risk of angering that one." The security chief's lip curled in a slight smile and Esper caught a twinkle of mischief in her eyes. "And besides, you have a soul filled with grace and a form pleasing to the eye. You fit in well here. I think I may enjoy looking after you."

Esper was not sure she had stopped flushing from before, but felt the blood rushing in her ears. She was beset by hedonists.

---

The planning room for what was being called the Operation RIBBIT looked like an executive board room that had been vandalized. It had the signature long, glossy black table, but it was covered in take-out containers and the chairs were a hodgepodge of different styles. All around the walls, there were posters for the Lewiston Black Barons, ad sprawls for popular holovids from the past few years, and a flatvid that flashed sports scores and betting lines from major events around the galaxy. Below the flatvid was the motto: "It's always game time on some world."

Carl sucked in the whole atmosphere in the few seconds it took for the door guards to let him and Tanny through. Mort was already seated inside, looking grumpier than usual, along with the rest of Janice's crew. "Good, you two are the last. Rudi, clamp down the door so we can get started." The door guard complied, and the conference room was sealed with an ominous thud.

"First things first," Carl said. "How'd our boy do?" The effort of trying to sound chipper fell flat. He was buzzing on too little sleep, a hangover, and three cups of coffee. He tried to tell himself he was wide awake and feeling fine, but for once he wasn't buying his own bullshit.

"You should be a squeaky-clean, upstanding citizen in a couple days," Janice replied. She had exchanged the slinky attire of the previous night for a black button-down blouse and slacks. One could have easily mistaken her for a legitimate businesswoman. "My guy, Marty, circled him like a vulture the whole time and gave him the all clear. If Bryce has the connections he claims, it's down to the waiting."

"How's he ride?" Tanny asked in a voice like lead. Unlike Carl, she was looking much better this morning, though he had noticed a look in her eye that disquieted him. When they met in the hall a moment earlier, she had looked right through him. He usually earned himself a glare or a frown or even a quick averting of the eyes to pretend she hadn't seen him.

"Excuse me?" Veronica spoke up. "That's no way to talk to Janice."

"This is business," Tanny said. "I want to know if we're bringing Bryce along because we can use him or because he can light you up. I saw you weighing him with those eyes of yours."

"You're out of—" Veronica began, but Janice cut her off with a raised hand.

"No, it's a legit question," Janice said, staring down Tanny like a gunfighter before a shootout. "I gave him a shot, but hey, he's a family man." She flicked a hand through her loose hair. "Says he kept them out of his official record, but he's got a wife and two kids. A new bed warmer might have been nice, but a family man's always a more reliable business associate."

The words hung in the air as Tanny and Janice glared at one another.

"So," Carl said. "I hear the holo-projector in here's top of the line."

"Yeah," Mikey Whistles said. He fished in his pocket for a remote and turned it on. The unit was mounted to the ceiling directly above the conference table, and the field hung in the air at the center of attention. "Boom! How's that for resolution? Smooth as ice."

A small fleet of ships appeared in the air, hanging in formation. The two-dimensional text markers all appeared to be facing Carl, though he knew through some techno-trickery it was making it look that way for everyone. The fleet was labeled: "Roy, Barnum & Toyoda Mining Expedition." The R, B, and T were highlighted, and below, the words Operation RIBBIT, with the R, first B, and T in matching blue.

"Here's our job," Janice said, pointing to the fleet as she began to walk around the table. Carl slid into a seat before she had to go out of her way to walk around him. Tanny did like-wise, scowling at Janice instead of watching the holo. On the table, one of the boxes still had some cold spicy chicken wings, and Carl helped himself to one. "This is the Roy, Barnum & Toyoda law firm's side business. One of those stuffed-suit Earthers got it into his head that the Platt System is ripe for an unregistered mining colony. Low profile. No paperwork. Real hush-hush. I only got the system name out of them when I said I couldn't bid unless I knew where I was going."

"So we're working *with* the mining lawyers?" Tanny asked.

Janice snorted, clearly amused with the appellation. "Something like that. They hired me—that is, us—to provide security in ARGO's absence. We get them there, hang around a couple days while they get settled and cozy planetside, then we get paid two hundred grand."

"What are they mining?" Mort asked. It was unusual for Mort to take an interest in operational details. It must have been the secrecy that gnawed at him.

Mikey spoke up. "Sssssssure don't know," he said, letting the long, sibilant 's' whistle. "Them boys is tight on that lock. They won't say. They people won't say. All's we know is it's gonna be a mint."

"So, they're just mining... somethingorother?" Carl said, waving his hands in little circles as if he was searching for the word.

"Don't matter none to us," Mikey said, grinning.

"I take it we're not going to Platt?" Tanny asked.

"No siree, Miss Tania," Mikey replied. He gestured to Carl with a beckoning finger, and Carl passed the cold wings.

"The mining fleet has three armed vessels," Janice said. She poked her finger into the holo-field and ships glowed at her touch. "Delta-grade military surplus. All obsolete. All retrofits.

Just guns welded onto the outside of heavy freighters, really. It's mostly a deterrent. Once we get out of secure space, *we're* their protection." Janice gave a smug grin that she shared around the table. There were nods and chuckles, but Carl knew a humoring-the-bosslady chuckle when he heard one.

"So where do we come in?" Carl asked. "Looks like your crew's got this covered."

"You brought me Bryce," Janice said. "He gets to clean up the registry on those vessels so I can resell them half legit. He flies with you; he's your responsibility. Since this is his first job, he gets a half share, and you and your crew can split the other half as a referral." She looked to Tanny. "Don't let anyone say I never done anything for you."

Carl furtively did a count around the table, trying to parse out how Janice would be splitting up the spoils with her own gang and estimating what one share was worth. That was when he remembered that it wasn't two-hundred grand that was going to split, but the profits from the stolen ships. At that point, he gave up.

The meeting delved into boring details on the ships, their crew complements, their defenses and weaknesses. Carl's eyes glazed over, and the dim light let him nod off through much of it. He knew his part. He owned a ship that was going to babysit a data-wrangler. Tanny would be flying it, and Mriy could handle the turret if it came to that.

Carl woke from his not-so-covert nap with Mort's hand on his shoulder. "Come on, Van Winkle, time to head back. There's something we need to talk about before Bryce finishes up here."

Tanny's mind was flat during the ride back to the *Mobius*. They had a ship to get back into shape, supplies to stow, and gear to purchase before they departed. Her thoughts were on none of that. Carl blathered away to Bill, who piloted the hover-cruiser for them, a conversation filled with his usual inanity. She paid it no heed. Mort stewed beside her, hunched in his sweatshirt and grim as she'd ever seen him. That warranted a passing inkling, but she had more pressing concerns: Janice was dragging them into piracy, and she was struggling to be bothered by that.

Tanny knew she didn't want to cross that line, taking her money over other peoples corpses out in the Black Ocean; it had been a hard rule she and Carl had agreed on when first putting together a crew for the *Mobius*. But she hadn't been about to get her hands on any Sepromax from her on-world contact. The little weasel, Branson, she had scrounged up as a supplier carried marine pharmaceuticals for buyers like her, but Sepromax wasn't standard issue; in fact, it ran counter to one of the marines' primary uses of Recitol. She *knew* she didn't want to murder a bunch of innocent spacers in order to steal their little mining fleet, but she couldn't actually care about it.

It was a frightening thing, realizing the control a drug can have over you, even as it tightens its grip. She wasn't afraid of getting caught. Odds seemed good they'd get away with the crime. She wasn't scared for her safety. It was as easy a job as they'd had in months. A lazy part of her brain said it wasn't worth arguing over and that she might as well get paid for once. It was only that memory of her resolve not to fall prey to the amorality side effect (if it truly wasn't intended by the chemists, which she questioned) of Recitol that kept her from caving.

The plan needed to be simple. It needed to be lazy. If she got frustrated or overwhelmed, Janice's Operation RIBBIT might just seem like the path of least resistance. Get back to the ship. Supplies. Repairs. Sneak off world when no one was looking and trust Mort to keep them below astral sensors. There would be hell to pay for it someday, but it was a price Tanny was willing to pay, she was pretty sure. It was hard to tell, when she couldn't give a spent fuel rod about the fate of those mining colonists.

The hover-cruiser arrived at the *Mobius*, leaving Bill to take a local shuttle back to the resort. She might have muttered a goodbye before he left, but a minute later she couldn't recall.

"Come on," Mort snarled through gritted teeth. It was odd for the wizard to be the first back aboard ship. Hurrying was one of a laundry list of activities that were beneath a wizard's dignity, according to him.

"How's the repair job going?" a chipper Carl asked Roddy as the laaku closed the loading ramp behind them.

"Good as you can expect, given our budget," Roddy replied with notably less enthusiasm. "Mort catch you up on what's gone on while you were in Ruckerland?"

"No," Mort snapped. "I didn't. I got a grand total of the walk up that blasted ramp without some drooling Rucker lackey dangling his ears in my way. These ninnies even let one fly us back here; Mr. Hangover and Mrs. Chemical Imbalance were in no shape to operate a hovery-wagon."

"Something I need to know about?" Carl asked.

"We can't do it," Tanny blurted. She shook her head both to clear it and for emphasis. "We're not pirates."

"Wait. What now?" Roddy asked.

"Yes, we are," Mort replied. "That's what I needed to tell you."

"You guys turned pirate since yesterday?" Carl asked. The look of bewilderment on his face would have amused her if she were capable of it at the moment. Instead, all she felt was a rising irritation. Unfortunately, anger, annoyance, and impatience were all quite intact despite the Recitol.

"As if Esper would have gone along with that," Tanny said.

"Actually, Esper's *with* the pirates," Roddy said.

Carl held up his hands for attention. "There's no way ..."

"Of course not," Mort said. "Esper's *with* the pirates. She isn't one of them."

"Why is she with the pirates?" Tanny asked. No one was making enough sense for her liking, and she wasn't certain that her off-kilter brain chemistry was the least bit to blame.

"There was an incident," Roddy said. "Esper and Mriy were out picking up supplies. Some dipweed local starts trouble, Esper kills him, Mriy gets beaten bloody, and the pirates took Esper."

Carl made a switcheroo motion with the index finger of either hand. "I think you flipped that around. Mriy killed someone, and Esper got roughed up."

"Nope," Roddy replied, crossing his arms and looking smug. The laaku was clearly enjoying this.

"Enough!" Tanny shouted. "Someone start making sense. I'm going to break a neck every time someone starts a story in the middle and leaves out the essential details. Starting with yours." She leveled a finger in Roddy's direction.

Roddy cleared his throat and backed in the direction of a toolbox. As if that would save him. "Mort. You tell 'em."

Mort described the events that had led to their being arrest and Esper's subsequent transfer to custody on the Poet Fleet's flagship. The killing being a magical accident and Mriy being subdued by a dozen armed sheriff's deputies added the necessary plausibility to quell Tanny's rising anger. The involvement of the Poet Fleet crystallized into focus: local politics. You just couldn't let folks inhabit star systems in numbers greater than a dozen or so without them fracturing off into factions and creating politics.

Tanny turned to Carl. "So it's the room that's cursed. It's not just tech specialists on the *Mobius*. It was always both until now."

"We're not leaving her," Mort said. Tanny had expected the first reaction to be Carl's, and had already prepared herself for an argument against him.

"I mean," Tanny replied. "How long have we really known—"

"Tania Louise Ramsey," Mort shouted. "Whatever gremlins are clogging your brain, you should be ashamed of yourself."

"Easy, Mort," Carl said, patting the air. "Tanny's not herself today. Cut her some slack. No, we're not leaving Esper."

"But we said 'no piracy,'" Tanny said softly. They weren't listening. She was *trying* to keep it together. Right and wrong were fuzzy enough just then without Mort and Carl changing the rules. "Years ago. We ... we won't be like my father. We've got standards."

Carl took a long, steady example breath, and Tanny followed suit. "It's going to be OK," he said. "We're going to get Esper back. We're going to get paid. Yes, maybe there might be something resembling piracy involved, but you heard your cousin ... that fleet belongs to lawyers."

"Well, shit," Roddy said. "Lawyers? Practically doesn't even count as piracy, does it? I mean, who're bigger crooks than lawyers?"

Tanny suspected they were having one over on her—there was too much grinning. But she couldn't put a finger on the hole in their logic. They were stealing from lawyers, whose job mainly consisted of using the law to screw with people. They would use law breaking to screw with them right back. Stealing their ships and killing the crews would serve them right.

"All right," Tanny agreed. She aimed her threatening finger at each of them in turn. "But you're not fooling me. This is piracy. But we're only going to do it a little."

---

"It's not like we can just knock off a ship or twelve, swing back to Freeride, pick up Esper, stuff our hands in our pockets and walk off whistling," Carl said, keeping his voice low. He leaned against the window of Mort's quarters, his back to the landing field. In the unlikely event anyone had a camera on them, they wouldn't get his half of the conversation by reading lips.

Mort rubbed a hand across his face as he paced. "Well, I don't see any paths except through the darkness. Esper's familiar with the concept of repentance. We can apologize afterward for resorting to wanton murder to save her."

Carl sighed and let his head loll back, wincing when it thumped against the glassteel. "I just get this nagging feeling that she might take that apology, then have us leave her in the first civilized place we come to. She still sees a lot of blacks and whites."

"Well, piracy's pretty black territory even if you're fluent in grays."

"Point taken."

"Tanny's going to be put out, too, once she gets herself

right," Mort said. He shook his head. "This is worse than the usual stuff you slip past her—I mean any of us."

Carl shook a finger at Mort. "This would be a lot easier if you had just rescued her instead of letting them take you both up to see Admiral Chisholm."

"What? You think I expected them to hold her hostage?" Mort asked. He paused his pacing and held up his hands to the sky, unseen through the ceiling and the hull of the *Mobius*. "This was all supposed to be a meat-fisted shakedown. She gets arrested on a bullshit charge when she was clearly the victim of an attack. I go up with her to see whatshername with the funny costume and Oxford vocabulary. She tries to shake us down. I tell her who I am. She blanches. I waggle my fingers and give her the squint-eye. She lets us go and apologizes."

"Well, your plan came off flawlessly."

"You can't tell me I haven't pulled that one off just like that a time or twelve," Mort said. "Besides, it was refreshing dealing with thugs who name their ships after Shelley and quote Napoleon over their doorways."

"Up until they said 'we're keeping Esper, now get the fuck off my ship,'" Carl said.

Mort nodded. "Yeah, that was about the point they lost me. Bugger me if that girl might not have really *had* some defense against wizards on that bridge of hers. Wasn't willing to risk it, not with Esper right there."

Carl frowned at Mort. He wasn't generally prone to over-protectiveness. "You and Esper really aren't..." He bumped his fingertips together. "...are you?"

"Yes, Carl," Mort said dryly. "I've seduced our resident disgraced priestess. The one who's younger than my own children and covers her eyes when there's nude scenes in a holovid."

Carl shrugged. "Prudes are the ones who snap and go wild. You gotta admit she's sort of drawn to you."

"It's the magic, not me," Mort said. "You never thought much of it, but she likes the feel. Mark my words, that girl's going to fall, and fall hard, from that One Church dogma of hers."

"Hard enough and soon enough to break herself out of a modernized Hades-class battlecruiser?"

Mort twisted his mouth aside in a puckered frown and scratched his chin. "Not likely."

"Then I think it's time we got ourselves used to the idea of kicking my dear ex-cousin-in-law out of the system," Carl said. "Once we figure out how."

---

Tanny lay on her bed cockeyed, her neck limp, head upside down over the edge. The windows on her side of the ship looked out at the mountains, which resembled nothing back home on Mars. They were dark gray crags jutting out against a lighter gray sky. A world washed free of color, just like the insides of her skull. There was an odd sense of detachment, knowing that her emotions were drowning under an ocean of chemicals whose exact workings went far beyond her under-standing. She should have felt horror, she knew. But she wasn't horrified. Horror was an emotion that those chemicals had punched in the gut and thrown out an airlock.

As she stared, she heard her own breathing, and that of Kubu, sleeping on the floor beside her. Tanny tried to take stock of what she could still feel and what was numb inside her. Anger—yes, that she had felt already. Fear—even the Sepromax only partially brought that back; she was bone dry.

Trust—that much was working, since she had taken Carl and Mort at their word. Surprise—she could think of no way to check that, but would watch for it if something came up. Disgust—she tried to picture Carl sleeping with Janice, but felt no reaction. Arousal—well, she wouldn't be perpetuating any species anytime soon. Sadness—she thought of Chip, Gandy, Maxwell, and a dozen other friends she'd lost in war or otherwise, and brushed a tear from her eye when the mountains outside grew blurry. Happiness—that was the big one. That was quality of life. There were different kinds of happiness. Blasting the last lutuwon drop ship out of the sky and whooping it up with her fellow marines was nothing like the simple joy of playing in the dirt as a girl on Mars.

It wasn't a happy day. She'd planned a pirate raid on a mining fleet and heard that a friend had been kidnapped. That was another emotions she'd check on when circumstances allowed.

Kubu yawned and looked up at Tanny, his face upside down to hers. It was an awkward reach, but she twisted an arm around to pat him on the head. "Kubu's glad to have Mommy back. Kubu loves Mommy." He nuzzled his head against her hand.

Tanny felt a twitch in her face. It was a smile. "Looks like that works. At least a little. Mommy needed that."

---

Tanny staggered out of her quarters in search of food, stretching to loosen tight muscles. She hadn't planned to fall asleep. It had just happened and not in the most comfortable position. Kubu followed at her heels, his repeated query of "Food?" told Tanny they were thinking the same thing. It was a worrying thought, that she had been reduced to the mental simplicity of a semi-sentient canine. Hopefully once they were both fed, the gap would widen.

"Hey, sleeping beauty," Carl greeted her. "We were getting ready to draw lots to see who'd have to kiss you awake. Looks like Kubu got to you first." He was sitting at the kitchen table with Mort, playing their stupid holographic monster game as Mriy and Roddy looked on, clearly bored.

"Nothing personal," Roddy said, perched atop the back of a chair. "But I wouldn't have done it. Those kids' stories from Earth are all sorts of fucked up."

"Sorry," Tanny replied. "I'm feeling a little more myself now. I think the worst is over." 'Little' was the operative word. She was a little optimistic, and the thought of Carl naked was a bit more arousing, but everything was muted. Her feelings were on the other side of fogged glass; she couldn't touch them, and she could only make out indistinct shapes for most.

The fridge was restocked, and sometime during her nap, Roddy had repaired the door. There was plenty beer, a better selection than they usually stowed, but nothing fancy. She pulled a six-pack of Moudren Pale Ale and checked to see what sort of sandwich the food processor could assemble for her.

"Hold still, boy," she heard Mort say. Tanny turned to find the wizard bent down in front of Kubu, with his back to the rest of the crew. He was whispering something to the dog, but she couldn't make it out. Kubu didn't seem to mind, whatever it was.

"What are you doing over there?" Tanny asked across the room. She glanced to the food processor controls and punched in a quick BLT. It was a light meal, but enough to keep her from getting drunk on an empty stomach.

"One second," Mort replied. "One... more... second."

Kubu yelped.

"Kubu!" Tanny shouted, "Are you all right?" She was startled to realize she was concerned about him and startled a second time when it occurred to her that she could be startled.

Mort stepped away, a smug grin on his face. Tanny hurried over as the processor grumbled, working on her lunch. Kubu pawed gingerly at his ear with a hind leg. "What did you do to Kubu's ear?" Kubu asked.

"Everyone," Mort said, "Say hello to Kubu."

"What do you mean?" Carl asked. "He's been here weeks now."

"Whatever," Roddy muttered. "Hello to Kubu."

"Why are we greeting him?" Mriy asked.

Kubu's eyes went wide and his jaw hung open. He stopped pawing at his ear, stood, and took a step back.

"Mort..." Tanny said. "What did you do?"

"You... you can all *talk*!" Kubu said. He craned his neck to look up at Mort. "You made everyone talk?"

"Shit," Carl said. "Those earrings work on dogs?"

"Why are we working bullshit jobs out in this wasteland when we can just sell those to dog owners on Earth and Mars?" Roddy asked.

"They don't work on dogs," Mort replied. "It does seem to work on whatever Kubu is, though."

"All this time..." Tanny said.

"Yup," Mort replied.

"I could have been bitching his ass out for shitting in the cargo hold."

"Any chance we can teach him to use a toilet?" Roddy asked.

Kubu stared from one speaker to the next, the same gape-eyed wonder in his eyes. "So... crazy..."

"Kubu," Carl said. "You know what we're saying?"

Kubu nodded enthusiastically. "Uh huh."

"If we showed you a magic water-filled hole that you can shit into, then push a button to make the shit go away, think you could manage that?"

"You can do that?" Kubu asked. "Kubu thinks that's the bestest thing ever!"

Carl turned to Roddy. "Sounds like a 'yes.'"

Tanny crouched down beside Kubu. "My name is Tanny. You can call me Mommy if you want, but Tanny is my name. And I want you to eat only food, not just anything you find."

"I'll teach him the controls for the food processor," Roddy said. He thumped a fist against the machine.

"Kubu can make food in the big noisy?"

Carl shrugged. "Sure. Saves us the trouble of feeding you."

"When did you figure this out?" Tanny asked. Mort had kept secrets before—he probably still had more than the rest of them combined—but this felt out of character for him. Letting an animal shit all over the ship as a joke seemed too crude for his humor.

"Only really came to me yesterday," Mort replied. "But I got sidetracked. Then I figured I could wait until Tanny got back so she could see him understand his first words. We got to spend a lot of time together while you and Carl were holed up in the luxury of Casa de los Bandidos."

Roddy chuckled. "I was thinking of the Rucker Resort as more of a Seroki Jyzak."

Everyone just looked at Roddy.

"What?" he asked, balancing on the chair back and raising all four hands in a uniquely laaku shrug. "Seroki Jyzak ... from

*Temple of the Scoundrel Mutant Prophets.* You all watched it with me. How could you forget a thing like that? The brothel that was a front for the Fifth Hand assassins."

Tanny shrugged.

"I liked that holovid, but I didn't pay attention to the details," Mriy said. "The Leaping Masters were good fighters."

Carl cleared his throat. "Once they introduced Master Gojeth's human sidekick, I was mostly watching her. You may have noticed I have a thing for tough girls."

"Anita Shau is a joke in laaku films," Roddy said. "Her accent is pitiful. They dub over her for the Phabian market. She's just there to get human eyeballs on the holos. A holo with a human in it makes twice on Earth what it does back home."

Kubu spoke softly. "Tanny? Mommy? What are they talking about?"

Tanny leaned down and replied low enough that none of the others would hear her. "Nothing at all. They talk a lot just to hear themselves. It's OK to ignore them."

Kubu nodded.

It was going to be a different world for him now. Tanny wondered how he would adapt. It gave her a moment's pause to wonder how Esper was faring in her own new world, as a prisoner. A little knot formed in her stomach. Things were coming back, and she wondered whether she was better off *not* feeling them.

---

Esper turned a page, relishing the sound of paper sliding against paper. Most of the books she'd ever handled had plastic pages, and the few paper books she'd seen were deemed too precious to touch. But she was growing accustomed to the faint musty smell, the texture of the pages, the curious weight. She had chosen *Oliver Twist* from among the pirates' eclectic library and was nearly finished with it. Time passed more quickly between the pages than it did in the throes of a holovid stupor. Besides, recent circumstances aside, she could watch holovids any old time. This was an opportunity.

The door warning chimed. Whoever was outside would wait ten, perhaps fifteen seconds for her to disentangle herself from any compromising position she might be in, then barge inside. It had been fairly consistent in the three days she had been 'held' aboard the *Look On My Works, Ye Mighty, and Despair*.

Esper set the book on the side table and looked around. The chair's abundant cushioning had engulfed her, forming around her delicate posterior like a mold. Her feet, propped bare on the ottoman in front of her, had tiny balls of cotton wadded between the toes. Each toenail bore a fresh coating of burgundy paint, still smelling of the alcohol-based evaporating agent as they dried. She hadn't painted her fingernails yet, loath to lose the reading time as she waited for them to dry before handling rare and valuable books.

Raising her hands in a helpless gesture, she waited for the door to open. She was simply in no position to get up and greet anyone.

"Miss Richelieu," Cormack said when the door opened. "The Admiral wants to see you." He was her favorite among her keepers—they hardly seemed to be guards. Fair hair, neatly cropped. A soft, high voice that could have been called prissy. He stepped inside as if hesitant to disturb her.

"Well, this is her ship and all," Esper replied. "But she picked an inopportune time." She waved a hand at her toes.

Cormack smiled and gave a knowing wink. "You have time. She's invited you for dinner. She expects formal dress."

"Let me guess..."

Cormack nodded.

Esper sighed. "Fine. She wins."

The very afternoon of her arrival, they had provided her a simple dress, cut almost perfectly to her size. It was a child's picture book image of what a dress should be and as blue as a crayon. It had just been a placeholder. After obtaining proper measurements, some madman tailor aboard the *Look On My Works, Ye Mighty, and Despair* had made her five more. Not a one of those five could have been described as plain. It was a far cry from Tanny's policy of functional, practical, inconspicuous clothing.

But there was one that had clearly been the formal option.

"Dinner will be at 19:30 Earth Standard Time," Cormack said. He set down a datapad and Esper's heart quickened. A datapad meant contact with the outside world. "I see the look in your eye, Miss Richelieu. It's a datanote. No omni, no comm. All it contains are dressing instructions and a reminder alarm. Sorry."

"A girl can hope," Esper said with a sigh. She liked Cormack. He seemed to understand. A dinner with him, she could have looked forward to. Someone she could talk with, laugh with, maybe take her mind off not being allowed to leave. And she could flirt with him until she was old and gray and never get him to like women. "How bad is it?" she asked, glancing from the datanote up to Cormack.

"You'll be stunning," he said. With a flippant, playful salute, he took his leave. Before the door closed, Esper just caught a glimpse of the *actual* guard, a thick-armed fellow with a stun baton clipped to his belt.

Her current attire was the nightdress she'd been given her first night in the pirates' custody. It seemed impolite to chance ruining a new dress with nail polish, even if she was technically a prisoner. Extracting herself from the cushiony nest she'd formed in her reading chair, Esper plucked the cotton balls from her toes and found the nails to be dry. The room's wardrobe was imitation Earthwood, oak grown on some arboretum world. She couldn't imagine even Admiral Chisholm could afford the real thing.

Inside the wardrobe, there were five dresses on numbered hangers. The Poets were the most detail-oriented pirates she'd ever heard of. The datanote's instructions made it clear that Dress 5 was the proper attire for the evening, though the included pictures made it impossible to confuse with the others. Checking the antique style hands-and-number-wheel chrono, she deduced that it was nearly two hours until dinner. She had time to paint her nails, take a long bath in the hot tub, and snack on chocolates in case dinner was something fancy and inedible.

By the time she was ready to dress, Esper had resigned herself to her fate. Dress 5 was a puzzling mix of the formal and risqué. Admiral Chisholm knew Esper had been a priestess, and had clearly passed the notion on to the ship's dressmaker (Esper still couldn't fathom anyone joining a pirate fleet in that capacity). The fabric was a somber black; it was smooth and soft without a trace of shine, trimmed around the edges with a few millimeters of white silk. There was black embroidery that only showed upon close inspection, swirling in patterns of ivy around a crucifix nestled over the stomach. From a meter away, it was all but invisible against the black fabric. The inside of the dress was all white silk and felt wonderful against her skin. It stretched a little as she pulled it up; there were no clasps, no zippers, not even one of those trendy self-sealing polymerized seams. It simply stretched as it went over her hips and snugged in against her waist once it was past.

There was a full-length mirror beside the wardrobe. The fabric came just high enough over her breasts that she could be shown on a family-friendly holovid feed, but no higher. Esper bounced and twisted, worried that she might have an unfortunate accident, but the dress clung to her modesty. It was like a chaperone that only allowed sex after a nice meal. The skirt came to her knees in a flare of petticoats, but left her lower legs bare.

"Computer, five more degrees, please," Esper said to the room, and she heard a whoosh of warm air begin flowing in to counter the chill that was more in her head than on her legs.

The datanote wasn't done with her yet. There was a silk neck ribbon specified as well. After that, in the top of the wardrobe, a black cloche hat with a white bow. The matching shoes were sixty millimeter heels, and Esper wobbled around the room for a few minutes getting used to them. She hadn't worn heels since she was eighteen.

She hadn't removed either her crucifix necklace or her bloodstone charm, which had turned a shade of pink that would be embarrassing if anyone recognized it for what it was. The color stood out against her pale skin—the only touch of color in her ensemble. Leaving it behind seemed foolish. The last thing she needed was weeks waiting for it to attune itself to her again if she was late in putting it back on.

The door warning chimed. It was time to go. Her escort was the thick-armed guard, who barely spoke a word and looked her square in the chest when he did. It was high school all over again. For a few minutes, once she had worked out the kinks in walking in heels, she had posed in front of the mirror like a glamor model, feeling ladylike and pretty for the first time in a long while. Thick-arms had turned her back into a piece of meat in an instant.

The admiral's private office was up a short metal stairway. Esper clung to the railings with an iron grip as she tiptoed in her heeled slippers, the soles so new they might as well have been waxed. But her relief at the top was fleeting, replaced by wonder.

They were at the top of the ship, in a clear dome, either glassteel or transparent metal, depending on whether science or magic had been used. Stretched out above them was Carousel. It was a dull, ugly world compared to many, but stretched out and filling the sky, it was breathtaking.

"I'm glad you like the view," Admiral Chisholm said. Esper blinked and turned her attention to her host and warden. Her eyes went wide, and her tongue stuck in her throat. The admiral had changed out of her uniform and into a dress better suited to sleepwear than receiving company. It was flimsy, diaphanous, and held up by two thin strips of fabric. The admiral's hair was unbound, still wavy from having been in braids. She wore a pair of gold-rimmed spectacles perched on her nose and held a wine glass.

Esper's first step cost her a stumble, her attention fixed on Admiral Chisholm and not on remembering to keep her toes pointed down. "Sorry," she said as she grabbed the edge of a side table set with a platter of cheeses.

"It becomes you," Admiral Chisholm said. "Even if you're not used to it. Go ahead. Ask. I see the question in your eyes. There can be no truth where questions are feared."

"I feel overdressed," Esper said. She made a gesture as if to point, but stopped short of actually aiming a finger at the admiral. "You... you seem rather relaxed, admiral."

"This is a place for getting out of yourself," she said, flourishing her wine glass. "For you, it's getting out of the drear and drudgery of your self-imposed life as a spacer. For me, it's getting out of prim and proper and being called admiral. In here, please call me Emily, Esper." She gestured to a seat across from her.

"Thank you... Emily," Esper replied, sinking gratefully into a seat and sneaking her feet out of her heels. How had she worn those to school every day for years on end?

A crewman in something resembling a tuxedo slipped in and poured a glass of wine for Esper and refilled Emily's glass. Esper sipped it, and found it more sweet than biting.

"If you are wondering about the occasion, I have good news for you," Admiral Emily said.

Esper pursed her lips into a dutifully expectant smile as she lowered her glass. She cocked her head.

"The data specialist you brought with you to Carousel is a mole. My people dug into his ... well, details are boring, but he works for an anti-syndicate task force. All your friends need to do is get themselves out of the crossfire, and the Earth Interstellar Enhanced Investigative Org will take care of Janice Rucker for me."

"So, I can leave?" Esper asked. She took another sip of the delicious wine.

Emily gave a sniffing chuckle as she drank, then wiped her mouth with a finger. "No, not yet. But soon enough, should your friends not get swept up in the whole affair."

Dinner came, and it was unlike anything Esper had eaten. Despite her family's rise to wealth and respectability, it had always been a secret shame that her parents had clung to low-class cuisine, preferring the taste and familiarity to the more stylish selections of their newfound peers. Esper had never eaten duck, let alone one basted in Earth-wine sauce, and her apple was infused with chocolate, a feat she had never heard of before.

Throughout the meal, Emily questioned Esper about her personal philosophy, and how one went about living within the teachings of a single school of thought. In return, Emily shared her commingling of Machiavelli and Augustus Caesar's views into the command of her own fleet.

"It's not as if I earned respect instantly," Admiral Emily replied. She waved a fork for emphasis, a bit of duck skewered on the end. There was a slur in her voice, not enough to sour its melody, but enough to suggest a saturation with wine. "I was handed the fleet from my father, who had gotten it from his mother. First I Machiavelli'ed the ones who refused to follow me... not suitable for dinner conversation. Then I set my sights on building, expanding, conquering. Do great things. Taking Freeride... all my idea."

Esper couldn't recall who Machiavelli was right then, and Caesar was the one who got killed in Shakespeare as far as she remembered. "That's impressive. Very impressive. You have the nicest bunch of pirates I've ever seen. And I've seen..." Esper frowned a moment. "...two."

Emily laughed, and Esper found it infectious. Crewmen came and cleared away their dinner plates, and refilled their wine glasses. Esper knew she'd drunk too much, but it tasted so good she was having trouble finding a reason to refuse more.

Emily took a long swallow of wine and sighed. It was the sort of emptying sigh that purges the lungs to leave you feeling clean inside. Esper grinned, and Emily locked stares with her.

"You know," Admiral Emily said. "I might enjoy spending a night in my own quarters." She licked the wine from her lips.

Esper giggled. "It's your ship. Who's going to tell you where to sleep?"

Emily stood and dragged the fingers of one hand along the table as she came around to Esper's side and stood behind her. Esper felt the warmth of hands on her bare shoulders and the whisper of breath on her ear. "Those are my quarters you're borrowing. I wouldn't think of imposing where I wasn't... wanted."

Esper blushed head to toe, and her breath quickened. This had suddenly become a sticky situation, with the risk of becoming stickier. The good idea/bad idea portion of her brain was submerged in a liter of wine. She was pretty sure there was sinning on the way—not that drunkenness wasn't a sin already. A lot of sins seemed to be chasing her down of late, and Esper was doing a poor job of sidestepping this one. Compared to murder, it seemed fairly minor. But that had been an accident, and this one might also be an accident. She hadn't had a man in her bed in six years, and this wouldn't even technically break her streak. Not to mention the other night when she'd had her engines revved up to full throttle before diverting emergency power to a harmless massage.

Esper stood, stumbling to her side and catching herself on the edge of a table with a helpless giggle. Emily bent down and looked her in the eye, laughing along. "I'm... I... flattered, but I... I can't."

Emily hadn't received the message any more clearly than it had been transmitted. "Sure you can. It's eeeasy. I can show you." She reached out and put her hands atop Esper's.

Esper pulled away, catching herself on Emily's chair. "No. Not 'no,'" she said, holding up her hands to ward off hurt feelings, then grabbing hold of the chair once more when wine and heels threatened to deposit her on the floor. "But it's a... philosophical thing. Core principle violation."

Emily straightened and sighed again, this time wistful. Her drunkenness seemed much less pronounced as she walked over and laced her fingers behind Esper's neck. "Such a shame. I had assumed, since you shunned Raimi—"

"Nope," Esper said, shaking her head emphatically, causing a sudden wave of dizziness. When the spell passed, Emily's lips found hers. She struggled briefly in her surprise, but the taste of sweet wine and the warm softness relaxed her. Alarm klaxons horned in her brain, warning of error codes and improper signals being received. Esper closed her eyes.

Emily released her with a gasp. "A pity. Your soul is a work of art. If your friends didn't make it back, I'd have gladly kept you as my personal attendant." With that, she turned and headed down the stairs.

Esper made the walk back to her borrowed quarters barefoot, leaning on Thick-Arms for support.

---

As soon as the door closed behind her, Esper collapsed against the adjacent wall. The room spun as she leaned her head back until it bumped against the faux plaster with a dull thump. With a push of willpower, she abandoned the support of the wall's presence, and let her heeled shoes drop to the floor as she staggered toward the dessert cart, freshly replenished in her absence.

Her stomach sloshed with wine, still being sucked into her bloodstream and her liver, continuing to exacerbate her drunkenness. If she didn't act quickly, she'd pass out, losing goodness only knew how much vital time. The *Mobius* crew was walking into a trap, and she was the only one who both knew and was inclined to inform them. The pastries were probably delicious when savored one by one, teasing out flavors from frostings and jellied fillings. Rammed into her mouth in pairs, with more to follow before she finished swallowing the prior lot, it was a sugary mush.

When the nausea of overeating threatened to overwhelm her, Esper used her magic. "Cuts close, bruises fade; three weeks healing done today; bones knit, pains ease; cleanse the body of disease." The rhyme was a comfort, a measure of control she had lacked when she killed Kenneth Eugene Shaw. The warm giddiness of her alcoholic stupor gave way to the fevered heat of her bodily functions kicking into overdrive. In seconds, the confusion of drunkenness had passed, along with the overfull sensation of a stomach crammed with jelly-puffs.

Bryce Brisson worked for the Earth law enforcement. Janice was being set up, and everyone was going to get fished up in the same net if she didn't warn them. She needed a way to contact them. Her first thought was the datanote on the table. Sure, they had *told* her it was limited to just a few select functions, but the easiest modification to a standard datapad would be to just lie about what it could do.

It was a Tooky-brand datapad, which didn't bode well. If anyone was cheap enough to sell datapads with all the functionality of a few slips of paper, it was Tooky Industries. The menu options were limited, letting Esper see the dress she was still wearing, along with a diagram of suggested accessories. It had an alterable alarm set for fifteen minutes before dinner, but which wasn't helpful in any other way she could imagine. There were standard functions as well: a calculator, calendar, a number of selectable background images, but nothing that transmitted.

The application of a butter knife was enough to pop the case open, the front and back halves popping neatly apart. The innards only took up two thirds of the interior volume, the rest being wasted space. Esper pored over the components, identifying each part as she was able. Processor. Screen. Microphone. Data Storage. There wasn't even a camera or motion sensors, let alone a broadcast antenna. She pushed the pieces off the table in disgust.

She had already checked the holo-projector, back on her first night with the Poets. It was a receiver only, and she knew she didn't have the know-how to convert it into a two-way. That left finding a transmitter somewhere else aboard the *Look On My Works, Ye Mighty, and Despair*. That meant getting out past the guard. Or did it?

The guards were regular crewmen. They were full-on pirates, with loot and plunder, probably. They could afford fancy clothes and shiny weapons that could do all sorts of interesting and horrible things to people. Her door guards only carried stun batons—which was a small comfort, not that she wanted to get beaten with stun batons—but the other Poets carried a creative array of weaponry. People who can afford expensive things don't carry around Tooky datapads; they'd have top-of-the-line OmniWalkers or Slashcubes, maybe one of the trendy laaku Yinswoos.

Esper stopped short. It was the second occasion in the past week where she'd considered stealing a datapad. "I must have some hang-up on datapads," she muttered. "I should probably buy myself a nice one when this is all over." That seemed like a reasonable compromise. Head off theft by indulging in palliative consumerism. Not quite a biblical solution to the problem, but that was a matter for later prayer and introspection.

A quick check of the wall chrono said it was nearing midnight. "What?" she gasped. She had dined and snacked and drank with Emily for hours. She felt a small pang of guilt for apparently leading the admiral on for so long. It was more effort than anyone had put into seducing her in a long time. But the late hour meant that a change of guards was due at any moment. Thick-Arms would hand her over to Paul, one of the few whose name she had learned.

Her hands shook. They knew what she was thinking before she even admitted it to herself. After cleaning up the broken datanote, she poured herself a glass of champagne. She hadn't touched the room's stock of liquors until just then, not wanting to turn into Roddy, who washed away his time in a liquid coma. But she was fully sober, and a sober Esper wasn't what her plan called for. She downed a half glass in two giant gulps, then refilled it halfway and took a seat in her reading chair. The hat got in the way of her lounging, so she tossed it on the floor nearby.

The door warning chimed. Her heart quickened. The plan had flaws, not the least of which was that of its several resolutions, the successful paths were all a choice between minor evils. She took another quick sip of champagne to dull that little voice that told her maybe her plan wasn't supposed to work.

"Good evening, Miss Richelieu," Paul greeted her when the door opened. "Anything you need, I'll be right outside until morning." He stepped back into the hall, and was about to close the door.

"Wait!" Esper said. "There is something." Paul stepped back in and put his hands on his hips. He was rugged, squarish in the shoulders and jaw, with a shaved scalp and pecks that showed through the fabric of his shirt. Esper licked her lips and avoided looking Paul in the eye, but let him see her looking over the rest of him. "Do you have a moment?"

"Sure." He looked over his shoulder, then hit the door control. They were alone together.

"What are your orders, specifically?" Esper asked.

Paul shrugged. "Keep you from going anywhere. Not let anyone in without the admiral or Indira's say-so. Pass along if you need anything."

"What if it was something you could do yourself?" Esper asked.

Paul shook his head. "Can't leave my post. I can get someone to bring you anything, pretty much. What do you need?"

"Are you breaking your orders right now, then?" Esper asked. "You're not outside the door."

"I can be in here," he said defensively. "Ain't nothing wrong with that."

"Long enough for drinks?" Esper asked. Oh God, please let her not sound like a blithering idiot. "Maybe... longer?"

Paul smirked. "I heard about you and the admiral tonight."

Esper swallowed, wishing she were a teensy bit more drunk for this. "A girl has needs, but it's... well, some locks just need the right key." Dear Lord, had she just said that? Where did that come from? Was it from some sappy holovid? Hopefully Paul hadn't seen it if it was.

"Oh yeah?" Paul asked, his smirk turning speculative. Men were such docile brutes. Esper fought back a wave of disgust over just how easy this was proving to be.

She stood and eyed the wet bar. Tipping back the remainder of her champagne, she asked, "Care to fill me up?"

She waggled the empty glass. That line she recognized the moment it escaped her lips. It was from *Daisy's Choice*, which she had watched more times than she cared to admit.

Paul was subtle, unhooking his stun baton and setting it on the table by the door. Nonthreatening. He knew that much, at least. He apparently knew the selection in the admiral's quarters as well, picking up an unlabeled decanter without hesitation. It was obviously not his first romp in this suite.

As he poured, Esper slipped around behind him, dragging a hand along the rippling muscles of his back. From the corner of her eye, she could see Paul's grin widen. But in her other hand, Esper held an unopened bottle of Chateau Descartes 2648; she brought it down on the back of Paul's skull with all her might.

Paul grunted and keeled over, stumbling to a knee. Esper hit him again before he recovered. He fell limp, and Esper breathed a sigh of relief, mixed with horror. She crossed herself, closed her eyes, and asked forgiveness. There was just no other way she could think of to save her friends. Sleeping with Paul *might* have worked, but she had chosen her lesser evil and she was going to stick with it. Besides, it was easier than sneaking around, hoping he didn't wake up.

Paul kept his datapad in a pocket at his thigh. Even limp, the muscle was stiff. Esper caught herself admiring his physique, but quickly shoved those thoughts aside. She had been right; his datapad was modern. It was an OmniWalker Tudor, last year's most popular high-end model—not that Esper had followed such trends, or quietly envied the Harmony Bay scientists' children who carried them. It was thumbprint locked, which proved to be an impediment for all of ten seconds. Paul limply obliged from the floor.

Tanny's safety drills came in handy once more. Esper had

memorized the comm code for the *Mobius*, the one that didn't show up in general directories on the omni. She punched it in and waited.

There was no response.

Frowning, and wondering why no one was answering when she really needed them to, she keyed the speaker override for the shipwide comm. Anyone on board would hear her now. "Hey, someone answer. It's Esper." She hissed out a frustrated breath. "Mort, if you're there, just push the red button below the speaker. Red. Speaker. Right below. Just push it and talk."

Mort could be dense about technology at times, but she *knew* he could work the comm panels. She was drawing a deep breath to shout through the ship's speakers when a voice came through the datapad.

"Kubu push button."

Esper nearly dropped the datapad. Her eyes went wide, her hand limp.

"Kubu good? Hello?"

"Kubu, find Mommy... Mo-mmy. Get Mommy." She could only hope he would go find Tanny for her.

"Mommy's not here," Kubu replied, his voice coming through admirably clear over the excellent speakers in the OmniWalker Tudor. "Everybody went out. Kubu can't go. Kubu is guarding the flying house."

Esper blinked. He understood her. That was a reasoned, direct reply to her command. She had to be sure. "Kubu, you can understand me?"

"Yes. Who is this?" Kubu asked.

"Esper. Mommy's friend. You know me."

"The one who puts flower smells in her hair?"

That would have been her lilac shampoo. Good gracious,

he *did* understand her. "Kubu, do you remember the new person? The one with short hair who sleeps in the front room?"

"Yes. He hides from Kubu."

"Kubu, you need to tell Mommy that he's a bad man. He works for..." She knew Kubu could understand her, but she doubted he was quite up to relaying 'Earth Interstellar Enhanced Investigative Org' in any cogent manner. "He works for the people who want to put Mommy and everyone else in a cage. He plays tricks on them, and he's not nice. You need to tell Mommy. Do you understand?"

"New man in front room plays tricks on Mommy and wants to put her in a cage," Kubu replied.

This was too bizarre. She was talking to a dog, and entrusting him with a mission. "Can you remember that until Mommy gets back?"

"Yes. Did you know Mommy has two names? Mommy's other name is Tanny." Kubu sounded so proud.

Esper swallowed past a lump in her throat. "You're a good boy, Kubu." She hit 'end call.' Quickly deleting the call record, she locked the datapad and slipped it back into Paul's pocket.

There was still a limp body on the floor beside her. It was time for the unpleasant part of the plan.

It took all her strength to drag Paul across the floor. If not for the polished floor, she might not have been able to manage at all. Admiral Chisholm's suite was equipped with a hot tub, and she left him at the edge of it. She turned away as best she was able and began removing Paul's clothes. But there were buckles and snaps, laces, and parts where she had to wiggle him around to get garments out from under his dead weight. There was just no ignoring him completely. She scattered his clothes around the bed as if they'd been discarded amid passion.

Paul's naked form was distracting. He was warm and a tad sweaty, not sliding along the tile floor around the hot tub nearly so well as he had across the hardwood. It took her nearly half an hour to wrestle him into a seated position in the hot tub. Turning on the water, she took a long breath and prepared for the embarrassing part. As the tub filled, she stripped off her own clothes and likewise discarded them by the bed.

Not looking at Paul was nearly as good as him not looking at her, and she covered herself with her hands despite being, for all practical purposes, alone. Admiral Chisholm was not the sort to deny herself girlish pleasures, and there was a selection of bubble additives. With a wince, she found one labeled in pink with claims of aphrodisiac properties. That was the right one; she had to play it up as best she could. As the bubbles filled the hot tub and the breeze from environmental controls chill on her bare skin, Esper crossed herself and climbed in opposite Paul.

It was a small hot tub, just large enough to be intimate with two or for one to relax and sprawl. Esper did neither. Even below the water level and bubbled, she covered herself with her hands, just on the off chance Paul woke. There was no getting away from touching him, either. Her legs ended up tangled with his, and there wasn't much to be done about that. Except wait.

An hour passed, then another. Esper had to reheat the water several times and refresh the bubbles once. The little jets of water were the only consolation—they felt wonderful on her back and legs. At long last, a few notes from an unfamiliar song blared muffled from Paul's pocket. It repeated, over and over, for a minute or more, then ceased. Paul hadn't answered; it was only a matter of time until someone came to find out why.

The door warning chimed. Esper was already touching Paul—she'd had quite enough of touching him, actually—so it was a simple matter to heal the wound she had inflicted. He began to stir just as another of the guards barged in.

"Paul, what the *fuck* you doing in there?" the guard demanded. A pillar-necked thug, he was the sort that most seedy organizations in holovids kept around to rough people up. The guard held a datapad up to his mouth. "Yeah, he's in here. He's been sticking it to the admiral's girl. ... Yeah, no, he's *right* here in front of me. ... No, you'd never know she was a priestess. Just get a couple guys down here, I'll take a picture and show you later." He took his datapad and angled it toward Esper.

Esper ducked as far down into the water as she was able, but Paul was taking up much of the free space.

"What's going on?" Paul demanded.

"I'm sorry," Esper said, loud enough that the guard with the datapad was sure to hear. "I didn't mean for us to get caught. You fell asleep. You got a comm on your datapad. I didn't want to wake you."

"How did I... did we... we didn't just ...?"

Esper nodded. It was easier lying without saying the words.

"Come on, lover-boy," the guard said, striding over to the hot tub. Esper hadn't planned this far ahead. She scrunched into a ball as the guard loomed over them, but all he did was grab Paul by the upper arms and haul him out of the tub.

"I... I..." Paul didn't seem to know how to put his evening back into a shape that made sense.

"Put yer clothes on," the guard said. "I don't give a shit if you're wet, I don't wanna drag your naked ass through the ship."

"Please," Esper said. "You don't need to tell Admiral Emily —I mean Chisholm. I... I don't want her to take this the wrong way."

The guard shrugged. "The admiral's a fine piece of lady. If that ain't your taste, that's your business. But really... this sorry scab was your back-up plan?" He looked to the floor shook his head. "'Who ever loved that loved not at first sight?' I get, but Paul?"

Esper kept her eyes averted as Paul dressed and the new guard escorted him away. Sleep couldn't come soon enough to put the day behind her.

---

Bryce Brisson strutted into the common room of the *Mobius* like he had just won the ship in a poker game. Fresh haircut. Clean shave. He carried a small footlocker by one handle, slung over his shoulder. There was a grin on his face as he shook Carl's hand, and he clapped Mriy on the shoulder as he walked by. He had a nod for Roddy and a wink for Tanny. He seemed about to pat Mort on the back as he passed, but a stern look from the wizard made him abort the attempt. Tanny tried to envision him undressed and was pleasantly surprised to find she liked the prospect.

She was feeling more like herself—her old self. Days spent in planning sessions with Janice's crew brought back memories of her time in the marines. Sure, her cousin's little splinter syndicate was nowhere near as hard-nosed and gruff as the 804th Planetary Insertion Division. But she felt a familiar rush of anticipation, like the hunger before a holiday feast.

"Quarantine looks like it treated you well," Tanny remarked. None of them had seen Bryce since Janice took custody of him, but with the mission launch coming up, he was entrusted to the *Mobius* once more.

"I've drunk more beer and watched more holovid sports than I did in college," Bryce replied. "How's it feel to be law-abiding citizens again?"

Carl chuckled. "You mean how's it feel having everyone else think we are?" he asked. "I'll let you know once we've had a chance to land someplace where they care."

"Fair enough," Bryce replied. "I assume I'm good for the same bunk? Can't wait to see what you've done with the place."

Tanny set aside the installation instructions for their new holo-projector, and shadowed Bryce as he sauntered off down the corridor to the front of the ship. She wanted to be there when he saw.

He opened the door and stopped short. "You gotta be shitting me."

Tanny slouched against the wall beside him and crossed her arms. "Just the way you left it." Despite ample time, the *Mobius* was still on a ramen-dinner budget when it came to luxury purchases, and that included upgrades to the guest accommodations. Their remaining funds had gone into restocking the fridge and pantry, patching up the *Mobius* to Roddy's satisfaction, and picking up a stolen holo-projector at a steep discount.

Bryce let the footlocker dangle from his limp arm, dragging it on the floor as he trudged into his quarters. It must have been a shock going from the Rucker Resort's classy three-star decor with wall-to-wall holovids and all the gambling you could stomach, to the bare walls and cot of the *Mobius*.

The controls of the *Mobius* felt good in Tanny's hands. The grips on the flight yoke were worn where her hands always rested, the seat cushion padding crushed into the shape of her buttocks and lower back. The subtle hum that vibrated throughout every surface when the engines were running was back, and that was a comfort all its own. The worst of the waiting was over. It was mission time.

How Carl had gotten Janice to go along with the plan, she didn't know. Mort probably knew. Roddy would have wheedled the details out of him. But when Carl had returned from the Rucker Resort grinning like a bandit, she had given him such a glare that he had kept his methods to himself. He had managed to keep his mouth shut about it even from the co-pilot's seat, where he monitored the comm and sensors.

Formation flying wasn't something Tanny had done much in recent years. It was like being back in the marines, in the cockpit of a drop ship. The controls were different. There were fewer crude comments from grunts racked up in the drop bay. But the low-intensity thinking of just following the other ships and waiting for updated orders was the same as ever.

"If this thing goes sideways, Mort's ready to drop us out of the convoy's astral depth," Carl mentioned. He just couldn't sit there keeping his mouth shut. It was downright psychiatric. Mort was *always* ready to try something stupid and dangerous to flex his magical muscle. She ignored him and hoped he would take the hint.

They were still in Poet-controlled space, using the fleet's astral gate out to the edge of the Freeride System. Twelve mining ships, including the large, clumsy colony ship, drifted along amid their escort. Janice's *Alley Cat*, a Shadow class blockade running, led the way. The *Mobius* took the port side of the formation, with the *Atlantis Dream*—a militia patrol craft under Bill's command—on the starboard. Taking up the rear was a temporary escort from the Poet Fleet, a pair of light cruisers that could dust the lot of them, the *Do Rhetorical Questions Require Punctuation* and the *It Tolls For Thee*.

It was only minutes to the astral gate that would take them back to real space at the outskirts of Freeride. Once they dropped out of the public astral space, the convoy would engage their own star-drives and head out of system. Tanny keyed the comm to the engine room. "Roddy, all systems check out?"

"No, that new holo-projector is a piece of junk," Roddy came back through the cockpit speakers.

Carl leaned across to Tanny's side of the cockpit. "Hey, it was the best we were getting in Carousel. You rather be stuck watching me and Mort play Battle Minions?"

"The *ship's* system, Roddy," Tanny said. "Engines, shields ... the stuff that matter *now*."

"Engines are 4 percent under ideal efficiency, probably due to fuel impurities, but it could be a misalignment in the ignition subsystem. Shields are iffy; the dissipation coefficient is only 29 percent, but it's not like we can power them up any higher than 30 or 35 with the engines and guns on line. Life support reports a pressure increase over nominal in the waste reclaim, and I'm pretty sure with Kubu around, that's going to need regular maintenance. Internal power distribution—"

"She just wants the military version," Carl said.

Roddy's snort carried clearly through the comm. "Okie dokie, cap'n. We're good as gum for a gunfight."

Tanny gave Carl a withering look, but he just smirked back with a silent laugh in his eyes. How could he keep the jester act when they were about to engage in a mission? Even with the Recitol telling her that worrying was for weaklings, she could feel her palms sweating.

*"Roy, Barnum & Toyoda Mining Expedition fleet, you are cleared for astral exit,"* Captain Jan Toivonen, commander of the *It Tolls For Thee,* said.

*"Roger that,"* came the reply from Commander Bilkken of the mining convoy. *"Thanks for the escort."*

Carl shook his head. "They actually sound grateful."

"They're Sol based," Tanny said. "They're probably pissing themselves being this far from an ARGO battle group. There's no Vendetta class interceptor cruisers to bail them out if they get in trouble. Those pirates probably looked like real protection to them."

"You're not getting cold feet, are you?" Carl asked.

"No," Tanny lied. This was all worked out and finalized. If they wanted their records to stay cleared, Esper back, and no one sentenced to decades of prison time, they had to follow through. "I just... they're like lambs to the slaughter."

"No slaughter," Carl replied. "I got Janice to buy off on that. We fuck this up in a 'prosecutor and judge' sorta way, it'll be simple piracy, not murder."

"What's that?"

"In years?" Carl asked. Tanny nodded. Carl was the one who normally worried about that end of things. "Fifteen for you guys, twenty for me as the ship's owner. That's if the big boys get us. If we got rounded up by local militias or someone besides an ARGO species, they'd probably dust us without hailing."

"I swore we'd never stoop to this," Tanny muttered. They'd done a lot of low jobs: theft, smuggling, illegal salvage. But this was the first time they'd ever attacked another ship preemptively.

Carl turned a shrug into an elaborate stretch, then laced his fingers behind his neck. "We've sworn lots of things, you and me. I've sworn to tell the truth, the whole truth, and nothing but. You've sworn to love, honor, and cherish. This shit slides. You want, I can have Roddy draw up some fake divorce papers to get you out of swearing never to become a pirate."

"Give it a rest." It was different, and Carl had to have known it was different. The fact that he could make one thing sound like another was part of the way he helped them on jobs. But Tanny was going to be damned if she was going to let him sit there and twist her around until she agreed with him. He was taking advantage of her tenuous mental state.

"I'm just saying, if it's the promise that's bothering you, we can—"

Her fist acted on reflex. She was already feeling the sting in her knuckles before she realized she'd done it. Carl fell across the console on the far side of the co-pilot's chair. He stumbled out of his seat, clutching a hand to his mouth. The sounds coming out were undoubtedly vulgar, but they were equally incomprehensible.

"I'm sorry, I—"

Carl ignored her and staggered down the corridor to the rest of the ship.

Tanny hadn't intended to hit him. She had just wanted him to shut up, or at least change the subject. He had been asking for it. She had warned him. It was *his* fault, really. Hadn't he known her long enough to realize that she was liable to haul off and hit him if he pushed her too far? Too far was just closer than usual these days. She had mellowed herself out by experimenting with mood-levelers over the years. But she'd had a quick trigger when they first met. He ought to have remembered.

"Oh God," Tanny muttered, alone in the cockpit. "Am I going back to what I was like when I mustered out?" Back in those days, she had no friends. Her marine buddies had stayed in the service or taken the free detox. Old acquaintances shunned her, afraid of how much she'd changed, and she didn't let new people close. Carl had put up with her out of an odd mixture of thrill seeking, a shared interest in drinking, and—if she was honest with herself—the fact that she was raging with suppressed hormonal needs that he positioned himself to benefit from.

"*This is* Alley Cat, *check in prior to astral drop*," Janice's voice from the comm startled Tanny.

"Alley Cat, *this is* Atlantis Dream. *Ready to dive*," Bill replied.

Tanny fumbled for the button to open the comm. "This is *Mobius*. We'll follow you in."

Switching to ship-wide comm, she continued. "Mort, when you feel the convoy drop, bring us with them."

---

Kubu watched Mort. When Mommy talked from the wall, she told him to drop them. Kubu wasn't sure he liked that, but it being dropped was probably better than being locked up in Mommy's room. Mommy's room was small and boring, and she didn't listen to him when he told her so. But he was only a good boy if he stayed and didn't chew on anything, so he stayed, and didn't chew on anything. Mort had said it was OK to come out, and had opened the door.

Mort danced and sang, but his words were silly and didn't make any sense. The words didn't hurt, but they made Kubu's ears feel funny. When Mort was finished his dancing song, he sat down on the couch. Kubu jumped up beside him.

"That was funny," Kubu said, opening his mouth in a wide smile with his tongue hanging loose.

Mort frowned. "Funny, eh? The flarngmoot ziffod of the gipgop is funny to you?" Mort used more silly words than anyone.

Kubu nodded. "You say funny words. Thank you for letting Kubu out."

"Well, it's Bryce's turn to get locked in a room, at least until we're done with this job," Mort said.

Kubu cocked his head. "Who is Bryce? Does someone else have two names, like Mommy?"

Mort laughed through his nose. "No. You remember Bryce. He was here before we landed. You scared him, so Tanny made you stay in the room."

Kubu's eyes went wide. "The bad man is back?"

Mort rubbed a rough hand on Kubu's head. "Oh, he's harmless."

"No," Kubu replied. "He wants to put us in cages. Mommy's friend in the wall said so."

"That's actually Tanny talking over the ship's comm," Mort said. "You get used to it."

"No, not *now*," Kubu said. "Before. Mommy's friend was talking from the wall, and the bad man is playing a trick to put us in cages."

Mort grabbed Kubu under the chin and looked him right in the eyes. The mustard on his breath made Kubu's tummy jealous and grumbly. "Esper called you?"

Kubu nodded. "Esper is Mommy's friend. She made the wall talk, just like Mommy does."

"Gadzooks! Esper sent us a warning," Mort said. "Why didn't you say anything sooner?"

Kubu hung his head. It seemed he hadn't been such a good boy after all. "Bad man was gone."

Mort jumped up from the couch and ran to Mommy's flying room.

---

Mort burst into the cockpit. "We've got a problem!"

Seated at the controls, Tanny would have leapt out of her seat if she wasn't buckled in. "God dammit, Mort! Get out of here!"

Mort waved away her concerns. "No time for that," Mort said. "That Bryce fellow is a plant."

"This is not time to get metaphysical," Tanny said. "Keep it together."

"You're not listening clearly," Mort replied. "Bryce isn't flora, he's a double agent. Think *The Three-Sided Coin* or *The Julian Affair*, except this time it's not on the holo and it's *our* keesters in the cross-hairs."

Tanny lifted her arms to an uncaring universe. "You just came to this revelation... how?"

"Kubu—"

"Good Lord, Mort! He's got the intelligence of an infant. You can't be taking him seriously."

"Esper left a message," Mort said. "Must have been while we were over at the resort. 'Bad man tricking us, wants to put us in cages.' Sound like something Esper might try to simplify to Kubuian comprehension."

"Shit." Mort was right. If any of them were going to trust a barely sentient dog with their lives, it would be Esper—though she wouldn't put it past Carl, either.

"Shit, indeed," Mort agreed.

Tanny keyed the comm to the engine room. "Roddy, get up here and fly this thing."

Mort furrowed his brow. "Doesn't Mriy usually take care of that?"

It was true, Mriy was their backup pilot, but that was almost by default. Roddy was needed elsewhere, whereas Mriy was dead weight in the Black Ocean if she didn't help mind the cockpit. But this time, it was Roddy whose skills could be spared. Tanny's thoughts were a blur, but there was one thing that was certain: they needed help, and it wasn't help they were going to find on board.

"Not this time," Tanny said.

---

As the door to her quarters slammed shut, Tanny allowed her frustration to show. She punched her mattress once, then again, then kept on punching it until her breath came in gasps. How could they have been so stupid? How could they have left the background check to Carl's "keen" eye? They needed to find out who Bryce Brisson really was, who he worked for, and some way that they might get some leverage to pry themselves out of the jam he had put them in. Tanny needed that background check, and someone who could do it *right*.

The datapad was the heaviest hundred grams she could have imagined. It took an act of will to lift it from her bedside and key in a code she had known since childhood, one she had to memorize, one she was only supposed to use in an emergency.

A cheery little waiting indicator swirled on the screen, informing Tanny that though nothing appeared to be happening, the datapad was hard at work in the background. They were a long ways from the Sol System, and the deepest, fastest astral omni relays were the most likely to be tapped by intelligence and law enforcement agencies. Even at nearly the speed of light, signals took time to travel at just four astral units deep.

"Hello?" a deep, puzzled voice asked. It was as familiar as her old bedroom, a voice filled with bedtime stories and promises of ice cream and ponies. Tanny's throat tightened. "Hello? Who is this? How's you get this ID? This comm is over—"

"Daddy, wait!" Tanny blurted.

"Tania? Is that you?" her father asked.

"Daddy, I've got a problem," Tanny said.

"You know you can—"

"I got caught up in something," Tanny continued. "I trusted someone I shouldn't have, and it looks like we're going to end up getting caught up with Janice and her crew in a bluehat trap. But my info might be wrong, and if it's wrong, I could sour a huge job, and maybe get some poor slob killed over nothing. We just didn't have the kind of resources to find out ahead of time whether—"

"Sweety, calm down," her father said. "I musta told you a hundred times; I don't care what you've done. I'll always be there for you. What do you need?"

Tanny sniffed. She wiped her eyes. "We picked up a guy," she said, clearing her throat. "Alias is Bryce Brisson. We did a background check, but nothing flagged as dangerous. Small-time data hustler; he did a little time. But we got a tip from someone being held by the Poet Fleet that this guy might be a mole. Can you dig him up good? Find out who he really is?"

"Sure, Tania," her father said. "Gimme an hour —two tops."

"Can you manage fifteen minutes?"

"You're that pinched?" her father asked.

"I'd try for five if I thought it was even possible."

"Hold on." The datapad went silent for a moment. "I got a guy on it. He knows this is important to me."

"Thank you, Daddy."

"Just one thing," her father said. "Can we put this on video comm? Just for a minute... please?"

Tanny closed her eyes and took a slow breath. She turned on the camera feed from her datapad. Don Rucker appeared on her screen, just as she would be appearing on his. He looked older. The last time she had seen him had been over a grudging invitation to her third wedding, but he'd been dressed to the nines and professionally styled. Now, his hair showed more gray than black, and the wrinkles around his mouth had deepened. But when he saw her, the familiar smile she had always remembered came back.

"There's my little girl," he said. A twinkle of mischief appeared in his eye. "You look like hell, though. Carl not taking good care of you?"

"I take care of myself, Daddy," Tanny replied. "And I'm just getting older, same as you. You look a little like hell, yourself."

"Maybe you oughtta finally quit that shit the marines got you hooked on," her father said. "If it's money, I can pay for the nicest place you'd ever want to dry out."

"It's not the money," Tanny replied. "That shit costs more

than detox would. It's just who I am now. Even Carl accepts that now, more or less."

"Well, maybe Carl just don't love you like I do," her father said. "My offer stands. You ever find yourself changing your mind, don't let money stop you. There's a place on the other side of Mars; they'd take good care of you."

"Let me know as soon as your guy runs his check," Tanny replied, shifting the topic back to the identity of Bryce Brisson.

"You got it, sweety," her father said. "It was good to hear from you, whatever the reason."

Tanny closed the comm. She wiped her eyes in earnest, and they welled up again in an instant. Dammit, she needed Sepromax! If she were herself, she never would have called her father for help. She certainly wouldn't have broken down crying like a five-year-old afterward. Thoughts of reporting back to the crew about the outcome of her call were abandoned, and Tanny let herself cry until the tears ran dry.

---

Bryce Brisson slammed into the wall, his toes just barely touching the floor. Mriy's grip around his throat was just loose enough for him to breathe. He tried to push the azrin away, but her arms were a quarter meter longer; he couldn't so much as reach her chest or face. Instead, he settled for grabbing onto the corded muscle of her forearm to support himself.

"It's all clear," Mriy called out. The rest of the crew filed into the converted conference room that Bryce had been given as quarters.

Tanny felt wrung out. Her eyes were still red in the mirror, but she was past the crying. When her father had called back, their brief exchange had been (almost) all business. Anger had prevented her from breaking down again, and her father's demeanor had reminded her why they hadn't patched things up between them. Don Rucker was one ruthless son-of-a-bitch, and it came across the omni loud and clear.

"Carl, Mort, one of you talk some sense into this crazy xeno," Bryce said.

"Trust me," Carl said, slipping inside and slouching against the wall by the door. He was still holding a hand to his sore jaw. "Mriy's the reasonable one here. Tanny would have broken both your legs if it weren't for Mriy handling you."

Mriy extended a claw on her free hand with a flick, gesturing to the floor. A broken stun blaster lay amid shattered pieces of its outer casing. "I got blasted twice in my broken ribs."

"If you'd let the doctors see you, they wouldn't still be broken," Carl replied.

Tanny approached within arm's reach of Bryce. If the snake wanted to take a swing at her, she'd have been more than happy to rupture his spleen in return. "Let's cut to the chase. "Your name is Martin David Morse, age thirty-eight, from Stockholm Prime. You are a captain in the Earth Interstellar Enhanced Investigative Org."

"Someone set me up," Bryce insisted, struggling for air.

Tanny shook her head. "No, they didn't. *You* set *us* up. Someone put a lot of effort into burying the link between Martin Morse and Bryce Brisson. But not enough."

Carl rubbed his forehead between thumb and forefinger. "Marty-boy, you've put us in a delicate situation. We vouched for you, and your bullshit backstory fooled everyone up until now. Janice still believes you. But we're bait in a trap now, thanks to you and your cronies. By all rights, we should dust you right now."

"We kill a member of the constabulary, we can kiss that records purge goodbye," Mort said, more or less just as they'd rehearsed in the common room minutes ago. "It's clever, really. I bet if he doesn't come back, those records mysteriously get put back the way they were."

Bryce managed a spasmodic nod. "Guaranteed."

"Of course," Carl said, sounding philosophical. "There's nothing that says they won't get restored even after this is over. That is, even if we don't get netted by lawmen before then. You've fucked us good."

"Simplest solution," said Mriy. "Kill him. Run."

Carl wagged a finger. "Don't be hasty. We still might come out of this with a clean rap sheet and our hides if we play this right. Everyone just give me a quiet minute to think this out."

Tanny glared holes in Bryce. Martian authorities had been trying for generations to bring her family down. They'd had their victories here and there. Plenty of her family had done time for one crime or another, and they had spent a fortune on lawyers over the years. As much as she'd have enjoyed breaking Bryce's neck herself, lawyers were the way to deal with EIEIO, and Carl was the closest they had on board.

Carl snapped his fingers. "I got it. Try this one on for size. You make a call, get your friends to drop their ambush, and we let you go once the hijacking is over."

Bryce managed a quick shake of his head. "They'd know something was up. The Ruckers would get arrested as planned, and you'd end up killing me."

"Jesus, Carl," Tanny said. "Weaseling out of our fuck-ups is supposed to be your specialty. Roddy could have come up with that plan."

Carl's eyebrows leapt. "Ooh, I've got a better one. This solves *our* problem, too. We don't jack the ships to sell them,

Janice takes them and settles a new headquarters with that colony ship and gets herself a little fleet of cargo ships, maybe sells off some of the mining gear and cuts us in."

"Uh, Carl," Mort said, standing in the doorway. "That still leaves us walking into a trap."

Carl began to pace. Tanny had seen him do it enough to know that it meant he was stumped. Carl didn't like pacing—probably didn't even realize he was doing it. "How are they going to intercept the fleet? Up until Janice orders the attack, it's just freelance work."

"We could just escort them to Platt, take their money, and worry how to get Esper free after," Tanny suggested.

Mort shook his head. "The Poets aren't the fools those Sol lawmen are. I'd rather deal with them and dupe Martin's buddies."

"You can call me Bryce, still."

Mriy snarled in his face. "No one asked you."

"I almost hate to bring this up," Tanny said. "But he wasn't lying when he told Janice he was a family man."

Bryce's eyes went wide, and he struggled in Mriy's grasp. "You wouldn't!"

Carl frowned. "I'm inclined to agree with him."

"Let's just put it this way," Tanny said. "My father knows what's going on out here. Half of Janice's crew is blood relatives, even if a few are a couple generations sideways of the main family line. You think he's going to just let this slide if Janice goes down? *We* won't have to do shit."

Carl folded his arms and leaned against the wall. "Don just seems like such a good guy, though..." A slow grin spread across his face.

Tanny gave a nod and Mriy dropped Bryce, who fell to his hands and knees. "Well, Bryce, looks like we're all in the shit one way or another. Your cover is blown to hell. You're as good as dusted, and I wouldn't want to be Trisha, Benjamin, or Todd right now." Naming his wife and boys seemed just enough to set Bryce into a full-on panic.

"You can't let him do anything to them," Bryce pleaded. "I'm doing my job out here, busting my ass to make the galaxy a little safer for them and everyone else. But they haven't done anything. They don't even know where I am for months on end. You've gotta explain that to your father."

"We've never seen eye to eye on how to handle family business," Tanny said. "Plus, why would I bail *you* out while we're still caught up on the cliff's edge?"

"Maybe we should kill him," Mort suggested.

"Mort talks sense," Mriy agreed.

"—same way we killed Esper."

"Wait? What?" Bryce spluttered, from the floor.

"OK," Tanny said. "This is going somewhere."

"You killed Esper?" Bryce asked.

Carl walked around and stood over Bryce as the double-agent squirmed into a seated position on the floor. "We faked it. I suppose we could fake it for you, too."

"How's that help us, though?" Tanny asked. That might spare Bryce the complications that fell out of the plan, for better or worse, but she couldn't see how it benefited any of them. If only she was balanced out; the right mix of brain chemicals would smooth out her jumbled thoughts until these connections made sense.

"He can help us," Carl said. "No, I've got this worked out. He calls in a last-minute update for whoever the hell is coming after us. New coordinates. Operational security meant that we altered the convoy's course so we couldn't be intercepted. Martin here sends them the updated course."

"But we go on the original course?" Bryce asked, a note of hope in his voice.

"No!" Carl shouted with a grin. He held up a finger to the ceiling. "We *do* change the course, but not to the one we feed you."

"Sounds like it could work," Tanny said, impressed. "But how do we convince Janice?"

Carl cracked his knuckles. "That'll be the easiest part. Leave it to me."

---

Alone in the astral gray. Or at least, as alone as fifteen ships can be. Traveling 2.5 astral units deep would earn a captain a hefty fine from any patrol vessel, but it was unlikely that anyone was going to stumble across the ships of Operation RIBBIT. The non-standard depth was just another precaution against someone taking a casual interest in their passing, but if Commander Bilkken of the mining convoy knew anything about fringe space, he would have known that the half depths were the highways of the undesirables.

"*Convoy, full stop,*" Janice ordered over the comm. "*Prepare to receive next-leg coordinates. Also, we have a maintenance issue on the Mobius. Please stand by to dock for a quick repair. We'll be underway in twenty minutes.*" This was it. Carl had been scant on the details, but his revised plan had the Mobius crew boarding the colony ship and spearheading the hijacking.

"*Alley Cat,*" Commander Bilkken replied. "*Is this repair urgent? We're only two days out from Platt.*"

"*Affirmative,*" Janice replied. "*It's an engine mis-ajustment that's going to leave a heavy ion trail if we don't get it corrected.*

*Anyone tries to track our course change, they'd be able to follow it."*

*"Very well, Alley Cat,"* Commander Bilkken replied. *"Just be quick about it. I don't like sitting idle in astral space."*

"Sissy," Tanny muttered. "We do it all the time."

Carl stood at the back of the cockpit, still nursing a sore jaw. "Yeah, but half the shit we do in the astral oughtta get us killed, so I don't know that it's bravery so much as desensitization. We're just too stupid to be scared of off-the-standards depths. Mort ever keels while we're down deep, we're just fucked."

Roddy slipped into the cockpit past Carl and stood on the co-pilot's seat. He pointed at Tanny and hooked a thumb toward the back of the ship. "Beat it, knuckles. I'm flying us into their hangar."

Tanny turned to Carl, ignoring the laaku. "What?"

Carl jerked his head, motioning for her to follow as he backed out of the cockpit. "Come on. You're not ready to be part of *this* little boarding party yet. Not dressed like that."

"What's wrong with how I'm dressed?" Tanny demanded. She was already in her ablative armor with a sidearm strapped at either thigh. Grab a helmet and blaster rifle on the way out and she was good to invade.

But Carl didn't answer. It was both a welcome change of pace for him, but the mischievous grin made it ominous all the same.

---

The three of them stood on the cargo ramp, ready to be lowered down as the ramp opened. Tanny felt ridiculous. Mort had magicked up a strapless red cocktail dress and a bowler hat with an ostrich feather stuck in the brim like an inkpot. If she hadn't been holding a blaster rifle, Carl would be snickering at her, and she couldn't have blamed him.

Not that Carl looked any less ludicrous in a black-and-white checkerboard suit and cowboy hat. To accessorize his costume, he carried his glyphed sword (which he had no business using in a fight), disguised to look like a gentleman's cane, and—of all things—a monocle. Where he had gotten the huge cigar he chomped down on as he waited, Tanny didn't know, but it wasn't a figment of Mort's magic. It would have taken special software to recognize him; Tanny's features were only disguised by a hooker's share of makeup, magically applied.

She didn't know if Mriy had gotten off easy, or if her disguise was the most humiliating of the bunch. She wore her usual vest with the high, hard back that protected her neck, and a worn pair of loose red slacks. But her fur was now a psychedelic swirl of colors, most of which didn't belong on a sentient creature. There was a striped pattern that peeked meekly from the chaos, reminiscent of a Bengal tiger's markings.

It was Carl's idea. It always seemed to be Carl's idea when things took a turn for the juvenile or self-abasing. Credit where credit was due, though: she barely recognized either of them.

Gas hissed as the atmospheric seal around the cargo ramp released. "Places, everyone," Carl sang, already in character. Tanny shifted her blaster rifle out of easy view as the ramp lowered.

A small team of personnel in drab gray coveralls were waiting for them. One held a datapad; the others carried standard issue tool and diagnostic kits. The apparent leader consulted his datapad. "Some sort of E-M leakage? We'll see what we can—"

"Nobody move!" Tanny shouted. She whipped her blaster rifle from behind her and aimed it at the one with the datapad. Without pausing for the mechanics to overcome their shock, she marched down the ramp, the red dot from her rifle's laser sight holding a steady position on the mechanic's sternum. Say one thing for the Recitol, it gave her fluid muscle control and balance.

One of the other two mechanics flinched. Maybe he was just nervous. Maybe he was reaching for a comm. But Mriy caught the man's hand as it reached for a pocket. With a twist and one of Tanny's takedown techniques, the mechanic was facedown on the floor in two seconds, with Mriy's boot on the back of his neck.

"That was moving," Carl pointed out cheerfully. He pointed to the remaining mechanic, stiff with fright. "See? He's got it right. Now if you'll excuse us, we're taking your ship. If you play nice, you'll be home safe and snug in a few days." He paused a moment and looked around the ship's hangar. "Unless you live on this tub, in which case you're being evicted."

Roddy scrambled down the ramp as soon as all the mechanics were rounded up with their hands bound behind their backs. He carried a plasma torch and a scan-all, with his own coveralls stuffed with smaller tools. "Give me three minutes."

"Comm first, then main power," Carl reminded him.

"You fucking idi—knave," Roddy shouted over his shoulder, correcting himself at the last second. He wasn't in costume, but there was still some degree of character to maintain. "I know my job."

Mort ambled down the ramp. "Am I my brother's keeper? Would that I could find one to become that brother?" he asked rhetorically. Mort, for one, had an ear for the archaic.

Tanny checked her wrist chrono. Two and a half more minutes for Roddy to bring down the colony ship's communications, then it would be time to play pirate. Three mechanics didn't count.

---

Tanny blew the reinforced door to the bridge off its hinges with a pair of Galex-B charges Janice had provided. That much, at least, had been in the original plan. The rest was new, and Carl's last-minute addition of a costumed frame-job was still being modified as they made their way through the corridors of the nameless colony ship, designation Roy Barnum Toyoda 001.

"Who do you think you are?" Commander Bilkken demanded. The commander of the mining convoy wasn't a fancy naval captain, but he had a crispness about his person, from his close-trimmed hair to his wrinkle-free uniform. He looked from Tanny in her nightclub costume ball getup to Mriy, painted like a tiger gone kaleidoscopic.

Of course, Carl wouldn't let attention linger anywhere but on him. "Some people call me the space cowboy," Carl said. Tanny furrowed her brow. "Some call me the gangster of love." He turned and winked his non-monocle eye at the ship's navigator, a woman with dark, tightly curled hair who shied away and looked at her console. "But you can call me Maurice."

"What is the meaning of this?" Commander Bilkken demanded. Tanny was impressed. For a guy without so much as a drawn sidearm, he was talking a good game. "We contracted with Janice Rucker for safe passage to Platt."

Carl gestured flamboyantly with his cane and the datapad he held in his other hand. "Ah, you contracted with Janice Rucker, but there's the rub. We don't work for her. Ships can wear false faces as easily as men. And ours are false indeed. You see, when you left Freeride, you thought you were escorted by two ships of the Poet Fleet, who said their 'fare you well' and 'God keep you.' But what if it were five, and but two parted ways with a wink and a share of mischief."

Carl whirled, datapad at arm's length. While Commander Bilkken was shielded from view of the screen, Carl took a quick glance, checking his cribbed notes.

"I got a guarantee from Admiral Chisholm herself that we would get safe passage through Freeride," Commander Bilkken snarled. "She..." Some realization seemed to dawn on the commander just then.

"We're not *in* Freeride, Commander Bilkken," Carl pointed out. "Words can mean very particular and precise things, and I should thank you to take better care with them in the future."

"What's your game, Maurice?" Commander Bilkken asked.

"This and this alone: a profit," Carl said. He twirled the cane in his hand, and Tanny winced, wondering whether he was going to forget it was a sword and cut off his own fingers. "But we wish no harm to you or your crew. If you would recall your crews and all pile aboard a single of the smaller vessels, we'll send you along to Platt without further delay."

"You're trifling with dangerous men, Mr. Maurice," Commander Bilkken said, lowering his voice to a threatening growl. "Misters Roy, Barnum, and Toyoda aren't men to rob."

Carl grinned and sidled up to Commander Bilkken, wrapping his sword arm around him, but carefully keeping the datapad out of view. "My good commander, many would have said the same of the Rucker Syndicate. In fact, many *more* than have ever heard of misters Roy, Barnum, and Toyoda combined. And yet, we Poets have removed Janice Rucker from this transaction, stolen the names of her ships, and shoved your eyes under the wool. You are welcome to inform your employers and anyone else you like of our part in this affair, once you're rescued. It would, in point of fact, greatly enhance our reputation. As Publilius Syrus once said, 'A good reputation is more valuable than money.'"

"Enough chatter, boss," Tanny said. Who knew how much thicker Carl was going to lay it on, or how many hollow platitudes he had loaded into that datapad? She wasn't going to wait for him to dig himself a hole deep enough for a grave. "Let's get these philistines onto a cargo ship and get out of here."

Carl gave a dramatic sigh and disentangled himself from Commander Bilkken. "If you would all be so good as to line up single file and not make any sudden movements, we can have you locked on autopilot to Platt by dinnertime."

---

Dozens of booted feet clomped down the steel hallway of the colony ship. Tanny had been assigned to herd the hijacked crew toward the docking port. Part of her dared any of them to make a sudden movement. These weren't smugglers, pirates, or military personnel, though, just spacers making a freight run in a bad neighborhood. They were probably scared *before* getting boarded.

Bilkken looked over his shoulder at Tanny as he walked at the back of the herd. "You're making a huge mistake."

"Keep it moving." Tanny jabbed him in the back with the muzzle of her rifle. She made a mental note to clean the weapon later; the commander's uniform was drenched in sweat.

But Bilkken kept talking, even as he faced forward. "You seem like the brains of this operation. Tell me what's really going on here. I had personal assurances from Admiral Chisholm that we'd have no troubles."

"Hey, we're doing you a favor. The Rucker Syndicate was going to dust the lot of you. Now, you just get a short vacation."

Bilkken hung his head. "I should have known something was up when Kristov got arrested planetside."

Curiosity peeked through the dull haze of chemicals. "Kristov?"

"My security chief. I knew that charge was bogus. I *knew* it! Kristov wasn't the sort to start fistfights. So some lowlife made a grab at her... she's handled that crap before..."

"Wait, your security chief—?"

When Bilkken turned, his furrowed brow showed genuine puzzlement. "You really are low down the flagpole, aren't you? You didn't know Chisholm had my security chief? Sprang her from lockup and kept her as a 'guest' on her flagship. Said we could swing by and pick her up on our way back after the delivery. None of this is deja vu?" He shook his head.

Pieces were falling into place. Esper had been set up. The run-in that resulted in her murder change was probably conceived as a simple assault. Chisholm had the whole system rigged, top to bottom. "Just what's the admiral supposedly do with these hostages? I only signed on a couple weeks back; this shit's all news to me."

He looked Tanny up and down. "Let's just say you and me aren't Chisholm's type. She likes 'em young and soft, from what I hear."

"But your security chief..."

"Kristov runs an explosive scanner and sweeps for trackers. She's a computer jockey, and since my wife's not here, I don't mind telling you she's a damn well-shaped one."

Tanny's mind raced. What was Esper caught up in? "What would she do to someone who rejected her advances?"

Bilkken chuckled, prompting Tanny to prod him with the rifle again. "Don't worry. Like I said, you're not her type. But if you're looking to grunt and sweat your way up the ranks, I'd lay off the gene splice and stims—whatever the hell you're on."

A few heads near the front of the crowd had turned to listen to their conversation. Tanny fired a shot into the ceiling over their heads. "Eyes forward."

"You don't sound like them... yet. Get out while you still can. That lifestyle just eats at your soul. Sex and wine. Theater and extortion. Easy living picking on the bones of someone else's hard work. It's like a drug."

He had a point about the lifestyle, but everyone had their drug. Maybe the Poets were helpless in the face of their own hedonism, but that was just their hangup. Mort had his magic. Carl couldn't help gambling. Roddy's alcoholism was painfully obvious. Esper was addicted to sticking her nose in other people's business. If Tanny's drug was literal, then so be it. The fact that she could acknowledge it meant that she had control, and the fact she noticed told her that the Sepromax was starting to kick in. This was Tanny thinking, not some chemical imbalance.

She had to give Bilkken credit, though. His ploy was a classic Psy Ops tactic. He had found a difference between her and the Poets and was driving a wedge into it as best he could. Too bad she wasn't really a neophyte pirate, or he might have had some luck.

"Well, buddy, maybe some of us like the drug."

The starport on Carousel was only slightly busier than the remote landing field the *Mobius* had used on its first visit. It wasn't used much for passenger traffic, serving mainly as an intermodal station for supply freighters and terrestrial shipping vehicles. Commerce of the blue-collar sort was going on all around the crew as they stood waiting at the bottom of the ship's cargo ramp.

Bryce was taking things better than expected. He stood motionless, staring out at the horizon beyond the chain-fenced boundary of the starport. A speck appeared in the sky on the approach vector they were expecting. Bryce swallowed. "I don't suppose this is negotiable."

"Bryce old buddy," Carl said. "You bought yourself a better bargain than you were in for, given the shit you tried to pull. But even if I was the fucking pope, I wouldn't be forgiving you like nothing happened."

"Suppose not," Bryce mumbled, then resumed his mute vigil.

It wasn't long before the speck grew large enough to be recognized as a spacecraft. Sleek, black, with lines like a racer and pristine as a showpiece, the ship landed fifty meters from the *Mobius*, sending up a wash of dust that had everyone but Bryce shielding their eyes.

Carl strode across to greet the new arrival. A side door opened, appeared from what had looked like a seamless panel of the sleek ship's hull, and two men exited. He clapped one on the back in a quick hug, and shook hands with the other. By the shake of their shoulders, Carl made both of them laugh.

"Which ones are they?" Bryce asked over his shoulder.

"My uncle Earl," Tanny said, deadpan. "And his son Jimmy."

"Earl Rucker..." Bryce repeated. His fists tightened at his side.

"If you're thinking of running... " Tanny warned.

Bryce shook his head. "I got your word. I go quiet, and you make sure your father leaves my family alone."

"This our vermin?" Earl asked in a bass voice as he approached. "Don't look like much." Earl was a wall, with shoulders nearly as wide as he was tall, and a neck like a tree trunk.

"Ain't that the point, pop?" Jimmy asked. Though smaller than his father, Jimmy was larger than the bouncers at most rough nightclubs.

"So this gray fuzz-top tried pinning that Lorstram hit on you guys?" Earl asked, poking Bryce in the chest with a hot-dog-sized finger.

Bryce cringed slightly. "Yeah," he replied, voice dry.

Jimmy laughed, and Earl chuckled along. Jimmy jostled Bryce with a forearm. "Lighten up, pigeon. We ain't sore winners. You got luckier than you even know, blowin' this job."

"Come on," Earl said, pinching Bryce by the cheek like an adoring aunt. "We'll take good care of you, long as you keep your yap shut and play nice."

They exchanged good-byes. The Ruckers remembered Roddy by name, but not Mriy. The two behemoths shook hands with Mort, but looked as if they were grabbing a blaster by the wrong end in doing so. Never had either of the two looked less intimidating. There were hugs for Tanny and handshakes for Carl, along with the ever-open offer to come work with them.

"Maybe next time," Carl said with a wink before they took Bryce and returned to their ship.

The sleek, black craft slid back into space like a sliver of night, disappearing into the darkness.

The crew of the *Mobius* went back inside and killed another two hours watching local system news on the holovid until it was time to reconvene. The sun was low in the sky when the sheriff's department shuttle touched down within meters of where the Rucker ship had landed. It was mere seconds before the ship's door opened and someone stepped out. It took longer for Tanny to realize it was Esper. She was wearing an ankle-length black dress and heeled leather boots, with an ermine stole wrapped around her neck against the cold. A sheriff's deputy followed her out, dragging a trunk with its own repulsors.

Esper waved a gloved hand and ran across the patch of dusty tarmac between the ships. Tanny had a sly curiosity as to who she'd seek out first. She'd an impression for a while now —two in fact—that both Carl and Mort had more than a passing interest in her well-being. Carl she understood. Esper's brain-fried mother had gotten her surgically sculpted into one of those dolls designed by mammary-obsessed creeps. The girl was practically designed to make drooling idiots like Carl into bigger drooling idiots. Not her fault; not even his. But Mort generally kept above that, clinging to the estranged family he'd left on Earth. If he snuck some on the side, he'd kept it discreet. Yet he doted on Esper in a frankly unfatherly manner, taking her faith as more of a challenge than a road-block. He was a wizard, but that didn't mean his self-control was iron.

As her run brought her closer, Tanny drew back in surprise. Esper was headed *her* way. They had gotten friendly, after all, but she had expected a couple weeks of captivity would have left Esper a little more ... pent up. But the impression passed quickly as Esper crouched low. Kubu separated himself from the crew and rushed forward the last few meters to meet her.

"Kubu, you did great!" Esper said. "You're a hero."

"Kubu is a hero?" Kubu asked. He licked Esper's face. "You are much nicer now that you're not a wall any more."

"I'm happy not to *be* a wall any more," Esper replied. She looked up to everyone else. "And thank you guys for believing him. I don't know how much longer I could have held out there."

"Yeah," Roddy said. "You're looking rough. Were the pedicures every *other* day, or every third?"

"Where should I put your trunk, Miss Richelieu?" the deputy asked.

"Just inside," Esper replied. "I'll unpack it myself." She seemed to realize the rest of the crew were staring at her. "What? They gave me clothes to wear. It's not like any of *them* are going to wear anything second-hand. Why let all those nice outfits go to waste?"

Carl scratched his head. "You *sure* you want to come back?"

Esper nodded vigorously. "It was like I was being hunted. It eventually got to the point where it felt like everyone on that ship was trying to sleep with me. It was Sodom, Gomorrah, and Vegas rolled into one."

"That's it," Carl said. "Next time, I'm getting captured by the pirates. You all can skip the rescue."

Mort snorted. "These pirates wouldn't have you. These are *educated* pirates."

"Sophisticated, even," Esper agreed.

"I could fake that," Carl said, sounding hurt.

"Yeah," Tanny said with a sigh. "He could."

---

Tanny sat on her bed, alone. Beside her was a digitally locked crate, given to her by Janice before they parted ways in the middle of astral nowhere. A gift, she had called it. Tanny would receive the combination to open it once Janice and her crew had gotten themselves to a suitable destination to drop the colony ship planetside. That had been four days ago. Tanny had been tempted to challenge Mort or Roddy to open it, as much to spite Janice as to discover the contents. If she knew Janice, it was going to be an insulting gift anyway. But every morning, she took the crate, set it on the bed, and kept it company as she waited for word from her cousin.

Today her vigil ended. She had set an alarm on her datapad for messages from Janice. It played a few bars of a heavy melody, filled with doom and dread. Janice had finally sent word:

*To Tania,*

*We found a place that's half shithole and set ourselves up in the half that isn't. No offense, but you don't get to know where. I know we butted heads for a lot of years, but you at least know how to work a job. If that Bryce had found dumber patsies, I'd be in lock-up right about now, or maybe dead. So I owe you for that.*

*To make things up, the combination is in the attached file. Oh, and I didn't fuck Carl when he stayed over at the resort. I just got him to play along and let you think I did. It would have been weird. Carl's family, after all. Anyway, go ahead and open that crate. You earned it.*

*J.R.*

Tanny opened the file appended to Janice's message, and fed the multi-layer encryption key into the crate. The lock popped with a soft puff of released pressure. Opening the lid, Tanny gasped.

Inside was everything she needed: Centrimac, Plexophan, Adrenophiline, Pseudoanorex, Zygrana, Cannabinol, and even Recitol. It had the mineral supplements she needed. There was even a supply of Sepromax. There was no way Janice could have gotten all that without Carl's help. Only the crew and a couple suppliers might have been able to pass that detailed mix along.

The song of doom played from Tanny's datapad once more, and there was another message:

*I figure you got it open by now. Just so you know, that's your cut. If you want a profit on this job, sell that shit at the nearest hellhole for marine burnouts. But if you want to stay hooked on that shit, it's none of my business.*

*J.R.*

An hour later, Tanny was beginning to feel like her *old* self again. Not her old old self, but the one she had been for most of her time serving on the *Mobius*. Things were starting to make sense again. She wasn't feeling as paranoid, unfocused, or inexplicably angry. She was feeling enough like herself to feel guilty about taking the crew's cut for herself, and but not enough that she was about to change her mind.

"I'll make it up to them," she told herself.

As far as offices went, Bryce Brisson had seen more impressive. He'd seen the section chief's office, with its so-new-they-sparkle holo consoles, polished glass desk and chairs, and oil portraits of Earth prime ministers and former section chiefs. He'd been to Oxford on an investigation once and seen a dean's office appointed with antiques that cost more than his annual salary. But those and others lacked one aspect that made this office more intimidating than all the others combined: it had Don Rucker sitting in it.

The syndicate boss looked just like the holos Bryce had seen for years working in Crime Disorganization. Take Don Rucker out of his expensive suit, confiscate his gold wrist-chrono, and remove him from his fawning associates, and you'd never tell him apart from a freight handler or a prison guard. He had the muscular shoulders of a man who once did his own leg breaking, and the ample gut of someone who'd had people for that sort of thing for a long while. But in the squareness of his jaw and the hard, disapproving glare, Bryce could see a lot of Tanny in him.

"So, this is the guy?" Don Rucker asked. It was a formality. Bryce knew the Rucker Syndicate had dug up everything they needed to undo him. There was no chance of mistaken identity.

"Sure is, Don," Earl replied. "He came nice and peaceful."

Don leaned back in his chair. "A man resigned to his fate?"

Bryce swallowed. He tried to say something, but no sound came. He licked his lips and tried again. "A man with everything to lose."

Don nodded with his lips pressed tight. "Yeah, you do. That wife of yours was a looker ten, fifteen years ago. I bet that's still the way you see her." He pressed a button on a console set into his desk. A tabletop holo popped up, showing Trisha walking down the street with an armload of groceries.

Bryce made a short, jittery twitch of his neck muscles meant to convey a nod.

"And those boys of yours..." Don let the holo finish his statement. With a press of another button, the holo changed, and it was Ben and Todd hopping onto the tram after school. They were heading home. Home. Bryce was never going to see home again. His lip quivered as he struggled to maintain his composure in front of the Ruckers.

"That's why you're standing here right now, isn't it?" Don asked, pointing less at Bryce and more toward the floor where he stood. "You coulda run. You coulda fought back. But you're just standing here—eyes welling up like your dog just died." Don hit a button and the holo disappeared.

"You've got me," Bryce said. "They don't know anything. They haven't done anything."

"Be a shame, seeing them scraping by on that ARGO widow's fund payout," Don said. The mention of his wife being a widow set the tears rolling down Bryce's face. "Oh, for the love of God. Jimmy, pour this guy a drink. What I was saying is that I don't see a reason she has to raise those boys on one salary and the chump change ARGO pays out for a killed-on-duty." Bryce felt a tumbler pressed into his hands and absently brought it to his mouth. The liquid burned from lips to throat, but he drank. He tipped it back, relishing the pain. He came up for air gasping, and doubled over. Someone took the glass when he offered it back.

Don, Earl, and Jimmy had a laugh at his expense. "Janice was right," Don said. "This one's not all bad. I tell you what,

Mr. Undercover Tech Sneak; today's your lucky day. I've got an offer for you, and you'd be wise to take it."

Bryce put his hand on his knees and pushed himself mostly upright. "An offer?" he asked, his voice hoarse.

"I like having people with inside knowledge," Don said. "You're going to come work for me?"

Bryce shook his head. "I can't. I won't betray ARGO."

"ARGO? What have they done for you?" Don asked.

"Nothing," Earl added.

"They ship you off to the cold, dark side of the galaxy. No backup. No bonus pay. You risk your life so some silver-spoon lawyers don't get their ships boosted," Don said. "You work for me ... well, let's say it's a safer life, believe it or not. New name, new digs, maybe a little cosmo so they don't catch you on a biometric scan. Life gets a little harder for those boys who hung you out to dry in Freeride; life gets a little easier for Trisha and your boys." Don popped the holovid up again, showing Bryce's family together at the tram stop, his boys just home from school. "Your little woman gets a patron in the form of a civic-minded individual who wants to help a widow make ends meet—and then some. Your boys get tuition to private schools, so they can get nice, safe, respectable jobs. Not like the jobs you just left, or the jobs you and me got now. Whaddaya say?"

Bryce used to wonder about the sort of weak, petty men who got dragged into organized crime. He understood now. When it all came down to it, all that mattered was family. And Bryce Brisson—or whatever his next alias would be—was willing to do anything for his.

"Deal."

# TO ERR IS AZRIN

MISSION 4 OF THE BLACK OCEAN SERIES

## TO ERR IS AZRIN

THE BOUNTY HUNTER's ship swerved around a derelict hulk, dodging fire from the *Mobius*. The chase had started out entertaining when the *Remembrance*, thinking he was making his exchange, dropped out of astral. It wasn't ten seconds before he opened fire, ignoring hails as he fled into the Kapos IV scrap yard. But once a lucky shot had knocked out the bounty hunter's auto-cannon, it had devolved into fox-hunt.

As near as Carl Ramsey could figure, the captain of the *Remembrance* had few options. Curious whether his quarry had the same list in mind, he keyed the ship-to-ship comm. "Vessel *Remembrance*, this is Captain Michael Jagger of the independent ship Rolling Stone. It's time to consider handing over that cargo of yours while you've still got some leverage to negotiate. You won't shake us long enough to go astral. You won't get us to crash in the scrap-yard debris. It's time to hand him over before we accidentally blow out your life support or breach your hull."

"*Burn in hell, Jagger,*" came the curt response.

Carl clucked his tongue and shook his head. "Such disrespect for a noble musician." Of course, with the comm closed, the captain of the *Remembrance* didn't hear that.

"Probably too busy evading us to care," Tanny replied from the pilot's seat. It was her handiwork that kept the *Mobius* on the bounty hunter's tail.

"He's wasting his time," Carl muttered. With his arms crossed and feet up on the console, he knew he was far from the model of efficient time use, but his ship was winning. Winning bought a captain a bit of leeway.

Tanny twisted the *Mobius* on its axis and they swung around the hull of an Earth Navy light cruiser. There was a hole the size of a small asteroid in the side—anti-matter torpedo, if Carl had to guess—and the *Remembrance* darted through it. The *Mobius* struggled to stay in the turn, but slipped through close behind. There was no sensation, no G-force tugging Carl from his seat—he wasn't even buckled in. Tanny flew with the safeties engaged. Between the thrust limiters and Mort's top-notch artificial gravity, her flying felt no different from sitting on a landing pad.

Carl yawned. If he were piloting, they'd not only have caught up with the bounty hunter's Osprey-class patrol ship, but they'd have had some excitement doing it. A staccato burst of plasma bolts shot across the forward window, narrowly missing the *Remembrance*. Mriy was picking at it with the guns, not wanting to destroy the ship outright. But it was damnably annoying to watch, knowing they were stuck giving chase until the azrin could land a lucky shot and take out the engines.

"Maybe we should give Esper a chance on the guns," Carl grumbled.

"Yeah," Tanny replied. "Same girl who won't fire a blaster and pulls her punches in Krav Maga sparring."

"I was joking," Carl replied deadpan. "Might not hurt letting Roddy have a crack at it though. He wouldn't—"

"Can you just shut up?" Tanny snapped. "This isn't as easy as it looks."

"Of course, you know," Carl said. "If you're having trouble, I can take over. You'd do a lot better than Mriy in the gunner's seat."

Tanny snorted. "We've got this won. We're just running him down now."

Carl cringed. It was the sort of thing that just wasn't said. Overconfidence bred carelessness. Thinking one step ahead could cause you to stumble over the one you were standing on. Plus, it was just plain old bad luck.

On the other side of the holey cruiser, the bounty hunter swung around. The cargo hold of the *Remembrance* opened, and something small and silvery tumbled out. Of course, at a quarter kilometer or so, "small" was a relative term. The fleeing ship changed course again, heading away from the vector of the cargo it had dumped.

*"All yours," the captain of the Remembrance snarled over the comm. "You can come after me or it, but it's headed for the munitions dump."*

Tanny checked the tactical sensors. "Shit! He's right. We can't—"

The *Remembrance* exploded with a plume of ignited oxygen as Mriy connected with a salvo of hits directly to the crew compartment. Tanny swung the *Mobius* around on an intercept course.

Carl leaned over and keyed the comm to the gunner's turret. "We were all set, Mriy. He dropped the pod and was making a run for it."

*"I know,"* Mriy replied. *"That was personal."*

Mriy strode through the common room, not pausing as she glanced at Mort's holovid. He was watching a historical recreation from his home world. It was factual, if she was any judge of human narrators. The good ones rarely interrupted the action to have someone tell old stories.

Mort looked up as she passed. "We get him?"

"Not yet," she replied.

Down in the cargo hold, Roddy was waiting with Esper, both standing ready in their EV suits. Roddy gestured with his upper set of hands as she approached, but with the EV helmet on, Mriy heard nothing of what the simian mechanic said. He seemed to realize this and removed the helmet. "You gotta either suit up or get out of here. We're intercepting the pod and bringing it in through the cargo bay door, not the airlock."

"Why wouldn't we just—"

"Out!" Roddy shouted. "We're on the clock. Get pissy later." She envied the laaku his ease with the human language, but her ears flicked at his tone.

Esper, still wearing her EV helmet, shrugged an apology. It was just like her to avoid confrontation. She was like a bird, quick to chirp and quick to flight. Mriy showed a quick flash of fangs to the both of them and made a hasty retreat back to the common room.

The door between had a small window, enough for Mriy to watch Roddy and Esper. Red light strobed, and a klaxon blared; it was loud even muffled by the steel door, warning that the air was being pumped from the cargo bay. Mort's holovid grew in volume as the wizard sought to drown out the annoying noise. Against the assault on her senses, Mriy flattened her ears against her head.

"... *the Roman senate was growing wary of Caesar's rising influence...*" the narrator droned on.

The klaxon faded as the air left the cargo hold, but the human-deaf wizard left the holovid blaring. "Turn that down," Mriy ordered. She fought the urge to attach a bodily threat to her command. Commanding Mort in the first place was an error of riled temper. The wizard's own counter-threats ran far fouler than her own, and she had little doubt he could carry them out.

"*Don't make me geld you, wizard.*"

"*I'd have your claws turned to butter before you cut through my jeans.*"

She shuddered at the memory of that particular threat. A declawed azrin was no longer fit to be a warrior. She might still fight with blades or guns, but her hand-to-hand fighting would make her a jesting target among her own kind.

Her own kind. Mriy returned her attention to the cargo bay, and looked out the open cargo bay as the *Mobius* matched speed with the cryostasis pod. The wreckage in the salvage yard was the only reference to show how fast they were traveling.

The pod was a silvery, flattened sausage. It tumbled through the darkness, shimmering with the light of Kapos, the sun of the system by the same name. The silver sausage grew larger as Tanny tapped the maneuvering thrusters, allowing the pod to catch up now that the *Mobius* was ahead of it. As it turned over, Mriy caught a flash off the glass window, covering a quarter of one side of the pod. The glare made it impossible for her to see in at a distance. Indicator displays glowed below the window, a good sign even if she couldn't make out what they said. At least the cryostasis pod had power.

Roddy and Esper prepared an inflatable mattress—one of

the useless wonders of the ship's clutter—and lashed it to the cargo ramp. Roddy must have been coordinating over the comm with Tanny, because the *Mobius* sped up, slowing the pod's arrival and lining it up such that it would not enter the ship so high above the mattress.

The pod landed without a sound, but the mattress burst beneath its weight as Mort's gravity took hold of it. Esper hit the controls to close the cargo door, and Roddy began harnessing the pod to attach the tow cable. Moments later, the klaxon began to sound once more, growing in volume as air returned to the cargo bay. Mort increased the volume of the holovid, but this time Mriy didn't care. She tore open the door and rushed down to check on the cryostasis pod and its occupant.

---

The metal of the cryostasis pod was cold enough to burn, as Mriy discovered when she reached out to touch it. The glass had frosted over with the ship's humidity. A status display panel was visible and functioning, but she didn't know enough about the device's workings to tell anything useful from it.

"So are you ready to tell us who's in it?" Esper asked. She tucked her EV helmet under an arm as she sidled up to Mriy.

"I don't know," Mriy replied. It was an answer she had learned from Mort, who could put so narrow an edge on a question that it would cut. Uncertainty was merely a form of ignorance.

"Come on. You can't expect us to believe you gave up a share of our next job when you had no idea who we were rescuing." Esper leaned around to interpose her face between Mriy and the pod. "Who do you *think* is in there?"

Mriy flattened her ears back. This one spent too much time listening to Mort. Esper knew the trick in that reply. "I would rather not say until I am sure. I would look foolish."

"Yeah," Roddy interjected. "That'd be a first around here." He hopped onto the pod, walking across its surface as if it were level ground. With one gloved foot, he wiped away enough of the frost to see the face of the occupant. There could be no mistake.

Mriy sighed and let her shoulders slump. The frozen form was azrin, with fur coloration not so different from her own. He was young, not quite yet adult, but few non-azrin would have been able to tell. He was large for his age and quite muscular. "This is Hrykii Yrris."

"Wait... as in Mriy Yrris?" Roddy asked.

"My nephew," Mriy confirmed. "Son of my brother Soora."

Esper swallowed. "The one you—"

"Killed," Mriy said, nodding. Now that she knew it was Hrykii, there was no avoiding the topic. "Yes, the same brother. Hrykii is the eldest of his generation."

"How'd you hear about this whole..." Esper paused, waving a hand over the cryostasis pod. In her quest for perfect words, she often resorted to gestures, which ruined the intended effect. Human languages had so many words that they tripped over one another. "Business."

"A friend of Hrykii contacted me," Mriy replied.

"Thought you were on the Class-A shit list back home," Roddy observed with his usual tact.

"I doubt I was his first choice," Mriy replied. She pictured Roddy bleeding on the cargo bay floor, his entrails sagging from a gut wound. The daydream helped her anger with him pass quickly. "How is he?" she asked, turning to Esper.

The human woman had already removed her EV suit's gloves, and was fiddling with a datapad, connecting to the cryostasis pod's computer. The thought of being sealed inside such a device made Mriy's stomach sour—access to your med scans, able to gawk at you, control over your very life.

"Hold on," Esper replied. "I'm downloading azrin metabolic baselines. The pod didn't have them installed. I mean, for starters, he's alive. Broken arm in three places. Most of his ribs are cracked. System is flooded with adrenaline and a..." Esper cleared her throat. "A zoological sedative."

Mriy nodded along with the overview. "He fought. He was not caught unaware."

A few quiet minutes passed, broken only by Roddy clearing space in the cargo bay and Esper continuing to poke at her datapad. "Aha! Here we go," Esper said. "Running your nephew's bios against azrin norms."

Mriy peered through the glass. "He was so small last time I saw him..."

"OK. Taking into account his stasis—which rules out metabolic readings—his toxicity results are clean aside from the two I'd noticed on my own. No brain trauma. No nerve damage. Estimated height... wow, 1.9 meters. Mass: 86 kilos. That sound about right to you?"

"He takes after his father," Mriy remarked absently. Soora had been over two meters tall and 130 kilos. Hrykii had time to catch up.

"Huh?" Esper said. "It says his estimated age is seven."

"Barely, at that," Mriy replied.

"I would have guessed more like fifteen or sixteen, honestly," Esper replied.

Roddy chuckled. "You don't know azrins, huh? Miss Omni didn't look up everything, I guess."

"What's that supposed to mean?" Esper asked.

"*I'm* sixteen," Mriy replied. "We don't waste half our lives in childhood like humans and laaku. It's a primate trait."

Esper's face went long, her eyes wide. "I had assumed I was the youngest on the ship."

"No," Mriy replied. She laid a hand on the cyrostasis pod. It was still ice cold, but the air in the cargo bay had begun to warm it. "Right now, that honor is Hrykii's."

"How do we wake him up?" Roddy asked, trying to peer over the edge of Esper's datapad.

"We don't," Mriy replied. "He is badly injured."

"I can just—" Esper began.

"No," Mriy snapped. "No magic. He is safe in the pod."

"Fine," Roddy said. "What *are* we doing with him, then?"

Mriy hunched over and turned away. "I need to speak with Carl about that."

---

Carl's quarters smelled foul, a mixture of seeping human fluids and improperly disposed meals. Her own quarters had a Devesson filter, which kept the air cleaner than anywhere else on the ship. Carl's habitat was particularly deplorable. It was only due to her pressing need that she ventured inside at all.

"You know," Carl said as soon as she opened the door. "You didn't have to fire on that bounty hunter. He'd already cut his losses and turned tail." He was sitting on his bed, tuning Roddy's double-necked guitar.

She closed the door behind her. "I slipped," Mriy lied.

"Bullshit, and we both know it," Carl replied. He was such an unusual human. Few sentients would confront an azrin in an enclosed space. Those who did usually had some plan for defense. Tanny kept a blaster by her pillow. Mort was a wizard, and the less said about how he might defend himself the better. Roddy had made it clear she wasn't welcome in his quarters. Esper and Kubu were too naive to be properly afraid of her. But Carl... he just seemed to operate with a certainty that she wouldn't lose her temper and tear his throat out with her teeth.

Today, at least, he was right.

"I need a favor," Mriy said, allowing Carl's pronouncement to stand. They were better off with the bounty hunter dead, and Carl realized that. He just disliked reminders of how little he was really in charge aboard his own ship.

"You're down a favor already," Carl pointed out. He strummed a chord on the guitar, wrinkled up his face, and resumed his adjustment to the strings.

"I can give up another job's share," Mriy offered. "We need to deliver Hrykii."

"Who?"

"The one in the pod," Mriy replied. "My nephew. I... assumed Roddy had commed you as soon as I left the cargo bay."

"Nope," Carl replied.

"Well, that's who it is," Mriy said. "I need to—"

"The answer is 'no,'" Carl said. He played a sad little series of notes on the guitar. "We're not your personal shuttle service, and we don't get work often enough for me to let you go two paydays in hock to the rest of us. It's not like we can just take out a loan, or buy on credit except a few places I'd really rather not. We don't get *paying* jobs, I can't afford fuel, and we're stuck planetside. Nobody wants to see it come to that. I'm sorry, but I hope you can see that—"

"Fine. Three jobs with no cut," Mriy said.

"Deal," Carl replied, accompanied by a grating rendition of the opening song of the Buy-or-Sell Show. "Where we taking Ricky?"

"H-Ri-kee-ee," Mriy pronounced for him. "And we're taking him home. Rikk Pa, Meyang."

Carl nodded. He leaned over and keyed the comm for the cockpit. "Hey, Tanny. New course. We're heading to Meyang so Mriy can get herself killed."

Mriy gnashed her teeth at Carl's flippant summation of their mission. She glared into his smirking face as she retreated from his quarters. If only he had been wrong.

---

Meyang VII, most often referred to simply as Meyang, hung in orbit around a white sun that appeared yellow from the surface and was in turn orbited by a pale moon. A ball of blue and green, with wispy white clouds swirling in the atmosphere, it was as familiar as a child's first picture book. It looked just like Earth.

Esper shook her head as she watched the planetary approach through the common room's domed ceiling. "It's practically deserted. Like everyone on Earth took a holiday out of system, and just a few people stayed behind to water the plants." Orbital space around Earth swarmed with traffic. At any given time, a hundred thousand ships clogged the space lanes between the thermosphere and Luna's orbit. And then there were orbital habitats, diplomatic embassies not allowed planetside, military posts, shipyards, astral gates, and solar collectors. But not Meyang. It was hard to pick out the occasional craft against the backdrop of the planet, the one exception being the massive Earth Navy battle cruiser that was the planet's main garrison.

Mort looked on with her. "Pretty, isn't she? You can almost forget it's the twenty-sixth century for a while, looking at a pristine world like that."

"You ever been to an Earth-like before?" Esper asked.

Mort shrugged. "A few. This is the least modern I've seen though. If it's possible, Phabian is worse than Earth; laaku have no cultural regard for nostalgia. Keru though, they had a nice little wizards' retreat out in the Ural Mountains... well, what Earth calls the Ural Mountains. Spent a week there, once, getting the processed air out of my lungs."

"I've never been," Esper replied.

Mort patted her on the shoulder. "It's nothing to be ashamed of. You grew up in Sol. Not a lot of cause to go out looking for other Earths when you've got the original."

"No, I mean I've never even been to Earth," Esper said, shaking her head. "I don't even know where the Urals are. I mean, I can find New York and Tokyo and maybe London—I think—but it's not stuff I think about much."

"Never been to Earth?" Mort echoed. "Good Lord, girl. We're going to have to fix that one of these days. Cradle of humanity. It's a weeping shame never to have been, especially for a girl from Mars. What were your parents thinking, neglecting your cultural education like that?"

"They were thinking that Earth was a pretentious, snooty, over-regulated museum, not fit for regular folks," Esper replied. "What's Earth got that Mars hasn't?"

Mort snorted and rose from the couch. "What's Mars got..." he muttered. "I could write a book..." He sulked off toward his quarters. "... damned Martian bigots."

Esper thought that she was going to be watching the rest of

the approach by herself. Meyang grew larger each minute. Such a grand sight seemed a shame to watch alone. Briefly, she considered seeing if Kubu wanted to come out and watch, but he was napping in Tanny's quarters.

"Here you go," Mort said as he opened the door from his quarters. In one hand he carried a cantaloupe-size ball that looked just like Earth. In fact, as Mort brought it closer, it might have looked *too* much like Earth. It wasn't plastic or fabric, but appeared to be actual rock and water, with a thin mist of clouds that spilled at the edges where Mort's hand held it.

When Mort pressed the orb into her hands, Esper found that it was no illusion. The surface was rough or wet in all the places it appeared it should be. The polar regions were even cool to the touch. "What is this?" she asked, hoping for an answer beyond the obvious.

"Best map I've ever owned," Mort replied. He leaned over the globe as Esper held it like a platter. "Ural Mountains."

The globe spun in Esper's hands, and a region that came to face Mort glowed softly.

"That's where they are?" Esper asked.

"Yup," Mort confirmed. "Go ahead and try it. You can't stump the thing."

Esper raised the globe to eye level. "New York Prime," she whispered to it. The magical map twisted around and a pinpoint of light brightened a coastal location.

"You don't have to add the 'Prime' on there," Mort said. "It knows you mean Earth. But watch... Phabian, Kethlet." The orb shuddered in Esper's hand, then twisted around and lit a small area on the far side from New York.

"What just happened?"

"I changed it to Roddy's world and his home district," Mort replied. "Roughly where Mumbai would be on Earth."

"Will it work here?" Esper asked. Mort's smile was all the encouragement she needed. "Meyang."

The globe vibrated, and this time she made sure to watch. The cloud cover reoriented instantly, and the colors changed, mostly to deeper greens. "Where's Mriy from?" she asked, not taking her eyes from the miniature planet in her hand.

"A place called Rikk Pa," Mort replied, enunciating with what sounded to Esper's ears like an attempt at an azrin accent. The globe spun around and lit a northerly area. "Looks like that would be somewhere in Norway, west of Oslo. Be cold as a polar bear's ass this time of year, too. They don't muck with the weather like Earth does."

Esper held the globe out to Mort, fearful of harming the priceless device if she kept it in her possession too long. "How's it work?"

"Damned if I know," Mort replied. "Probably some sort of magic."

---

The church held that the existence of Earth-likes was incontrovertible proof of God's hand at work. Every Earth-like's sun was a twin of Sol. Every moon identical to Luna. The extraneous orbital bodies in the system varied from one to the next, but every Earth-like spun in perfect synchronization. Mid November on Earth was still late autumn on Meyang's northern hemisphere, and it was indeed cold enough to warrant Mort's comparison to ursine posteriors. Getting used to different worlds was becoming a habit now, with how restless the *Mobius* was. Esper had no basis for comparing how close it felt to Earth, but it was a solid winter by Martian standards. Most spacers didn't risk damaging their EV suits by wearing them planetside, but she was glad of the warmth, despite the potential cost.

The ARGO-secure landing area was reserved for off-world vessels from ARGO member systems. With its Earth registry, the *Mobius* had no trouble passing the orbital security checkpoint or acquiring ground clearance for their choice of landing sites. After their adventures in the Freeride System and Hadrian IV, their easy entry to the system was something of a surprise. Meyang was an occupied world. Officially it was an ARGO protectorate, but that only meant that the Allied Races of the Galactic Ocean had claimed them before any of the galaxy's other powers could gain a foothold. The azrin had no status within ARGO in terms of citizenry or representation on the ARGO council. All around the landing area, there were reminders of that fact.

The landing zone was a roughly six-square-kilometer area, surrounded by a ten-meter wall and dotted with security towers. Patrol craft were in constant sight overhead, drifting around at low altitude; eyes looked down on all the naughty creatures below.

The crew piled into the hover-cruiser, an open-topped flatbed conveyance they had liberated from a previous job. Kubu was appointed Official Ship Guardian, which seemed appropriate, given that he was basically a sentient dog. There was a fine tradition back on Earth of using dogs to guard things, even if Kubu had the mental faculties of a preschooler. Convincing him to stay behind (and out of trouble) seemed the prudent course until they had a better idea of how he would be received on Meyang. The rest of them, along with the cryostasis pod, headed out to see Pikk Pa.

It was a short trip through the maze of parked starships and other small on-world transports. For that short while, there was the flickering possibility of an uneventful trip. But the security checkpoint at the exit stopped them.

"Sorry," an ARGO sergeant in articulated power armor informed them. He gestured to Mriy with a stun baton. "Cat's on the wrong side of the fence. This gate leads to the Humantown. No locals allowed." Esper could only imagine the security situation on a world like Meyang, where half the populace was deadly to even a seasoned soldier. Tanny's marine stories mentioned such armor for shock troops and front-line combat engagements.

"She's not technically a local," Carl replied from the front passenger's seat. He wore his battered leather jacket, but was otherwise girded against the cold in over-sized woolen mittens and a fur-lined hat with ear flaps. "She's part of the crew. And the popsicle isn't even conscious."

"I didn't notice your prisoner was azrin," the sergeant replied. "But in stasis, you can transport it. We're going to have to bring a shuttle for transporting your crewman. Can't have it in Humantown, whatever your relationship."

Mriy muttered something that Esper couldn't quite hear, but the guard obviously did. "Fine, you're a 'she.' Go ahead and fucking report me. I speak the local just fine, thanks."

"Sorry," Mriy muttered in English.

That drew a smile from the guard. "Well, at least you learned the language. Better than most of your friends around here. Fifty years... you'd think the schools would do a better job teaching it."

They waited fifteen minutes until a small official craft arrived, and Mriy transferred aboard. She went without complaint, climbing into the back of a craft with separate cockpit and passenger compartments. Even an angry azrin would have had difficulty disrupting the flight. The ARGO shuttle lifted off, and Esper watched to see whether Mriy might wave, or at least look down at them from the window. She didn't.

"Think she'll be all right?" Esper asked to no one in particular as the hover-cruiser zipped through the security checkpoint. They were cleared as soon as they were rid of the unauthorized azrin.

"Nothing to worry about," Roddy replied. "Just life on an occupied world."

Esper found it odd that no one gave a second look to the laaku as they headed for Humantown. Laaku were nearly human, and azrin were not.

---

Mriy sulked in the back of the shuttle. Her fur bristled in embarrassment, and she was glad that her crewmates were largely oblivious to those sorts of azrin subtleties. This was her world, not theirs. Yet because their ancestors had develops starships and plasma rifles and energy shields before her own, she was the one barred from certain areas of her home world.

The temptation to look down at Rikk Pa from the air nagged at her. The view from the *Mobius* on approach had been all too brief, and she didn't have a good vantage from her quarters. But the shuttle had a camera in the passenger compartment, watching her. She didn't want to look like a homesick reverse tourist, drooling at the evergreens and smoke-puffing chimneys through dingy transparent titanium. It was a matter of personal dignity, something that was all too hard to come by in the custody of the occupation force.

Had she been gone so long? Three years was a solid bite of her adult life, and she had grown used to human company. She understood their main language. How had she forgotten the feeling of being on the wrong side of the wall? How could a weakling race cordon off a tiny portion of Meyang, and yet make it feel like the azrin were the ones trapped? Smug tourists on her world, venturing into the azrin cities and building shops, hospitals, factories—as if they were some great force of civilization. Carl wasn't so bad. Tanny was nearly azrin, in some ways. Even Esper was more like a kitten than the invaders she had grown up around.

The pilot of the shuttle could mate with cows for all she cared. Mriy looked. Spread out below were water and mountains, with snow-dusted valleys in between. It should have come as no surprise, but she smiled at the realization that she knew the names of these places. Kinna Peak, gray and imposing. The Godswash, flat as a mirror, reflecting the clouds above. Here and there, little clusters of homes and businesses—a dozen here, a hundred there—with forest and roads stitching them together to form Rikk Pa.

"Down in two," the pilot's voice buzzed over the comm. He was just three meters away, but on the other side of a safety-grade wall of composite steel and transparent titanium. She'd be rid of him in two minutes, plus however long the departure sequence took.

Public terminals were a good deal shabbier than the landing site for ARGO-registered transports. Asphalt tarmac instead of evercrete. No security fence. Just a lone navigation control tower and ground tram service up and down the rows of mismatched ships. In fairness, the *Mobius* would have fit better here than among the up-to-spec vessels in the high-security zone, but registry was everything. As for Mriy herself, she was of Meyang origin; her registry said this was where she belonged, locked out of the safe zone for humans.

As she hopped down to ground level, Mriy wished she had taken some personal effects. This had only been intended as a drop-off followed by a quick return, but Rikk Pa tugged at her. She might not be welcome, but she was in no hurry to leave, either. Returning to the *Mobius* no longer promised to be such a quick trip. Carl was likely going to have to come back and pick her up outside the security zone when it was time to leave.

If she was going to leave.

It wasn't a foregone conclusion that she was going to survive her homecoming. Bad blood among humans might run cold under the watchful stare of the law. But here she was under no such protection. There were several azrin who were well within their legal rights to kill her, including Hrykii, once he was thawed.

But none of that was worth dwelling on. It would happen, or it would not. She couldn't very well show up to the family compound without her nephew, which meant meeting up with the rest of the crew. Tanny's tactical brief before they arrived had included Mriy selecting a rally point in case they became separated. This wasn't the circumstance Mriy had envisioned when planning things out, but then again, that's what Tanny's contingencies were for—dealing with the unforeseen.

Following signs written both in Jiara and English, Mriy made her way to the ground transport station. A brown-furred attendant greeted her.

"Where will you be when you arrive?" he asked. He had an odd accent and manner of speech. He was Ruuthian, a long way from his home on the far side of Meyang.

"Nowhere far," she replied. "There's a cluster of off-worlder restaurants by Humantown. How much?"

"Eight dreka," the attendant said.

Mriy dug in her pockets for local currency. It had been a long time since she'd bothered carrying drekas. Filtering through a pile of cubic metal blocks, she found a two-by-two-by-two and passed it across the counter. The attendant picked up the coin, looked it over, and tossed it into a jar with a clink. A digital display read 008 momentarily, before going blank.

"Bay Three," the attendant told her.

The vehicle that awaited her was an old model Capchak dirt-roller. Its metal tracks were rusted and pitted, but otherwise looking sound. It didn't matter much how badly it ran. If a dirt-roller broke down, the riders could just walk away. It wasn't like a starship, or even a hover-cruiser in that regard. The engine growled like a warrior's challenge, and the driver popped out of the forward hatch to wave. "Climb on. Ziyek called ahead. Ready to roll when you're up."

The driver was all black, with three links of chain dangling from one ear. His fur bushed out at the neck, making him look stronger than he probably was. But right now, Mriy found her chest heaving. It had been a long time with no male companionship—non-azrin hardly counted. The driver obviously had no idea who she was; he was probably barely grown when she'd left. If they had known one another before, both had changed in the intervening years. It was possible... no, as soon as he discovered who she was, it would end badly.

Slowing her breathing with a human concentration technique, Mriy hauled herself over the side railing of the dirt-roller. "Roll when you wish," she shouted. The wind of speed and weather combined to cut through her vest and fur, straight to the bones. The dirt-rolled gouged its way across Rikk Pa's landscape, and Mriy's body let loose the heat of anxiety, anger, and starship environmental furnaces into the Meyang atmosphere. Throwing back her head, she let out a roar. Whatever lay ahead for her, at that moment, she felt more alive than she had in years.

---

"You've got to be kidding me," Esper said as they reached the rendezvous point.

Carl chuckled. "You've got to get planetside more often."

The location Mriy had chosen was just outside Humantown, in an area where human-curious azrin congregated. The restaurant where they would wait for her was called Human Joe's Cow Ranch. It featured an actual ranch out back, with doomed bovines milling around and a gaudy holovid of an azrin in a cowboy outfit playing on loop over the roof.

Esper ended up at the front of the group and pushed her way through the saloon doors. "I'm just going to take a wild swing and say that azrin's name isn't really Joe," she said, raising her voice over the piped-in frontier music. The inside of the eatery was just as overblown and tacky. Giant cow and bull heads adorned the wall, mounted like hunting prizes in old-Earth fashion. The tables and booths surrounded a dirt-floor arena, where a robotic bull stood idle. "What's going on down there?"

"Looks like we're about to find out," Tanny said. There was a queue of azrin at the entrance to the arena, and the attendant opened the gate to allow a lone azrin through.

"Can I seat you, partners?" a white-furred azrin asked. His accent was a distinct attempt at an old-Earthish dialect consistent with the décor. With his cowboy hat, holstered six-shooters, and spurred boots, he didn't look much like a restaurant host. The stack of menus he carried said otherwise.

"We're meeting someone," Carl replied. Having spent time around Mriy, Esper picked up on the subtle shift in the host's ears, signaling annoyance. The polite smile never left his face though—probably part of his training for dealing with human customers.

"Got a bar?" Roddy asked.

Whether it was an intentional effort on Roddy's part to appease the host, or—more likely—simply a desire for a beer or five, the host perked up. "Of course, sir. Follow me."

The bar was packed, and despite a preponderance of azrin customers elsewhere in the restaurant, most of the barflies were human. Drinking for the sake of it was a cultural export that just hadn't caught on, at least on Meyang. Roddy pushed his way close enough to get the barkeep's attention and bought a round for the crew.

Down in the arena, a tan-furred azrin was stripping off his vest and approaching the robotic bull. A loudspeaker blared overhead. "Next contestant, Uajiss Finnu." It was hard to get a sense of scale with nothing near the lone azrin besides the bull. The would-be bullfighter was heavyset, with a swaggering walk that suggested confidence. He raised his arms and spread his fingers with claws extended—not that those thirty-millimeter blades would help against his robotic opponent.

A horn sounded and the bull charged. Esper had never seen a live bull up close, but this false one acted enough like a living creature that she was willing to give it the benefit of the doubt as a plausible reproduction. It shook its shoulders and thrashed its head as it bore down on its azrin challenger. The bullfighter sank into a ready crouch, an easy posture for the feline legs of an azrin. With whisker-thin timing, the challenger dodged aside as the bull careened past, angling stainless steel horns to gore.

Esper gasped along with a good portion of the human crowd. The azrin spectators hissed or looked on in silence. "What would happen if he didn't get out of the way?"

Tanny shrugged. "They got medics around here somewhere."

The bull pulled up and twisted around, aiming itself once more in the azrin's direction. With less room to build a head of steam, the robot came in slower, though exhibiting no less ferocity. This time when the azrin dodged aside, he grabbed one of the horns and held on. The bull flung its head back and forth, seemingly unsure whether to shake loose its opponent or try to impale him on the held horn. Despite the erratic movements, the bullfighter managed to catch hold of the other horn as well, holding the bull as if it were a bicycle or an anti-grav sled.

"Boo," Roddy muttered, slipping onto a seat at the bar while one of the patrons was distracted. "This guy's a pro. I was hoping we'd see some idiot get himself skewered."

Down in the arena, the robot and azrin wrestled for leverage. The bull pushed; the azrin put his feet back to maintain balance as he skidded along the dirt. The bull tossed his head; the bullfighter stretched long arms and legs to keep both his footing and his grip. The crowd cheered—a mix of human hoots and azrin yowls. Uajiss Finnu was putting on a show. Through remarkable programming, the robotic bull appeared to grow frustrated. It snapped its head from side to side, unable to shake its prey-turned-tormentor. On one pass, the bullfighter shifted his weight, overbalancing the robotic beast to one side. Hanging from the horns, he swung under the bull, kicking out one of the robot's legs with both of his and toppling the machine to the dirt.

The crowd's cheering reached a crescendo. Esper let out a sigh. "At least he didn't get hurt."

"Cut his arm," Tanny replied. The azrin stood atop the now inert beast. There was no thrashing, now that the program had run its course. Against the tan fur, there was a matted smear of red on one upraised arm. "Doubt he cares though."

Esper gave Tanny a narrow-eyed glare. "You're not thinking of—"

"*Hell* no," Tanny replied. "I don't think I've got the mass for it. And I certainly don't have anything to prove to *this* lot."

"I saw a sign at the entrance," Esper said. "There's prize money. Works out to about 7800 in terras."

Carl's eyes widened. "You know, Mort..."

"The answer is 'no,'" Mort replied before Carl could even get the question out. "I could reduce that bull to a flopping sack of loose parts, but I don't think anyone would believe I hadn't cheated. For Chrissakes, just look at me. Now look at the fella with his furry arms up in the air. Which of us looks like a likely candidate to flip robo-cattle on their asses?"

"Bet we'd get good odds," Carl replied.

"And get ourselves arrested. It's not even subtle," Esper said. She lowered her voice and tried to spice it with an angry edge. "And I'd thank you to keep those larcenous thoughts bottled up when we're out in public."

"Where's Mriy anyway?" Carl wondered aloud. "Shouldn't be taking her this long to cut across town. Where the hell'd those patrol twits ditch her? Off-world?"

Carl's answer came in the quieting of the crowd. There were places where the buzz of voices ebbs and flows to the point where an occasional quiet moment might have gone unnoticed. Human Joe's wasn't one of those. Curious eyes turned toward the entrance, where a lone azrin entered. White furred except for a few spots of orange, she stood tall and towered over most of the azrin around her. Esper hadn't realized that Mriy was so large a specimen among her own kind.

Mriy scanned the crowd until her eyes fell on the *Mobius* crew, then she headed their way. The crowd parted for her as whispers spread around the eatery. One brown-furred azrin stepped into her path, but a twitch of Mriy's lip to show fangs was enough to move him out of her way. Esper could only surmise the azrin's gender, of course. Accustomed to primate anatomy, she was largely ignorant of the clues to tell azrin sexes apart.

"Quite an entrance," Carl remarked as Mriy joined the group.

Mriy kept her voice low. "I hadn't expected to be recognized so quickly or easily. Can we get out of here?"

"Looks like you can clear us a path," Carl said. "Lead on."

Esper fell into step near the rear of an impromptu parade to the exit. Only Roddy came after her, carrying one of Human Joe's mugs as long as he could to drain its contents. It seemed as if the restaurant had paused while Mriy was inside. Whether it started up once more upon their departure, Esper could only speculate.

No one questioned Mriy when she took the controls of the hover-cruiser. This was her world, after all.

---

Dusk had settled over Rikk Pa by the time they arrived at the Yrris Clanhold. Mriy had hardly said a word on the trip, answering brief queries about the landscape and their destination with even briefer replies. Human Joe's had put her on edge. A whole restaurant full of people all knew she was back. Whether a few keen observers had spread word like an avalanche or every person on Meyang recognized her on sight, the effect was the same. Word would reach her family before Mriy did.

From the outside, the clanhold appeared unchanged since her youth. Evergreens along the winding road hid the compound from view until they were almost upon it. A dozen squat, conical buildings poked through the snow that coated the mountain lowlands, chimneys belching woodsmoke into the evening sky. It had been springtime when she'd last seen it; the herd grass was green and soft on bare feet. It should have changed more since then. There should have been a new house built, or one of the old ones burnt down. Even a few darkened buildings with no fires burning would have shown that the Yrris Clan had fallen on hard times without her.

"Looks cozy," Carl said, his words coming out accompanied by puffs of fog. He huddled in his jacket with his arms hugged close. "We gonna just look at it all night?"

Mriy bit back a snarl. It was no good arguing with Carl when he was wrong, let alone when he was in the right. She hit the accelerator and started the hover-cruiser toward the hearth hub, center-most building in the clanhold. The cheerful, inviting, mocking, spiteful lights from the windows grew closer.

Floodlights snapped on, blindingly bright, forcing Mriy to slow the hover-cruiser. Engine hums came from left and right, approaching and surrounding them. Snow-rollers revved their engines as they encircled the *Mobius* crew and Mriy was forced to either stop or risk hitting someone. She might have been able to put enough air under the craft to jump it over the snow-rollers, but that was a trick better suited to Carl's skill set, not her own.

"Heard you were back, Mriy," a voice shouted over the growls of combustion engines. "You're going to regret it."

"I came to bring back Hrykii," Mriy replied in the direction of the speaker. "You defend the clan now, Yariy?"

"Of course it fell to me," Yariy replied. "Who else? Soora? You?"

"Graida," Mriy answered.

"Dead."

"Seris?"

"Offworld, earning for the clan," Yariy said. "You said you had Hrykii. All I see are humans with you."

Mriy elbowed Roddy to keep him quiet. The last thing they needed was his surly tongue. She pointed to the back of the hover-cruiser. "In the tube. We rescued him from a bounty hunter. He is too badly injured for us to wake from stasis with no doctor. We brought him straight here."

A single snow-roller revved its engine, and Yariy pulled alongside the hover-cruiser. Standing on her vehicle's seat, she looked at their cargo and ran a hand along the smooth surface. "Get him inside. We'll see about you when we get the tale from him."

"But I thought—" Mriy said.

"You thought wrong," Yariy replied. "Seerii speaks here. I serve. You have no standing. We'll find you if Hrykii thinks you've earned a voice."

Mriy fumed in the night air. She would not have been surprised if the snow melted under her glare. Yariy had been a child when she left, and now gave orders like a guardian. For once the *Mobius* crew kept a respectful silence. She had dragged them into this, but they had no stake in Yrris clan matters. Two younger cousins hefted Hrykii's stasis pod between them and loaded it onto a snow-roller driven by someone Mriy had never met. The latter might have mated into the clan recently, or may have been a hired claw for all she knew.

The snow-rollers grumbled and kicked up white, powdery wakes as they sped off into the security of the clanhold. When they were out of sight, the floodlights went dark and the mystery of night set in.

"So, we done here?" Carl asked, shivering.

"For tonight," Mriy answered. "I can't easily go back to the ship, but the rest of you can. I'm going to stay in Rikk Pa."

"For how long?" Esper asked.

"If Hrykii vouches for my actions, perhaps forever."

---

As Earth-like worlds went, Meyang was sparsely populated. Carl might have gone so far as to call it deserted. While humans had bred Earth to the brink of ruin before spilling out into the stars, the azrin people had kept their numbers down to levels of pre-industrial Earth. There was unspoiled land between cities, and even a fair amount within them. Rikk Pa was more of a patchwork collection of villages, shopping centers, and civic hubs than any city Carl had seen. As Tanny parked the hover-cruiser, he and the crew prepared to do a little local exploration.

"Remember, keep your comms handy at all times," Tanny said, part of her standard security briefing for planetside romps. The reputation of the locals aside, Meyang ought to have been as safe as anyplace they'd been in a long time. As a protectorate, the planet warranted direct protection of the

ARGO fleet. And since the azrin central government wasn't too keen on the idea, there were ground forces aplenty on the surface.

"Not it," Roddy called.

"Not it," Carl quickly echoed.

"Looks like it's your turn," Tanny said to Esper.

"Me? My turn for what?" Esper asked.

Mort chuckled. "You ever seen me carry a comm?"

"I'm babysitting?"

"Egads, girl, I could be your—well, I was about to say grandfather, but that might be stretching it a bit. Let's just say that I could be your father, and I don't need babysitting. Think of it as being a caddy for me, carrying a comm around in case Mother Hen needs to check under her britches to see if we're all still breathing and unmolested by the local constabulary."

"Fine," Carl said, interceding between the two. "I'll tag along for a while. Not like I've got money to blow on anything fun."

In daylight hours, Rikk Pa was brisk, not so bitterly cold as the night before had been. So while Roddy slunk away to find a bar with wide hours and Tanny flitted off on errands she wouldn't share, Carl fell into step behind Mort and Esper, taking his amusement in watching the two of them together.

"If this is the azrin section, why do all the signs have English, too?" Esper asked as they passed the civic tram depot.

"ARGO rules with an iron clipboard," Mort replied. "Rules with rules, so to speak. I doubt one in five can read them, but they put the signs up with both languages all the same. Next generation it might be one in four, then one in three. Sooner or later, grandparents will be teaching their children azrin so that they remember the old ways, and not the other way around."

"Worked for Roddy, I suppose," Esper said.

"Not hardly," Carl piped up. "Laaku are nearly all bilingual. They didn't give up their native languages; they just all decided to learn ours so we'd leave them alone about it. I think Roddy's got to know at least three or four."

"Six," Mort said. "English, plus three from his own world, a smattering of setrine, and he's picked up the major azrin dialect from Mriy. Ask any laaku and they'll tell you the same: they're smarter than us."

"Wow," Esper whispered. "I had no idea."

"Well, correct him on his grammar sometime," Mort said with a sneer. "Rotten monkey speaks better English than the lot of you when it suits him. He doesn't like people thinking he's stuffy, but you can egg him on until he proves it."

"Forget that crap," Carl interrupted. "Where we going?"

Esper looked back at him with a frown. Carl returned a sanguine grin. "I looked at the local map this morning, and there's a cathedral nearby that—"

"Oh, come on," Carl griped.

"That belongs to the One Church," Esper continued. "It's Saturday, so there won't be Mass. I'm just going to confession."

"Well, since you've been traveling with us for what, four months or something?" Carl asked. "You'll be in there a while."

"Very funny," Esper replied. "I'd say you need it worse than I do, but you don't care, and they wouldn't listen to you anyway. You have to actually be penitent to confess. You'd just be bragging."

Carl shrugged. She was right of course. "How about you, Mort? Anything you want to get off your chest?"

"If I'm of a mind to discuss my immortal soul, I'll address the man in charge directly," Mort replied with a huff.

The Cathedral of Saint Hubertus stood out amid the

largely azrin architecture. Near as Carl could figure, every-thing around Rikk Pa was built to deal with heavy snowfall—steep roofs, elevated main floors, and underground passages to nearby buildings. The Cathedral of Saint Hubertus was Old Earth Gothic, complete with flying buttresses and gargoyles perched around the roof. If Mriy was any indication of her peers, that last detail was bound to go over well with the locals.

"Will you two wait for me?" Esper asked before heading inside.

Carl looked to Mort with a shrug, and the wizard shrugged right back. "Sure," Carl replied. "Make us wait long enough for my feet to start hurting though, and you're finding your own ride back to the ship."

They waited until the oak doors closed behind Esper. "So, what do you want to do while she's in there?"

Mort cleared his throat. "I think I'm going to see if they've got a washroom in there."

Carl watched Mort with a suspicious eye, wondering what he might be up to.

---

Esper stepped from an alien world into an embassy of peace and infinite love. It was unfair to say that if you had been to a single One Church cathedral you had been to them all, but there was a certain consistency to them. Same stained-glass iconography, even if the images varied. Same pews, with velvet upholstered kneelers. Same hymnals and Bibles. Same confessionals.

Esper's boots echoed on the polished floor, the marvelous acoustics carrying the sound throughout the nave. She gawked and meandered, letting a smile slip across her face as the warmth of home seeped into her. This was the real reason humans built cathedrals. They were old, solid, dependable. One cathedral was as close to the Lord as any other. He was always present, cathedral or no, but this was the reminder that He was omnipresent. You couldn't forget or dismiss His presence from within these sanctified walls. After months adrift and conflicted, Esper Theresa Richelieu felt her feet beneath her.

She was far from alone. There were worshipers scattered among the pews—mainly human, but a surprising number of azrin mixed with them. There was a confessional with the door slightly ajar, and she headed straight for it. The inside was darker than she was accustomed to, but that quaint musty smell of old wood in tight spaces brought a twitch of a smile.

A moment later, a priest sat down on the other side of the screen. "How long has it been since your last confession?" he asked.

Esper knelt and made the sign of the cross. "Bless me Father, for I have sinned. My last confession was six months ago."

"I hope you may find an easing of so long a burden," the priest replied.

Esper began with the gravest sin she had committed. "Father, though it was not my intent, I have killed a man." That was where it began. From there, the dam burst. Everything she had done since joining the *Mobius* and even the short while before poured out of her: her use of magic, her crimes against secular law, and her brushes with temptation of the flesh. The priest made scant comment throughout, allowing her to continue until she had to pause for breath.

"Of all these sins, which do you most fear?" the priest asked.

"Fear?" Esper echoed, not quite understanding this unexpected line of questioning.

"Did you find killing gave you pleasure? Did it sit easily on your conscience?"

"Of course not, Father!"

"Did you regret not acting when offered the pleasure of the flesh? Do you fear that you will succumb the next time, or the time after that?"

Esper paused. "Maybe a little. I try though, and so far trying has been enough. I pray for that strength."

"Did you enjoy the feel of handling God's power?"

"I... I've used it twice to save lives and once to take one," Esper replied. "I felt guilt each time, but maybe not as much when I helped people. I may have also overlooked this one, but I've also taken to using the hunger side effect of the healing spell to burn off chocolates so I can eat more of them. That one I always feel guilty about too—more for the magic, a little less for overindulging in chocolates."

"I will tell you something that may set your mind at ease," the priest said. "The powers you possess are a gift from God. The misuse of them is certainly a sin, but there can never be a more proper application of them than the saving of a life. But since you have also killed by negligence, I will enjoin you to study. If you would continue to serve your fellow man in the manner of Christ, you must separate the beneficial from the malignant. It is a burden you carry and a responsibility. Find a way to control and harness the goodness that resides within you, and be not ashamed of doing the Lord's work."

"That's my penance?" Esper asked.

There was a soft noise from the other side of the screen, too polite to be either a snort or a laugh, but suggestive of both. "I never said that. This goes beyond, and it will carry with you far longer. You must either give up the use of this power entirely, which would be a pity, or learn to use it with the certainty that it will do the good that you wish."

After that, the priest gave a long overview of the prayers she would need to recite, starting right then. He left her to her Hail Marys and her rosaries with an admonition to consider her choices when it came to giving up magic.

---

Mort strolled out of the cathedral with a grin that threatened to split his face in two. Carl checked the chrono built into his comm. "You get lost looking for that washroom, or did you get a little sidetracked along the way?"

As he walked by on his way to a wooden park bench, Mort snickered.

"You did it, didn't you?" Carl asked.

Mort shrugged. "I'm going to hell anyway."

---

*"Come home."*

That was all the note said. Mriy had waited all morning in her rented room at the Taste of Sol boarding house. It wasn't until she checked an old comm ID that she hadn't used in years that she finally discovered it. It was unsigned, and from a comm ID she didn't recognize—she wasn't the only one who had moved on in the years she'd been gone.

She considered calling Carl and letting him know where she was going, but decided against it. This was her business, not his. Besides, Carl wouldn't be pleased that she had a recording of their encounter with the *Remembrance*. But as Mriy clutched the data crystal, she knew it had been a wise precaution. Without her recording of the sensor feed from the chase and stasis pod recovery, it would have been her word alone as to what happened; Hrykii had been in stasis through the whole ordeal.

Without access to the crew's hover-cruiser, she booked a quick intra-city livery service to pick her up and take her home. It was human owned, but azrin operated. QuickRide hadn't been operating in Rikk Pa when she'd last been there, and it felt odd being chauffeured by a handsome young azrin in a human-styled suit, complete with sleeves.

There were no floodlights when she arrived at the Yrris Clanhold, no swarm of snow-rollers. Her boots crunched the snow as she waded to the main building's front door. How long had she lived there? How long had she lived away? Weighing her childhood against her professional travels and her exile, she had spent more of her life there than anywhere else. But those early memories were hazy. There was no warmth waiting for her, despite the chimney smoke that foretold a hearth fire.

She pounded her fist four times on the door. Four was the Yrris number, telling the door guard she was family. But Yariy was the one to open it, and Mriy wasn't sure Yariy considered her to be family at all. "You came after all," Yariy said, stepping aside to allow Mriy in.

"The message went to an old ID," Mriy replied. As she stepped past, she made sure not to slouch low enough to let Yariy seem even close to her own height. Though her cousin had a reputation in her own right, it was no time to let Yariy think she could be bullied.

"You left a lot of old things behind," Yariy replied. "Seerii didn't wait for you. She's out hunting for lunch."

"I haven't eaten," Mriy replied, dangling the implied offer to join the hunt. It was encouraging to hear that her mother was still fit to kill her own food.

"Maybe you should have thought of that before you came," Yariy replied, slamming the door. "We're not here to feed you. The hunting grounds are for the family."

"But I thought—"

"You thought wrong," Yariy snapped, taking a step to close the gap between them. It was a bold move, considering their difference in size. Mriy had come unarmed as a sign of good faith, and Yariy had two knifes at her belt. Mriy still liked her odds. Her cousin was shouting to tempt an avalanche. "Whatever Seerii decides, she hasn't told me anything about treating you like family."

Mriy took a step of her own. She loomed over her cousin and had the satisfaction of watching Yariy's ears flatten back. It was an easy thing to talk like the clan guardian when no one threatened to convert those words into actions. "A life for a life. Mother can't deny that. She might not forget, but she will forgive. And when she does, I'll be in my rights to challenge for your job as guardian. Think on that." She gave Yariy a shove and knocked her cousin back a step.

Yariy was a finesse fighter and a good one. She'd obviously improved in the years Mriy had been gone, or she wouldn't have risen to guardian. But that didn't mean she was a threat to Mriy. Yariy wouldn't have taken the guardian's job from Soora. Mriy had been nearly as strong as Soora, but too quick for her brother. She suspected she was just as nimble as Yariy and could throw her around like prey.

Yariy glared at Mriy, but took another step back. "What's wrong with you? You think you can barge in here, talking with a human accent, and buy forgiveness? You'd destroy the clan. No one would stay if you became guardian."

Mriy had never considered that she'd picked up an English accent.

"By rights, the job is mine," Mriy replied. She'd defeated Soora, and the unfortunate confrontation at the conclusion had earned her exile. But in that brief interim, she had owned the position. "If you don't win it from me, it's a hollow title."

Yariy flashed her teeth. "We'll see about that." She whirled and stalked out of the room. Over her shoulder, she called back, "Yesterday's kill is in the cold room. Stay out of the hunting grounds."

It was another hour before the hunting party returned. Mriy had pillaged a lunch of venison after trying without success to discern by claw marks who had killed it. She used to know the habits and hand spans of every hunter in the Yrris Clanhold. Soora's handiwork was plain by the massive deep cuts in the prey's flesh, claws spread wider than any other Yrris. Her father had a penchant for snapping necks without leaving a scratch. Some younger cousin likely killed deer that provided her meal.

There were a lot of young cousins in the party that arrived back at the clanhold. Seerii led them. It gladdened Mriy to see Hrykii was well enough to have gone along. But aside from Meriik and Seninshee, the rest were strangers to her, grown children she no longer recognized. They walked past, ignoring her; four of them lugged a brown bear in a litter, already skinned. The four carried the animal into the butchery for preparation, without so much as a sidelong glance in Mriy's direction. It was Seerii who finally broke the shunning.

"You came back," her mother said. "I thought perhaps you would not."

Mriy stood and hung her head. Contrition was her best ally, now. "I belong here. This is home."

Seerii hissed softly. "Home is family, not a place. Soora understood, but never you. Settle down. Take a mate. Raise your children. Then you'll understand, too."

Mriy felt her hackles rise. "I'm too old to find a mate." It was a hard thing to admit with so many strange faces watching. She had wasted her best years away from Meyang, first fighting for money, then in exile. A family of her own was always a plan for later, until later became too late.

Seerii looked her over, stepping around to view her from all sides. Mriy looked much like her mother, except larger and with far more muscle beneath her fur. Watching Seerii as she was inspected was like a mirror into her own future. This is what she would look like in twelve years' time.

"Still fighting shape," Seerii said while she stood behind Mriy. "Carrying human guns hasn't softened you—much."

Mriy jerked her head toward the hunters' kill. "Stronger than that bear you brought. Strong enough to protect the clan."

"So that's the trick," Seerii said. "You want the guardian's job again. That title sat poorly on you last time. No sooner had you won it but you betrayed the clan."

"Soora spat at me," Mriy snapped. "He lost; the job was mine. My blood was still hot and he spat at me. My moment of triumph, and he spat on it. If he was half the fighter he claimed to be, he should have known to defend himself if he was going to do that."

Seerii turned away, but her claws were extended. "You

broke most of his ribs and his right arm in three places—all fair, of course. But spitting was all that was left in him. I'm amazed he managed in his condition."

"You talk like he did nothing wrong," Mriy replied. She grabbed Seerii by the shoulder and turned her mother to face her. Five of the hunters flinched toward them, prepared to intervene, but Seerii cut them off with a raised hand. Mriy put her face right in her mother's, looking down the head's height difference between them. "You talk like I deserved to be spat on."

Seerii jerked her shoulder free of Mriy's loose hold. She was still an old woman, so Mriy hadn't dug in her claws. "You'd have made a poor guardian then, and you'd make a worse one now. For two years, you'd spent more time away than home—no harm in that alone. You'd fought and won, but what about the prize money? We didn't send you off-world to fill your hands with gold. You were out there to support the clan."

"I sent back plenty," Mriy replied, flashing her teeth without meaning to. They had always overestimated the winnings from the Silver League.

"Not enough," Seerii countered. "Not enough for how much you were gone. You squandered your time and the clan's money."

Mriy turned her back on her mother, and a pair of younger clan members scrambled to remove themselves from her line of sight. "Same river; new water. I'm here because I brought back Hrykii. A life for a life. Talk of now."

Hrykii spoke up. His voice had deepened in the year since Mriy had last heard him. "So you claim. How do we know it wasn't *you* who kidnapped me? The hero's shadow is the easiest villain."

Mriy grinned. Seerii was being dense, but Hrykii had put rock to steel and made a spark. She slid the data crystal from her pocket, knowing that all eyes in the room followed her movements. "Come to the viewing room. I have proof."

---

Esper laced up the rented shoes and wondered how many wizards' feet had been inside them before hers. They were garishly striped, smooth-soled, and didn't fit perfectly. Who would think of such a bizarre ritual? "Why can't we just bring our own shoes?" she asked.

Mort had changed into his bowling shoes already and was selecting a ball from the racks. "Tradition. Golfers wear plaid knickers, polo players ride live horses, and bowlers wear rented shoes."

The rack was as daunting as it was confusing. Every ball looked a hair different from the others, but identical in all the ways that probably mattered. She picked one at random and was shocked at the weight. "We're going to be throwing these around all afternoon? This thing weighs a ton."

"Sixteen pounds," Mort replied, waving his own in one hand. He had three fingers jabbed into matching holes in the surface. Esper did likewise, but found the spacing uncomfortable.

"What's that in kilos?" she asked.

"It isn't," Mort said. He plucked the ball from her hands, browsed the rack, and handed her another. This one fit her fingers more readily. "Pounds are weight; kilos are mass. Gravity is the difference. Any respectable bowling alley uses Earth gravity. Since this planet is identical, that's a non-issue.

But you'll do better if you don't tie your mind up in knots with numbers."

"Why am I doing this to myself?" Esper muttered. The priest was half-baked. She had a mind to report him to the Vatican. Though she had never stopped to consider it before, the Seal of the Confessional probably worked both ways. Whatever cardinal oversaw Meyang likely wouldn't even listen to her grievance.

"Because you said you wanted to keep your magic under control," Mort replied. "And because I am a kindly old wizard, I agreed to help you. This is the place to learn." He took a short, measured walk to the line and rolled his ball down the lane, knocking over every pin.

"I can't compete with your magic," Esper said with a huff. She'd never bowled in her life, and Mort was an experienced wizard, capable of magicking the ball to anywhere in the lane he liked—hers too.

Mort clucked his tongue and wagged a finger. "Not today. Today is all about you. Anything you can to do my ball or yours, do it. I won't try to stop you."

"But you just—"

"Bowled a legitimate strike," Mort finished for her. The primitive mechanics at the end of the lane set up a new rack of ten pins. "I don't need magic to hit a bunch of plastic pins with a ball. You figure out some magic today and you can make me miss, but if you don't, I'm going to mop the floor with you."

Esper mimicked Mort's approach to the line, but skidded to a halt before she was ready to roll. Recovering her balance, she crouched low, set the ball on the floor, and gave it a push. Sixteen pounds of polyurethane wobbled down the lane at the pace of a baby's first steps. Two thirds of the way down, it slipped into the gutter.

Moments later, her ball rolled back to the head of the lane along a pair of polished steel rails. Mort picked it up and brought it back to her. "Practice ball," he said. "This time, tell it where to go. Gesture at it. Use body language. Technique only matters if your opponent can stop you from using magic. Push it with your foot if you want. Just steer it."

Esper gave Mort a wary look as she stepped past him to the line. She took a deep breath, set the ball on the floor, and shoved it with both hands. It took off down the lane, and she could see already that it was heading for the right gutter once more. "Left. Come on, left," she coaxed it, waving a hand for emphasis.

"There you go," Mort said. "Keep at it. Try Latin. The older the language, the better."

"*Sinister. Sin-is-ter... SINISTER!*"

The ball was turning as she waved it over. Esper leapt to her feet, swinging both arms as she cajoled the ball toward the pins. It was hanging on the edge of the gutter. She was almost out of time.

It clipped the rightmost pin. "Yes!" she shouted, clenching a fist in the air.

Quickly she glanced around the alley. There were just four lanes, and only theirs was in use. The attendant ignored her outburst, and the young azrin at the snack counter gave her a thumbs up. Esper offered a self-conscious smile in return.

"Sorry," she whispered to Mort as she got out of his way for the next round.

"Sorry schmorry," Mort replied. "It's a game. Have fun with it. Now let's see what you can do to *my* shot."

The viewing room had been upgraded while Mriy had been away. The azrin-made Ruaka Pik holo-projector had been replaced with an authentic Reali-Sim 2655. The holographic field filled half the chamber, and there was no graininess to spoil the illusion of real ships flying overhead. It was odd seeing the *Mobius* from the outside, as the sensor replay simulated the encounter from a third person perspective. There were occasions where bits of debris from the scrapyard faded from view or appeared suddenly as the ship's sensors picked up and lost track of them. Other than that, Mriy and her clan saw the battle just as it had taken place.

"Look at her," Yariy remarked. "If Mriy was at those guns, I wouldn't trust her with a thrown knife. How many shots has she missed?"

"Hrykii was inside," Mriy reminded everyone. "The idea was to maim the ship, not destroy it."

"Better to die than be kept as a trophy, or as a thing to torment," Yariy said. "What if that ship had gotten away?"

"Keep watching," Mriy snapped. Though watching it herself, she had to admit that her aim was wider of the mark than she had remembered.

The critical moment was coming up. The bounty hunter's ship slowed and swung its tail end around. A small object, barely more than a sliver in the holo-field, drifted off in the direction of the *Remembrance*'s momentum as the bounty hunter changed course.

"*You can come after me or it, but it's headed for the munitions dump.*" Mriy glanced around the room, wondering how many of her clan understood human well enough to follow the conversation. They didn't have the benefit of a translator-charmed earring like hers.

The turret gun of the *Mobius* flashed, and this time the

shot was a direct hit. The *Remembrance*'s oxygen burned off into space in a fraction of a second.

"*We were all set, Mriy. He dropped the pod and was making a run for it,*" Carl's recorded voice said.

"*I know,*" recorded Mriy replied. "*That was personal.*" She wondered if Carl had even noticed that she had stopped speaking his language and swapped back to her native tongue. Wearing a translator charm of his own, Carl would have heard her in his own language either way.

"What did he say?" Seerii asked. "I heard one of them speak your name." Her mother understood human, but Carl wasn't the clearest speaker.

Yariy provided a somber translation. There was a grudging respect in it. Hard to argue when Mriy had disobeyed an order to enact vengeance for the clan.

The holovid continued to the point where the cryostasis pod was secured inside the ship. There were no sensor logs of what took place within. Carl would have been furious to know she had even made a recording of what had gone on outside.

Hrykii stood. "I thank you for my life." He gave a stiff nod and reclaimed his seat.

A quiet followed. Eyes turned toward Seerii, awaiting a decision. "How certain are we that this is authentic?" her mother asked Yariy. Mriy's fur bristled at the implication.

The guardian of the Yrris Clan narrowed her eyes. "It's possible she rigged it. We'd need a specialist to analyze it." The implication was clear. Specialist meant human, or possibly laaku. Even Yariy didn't trust her fellow azrins to out-puzzle an ARGO tech specialist. The universities, the ARGO navies, all the best training grounds for tech wranglers were off limits to her people.

"No," Seerii said. "We have Hrykii back. We have this

recording. We will not bring this in front of the humans, even paid ones. Mriy destroyed one of their kind. The occupiers would pay more for this as evidence than the clan could afford to pay to keep a human quiet. Your exile is ended, Mriy. You are welcome here once more." She stood and opened her arms.

There were murmurs of quiet conversation around the viewing room, not all of them sounding friendly. But Mriy ignored them and stepped into her mother's embrace, nuzzling against the fur of her neck. How loose the skin there; how slack the sinew. Her mother was old indeed.

"Thank you," Mriy whispered. "I will keep the clan well when my time comes."

Seerii stiffened. She pushed Mriy away firmly, though Mriy did not dare resist for fear of hurting her. "No, you will not take over the clan when I pass. Hrykii is the heir. He was given the title when you were exiled, and it has not been taken from him."

Mriy drew a deep breath. She wanted to scream, to roar, to shake her mother until her senses returned. What good was returning to the Yrris clanhold as neither guardian nor heir? She had not come back to slink into the rank and file of the cousins and mates. She had been second heir after Soora, and Soora was dead.

"Then I challenge, Hrykii, and he will take no shame in backing down," Mriy replied.

"Hah!" Hrykii shouted. "You think you can pay me life for my father's then bargain it away again for leadership of the clan after grandmother? You dragged me here half dead, but we paid a human doctor's ransom. I'll be myself in a day or two."

Mriy gave a soft, hissing laugh. "I could give you two days to heal plus two years to grow muscle on those skinny arms of yours. The day you step into the pit with me, we find you another human doctor."

Several of the Yrris Clan cousins stood and flexed their claws, taking a stand beside Hrykii. But Hrykii smiled. "You could. No doubt, you are a brute. My father learned too late. But since you challenged me, I set the contest. It's my right as heir. I choose the pack hunt."

Mriy's ears flattened. "Getting the clan to do your work for you? Coward."

"My father taught me that the clan isn't about the one, it's about the all. Leading is more than being strongest. Packs of five, in three days' time. See who will follow *you*, brother-killer." Hrykii strode from the room, taking most of the clan with him, including Yariy. She would have been a long shot to join Mriy's pack for the hunt, but sometimes picking the winner is more important than picking the friend.

A minute later, Mriy was alone in the viewing room with Seerii. "It is possible that you might find no one to follow you. If you are alone against a pack of five, maybe you will learn that friends are earned, not won." With that, Seerii left as well.

---

Seerii's words proved prophetic. Two days scouring the clan-hold and making calls on her datapad, and she had a pack of one—herself. Simkin had already agreed to join Hrykii. Tamrau was planning to. Mriy hadn't bothered to ask Yariy. Renyau told her flatly that he hoped she would lose. A dozen weaker hunters had made excuses, avoided speaking with her, or chosen sides against her. Even when she began asking outside the clan, her old acquaintances wanted no part of the hunt.

It was a hard thing to stomach, taking the tally of allies and coming up empty. For a ritual hunt, there could be no payment, no exchange of favors. Mriy had to find hunters who were loyal to her, who wanted to see her win badly enough to spend days in the remote wilderness helping secure her victory. Mriy just didn't have those sorts of friends, it seemed.

Mriy had never found much use for the chapel when she was younger. Years had changed her, not to mention the constant exposure to Esper of late. The Yrris chaplain was still Auzuma, black as the night sky and thin as the crescent moon. He greeted her at the door, as if he had expected her visit.

"Come in Mriy," Auzuma said, his voice smooth and soothing. Auzuma wasn't Yrris; she didn't know how he came into the clan's service. He had been a friend of her father's; that much she knew. The old azrin put a hand on her back and guided her inside the chapel.

Mriy bristled at the touch. As a fighter, she had instincts to suppress any time someone put a friendly hand on her. Caught unawares, she might have broken Auzuma's arm before she could stop herself. Maybe he felt her stiffen. Maybe her ears twitched back. But he let Mriy alone just after she cleared the doorway.

The insides of the chapel smelled of cut evergreen boughs. The pine and spruce resins made the chapel smell like an entire forest had been compressed inside. Mriy took a long breath and let the tension ease out of her—though much of it clung stubbornly.

"I need advice, Father," Mriy said. She sat on a floor cushion in one of the cubbies along the wall, just large enough for two.

"I get few visitors who don't," Auzuma replied, taking a seat beside her. He must have been approaching thirty, but he still moved like a young man. He stretched, and she heard the crackling in his spine as he settled in, spoiling the illusion of youthful vigor.

"Mother has allowed me back home," Mriy began. It was obvious, of course, but it was a hard enough subject even with proper preamble. She couldn't just blurt it out. "But Hrykii is heir. I've challenged him, and he chose the pack hunt."

"Wise of him," Auzuma said, nodding. "A promising sign in a young heir."

"But I can't gather a pack."

"The Mriy I remember was always willing to take on a challenge," Auzuma said. "Would not winning a hunt, alone against five, prove your worth beyond doubt?"

Mriy growled. "No! It would prove me for guardian maybe, but not heir. I could snap Yariy's neck and take the guardian's job any day."

"Then step back," Auzuma said. "Become humble. Show respect for your mother's decision. Ask to be named heir after Hrykii and guard his life more dearly than your own. That would show respect for Seerii and for the good of the clan."

"If I show I can gather a pack, I can prove to mother than I am worthy of being heir, even if not more worthy than Hrykii," Mriy said. "I have to show mother that I should never have had my position taken from me."

Auzuma sighed and stood. "Redemption is a powerful motive, and one I can approve. If you will have an old man, I will join your pack for the hunt. No one who comes to the chapel begging aid is turned away without it. If you lose, you will not be shamed by losing alone."

"Thank you, Father Auzuma," Mriy replied, bowing her head.

"But you will want three more," Auzuma said. "I'm too old

to be much use. It will take all my strength just to keep up. There are charitable hunters who may take pity on you, but I suggest you set a wider snare. You would not have come to me before looking all the likely places. Time to look in the unlikely ones for hunters."

---

It was, according to the local omni, the best azrin restaurant for off-worlders in Rikk Pa. The sign outside was lettered in a jumble of azrin script in red chromaglow, but everyone called it by the English translation: Fleshfire. It would have been an unappealing name on a more civilized world, but on Meyang, it carried the comforting connotation of cooked meat, as opposed to the local preference for raw.

The restaurant was a quarter kilometer outside Human-town, and was fancy enough that Esper made sure to shower and change out of her sweaty clothes from bowling. She hadn't come close to catching Mort in any of the eight games they played, but by the end, she was at least rolling the ball with proper form, and adjusting the aim on her throws by a few centimeters. Mort's sure, heavy rolls moved too quickly for her to exert any noticeable influence.

Everyone but Kubu had been invited. He looked so sad when they said goodbye to him at the cargo ramp, but he didn't try to follow. He really was trying to be a good boy. Whether he would ever be accepted into restaurants or any other place of business remained to be seen. For now, he was a rowdy child and far too big a risk to bring along. Not to mention the fact that he looked like a house pet, and it took magic to understand him.

Their booth was in a quiet corner. Whether Carl had said

something on the sly to the host or whether Mriy had arranged it in advance was anyone's guess. The dining hall flickered with torchlight. It wasn't the false effect created by software-controlled diodes or even magic, but actual burning wood-and-pitch torches, changed by the waitstaff at regular intervals. A hearty ventilation system sucked the smoke up through the central chimney before it choked the diners.

"Place has some atmosphere," Mort said as he slid into the booth.

Roddy snorted. "Just hope they know how to cook meat. I've seen enough of Mriy's dinners not to want mine raw."

"Hey, according to DinnerBlab, this place is the real deal," Carl said. He took an end seat and slouched down, letting a hand dangle toward the floor.

Mriy was not long behind them, arriving before they had even finished sorting themselves into the booth. "Good. Glad you all made it. I was worried you might have spread over half Meyang by now."

"Nothing personal," Tanny said. "But Meyang isn't exactly bubbling over with tourist spots."

Mriy shook her head. "No time for that now. I have a favor to ask. A big one."

Carl sighed and let his head loll back. "Can't keep cutting you out of future jobs, Mriy."

"Good," Mriy replied. "Because I'm not allowed to pay you for this favor. Not in any way."

"This is sounding promising," Roddy said evenly. "I love not making money. We're getting to be fucking experts at it."

"Hrykii wants a pack hunt, his pack of five against mine," Mriy said. "Win, and I become heir to the clan again. I would take over when my mother passes. But to win, I need a hunting pack."

"That's nice," Esper said. It was like listening to her older brothers talking about sports. What else was there to say? "But what do any of us know about hunting?"

Carl held up his hands and gave a magnanimous smile. "You provide me a Typhoon, and I'll hunt you anything from squirrels all the way up to local patrol ships."

Tanny cuffed him in the shoulder, reaching over Roddy to get at him. "I've had survival training, for what it's worth."

"Much," Mriy replied, nodding. "I was counting on your help. I was also thinking of enlisting Kubu, since he has such an excellent nose."

"Does Kubu know how to track?" Esper asked, not directing the question to anyone in particular.

Tanny laughed out loud, drawing attention from the nearby tables. She tossed a datapad on the table. "Sorry, just struck me. I heard back from that professor today, the one who was going to figure out what Kubu is."

Mriy picked up the datapad first, her expression unreadable as her eyes flicked back and forth. "Blessed God," she whispered. Her eyes went vacant and she stared off in the direction of the *Mobius*, as if it could be seen through the walls of the restaurant.

Roddy snatched the datapad from her hands and began perusing it himself.

"What's it say?" Esper asked.

"Holy hell," Roddy muttered. "Dog's put on twenty kilos since we got him, and this says he hasn't hit a growth spurt yet. He's looking at two or three *tons* by the time he's full grown. By then, he could take that robotic bull over at Human Joe's and use it as a chew toy. His world's got megafauna, and his kind *eats* them."

"So that's a 'yes' on the hunting, I take it?" Esper asked.

Roddy pushed the datapad in Esper's direction. "Let's just say I'm gonna be a lot nicer to that mutt starting now."

"Will they let you bring a dog?" Mort asked.

Mriy shook her head. "No dogs, but I can convince them he's sentient. That will make him a willing pack member, not an animal."

"So, with me and Kubu, you'll have three," Tanny said.

"Four," Mriy corrected her. "My clan's chaplain is part of my pack. His name is Auzuma." Mriy grinned, showing teeth. "Since Hyrkii's pack includes a smoke seer, I have no reservation about bringing a wizard of my own. I would be honored if you would be our fifth, Mort."

Mort leaned back and crossed his arms. "Nope."

"What?" Mriy gasped.

"Feels too much like cheating," Mort replied. "I don't mind the stuff we do, generally. But this is family. I won't be a party to that sort of thing. Besides, it's like I'd be doing all the work for you."

"The prey wears a charm, an heirloom of my clan," Mriy said. "It can't be tracked by magic or science. It has to be hunted by guile and senses."

"Magic's magic," Mort replied. "You think your local witchdoctors are going to fool *me*? I'm sure that charm can discombobulate scientific whosamajiggers, but you're daft if you think I couldn't sniff that charm out from miles away if I was of a mind."

Mriy sank back in her seat. "Auzuma may know a protective charm or two, but I could use a proper wizard."

"Take Esper," Mort replied. "I spent all day giving her a rundown of the basics."

"Esper?" Mriy asked, confusion clear in her tone.

"Esper?" Esper asked, clearly not having heard correctly.

She was no wizard. She knew one spell and knew it badly enough that she'd accidentally killed someone with it when it was supposed to heal.

Mort shrugged. "You're young. Got healthy lungs in you. Getting away from science for a few days'll do you some good. Practice away from the heavy expectations of civilization. Magic's harder where people rely on techno-gizmos. Breathe some fresh air, levitate twigs, make the birds fly funny."

"I need a wizard, not..." Mriy struggled for a word and settled for gesturing to Esper.

"Me."

"You," Mriy confirmed.

Esper looked down at the menu in front of her, but the words didn't register. They were English, but her mind was on Mriy's opinion of her, not the food selection. She just couldn't look the azrin in the eye.

"Don't even *think* about looking at me," Roddy said, breaking the awkward silence. "A few days without booze or tech, I'd be ready to fucking kill myself."

Carl looked off into the restaurant, for all indications taking in the ambiance. "You know, there's more to being a leader than picking a bunch of ringers. Sometimes, pack leader —or a captain—might just have to take the ones she's got because they're the only ones who'll have her. Esper's no wizard like Mort, but who the hell is? She's a quick learner, and she'd be better use in the woods than I'd be. I couldn't sneak up on a cow unless it was in a bun with ketchup and bacon."

"We will hunt an elk, not cow," Mriy said.

"Point is," Carl said. "I'd suggest you ask Esper nicely, else you might be running with a pack of four. I'm guessing we were your last stop."

Mriy was silent. Esper listened, and all she heard was breathing and the rustling of clothes as the *Mobius* crew shifted uneasily in that silence. She spared a glance up and saw that Mriy was staring at her. The azrin had been waiting to make eye contact. "Will you help me?" Mriy asked.

There were a dozen reasons to refuse. Mriy obviously hadn't wanted her along. Mriy didn't think she would be any use, and who could blame her. Esper didn't know anything about hunting and had never eaten anything she'd killed herself. She'd even gone through a phase where she didn't eat meat. The seminary had taught her that animals were God's gift to mankind, meant to be eaten, used to carry burdens, or kept as pets. This wasn't wanton sport; it was a time-honored azrin ritual, and she had no place mucking it up. And as much as she hated to admit it, she liked datapads and holovids, food processors and voice-activated environmental controls. The woods had none of that.

But Mriy needed her. She hadn't asked because Esper was any good. Mriy needed her because she was all she had. How could Esper refuse? "I'll help you."

Hopefully there would be enough time before the hunt to look a few things up on the omni, starting with "how to hunt."

---

The *Mobius* lifted off as soon as Auzuma was aboard. Tanny hadn't waited another minute before she got them out of the Yrris Clanhold. The *Yinnak* had a minute's head start en route to the hunting grounds, and hadn't left them any coordinates. She had no idea what the azrin custom was for forfeiture or concession in regard to tardiness or never finding the hunting grounds, but she'd be damned if it was going to be her fault that they lost track of the clan's ship.

Tanny had been to Earth-like worlds before. The similarities had always comforted her—familiar geography, familiar climate, familiar gravity. But Meyang was a bit spartan. It was like someone had taken Earth and stripped away civilization. Cities were pockets of modern life amid primordial forests and trackless seas. The hotbeds of culture and the population centers so common on Earth-like worlds were barren. The *Yinnak* took an erratic course, wandering the planet from the upper atmosphere.

"Are they giving us a tour, or are they just lost?" Carl wondered aloud. He stood behind the copilot's seat, leaning his forearms on the headrest.

"Maybe they're trying to keep us guessing," Tanny ventured. "Jesus, this place is empty. It's like someone turned a natural history museum inside out, and they've got a planet full of people stuffed in an old building somewhere."

"Weird seeing the British Isles uninhabited," Carl said. "We ever look at the population survey?"

"Less than forty million," Tanny replied. "They can afford to pick and choose."

The *Yinnak* sped over Africa and across the southern Atlantic—or at least Meyang's equivalents. They crossed into South America and followed the Andes Mountain range north. The greens were so green, the blues so blue. Earth and Phabian, pillars of ARGO, were monuments of silver and glass, inhabited to the point of bursting. Meyang was an arboreal world, ripe for lumbering. Even the moon above was a pale white rock, with no sign of cities or orbital traffic.

It was in the northern part of Meyang's Rocky Mountain

analogue that the Yinnik finally landed. Tanny set the *Mobius* down a hundred meters away.

"You take it easy with this thing while I'm gone," Tanny said, giving Carl a stern glare. "No racing, no daredevil bullshit, nothing that'll get the *Mobius* impounded."

Carl held up his hand for a courtroom oath. "I will be a model citizen." The smirk didn't make him convincing.

She cringed as he slipped into the pilot's chair before she'd even left the cockpit. He wriggled into position, as if trying to form the seat to his backside.

"Not even going to wish us luck?" she asked.

"Since when have I ever been good luck to anyone?"

Tanny thought a moment. "Fair enough."

"Just keep them as safe as you can," Carl replied. "This isn't a fight, it's a hunt. Worst thing if Mriy loses is she gets written out of her mother's will, or however the hell that works around here. Not worth anyone getting hurt over."

Tanny shouldered the knapsack with her survival supplies. "Tell that to the Yrris Clan."

The rest of the hunting pack was waiting for her in the cargo bay, with Mort and Roddy there to see them off. It was a motley bunch. Mriy was the only one who looked like a proper hunter. Auzuma was an old man, though Mriy had told her that he was a year younger than her thirty-one years. Tanny wasn't quite sure how to take that, but it made her glad she was human. For all the times that she'd occasionally envied Mriy's easy strength and feline reflexes, she'd outlive the azrin by decades. Esper looked like she'd packed for a holiday camping trip, all store-bought new. It was going to be a chore just getting her to contribute, let alone be an asset. Kubu was the only one who looked excited.

"It is time to go now?" Kubu asked. "Kubu wants to go hunting."

Tanny eyed the canine—or *canis ultra poltidae* as scientists had dubbed his species. "Extreme dog from Poltid" was the translation. Was he bigger than yesterday? She needed to start scanning him more often.

"Yes and no," Tanny answered. "Yes, we're going outside now, and that's where we'll be hunting. But hunting is going to take a long time. We won't find what we're looking for right away."

"You can really understand that beast?" Auzuma asked, eyeing Kubu. The old azrin and Kubu had fur the same shade of black, but could not have looked more distinct otherwise. Auzuma was tall and wiry, and moved with a statesman's grace. Kubu was a barrel with legs and jaws that boiled with eager energy.

"Same as I understand you," Tanny replied, flicking her earring. Auzuma understood English just fine, thankfully. Mort wasn't going to provide another translator charm just so the azrin could understand Kubu. "Mort and Roddy understand your language, but they're not part of the hunt."

Roddy reached up and slapped the button that started lowering the cargo bay door. "May the wind blow your way," he said. Some funny cadence in the words suggested to Tanny that she was hearing the translator charm's interpretation of Roddy's azrin. Showoff little smartass.

The wind was indeed blowing as Mriy and her pack exited the *Mobius*, but it wasn't blowing any way Tanny wanted to claim as her own. If Rikk Pa had been cold, this area was frigid. On Earth, they'd have been a few hours walk outside Calgary Prime. She didn't know what it was called on Meyang, but she had a few colorfully vulgar suggestions.

The *Yinnak*'s passengers were disembarking as well, none so bundled against the cold as Tanny and Esper were. The azrin wore heavy vests and leggings, but still left much of their fur exposed. Kubu wore nothing and didn't show the first sign of being bothered by the weather. His breath came in steaming bellows as his tongue lolled and he bounced on front and hind legs like a bucking horse.

"There is our prey," Mriy said, pointing. The Yrris Clan was unloading a beast from their ship. Tanny was no expert on tundra wildlife, but Mriy had informed them that they should be hunting elk. It was as tall at the shoulder as its azrin handlers, with a rack of antlers that rose to twice that height. Unless the local fauna had taken a drastic twist from Earth's, its green and orange coloration was painted on.

"What're those symbols?" Esper asked, saving Tanny the trouble of looking the fool for not knowing.

"It marks our prey," Auzuma answered. "No azrin will interfere with the challenge by killing it. The medallion around its neck conceals it from science and magic alike. It is for us to find and kill, no others."

"We hunt that?" Kubu asked. He took off at once, accelerating to a full run in three strides, sending up a wake in hip-deep snow that seemed to do little to slow him.

"Kubu, stop!" Mort shouted. They all turned to see the wizard following them. Kubu skidded to a halt in a self-made snowdrift. "Not now. They'll tell you when it's time."

"Mort, what are you doing out here?" Tanny called out.

The wizard trudged through the snow in sneakers and jeans. His only concession to the cold was keeping his hands in the front pocket of his hooded sweatshirt. "Decided I'm going to keep an eye on things. Mriy's clan might play things on the level; they might not. With me around, they won't dare slant things Hrykii's way."

Mriy's ears flattened back. "I don't think my mother will approve."

"Then I'll just point out that we're a long way from things out here," Mort replied. "And there's more than one way to inherit a clanhold."

"You will not threaten—"

"I won't have to," Mort snapped. "I *am* a threat. You've gotten used to having a wizard around, but most azrin haven't. They're sensible, superstitious folk—smart enough to take heed of a wizard. They'll worry about me wilting their crops or sickening their herds, when they should really be wondering whether I'd incinerate them or crush them into a grapefruit-sized ball of meat. But the result's the same. They'll let me oversee."

Mort hung back as they approached the *Yinnak*. There was a brief ceremony where strips of cloth were rubbed against the elk's hide, then passed out to each member of both packs. Tanny tucked hers away without giving it the elaborate sniffing that the azrins did. Her human nose had no use for scent in tracking. Not her job on this expedition.

"Most of you know the rules," Seerii said. "For the outsiders, this is a traditional hunt. No weapons that shoot. Anything that harms the prey must be a part of you or held in hand. The prey will be left in the mountains. None of the hunters know where we will leave it. It will be at least one day's travel from here; beyond that I will not say. The prey must be returned to this spot, dead, for the bearer to be declared winner of the challenge."

Seerii did not ask if anyone had questions, or whether they were unclear on the protocol of the hunt. Tanny had the impression that even the little she said was a concession to Mriy's odd pack. The members of the Yrris Clan loaded the animal back into the *Yinnak*, and Mort followed them. There followed a quiet but heated discussion, and at the conclusion, Mort joined the azrins in the ship.

"We move," Mriy ordered. Hrykii's pack was already starting out, following the general direction of the *Yinnak* as it headed off to the northwest. Kubu bounded to the front of the group, running ahead and circling back to Mriy. He was clearly unfamiliar with the concept of conserving strength. Tanny waited until Auzuma and Esper fell into step behind their pack leader, and then took up the rear.

Just then, the engines of the *Mobius* roared to life. It lifted skyward, kicking up a storm of powdery snow that coated Mriy's hunting pack. The ship rolled over so that the landing gear faced deep space and tore across the evergreen forest at treetop height, threatening to topple the ancient pines. In the distance a moment later, the *Mobius* headed straight up, spinning like a corkscrew before taking an orbital trajectory and disappearing from sight.

Tanny's footsteps crunched in the snow, audible with the departure of the two ships and the increasing distance between the members of the pack. She didn't worry about keeping up so much as she did what would become of the ship with just Carl and Roddy looking after it. "Maybe I can work for Mriy after they get it impounded."

---

Mriy's kinfolk gathered around Mort as if he were a zoo exhibit. He let them look. None approached within arm's reach of him, but they conversed among themselves.

"Why did Seerii agree to this?" one muttered out of the side of his mouth, never taking his eyes from Mort.

"I don't know, but I don't like his look. Could we throw him out the door and be done with him?"

"He's a wizard."

"He's scrawny."

"Still a wizard."

"And can understand every word you're saying," Mort added, speaking in Jiara. This had the effect of splashing cold water on the group. They flinched back and looked at him in shock.

"You speak our language?" one asked. He had a dim look, even if Mort wasn't generally one to judge intra-species facial expressions.

"No, you gigantic floor mop," Mort replied. "I'm just speaking random words and got lucky."

"What did you call me?" the floor mop demanded.

Mort held up a placating hand. "Perhaps the comparison was out of line. But you're a horse's ass for talking about me like you just were. I'm here to keep this contest on the straight and narrow. No funny business. No sticking our noses in. Just let the chips fall where they may."

"I think he was telling the truth about guessing," one of the smaller azrin said. "Those are all words, but they make no sense."

Mort seethed out a long breath. Idioms might as well have been riddles. "Idiots, I am here to make certain the contest is fair." He spoke slowly, as if they were new at understanding their own language.

"Wasting your time, then," an orange-furred Yrris said. "No fair contest between Mriy's pathetic pack and Hrykii's hunters."

"Ignoring that," Mort said. "I want no interference. We drop this beast off, then go back and wait for them to bring it."

"We didn't bring human food."

"Shit," Mort muttered, remembering to use English. He had no reason to insult their food, though in truth the whole planet's cuisine could use a good insult or two. A whole species had managed to have an industrial revolution without inventing baking, sausage, or soup. Spices had been introduced by human conquerors. "I don't suppose you lot can order take-out wherever we are?"

---

Roddy vaulted over the armrest and into the copilot's chair. "What's the plan, Captain?"

Carl smirked. It wasn't often that Roddy got all naval with titles. "Haven't decided yet. Plan on enjoying a little flying though, while I've got the ship to myself—present company excepted, of course. Meyang's not really my cup of tea."

"Yeah," Roddy agreed. He slouched down in the seat and reached for the console with one of his feet. He turned the volume on the sound system down to a whisper. "Listen, I got a thing."

"A thing?"

"You know, an idea," Roddy replied. "For you."

"Just spit it out." Carl started to wonder what sort of plans Roddy was hinting at.

"You know that sword? The magic one we all keep telling you you're going to kill yourself with?" Roddy asked.

Of course, Carl knew it. It had set him back 4,000 credits and had seemed like a bargain at the time. It was sharp enough to slice steel like a ripe tomato and weighed next to nothing. "What about it?"

Roddy tossed Carl a datapad. "They've got this guy, a local. Real whiz with weapons. Ancient azrin techniques and all that shit. He's the only one teaching these secrets to off-worlders."

Carl glanced over the advert for Master Yuuwai Viyaa. It was flashy and slick, the sort of thing that Martian ad agencies cranked out for borderlands companies, where the locals weren't as sophisticated as back in Sol. "Sounds like a scam." People of every race and species had been pulling stunts like that for as long as explorers had been discovering new lands. Some rich bastards plunked themselves down on your land, and if you couldn't fight them off, you soaked them for every terra they had.

"You're signed up starting tomorrow, dawn local time," Roddy said.

"What?" Carl scowled at the laaku mechanic, searching that simian face for any sign that he was joking. But if there was one thing Roddy was awful at, it was keeping a straight face while making a joke. With his dead calm, he could have been at a funeral.

"My dime," Roddy replied. "You don't like it, bail after the first day. But it's on a tropical island, and you might come back a badass swordsman. So you might think twice before spending however-the-fuck long that hunt goes joyriding."

"What's the catch?" Carl asked. "You've got an angle."

"I'm lazy," Roddy admitted. "You with a few days behind the yoke on this baby, I might never be done putting it right. I'd be overhauling every maneuvering thruster, replacing coolant lines, and patching up stress cracks in the hull for months. It's worth a few hundred terras out of my own pocket to ground you."

"I could say 'no,'" Carl suggested, probing for a reaction.

"Badass. Swordsman. Tropical. Island. The Earth name for the island is Fiji, by the way."

"Fucker," Carl muttered. "What time is it there now?"

Roddy took back his datapad and checked the built-in chrono. "4:33 AM. You're gonna want to get a move on."

---

"Get a move on," Tanny shouted.

Esper had lagged behind the rest of the pack, and Tanny had slowed to stay behind her. Her knapsack was heavier than it had been earlier in the day, despite containing one less meal and a liter or so less water. The snow was harder to force her feet through, even though it wasn't as deep.

"I'm trying," she replied, not caring whether Tanny could hear. Esper couldn't spare enough breath to shout back. Dusk had come and gone, and a clear sky with a bright half moon was the only reason they could see ahead.

The stars poked out through the darkened atmosphere, taunting. *You could fly if you were on a ship*, they whispered down to her. *You've barely gone twenty kilometers*. Esper knew she was imagining it, that it was her own voice she was hearing. That didn't make her any less cross with the stars.

Tanny's steps drew closer, their pace quicker. A hand reached out and unclasped the buckle that secured Esper's knapsack around her waist. "Hey, what—"

"No time for this," Tanny muttered as she slipped the knapsack off Esper's back and slung it over her shoulder. It was an awkward fit with Tanny's already in place, but the ex-marine managed. "Hrykii's pack is probably five klicks ahead of us by now."

"Sorry."

Tanny shook her head. "It's not just you. Auzuma's not doing much better. We're going to have to stop soon for camp, even if we lose ground in the night."

"You think they'll push through?" Esper asked.

"No idea. But I bet they could if they wanted to. Look at Mriy. She'd be good to go all night. Kubu, too." The canine's energy was inexhaustible out in the cold. He puffed and panted, breath fogging the air like an old-timey steam locomotive. But he kept going without complaint. In fact, it was the happiest she'd seen him.

If nothing else, the scenery was spectacular. When Esper wasn't watching where her feet were landing, trying to follow the trodden snow where Mriy and Auzuma had passed, the mountains loomed majestically around them. She had to look away and ignore them for a while for them to ever appear any larger. Watching them the whole while, they never seemed to grow or come any closer.

Night had settled in fully by the time Mriy agreed to call a halt. The pack had been following a creek for the last few hours and settled into a bend where it wound around one of the foothills. Their campsite had them sheltered from the direction of the wind. Esper had lost track of the compass direction when the sun had finished setting, so she didn't know quite which way that was. But it was welcome having some protection from air that cut through the gaps between her hat and scarf to rob her body of heat.

"Auzuma, Esper, set up camp," Mriy said, dropping her load of supplies in the snow. "Tanny, Kubu, let's patrol the area to make sure we're alone out here." There was an unfamiliar hardness in her words. Mriy hadn't done much commanding on the *Mobius*. Carl was in charge—to a degree. Tanny did most of their tactical work on the ground. Everyone listened to Mort. Roddy obeyed orders when he chose. Mriy mostly went along, at least as long as Esper had known her. If she ever expressed a preference, it was for expediency, not for getting a job done right.

The old azrin stepped beside her and they watched side by side as the patrol departed over their sheltering hill. "Have you set up a camp before?" Auzuma asked.

"No," Esper admitted.

"You don't belong out here, do you?"

"No."

"Then I give my deepest thanks," Auzuma said. Esper gave him a furrowed glare. If the azrin could read human expressions at all, hers was likely lost under thick-bundled outerwear. "It's an easy thing to help someone when you know how. It is the act of a friend to help when the helping is a burden."

"She didn't want me along," Esper said, hanging her head. "She didn't have many options."

"You came for the same reason I did," Auzuma said. He put a hand on her shoulder, heavy even through three layers of fabric. "You have compassion. It is a trait that runs thick in God's servants."

Esper looked up. "She told you?" The azrin nodded. "I'm not anymore, you know. I ran. If I was any sort of priestess, I'd have gone back and faced the music."

"Music?" Auzuma echoed. He waved aside his own puzzlement as if it was of no consequence. "You left a church. I can tell you haven't left His service."

"You sound more sure of that than I am," Esper replied.

"I must be a better judge of character, then," he said. "I'm no fool. Mriy doesn't deserve our help in this. She was wrong to make her challenge. Hrykii is a fool, too, but he is young and less set in his ways. It is Seerii that Mriy disrespects by this quest for the title of heir."

"Then why did you come?" Esper asked. "I felt pity for Mriy and figured if I didn't help her, no one would. She didn't want me. She might even have been better off without me."

"God's word reached your world, same as it did mine," Auzuma said. "So I know you understand redemption. Mriy is not worthy to win, but by the end of this challenge, perhaps she will be. Now, let's get started putting a camp together."

---

Cold wind cleared the head. Seerii had taught her that. Mriy had a lot of time on the hike for thinking, but not much for discussing strategy for the hunt. There was little need for a patrol. That might have been a sensible precaution if Hrykii's pack was within an hour's hike of them, but Mriy couldn't imagine that to be the case.

"We need to talk," Mriy said, letting Tanny draw close. The human had kept up well. She hadn't sagged under the pace or the burden of taking on Esper's gear. She was a boon to the pack.

"I figured as much," Tanny replied. "We're up shit's creek, aren't we?"

"The creek's name escapes me," Mriy replied, glancing in the direction of the rushing water, even though the terrain hid it from direct view.

"No, I mean we're not winning this," Tanny clarified. "Those two are slowing us down. Your nephew's going to have the prey back to your mother before we get halfway to them."

Mriy stretched and flexed her back, looking up into the night sky. "Normally the slow pack sets an ambush to steal the prey. I'm worth two of them, and you might hold your own, but that won't be enough."

"You're allowed to fight each other on the hunt?" Tanny asked.

"Of course," Mriy replied. "You heard my mother set out the rules. She said nothing about our conduct. The mountains are vast and quiet. We won't kill them, but leaving them maimed and taking the prey is a valid tactic."

"Might have mentioned that *before* we signed up."

"You would have come anyway," Mriy replied. Tanny didn't shy from fights. Mriy knew she secretly relished combat, which humans found unbecoming.

"Maybe, but not Esper."

"No," Mriy agreed. "And I think it is time to fix my mistakes."

"Send her back? After a full day out here? She's going to be pissed."

"Her and Auzuma. Neither belongs. We are too slow to race Hrykii's pack and too weak to fight them."

Kubu made a curious noise, a whine that rose in pitch. Nothing came in translation, so it was not meant to be any sort of word. He cocked his head and sniffed the air. Mriy sniffed along by reflex, but picked up no scent on the wind.

"Kubu is hungry," Kubu said, using a quiet voice she had rarely heard him employ. He bounded off into the low brush, little more than a thicket of spindly twigs devoid of leaves. He disappeared from sight.

"Kubu!" Tanny shouted, starting off after him. "Kubu, get back here!"

Mriy followed Tanny, but knew that neither of them was

going to catch Kubu unless he stopped or doubled back. Azrins were faster than humans in short bursts, but not by nearly the margin that Kubu exhibited. A snarl sounded from the darkness, followed by barking and a ferocious growl. Tanny quickened her pace, rushing headlong and drawing a hunting knife in stride as she ran.

A pained shriek split the night air, followed by more growling. When they caught sight of Kubu, he had a lynx by the neck; the creature dangled limp from either side of his jowls. He shook it like a chew toy, then dropped it in the snow. Wasting no time, he tore into the kill and ripping open the lynx's belly. The carcass steamed in the moonlight.

Mriy had killed with her bare hands before. She had torn out a deer's throat and tasted the warm blood. She had even eaten a hot kill in the wild once or twice, despite the mess and having to eat around the hide and unsavory organs, not to mention bones. But she had never seen a hunter eat like Kubu. His meal started like a wolf's feast, with the easy, the juicy, the nutritious. But he didn't stop there. He didn't strip flesh from bone, didn't tear away the skin and fur. He bit through limb and torso alike, crunching great mouthfuls of anything he could fit between his jaws—which for the lynx, happened to be everything.

It took two minutes, perhaps as long as three. Mriy spared no attention from the spectacle to check a chrono. The lynx was gone. Kubu even gobbled up several mouthfuls of snow that had been spattered with blood, and a few more that hadn't, just for the water.

"How much do you think that thing weighed?" Tanny asked quietly.

Mriy did some quick figuring in human units. "Eight or ten kilos. It wasn't a big one."

Kubu ambled over to them, tongue working around the edges of his muzzle to clean the mess from his face. "Kubu not so hungry now."

Mriy remembered a time, not so long ago at all, when she'd had to wrestle Kubu to the ground. He had gotten into Tanny's chemical supplements, the ones that humans gave to their soldiers to make them strong, fast, and aggressive. She had overwhelmed him with leverage and technique. But she remembered the strength, the corded, sinewy muscle like iron, just below his fur. He was growing by the day. Even now, could she have managed the same feat?

"You sure we can't fight them?" Tanny asked.

"Even if we could, I'm not certain we should," Mriy replied. "I don't see a middle ground between defeat and a distasteful meal. But we're keeping Kubu with us. Lose Esper and Auzuma, and we become the faster pack."

---

By the time the patrol returned, Esper and Auzuma had erected the tents and gathered firewood. The two azrin tents were little more than large, droopy umbrellas with the lone occupant meant to curl around the pole and pull it down until the dome touched ground. Esper and Tanny were to share a traditional human-style camping tent that might have fit Kubu as well. Fortunately, the canine had happily dug himself a hole in the snow and curled up outside.

Esper had chopped some small branches into firewood with a carbon-bladed hatchet and was trying to get the green wood to catch fire. "This is stupid," she muttered. "Why can't we just have a little fire-starter laser? It's not like we could hunt anything with it." She struck the rock against the steel blade of her hunting knife and watched the sparks die on the bark of her branches.

It was Mort's idea for her to come out here. Get away from technology, he'd said. She was supposed to be practicing, learning to control her magic. Learning not to kill people, was more like it. Esper had insisted everyone go through a medical scan before the hunt, to make sure they wouldn't grow anything malignant if she had to use her one reliable spell on them. Speeding the body's natural healing seemed so innocuous—until you considered that cancer was going to thrive as well. What could she do wrong trying a little fire? The possibilities seemed exponentially greater.

Still, it was deathly cold with deeper temperatures to come before morning. "You are on fire," she whispered to the twigs. Nothing happened. "Fire." Nothing happened. She tried to picture the twigs aflame. "Fire." Nothing happened. "*Ignis.*" She thought for a moment that the switch to Latin had done it. But the wisp of smoke had been her imagination. She tried to recall the word Mort had taught her, one of a handful he'd made her memorize before embarking on the hunt.

Remembering another bit of Mort's advice, she stopped trying to remember the word and just spoke it. It lacked form and shape on her lips. She could not have written it down or explained how to pronounce it. Mort had spoken it to her, and it had wormed its way into her head. But the language of angels and demons combined with her imaging of burning twigs turned that wish real. She leapt back, falling onto her backside and hands in the snow as the campfire caught.

"Nice work," Tanny said. "I was never much at starting fires. Glad you figured it out. Find a tutorial on the omni or something?"

"Or something," Esper muttered. From the corner of her

eye, she caught Auzuma watching her with interest. Was he smiling?

They ate a quiet meal, all except for Kubu, who slept. They talked about the day's hike and where Hrykii's pack might have ventured. Mriy mentioned the hardships that lay ahead, and Tanny talked about how much ground they were going to have to make up. By the time everyone settled into their tents, Esper had grown suspicious.

Curled up in a sleeping bag, just a few centimeters from Tanny, there was no room for secrets. "You two don't want me here," she said.

Tanny faced away from Esper, not bothering to roll over to address her. "What Mriy and I said was true. How you take it is up to you."

"You don't have Carl's talent for it."

"Huh?"

"For lying," Esper said. "You're as subtle as a sermon. You want me to volunteer to go back, so you don't have to tell me I'm not welcome."

"Mriy hadn't said anything before, but it can get rough out here," Tanny said. "If we don't get to the prey first, we're expected to try to ambush Hrykii's pack to take it from them. People are going to get hurt out here."

"All the more reason you need me," Esper reasoned. After all, healing was the one thing she seemed to have tidied up in her repertoire. "I won't give up."

"Then you'd better keep up tomorrow," Tanny said. "And you'd better get to sleep. You're going to need the energy."

---

In the end, Mort and the Yrris Clan found a human-food

restaurant with a 500-kilometer delivery radius. In an act of magnanimity, he offered to introduce them to one of Earth's most azrin-friendly cuisines. He sat surrounded by azrin in the *Yinnak*'s dining hall, which was smaller than the common room of the *Mobius* and designed for creatures with their feline legs pointing the wrong way. He thought it gave him some insight into the trouble Mriy must have had with human chairs.

"What is this?" Yuanan asked. He had gray-fur was missing the tip of one ear. His coloration was natural, not a sign of age, Mort had learned.

"We call it sashimi," Mort replied. "It's got all sorts of fancy names by the meat inside, but damned if I know most of them. This place had a menu with azrin dishes, light on the vegetable components. Mine's the stuff in the yellow plastic container. The rest is for you fine folks to share."

It had cost a small fortune between feeding a dozen azrin and paying some poor slob to trek it out to them, but Mort was looking for some way to break the ice with Mriy's family. He might be holed up with them for days, so friendly terms were a lifestyle improvement over their cold silence and blank looks.

Frouniy opened the much larger white package and unwrapped several bundles. "Shrimp. Tuna. Some other fish. Is this all ocean food?"

Mort gave Frouniy a nod of confirmation. "There are some specialty dishes that use other meat, but since this is your first time, I'm sticking to the traditional."

"Traditional is good," Yuanan agreed. In the absence of Yariy, he had been acting as guardian. Mort had overheard two of them talking in the next room.

"Before Seerii eats, you eat," Ryhma said, narrowing her eyes and leaning in as if Mort was going to flinch or blanch or make some other damned fool slip-up in the commission of betrayal. It would have been funny if they weren't so deadly serious. Not one of them had an ounce of guile for human deception.

Mort snickered. "I took the precaution of only ordering things I'd eat. Figured you lot might be paranoid." He picked up a tuna roll and popped it into his mouth. It tasted funny with a thin wrapping of beef jerky in place of seaweed, but not a bad sort of funny. Just wasn't what he'd expected. "How many you want me to try?"

"All of them," Yuanan said.

"Fuck that," Mort said. "I got my own to eat, and I'm not a bottomless pit. Use a science thingy to check it, or have one of your own taste the food. You don't trust it, pitch it in the snow."

"You *will* eat it," Yuanan snarled, rising to his feet.

"Listen, Fluffy, if you think you can bully me, give it a go," Mort replied. He reached out and picked up one of his tuna rolls and popped it into his mouth. He chewed as he continued. "But I'm not in the mood for your shit."

"If you were a hunter, you'd have gone with Mriy, if you're so worried about her," Yuanan reasoned. "I think you are a warm wind."

Mort leaned over to Seerii, who had stayed out of the confrontation thus far. "Did he just accuse me of flatulence?"

Seerii shook her head. "He accuses you of talking more than being. He thinks you bluff."

"Oh."

Mort swallowed his tuna roll and stood. Yuanan must have seen something in his unconcerned posture that gave him pause. The azrin cringed back, but held his ground. Mort stepped forward, put a hand on the azrin's chest, and shoved him through the nearest wall. There was no crash, no splatter; Yuanan simply passed through solid steel—or whatever azrins made ships out of. Mort wasn't sure on that front.

"What did you do to him?" Seerii demanded. The other Yrris bystanders scrambled to put distance between themselves and Mort. Warm wind indeed.

"I threw him outside into the snow to cool off," Mort replied. "And Mriy asked me to join her pack, but I refused. Wouldn't have been fair. I could sniff that ox of yours out by the magic—don't tell me I couldn't. Then I could have ridden it back here, killed it at your feet, and been back sleeping in my own bed by nightfall. But I didn't. Wouldn't have been fair. I'm *very* interested in this contest playing out fair."

The azrins watched him in silence. They seemed not to know whether to attack him en masse or offer a surrender, exchanging glances that may have carried more communication than met the (human) eye.

Yuanan burst back into the room, throwing open the door in the process. He was dusted with snow, and his boots were leaving wet prints on the floor as he strode over to Mort, teeth bared. "How dare you—"

Mort didn't move, except to stuff another tuna roll in his mouth. Yuanan reached for him, but found his footing gone from beneath him. Without so much as the shove he'd given the last time, Mort levitated Yuanan and threw him through the wall yet again. Ryhma crept over and pressed a hand against the wall, but it was fully solid.

"I can keep this up all night," Mort replied. "I haven't even broken a sweat." He glanced around the dining hall. Mriy was a tough nut to crack when it came to reading facial expressions. Her clanmates were not so reserved. Mort found a mix of fear, anger, confusion, and hints of amusement at Yuanan's plight.

He held out the white container to Seerii. "Grab some sashimi. I didn't poison the goddamn things. I've killed more people than all of you put together, and I'm long past being shy about it."

Seerii reached a tentative hand and picked up a shrimp roll in two extended claws. "This will be a fair contest."

---

The *Mobius* climbed into orbit at a leisurely pace, leaving the azrins' take on Fiji far below. The crew was gone, off playing savages in the snowy wilderness. Carl was checking into his sword-fighting resort. Roddy had the ship to himself. All he heard were the mechanical sounds of the engines, the life support, the hum of the computer coolant system. It was bliss.

He'd never liked the ship's control layout. It had come as-is and configured for human comfort. The seat was too long and too far back from the yoke, and everything just seemed to be spaced wrong on the panels. It was hard to pin down exactly why, but the ship clearly had not been built with laaku ergonomics in mind. Ignoring the mild annoyances, he keyed the comm for the local ARGO patrol fleet.

"Orbital control, this is Earth-registered vessel *Mobius*. Request long-term orbit."

"*Vessel Mobius, state your reason for orbital clearance.*"

Roddy shrugged, though the comm was voice only. "I've got some maintenance to do, the ship to myself while the crew's planetside, and I just wanted the view."

"*Will your maintenance interfere with your ship ID broadcast, engine signature, or involve deviation from a proscribed orbit?*"

"None of the above," Roddy replied. "Sub-system over-hauls and preventative maintenance only."

"*You are cleared for long-term orbit. Transmitting a trans-polar orbital path. Enjoy your sightseeing.*"

"Thank ya kindly," Roddy replied and shut off the comm. "I give those boys too much shit sometimes. This garrison seems pretty laid back." He followed the transmitted heading, then rolled the ship up so the forward windows looked down on Meyang.

By the side of the seat, Roddy found his guitar case. Of late, it had seemed more like Carl owned it—he certainly played it more these days. But it belonged to Roddy, and it was past time to brush the rust off his fingers and play it a little. It was a double-neck, a style invented by humans even though they couldn't play both at once. It was the laaku that had taken the design and made a proper instrument out of it. His guitar had been made on Phabian, in a little factory just outside Keth-let. It was as old a friend as he had.

He strummed both sets of strings and cringed. Carl had an ear for good music, but he was as good as tone deaf when it came to playing it. Roddy spent the next few minutes with an acoustic analyzer, tuning each string to mathematical perfec-tion. Each chord he tried rang beautifully. "There ya go, baby. That's the guitar I know."

He reclined the pilot's chair and slouched back until he could comfortably balance while all four hands played. He picked a human song. He'd grown up on human music, thanks to his old man. It wasn't one that was supposed to have a guitar part, but it was the first thing that came to mind, so he made it work. Before human contact, laaku music hadn't had lyrics except for hymns; it had just seemed sacrosanct to those laaku from way back.

"That's just one damn pretty ball of rock down there," he mused as he played. Phabian had looked like that once, a long, long time ago. There were still a few nature preserves; it wasn't Earth, after all. But the blue-green orb covered in wispy clouds only existed in pictures, in museums, and on the Earth-likes. It grated a little that the term had caught on. They were Phabian-like, to Roddy's thinking.

He strummed with his feet for a moment while he grabbed a beer from a six-pack he'd brought with him to the cockpit. After a long pull and a refreshed gasp, he set back to playing with all four hands, this time singing along with his own accompaniment. He picked up midway through.

"...and I think to myself, what a wonderful world."

---

Whatever Tanny had said to Esper in the night, it had not been to give up and return to the *Yinnak*. Every time Mriy looked over her shoulder, she expected to see the human fallen hopelessly far behind. Each time, she was surprised to find her keeping pace. It was Auzuma that was the trouble. He was lagging, and Mriy didn't know how to get rid of him in any way that would save face.

Auzuma had been with the Yrris Clan since before she was born. He might outlive Seerii, if their relative health was any measure. How could Mriy win back the title of heir, then take over the clan while Auzuma was still chaplain? He would oversee the blessing of inheritance—or would he refuse to perform it? The old man was as beloved in the clan as any blood relative. How could she shun him in taking the title and keep peace in the clan afterward? He would be within his rights to leave.

"Meal," Mriy shouted, judging that the sun was high enough to be called noon. She had to admit, it was refreshing not to look at a chrono to tell the time. She slung the knapsack off her back and rummaged around to find her jerky. It was poor fare, but sat easy in the stomach. With wild game, there was always the risk that the animal was sick or had some foulness to it. Not to mention the wasted time in hunting quarry beside their prize.

"Kubu hungry!" Kubu chimed in, bounding back from one of the side excursions that had become his hedge against boredom.

"You've eaten twice since breakfast," Tanny replied. "Remember the snow hare? Remember the beaver?"

"The beaver was very wet," Kubu replied, nodding. "The bunny was yummy. Kubu still hungry."

"Well, you'll have to find your own while we walk, because I don't think we've got enough in the supplies to keep up with you."

"Who'd have thought he'd get fat running fifty kilometers a day and hunting for his own meals?" Esper asked. She dropped her knapsack, and it barely dented the snow.

"He's not getting fat," Tanny countered. "He's growing."

"What is that?" Mriy asked, ignoring the discussion of the dog and pointing to Esper's knapsack.

"My gear," Esper replied. "I couldn't make Tanny carry it two days in a row."

"Let me see that," Mriy said. She stalked over and hefted it by the straps. It was feather-light. Then she unclasped the flap and looked inside. It carried all that it ought to have; Esper hadn't ditched her supplies in a gully somewhere as Mriy had initially suspected. "How?" She shoved the knapsack into Esper's arms.

Esper dropped it in the snow once more. "Magic."

She had been speaking too often with Roddy and Carl. Their snide sarcasm was rubbing off. "We are not allowed modern devices on the hunt. Whatever anti-grav you snuck into it, turn it off."

"Ma-gic," Esper replied. "Hocus pocus. Dark arts. Mort was exaggerating when he called me a wizard, but he *has* started teaching me a few things."

Mriy picked up the knapsack once more. "You did this? Not Mort?"

"Last night it weighed a ton," Esper said. "After I got the fire to work, I figured I'd have a go at making the gear lighter. It's not so hard keeping up anymore, but I must say, you've got awfully long legs."

The human pulled out a food bar from her pocket and unwrapped it. The contents let out a whiff of factory-processed chemical flavorings that seemed out of place in the mountains.

"What is that?" Mriy asked, leaning in to sniff at it. "It smells like fruit." She was no expert at non-protein foodstuffs, but had grown accustomed to some of the smells while aboard the *Mobius*.

"It's actually six kinds of fruit, plus all the vitamins and minerals a woman's body needs," Esper recited. "It's a delicious part of a balanced diet."

Mriy's eyes narrowed. "I've heard the adverts," she muttered. It was a Snakki-Bar, one of those lazy human foods. They supposedly did all the work of three meals, but tasted awful and weren't satisfying.

Esper shrugged. "I know you don't like them. Trying one was enough. But I can't eat that stuff you brought, and I can hardly think about Kubu's meals without losing mine."

"How much of that magic did Mort teach you?" Mriy asked. A plan was forming. Maybe they were not the weak pack after all.

Esper backed away a step. "Ooooh no. I see that look. I'm not a *wizard* wizard. I'm not even a pretend wizard. I'm just learning a few things. I'm not making anyone's fur fall out or pulling knives out of people's hands. I can still lose an argument with a campfire."

"You can still cause painful hunger with a touch," Mriy said. The human was speaking in false modesty; she had killed with her magic.

"As a last resort," Esper replied. "For defense only." She took another bite of her Snakki-Bar.

"Right," Mriy said. "Defend the kill. Defend honor. Win the hunt." She clapped Esper on the shoulder. "You'll do fine when the time comes. Eat up. This won't be a long break." Esper coughed something in response, but it was lost in a mouthful of mealy, meatless food substitute.

---

The holovid was in azrin, which made it hard to follow. One of the occasionally annoying features of the translation charms that all the crew wore was that they didn't translate what the wearer could already understand. Since Mort's understanding of the Jiara dialect was better suited to slow conversations, he was having trouble keeping up. It wasn't that he cared what happened to the two azrin mercenaries trapped behind enemy lines on some generic extrasolar planet—well, maybe he cared a little—it was that everyone else in the room understood and he didn't.

Being the dumbest one in the room was a splinter in Mort's

craw. It didn't matter that it was the dialog to a holovid with a title that translated roughly to "Two Deaths Died Well." Mort had written off the two main characters from the opening title shot. It was more that these brutish, oafish savages had one up on him in the brains department. He had always preferred a shutout victory, especially when dealing with people he had already cataloged among his mental inferiors.

"How long these hunts usually last?" Mort asked in a down moment. The two protagonists were reloading science thingamajigs into their guns.

"Hmm? What?" Frouniy asked. He was the nearest Yrris to Mort, at the back of the viewing room.

"I said—"

But there was a huge explosion in the holo-field, and the noise drowned him out as the Yrrises cheered. Mort tucked his hands into the pocket of his sweatshirt and slouched down. He didn't care what happened to the two doomed azrins on the holovid. Given the unimaginative title, they were going to die well, and that was apparently the important thing. Mort didn't need to see the ending.

With a subtle suggestion to the universe that electro-whozamawhatchits didn't need to be shooting light all over the place, the holo-projector flickered and gave out. There were mixed groans and shouts of outrage from Mort's fellow view-ers. One whose name Mort hadn't asked got up and popped open the access panel to check inside as his kin badgered him with questions and suggested methods of diagnosing the prob-lem. After a minute or two, the suggestions died down and left a sulking impatience in their wake.

Never one to let an opportunity pass, Mort struck up a conversation to fill in the silence. "So, how long is everyone expecting this hunt to last?"

This time, Frouniy was not too distracted to answer. "Tomorrow. The day after at the latest. Yariy has a good nose and can think like the prey."

"How long would it take for Mriy, if her pack was going to win?" Mort asked.

A few azrin laughs—the same hissing chuckle that Mriy used—told him that other ears were listening in. "A year," Frouniy replied. "Maybe if some poacher found our prey and didn't respect the ritual markings, they might stay out long enough that an elk might be born that looked like it. Mriy could paint it up and bring it back as a winning kill."

"Is that legal?"

"Of course it's not," Seerii said. "He jokes at you. Mriy hunts for the kill, not the track. She was four days in her ascension hunt, while her cousin Yariy did hers in an afternoon. She'll kill anything she finds, but this prey isn't a challenge for a killer. It's a tracker's race."

"What about the old fella?" Mort asked. It was odd calling Auzuma old, since he was about the age of Mort's children, but from an azrin perspective, he qualified.

"Auzuma's nose isn't young," Seerii replied. "You are old among your people. Have you not noticed the loss of scent since your youth?"

Mort chuckled. "I'm not *that* old and blast me if I'd notice the difference. If I can tell the difference between bacon, beer, and the perfume at a woman's neck, I'm all set in the scent department."

"Well, Mriy's pack is scent-blind," Seerii said. "They'll be guessing as much as anything. Mriy will be lucky to track Hrykii's pack, let alone the prey. And outnumbered five to two, even Mriy can't fight those odds."

Mort gave Seerii a shrewd squint. "You got one of those

datapads that gets the omni on it? Look up a critter called *canis ultra poltidae*. I can spell it if you need; that's an old Earth dialect. I'll wait. Then you can give me a better answer about how close this contest will be."

---

By evening, Mriy was ready to strangle Auzuma and leave him in the snow until the thaw. While Esper was managing not to fall behind, the chaplain's feet dragged slower by the hour. Hunting was a point of honor; Seerii hunted well beyond her years, but for her health and as a point of pride. A challenge was no place for the old. Desperate though she was, Mriy would have fared better with four or even three, than be weighed down with pack mates like these.

She waved to Tanny, summoning the human warrior to her side. At least Tanny would be fine for the whole of the hunt. Mriy had never seen her tire, not while she was flush with the effects of her chemicals. Though it might have been a stretch of the rules, Tanny had brought her daily doses along as part of her rations. She was the one Mriy would have to count on most until the end of the hunt.

"How is Esper?" Mriy asked as Tanny drew near, careful not to let Esper overhear.

"Tired, but holding up," Tanny replied. Mriy could hear the short breaths she took, but it was the only visible sign of Tanny's fatigue. "I'm worried about Auzuma though. I think he'd die on his feet, just to prove he won't quit."

Mriy nodded solemnly. "He might, at that." The last thing they needed was to lose more ground on Hyrkii, but she couldn't kill Auzuma either. "Break!" she shouted.

Esper slumped into the snow and looked up into the feeble sun, which gave light but little warmth. Auzuma trudged several more paces and settled in beside her. Kubu, who had disappeared more and more often as they traveled, bounded out of the forest moments later.

The five of them settled in and took a meal. Esper and Auzuma spoke of God and churches and duty. It was good to keep the two preachers facing one another, to cancel out all the noise they made. Better than them bothering her with it. Kubu had eaten something with feathers and spent the mealtime working one loose from his teeth.

"You're showing frustration," Auzuma said. They were the first words he'd spoken in her direction all day.

"We lose more ground every hour," Mriy replied.

Auzuma pointed to a mountain in their path—simple enough as mountains loomed all around. "Which one is Hyrkii's pack on now? That one? The one beyond? And which mountain hides our elk? Do you know? Does Hrykii? The hunt isn't about speed; it's about guile. Think like the elk, and be where it will be."

"Do you know where it is?" Esper asked between bites of a Snakki-Bar.

Auzuma chuckled. "I'm no elk."

"Then how do we—"

"This is pointless," Mriy snapped. "We finish eating, then get back to catching up with Hrykii. His pack will find the elk first, and we need to be there to intercept them."

Auzuma shook his head. "You sound like the fisherman who lost his spear."

Mriy huffed and swallowed back her temper. "I don't know that one," she grumbled. She knew from Auzuma's tone that she was going to hear the story or be questioned on it. Denying her ignorance would only make her look foolish.

"A young fisherman missed his thrust and hit a rock. His spear broke, and he could not find the tip. He pulled his boat onto shore and found the nearest village. But no one in the village would sell him a spear—they had no spears to sell. He asked if they could make him one, but the price they asked was more than he could afford. When he despaired of finding a replacement before the day was lost, an old man took pity on him. *I was collecting these to line a garden, but you have more need than I.* He handed the young fisherman a loose-weave bag filled with rocks. Each rock was white and smooth and big enough to fill the palm of the hand. The young fisherman thanked the old man and took the bag because he was too polite to refuse a gift. None of the rocks would make a spear tip. The bag and all the rocks inside were not worth the cost of one in trade.

"So the fisherman went back to his boat, and set off downstream toward his home. But on the way, he found a spot where fish danced at the surface, enough for three meals for his family. He anchored his boat and tried to catch them with his claws, but the fish fled when his shadow cast across the water. He tried the broken shaft of his spear, but the end was not sharp enough to skewer a fish. Then he thought of the old man's gift and tried the rocks. The bag had a woven loop for a handle, and it tied shut at the top. The fisherman tried swinging it like a club, but only splashed water over himself and into his boat. He took rocks one at a time and threw them at the fish, thinking that if he stunned one, he could pluck it from the water before it recovered. Emptying the whole bag, he hit just two fish, and both recovered before he could snatch them from the water.

"That was when he noticed that the bag was loose weave and empty, and it had a long woven handle. He dangled the bag in the water, and netted fish after fish. The old man had given him just what he needed, but the fisherman had not noticed."

"Fish come from the water?" Kubu asked. He had sat in rapt attention during the story.

"Live ones, yes," Tanny said. "The dead ones Roddy likes on his pizza come from a can."

"Are we the net?" Esper asked.

Auzuma smiled. "We are either the net, or the rocks."

"That doesn't help us," Mriy replied.

"You're using us like a spear, when we're not a spear," Auzuma said. "Knowing that must help somehow. It was exactly what a pack leader needed to hear. We are not faster than Hyrkii's hunters, nor are we stronger in a fight."

"I'm not sure of that," Mriy muttered. She was regretting bringing Auzuma along more each second. Being useless was bad enough, but to lecture her as well...

"What do we do better than him? Than his pack?" Auzuma asked.

"God's grace?" Esper guessed.

"Possibly," Auzuma allowed. "But I don't expect Him to intervene."

"Better tactics," Tanny said.

"You've hunted before, then?" Auzuma asked. "You are an expert?"

"Bet your ass I am," Tanny replied. "Not elk, either. I've been up against the Sishaji, the Plouph, and even a few Zheen. Enemies that think back at you."

"We have Kubu's nose," Esper said, straightening in her snowy seat. "We must be able to out-sniff them."

"The black beast knows how to hunt," Auzuma said. "It's in his blood. You can see it plainly."

"You're saying we should let Kubu lead?" Tanny asked.

"No," Mriy replied. She stood and looked out into the mountains, in the direction she had been expecting to find the elk. "Kubu, can you smell the elk? The one with the paint on it by the ship. The one Mort told you not to hunt yet."

Kubu nodded. "Yes. Kubu smelled it since last night. We go the right way, so Kubu thought you smelled it too."

"Well, there's that," Tanny said. "Least we're on the right track. How about we get back on it." She climbed to her feet and brushed the snow from her pants.

A slow grin caught Mriy by surprise. It was the first time since the outset where she realized a path to victory in the challenge. "No. The four of us rest. Kubu, I want you to run ahead and find the elk. Find it, and come back with it."

"Come back with it?" Tanny scoffed. "It's twice his size."

"Look at him," Mriy said, pointing to the alien canine. "He bursts with energy. There's more muscle on him than you or me. Kubu, try to bring it back, and if you can't, come back and lead us to it. Understand?"

Kubu nodded. "Yes. Kubu can't eat it, right?"

"Maybe after we give it to my mother," Mriy replied. "Now this part is important. If you run into azrin—people like Auzuma and me—run away. Don't let them catch you or hurt you. If you can prevent it, don't even let them see you. Just come right back to us; leave the elk if you have to."

"Kubu can," Kubu replied. "When can I go?" He bounced from front legs to back, tail wagging.

"Now," Mriy said.

Kubu shot off like a blaster bolt into the forest.

Kubu scooped up a mouthful of snow in full stride. Snow was the best stuff ever. It kept him cool no matter how much he ran, and it melted in his mouth so he didn't have to stop to drink. Everywhere around this place was cold, and there were yummy little animals whenever he got hungry. It was like being inside a giant refrigerator, except without the beer cans.

Kubu wished Mriy had said earlier that she didn't know where the elk was. Kubu could have told her that. The elk didn't just smell like animal; it had paint on it that smelled so different that Kubu couldn't help but notice it. There were a lot of animals around, hiding in the snow, in the trees, under the ground; but only one had the paint smell.

It was going to take a long time to get to the elk. Mriy had been going in the mostly right direction, but not the best direction. Kubu had to go around a mountain, after several failed attempts to find a way over it. There was a break for eating a bunny and another for eating a funny little animal with sharp, pointy fur that was sleeping under the snow. The sharp, pointy fur had taken a lot of chewing, and Kubu had spit some of it out for being too much work for not enough taste. But now he was moving again, and slowly closing in on the elk.

Kubu was being such a good boy. He was going to be everyone's hero when he found the elk for them. Mriy was worried that Esper and the new kitty-person were too slow, and that they'd have to go back. But now Kubu was fast, and they all could just wait for him to get the elk. Everyone was going to be very happy because of him.

There was a scent of smoke in the air. Smoke meant cooked food. Kubu had liked finding food all over the forest and the low parts of the mountains. Fresh animals were juicier, and some had surprise foods inside them. But cooking was nice, too, and the smoke tickled Kubu's nose and tugged at his attention. It wasn't as if he was going to forget about the elk; there was just a smoke smell to follow first.

As it turned out, there was more than just smoke; there were kitty-people, too. They looked like Mriy mostly. They walked on two feet, had pointy-up ears, little pink noses, and big eyes with pupils like slits. Kubu saw them before any of them looked like they noticed him. They had a pointy little house, and the smoke was coming out the top.

"Hey! We got a stray wandered in," one of the kitty-people yelled. Kubu had been wrong; at least one of them had seen him.

"Hello!" he shouted back. "It's just Kubu! You aren't the kitty-people hunting the elk Kubu is hunting. Sorry. Kubu goes now."

"Shut that damned thing up," a different kitty-person said. "Probably belongs to the humans. They keep those as pets and use them for hunting."

"Kubu isn't a pet," Kubu replied. "I stay with Mommy because she loves me, but I *am* hunting with her and Esper. I'm hunting with Mriy, too, but she isn't a human."

"Noisy creature," the first kitty-person said. He sounded mad.

Kubu realized something. They didn't have Mort, so they didn't have Mort's through-the-ear magic that let them understand Kubu. Esper had one. Mommy had one. Everyone on the ship had them—even Kubu. Kubu had gotten used to the idea that people could understand him, but these kitty-people couldn't.

One of the kitty-people had a gun. Mommy had guns, and he wasn't supposed to touch them because they were dangerous. Now the kitty-person was aiming a gun at Kubu; it was time to do lots of running.

"Get after him," one of the kitty-people shouted. "If that thing gets back to his human masters, we're dead. Break camp and be ready to ride."

Kubu didn't know what a lot of that meant, but he gathered that they were very interested in getting him. He only hoped that they were as slow as Mriy.

---

The *Mobius* touched down on a strip of beach, the internal gravity not even allowing a gentle thump to jostle the lone occupant. Roddy found the remote trigger for the cargo bay door and hit it, then reclined in the pilot's seat with his fingers laced behind his head. So much for his vacation. So much for peace, quiet, and solitude. The comm had come less than an hour ago; that was about as long as Roddy had been willing to let Carl stew before picking him up.

There was a rumble of pumps and hydraulics as the cargo bay ramp lowered. No one else seemed to be able to do it, but Roddy knew the ship's systems well enough that he could tell by feel or by sound when subsystems kicked on. The sound stopped, then a moment later, started again—raising the ramp.

Roddy waited.

Booted footsteps approached, slower than Carl's usual pace. "Get us out of here," Carl said in a dead-tired voice.

Roddy fired up the engines and lifted off, operating the controls with his feet. His fingers were still laced behind his head when he twisted around to face Carl. "Kicked out or quit?"

"Kicked out."

Something seemed out of place. Carl wore his usual battered leather jacket and had his stupid magic sword sheathed at his hip. But he was wearing a hat with earflaps and a pair of dark glasses. "What's with the getup? They blacken those eyes of yours, or were you training to fight in the dark."

"I'm in no mood right now to—"

"Holy shit," Roddy said, sitting up straight. "Are your eyebrows blue?"

Carl sighed and took off the glasses. His eyebrows were indeed a rather atmospheric shade of blue.

Roddy couldn't help himself; he doubled over laughing. Carl just stood there, waiting for the fit to pass. His blank, weary face made it all the more amusing. "Let me guess," Roddy said, gasping as he recovered his breath. "This is part of the sword master's teachings?"

"No," Carl said. He pulled off the hat to reveal hair that was a matching shade of blue. "I pissed him off, and he put some fucking mystic curse on me."

Roddy hardly heard the explanation, because his laughing fit redoubled. Carl looked like a cartoon character, or one of those teenyboppers who goes to pop concerts—Esper had probably dyed her hair that way when she was a kid, he guessed. And that's what Carl looked like, some teenage girl who wanted to stand out, except he still had the face of a rough-cut spacer.

"It doesn't wash out, either," Carl said when Roddy had calmed down. "I'm gonna have to ask Mort to fix it."

Roddy squinted, angling his head to catch Carl in the natural light from outside. "Is that... it is! He got the hair on your peach-fuzz face, too. It's like you're growing blue lichen."

"Oh yeah," Carl said with a sigh. "*All* my hair turned blue. The blue-fur curse, he called it. Threatened me with it when I called bullshit on some of the stuff he was teaching. Straight out of the holovids, the lot of it. If I wanted to learn dispy-do sword fighting like they do in the vids, I could download a manual from the omni. Anyway, I said I didn't have fur, so he could take his curse and suck on it. In retrospect, not a good call on my part."

"So the guy's a legit wizard?" Roddy asked.

"More wizard than swordsman, if you ask me," Carl replied. He scratched at his emerging blue stubble. "Still, once Mort gets back, I can't see him having any trouble fixing me up."

"So, what's next on the vacation tour?" Roddy asked. Hopefully, Carl would want to move on to a more relaxing pastime and leave the *Mobius* to him again.

"You kidding?" Carl asked. "No way in hell I'm going anywhere like this. Until we get Mort back to fix me up, I'm parking right here. Could use a bit of a blow off though; thinkin' maybe a little guitar might ease my troubled mind."

So much for that. "Yeah, sure," Roddy said. The ship's orbital path was already locked into the autopilot—that was about as much as he trusted the worthless computer to manage on its own. He slipped out of the pilot's chair and left the controls unattended. There would be no music to play, no peaceful view. If he was going to have any time to himself, it would be fiddling with the engines. "I tuned it. Lemme just grab it for you."

---

Somewhere along the way, Kubu had mostly forgotten about why he was running. It was important to get back, and he was in a big hurry, but the running was fun. Following his own scent back to Mommy was so easy that he didn't have to slow down to check which way to go. The wind in his face cooled him just as the running heated him from inside. An occasional mouthful of snow evened things out when the warming started to win out.

It was dark. The sky had lots of little lights, and the ground was all bright white, so Kubu could see. But it was time to get sleepy. The flying house didn't have good day and night like outside did. It was nice to have day and night, and night was for sleeping. Once Kubu was done running, he was going to have a nice, big sleep. Hopefully Mommy wouldn't mind sharing her food. Kubu was hungry.

Kubu couldn't remember the last time he had run so much. It was a long way back to Mommy, he realized. It had taken him a lot of time to find the little house with the kitty-people— oh, that was why Kubu was running!—but he hadn't realized how far it was all in one run.

Two growling buzzes approached from somewhere behind Kubu. He had never heard anything quite like them before. They sounded like big bugs, the kind that fly and sting, but much louder. Kubu hadn't seen any bugs. Mommy had said that bugs don't like the cold, which was another reason that the big outdoor refrigerator was the best place ever. Kubu had never liked bugs, especially the ones that flew and stung. They were hard to catch, stung the inside of his mouth, didn't taste good, and didn't fill the tummy much. There was just nothing good about bugs. With two bugs—probably very big ones— coming from behind, Kubu ran even faster.

---

Dawn was breaking when Kubu arrived back in camp. Mriy

had been just about to wake Esper and Auzuma for breakfast when the huffing and panting of the noisy beast approached. To her chagrin, he was not dragging a painted elk in his jaws. It had probably been optimistic to think Kubu could haul a creature three times his size for kilometers over snow-covered terrain.

"Mommy-mommy-mommy," Kubu shouted as he came within sight. Tanny was already awake and raised an arm in greeting. At least *she* had the good sense not to give her location away by shouting.

"Did you find it?" Tanny asked.

Kubu pulled up a few meters from camp and cocked his head to the side. "Find it?"

"The elk," Mriy clarified. "The painted elk you were looking for."

"Kubu found kitty-people," Kubu replied. His tongue lolled from his mouth, and he hung his head.

Mriy flattened back her ears. "Az-rin. Not kitty-people." She had told Kubu a dozen times at the least. "Where are they?" This could be decisive news. If Kubu could lead them to Hrykii's hunting party, they could set up a distraction and ambush to separate them from the elk when Hrykii found it— if he hadn't already.

"They had a pointy little house with smoke," Kubu said.

Mriy felt a chill that her fur and vest could do nothing to ward off. "They had a house?"

"Who'd be living out here?" Tanny asked.

Mriy shook her head. "No one should be. This is a public hunting ground, an area a hundred times the size of Rikk Pa that should be only for hunters. Come, hunt, leave: those are the rules."

"Kubu, did they see you?" Tanny asked, bending down to one knee to look Kubu in the eye.

Kubu nodded. "Oh yes! Kubu tried to talk to them, but they didn't have through-the-ear magic, so they couldn't understand Kubu. Then they got mad and pointed guns at Kubu, so Kubu ran away."

"Well, that was smart—the running part, I mean," Tanny said. "You know you're not supposed to be talking to strangers."

"Did they follow you?" Mriy asked.

Kubu shook his head. "Just bugs. Kubu had bugs chase him, but he got away."

A sound that had no place in nature prickled Mriy's ear. It was distant, but grew louder by the second. It was a buzz, and as it drew closer she identified it. "Those weren't bugs," she snapped. "Those are snow-rollers. You led them back to us!"

"What are we up against?" Tanny asked, drawing a hunting knife. It was a soldier's reaction, and a good one, but likely inadequate.

"Poachers, trappers, squatters, fugitives," Mriy listed them off as possibilities came to mind. "If they were traditionalists, they wouldn't have vehicles. If they're not, then they'll be armed with more than knives."

"Options?"

Mriy shook her head. "Even if we had Kubu start a false trail, he still left tracks straight to us. Wake Esper and Auzuma; get them to cover."

This wasn't good. Hrykii pack was already more than a match for them. It was going to be a battle of guile against a superior force. This was more than anyone in the challenge had bartered for. Mriy headed back along Kubu's trail, taking a position on a ridge a quarter kilometer outside camp on a low rise. There just wasn't enough tree cover. Snow-rollers would slice through camp at full speed, and gun-armed occupants would have every advantage. Except possibly surprise.

Mriy worked quickly. She took rope from her knapsack and tied one end around the stump of a fallen pine. The whine of the engines continued to draw nearer. The mountain echoes played tricks with the ear that prevented her from pinning down their exact distance, but time was at a premium. Crossing Kubu's tracks in the snow, she found a standing pine and looped the rope around that as well, tying it off with a bit of slack. There was just enough play in the line for Mriy to wiggle the rope below the snow's surface and be able to pull it back up to just about the height of a snow-roller's tracks.

The snow was knee-deep and powdery. Mriy grabbed a branch as long as her body, then hunkered down in the snow. White fur was uncommon in azrins. When she was young, children had teased her about it—before she grew larger than her tormentors—but now she was thankful for a bit of natural camouflage. The buzzing continued to grow, until she could clearly make out two distinct snow-rollers. She had been off-world too long; the engines were newer models that she didn't recognize by ear. They sounded heavy duty, possibly six- or eight-seaters—if she was lucky, perhaps just four.

With the size of the approaching snow-rollers, Mriy began to worry about the rope. It was a glass-fiber composite weave, but far from indestructible. It wasn't often that she wished Roddy were around, but the laaku mechanic had a quick mind for such problems. Assume a speed for a snow-roller, its weight, its durability. The rope had a tensile strength, which Roddy would know or could estimate. Which would prevail? Would the rope halt the snow-roller, or at least slow it violently enough to eject the occupants? Would the trees even hold up to the strain?

Mriy's slapdash plan was to disable one vehicle, scavenge a weapon from the dead or injured crew, and take on the surprised survivors in the second snow-roller. Best case, the second vehicle would crash into the first, but that was asking much from a benevolent god. More likely, Mriy would die a good death, taking enough of Kubu's pursuers with her that Tanny could find a way to deal with the rest.

The engines grew thunderous as the snow-rollers sped toward her position. They must have been following Kubu's tracks, with no effort to head him off or circle around. Good. She had counted on that. Just as she prepared to use her branch to lift the rope into place, one of the engines cut to idle, then the other.

"Come on out," a voice called, echoing in the mountain air. "Got you on thermals. You'd have to be down there long enough to freeze to hide from me."

Mriy let go of her branch and drew her fighting knives. She had bought them off-world, and had never gotten a chance to use them on prey. It looked like today was not going to be the first, either. "Who are you?" she shouted back over her shoulder, her back against the base of her rope's anchor tree.

"We are the sons and daughters of Meyang," came the reply. "I am Hraim."

"Shit!" Mriy muttered in English. It was such a rich language for cursing. But now wasn't the time to panic. These were rebels, the self-proclaimed saviors of azrin-kind. They were dedicated to evicting the human occupation with a mixture of stubborn disobedience, propaganda, and a charmingly naive misunderstanding of planetary logistics.

It wasn't time to fight. She was outnumbered, and her

ambush had failed thanks to a pair of thermal-imaging lenses. It was time to Carl them. Unfortunately, this meant Mriy would have to play the role of Carl. *Lie, and if the lie doesn't work, lie some more.* It was worth a shot. "I'm on a ritual hunt," Mriy answered back, still not emerging from behind her tree. It was one of Carl's tenets not to lie about the obvious and easily verified. *Motives. Lie about motives.* "My chaplain and I found a pair of humans and took them prisoner."

"Where are they?" Hraim demanded.

"Don't shoot," Mriy said. "I'm standing up. I am armed only for the hunt." She stepped from behind the tree and showed the rebels as she sheathed both knives. There were eight of them traveling in a pair of six-seater snow-rollers. Each was armed with a blaster rifle, some off-world brand she didn't recognize—probably from a non-ARGO world, if they weren't hypocrites. All, of course, were azrin.

Mriy turned her back on the rebels, facing camp. "Auzuma, you can come out. They're our people. Bring the human prisoners." Hopefully at least one of the three of them had the sense to play along. Tanny probably. She had known Carl and his ways for a long time.

A minute later, Auzuma emerged from the distant trees, herding Tanny and Esper in front of him. Neither of the humans were wearing the sheathes for their hunting knives. Good. Hopefully they had hidden the weapons under the snow and concealed them well.

Hraim's rebels aimed weapons at the pair of humans. That was when things went over the ledge. "What were they doing when you—"

His question was cut off by a snarl that had Mriy reaching for her weapons by reflex. She dropped into a ready crouch before she saw Kubu charge from the forest, teeth bared. "No, guns at Mommy!" What it must have sounded like to the rebels, Mriy couldn't imagine.

"Turn to stone, dog!" Hraim shouted, his rifle aimed in Kubu's direction.

Whether it was a poor understanding of idiom, a protectiveness of Tanny, or simple canine bloodlust, Kubu didn't falter. Neither did Hraim. The rebel fired a single shot, and a splat of plasma caught Kubu in the shoulder. But Kubu only stumbled into the snow for a second. He came up howling, hobbling, and heading straight for Hraim. Mriy had never seen a human get up after being shot with a plasma bolt, even a nonlethal blast to a limb. She doubted she could muster the strength to stand after taking a shot like that, and she'd never have been able to run.

A second shot caught Kubu in the chest. He let out a lone, shrieking whimper and collapsed, skidding to a limp halt in the snow.

---

Carl settled into the copilot's seat. His guitar sounded all wrong thanks to Roddy fiddling with it—too perfect, no soul— but it was technically the laaku's, so he couldn't complain. Without a few riffs to relax him, Carl decided to see about scrounging up some work for the *Mobius*. Meyang might have been a backwater with an ARGO garrison parked in orbit, but sometimes those were just the right ingredients for someone to need the sort of service the *Mobius* offered.

But the first thing that struck Carl as he looked out the cockpit window was the ship's attitude. They were nose first to the planet, pointing like a hunting dog with a gift for stating the obvious. Meyang filled the view, like a naked Earth without its cities. Carl leaned over to the pilot's controls and feathered the maneuvering thrusters, flipping the *Mobius* around without altering their orbit. He took a long, deep breath as the welcoming stars greeted him. "We'll be back out there soon enough. You fellas aren't going anywhere, right?" Carl had been born on a starship and lived most of his life on them. A planet was just an asteroid with pretension.

"Now, let's see," he mumbled to himself, browsing the ship's computer from the copilot's terminal. "Meyang, Meyang, Meyang—what do you people need to get off-world?" The omni was filled with every bit of useless information anyone felt compelled to share over public computing. From ancient historical translations, to ARGO treaty terms, to complaints about the local music scene—if someone saw fit to log it to an unsecured network, it was on the omni. Slogging through the mush of data wasn't Carl's specialty, but anyone with a decent education could muddle through it.

It was boring. Carl was bored. The omni went on and on forever—that was sort of its thing. Over the two hours he searched, he learned fact after useless fact about Meyang and azrin culture. It went in through his eyes and leaked out his ears. For the most part, azrins were retroverts, xenophobes, and paupers. Anything new, expensive, or off-world was a tough sell. They resented ARGO—though who could blame them. The ones who worked closely with the "occupiers" were widely derided. A tech-free lifestyle was considered the ideal —which Carl found an ironic sentiment to be posting on the omni.

With nothing better to go on, Carl reverted to the old-fashioned method. He took out an ad. There was an art to advertising illegal services. As with many cons, it relied on the way a potential customer would read it, as opposed to an honest citizen. Turn your back on a stack of hardcoin terras, and a corrupt bureaucrat knows to take the bribe. Tell a potential client that you can "get anything he needs," and he'll know you're willing to ship contraband. But the same way an honest filing clerk will leave your terras alone, an honest client will just think you're being enthusiastic and accommodating.

But with savvy ARGO agents out there watching, it took more care to craft an advert. They *weren't* the honest sorts, which is how they did their job. Overplay it just a little and a captain could end up with a ringer on board—like one Mr. Bryce Brisson, or whatever-the-hell his real name was.

*Light freighter leaving orbit soon. Space left in hold. Prefer small, high-value cargo.*

That sounded about right. It sounded like a captain wanting to squeeze some terras into the last few cubic meters of his hold before heading off-world. Really, aside from tremble-handed cowards, who *didn't* want to carry small, high-value cargo? But to someone desperate to get a quarantined plant or a thousand-year-old cultural artifact out of the system, the implication was clear: *pay me enough and I'll sneak something past customs for you.*

Carl smiled to himself, satisfied with a job well done. Let the suckers planetside do the work themselves. He had a guitar to tune until it had some soul back in it.

---

"Kubu, no!" Esper shouted. He fell into the snow and didn't move. All thoughts of their ruse of being prisoners fled her mind. She rushed through the shin-deep snow, stumbling to her hands and knees twice on her way to reach Kubu's side.

He was breathing quick and shallow. A gaping hole in his

chest, charred around the edges, leaked red blood onto the snow. Another in his shoulder did likewise. Esper wanted to be sick, but there was no time for that. She shut her eyes and placed her hands on Kubu's side. "It's OK. It's going to be OK," she whispered.

He whined softly. "Kubu hurts."

She had learned her healing spell in a rhyme as a girl. It seemed silly at the time, but she knew from Mort that asking was a part of receiving. *"Cuts close, bruises fade; three weeks healing done today; bones knit, pains ease; cleanse the body of disease."* She repeated it in Latin, remembering Mort's advice that the universe responded better the older the languages. *"Comprimare vulnus, livores defluet; tres septimanas sanando fit hodie; os implexae, lenire dolores; purgare corpus morbus."* In church Latin, it felt like an invocation to God.

Kubu writhed beneath her hands. His whining grew stronger, pained. "Hungry! Kubu hungry." She looked down and saw a pair of blood-crusted scars with missing fur, stark pink against Kubu's black fur.

Esper plunged her arms into the snow and wrapped them around Kubu's neck, engulfing him in a hug. "Oh, Kubu. You're going to be all right."

He squirmed in her grasp, his high-pitched keening causing a pain in Esper's ears. "Hungry."

"Of course," Esper mumbled. Fumbling in her pocket, she pulled out two Snakki Bars she'd been keeping handy for mid-hike snacks. Kubu took a quick sniff and gobbled them from her hands before she could even take her gloves off to unwrap them.

"What did she do?" Hraim demanded.

"She is holy," Mriy replied. "A priestess among the humans. God listens to her prayers."

That might have been a bit of a stretch. By Esper's quick count that was a lie, a used-to-be, and an I-don't-know. Had it been God she'd just spoken to, or some less deific entity that held sway over physics and impossibility.

"We are on a ritual hunt," Auzuma said, drawing the attention of the rebels, but not the aim of their rifles. "We did not come to hunt humans, but humans are what we found. I am a chaplain, so I couldn't abide the killing of a priestess."

Hraim nodded. "I won't keep you from your hunt. We have contacts. We can get a ransom for them. But not for the dog. Those things are good for nothing but hunting our people. One fewer bloodhound, one less worry for us." He strode through the snow like a king—or a warlord—his head high, weapon held ready to pronounce sentence.

Esper threw herself over Kubu, who still lay in the snow after devouring his snack. "You won't hurt him!"

Hraim stood right over her, prodding with the muzzle of his blaster rifle. "Move aside. Obey and you'll see your people again. Defy me, and holy woman or not, I'll shoot him right through you."

Esper hadn't been a criminal long enough to be used to people pointing weapons at her. The image of Kubu's charred wound flashed across her mind. She wasn't built like him, wasn't half muscle, half sinew and bone. A blaster wound would be fatal before she could even begin to heal herself.

"*Ignus,*" she muttered. Tempting as it was to take out her wrath on the azrin rebel, she turned her thoughts to melting the snow around her. "*Ignus,*" she repeated. A thin fog rose around her.

"What are you doing?" Hraim asked. "Stop it. Stop it at once."

"Shoot me," Esper said, neither raising her head nor

looking at the azrin. She continued to shield Kubu with her body.

"Dumb human, I don't want to—"

"God will protect me!" Esper shouted. She wondered how many of the rebels understood English, the language of their enemies.

Hraim hissed a long sigh, heavy with disgust. "Fine."

*Click.* Esper cringed, but nothing happened. *Click. Click.* Esper's use of magic so close to the rifle had fouled the scientific principles it replied upon.

"What's going on?" Hraim demanded. "Zaulau, toss me your gun." Another of the azrin rebels complied, and the weapon slapped into Hraim's waiting hands.

Esper buried her face against Kubu's flank. "*Ignus.*"

*Click... click click click.* "Blasted things. What's—"

"Going on?" Auzuma asked. "Just as she said, Hraim: God protects her. See why we did nothing to them?"

Esper let out a sigh and was glad not to have been standing. She likely would have toppled to the snow with her legs turned to rubber beneath her.

Hraim gestured with his rifle in Tanny's direction. "What about the other one?"

"Who's to take a chance like that?" Auzuma replied. "Not me. Not Mriy. This is a ritual hunt, not a rebellion. We stand together, but in two different places. This is your battlefield, but our hunting ground."

"We'll take them off your hands, so you can continue your hunt," Hraim said.

"Do you have a fire we could share?" Mriy asked. Something in the way she said it sounded stiff and formal. What Esper didn't know about ritual hunts could have filled a book—and somewhere on the omni, it probably did. New aspects popped up every time the wind shifted. Did a fire hold special significance, or was Mriy simply begging for hospitality?

Hraim glanced over at the snow-rollers. "We have a permanent camp set up. You can sleep in beds and have a fire for the night. Make your human prisoners understand that their lives depend on their behavior. And if that mongrel so much as looks at me, I'm shooting it and leaving it for the crows."

Mriy repeated the instructions in English, knowing full well all of them had understood Hraim just fine. Of course, the less he knew about them the better.

As azrin hands hauled her into the lead snow-roller, Esper wondered just how much Carl might be willing—or able—to pay for her release.

---

The call wasn't long in coming. "Yo, *Mobius* here," Carl said into the comm. He set down his guitar between the pilot and copilot's seats. He couldn't remember how to play the outro to "Layla" anyway, so nothing of value was lost.

"*Is comm secure?*" a voice with a thick azrin accent asked.

"Sure," Carl replied, kicking his feet up onto the control console. "How about your end?"

"*As well, mine is,*" the azrin replied. "*I see face. You transmit.*"

There was an old belief among humankind that you could tell a man was lying by looking into his eyes. You wouldn't do business over a comm or with a guy wearing dark glasses. That was for suckers. Modern psychology said that was all bunk, and Carl knew just *how* bunk better than most. Apparently that tidbit of modern thinking hadn't reached Meyang just yet.

"I really prefer voice only," Carl replied. If no one saw

your face, you could claim in court that it could have been anyone forging your voice imprint.

"*My job, eleventy thousand terra,*" the azrin replied. Carl supposed that was a lot like 11,000. "*You. Face. Or no terra.*"

Carl rolled his eyes and reached for the button to switch on the vid feed. "You're the boss. Happy now?"

"*Your fur. Blue?*" the azrin asked.

"Yeah, it's a funny story. I was—"

"*No cursed fur,*" the azrin replied. "*Deal off.*" The comm went dead.

"Yeah, well you're no prize yourself," Carl snapped, addressing a comm panel that was no longer transmitting. "Fuck. He probably wanted us to transport sentient eggs, or cloned scientists, or some other bullshit. When the hell is that azrin cultural enrichment field trip going to end? I'm sick of this flea-trap planet and its superstitious felid residents."

He looked around the cockpit. "Where the hell did I leave that hat?"

---

The rebels' refuge was nicer than Kubu had let on. Given Kubu's communication skills, that might have been expected, but this went beyond understatement. The rebels had built along a hillside, using the soil for insulation. Despite needing a chimney for their fire, they were reasonably hidden from thermal scans.

Mriy and Auzuma were led inside, while Tanny, Esper, and Kubu were herded into one of the pens where the rebels kept wild game caught alive. The lone mountain goat that had occupied it before their arrival was slaughtered and brought inside for the night's meal.

Hraim's rebels gave Mriy a wide berth, but a few spoke briefly and quietly with the chaplain. It seemed that he was the less intimidating of the two, or perhaps Hraim had wanted to handle her himself. He came to sit with her, bringing two goat legs. He offered one to Mriy and took a bite from the other. "So, what sort of hunt was this?"

Mriy saw no reason to lie, this time. "My nephew was appointed heir while I was away. Three years off-world is not abandonment of my duties. I challenged to make the claim my own."

Hraim pointed to Auzuma with his dinner. "And him? Seems old for a hunt."

"My nephew brought the clan's guardian. I wanted an even match. If we fight for the prize elk, let him match against the chaplain, while I face the guardian."

"Bold," Hraim replied, nodding. "Very old thinking. Sounds like something I'd expect one of mine to do."

"What about them?" Mriy asked. "What are the sons and daughters of Meyang doing so far from cities? These lands are meant for hunts."

"And we hunt them," Hraim replied. "That goat you're gnawing is no pen-raised cattle. You can feel the strength in those muscles as your teeth tear through. We're too few to fight back against the humans, but we won't let them turn us into their kind. Weak. Store fed. Reliant on technology. Not us."

Mriy noticed that many of the rebels were young, not much older than Hrykii. They hung on Hraim's words, though none moved close enough to join the conversation. They hung on the fringes of the common dining hall, watching.

"How much do you make selling hostages to the occu-piers?" Mriy asked. It was a question she'd never have considered three years before, but the *Mobius* and her wandering times had taught her to think of the costs of things. The worlds made much more sense when you saw how money flowed. Desperate thieves and dishonest businessmen had seemed such strange creatures before she had met so many of them in person.

"Most of them get 10,000 terras per head," Hraim replied. "Hard to spend, though, since they look for us in the cities. This holy woman, maybe we'll get 20,000 for her. Some church must miss her by now."

"The One Church," Mriy added.

"All the better," Hraim replied. "Those fiends spit on God's commandments and have more wealth than the Profit Minya, blessed is his name. Be good to have some of that back from them. They owe more than they can ever repay."

"What of food, shelter for the night?" Mriy asked.

Hraim yawned. He had finished most of his goat leg as they spoke, and the weight of sleep was heavy on his eyes. "We've penned humans overnight before. They're dressed for it. We've never had one freeze, yet. And they won't starve in a single night. I don't want the dining hall smelling like burned meat."

Mriy finished her meal, and a young rebel with lusty eyes led her to her borrowed sleeping quarters. The offer of his own was plain in his manner—the low growls, the touch of his hand on her back—but Mriy ignored him. She had bigger problems, because no one was going to be paying for Tanny or Esper's rescue.

---

Carl woke to the sound of the comm built into his datapad. He hummed along with the opening bars of "Smoke on the Water" as he fumbled to accept the call.

"Whazzit?" he mumbled, rubbing his eyes.

"*This the* Mobius?" a voice on the other end asked. It was human, which was a damn sight better than fur-fearing locals.

"Yup," Carl replied. There was a long pause. "This is the part where you tell me why you called."

"*I... I've got an object—let's call it an item—and this item needs delivering,*" the voice on the comm said.

"Listen, pal," Carl said, stopping to yawn and stretch. "I can tell you're new at this, so let me help you out. You tell me what you've got—a box, a sack, a herd of somethingorothers, a person—how big it is, how much it weighs, whether I need to feed it or keep it cold or whatever. Then you tell me where to bring it and how soon you need it there. You offer me a price and we haggle until we agree on a number. This isn't a holovid; it's just business."

"*Oh.*"

"Take a minute," Carl said. "Collect yourself. I just woke up, and I gotta piss." Carl muted the comm.

*When he came back, his contact was better prepared. "It's a box. Weighs 0.65 kilos. Fits in hand. I need it delivered to a ship waiting at an astral depth of 3.80, just outside the Meyang System."*

"Sounds easy enough," Carl replied. It was a local drop-off. The poor slob on the other end of the comm probably worried that he'd get searched at customs, and his buyer probably had warrants out on his ship and crew.

"*I need it there by 7:00 tonight,*" the voice said.

Carl blew out a long breath and scanned the datapad for the time. It was 9:32 AM, but the *Mobius* kept to Earth Standard Time. "That local? What's it in Earth Standard?"

*There was another long pause. "I'm two hours ahead of Earth Standard, so 5:00 PM for you. Can you manage by then?"*

"Sure," Carl replied. It was seven and a half hours for a quick pickup and drop-off. "What's the job pay?"

*"How does 50,000 sound?"*

It was times like this that Carl was glad he didn't leave the comm open while he listened. Otherwise his client would have heard him choke on the beer he had just cracked open. He finished coughing and sputtering and composed himself. Fifty thousand was just another day scanning in on a time clock, he told himself. "Yeah, I guess it's easy enough. I don't have anything else going on today. Transmit coordinates, and I'll come make the pickup."

Carl brushed his teeth as the client worked on that, then called down to the engine room and woke Roddy up, letting him know about the job. A pickup the two of them could manage just fine. For the delivery, they were going to need Mort. The edge of the system at a weird astral depth was child's play with Mort along. Without him, they might as well have been sitting atop the ship's hull with oars for all the good it would do them.

Settling into the pilot's seat, Carl put them on a heading for a place the azrins called Ishiy Pa, but which ancient Earth-lings had named Athens—give or take a hundred kilometers. They'd be there in minutes, but that end of the trip wasn't the trouble. He found a comm ID for the *Yinnak* and put in a call.

"*Who calls?*" an azrin voice demanded.

"I need to speak with Mort, the human wizard you've got staying with you," Carl said.

"*Who. Calls?*" the azrin said more slowly.

"Shit. Doesn't speak English," Carl muttered. Not for the first time, he wished more people wore translator-charmed earrings. Understanding people who didn't think you knew their language came in handy once in a while, but nowhere near as often as it was a royal pain in the ass. He dusted off the few words of azrin he'd picked up and keyed the comm. "No. Azrin. Speak. Human."

"*You wait,*" the azrin replied. Carl breathed a sigh of relief.

"*Who is this?*" a new voice asked.

"This is Carl Ramsey, captain of the *Mobius*. I need to speak with Mort, the wizard that—"

"*Mort!*" the azrin shouted. Carl flinched and pulled the datapad away from his ear, though by the echo, it had not been shouted directly into the comm. "*Some ship captain wants to speak with you.*"

"*Bleeding blue blazes, Carl,*" Mort's familiar voice carried annoyance clearly over the comm. "*We were watching a holovid of the Mongol invasion of China. I finally convinced them that their local fictional productions were shit. I still think they're mostly watching to see gruesome human deaths, but it's an improvement over the wooden acting and fairy-tale plots their holos are crammed with.*"

"Glad you're having fun, but I've got us a job," Carl said. "It's hot to go, and I need a wizard for it. Delivery is in astral space, just outside the system. There's always a chance we might wear out our welcome in the process, so I'd like to get everyone rounded up before we head off. We've got just over seven hours left to make the drop, and I'll be picking it up in the next fifteen minutes. I can get to you in under an hour."

"*Don't rush on my account. Our intrepid hunters aren't back yet.*"

"They've got to be just about done by now. Any chance you can prod things along?"

"*I came down to prevent that sort of thing, not cause it.*"

"Yeah, but this is just a family matter," Carl replied. "I've got business up here."

*"Head on over,"* Mort replied. *"But I'm not leaving until they get back—on their own."*

Carl punched the comm hard enough that he worried he might have broken it. "Dammit! Why do you have to act like such a fucking..." Carl searched for the word, but nothing described a wizard who gummed up the works. If Mriy wanted to inherit a chunk of this blasted planet when her mother died, fine. But it was getting in the way of easy money —which was never as easy as advertised.

---

Esper had never been in a cage before. It was nowhere to be found on her list of things she wished to experience in her lifetime. She might have listed setting foot on an Earth-like world or two, but not setting face on them. If there was one good thing to be said about the animal pen where she and Tanny had been locked up, it was that it had been kept clear of snow. That and the wall of snow that came right up to the bars on one side shielded them from the worst of the wind.

"Hold still," Tanny scolded. They were lying back to back, where Tanny could reach the cord that tied Esper's wrists together while her own were similarly bound. "I've almost got a grip on it... almost... shit!"

Tanny was breathing hard, her huffing as loud as Kubu's panting from the next cage over. He seemed none the worse for wear after his ordeal, other than being hungry—not that he wasn't always hungry. A part of Esper had doubted he would survive those horrible wounds. She wasn't a miracle worker; her magic only sped natural healing. That meant that if someone had kept Kubu from bleeding to death or suffering infection, he'd eventually have pulled through on his own. She could hardly imagine running into a full-grown version of him, wild and hungry, and fully able to devour her in a bite or two.

"Give me a minute, and I'll try again," Tanny said. She twisted and rolled to face Esper's back. "I need another look at those knots."

"Maybe it's special cord," Esper said. "It might be meant to cut and not untie."

"I don't care what it's meant for. I just want to get loose."

"What do we do if we get ourselves untied?"

Tanny heaved a sigh. "We'll figure that out if we get that far."

"I could try magic," Esper suggested.

"Mort showed you a trick for getting loose from something like this?"

"Not exactly," Esper replied. "But he showed me the general principles of arguing with the universe. I could improvise."

"Let's save that as a last resort, all right?"

Tanny flipped back-to-back again with Esper, and the tugging at her wrists resumed. Esper gritted her teeth as the cord dug into her flesh and rubbed the raw wound. She didn't say anything about it to Tanny; Tanny was doing everything she could to help them escape. She didn't need Esper whining and complaining the whole while.

"Mort did teach me how to set things on fire," Esper said softly as Tanny worked. "But I don't think I could to it to a person. I... I just thought you might need to know that."

"Figured as much," Tanny said between grunts of exertion. Esper could barely feel her hands, with the cord cutting off circulation. She could only imagine Tanny's struggles to untie a knot with hers still bound. "Just wish they'd used a fiber rope instead of this synthetic shit. I'd stomach some burns to get loose, but not the temperatures it would take to melt this stuff."

Esper kept quiet and tried to focus her thoughts anywhere but on the pain in her wrists and ankles, but the latter wasn't so bad through the fabric of her pants. She couldn't tell whether the numb feeling down in her feet was lack of circulation or the cold. The azrins had taken their boots.

The tugging at Esper's wrists finally stopped. Tanny fell back, panting. "Not gonna happen. Even if I could get a grip, my fingers are too numb to loosen the knot."

"Magic's turn?" Esper asked. "What should I try?"

"Nothing that can explode or burn," Tanny replied. "I dunno, maybe make the cord stretchy or brittle. Mort doesn't usually go in for half-measures, so I'm guessing here."

"I'll try stretchy," Esper replied. She closed her eyes and envisioned the cord being rubber—soft, pliable, elastic. She described the imagined cord in detail, the words kept inside her head. The universe would hear her either way. When there was no immediate effect, she began again. Then a third time and a fourth. By the fifth she was growing cross with the universe, and told it so. By the sixth recitation, the universe had just about had it with her nagging.

A jolt shook the ground and rattled their cage, though not enough to damage it or break loose the lock. Esper flinched; she would have jumped if she hadn't been tied hand and foot.

"What was that?" Tanny asked. It was the first time Esper had heard a tremble in her voice.

"I argued with the universe, and I think it just said 'no.'"

Mriy crept through the darkened hideout. The rebels kept no sentry, no night watch. And why should they? Their prisoners were caged and secured. Their two guests were on a ritual hunt. At worst, they might have suspected Mriy and Auzuma to depart before dawn to resume their hunt. Waking their hosts would have been far more rude than departing without a farewell.

Mriy's makeshift room had been a corner of a supply closet. Auzuma had been given space in the dining room, with a bed of blankets not far from the hearth fire. It was a concession to his old age and a sign of respect from the rebels. A young warrior enjoyed cold air for sleeping, but old bones liked to feel a fire's warmth.

Auzuma snored, curled up head-to-feet, with one arm over his face. Mriy approached with a hunter's stealth, as if he were prey. Her first instinct was to clamp a hand over his mouth to silence him while she assured him who she was. It was a human's holovid plan. It might have worked on human sleepers, but if she did that to Auzuma, old warrior instincts might have taken over and she could have found herself brawling in the middle of the room before Auzuma realized what he was doing. Instead, she whispered.

"Auzuma."

An ear twitched, but he showed no other reaction.

"Auzuma," Mriy repeated, leaning closer but not daring any louder voice. He stirred, and she spoke his name once more.

An eye opened, the wide pupil narrowing to a slit in the firelight. "What is it?" he asked in a whisper that matched her own.

"The hunt is over. I have failed. We're going to release the humans and get out of here."

Auzuma twisted his head until both his eyes could look into hers. He held her gaze for just a moment, then gave a solemn nod. Mriy swallowed back a lump in her throat, knowing that she hadn't admitted until then—even to herself—that she would not prevail over Hrykii.

Auzuma followed her without another word. When the old chaplain reached for his knapsack, Mriy put a restraining hand on his shoulder. She shook her head when he turned a questioning look in her direction. The gear was not worth the risk of the noise it might make in the taking.

The night air was calm, but cold enough to cut through fur. By the moonlight, the live-prey cages were easy to spot, some fifty meters from the nearest building, where the smells and sounds of the animals would be less distracting. Out in the open air, there was less need for quiet.

"You find the snow-rollers," Mriy said. "However many they have, we take them all or disable any we have to leave behind. I'll release Tanny and Esper."

"Kubu too!" Kubu shouted, his deep voice echoing in the mountain air. Mriy had forgotten how keen Kubu's ears were. He had overheard her hushed voice from forty meters away.

"Yes, you too," she hissed. "Be silent."

She hurried through the snow as Auzuma disappeared around the side of the rebels' main domicile in search of snow-rollers. There were a dozen cages, each a mesh of composite steel bars with gaps barely large enough to fit a finger through. The animals occupying the rest of the cages stirred as Mriy approached the cage with Tanny and Esper bound on the cold ground within.

"Mriy, praise the Lord," Esper whispered. "Get us out of here."

"What did you think I was out here for?" Mriy muttered as

she examined the lock. It was a simple padlock with a DNA reader. Such trivial security seemed negligent, but the cages were mainly used for livestock. Mriy pressed a finger to the pad of the reader, and the locked opened.

Dragging Tanny and Esper out into the open to get better access to their bindings, Mriy drew a hunting knife and sawed through the cords. Esper gasped in relief when the pressure came off her wrists, twisting and stretching and flinching when she rubbed at the raw, bleeding wounds that were left. She stood clumsily, shaking feeling back into numb feet. Tanny was more stoic and less patient. She grabbed a spare knife from Mriy as soon as her hands were free and quickly snapped the cord tying her own ankles together.

"This one won't open," Esper whispered loudly. She was crouched at Kubu's cage, pressing her own finger to the lock as Mriy had done earlier.

"Azrin DNA," Mriy said. She crossed over and pressed her finger to the reader. The lock popped. "Anyone here can unlock it except you two—three." She added the last after Kubu opened his mouth to object.

The canine had not been bound. Given his quadrupedal anatomy and the fact that his dewclaws barely functioned as thumbs, there was little need to bind him. He sprang from his cage with his tail wagging, but remained obediently silent.

A knife blade caught the moonlight, flashing a signal that caught Mriy's eye. Auzuma waved to her, summoning the group to his location around the side of the compound. But Mriy's keen eyes caught something else as well, approaching from the woods. An azrin form was watching them from behind a tree. It seemed that Hraim might have been cautious enough to post a guard, after all.

"Run for it," Mriy whispered. "I'll catch up." She pointed

toward Auzuma and hurried Esper along with a shove in that direction.

"We won't leave without you," Esper insisted, catching her balance and stopping dead in her tracks in the snow.

"You're not fit to stay and help," Mriy replied. "You have no boots. You'll freeze if you don't get to the snow-rollers and get out of here."

"Just hurry," Tanny said, grabbing Esper by the arm.

"Don't worry. Leave without me if you must. They won't kill one of their own kind," Mriy said. She dropped into a crouch and headed for the tree line.

It was then that the sentry must have realized he had been spotted. "Turn to stone, traitor!" he shouted. When he came up from his crouch, the sentry was aiming a blaster rifle at her.

Mriy did as ordered, stopping in her tracks. He was too far to rush, too close to miss his shot. Only seconds earlier she had claimed that these rebels—these sons and daughters of Meyang—would not kill her. She still believed that to be true. But what she couldn't admit in front of Esper was that, short of killing, there was no limit to the harm they might do a traitor. Mriy's best ally was the sentry's own reluctance to fire what was undeniably a deadly weapon at her.

"I tried to stop them," Mriy said, carefully keeping her hands out wide and in plain sight. "The holy one used some spell on me. She's only just now far enough that I could break free of it."

The sentry stepped out from behind the cover of his tree and into better light. She struggled to recall his name—Rrumlau, the quiet one with the shoulders like an ox. He kept his rifle aimed at Mriy's midsection, but remained silent.

The growl of a snow-roller's engine echoed in the night. It

was joined by another a second later. Those engines revved and hummed, then quieted.

Mriy turned her head in the direction of the noise. "They're getting away!" she shouted. "They won't come past us. They'll go the long way around. Hurry if you want to get a shot off before they're gone."

Rrumlau looked from Mriy to the distant sound of the snow-rollers and back again. He snarled. "Try nothing foolish." With that, he rushed off in the direction of the fading engine noise.

Mriy drew a hunting knife, took aim, and threw. The blade flipped end over end, catching Rrumlau a glancing blow on the back of his shoulder, but it drew blood. Mriy was already in full run by the time the knife hit. Rrumlau yelped and lost his grip on his rifle with his trigger hand. He dropped it to the snow when Mriy barreled into him as he tried to turn.

Rrumlau was a classic brute. He had twenty kilos on Mriy at the least, and was younger by a full hand of years—his fighting prime. But Mriy had stolen the initiative, first blood, and the upper position in the brawl. Soora had been built like Rrumlau. As he tried to buck and shove at her shoulders and hips, she realized that he fought much like her brother as well. Mriy let him push and struggle beneath her, shifting her weight and leverage so that he could not rise from the snow. With gravity aiding her, she landed heavy swipes to the sides of Rrumlau's head, narrowly avoiding the bites he attempted in defense.

They grappled in the snow for minutes, until Mriy managed to kick off her boots and get her hind claws into Rrumlau's flanks. That rendered his legs flailing and useless and started to compress his abdomen, robbing him of breath. The larger azrin tired quickly from that point, struggling for breath and clawing effectually at Mriy's arms and face. With her toe claws dug in, the battle of arms only needed a stalemate from her end. As Rrumlau fought for air, his struggles turned entirely defensive. Mriy picked her way through his guard and pounded him until he was dazed and limp.

Rolling off the heavier fighter, Mriy fumbled in the snow until she found the dropped blaster rifle. It was cheap and lightweight, nothing like the ordinance Tanny procured for the *Mobius*. She crawled over to Rrumlau, who was now helpless on his back, trying to regain lost breath and staunch the bleeding in his sides. She aimed the rifle down, right where she judged his heart to be.

Mriy listened. For the first time since the blood rush of combat began, she noticed her surroundings. The hum of snow-roller engines had faded into the distance and was gone. If she was lucky, she could follow the trail. They might double back for her, or stop and wait if they thought pursuit was lost.

Rrumlau spat up at her. Given his struggles to fill his lungs, she gave him the barest credit for managing to spit into her face. But it was a mistake. Mriy hissed and tightened her finger on the trigger. But it didn't fire. The last little bit, the final squeeze that would send a burst of plasma to incinerate Rrumlau's heart, would not come.

Light poured from the door of the domicile, spilling across the snow. Azrin voices shouted demands and threats. Mriy tried once again to pull the trigger, but couldn't bring herself to do it. She had counted on the rebels' beliefs to protect her— that they would not kill one of their own kind. How could she show clear proof that she was less noble?

Mriy flipped the rifle around and brought the butt end down on Rrumlau's upper jaw. The crack that sounded was payback for his spitting on her. A glance at the rebels pouring from the domicile told her that there was no escaping. She might kill a few, but they wouldn't hesitate to kill her in self-defense at that point. Letting the rifle slip from her grasp, Mriy collapsed onto her back in the snow.

Footsteps crunched through the snow toward her. "By your place in God's heaven, what came over you?" Hraim asked as he loomed over Mriy.

"They were my pack," Mriy mumbled, too exhausted in mind and body to lie. "They were *all* my pack. Even the damned dog."

---

"We have to go back for her," Esper insisted. Her stomach lurched as the snow-roller took a turn, while she was twisted around watching behind them.

"We can't," Auzuma replied. It was just the two of them; Tanny drove the rebels' only other snow-roller and had Kubu with her.

"They'll kill her," Esper said. "She betrayed them."

"Those rebels are true believers," Auzuma replied. "They know their Book. 'You shall not kill kin.' Most of my people take it to mean not to kill within the clan. But those rebels, they hold to the old interpretation. We are all God's children, so they won't kill another azrin."

"My species has that one, too," Esper replied. "It's worded a little less ambiguously, and they still break it all the time."

"I've met few pious humans," Auzuma said. He swerved the snow-roller around a fallen tree, causing Esper's gorge to rise. She gave up on watching the second snow-roller and the path behind them. "We heard the word of the same God, but we followed it better. We have had no flood, no great plagues—

yes, I've read your Bible. Our commandments numbered just six, and we followed them better than your kind ever did."

"But what if they're not as pious as you think?"

"Then Mriy will die."

"Right! So we have to go—"

"No," Auzuma said. His easy banter was gone. His pronouncement carried the weight of finality. "If Mriy needs saving, it will be the Yrris Clan who goes back for her—with a ship. Not us."

---

Mriy didn't remember being dragged indoors, but she recognized the scent of the rebels' hearth fire before she opened her eyes. The sap from the green pine wood gave off a distinctive aroma. She would have liked to take a good sniff of the room, but feared that she might alert her captors that she was awake; instead she let the smells around the room waft to her. Hraim was here, along with Rrumlau and four other rebels.

She lay facedown on the dirt floor, arms pinned behind her. Ropes at her wrists and elbows kept her forearms pressed together and her shoulders straining in their sockets. Her legs were splayed, pulled in opposite directions—probably tied to stakes. It would have been a comical parody of some of the worst locally produced holovids if it weren't so painful. The only solace she could take was that they left her arms—and claws—facing upward; it meant they didn't intend to violate her before she died.

A bare toe prodded her ribs, and Mriy realized she was unclad. "She's awake."

Hraim knelt beside her. "Well, well. Looks like our friend

is faking." A thin-clawed slap left trails of fire across Mriy's face.

She opened her eyes. "You are sad relics, living in dead days."

"And you're a traitor to your kind." Rrumlau spoke with his jaw clenched. Mriy took grim satisfaction knowing that she'd broken it.

"What do we do with the human-lover?"

"She's as good as human. Just kill her."

"Make her pay, first."

Hraim pressed her head to the floor and stared into Mriy's eyes. "No. She's still azrin. We don't kill kin. But I think, if she wants to be part of a human pack, we oughtta help her."

Rrumlau strutted into view. He bent low and held out a hunter's tool, a pair of iron pliers that looked old enough to have been in his family for generations. They were used for taking trophies from a kill. Speak to any hunter who wore a necklace of teeth or claws, and he could pull such a tool from his pocket to show you. Mriy owned a little-used pair that she kept on board the *Mobius*.

Hraim held out a short piece of a tree branch that hadn't been stripped of bark. It was thick as her forearm. "Open up. This is the last favor we do you."

Mriy felt an instinctive urge to resist, to thwart any effort her captors made. But she knew the truth of it, and realized why her hands were tied behind her, where her captors had easy access. It was accept their offer, or suffer through the pain with nothing to bite on while they declawed her.

With a growl, she snapped her jaws down on the wood, giving a resentful glare as she did. But Rrumlau just laughed, and Hraim tied a cord around one end of the wood and looped it behind her head before trying the other. He wasn't securing it so Mriy didn't spit it out; he was forcing her jaws wide until she could barely bite down at all. Her protests came as inarticulate grunts.

Rrumlau turned and swiveled an ear toward her. "What's that? I don't understand human."

Her captors pressed Mriy firmly to the floor. Try as she might, with no leverage she couldn't stop them from unclenching her fists and forcing her claws out, one by one. In gentler fashion, it was the same trick a mother used to file a child's claws. But one by one, those pliers clamped down and pulled. Mriy screamed into the wooden bit between her teeth as searing pain blazed at each finger, each adding to the misery of the last. One by one, bloody claws were pitched into the hearthfire as Mriy watched through eyes swimming with tears.

Ten fingers. Eight toes. She could barely whimper by the time they finished.

Rrumlau patted her on the cheek. "That wasn't so bad, was it?" He opened and closed the pliers with a rusty grating noise. The wet tips gleamed in the firelight.

Mriy grunted. Her jaw ached, and she was dribbling spittle onto the dirt. She wanted to goad them into hearing what she had to say, just so they would take the bit away.

Rrumlau cocked his head. "What's that? You say humans don't have fangs? Why... I think you may be right about that."

Mriy's eyes went wide. She'd had enough. Hadn't they done enough?

With frantic urgency, she struggled against her bonds. A knee came down hard on her back, across her already-strained shoulders. Hands gripped either side of the wooden bit and pulled her head back. Mriy might have been stronger than any one of them, maybe even Rrumlau. But tied up, beaten, and exhausted, she offered only feeble resistance.

Her breath quickened as she saw the pliers coming. Rrumlau took his time. She felt the wiggle in her jaw, the tug, the pain. The pulling brought her head forward despite the rebel holding her back. Then her head bobbed back and she tasted hot blood in her mouth. Spots swam before her eyes. Rrumlau waved the tooth with its bloody roots in front of her eyes before tossing it into the fire.

Three more times, and each time Mriy wished she was weakling enough to pass out from the pain.

When they finally untied the bit from her mouth, it slid out easily; no canine fangs impeded its exit. When they cut her bonds, she lay limp; no strength remained in her muscles.

"Kill... me."

Hraim hooked a foot under her side and rolled Mriy onto her back. "You're going to die, but we won't kill you. You're going to die like a human. Alone in the wilderness. Unable to hunt. I'd have shaved you bare like a human, but freezing's an easy way to go. You'll find water, if you don't lie there and give up. You're going to starve—starve in a forest filled with game you're too weak and harmless to kill."

Rrumlau dragged her outdoors by the wrists. The cold felt wonderful, the snow numbing her wounds. She made a point of hiding that revelation, lest they bring her back inside. But it appeared that they had other plans for their shelter. Mriy watched the smoke as it burned.

Hraim was the last to address her before the rebels left. "Mriy Yrris, in your last moments, I hope you repent. Think about what you've done, and the mistakes that brought you to this end."

Mriy knew already. Hraim, Rrumlau, and all the rest had shown her with perfect clarity. She should never have come back.

Carl stood at the back of the viewing room in the *Yinnak*, killing time along with a host of Mriy's relatives and his own goddamn wizard. The box he flipped idly and caught, again and again, was worth 25,000 terras to whoever was slumming around astral space at the edge of the system. Mort could trust the azrins for a few hours—tops—and be back to watch the end of the contest. Instead, Mort sat there stuffing local sushi in his face, explaining the nuances of Napoleonic warfare as the holovid showed the Battle of Waterloo.

The only thing that kept Carl from losing his cool and screaming Mort's bloody head off was the fact that the other 25,000 had been paid up front. It took a lot to upset the captain of a ship who'd just put 25,000 terras in his pocket, but a thin thread dangling the other half toward a black hole was enough to do it. Just then he wished Mort actually worked *for* him, so he could threaten to fire him.

Carl had always hated any math more complicated than a split of loot from a job. He piloted by gut and let the computers handle the fiddly bits with numbers. But there was an answer to one question he needed: how long did he have before he couldn't make his drop on time. The nameless weasel who'd given him the box and paid him had insisted that late was as good as never delivered. That meant that the ship out there waiting was on a tight deadline. Get to the coordinates and astral depth any later than 5:00PM, November 21 Earth Standard, and that ship would be gone.

It was 3:21PM. Less than two hours away. Planetary rotation kept it from being much past daybreak locally, but Earth Standard didn't care about local sunlight. The box was as light as the client had claimed, made from some advanced plastic composite without any locking mechanism visible. Whatever was inside was probably a lot of trouble, as were the nameless weasel and whoever was paying him the other half of his 50,000. But whatever was inside was also probably pretty damned valuable—maybe even worth more than the 25,000 even accounting for whatever trouble it brought with it.

Carl made an executive decision. He nudged one of the glass-eyed azrins watching holovids with Mort. "Hey, got a comm I can borrow?"

He'd guessed well, and this Yrris understood English. "Sensor station, door before the cockpit."

"Thanks," Carl replied, patting the azrin on the shoulder as he left the viewing room. Sometimes a vague, offhanded request with no context could get people to agree to pretty stupid things.

Carl settled himself into the seat at the sensor station. It took a couple minutes to reset the language to English, but it was a variant of a computer system used across half of ARGO space, so Carl muddled his way through it. Relays, proxies, and ghost comm IDs didn't fall under Carl's list of skills. He settled for opening an account on a local omni exchange under a false name and residence, then began his text-only message.

*AGRO patrol. I hav loyal message. Smuggel ship wait on border. Much wanted. I am loyal, no criminal. You find, keep Meyang saif. Love For Meyang!*

Cross-referencing with his own datapad, Carl attached the coordinates and astral depth the nameless weasel had provided. Hopefully the false ID and crummy spelling and grammar would convince the garrison busybodies that it was a local ratting someone out. They'd never believe that whoever sent the message was innocent, but that made it all the more likely they'd send someone to check it out.

Carl reset the comm panel to azrin and headed back to see who won the Battle of Waterloo.

───────

It was approaching noon local time when Roddy caught Carl on the comm.

"*Boss, we got a problem,*" Roddy said. Carl could hear the nerves in his voice. Either that laaku wasn't drunk enough, or something was going badly.

Carl looked around the room at his azrin hosts; none of them were paying attention. "Dump it. Line's clear enough."

"*You remember those Harmony Bay bastards?*" Roddy asked.

"How could I forget them?" Carl replied, covering his non-comm ear with a hand to block out the noise of the Yrris' latest selection, a pre-ARGO laaku martial arts vid. "Not every day someone comes that close to dusting us."

"*The Bradbury just entered orbit around Meyang.*"

"That's..." Carl struggled for a word. "...ominous. How much of a signature have we got on the ground?"

"*This comm is about the only thing running right now,*" Roddy replied. "*I even opened the Mobius up and turned off life support. We'll be scrubbing local air through the filters for weeks, but our EM signature is zilch.*"

"Good call," Carl said. "We can hang tight until the crew gets back, wait for them to be on the other side of the planet, then—"

"*Is that Eight Fists, No Waiting I hear in the background?*"

"Yeah."

"*I'll be right over,*" Roddy said. "*Haven't seen that since I was a kid.*" The comm clicked and went silent. Two minutes later, the laaku was parking himself between two of Mriy's cousins, buying a welcome by sharing from his six-pack of Earth's Preferred.

Carl stewed and watched the laaku join his wizard in thrall to the holovid. Under normal circumstances, he'd have been all for leaking some coolant pressure over a few hours of mindless holovid action. It was early laaku holovid, so the quality was low, but the action was top notch. Unfortunately, there was too much action in real life hanging over him for Carl to let loose. It came as a relief when the Yrris hunting pack arrived back. Everyone went outside to witness the return.

There was a hullabaloo, with all the Yrrises celebrating Mriy's nephew and his pack of ringers. When Carl saw the size of the azrins who'd gone with him and then considered who Mriy had dragged along, he realized she probably never stood a chance. The elk was a dead elk. It looked stupid, colored up like some cave painting. Its neck lolled and was clearly broken. Carl's stomach was just as glad that it wasn't drenched in blood.

Carl pulled Seerii aside as the initial jubilation died down. "So, Mriy loses. Can we go round up her pack and get out of here?"

"She might not forgive you," Seerii replied, keeping her voice low. "But you should take her from here when she returns. By law she is welcome. By all other measures, she is not."

"We just wait here?" Carl asked. "How long should they be?"

"There is no way to be sure, but they should have been tracking the winning pack. Not long, I imagine."

Seerii was right, but for all the wrong reasons. It wasn't

long before two snow-rollers thundered into the base camp, pulling up beside the *Yinnak*. There were two occupants in each, which by Carl's simple math, put them one pack member short. "Where's Mriy?" he shouted over the noise of the combustion engines, before someone cut power to them.

"We ran into rebels hiding out in the hunting grounds," Tanny replied, hopping down from the snow-roller. She wasn't wearing any boots.

"We've got to go after her," Esper added. She wasn't wearing boots either, and there was blood at her wrists.

"The hell happened to you girls?" Carl asked.

"We got captured," Tanny said. "They're not exactly pro-human, if you know what I—is your hair *blue*?"

Carl's face froze. "That *bastard*! He said he fixed it." Carl looked at the backs of his hands—brown. He squinted and pushed an eyebrow into his field of view—brown. He tried holding his datapad up as a mirror, but the black surface didn't deal well with color in reflections.

"Quit it," Esper scolded. "Those rebels have Mriy. She was holding one of them off to cover our escape. She said they won't kill her, but she needs *us* to rescue her."

"Roddy, fire up the engines," Carl said. "Everyone else, get on board. Seerii, I'd love to say it's been nice, but your planet is a shithole and its inhabitants have been pissing me off since I got here."

"How dare you—" Seerii snarled, flexing her claws.

Mort put a warning hand on her arm as he passed by. "Wouldn't try that," he cautioned.

"What about that Harmony Bay ship?" Roddy asked.

Esper's eyes went wide. "What Harmony Bay ship?"

"We'll worry about the *Bradbury* if we have to," Carl said. "I don't believe in coincidences, but that doesn't mean we can't get lucky once in a while. We're finding Mriy and getting the hell out of this system."

They didn't have much to retrieve before lifting off. Mort had brought a few personal effects that he refused to depart without, but that was the bulk of it. They were closing up the ship minutes later.

"Wait," Auzuma shouted as the cargo ramp went up. Roddy hit the control button and stopped it. "Give this to Esper." He handed Roddy a book in Jiara script. The title just said: Book.

"Will do," Roddy replied and closed the bay door.

---

Tracks led from the burned-out ruin of the rebel compound. One set were azrin footprints, another the twin lines left by snow-rollers. Mriy followed the latter. Though there was little chance of the rebels coming back for her, Mriy didn't want to wait for rescue. She had enough fat on her to weather the cold without winter gear; under the daytime sun, it was even refreshing. The wind whipped a dusting of snow from the ground. Tiny crystals of ice caught in her fur and froze there.

Years of training as a hunter, a warrior, and a Silver League fighter went into simply keeping her balance as she set down one foot, then the other. That two-step repetition was all she needed to follow the tracks. They would hate her at the Yrris clanhold. Hrykii would mock her. Yariy would gloat. Seerii would send her away. And she would go. And she would not return. Never return.

One foot. Other foot.

It had been foolhardy to return and try to wrest her old position back.

One foot. Other foot.

But Esper, Tanny, and Auzuma had gotten away. Or at least she hoped they had.

One foot. Other foot.

She caught the scent of a hare on the wind. In daydream, she would catch it, crush it between clawless fingers, tear at its flesh with her incisors, carefully avoiding the tender, bloody holes in her mouth.

One foot. Snow.

The ground rushed up and slammed into Mriy. The powder cushioned her fall. Her breath melted a tiny area around her mouth and nose. Blood stained the snow.

---

Tanny took the pilot's chair, adjusting it mid-flight and complaining all the while about what Carl and Roddy had done to it in the three days she'd been gone. Carl had offered to fly, since Tanny was half-frozen, wounded, and didn't have any boots. In typical marine fashion, she'd brushed those concerns aside as inconsequential to the mission.

"How far is it?" Carl asked. He stood behind the copilot's seat, where Esper had taken position, watching out the forward window as the *Mobius* flew with its nose angled down for better visibility.

"Not far," Tanny replied.

Esper pointed. "I recognize that hilltop. We camped within sight of it the first night. But we just took off." She was chewing on some of Mort's leftover sushi after healing her wrists.

"There's a reason they build these things," Carl said. "Walking long distances outdoors is for animals. Just ask

Roddy about Phabian; you can live there your whole life without setting foot outdoors. That retrovert stuff is bullshit."

Esper held a hand over her mouth as they ducked over hills and mountains with the ship's attitude and altitude making it appear they were going to crash any second. She was still new to this whole business. Motion sickness was something she was going to have to learn to deal with.

"There it is," Esper said. To her credit, she'd kept her eyes open when shutting them would have made the effects go away. After all, none of the G-forces were overcoming the ship's gravity.

A plume of smoke rose through the trees. "I'll man the guns," Carl said. "Esper, take Mort to the cargo bay. We might need unconventional firepower, and you might need to heal Mriy, depending on what kind of shape she's in."

"What if they're not willing to negotiate?" Tanny asked.

"With Mort?" Carl scoffed.

"Right," Tanny replied. A failed negotiation with the ship's wizard wasn't something one walked away from.

But all their preparations were in vain, except for Esper's. The camp was burned and abandoned. Tracks led off deeper into the mountains, and if they had wanted to, the *Mobius* could have hunted them down. But the crew spread out along the compound and found what they were looking for.

Mriy had collapsed in the snow, less than a kilometer down the trail left by the snow-roller escape. It was Kubu's nose that found her; the white of her fur made her nearly invisible. When Tanny rolled her over to check her vitals, they noticed the blood. There were gashes on her sides and face, and all along her arms. What drew attention their were the bloody tips of each finger and the red all around her muzzle. Her eyes fluttered open, then shut tight against the glare.

"Get her something to eat," Esper ordered, putting her hands on Mriy's chest. But Mriy shook her head. In obvious pain, she opened her mouth and showed the raw sockets where her canine teeth had been pulled. "Oh Lord!"

"Mort, levitate her and be gentle about it," Carl ordered. "We'll get this sorted out in the Black Ocean. We've got a ship up there that's getting closer by the second."

---

"The *Bradbury* is closing on us."

Carl swore under his breath. "How long to break atmosphere?"

With a quick check of the scanners, Tanny shook her head. "We're not winning this race."

Carl ran down the hall to the common room. "Mort! What are the prospects of astral from atmosphere?"

The grizzled wizard hung an eyebrow low as he scratched his chin. "I don't like that prospect one bit. Rather get boarded and roll up my sleeves for the fight."

At that moment, Esper backed out of Mriy's quarters, shutting the door softly behind her. "She's in bad shape. If she was human, I think she might have died already. I gave her a trickle of healing, just enough to stop the bleeding. But she's in no shape to eat anything right now."

Carl held up a hand. "Great. You keep on that. We'll figure something out once we get away from the—"

"No!"

Carl blinked.

Esper stood toe to toe with him. "Harmony Bay is the leading medical supplier in the galaxy. The *Bradbury* will have better medical staff than anyone planetside or most of the colonies we visit. I can't magic Mriy up new teeth or claws. She needs a med bay."

Carl shook his head and headed for the cockpit. "I don't have time for this right now. We'll get Mriy to a med facility... maybe Sindra III. She's tough. She'll pull through."

*Esper followed him to the cockpit. A comm came in just as he settled into the copilot's chair. "Vessel Mobius, this is Captain Yasmira Dominguez of the Bradbury. You are in possession of property that belongs to us. Cut your engines and prepare for docking."*

The ship shook gently. Tanny twisted the flight yoke left and right, but the *Mobius* didn't maneuver. "Shit. They locked on a tractor beam."

Carl reached for the comm, but Esper leaned past and put a hand over it. "Hand over their thingy, the one we were supposed to deliver."

"If I'd have known it was them, I never would have taken the job."

Esper raised her voice. "That doesn't matter. Give it back and bargain for them to fix up Mriy."

Tanny pulled her hand away. "It's a nice thought, but we can't trust them."

"I thought Captain Carl Ramsey could talk his way out of anything. Huh?"

He met her glare, and she must have seen something there, because the bluster drained from her in an instant. Not taking his eyes off hers, Carl reached out and powered down the engines. "Yeah. I can."

---

They always underestimated her hearing. Days spent planetside had sensitized Mriy to the various noises on the ship. Before the hunt, her ears had learned to ignore the droning of the holovid, arguments in the common room, and Mort's snoring. It was the key to staying sane in close quarters aboard ship. But hunting brought back that sharpness of ear that listened for cracking of twigs and the sudden change in birdsong that signaled a predator's presence. Even through the door of her quarters, she could strain and make out every word of the argument in the cockpit. God's favorite niece was going to convince Carl to surrender so that Harmony Bay could treat Mriy's wounds.

The wonderful thing about every part of Mriy's body hurting was that nothing she did could make her feel worse. Pains would shift and vie for attention, but overall the effect was the same. With a grunt of effort, she sat up. From there it was easy. A few shuffling steps to the door. A ginger grasp to turn the handle. A shoulder to shove it open.

Mort stood waiting in the common room, staff in hand. "Egads! Are you delirious? Get back to bed. You're in no condition to—"

"Must. Stop. Carl."

Mort played the old fool much of the time, but he was not. Instead of arguing with her, he offered his shoulder and helped Mriy's faltering footsteps up to the cockpit.

The argument over whether to surrender continued as they approached. The hum of engines died away. "Yeah, I can," Carl said with typical smugness. He thought himself without peer. He thought he could lie away any trouble.

Had Mriy not been just like him with similar blind faith in her prowess? "Don't. Not worth... it." Speaking with missing teeth, she sounded like a child. She wiped at her mouth and found blood on the back of her hand.

"Good heavens! Mriy, what are you doing up?"

Mriy shrugged aside Esper's attention and put her face close to Carl's. "No."

To his credit, Carl didn't shy or look away, not even when Mriy parted her lips to let him see the bloody wreck left from the rebels' handiwork. "You sure about this? These bastards have the tech to fix you... real teeth, real claws, good-as-new fixed."

There was a nagging temptation. A good half of Carl's schemes worked out. He might be able to convince them to patch her up, to let them all go unharmed—though probably without payment. From the bits and pieces, she had gathered there was something Carl owed them, but that wasn't the point. The question was whether she could ask them to stand in the line of fire for her... again. "Not. Worth. Don't trust."

Tanny cleared her throat. "Well, that's just peachy, but we're still caught in their tractor beam."

"Esper, get Mriy back to bed. Mort, think you can disrupt that tractor beam without killing off half the ship's systems?"

"No, but I may be able to do one better. Let them drag us close." Mort pushed past Esper and Mriy, staff tapping along the ground as he strode back to the common room.

Carl called after him. "I hope you know what you're doing!"

"Of course he does," Esper muttered, so softly that she probably didn't expect even Mriy to have heard her.

Mort began his chanting. Whatever language he used, the earring that translated every other language in the galaxy threw its hands up in despair. The light changed in the common room. Though it took a great effort to crane her neck, Mriy peered up through the domed ceiling to watch astral gray replace the black and stars of realspace. The sight had never failed to unnerve her, but this time she was too weary to care.

The *Bradbury* was oriented so that it was visible through the canopy. Even as the *Mobius* sank into the astral, it never wavered. It couldn't have been more than a hundred meters away.

Carl shouted from the cockpit. "Mort, you daft old shit! You're bringing them with us! This isn't how escapes work!"

Trusting that Esper would mind her footing for her, Mriy kept watch on the sky. The gray deepened and darkened. It took on an aspect of violet. All the while, the *Bradbury* remained fixed in place, towed along with Mort's magic.

*From the cockpit, the comm blared. "Vessel Mobius, I don't know how you're doing this, but you have thirty seconds to return us to realspace or we will open fire, cargo or no cargo."*

Mort gave a wave at the ship on the other side of the glassteel dome, and the tone of his chanting shifted. The purplish tinge of astral space faded to the accustomed gray, and this time, the *Bradbury* faded from view, no longer following in their wake.

Cupping a hand to his mouth, the wizard shouted to the cockpit. "All clear. Let's see their star-drive gizmo dig them out of *that* mess!"

As Mriy let Esper settle her back into bed, she could hear Carl and Tanny arguing over the course to plot that would put them farthest from Harmony Bay's influence. Or the nearest medical facility. Or someplace remote. Or a place with xeno-cosmetic facilities. Mriy let her head sink into the pillow and closed her eyes. Not everything hurt. Her heart was at peace. She was home.

Mriy looked at herself in the mirror. Everything in her mouth was sore, and the taste was strange. She opened wide and inspected the ceramite implants, trying to remember what her natural teeth had looked like. If there was a difference, she couldn't tell. The cosmo-surgeon had done his job.

She flexed the claws of her left hand, wincing as the sheaths flexed around tender tissue. Her false claws were a silvery black, made of a material she couldn't pronounce in English. They were sharper than her old ones, and would need to be replaced every few years, depending how roughly she treated them. It would be days yet before she was willing to try them on anything tough like fresh meat. It was strange to think that there were parts of her that were no longer her own.

A tentative knock at her door meant that Esper had come to check on her again. "Enter," Mriy said, wincing in anticipation of a pain that didn't come as she spoke. It was a promising sign.

Esper opened the door and smiled. "You're looking much better this morning."

"I am feeling better. But the answer is still 'no.'"

"You'd feel ship shape after a big meal," Esper countered. It was a sweet gesture. While useless to the point of infuriating in the wild, Esper was of great use elsewhere. Simple kindness was something Mriy had taken to underestimating.

She sat down on the bed and gestured for Esper to join her. The human joined her, sitting a meter away. Being shirtless was taboo among human women, but not at all so for azrin. She slid over and wrapped her arms around Esper, who stiffened for a moment before relaxing. "You have been a better friend than I deserve. Young as you seem at times, you are my elder, and wise in ways I don't see easily. My wounds pain me, and I know you could ease them. But I will recover, and my recovery will reinforce the many lessons I've learned since the hunt. I have no mother who wants me. My clan is foreign to me now. But I have two sisters and three brothers instead—and a dog, I suppose."

Esper tried to put her arms around Mriy but could not come close to reaching. She stopped trying and settled for being held, leaning against Mriy's chest. "I've thought about going home, too. I don't think it would go well. For better or worse, this is my home now. You all are my family."

"I only wish I could have seen Neep while I was there," Mriy said softly. She winced and her ears twitched. That was something she hadn't meant to mention.

"Who is Neep?" Esper asked.

Mriy swallowed. Esper was family; she would understand. "He was my pet. I was two when I named him; Neep is a childish name."

"What kind of pet?" Esper prodded. There was a sweetness in her question; humans had such weaknesses for pets. It explained much of what Kubu got away with, despite being able to speak and understand.

Mriy sighed. "A hyoba—a tiny hominid. They... they look like little humans, just knee high. Neep is the noise they make, like a dog's bark. I don't mean anything by having one. I know they're illegal, but I was only—"

Esper laughed and pulled herself from Mriy's embrace. "That sounds adorable."

---

Captain Carl Ramsey slumped down onto his bed and leaned back against the wall. With datapad in hand, he got back to a little side project he had started working on. It was time to update the notes for his eventual memoir.

*We cleared out of Meyang before those shits from Harmony Bay found their way out of astral. I never imagined that the ship I ratted out to ARGO would be one of theirs. I get plenty of shit around here for bad plans that we pull off anyway, but this was a damn fine plan if I do say so... we just got unlucky.*

*Mriy was in bad shape, but she's tougher than composite steel. We needed to get her to a medical facility, someplace where we wouldn't worry about Harmony Bay grabbing us. Normally we stick to the edges of society—the borderlands, the systems just outside ARGO space, the little pockets of savage space without inhabited systems. Even Meyang was uptown for us. But Roddy figured that with our scraped-clean records, we could afford a trip to Phabian and found a doctor on one of the outer worlds that was willing to work for cheap on an azrin. I hope we never have to tell Mriy that he was a veterinary specialist. Since we blew our stolen take from the delivery for the weasel, she shouldn't be asking too many nosy questions about how we pulled it off.*

*I'm thinking that it's time we lay high for a bit, since lying low's gotten us in so much trouble lately. We can take our respectability and see how far we can push it before we piss someone off.*

*Mort's beside himself with glee that Esper managed to summon fire while she was out hunting with Mriy. I guess it goes to show that wizards get what they want. I just hope she never finds out who was in that confessional. Maybe I can hold that over him to get him to finally turn my hair back to its original color. I just hate to think what he'll come back with if I start fighting dirty.*

*Kubu's going to be a problem, sooner or later. He's behaving better, but he's going to bankrupt us on food alone. Not to mention the fact that he's putting on ten kilos a week and it's all going into muscle and bone. There isn't a flabby bit of that mutt. In a month, he's going to be bigger than Mriy, and in three I'm wondering how he's going to fit through doors. I think "Mommy" is going to have to make a hard choice soon about his future.*

*I've still got my suspicions about how this whole business started. It was so seat-of-the-pants at the time that none of us had a chance to pick it apart and see if the pieces fit. Damn convenient that Mriy had someone point her to a relative in need of rescue, one who just happened to be the perfect key to unlock her old life if it had played out like she expected. She never said who tipped her off. I wouldn't be half surprised if it was Mriy who hired that bounty hunter in the first place. I'd never be able to prove it, but if she did, she's been learning something around here.*

Carl paused and reread the last few paragraphs. With a frown, he scanned back and reread a few previous entries. Dreams of publishing his life's story someday and living off the holovid deal evaporated before his eyes.

"If anyone reads this, I'm a dead man," he muttered to himself, then deleted the file.

# GUARDIAN OF THE PLUNDERED TOMES

## MISSION 4.5 OF THE BLACK OCEAN SERIES (BONUS SHORT STORY)

## GUARDIAN OF THE PLUNDERED TOMES

Eleven wizards bore down the weight of their ancient eyes upon the twelfth of their number. Mordecai The Brown swept his gaze around the vast table's circumference, seeking pity or sympathy in any of his fellows. He found nothing but scorn. The air hung heavy and still in the Convocation's Grand Council Chamber, the echoic reaches of the vaulted stone ceiling finding no sound worth magnifying or repeating. Sunlight poured through stained glass windows depicting Merlin bestowing Excalibur upon Arthur, St. George slaying the last dragon on Earth, and the sinking of Atlantis. The beams caught motes of dust in their trails and made time flow like cold honey. Everyone waited for him.

"I can offer no explanation," Mordecai replied. He sat with his arms resting on the table's timeworn stone surface, hands tucked within opposing sleeves, wet with perspiration. There was no wizard among them who was his junior, but he was not the least of their number. He held his chin high and fought to keep his breathing steady.

"Do you dispute the library census?" Bertram Hancock,

the holder of the First Chair, asked, shaking a leather-bound ledger. It had a listing of every book in the Convocation's libraries, from the memoirs of long-dead wizards to mundane works of history and mathematics. It also contained listings of the books known as the Plundered Tomes, volumes confiscated from wizards who once opposed the Convocation. A few were harmless, but most were forbidden to even open, for the dark magics described therein contained the roots of the malevolence that had spawned those ancient enemies.

One of those tomes was missing.

As Guardian of the Plundered Tomes, responsibility fell to Mordecai. "I've verified it myself. The census seems to be correct."

"No one gets in or out of the vault without your knowledge," said Pao Wenling, the holder of the Third Seat and Inquisitor of the Convocation. Her statement had the vague sense of a question lingering about its edges, but stung as an accusation.

"I had always presumed so," Mordecai said, "but I admit the possibility that someone has."

"You're couching your words carefully, Mordecai," Bertram said, tapping the fingertips of one hand on the census ledger. It wasn't as if Mordecai was going to forget that it was there.

"Too carefully, perhaps," Wenling agreed. The rest of the wizards looked on, mere spectators. They were there to witness, to add gravitas... possibly to lend aid in overpowering Mordecai if things turned impolite.

He searched for a sign that anyone disagreed with Wenling's assessment. In the Fourth Chair, Ronald Sternenlicht wouldn't meet his eye. In the Sixth Chair, his cousin Ezekiel knit his brow and tried to make Mordecai look elsewhere. Diane Smythe, in the Eleventh Chair, spared him the twitch of a smile, and that was the best he was going to get.

"So what is it, then?" Mordecai snapped. "Vague accusations? Discrepant reports? A bloody book is missing, and we all know it. What are you more interested in, having someone's eyes out for reading a forbidden tome, burning me at the stake for letting him, or finding the damned thing and getting it back?"

In the silence that followed, Mordecai began to worry that perhaps retrieval of the book was *not* their highest priority. Options swirled in his mind, contingencies for avoiding a stake-burning that would only be figurative in the sense that outdoor human barbecues were illegal on Earth. Wenling and Bertram exchanged a look across the table. Mordecai held his next breath, wondering how many more like it were left in *him*.

"Very well," Bertram said. "As the guardian responsible, I charge you with finding and returning the book, and dealing with the perpetrator of the theft. You have three days. Come sunset Friday, we will have either the book or your resignation."

"Thank you," Mordecai said. "Three days will be plenty." Plenty of time to get away.

"I will conduct my own investigation as well," Wenling said. She graced Mordecai with a smile that said she was trying to help, but the look in her eyes made him suspect she would be investigating him.

"Well, then," Bertram said. "There is much to be done. I see no reason to detain either of you. Council is adjourned."

The air outside Convocation Hall was crisp and fresh with the scent of autumn leaves. Boston Prime was one of the few urban areas left on Earth with tree-lined parks, thanks to the wizards who paid exorbitant taxes for land with nothing but dirt and flora. Mordecai savored the walk back to the churning bustle of the surrounding city.

Nancy was waiting for him on a bench, watching the sunset over the cityscape. She turned at the sound of his footsteps. "Hey there, handsome," she called out as he approached. She was dressed for the weather in a baggy wool sweater and her hair pulled up under a matching knit hat.

Mordecai reached down and offered his hand to help her up, and she kissed him as he pulled her close. "Let's get out of here," he said.

"Ooh, that doesn't sound good," Nancy said, falling into step beside Mordecai and taking three steps for every two of his. "I'd hoped you'd clear everything up in there."

"Didn't shake out like that," he replied. "They gave me three days. I've got to find the book and bring it back by Monday night."

"Oh," Nancy replied. Then after a moment's pause, "I guess you'll have your hands full this evening."

Mordecai could read her like a written page. "What'd you have planned?"

"The kids are staying with your parents for the weekend. I got us tickets to a show... it was a birthday surprise."

Mordecai snorted. "It's not my birthday. But you knew that."

Nancy's smile cut through the knot of worry binding his guts. "I can't surprise you *on* your birthday anymore. You get all defensive and paranoid, and I wanted a real surprise this year. But now..."

"Aw, hell," Mordecai said, kicking a twig off the flagstone path. "The damn book can wait. Where we going?"

"You sure, Mort?"

"Absolutely." Since his investigation was going to be a farce, losing time wasn't a concern. "Anything to clear my head. Just... well, it's not some singing show, is it?"

She laughed. "Yes, Mort. I'm dragging you to the opera. I always torment you for your birthday, don't I?" When he raised an eyebrow in mock alarm, she relented. "It's a comedy show, as hokey and old fashioned as I could find."

"More like it..." he muttered.

They passed under a wrought iron archway that allowed passage through the ivy-laden red brick wall surrounding the Convocation grounds. Beyond the reach of the subtle magic that kept the peace and solitude of the wizards undisturbed, the modern world rushed in. The air swarmed with the repulsor lights of uncountable cars, freighters, and patrol ships. Luna was visible in the sky above, the blue-green surface of Earth's only moon half full.

At the sidewalk's edge, a line of taxis bobbed, waiting for passengers. Mort picked one at random and opened the door for Nancy.

"Good evening," the driver said. "Fifty terra, anywhere in the city. One hundred for the region. Five for anywhere planetside. I don't do off-Earth. Where are we heading tonight?" The spiel was well rehearsed and fluid, with no polite point for a passenger to break in with a question.

Mordecai looked to Nancy, since he had no idea where they were going. "Orpheum Theater," she said to the driver. "See? Oldest theater in Boston Prime. Plus we don't even cross an ocean tonight." For a notorious homebody like Mordecai, being stuck in a science-powered vessel for half an hour or more always fouled his mood.

"Excellent, ma'am," the driver said. "Fifty terra, digital or hard coin?"

Mordecai held up the palm of one hand and a symbol appeared between his outstretched fingers, the stroke of lightning crashing through the letter C. The symbol of the Convocation. "Convocation's tab," he said gravely. It always helped to keep a serious tone when acting the part of a wizard, lest regular folk get the impression that wizards were people just like them.

The driver straightened in his seat, his easy friendliness turned formal in an instant. "Yes, sir!"

Mordecai and Nancy tucked their hands into opposing sleeves and settled in for the ride. It was a gesture, more than anything—reassurance to the driver that they would work no magic. Few wizards were foolish enough to try spells while aboard a moving vehicle, but it never hurt to show good faith and good manners.

---

The Orpheum Theater had a pleasant weight of age. It was almost seven hundred years old, and Mordecai imagined that he could feel the ghosts of performers long dead watching over the place. It had been refurbished a number of times, but always with an eye toward preservation rather than modernization. A wizard's critical eye could pick up a holoprojector here, or a security scanner there, but looking past those, it was easy to let the mind drift back to a simpler era. The seats were upholstered patterned cotton, the curtains red velvet. The ionic columns were a throwback to ancient Greek times even when the place was new, and the vaulted ceiling hearkened to Renaissance architecture.

Nancy caught him gawking. "You like it?"

"How is it that you've never taken me here?"

"You're the most curmudgeonly thirty-two-year-old anyone's ever been," she replied. "If I'd have known old theaters would pique your interest, I'd have tried them years ago."

Mordecai said nothing in reply. He wanted to tell her that she could take him wherever she liked. That anywhere would be fine. That she was all he needed to be happy wherever he was. But he didn't trust himself. He risked ruining the night if he let slip how desperate he was. There were three days, and Convocation be damned, he was going to milk them for all their worth.

Their seats were mezzanine level, front and center, looking down at the stage from so close that he could loft a paper starship down at the performers. As the audience filled the theater, ambient music rose from unseen sources. "What's this?" Mort asked, unfamiliar with the tunes.

Nancy pressed a program into his hands. "It's a twentieth-century themed show. The music is period. To set a mood, I imagine." It was twangy and fuzzy, with a pronounced rhythm and up-tempo beat. There were lyrics, but Mordecai would be damned if he could tell what language they were. It *sounded* Earth-like. After a moment's devoted listening, he picked out a word here or there and realized that the whole bloody thing was sung in English, but with the most horrid enunciation imagined.

As the crowd packed in around him, Mordecai grew tense. Something felt wrong, but he couldn't place it. Nancy put a hand on his knee. "What's eating you? Did that hearing go worse than you're letting on?"

"Yes," Mordecai murmured. "Much. Someone's following us. I can't place them, but feel the air. Someone's steadying the room, down in the lower seats." It would have been a hard concept to explain to a non-wizard, but Nancy's arcane powers were nearly as strong as his. A wizard not working magic kept an area of the universe stable around himself. The laws of physics did not bend so easily when someone else believed strongly in the status quo. A subtle mind could sniff out when such supernatural stability was in play.

"Mort..." Nancy said. "Why are you being followed?" Damn. He had let too much slip.

He patted her hand where it rested on his knee. "Nothing that will spoil a show," he assured her.

When the show began, headlining comedian Chuck Ramsey came onto the stage, smiling and waving, an old-fashioned handheld microphone clutched in one hand. "Good evening, everyone! Great to be back on Earth. It's been so long, I feel like a xeno on my own planet. Did you folks evolve while I was gone? Everyone seems to have more hair than me. I've been touring the borderlands, and let me tell you, the food is nothing like what we get here on Earth. I mean, where else can you get a snyth-meat hamburger with chemically simulated cheese and bacon, soy byproduct fries, *and* medical treatment for it the same night...?" The audience laughed, and Mordecai chuckled along with them. The comedian was making fun of modern Earth. It was stupid, childish humor, and it was funny.

Chuck Ramsey introduced several other comedians for short bits, then put on an hour-long show himself. Topics ranged all over the spectrum. Why couldn't Earth stop itself from invading smaller planets? Poor service on interstellar transports. Child-rearing tips and the best threats to use on children, as learned from his father. Seven words that you couldn't say on Mars. How Luna was terraformed just to get all the lunatics to move there. He even went back to his burger joke from earlier and expounded on how the iconic meal differed throughout Earth-controlled space.

Mordecai couldn't get enough. It was low-science, low-complexity humor filled with an overriding folksy wisdom that felt timeless. He laughed along with Nancy, and thanked his lucky stars that he had a wife who understood him. It took his mind off his troubles, at least for a little while. After Chuck Ramsey took his bows and the spotlight disappeared, house lights came up. It was just an historic building in the theater district of Boston Prime again. Mordecai stood and let out a long, wistful breath that carried that momentary sense of wonderment along with it.

"You seemed to enjoy yourself," Nancy said. "See what happens when you leave the house to go someplace besides work?"

Mordecai nodded. "I needed that. How would you fancy a walk home? It can't be more than a couple miles."

"Actually, I've got one more surprise for you," Nancy replied. "But I wanted to see how you liked the show first. I got us backstage clearance."

Mordecai raised an eyebrow. "You know, I wouldn't half mind meeting that Ramsey fellow."

---

The dressing room for the comedy show wasn't quite what Mordecai had envisioned. He had assumed it would be a bustle of production assistants and comedians half changed between stage attire and what they wore about town. What he hadn't anticipated was a childcare center. The comedians were in the anticipated state of dishabille, but the rest was a mass of yowling children and the wives and husbands trying to wrangle them.

"You must be the Browns," Chuck Ramsey greeted them, sticking a hand out for Mort to shake. He had removed his suit coat and tie, and his brow glistened with sweat from standing under the house lights for an hour. "Wizards, I hear. I always wondered what sort of nutter paid extra to meet me. Guess now I know."

Mordecai couldn't take offense with Chuck's rough assessment. In truth, he had always found that he and his fellow wizards *were* proper nutters. "I'm Mordecai, but anyone without a stick up his ass calls me Mort. This is my wife, Nancy."

"Pleased to meet you," Chuck said. He twisted around and checked over his shoulder in the dressing room mirror. "Mort." He winked at Nancy, who giggled. Mordecai couldn't even fault the man's flirtation—he was a showman, after all. It came with the territory. "This is my wife, Becky. My two youngest, Mike and Rhiannon. My oldest is around here somewhere, too."

"Hi!" a voice caught Mordecai's attention from behind. "My name's Bradley Carlin Ramsey. Pleased to meet you, Mort." The boy was eleven, possibly twelve years old, with an unruly mop of hair and bright green eyes that look like they were aimed at something. Most children had eyes that wandered—even his own were prone to inattention—and few gave a thought to looking square at an adult. The boy stuck a hand out in imitation of his father. The young Ramsey gritted his teeth as he squeezed, but it was a boy's handshake, however much he tried.

Mordecai gave the boy a fearsome mock scowl. "Shouldn't that be *Mr.* Brown?"

The boy shook his head. "I don't have a stick up my..." The boy glanced to his mother, whose face bore a more threatening scowl. "...bum."

Mordecai tousled the boy's hair and turned his attention back to the father. "So, what gets a man into comedy?" Mordecai asked. He eyed the backstage setup critically. "Doesn't look like it's a path to riches."

"Mort!" Nancy exclaimed.

Chuck laughed. "Don't worry, Nancy. Gotta have a thick skin in this business. Besides, Mort's right. It keeps fuel in the engines and food on the table. All you need really. I get to set my own hours and captain my own ship... see the galaxy on my own terms. You can join the navy and see the before-and-after from a bomber's window, but I like my way better. Plus, I can have my family along."

"You own your own ship?" Mordecai asked. His opinion of the man rose. "Must make things easier for your line of work."

"Can't break even these days paying other people to fly you around planet to planet, gig to gig," Chuck replied. "Just not enough money in it. Worst I gotta pay now is fuel costs and star-drive repairs. Damn things break down every five drops or so."

"Magic and science shouldn't mix," Mordecai replied. "Those things are fundamentally flawed. Constantly at odds. There's a whole legion of drooling half-wizards employed in fixing them. That ought to tell folks all they need to know."

"Mort, don't go on one of your tirades," Nancy scolded him.

Chuck waved a lazy hand. "Naw, let him go. Comedians are the philosophers of their time. Meeting people from all walks of life and getting snips of the galaxy through their eyes, that's what it's all about. Maybe one day I'll do a star-drive mechanic bit."

"You're... going to make a comedy skit based on me? On what I just said?" Mordecai asked. He turned to Nancy. "We didn't agree to any of that, did we?"

"Woah, woah, big guy," Chuck said, holding up his hands. He grabbed a bottle from the dressing room table and popped it open. "You don't want to be in a joke, fine. Can I interest you in a bottle of Chateau Noir, '40?"

Mordecai eyed the bottle. "I assume that's this year's vintage and not some number of hundreds of years old."

Chuck grinned. "Stuff's not even old enough to walk."

"Got any beer?" Mordecai asked.

"I'll have glass," Nancy replied politely.

"Becky, we got anything like a glass?" Chuck asked over his shoulder.

"Spill-proofs for Rhiannon," Becky suggested.

Chuck dug into a cooler and tossed Mordecai an Earth's Preferred, the cheapest dishwater suds the planet exported.

"I didn't even know they sold this stuff on Earth," Mordecai said.

"They don't, far as I know," Chuck replied. "We always pick up extra when we're heading for Earth." He took a second can for himself.

"This is lovely," Nancy said, sipping newborn wine from a bright red plastic cup with a molded-in straw. She forced a smile.

Chuck shrugged. "Nothin's fancy in this life," Chuck said. "But I wouldn't trade it for the world. I scrape by, raise my own kids, and don't have anyone looking over my shoulder all the time."

"You have quite the interesting life," Nancy said, and Mordecai knew she was saying it just to be nice. For all the rough edges though, Mordecai could see the appeal.

---

Morning had neither crept up, nor sprung upon him, but Mordecai was awake before the dawn. Nancy still clung to her slumber, wrung out to exhaustion the night before by their invigorating walk home in the small hours and the lovemaking that followed. The house was quiet with the children away at their grandparents'. Too quiet. This wasn't how he wanted to remember it. He wanted to bump into Cedric's blocks levitating in the hall, or catch Cassandra trying to curdle the milk in his cereal without him noticing.

"What's wrong, grumpyface?" Nancy mumbled half into her pillow. She had one heavy-lidded eye focused on him.

It was time. The darkened hours alone with his thoughts had assembled the disparate pieces of a plan that had floated within the twisted halls of his mind. He had to tell Nancy. "I have to go," he said.

"Go where? It's Saturday, Mort," Nancy replied. "Sleep in."

"I'm not going to find that book," Mordecai replied. "Neither is Wenling."

"Hmm?"

He threw off the blankets and stood. Warmth from the magically heated oak floor seeped into his cold feet, soothing them as he walked to the bureau. "Last night was wonderful, but I can't afford to lose more time. Those three days were a reprieve, a farewell."

"Mort, you're scaring me," Nancy said, sitting up in bed and pulling the blanket to cover herself.

"I'm sorry," Mordecai replied. "But you might need to be, at least for a little while. But be scared for me, not yourself. After I've left, go stay with my parents until things cool down. My father won't let anything happen to you or the kids. You're innocent in all of this."

"You lost a book," Nancy said. "Even if it never gets found, what's the worst they're going to do, make you resign? You're over—"

"It was *me*," Mordecai snapped. "Everyone who's ever held my post sticks their nose in the forbidden texts once in a while. It's no big deal. Builds character, resisting those nasty old words left by dead wizards of old. But this one got to me. I read every word of it, and it still haunts me. I *burned it.*"

"You didn't..."

"I've covered my tracks. Fudged a few records. I thought I might get past the book census, but those buggers under Kramer were thorough. I don't know how long I have before the Convocation figures it out, but if I'm here when they do, I'm done for." Mordecai stuffed garment after garment into a knapsack, long after it should have been stuffed to overflowing.

"This is crazy, Mort. Go see your father. There's no need for this to get blown out of proportion."

"My father?" Mordecai scoffed. "The great Alastair The Brown, defend a book-burner? Only three copies of that book ever existed, and the other two are lost. I've destroyed priceless history, and the only thing that might stop them reducing me to cinders is the fact that it carved its wicked words into my mind. I might be the last copy out there."

"What book was this, anyway?"

"I won't speak its title aloud. The less you know, the better." Mordecai scanned along his bookshelves, picking out a selection to shove into the pack with the rest of his travel supplies.

"So you're going to run away?" Nancy demanded, letting go of the blanket and folding her arms. "Abandon me and the children? Think this through, Mordecai The Brown."

"I have," Mordecai replied. "I was up all last night and for weeks since the census was announced. I've wondered what I'd do ever since I put that book to the flame. You had no part in this. You and the children will live with the shame of what I've done, and I'm sorry for that. But life will go on."

"And what am I supposed to tell Cedric and Cassie?" she asked. "That their father is a criminal on the run? How will they face up to their mistakes if *you* don't?"

"Well, if anyone is ever after them to carve the eyes out of their skull to see what they've seen, I won't hold it against them if they tuck tail and run," Mordecai replied. He took his best staff made from ancient oak—from the days when Earthwood was still legal—and packed it away, along with his pendant of office.

"Good god, Mort. Really?"

"If I'm lucky, they wouldn't kill me in the process," Mordecai replied. He snorted. "Lucky..."

"But where will you go?" Nancy asked.

"If I told you, you'd only have to worry about letting it slip. There'll be hell enough to pay when you don't run straight to Bertram and tell him everything I've just said to you, but *that* I think my father can protect you from."

"How long will you be on the run?"

"I'll look for another copy of the tome," Mordecai said. It

was a lie, but one Nancy needed to hear. He could have written the book from memory if he chose, but there was no way he could bring himself to recreate it. No, if he were to look for the other two copies, it would be to burn them as well. "If I can replace it, maybe I can gain a reprieve. Or maybe Bertram's successor won't be such a hard-ass, and I can get clemency. Until then though? I'll keep moving."

---

Nancy stood at the doorway as Mordecai crept into Cassandra's room. The soft glow of conjured fireflies kept the worst of the darkness at bay. She had been afraid of the dark once, and Mordecai had created them to make her feel safe. There had been hundreds at first, but night by night, Mordecai had reduced the fireflies in number until only a handful remained and Cassandra no longer feared the night. For her last birthday, she had asked for them back because they were pretty. As Mordecai navigated an obstacle course of scattered toys, he was thankful that he had obliged her.

He hadn't known Nancy at that age—they had met while both attended Oxford—but he had seen old pictures of her, and Cassandra was her time-lost twin, separated by a mere twenty-four years. His daughter slept heavily, worn ragged by a day spent horseback riding with her cousins. Touseled hair lay splayed across her pillow. A bruise darkened one cheek where Cedric had struck her with one of his alphabet blocks. Mordecai smiled—the simple, innocent dangers of childhood.

Without a word, he bent over the sleeping Cassandra and brushed the hair from her face. She stirred and rolled onto her side, but didn't wake. Mordecai planted a gentle kiss on her forehead. He whispered, too softly for Nancy to hear him from the doorway. "My little angel. Mommy's going to need you to be strong and brave. Just remember I love you, and want nothing more than for you to be happy and safe."

He kissed her once again, and added a kiss for Nancy on his way out the door. By the light of the fireflies, he could see the wet streaks down her cheeks.

Cedric's room was simpler, kept tidy by the nanny. An arcane orb lit overhead at a gesture from Mordecai. The boy had outgrown his crib, but still slept in a tiny bed, low to the floor. Mordecai knelt beside his son's sleeping form. The blankets were thrown aside, and the sheets tangled themselves around Cedric's legs; even in sleep the active lad couldn't keep still for long. Family stories said that Mordecai had been the same way at that age.

Same as he had done with Cassandra, Mordecai kissed Cedric on the forehead. But he was no sleeping dragon like his sister; he was a watchdog. In an instant, Cedric's eyes were open. "What is it, Daddy?"

Mordecai swallowed past the lump in his throat. "I have to go away for a while, Ceddie. You'll have to be the man of the house while I'm gone."

Cedric rubbed one eye with his fist. "When are you coming back?"

"Not for a long time," Mordecai said. "But every time you ask how long, or even think to wonder, I'll be gone a little longer. Can you hold your tongue and still your thoughts about something you can't change?" It was a horrible thing to ask of a four-year-old. But Nancy would go mad with worry if persistent little Cedric badgered her about him.

"Yes, Daddy," Cedric replied. Despite the yawn in his voice, and despite his tender age, Mordecai knew he would remember. Cedric was brighter than fire, even laying aside fatherly bias.

"Good boy," Mort said, stroking his head. "Now go back to sleep. Tomorrow is a big day."

Cedric smiled sleepily. "Every day is a big day." Mordecai had taught him that one. But this time it was more true than usual. Tomorrow would be the day that Cedric lost his father. There was never any guarantee that a big day was a good one. It hurt in the pit of his stomach to know what was coming for the boy.

As soon as the door shut, Nancy collapsed against his chest, sobbing quietly. Mordecai just held her there, waiting. There were words brewing, he could tell. Best to let them steep until they were ready.

"Stay," Nancy said, her voice trembling.

"I wish I—"

"You can," she said. From within his embrace, she looked into his eyes, craning her neck as he towered over her. "You can beat this. You've got friends, connections. It'll be ugly, but—"

"No," Mordecai said. "I have nothing... nothing but a family I need to keep safe from this business. Those friends, those political allies of convenience? The wind has changed, and their sails are already set for it. Lie to the children, or trust them with the truth. You'll can judge which will be better for them, and I've got no right to a say. Just... never let them forget that I love them."

How long the stayed in each other's arms, Mordecai couldn't say. Forever would have been too little time. And then it was time for him to disappear.

On the streets of Boston Prime lurked no fewer than eight Mordecais. None of them would notice it, of course, but everyone who saw them perceived them as a tall, scrawny wizard with a baggy-sleeved shirt and a pack slung over one shoulder. Only someone as talented as Mordecai would be able to tell which was which without resorting to vulgar displays of revelatory magic. Every time he found himself at a crossroads or crowded terminal, he found a likely candidate heading in another direction and deputized them as a new doppelganger. Yet every time he sent another false Mordecai to muddle his path, he was still left with the pervasive feeling of being followed.

If he could not buy himself a moment's peace from whoever was pursuing him, his plan might fall dead at his feet. Mordecai tried something more creative. He stopped at a shuttle terminal—nothing fancy, just a simple intra-hemispheric depot. Giving a paranoid look over his shoulder, he ducked into the mens' washroom. In the privacy of his stall, he paused to collect his thoughts, counting to one hundred with a slow, even cadence in his head. He emerged and washed his hands, studying a gentleman at the sink beside him—tall, wide shoulders, with a gray suit and matching hair, receding from the brow. The man carried a business attaché case.

When Mordecai left that washroom, he was the one with the grey suit and hair, his knapsack transformed to appear as an attaché case. The false Mordecai who followed him out sported a beard and glasses that Mordecai lacked, and wore different clothing, but in all other ways look just like him, right down to the case that appeared as a knapsack, dangling casually from his hand.

Mordecai never discovered his pursuer. He stood by a

departure and arrival board and watched as his body double boarded a flight to London Prime. By the time the shuttle to London lifted off, the sensation of a wizard concealed in close proximity vanished. It had to have been one of Wenling's lackeys, he had assumed initially. But the more he thought about it, he wondered if it had been Pao Wenling herself following him. It certainly would have explained his inability to pinpoint his pursuer. As he watched the shuttle disappear into the distance, he raised a finger to his temple in a quiet salute.

Free from his tail, Mordecai made for the theater district, resuming his own form. At the Orpheum, he slipped past two magic-befuddled doormen and made his way backstage. "Where can I find Chuck Ramsey?" Mordecai asked a flunky who stood with datapad in hand, updating the flatvid boards that showed what was playing at the theater.

"That lot's shipping off-world," the flunky replied. "Try Logan Starport. His ship is the *Radiocity*." The lad pronounced it like some sort of chemical process, but being a wizard, Mordecai's mind parsed things differently. He instantly saw a likely spelling in his head, pulled it apart, and reattached it as *Radio City*, a New York Prime theater just as famous as the Orpheum. Ramsey had a consistent style; he'd give him that much.

Mordecai reached into a pocket and grabbed a ten-terra coin. He muttered a few words over it and tossed it to the flunky. "I was never here," he said, as the coin was in mid-air. By the time the lad caught hold of that coin, he had no inkling of having met Mordecai The Brown. For all that theater worker knew, he had found the coin along the back alleyway.

Logan Starport was the hub of Boston Prime, despite being located on the waterfront. Mordecai hopped into the first taxi he found and paid hardcoin to get there. He wasn't about to risk using his Convocation tab for anything... perhaps ever again. As the city blurred by, Mordecai fought the impulse to hide his hands in his sleeves. He went so far as to roll them up to the elbow to hide the wide, conspicuous openings.

At the starport, Mordecai was whisked into a world rife with science. Holovid advertisements, security-scan checkpoints, self-propelled luggage transports, and voice-interactive information kiosks. He held his breath as he passed by the worst of the scientific devices, keeping even his most casual uses of magic at bay lest he set one of them malfunctioning and draw attention to himself. Finding a lone starship in the jumble of humanity and blaring holovids was more daunting than he expected. For a moment, he considered striking up a conversation with one of the kiosks, but he had never spoken with a machine before. Would one even talk to a wizard? He hated them; would they hate him right back?

Security cameras throughout the starport would be recording him every step of his search, but one magic that he would not relinquish was the one that kept his features indistinct to science. No techno-gadget was going to do better than a finger-painted picture of Mordecai while he was in the starport. Humans were another matter. A lone traveler might not attract attention, but one who asked for directions might stick in someone's mind. Wiping memories was a simple enough task in an empty theater, but there were wards against those sorts of magic in high-security areas.

Mordecai's eyes widened. There was a group of laaku passing by, wearing uniforms for Phabian Starways, the major interstellar passenger service of their homeworld. The laaku were chimp-like, resembling those distant ancestors more closely than humans mirrored the great apes from which they diverged in pre-historic times. Shorter, quadridexterous, and covered in short fur, they were the only xeno-species allowed to freely roam Earth. Despite being humanity's closest ally and a founding member of the Allied Races of the Galactic Ocean, there was a common perception that all laaku looked alike. Among laaku, that perception was inverted, and they found all humans more or less identical. Mordecai could use that.

"Excuse me, sir?" Mordecai asked one of them. The laaku stopped and craned his neck up at a human twice his height. He wore a name badge that identified him as Korvin, with some laaku script beneath that likely said the same thing.

"Can I help you?" Korvin replied in English with just the barest hint of a laaku accent. Master collaborators, the laaku had largely embraced Earth culture, and many spoke English better than their native tongue. It was a survival technique that had made them prosperous where other species saw their worlds bombarded from orbit and occupied.

Mordecai smiled. "This is my first time in a starport, and I'm lost. Can you show me where I can find the *Radiocity*?"

Korvin exchanged an amused glance with one of his co-workers and took Mordecai to a holovid map, buzzing though a rapid-fire explanation that ended with a simple instruction on which way to go. Had Mordecai been able to grasp the process, he was sure Korvin had showed him enough to find any ship he ever needed to, but all that he had gotten from the exchange was a concourse number and landing pad. It was enough.

Logan Starport might have been a Byzantine labyrinth, but it had good, plain-painted signs. Permanent. Non-digital. Non-holo. Just words on flat panels, dangling over every intersection. Mordecai followed them to Concourse J, Pad 1172.

Given all the gadgetry scattered around the starport, he was sure he had been scanned a dozen or more times on his way, but nothing made a fuss. He came out into the open sky to find a starship that looked... well, very starship-like to Mordecai. It was dishwater gray and bigger than his house, though not by much. The side of the front bit was painted with the name *"RADIOCITY"* in bold letters, flaked away in spots but clearly legible.

Music came from the ramp around back, where men with hovering skids and robotic arms carted things aboard. Mort listened to Chuck Ramsey's voice singing along as he made his way around the ship—some sort of backhanded ode to Boston Prime that he had never heard. The comedian was playing an acoustic guitar that sounded like it might have been half a note out of tune. When Mordecai rounded the corner, the song stopped.

"Well, how's about that?" Chuck said, standing and setting aside a guitar with a frayed strap and the cherry wood buffed smooth where the player's hands rubbed over the years. "Mort! Didn't expect to be seeing you... well, ever, frankly. We don't get back to Earth much, and what're the odds, you know?"

Mordecai stepped onto the ramp, glancing over his shoulder to see if any of the freight loaders might be listening. "Hey, Chuck. Any chance you might take on a passenger?"

Chuck pulled back and narrowed his eyes, but a smirk spread on his face at the same time. "Thought you were some fancy-pants *real* wizard, not some star-drive mechanic. Never heard of wizards traveling off world much, except for navy attack dogs or terramancers."

"I have pressing business with the Convocation that involves being anywhere but here."

"I see," Chuck said. Their eyes met, and Mordecai had the impression that Chuck Ramsey was sizing him up, weighing him, and deciding whether there was room aboard his ship for both Mordecai and the trouble he was bringing with him.

"You told me you had troubles with your star-drive," Mordecai said.

"You gonna sign on as a mechanic?" Chuck asked, crossing his arms and cocking his head.

Mordecai harrumphed. "Please... with *me* aboard, you won't *need* a star-drive. All those gizmos do is imitate what a real wizard could manage. You not only won't have to pay for constant repairs and getting towed back to real-space, you'll be able to outrun... well anything without a wizard as good as I am."

Chuck gave him a shrewd look. Terras floated in his eyes, weighing against whatever trouble Mordecai might be running from. "Deal. Come on aboard. I gotta watch these lift-loaders, but Bradley can show you around." He stuck out a hand, and the two men shook.

Bradley Carlin Ramsey looked ecstatic to have a live wizard aboard. "You can bunk with me," he insisted. "You're old, so I'll take the top bunk so you don't have to climb so much. You know... I always wanted to be a pilot, but if you could teach me to be a wizard, that would be far out!" The boy had obviously been listening to too much of his father's old twentieth century material and picked up the archaic lingo.

"Whatever you grow up to be, just don't become what everyone expects of you," Mordecai said, wagging a finger and trying to sound sage. "People like that are boring as shit."

Bradley looked around, ducked his head, and whispered. "Shit's a bad word."

"Kid, I'm an expert on bad words, and trust me, 'shit' doesn't make the top one hundred." Every word of the *Tome of Bleeding Thoughts* qualified, he thought bitterly, the book that had cost him his life on Earth.

[Fifteen years later]

Mort arrived at the shipyard in a foul mood. The taxi had refused his hardcoin, and he had to take a public tram from the starport to a tram station a half-hour's walk from his destination. Granger III was backwater, but not backwater enough that all the colonized regions were clustered together. Three days on a starliner to Granger VII, intra-system shuttle to Granger III, and now this mess of planetside transportation. Bradley had better have something planet shattering to show him.

The man who met him at the shipyard entrance was not the same young man who had left his father's ship at eighteen to join the navy. Brad had filled out a little, turned scruffy, and had a cocky veneer painted over his face that he had lacked as a boy. Somehow, it had taken nine years away from Chuck for Brad to turn into his father.

"Brad," Mort called out, raising a hand. "Good to see you, boy. I'd have sworn you dropped through the astral plane and out the other side."

"Hey, Mort. I've taken to going by Carl these days," Carl replied. "We had another Brad in my squadron, and he was there first. Besides, now I can tell who knows me from where when someone shouts my name across a room."

"Well... Carl, what did you drag me out to Merlin's privy for?"

Carl's eyes lit up. "Come on. I gotta show you." He beckoned Mort along as he backed toward the shipyard.

After following him around the hulking masses of a dozen derelict used starships, Carl stopped at one and spread his arms. "What do you think?"

"Is this one you shot down as a fighter pilot?" Mort asked. "It's a sweet gesture, boy, but I don't have a mantelpiece big enough—"

"I just bought it," Carl replied.

"You own this... device?" Mort asked carefully.

"Yeah. If anyone asks, I won it in a card game."

"And the truth?"

"Me and some guys in my squadron saw some shit," Carl said. "Navy bought us out of our pensions to shut up about it and go away. Sweet deal. If I refused, next on their list was probably a series of suicide missions until one of them took."

A clang from inside the ship caught Mort's attention. "Who's inside?"

Carl held up a finger and retreated up the ramp, grinning. "Tanny!" he shouted into the ship's interior. "Mort's here." There was more clanging, and the clatter of something metal dropping to the floor. A woman emerged from within. She was Carl's height, with close-cropped dark hair and muscular arms bared under a sleeveless top that showed a marine insignia tattooed on her shoulder.

She eyed him up and down. "This wizard of yours looks a lot like an out-of-work accountant. You sure this is the right guy?"

"Mort, this is my girlfriend, Tanny," Carl said. "Tanny, this is Mordecai The Brown."

"Charmed," Mort muttered.

"Tania Rucker, officially," Tanny offered, extending a greasy hand after a quick wipe on her dungarees. "Tell me something. That really your middle name? Carl said it was, but he's full of shit half the time, so I couldn't be sure."

"Family tradition," Mort replied. "My ancestors had a

sense of humor, and my parents lacked imagination. How do you and Carl know each other?"

"Frequently," Carl quipped. Tanny gave him a back-handed slap to the chest without even looking. It appeared they have been together long enough for her to be ready for Carl's off-color jests. Nine years in the navy had done nothing to undo the bad influence Mort had been on him growing up. If anything, it appeared to have fertilized him.

"Back from a mission, I had this hotshot pilot track me down and brag how he'd blown six Zheen fighters off my tail," Tanny said. "I was flying dropships, ferrying troops down to the front lines on the surface. Never noticed any heat, and I told him so. Turns out it was some other dropship he'd bailed out, and he bought me dinner to apologize. Well, one thing led to another—"

"And another ... and another ..." Carl added.

"Anyway, when Carl left the navy, my tour was almost up," Tanny replied. "He had this half-cooked idea about running his own starship and convinced me to come out here with him and sign on to the crew. How'd he get you?"

"He hasn't... yet," Mort replied.

"Lemme show you around," Carl said. He took Mort on a tour of the ship. It was larger than the *Radiocity*, bulkier, block-ier, and far, far emptier. The main feature Carl kept dangling before him like a mule's carrot was the fact that it was an old diplomatic shuttle, Turtledove class, as if that was supposed to mean anything to him. But because it was designed to ferry diplomats around, it had multiple crew quarters, enough for everyone to have their own private space.

"I don't know..." Mort hedged.

"Mom and Dad aren't touring the galaxy anymore," Carl said.

"You want to join up, maybe one of these days we'll stumble across that book of yours, and you can get home to see your family. I don't plan on running things like Dad did. He only ran cons here and there to fill in the gaps between gigs, but we plan on cashing in however we can, short of piracy. We're going to go places and meet people Dad was never going to with a family in tow. If you're up to it, we can take on the galaxy and make our own rules."

Carl's choice of words was calculated. He told Mort much between those lines. Carl knew the whole story behind that book, of course, even things Mort had kept secret from his wife. He knew that Mort was never going back; but he must have told Tanny the fairytale version with the happy ending still pending. That meant that Carl had kept Mort's darker secret safe. As for the bit about Chuck Ramsey, Mort had always enjoyed the challenge of matching wits with two-bit criminals over the steady tedium of hearing the same old comedy routines, system after system. Carl could be masterful when he put his mind to it—carrot and stick, held out for Mort to choose with Tanny none the wiser.

Mort gave Carl a rueful grin. "Let me guess: the star-drive on this heap doesn't work."

"Oh, the star-drive works fine," Carl replied. "Maybe the newest system on this old bird." He picked up a wrench big enough to twist a man's arm off and proffered it to Mort. "You join up, you're welcome to smash it to scrap."

"You're such a fucking salesman," Tanny muttered.

"Deal," Mort said. "This bucket of scrap star-drives have a name yet?"

"Carl keeps trying to name it Star Ghost," said Tanny. "But I like Trident. Seems a bit less... kitschy."

"Better than naming it after a spear," Carl countered.

Mort looked the vessel over and considered its prospective

crew. It was less in need of a name than a philosophy. "No, those won't do," he said. He imagined a strip of white cloth into being. It was only a temporary prop, destined to oblivion the moment he stopped devoting attention to it. He gave it a twist and connected the two ends, fusing them with no sign of artifice or technology. Tanny's eyes widened; Carl's narrowed. "Do either of you know what this is...? It's a mobius loop. It has a single side, the only object in existence to exhibit that peculiar property." He handed it to Tanny and watched her trace a finger around it, coming back to the start without ever leaving the same surface. "That should be this ship's name: *Mobius*. That way we'll always be on the same side, and no matter how long it takes, we'll all eventually get back to where we started."

Carl looked somber. It was the first time since Mort arrived that it looked like thoughts might be going on inside Carl's head that weren't spilling directly out his mouth. He glanced to Tanny, who nodded. "Yeah, let's do it. We've still got a crew to fill out and a million repairs, but at least we've got a name now: *Mobius*."

The three of them tromped up the ramp and into the newly christened vessel, Mort taking up the rear. "What have I gotten myself into?" he asked too softly for Tanny or Carl to hear. "Climbing into the belly of a starship again, to fly with a Ramsey."

---

---

Ready for more? *Mission Pack 2* is available for you right now! Get your copy *here!*

## EMAIL INSIDERS

You made it to the end! Maybe you're just persistent, but hopefully that means you enjoyed the book. But this is just the end of one story. If you'd like reading my books, there are always more on the way!

Perks of being an Email Insider include:

- Notification of book releases (often with discounts)
- Inside track on beta reading
- Advance review copies (ARCs)
- Access to Inside Exclusive bonus extras and giveaways
- Best of my blog about fantasy, science fiction, and the art of worldbuilding

Sign up for the my Email Insiders list at:
    jsmorin.com/updates

BOOKS BY J. S. MORIN

## Black Ocean

*Black Ocean* is a fast-paced fantasy space opera series about the small crew of the *Mobius* trying to squeeze out a living. If you love fantasy and sci-fi, and still lament over the cancellation of *Firefly*, *Black Ocean* is the series for you!

Read about the *Black Ocean* series and discover where to buy at: blackoceanmissions.com

## Black Ocean: Astral Prime

Co-written with author M.A. Larkin, *Black Ocean: Astral Prime* hearkens back to location-based space sci-fi classics like *Babylon 5* and *Star Trek: Deep Space Nine*. *Astral Prime* builds on the rich *Black Ocean* universe, introducing a colorful cast of characters for new and returning readers alike. Come along for the ride as a minor outpost in the middle of nowhere becomes a key point of interstellar conflict.

Read about the *Black Ocean: Astral Prime* series and discover where to buy at: astralprimemissions.com

## Black Ocean: Mercy for Hire

*Black Ocean: Mercy for Hire* follows the exploits of a pair of do-gooder bounty hunters who care more about saving the day than securing a payday. The series builds on the rich *Black Ocean* universe, centering on a couple of fan-favorites and introducing a colorful cast for new and returning readers alike. Fans of vigilante justice and heroes who exemplify the word will love this series.

Read about *Black Ocean: Mercy for Hire* and discover where to buy at: mercyforhiremissions.com

## Twinborn Chronicles: Awakening

Experience the journey of mundane scribe Kyrus Hinterdale who discovers what it means to be Twinborn—and the dangers of getting caught using magic in a world that thinks it exists only in children's stories.

## Twinborn Chronicles: War of 3 Worlds

Then continue on into the world of Korr, where the Mad Tinker and his daughter try to save the humans from the oppressive race of Kuduks. When their war spills over into both Tellurak and Veydrus, what alliances will they need to forge to make sure the right side wins?

Read about the full *Twinborn Chronicles* and discover where to buy at: twinbornchronicles.com

## Robot Geneticists

*Robot Geneticists* brings genetic engineering into a post-apocalyptic Earth, 1000 years aliens obliterated all life.

BOOKS BY J. S. MORIN / 657

*These days, even the humans are built by robots.*

Charlie7 is the oldest robot alive. He's seen everything from the fall of mankind at the hands of alien invaders to the rebuilding of a living world from the algae up. But what he hasn't seen in over a thousand years is a healthy, intelligent human. When Eve stumbles into his life, the old robot finally has something worth coming out of retirement for: someone to protect.

Read about all of the *Robot Geneticists* books and discover where to buy at: robotgeneticists.com

## Sins of Angels

Co-written with author M.A. Larkin, *Sins of Angels* is an epic space opera series set 3000 years after the fall of Earth. With the scope of *Dune* and the adventurous spirit of *Indiana Jones*, it delivers a conflict that spans galaxies and rests on the spirit of brave researcher Professor Rachel Jordan. Follow the complete saga, and watch as the fate of our species hangs in the balance.

Read about *Sins of Angels* and discover where to buy at: sinsofangelsbooks.com

## Shadowblood Heir

*Shadowblood Heir* explores what would happen if the writer of your favorite epic fantasy TV show died before the show ended—and the show was responsible. If you wonder what it would be like if an epic fantasy world invaded our world, this urban fantasy story might give you that glimpse.

Read about *Shadowblood Heir* and discover where to buy at: shadowbloodheir.com

## ABOUT THE AUTHOR

I am a creator of worlds and a destroyer of words. As a fantasy writer, my works range from traditional epics to futuristic fantasy with starships. I have worked as an unpaid Little League pitcher, a cashier, a student library aide, a factory grunt, a cubicle drone, and an engineer—there is some overlap in the last two.

Through it all, though, I was always a storyteller. Eventually I started writing books based on the stray stories in my head, and people kept telling me to write more of them. Now, that's all I do for a living.

I enjoy strategy, worldbuilding, and the fantasy author's privilege to make up words. I am a gamer, a joker, and a thinker of sideways thoughts. But I don't dance, can't sing, and my best artistic efforts fall short of your average notebook doodle. When you read my books, you are seeing me at my best.

My ultimate goal is to be both clever and right at the same time. I have it on good authority that I have yet to achieve it.

*Connect with me online*
jsmorin.com

facebook.com/jsmorinauthor

twitter.com/jsmorinauthor